THE FATE OF THE
DWARVES

MARKUS HEITZ

Translated by Sheelagh Alabaster

www.orbitbooks.net

ORBIT

First English-language edition published in Great Britain in 2012 by Orbit

5 7 9 11 12 10 8 6

Originally published in Germany as *Das Schicksal der Zwerge* by
Heyne Verlag in 2008

A CIP catalogue record for this book
is available from the British Library.

ISBN 978-1-84149-936-9

Typeset in Sabon LT Std by Palimpsest Book Production Limited,
Falkirk, Stirlingshire
Printed and bound by CPI Group (UK) Ltd, Croydon, CR0 4YY

Papers used by Orbit are from well-managed forests
and other responsible sources.

MIX
Paper from
responsible sources
FSC® C104740

Orbit
An imprint of
Little, Brown Book Group
100 Victoria Embankment
London EC4Y 0DY

An Hachette UK Company
www.hachette.co.uk

www.orbitbooks.net

*Dedicated
to all the friends of the "small folk".
You have earned this!*

"Word goeth that ye dwerffes be greyt relayters of riddles and wit. One of ye most famous is sedd to be the tayle wheyre an orc asketh a dwerff ye way and ye dwerff answereth.

Ye tayle goeth lyke this: One ~~aurbit~~ orbit an orc was strollyng along a road, its eyes fixed on ye path, but still not knowyng whych way to tayke.

It so happened that a dwerff was standing at that very crossroads seeing what was to be seen. Ye dwerff bore an axe of pure vraccasium, his chayne mayle tunic was strong and fynely wrought, fit to withstand ye arrows, swords and blaydes of all kinds.

And it was clear from his stature that he fain must be one of ye fiercest and most valiant warriors among all ye tribes of ye dwerffes. His beard was brayded and oiled. Tiny pieces of gold were to be seen thredded into sed beard, whych was twisted around with fyne silver wyre to keep it in form. A very master among dwerffes, to speak true, with his hair and his weapons and his armour!

~~And so the orc comes and sees the dwarf . . .~~
~~And then the dwarf comes . . .~~

And ye orc comes up to him and asks ye ~~twerf~~ dwerff whych road ~~where long~~ to tayke"

Taken from "Descryptions of ye Ffolk of Girdlegyrd: Manneris and Karacterystycks" In the Great Archive of Viransiénsis, drawn up by Tanduweyt, collected by M.A. Het, Magister Folkloricum, in the 4300th solar cycle, a fragment, much of the document having been destroyed in fire.

"To be totally honest, I don't care for the story at all. I still don't understand why the whole world seems so keen to know the punch line. In my view the whole thing is a complete waste of time. But, you know what? They all laugh. It's beyond me."

Hargorin Deathbringer, Leader of the Black Squadron

"If I have to tell the joke about the orc and the dwarf one more time, even ONE SINGLE TIME, I'll go dwarfingly fighting mad, and I shan't rest till all the idiots who want to hear the stupid thing are slaughtered. I swear this on my crow's beak!

And I don't care if it's a twenty-headed dragon asking for it or a singing dancing talking unicorn or a shiny fairy who's got a thousand wishes to grant me. I DON'T CARE! I'll kill them all, no matter who they are! No more jokes, got it?"

Boïndil "Ireheart" Doubleblade from the clan
of Swinging Axes, of the secondling folk, spoken
at a banquet held in Mifurdania in honour
of the comedians and descendants of Rodario.

Prologue

The air was filled with the smell of bone dust, ice-cold stone and frosty damp. The thin-armed creature stepped cautiously out of the shadow of a rock and blinked. Ten paces ahead the shimmering made everything on the far side appear hazy. The same as always.

The nameless creature sent a long green tongue over the skin of its doglike face, revealing needle-sharp teeth. With two of its sixteen fingers it explored the short dark fur under the dirty armor, scratched itself and yawned. It adjusted the armor that was pressing uncomfortably on its balls.

It gave a sigh of relief and then another yawn.

On the orders of the Strongest One it had to keep watch from dawn to dusk and immediately report any changes to the quivering vibrations in the air. It was a boring task. Thankless and boring.

After a while it picked up and ate a yellow beetle emerging from under a moldering thighbone on the ground. As it chewed it occurred to the creature that not one of the hundreds of its own kind could remember a time when the air had *not* shimmered.

It grunted and kicked at the black wall of rock, then strolled up to the edge, trailing an over-long sword. As the rusty brown metal blade scraped against the rock floor, it collected yet more dents and notches.

The creature sat down on the ground next to the shimmering. Yawning, it picked up a pebble and idly chucked it. The air hissed and flashed, for a second turning opaque like murky water and stopping the pebble's flight. The little stone bounced back and landed at the tip of the creature's boots. Another sigh. This was a ritual that never ever changed. It was obvious why the pebbles were being chucked: They did not disappear straight away when they met the shimmering.

There had been times when the invisible barrier had simply been an indestructible wall. It would hurt if you ran into it, but nothing else happened. Then, all of a sudden, the wall would destroy whatever touched it: There'd be a crackling flash and you'd be drenched in fire and burned to a fine cinder ash that blew away in the wind. But for about seven world-ages now, the wall had been taking quite a long time to actually kill you. If you were quick and tore yourself back off it you'd get away with a burn.

On the other side the creature could pick out a strange vertical structure composed of metal rings. When the sun stood high there'd be a bright light in the center. Every so often a few small chunky two-leggers could be seen going up to the rings, walking around and then disappearing again. You could just see strong high walls with colorful flags atop square towers, but the shimmering made everything indistinct. The towers were quite a way off.

If it tried very hard, the creature could make out two-leggers walking to and fro on the battlements. They looked different from the ones that marched round inspecting the interlocking iron rings. Bet their job was just as boring—and would remain so until some time in the future the air no longer made waves like on a hot summer's day.

That was the moment the Strongest One had been waiting for, along with so many others, big and small, two-leggers and many-leggers, screech-phantoms and soul-rippers alike—and the kordrion, of course. Even the Strongest One was afraid of the kordrion—the flying horror was obeyed by all.

When the shimmering stopped a new empire would open up, the Strongest One had told them. There'd be delicious fresh meat and rich pickings for all. The Strongest One before the Strongest One had promised that as well. And the one before that, the Strongest Ever, had said the same.

The creature didn't believe it any longer, but wasn't going to let on. You died soon enough if you stepped out of line. A single life was nothing—the Strongest One had thousands of nameless foot soldiers at his beck and call.

Another pebble was chucked, half-heartedly. The large brown beetle crawling out of its rocky hiding place was really much more interesting.

Moving swiftly, the creature grabbed the beetle, pulled off the poisonous mandibles and sucked out the entrails, which tasted of rotten wanko berries. There was a lot of satisfied chewing. The empty beetle case was discarded and the creature bent down. Where had the pebble fallen this time?

Long fingers searching the ground found—nothing.

Curiosity now aroused, it lifted its head and saw the small stone lying out in the sunshine.

Snorting in disbelief, the creature got up and stared: The shimmering had stopped.

It hardly dared to move. Its whole body was tingling. Its nostrils widened to catch new scents. For the first time you could smell the land on the other side without the stupid filter: Flesh, iron, dust, stone—the smells of excitingly different things in your nose. Freedom! Booty! Meat! And untold treasure!

Looking back at the entrance to the underground empire of the Strongest One and the kordrion, the creature knew it had to make its report as quickly as anything, but . . . It turned its narrow head again, long pointed ears erect. Why not take another look before anyone else turned up? What was the world out there going to look like without that shimmer effect? Might there be some rich pickings to secure for personal use?

You'd have to inspect it properly, or your report wouldn't be accurate. There was a big chance they'd call you a liar if your description wasn't specific enough. Liars got treated the same way as the ones who stepped out of line. A *very* good reason for not racing off to the Strongest One's lair in the abyss, quite apart from the rich-pickings possibility.

Carefully, one step at a time. Here's the edge of the rocks now, and then out into the sunshine.

Any hope of a bit of secret pillaging died a death. Those fortress walls couldn't possibly be scaled. The Strongest One's help would be needed there. The kordrion's, too. Tough . . . Without the distortion caused by the shimmering those square towers appeared even more invulnerable than ever. The creature's dreams of rich pickings and fresh meat faded fast. The stonemason's art up there—you wouldn't get that type of thing back home.

But the creature's approach had been noted. Vast numbers

of weapons were heard rattling. Shouts came from the battlements. Then the dread sound of alarm horns.

This was scary. Best duck down!

Still trying to get a good look at all the colors and the patterns on the banners, the creature turned tail and made for the rocks—but a hefty blow on the back hurled it to the ground. The sword slipped out of its grasp.

It could scarcely breathe. It spat and saw its own green blood! But then the pain flooded through from the wound.

Yowling and whimpering by turns, it clutched at a thin wooden shaft sticking in its back.

From the right-hand side something came hissing, striking the creature in the face, shattering the upper jaw and adding to the torture. The howls grew louder and stopped, suddenly, when a dozen arrows whirred in from all directions.

One arm pierced and anchored to the flank, the creature dragged itself steadfastly on, groaning and spluttering. The Strongest One must get the report and avenge the death. Let the storm break!

Once back in the shadow of the rocks, past the place where the air normally shimmered, everything felt safer. Now the report would be made!

All at once the smell in the air changed.

In spite of all the blood and the mashed nose, you could sense it clearly: It was the smell you got just before a thunderstorm. Invisible energy was gathering, crackling all around.

Shrieking in terror, the creature clutched at the floor of dust and ground-up bones, trying to get a hold to pull itself forward . . .

The magic sphere flared into being once more, cutting the creature in half at the hips.

One last ghastly scream escaped its throat before it died; the legs convulsed for a time before falling still.

"Praise and thanks to Vraccas! The shield is up again!" Boïndil Doubleblade, known by friends and enemies alike as Ireheart on account of his ungovernable rage in combat, had observed the fate of the thin-armed creature. Putting the telescope down on the stone parapet, he watched the glittering shield that enclosed the Black Abyss. "The artifact seems to be running out of power." He turned a quizzical gaze on Goda. "Can you tell me anything about that?"

He was standing with his beloved consort on the north tower of Evildam, which had defended these parts for the past two hundred and twenty-one cycles.

Built by dwarves, undergroundlings, ubariu and humans, the four walls of the fortress formed a square thirty paces high and, at the widest points, over fifteen paces thick round the Black Abyss. The structure was simple in form but masterful in execution. The cooperation of the various participators had ensured the creation of something unique, even if the dwarves' contribution had been the greatest part. Ireheart was proud of it. The runes on the towers praised Vraccas, Ubar and Palandiell.

Catapults installed on the broad walkways, the towers and the levels beneath the roofed platforms could launch stones, arrows and spears when needed; there were enough missiles in store to contend even with attackers outnumbering them by many hundreds to one. A garrison of two thousand warriors manned the defenses of Evildam, ready to take up arms and fight back dark armies.

But for two hundred and twenty-one cycles this had never been necessary.

The creature that lay there in its own blood was the first ever to leave the prison: A dark cleft half a mile long and a hundred paces wide was a blemish on the surrounding landscape and marked where evil would emerge if the magic barrier and the fortress allowed it.

Goda turned to her warrior husband—a sturdy secondling dwarf with such a reputation and so much combat experience behind him that he had been appointed commander of the fortress. She tilted her head to one side; dark blond hair poked out from under her cap.

"Are you *afraid* the shield won't hold, or are you *hoping* it won't?" In contrast to Ireheart, who was sporting a chainmail shirt reinforced with iron plates, she wore a long light gray dress, simple and unadorned apart from the gold thread embroidering the belt. Goda wasn't even carrying a dagger, showing plainly that she eschewed conventional fighting. Her arsenal was a magic one.

"Oh, I'm not afraid of what's out there in the Black Abyss! It can't be any worse than what's abroad in Girdlegard," he growled, pretending to be offended as he stroked his thick black beard, now exhibiting its fair share of silvery gray. It was a sign of his advanced age. But really he was in the prime of life. Ireheart gave his wife a sad little smile. "And I've never given up hope from the day *he* went to the other side." He turned his head back to gaze at the entrance to the Black Abyss, over behind the shield. "That's why I'm waiting here. By Vraccas, if I could only glimpse him behind that shield, I'd be off like a shot to help! With all the strength at my disposal." He slammed both fists down on the top of the wall.

Goda looked over at the artifact with its impenetrable

sphere enclosing the abyss. The artifact stood at the entrance to the Black Abyss and was composed of four interlocking vertical iron rings which formed a kind of ball with a diameter of twenty paces. The metal circles showed runes, signs, notches and marks; horizontal reinforcements connected to the central point where there was a fixture decorated with symbols. And it was there that its power was to be found: It drew its strength from a diamond in which enormous amounts of magic energy were stored.

But the stone was developing defects; each orbit would bring yet another fissure. When that happened you could hear the cracking sound echo from the fortress walls. All the soldiers were aware of it.

"I can't say how much more it can take," Goda told him quietly, her brows knitted in concern. "It could give at any moment or it could last for many cycles yet."

Ireheart sighed and nodded to the guards passing on their rounds. "How do you mean?" he growled, rubbing the shaved sides of his head. Then he adjusted the plait of dark hair that hung down the length of his back. It was showing just as much silver now as the beard. "Can't you be more specific?"

"I can only repeat what I always say when you ask that, husband: I don't know." She didn't take his unfriendly tone amiss because she knew it stemmed from worry. Over two hundred and fifty cycles of worry. "Perhaps Lot-Ionan could have given you a better answer."

Ireheart's laugh was short, humorless and harsh. "I know what he'd give me if we met now. I expect it would be an extermination spell right between the eyes." He picked up and shouldered his crow's beak, the one his twin brother

Boëndal Hookhand had once carried into battle. He made his way along the walkway. He used his twin's long-handled weapon in honor of his memory: It had a heavy flat hammer head on the one side and a curved spike on the other, the length of your arm. No armor could withstand a crow's beak wielded by a dwarf.

Goda followed him. Time to do the rounds.

"Did you ever think we would spend so long here in the Outer Lands?" he asked her pensively.

"No more than I ever thought things in Girdlegard could change like they have," she replied. Goda was surprised by her companion's thoughtful mood. The two of them had forged the iron band together many cycles before.

Their love had provided them with seven children: Two girls and five sons. The artifact had not objected to its keeper no longer being a virgin, as long as her soul was still pure. Goda had retained this innocence of spirit. Nothing dark had entered her mind. She had remained free of deceit, trickery and power lust.

The fact that she had abandoned Lot-Ionan made this very clear. Many others had remained with him. She had gained herself a powerful enemy by leaving him. "Don't you think it's time to go back and support them? You know they've been waiting for you. Waiting for the last great dwarf-hero from the glorious cycles."

"Go back and leave you alone, when the artifact may burst at any moment? Give up command of the fortress?" Ireheart shook his head violently. "Never! If monsters and fiends come pouring out of the Black Abyss I've got to be here to hold them back, together with you and our children and my warriors." He put his arm round her shoulder. "If this evil were to flood over into Girdlegard there would be no hope at all anymore. For no one, whatever race they belong to."

"Why stop Boëndalin going back to our people? He could go in your place," she urged him gently. "At least it would give the children of the Smith a signal . . ."

"Boëndalin is too good a fighter to be spared," he interrupted her. "I need him to train the troops." Ireheart's eyes grew hard. "None of my sons and daughters shall leave my side until we've closed up the Black Abyss for all time and filled it up with molten steel."

Goda sighed. "Today's not one of your best orbits, Ireheart."

He stopped, placed his crow's beak on the ground and took her hands in his. "Forgive me, wife. But seeing the shield collapse like that, and then seeing how long it took to repair itself, it's really got me worried. I can easily be unfair when I'm troubled." He gave a faint smile to ask for forgiveness. She smiled in her turn.

They marched to the tower and went down in the lift, which worked with a system of counterweights and winches.

One hundred heavily armed ubariu warriors were waiting for them at the fortress gates.

Ireheart scanned their faces. Even after all those cycles they were still foreign to him. It had never felt right to forge friendships with a people who looked for all the world like orcs. Only bigger.

Their eyes shone bright red like little suns. In contrast to Tion's creatures, the ubariu kept themselves very clean and their character was different too, because they had turned their back on evil and on random cruelty to others—at least that was what the undergroundlings claimed. The underground-lings were the dwarves of the Outer Lands . . .

And even if there had never been cause for doubt, Ireheart's nature would never allow him to lay aside his scruples and accept them as equals, as friends. For himself, in contrast to how his wife and children felt, they would never be more than military allies.

Goda gave him a little push and he pulled himself together. He knew his reservations were unjustified, but he couldn't help it. Vraccas had hammered a hatred of orcs and all of Tion's creatures into the Girdlegard dwarves. The ubariu had the misfortune to look like evil—and yet there was no way round it: They had to work together to guard the Black Abyss.

Ireheart gave the gatekeeper a signal.

Shouts were heard, strong arms moved chains and pulley ropes to set the heavy cogs in motion to open the main door. With a screech of iron the massive gate, eleven paces by seven, rose up to make a gap through which the column of soldiers could march out toward the artifact.

"We'll check the edges of the shield today," Ireheart told Pfalgur, the ubari standing next to him. "I wouldn't put it past these beasts to have dug an escape tunnel. You go one way, we'll take the other. I'll start at the artifact. You get along."

"Understood, general," the ubari's deep voice responded, passing on the orders.

They traversed the basin that held the Black Abyss. The sides were smooth and black as colored glass, and steep paths led off to the right and left, ending at the protective sphere.

Ireheart turned right toward the artifact; the ubari led his troops in the other direction.

While Goda used her telescope to inspect in minute detail both the diamond and the structure, which was enclosed in the same kind of energy dome as the abyss itself, Ireheart went over to the corpse of the abyss creature. On this side of the barrier lay the ugly thin legs that didn't look capable of ever having walked properly in those heavy boots. On the other side Ireheart could vaguely make out its upper body, pierced with arrows. Greenish blood had formed puddles and little rivulets.

"Stupid freak," he said under his breath, kicking the creature's left leg. "Your moment of freedom only brought you death." Ireheart looked up and stared into the chasm. "Did you come on your own when you saw the shield was failing?" he asked quietly, as if the creature could hear him.

"Boïndil!" he heard Goda call, her voice excited.

Something wrong with the diamond? He was just about to turn round to speak to her when he thought he noticed a movement in the darkness.

Ireheart stopped and stared fixedly.

The strength of the magic barrier was making his mustache hairs stand on end. Or was it that feeling of unease?

"Boïndil, come on!" his wife called, attempting to get his attention again. "I've got something to . . ."

Ireheart raised his right hand to show he had heard her but that he needed quiet. His brown eyes searched the twilight for vague figures.

Once more he noticed a slight scurrying movement—something going from one rock to the next. There it came again. And yet another!

There was no doubt in his mind that more monsters were creeping up. Had they sensed the poor state of the barrier? Did they have the advantage here with their animal instincts?

"I want . . ." he called over his shoulder. Surprise cut off his words. Wasn't that a *dwarf helmet*?

"This confounded distortion!" he yelled, taking a step forward. Standing dangerously close to the sphere, such that he could hear the humming sound it made, its pitch varying, he called out in a mix of hope and expectation. "Tungdil?" He nearly laid his hand on the energy screen; then gulped in distress. His throat had never felt so constricted before. "Vraccas, don't let my eyes be deceiving me," he prayed.

Then a huge pale claw, as broad as three castle gates, appeared out of the shadows, and gave a thundering blow to the sphere, producing a dull echo. The ground shook.

Ireheart jumped back with a curse, hitting out with his weapon as a reflex. The steel head of the crow's beak crashed against the barrier, but ineffectually. "The kordrion is back!" he bellowed, noting with grim satisfaction that the alarm trumpets on the battlements immediately sounded a warning to the soldiers to man the catapults. All those drills he made them do were paying off.

The pale claw curled, its long talons scraping along the inner side of the shield, creating bright yellow sparks. Then the kordrion retreated and a wall of white fire rolled in, slapping up against the barrier like a wave and washing all around.

Ireheart retreated, dazzled, stumbling backwards to the artifact. "It won't hold for long," he shouted to Goda. "The beasts know it and they're gathering."

"The diamond!" she called back. "It's crumbling!"

"What? Not now, in Vraccas's name!" At last he could

see again: Behind the force wall stood a range of monsters brandishing weapons! "Oh, you fiendish . . ."

Most were like that creature that had been cut in half; but there were others, significantly broader in the beam, much stronger and terrifying in appearance. No nightmare could have come up with better.

"By Vraccas," Ireheart breathed, bereft that his friend, Tungdil, had not come, after all. He issued brisk orders to the ubariu, telling them to spread out in front of the artifact to protect Goda. The warriors formed a wall of bodies, iron and shields, their lances pointing forward like so many defensive tentacles. Ireheart turned to Goda and saw that she was touching the shimmering sphere. "What's happening?" he called.

She was deathly pale. "A piece . . . of the diamond has come away," she stammered. "I can't hold it . . ."

There was a loud crack, like the noise of ice breaking. They all stared at the jewel. It had suddenly gone a darker color and there was a distinct fissure on its surface. The barrier fizzed and flickered. Layer upon layer was flaking off the edges of the diamond and falling to the ground. It was nearing the end.

"Get back!" commanded Ireheart. "Get back to the fort! We stand no chance here." He took Goda's hand and ran with her. In recent cycles he had grown to know the difference between courage and the insanity that used to overtake him in battle. His sons, too, had needed to learn the same lesson. The madness wasn't something he was proud of handing on to them.

The ubariu warriors kept pace with them, even though they could easily have covered the distance much more swiftly than the dwarves. Goda found it well-nigh impossible to tear herself away from the artifact, but was dragged along by her colleagues.

With a brilliant flash and an ear-splitting detonation the diamond burst apart, the force of the explosion bringing the whole structure down. Parts of the vertical iron circles broke off and flew through the air to bury themselves in the ground several paces off. The ends were glowing. There must have been incredible heat involved.

At the same time—the barrier at the Black Abyss fell!

The maga could clearly see the army of beasts—there was no immovable power to hold them back now. The wind carried an unbelievable stink over to her, a mixture of excrement, stale blood and sour milk. Grayish white clouds of dust and bone meal flurried up like mist in front of the somber rock face. Figures appeared out of the fog.

Behind the army the pale dragon-like head of the kordrion reared up out of the chasm, horns and spikes erect. The four gray upper eyes were assessing the walls of the fortress as if to judge what weaponry might be used against it and its followers. The two lower blue eyes beneath the long bony muzzle were fixed on the ubariu and the fleeing dwarves.

"Vraccas!" exclaimed Goda, who was gathering her magic powers ready for defense. She had spotted a helmet among the first row of smaller monsters—a helmet as worn by children of the Smith.

Then a dwarf stepped forward, head to foot in dark armor made of tionium; glimmering inlay patterns glowed in turn. The creatures all drew back in respect.

In his right hand he held a weapon that was a legend in Girdlegard and the Outer Lands alike, black as the blackest shadow and longer than a human arm. On one side the blade was thicker and had long thin teeth like a comb, and on the other side it thinned out like a sword.

"Bloodthirster," breathed Goda and stopped in her tracks.

Ireheart was brought to a halt. He turned—and froze. Words failed him.

The dwarf in the night-colored armor raised his left hand to lift his visor. A familiar face with a golden eye patch could be seen, but the features were hard and marked with bitterness. His cold, cruel smile promised death. Then he held his weapon aloft and looked to the right and to the left. The creatures responded with shouts.

"Vraccas defend us: He *has* returned!" whispered Goda in horror. "Returned as the Commander of Evil!"

At that moment discordant trumpets blared out from the abyss, echoing off the bare rock. The kordrion opened its muzzle to utter a furious roar.

I

Ireheart stared at his friend, so sorely missed and so eagerly awaited, and now there he was at the head of an army of fiendish demons. With his black armor on his back, Bloodthirster in his hand and an icy expression on his face, Tungdil seemed to have found his ideal setting. He *belonged*.

"But it can't be," Ireheart exclaimed, unable to take it in. "That's not him! May Vraccas be my witness. *That* isn't my Tungdil Goldhand!" He looked at Goda helplessly. "It's not him," he repeated, as if he were trying to convince himself. "It's a hallucination—a specter sent to scare us." As his despair turned to fury he raised his crow's beak, powerful rage getting the better of him again like in the old days. He was not about to resist the urge. "I'm going to smash it to pieces!"

This time it was Goda's turn to calm him. "No, Boïndil!" She faced him courageously, taking his face in her hands and staring into the brown eyes that flashed with madness and hot temper. "Hear my words, husband! This is not the time. We must get back to the fortress. Out here we're . . ."

Her speech was swallowed by the crashing of the catapults. Stones, arrows and spears were hurtling from fortress platforms and battlements; they flew over the heads of ubariu and dwarves, darkening the winter sunlight and casting shadows on the handful of defenders by the gate, before finding their mark in the ravine.

Metallic clashes rang out as iron spears rained on shields or penetrated helmets and armor; then came the victims' screams and the thud of missiles landing among the serried ranks of beasts. This was the very essence of battle, overlaid as it was with the intense smell of blood.

Goda knew this was only the beginning. Worse was to come. Soon the defending garrison would be adding their screams to the cacophony of death.

"Come with me," she begged Ireheart, pressing a kiss on his brow as missiles flew overhead. Smoking firebrands were launched, hissing into the air to burst against the steep walls of the Black Abyss and drench the monsters and the raging kordrion with burning liquid.

Believing Boïndil's spasm of fury had subsided, Goda slackened her grip, but he pushed her aside and raced over to the enemy lines with a bloodcurdling yell and the crow's beak raised high.

For the dwarf-woman this was all too fast—she tumbled to the ground. "No!" she shouted in her fright, trying in vain to hold him back. She turned. "Yagur, after him! Keep him safe!" she commanded. Without a moment's hesitation, the ubariu leader charged after the general to give backup; no easy task given the enemy's superior numbers.

Goda got to her feet and gathered her magic power so that she could help her husband from a distance.

Ireheart wasn't thinking anymore.

He was seeing his world through a blood-red mask and the only spot in the whole scene that he could clearly distinguish was the hideous phantom impersonating his best friend, Tungdil. He was not going to allow this vile infamy to persist. *You must not be Tungdil! Not on their side!*

The ringing in his ears masked the noise of battle. He was so overcome with the need to destroy the phantom and then to hurl himself on the opposing forces that he could no longer think clearly. It was too much for a warrior like himself, whose hot blood surged through his veins like molten rock through underground tunnels. And he did not even want to control himself.

Some of the spears and arrows landed near him, falling short of their intended targets. The soldiers at Evildam were sticking to the letter of their commander's instructions, even if he himself was acting contrary to his own orders. He was seeking to engage the enemy on open ground instead of running for the fortress to repel the approaching army of beasts from the safety of the stronghold's mighty walls.

Ireheart found himself less than ten paces away from the enemy. They hadn't stirred from their positions and were waiting at the exit to the ravine.

Enemy reinforcements clambered out over the bodies of fallen comrades, putting out fires with sand and bone dust. As soon as one creature fell, another ghastly monster took its place. The chasm apparently held an endless number of them. It was a nest of horrors.

As far as Ireheart could see, they were keeping their distance from the false Tungdil figure, as if he were surrounded by an invisible dome of respect and awe. "Whatever you are, I'm going to wipe you out!" he yelled, and with an ear-splitting cry of fury he swung the crow's beak high over his head.

The two blue eyes on the underside of the kordrion's muzzle focused on Ireheart for a moment and then turned on the black-armored form of Tungdil, who swiveled away from the fighting-mad Ireheart to face the gigantic monster, the runes on his armor glowing.

The kordrion screamed, and it sounded . . . afraid?

Before Boïndil could reach him, Tungdil had leaped forward onto one of the monsters' corpses; he jumped onto another close by and used a thick spear jutting out of the body as a springboard to reach a position on top of a huge boulder. From there his path took him to the next boulder and the next until he had passed along to the head of the army as if on stepping stones in a stream. Now he was close to the kordrion's throat. The cowering beast recoiled, hissing sharply.

Unable to hold back the blow he'd been waiting to deliver, Ireheart released it against one of the monsters racing toward him. This one seemed like a cross between an oversize reptile and a very fat orc, with the arms of a gnome stuck on to its sides. But it was still wielding a sword and shield with aplomb.

The flat head of the crow's beak shattered both shield and thin arm holding it, then smashed right into the ribcage; the beast fell dead in the dust.

Ireheart held off his next adversaries by whirling his weapon round in circles, liberally dealing out injury and death among them. All the time he ensured that the supposed Tungdil remained in sight. He was steadfastly refusing to assume that it might yet be his battle companion from the past but his confidence was starting to fade. *What in the name of Vraccas is he up to?*

Suddenly Yagur and the other ubariu were at his side fighting evil's misbegotten monsters, which in spite of their superior numbers seemed to be holding back, awaiting the order to storm the fortress *en masse*. Only a few of the creatures were venturing to attack and they paid with their lives. Some arrows, meanwhile, glanced off the huge shields the ubariu carried while others were halted in mid-air, falling ineffectually to the ground. Goda's magic.

"We'll have to go back, General," Yagur insisted, as he sliced his opponent down the middle with a wild sword thrust; Yagur jabbed through the falling body to reach the next oncomer. The second ubariu patrol joined them, strengthening their numbers.

Ireheart looked up at the black-clad dwarf wielding Bloodthirster in both hands to attack the kordrion. The strangely shaped blade cut through the creature's putrid grayish skin to release a river of blood.

The kordrion emitted a roar that shook Ireheart to the core and almost paralyzed him. The thunder of the creature's mighty voice all but caused the work of battle to cease and the walls of the ravine shook under its reverberations.

Everything was still . . .

. . . apart from the dwarf in the dark tionium armor!

He clanged the visor on his helmet, not caring about the blood streaming over his head.

It is him after all! He was just waiting for the right moment to show us who he is! At the sight of the dwarf's face Ireheart could no longer doubt this was his best friend returning at last to his side. He had missed him so badly. He wanted nothing more than to believe that this was Tungdil. The heroic and selfless conduct displayed in the assault on the kordrion was typical of the dwarf who had triumphed in the past in so many battles for Girdlegard. And there was probably a very good explanation to account for Tungdil's completely different set of armor—armor that reminded Ireheart of Djerůn. Time for all that later. Now for the fight!

But when, next moment, Tungdil was bathed in the kordrion's white fire and swallowed up by bright flames, Boïndil gave up the hero for lost. He knew exactly what those flames would do, even though his experience of them had been over two hundred and fifty cycles previously. Even if the tionium withstood the fire, the heat inside the armor would roast the wearer alive. He remembered finding the body of his twin brother . . .

"No!" Ireheart bellowed in despair, hacking through helmet and skull of another enemy with the curved end of the crow's beak. There was a crack and then the sharp point appeared again through the breastbone under the throat. Boïndil hurled the creature to the ground, placing his right foot on its shoulders to pull the weapon back out through the ugly face. "Vraccas, don't let me have found him only to lose him again so soon."

The ball of fire spread and swelled to form a cloud in which a black shape could be seen. Tungdil seemed to have survived!

The black-armored dwarf had sunk onto one knee. He held Bloodthirster protecting his face, his other arm at his back. As the flames ebbed away he sprang up and stabbed at the lower eyes of the kordrion, taking it by surprise.

Tungdil managed to hit one of the eyes. It sounded like a leather wine pouch bursting.

Bluish liquid poured out, swiftly followed by a stream of

dark-red blood. Veins and sinews tumbled out as thick as a man's arm; more liquid fountained out of the wound and the creature convulsed with pain.

Ireheart couldn't believe his eyes: Spraying blood from a gash in its side and the injury on its head, the kordrion was slinking back into the ravine!

The enormous feet squashed dozens of monsters, pressing them into the ground. Bodily juices squirted out in all directions. Then it was gone, leaving a wet trail on the rocks. A final flurry of arrows and spears accompanied it to its lair, then the stronghold catapults fell silent.

Quiet returned, so that the sound of the wind along the battlements and on the slopes of the Black Abyss—not heard amid the noise of battle—was loud in comparison.

Ireheart commanded the ubariu to watch the murky path down into the chasm while he stepped forward, lowering his blood-smeared crow's beak.

He gestured to the armored dwarf to come down. "Show yourself, so that I may see if you are an old friend or a new enemy," he called out. He could not control his excitement, but was yo-yoing between joy and suspicion, his belief that this might be his old companion not quite being enough in itself to convince him.

Trumpets blared from the battlements, the great gate was opened and an army of two hundred dwarves and undergroundlings issued out under Goda's command. They took up their positions behind Ireheart and the ubariu and waited. Ready to fight.

The dwarf that was possibly Tungdil sprang down with remarkable agility, belying the weight of his armor, then ran along the stepping stones until he reached ground level. As he jumped down, a cloud of white dust rose, covering the black metal knee protectors. He held Bloodthirster in his right hand, with the blade resting up against his shoulder. Step by step he approached the band of warriors. The helmet stayed shut.

Boïndil gulped in apprehension, his throat dry. "Visor up!" he barked, his right hand flexing in readiness around the handle of the crow's beak. The leather grip creaked. "I want to see your face by daylight." Behind him the dwarves were raising their weapons, as the armored figure continued on his way, impervious to the command.

Now Ireheart could see the armor clearly. It was covered in runic signs and symbols he had never come across before.

A quick glance at Goda told him that the maga was equally bemused. She shook her head briefly, unable to interpret the meaning of the glimmering silver inlay or engravings any more than he could.

What bothered Boïndil was that there was no hint there of allegiance to Vraccas or of any dwarf origins, even if the suit of armor itself had unquestionably come from the hand of a child of the Smith: The work of a dwarf-master smith indeed.

Would Tungdil do that? Would he deny his own people? "Stand and show yourself!" he ordered resolutely, lifting his weapon. "If you are Tungdil Goldhand, show us your face. Otherwise . . ." Ireheart whirled his crow's beak round his head ". . . otherwise I shall smash your face in still inside the helmet!"

The other dwarf stopped in his tracks. Legs wide apart in a supremely confident stance he faced the gathered force, then—in a movement that was neither hasty nor frightened—his left hand went slowly up to his helmet. Bit by bit the dark grating was soundlessly lifted.

Boïndil was breathless with anticipation, his heart pounding. *Vraccas, let the miracle have happened!* he begged, closing his eyes to make the prayer to his god more fervent still. It was all he could do to open them again in order to look at the face before him. Hearing Goda's sharp intake of breath didn't make things easier.

At last he dared open his eyes.

He saw a short brown beard surrounding the familiar features of a dwarf who had certainly aged. But this was a face he would have known among a thousand.

The left eye was hidden behind an engraved patch of pure gold held in place with gold thread. The remaining brown eye was focused steadily on Boïndil. In that gaze Ireheart saw curiosity, little joy and . . . something else he could not fathom.

Visible through the beard the lines around the mouth and nose had grown deeper and gave the dwarf's face an authoritative air that many a dwarf-king would have envied. There was a scar running up the forehead from above the right eye and disappearing under the helmet—healed over, but very dark.

Ireheart gave a deep sigh. It definitely looked like his old friend standing before him once more. He took a step forward, but thought he could sense rejection from Tungdil.

"What sort of evidence do you want to prove I'm Tungdil Goldhand?" he asked, loosening the chin strap and tugging the helmet off the shock of shoulder-length brown hair. The scar on the brow went all the way up to the crown.

Tungdil cast the helmet down on the ground and shook off a gauntlet to show the golden mark on his hand. "Touch it, if you like, Boïndil. It's my everlasting souvenir from the battle for the throne of the high king, although I never really had a claim to it." He stretched out his hand in challenge.

Ireheart passed his fingers across the yellow-gold spot on the palm, then looked enquiringly into Tungdil's countenance.

The dwarf smiled and *it was the old smile*! The familiar smile he had so longed to see once more.

"Perhaps I should tell you how you tried to make me believe that the best way to seduce a dwarf-girl was to rub them from head to toe in stinky cheese?" He leaned forward with a wink. "I never used the method. Did you need it with Goda?"

The maga laughed out loud.

"So it's really you!" exclaimed Ireheart. He dropped the crow's beak, and pulled Tungdil into his open arms. "By Vraccas, it's really you!" he exclaimed, his eyes stinging with tears. Nothing could stop the flood of emotion. Such was his joy as he hugged Tungdil that he failed to notice the embrace was not being returned.

Tearing himself loose from Tungdil, Boïndil turned to the dwarves watching him with bated breath. "See!" he called enthusiastically, raising his head so that his words might carry to the battlements at Evildam. "See, our hero has returned! Girdlegard will soon be free of the yoke of manifold evil!" He tapped the black armor. "Ho, Lohasbrand, Lot-Ionan and all the rest of Tion's cursed issue; expect no mercy now—there's no escape for you!"

Goda was radiant and wiped tears of joy and relief from

her eyes. The dwarf-warriors behind her stared in deepest respect at the hero most knew only from hearsay. A legendary figure had returned to them and had, moreover, just seen off the most terrifying monster ever to emerge from the Black Abyss.

The garrison at the fortress had heard Boïndil's announcement. Drums and trumpets filled the air, heralding the news through a special melody composed specifically in anticipation of the long-awaited orbit when Tungdil would return. All should learn that the day had come.

Ireheart grinned: "I can imagine some will be thinking the trumpeters have got the fanfare wrong and were intending to send out quite a different set of orders." He thumped Tungdil heartily on the shoulder and couldn't wipe the smile off his face. "Let's go into the fortress and forget about the Black Abyss for now. It's time to bid you properly welcome. You'll have to tell us what you've been up to, all these long, long cycles. And we'll have a lot to fill you in on, too." He bent down to pick up Tungdil's helmet and gauntlet. Looking him straight in the eye, he told him, "You've no idea how happy I am to see you, Scholar."

Tungdil took his things and half turned, still watching the Black Abyss. "They'll be back, you know, Ireheart. I took the kordrion by surprise; as soon as its wounds are healed it'll come creeping out of its hiding place again. And word will soon get around that the barrier has lost its strength. The monsters will form an army and break out again . . ."

Boïndil pointed up at the massive walls of the stronghold. "That's why we've got the fortress and why we called it Evildam," he interrupted. "They won't escape, not a single ugly one of them. And we'll spike the kordrion all over with our heaviest spears till it looks like a hedgehog and collapses, dead." He looked over proudly to Goda. "She is now a maga. Our strongest weapon."

The dwarf-woman had taken a step forward and Tungdil observed her with a strange look in his eye. "You will need her," he said quietly, looking back at the cleft in the rocks.

Ireheart smiled. "We are more than confident, Scholar. Now you are with us again, nothing can frighten the children of the Smith." He set off, and the crowd of ubariu, undergroundlings and dwarf-warriors drew back to form a guard of honor to let them pass.

Goda stared at Tungdil as he passed. She had the impression that he didn't recognize her. His one brown eye had shown no reaction when he had looked her way. *And he never once asked about Sirka*, she said to herself, her face clouding over. Even if her husband was a pushover, bathed in joy and nostalgia as he was, she was going to be harder to convince. Suspicion had taken hold in her mind.

Goda followed them and the warriors stood guard while they withdrew into the stronghold behind the mighty doors. In the coming orbits, she decided, she would subject this dwarf, whom everyone seemingly held to be Tungdil Goldhand, to closer examination. Even as they entered the fortress to the accompaniment of triumphant fanfares and the acclaim of the troops, she was busy thinking up questions, because if the evil had sent them a false Tungdil there was unquestionably something terrible in store for them all.

Keeping her eyes on Tungdil's suit of black armor with the mysterious engravings, the dwarf-maga became more and more sure with every step she took that this was not their old friend they were welcoming here. They were letting evil into their midst and were celebrating its arrival!

She looked right and left and up to the towers, where shouts of wild rejoicing could be heard, loud enough to prevent any conversation.

Goda realized she seemed to be the only one in the fortress worried about this Tungdil figure. All the rest were in ecstasy because—despite his not having spoken a single word to them—they were convinced their long-awaited champion had returned to rid them of the evil.

She sighed, and her gaze drifted over to where Yagur, the ubariu leader, stood—and she recognized a similar concern on his face.

Girdlegard,
Former Queendom of Weyurn,
Mifurdania,
Winter, 6491st Solar Cycle

"And here, highly esteemed spectators, *here* at my left at the end, we have another legitimate descendant of the unique, incomparable and, for countless decades, never bettered, Incredible Rodario!" announced the man in opulent white attire standing on the same stage that normally saw service for executions. If you looked carefully you could still see the odd tuft of hair stuck in dried blood in the notches on the block. Nobody minded.

Or rather, nobody was allowed to mind.

There was not an inch of space in the square in front of the theater known as the *New Curiosum.* The covered tribune for the nobles and rich merchants or other privileged burghers was also filled to capacity.

Only the tribune's first row, reserved for selected notables, was still empty. Such dignitaries seldom if ever came to light-hearted events like this, preferring public beheadings, and the punishments and humiliation ordeals usually meted out here.

A pretty young woman sat in the second row. She had bright tawny orange eyes and, covered by a flimsy veil, beautiful black hair reaching down to her waist. She wore a mantle of black wolf fur wrapped round her and held a cup of mulled wine.

Round the edges of the square, stalls were selling various comestibles ranging from hot sausages and sliced pork to waffles and sweet chestnuts in cream. If anyone was cold they could grab a warm beer or a hot mug of wine, served with honey or spiced to taste. White clouds of steam rose from the many stoves in the market booths and there was music and song coming from the inn.

The young woman smiled as she inhaled all these smells. At last there was a reason to be cheerful, rare enough in these times of occupation by Lohasbrand and his henchmen.

"Is there anything else you'd like, Princess Coïra?" asked her companion, who was of an age to have been perhaps a brother. Under his open brown fur coat he wore leather armor, and a short sword hung at his side. His hair was hidden by a flat padded woolen cap that gave him a harmless appearance. That was the intention.

"Yes, I'd like you not to use that title," she hissed, flashing her eyes in reproach. "You know what they'll do to you if they hear you addressing me like that, Loytan."

Her companion scanned the empty front bench. "There's nobody here to take me to task for speaking the truth," he answered quietly but firmly. "You *are* the princess and your mother would be queen of Weyurn but for the accursed Dragon . . ."

Coïra placed her hand over his mouth. "Be quiet! You're risking your life, talking like that! They have eyes and ears everywhere!"

In her mind she could see her mother, imprisoned in her own palace, the Ring of Shame around her neck. Every hour of the orbit she was watched, humiliated and robbed of her authority. If the Dragon decided she should die, his servants would pull the ring tight to strangle her slowly until she suffocated. The princess sighed. "Look at the stage and enjoy what the Incredible Rodario's descendants have to offer us this time, when they choose their best competitor."

Loytan smiled obediently and turned toward the stage.

The master of ceremonies was pointing his cane to the end of the line. There were no less than eleven men and six women this cycle.

They were all dressed in showy and extravagantly tailored garments. The fabrics chosen were, one and all, scintillating and amazingly brightly colored. And yet the clothes had been selected in each case—coats, dresses, hats and boots—expressly to make each competitor stand out from the others.

The only one who didn't conform to type was the fellow at the end of the line.

He was the only one the tailor had provided with togs that didn't fit. Or perhaps he was standing so poorly that everything he wore seemed to crease and sag in the wrong places.

As appropriate for a descendant of the Incredible Rodario, he had brown hair, worn to his shoulders, and a good bone structure, but his cheeks were rather plump and this detracted from the promise of aristocratic features. The goatee beard, a distinctive mark of the original Incredible Rodario, founder of whole dynasties of renowned actors in many regions of Girdlegard, was disappointingly wispy and badly groomed.

"He calls himself—and I admit it's one of the more predictable choices—Rodario the Seventh! Applause, if you will!" The master of ceremonies raised his arms to encourage the audience, but the clapping was sporadic and died away quickly.

"By all the gods," said Loytan, amused. "What a miserable figure he makes in the midst of all those peacocks! He won't even get a consolation prize."

"I think it's . . . quite clever," Coïra said in defense. She felt some sympathy for this particular descendant of Rodario. He bore a certain tragic charm. "He's . . . different."

"He's definitely different." Loytan laughed out loud." In my opinion he'll be the first of the last again. Shall we have a bet, Princess?" He smiled at her happily, then something caught his eye just past her and his expression lost its merriment.

A broad shadow fell over them; Coïra swirled round in fear.

Behind them, four of the Lohasbrander henchmen had entered the tribune unnoticed and were making their way to the first row. They had heavy armor hung with discs of metal under their cloaks and their helmets were in the form of a dragon with folded wings. Each wore an amulet on a silver chain—a dark-green dragon scale, the sign of undisputed power in Weyurn. Thus they outranked all except for their master.

Coïra leaned forward searching the crowd in the square until she located the orcs. They belonged to the Lohasbranders and were their devoted servants. There they were, hanging out in one of the side streets, stuffing their faces. Because of the cold, the meat they were eating was steaming. Coïra didn't want to know whether it was freshly stewed or just very fresh.

The man at the front grinned at Loytan. He was fat and muscular at the same time; his broad face sported a light blond beard. "Did I just hear you say something you'd better have left unsaid? You know the law, Count Loytan of Loytansberg. It holds even for nobility like yourself. Or especially for nobility like yourself." He gathered a mouthful of saliva and spat at the young man. "But I'll overlook it for now. I don't want to spoil the atmosphere." He thumped down the steps to take his place straight in front, so that his helmet spoiled Loytan's view of the stage. "I recommend that you are no longer there when I get up to go. If you're still there I shall be implementing the orders of Master Lohasbrand." His comrades laughed as they took their seats.

"Here comes the first round, ladies and gentlemen. You love this part of the contest," announced the man in white. "It's the quick-fire slander session that starts here in Mifurdania, where the Incredible Rodario had his theater for so long." He surveyed the audience, hands on hips. "I can see from quite a few of your faces that your great-grannies used to enjoy going to the *Curiosum*, but going *backstage*, of course, I mean."

The crowd loved it.

Coïra restrained Loytan's hand, which had wandered to the sword at his belt. "Don't," she whispered urgently.

He was shaking with anger. "But . . ."

"You might get him, but the orcs will finish off your entire family. The Dragon will punish everyone, not just the individual—have you forgotten that?" Coïra took her handkerchief to remove the globule of green spit from Loytan's face, but he turned aside and wiped it on his own sleeve.

"One day nothing will save him from me," Loytan growled.

The woman released her hold. The danger was over for the moment. "Leave rebellion to others," she said quietly. "To those who don't have families."

He turned his eyes to the stage again. "You mean leave it to that cowardly rhymester?"

"He's a proper *poet*, not just a ballad writer, and he's certainly not cowardly. The writings he puts on Weyurn's doors at night have done more to change things than any sword or arrow." Coïra had noted the jealousy in Loytan's voice, but it was quite unfounded. Loytan already had a wife of his own and Coïra regarded him more as a big brother and protector. She had so far not met anyone to whom she could give her heart and her innocence.

"What he writes brings only death to those that read and follow it," Loytan retorted promptly. "I can see the tufts of hair stuck in the blood. The poor wretches had their heads cut off for demanding freedom for the kingdom and for your mother."

"One more word from you, Loytansberg," threatened the Lohasbrander in front of them, "and you'll be the next candidate for the block. Enough of your stupid nonsense.

Keep your mouth shut or I'll make sure you never open it again." His comrades laughed.

Loytan snorted and grabbed his cup of wine, drowning his response in it.

The master of ceremonies continued, "So let the proceedings commence and let the insults fly. Sons and daughters of Rodario, let's hear what you're capable of."

A young woman was the first to take the stage. She'd stuck on a large mustache and goatee beard, and stepped to the front with an exaggeratedly masculine gait. Standing there, she stroked her artificial facial hair and tapped herself proudly on the codpiece. Her gestures took a rise out of all the men and the audience roared with laughter.

Abruptly she tore off the false beard. "Oh, trapping of man's vanity—away with you!" she cried. "I'm Ladenia and I'm a woman, as you can plainly see, but I'll be more of a man than the rest of you!" With an impudent grin on her face she walked along past the other Rodarios until she reached The Incomparable One. "They told me you wanted the title and had the best chance because you were so good-looking." She emphasized the word and fluttered her lashes, "Because you are so clever" (here she placed her hand at her own brow) "and because you sleep with most of the women in the town and they'll all be voting for you." She laughed. "But I can see more men than women in the audience: I was better than you!"

The crowd yelled out and laughed.

"You all know the joke about the orc asking the dwarf for directions, but I know one that's much funnier," Ladenia told them. "How many of these useless Rodarios does it take to lift up an orc?"

The Lohasbrander leaned forward expectantly, his left hand raised.

Coïra looked over to where the greenskins were standing. They'd stopped chewing and had drawn their weapons. There was a catastrophe about to happen. As soon as the Lohasbrander completed the signal he was giving they would come charging across the square and put a stop to the show. Just because of a single joke. Ladenia had no idea what she was doing.

"So, what do you think?" continued the woman on the stage. "What's the matter? Does nobody dare to say?"

Coïra was trying to think how she could distract the Lohasbranders without putting herself in danger. It would be difficult because the Dragon's men would be delighted to have an opportunity to arrest the daughter of the rightful sovereign.

She was opening her mouth to say something harmless, when Ladenia supplied the punch line. "I'll tell you then: five. Four to hold him fast and one to dig a hole, because otherwise you couldn't get the orc's feet off the ground. None of the weaklings would be able to take the weight."

Coïra saw the corner of the Lohasbrander's mouth twitch. He dropped his arm. It wasn't an insult that had to be punished. It wasn't even a good joke.

Ladenia realized this herself when a leaden silence fell over the audience. She hastily executed a few nifty dancing steps, circled round and then sang a song until the announcer came up and pushed her back.

"Ladies and gentlemen, we've seen that at least this female descendant of the great man can't hold out much hope of the title," he said, laughing at her performance. "She's shown us there's not much difference between singing and pain."

The man earned laughter for his cutting words and he invited the next contestant to step forward.

One after another they took the floor, launching viciously satirical attacks on their fellow contenders for the title of "Worthiest Successor of the Incredible Rodario," the most scurrilous contributions being greeted with uproarious applause; only three contestants attempted black humor or even wit, and they did not go down so well with the audience.

Coïra followed what was happening on stage, but kept her eye on the orcs and the Lohasbranders at the same time. She would have liked to be able to enjoy the performances, but the presence of the hated occupying forces spoiled any pleasure she might have taken. As long as she could remember, they had always been there in the background, the ones who served the Dragon.

She had never seen the Dragon itself, but she'd noted the fear in the faces of the oldest inhabitants of Weyurn when the subject of the winged monster came up. When it first appeared in Weyurn two hundred and fifty cycles ago, the Dragon had laid waste to the kingdom with his white fire and had forced the queen to leave her throne. Wey the Fifth had subjected herself to the Dragon's rule, not out of cowardice but in order to protect her people.

After that it had been the orcs, the Dragon's henchmen, who had come to keep watch on activities in the provinces on his behalf. Humans, too, had turned up, willing to serve the Scaly One. These humans gave rise to the present day Lohasbranders, Weyurn's nobility, devoid of decency or dignity.

Coïra knew that Lohasbrand was intent on taking over

the rest of Girdlegard, in order to fill its legendary hoard
in the Red Mountains with yet more treasures, but there
were too many rivals. Rumor had it that the four enemies
had agreed an armistice, but she didn't think this would be
long-lasting. Lohasbrand had extended his sphere of influence
until he came up against Lot-Ionan and the kordrion. He'd
be sure to make a further attempt soon. She reckoned that
was why the guards holding her mother had seemed particularly nervous recently.

Coïra craned her neck to watch the guy calling himself
The Incomparable: A good-looking man of about twenty
cycles, and the spitting image of the original Rodario, judging
from pictures. "He ought to win," she told Loytan. "He's got
style."

"And absolutely no chance of success," he cut in. "Don't
you hear what the plebs are calling for? They want mockery
and spite, not clever words and convoluted sentences where
you can never tell where the meaning is going."

Coïra leaned forward in her seat to have a closer look at
the actor of her choice. "Where's he from?"

Loytan consulted one of the flyers that had been handed
out. "Here we are, *Rodario the Incomparable*. He's from the
next-door kingdom of Tabaîn. He apparently runs a theater
there and appears in Gauragar and Idoslane on tour." He
looked at the man. "Good figure of a man. For an actor."

That was exactly what Coïra was thinking. In her imagination he was taking on the persona of the unknown poet
who held the occupying forces up to ridicule and scorn and
was encouraging the people of Mifurdania to rebel against
the Dragon and the Lohasbranders, reminding them there
had been a time when their nation had not been oppressed

and forced to pay tribute in this way. And he gave them hope for a future in which they would again be free of fear.

He represented a danger to the Lohasbranders and the orcs. He was held to be responsible for at least thirteen killings. It was not just a sharp tongue he wielded.

The Incomparable One from Tabaîn exactly fitted her idea of the unknown poet, on whose head a price was set—a price large enough to keep a hundred Weyurn citizens in comfort until the end of their days; be that as it may, no one had tried to denounce him to the Dragon yet.

Now it was the turn of Rodario the Seventh to win over the crowd with his ready wit. But the very way he moved when he stepped to the front of the stage was enough to tell the audience this was going to be embarrassing. Horribly embarrassing.

"Oy, lad," someone called out. "Hope you've rehearsed a bit this time, or we'll have you back in the tar barrel and cover you with sawdust!"

"Or dunk you in the privy," came a second voice. "Then at least you'll be the champion when it comes to stinking."

The people laughed and the hecklers were applauded. The white-clad master of ceremonies called for quiet. "Let him make a fool of himself without being interrupted, ladies and gentlemen," he said with a smirk. "At least he has shown us every cycle so far that he's really good at that." He pointed at the Seventh Rodario with his cane. "We're waiting!"

Coïra hoped for his sake for some distraction to prevent him starting his performance. A lightning strike, a snowstorm, even maybe a house catching fire. She looked at Loytan, who grinned and stood up in order to hear better and see over the Lohasbrander's helmet.

"Behold the handsome Uncompared . . ." he started with a quivering voice, and the audience in the front row were chortling already.

"Excuse me, but the name is *The Incomparable*," corrected the man himself. His interruption was friendly but assured. "Start again."

The Seventh Rodario cleared his throat but sounded more like a woman than a man when he spoke. "Behold the handsome Incomparable," he said, addressing his rival, who gave him a friendly wave and made a winding-up gesture to indicate he should speed up. However, The Seventh suddenly lost all the color from his cheeks. "But like that it won't rhyme with the next line," he said, horrified. He scratched his beard feverishly. "What shall I do?"

The audience were in stitches.

Coïra sighed and pitied his senseless courage. He'd be leaving the competition in humiliation and disgrace—and next cycle he'd be on stage again.

Rodario the Seventh went red. The laughter brought him to his senses and he clenched his fists. "There he stands, all long and tall," he shouted above the noise of the throng. "But he'll be feeling ever so small. When he sees my act. And that's a fact." He gave a hurried bow to the audience and stepped back to join the other contestants.

Loytan looked at Coïra and laughed. "Was that it? That can't have been the whole performance?"

"I think maybe it was." She looked at her hero, The Incomparable One, who was grinning to himself. He was enjoying his victory quietly, not making a triumph out of it. This endeared him to her even more. She was surprised to find her heart beating wildly when she looked at him.

People started chucking rotten vegetables and snowballs at Rodario the Seventh. He put up with it just like he endured the catcalls and abuse.

The Incomparable stepped forward unexpectedly and raised his arms. "Stop that!" he ordered the crowd. "He doesn't deserve to be treated like that. He may not be a word-acrobat and he may not be the best-looking, but he's still a descendant of the great man himself. Same as me."

"Are you sure of that?" yelled a woman.

The Incomparable had made her out straightaway and pointed. "Who are you to poke fun at him?" he rebuked her. He no longer had a genial air about him. "You can't even read or write, can you?"

"It's enough if I can see and hear this idiot!" she countered. Her response was greeted with renewed laughter.

Rodario looked at his defender, who was just about to make a barbed retort. "Let it go," he said, smiling sadly. "She's right, after all." He brushed the rotten lettuce leaves from his shoulders onto the floor, and shook the bits of ice out of his hair. "I'm as bad at this as ever."

"Stand tall, you're a descendant of the Incredible Rodario!" said The Incomparable. In a dramatic gesture he whirled around, swinging his wide mantle effectively—and as he did so some papers fell out onto the ground.

Most came to rest on the stage, but a couple were caught by a gust of wind and wafted out of reach before the actor could grab them.

The same gust blew one of the papers over the heads and outstretched fingers of the excited mob toward the tribune, where it fell directly into Coïra's hands.

The first line alone, in its extravagant handwriting, was

enough for the young woman to know that her wishes had become reality. The text began: "Citizens of Mifurdania, stand up to the evil that comes from the mountains!"

An armored gauntlet grabbed at the paper; the Lohasbrander had snatched it out of her grasp. "Read it out," he told his comrade, passing him the leaflet. "I want to know what else The Incomparable has prepared in the way of speechifying."

Coïra looked at Loytan, who understood immediately that what was written on the paper was not harmless scribble.

It seemed even the second Lohasbrander wasn't able to decipher the words.

"Perhaps I can help?" Coïra offered her services in a flash of inspiration.

The leader of the Lohasbrander turned to his companion, retrieved the paper and handed it back to the young woman. "What does it say?"

Coïra pretended to be reading out the text, inventing some trivial speech sufficiently poor for the Lohasbrander not to want to hear it again from the actor's mouth.

Hardly had she finished speaking when the Lohasbrander turned back toward the stage. "Load of rubbish," he said. "No better than La . . . what's her name, that girl, earlier. Stupid competition."

Coïra looked at The Incomparable Rodario, took the paper and folded it carefully. The actor made a deep bow. He didn't know exactly what she had done, but as the armored men had not leaped on to the stage to arrest him and cut off his head, he assumed she had lied to save his skin.

"Ladies and gentlemen, that was the first part of our entertainment," announced the master of ceremonies. "A ballot of rotten vegetables and snowballs has decided that Rodario the Seventh will not be taking part in any further competitions. He has withdrawn with dignity. That's good news for Ladenia, the mistress of Un-wit." The audience laughed again. The man in white jumped down from the dais and walked over to the Seventh Rodario to congratulate him on withdrawing from the contest. He took out a dried flower from under his coat and handed it to him. "Here, for you, a stink-rose."

"He'll have a whole bouquet of those at home!" joked one of the audience. "He can put them in . . ."

"Am I the master of ceremonies or is it you, Big Mouth? That's enough now!" The announcer cut the heckler short, waving his cane. "Tomorrow we have performances in the *New Curiosum* and you can get your tickets at the stall on the square." He bowed and was applauded for the way he had run the contest. He thanked the audience with a series of theatrical bows.

Rodario the Seventh stood next to the steps looking rather lost with his dried flower. Studying it sadly, he failed to see members of the audience moving bad-temperedly out of the way to make room for a troop of orcs moving over through the market square. Twenty of them surrounded the stage, and four climbed up.

Anyone acquainted with the history of the orcs in Girdlegard would have been surprised to see these particular specimens. The difference in their appearance, it was said, came from the fact that they were from the western part of the Outer Lands and had always been followers of Lohasbrand.

Their height was impressive, and though the ugly shape and greenish-black skin characteristic of orcs showed no change, they certainly didn't stink the way others did. They looked after their weapons better than in the past and didn't go about the place yelling and grunting. They were clever and behaved sensibly—all of which made these Dragon-serving monsters much more dangerous.

They clanked and stomped their way over the boards and their captain positioned himself face to face with The Incomparable One. Coïra was horrified to see that he was holding one of the papers in his hand.

"Damnation," Loytan cursed under his breath. "Your trick nearly worked, Princess." He placed one hand on the pommel of his sword and with the other took her by the elbow. "Time for us to leave."

Coïra was about to object. "I . . ."

"You told lies for the man," he whispered to her. "What do you think the Lohasbrander will do to you when he realizes? The Dragon has been waiting for an opportunity like this!"

She turned pale and got up cautiously from her seat. Loytan did likewise and followed her to cover her back.

The leader of the Lohasbranders had got up and was looking at the stage. "What's that, Pashbar?"

The orc held up the paper in his fist. "A scurrilous leaflet in this man's writing; this criminal who calls himself the Poet of Freedom." He pulled out his shining jagged-edged sword and placed the blade at The Incomparable One's throat. "It came from him. Everyone saw it."

"What?" The Lohasbrander looked over his shoulder for Coïra but saw she had left. "So that's it!" He drew his sword from its scabbard. "Arrest the actor and throw him in prison. And find the queen's daughter! She tried to protect him!"

"But . . ." The comrade on his right was unsure. "She's a maga, they say, just like her mother, and I . . ."

"I don't care what she is," he shouted furiously. "Find her! And if you can't catch her, then kill her. The fact that she's run off is proof enough of her guilt. She and that criminal are in cahoots." He ran down the steps of the tribune and rushed through the throng with his companions.

The Incomparable Rodario did not dare to move. The sharp blade was too close to his throat, so he had to allow himself to be taken captive. The orcs tied his arms behind his back while their captain stared at him intently.

"So it was you ambushing and killing our soldiers," growled Pashbar, baring his fearful teeth. "I shall ask Wielgar to let me eat you alive, so I can hear you scream at each bite."

The Incomparable One wasn't intimidated. He smiled and allowed the orcs to lead him away.

It had grown eerily quiet in the market square.

As The Incomparable One passed Rodario the Seventh he turned his head and said, "Stand tall, my friend. That's what's important, whatever you do. Never forget that. Next competition you'll make the grade." Pashbar gave him a shove and he moved on.

Nobody could remember a cycle when two contestants pulled out of the competition within minutes of each other.

And certainly not under circumstances such as these.

II

Girdlegard,
Protectorate of Northwest Idoslane,
Winter, 6491st Solar Cycle

The squad of black ponies was well known in Idoslane's northwest province and their one hundred and fifty riders were known even better: *The Desirers*. These armored and helmeted dwarves were associated only with loss and pain in the minds of the inhabitants. The residents of Hangtower, the small town the band was heading for, were no exception.

The name of the unit had no romantic connotations. It had purely practical origins: Whatever they desired, they had to have; no ifs, no buts.

The watchtower bell sounded the alarm and Enslin Rotha, the burgomaster, hurried over accompanied by the town's leading citizens to receive the dwarf-squad at the main gate. News of their approach had interrupted Rotha's siesta, so he had hurriedly flung a mantle of rough sheep's wool over his disordered clothing. He was not concerned with appearances.

"They're too early," he murmured, waiting for his fellow councilors to join him before the gate was opened up.

He signaled for the wagon with the tribute to be brought over and positioned himself in front of it. That way the dwarves would be assured at first glance that their tribute was going to be paid, but he could discourage them from actually entering the town.

In spite of the chill, Rotha was starting to sweat. Recent winters had been colder than ever. He saw it as a sign of how badly things were going for the peoples of Girdlegard, although, as the protectorate of the thirdling dwarves, Hangtower had got away comparatively lightly. The regions in Gauragar where the älfar held sway or where they had delegated authority to power-hungry despots were in a more parlous position, it was said. Rotha had no reason to doubt the truth of such rumors. In all probability the details of cruel treatment were spot on.

One of the councilors, Tilda Cooperstone, a long-standing close friend, joined him. She was as tall as he was, with blond hair peeking out from under her cap; her green eyes were full of concern. As were his own. "They're much too early," she nodded over to him, pulling the belt of her white bearskin coat tight and putting the collar up.

"My thoughts exactly," replied Rotha, wiping his brow. It was fear, fear pure and simple, that was making him sweat. It was a wonder the perspiration wasn't turning to drops of ice.

Cooperstone's face grew more worried still. "We haven't done anything wrong, have we?"

Rotha shook his head. "No. All the time I've been burgo-master we've complied with the thirdlings' demands. To the letter." He raised his arm and the gate was pushed open. A cold wind blew in, finding any gaps in their clothing and making them all shiver.

When the gate was fully open they could see the squadron of thirdlings less than one hundred paces off. And this time they were accompanied.

"The älfar!" Cooperstone exclaimed. The black armor of

the three tall riders contrasted sharply with the white of the falling snow. Each time a night-mare hoof hit the ground, sparks flew, making the whiteness fizz and disappear.

The älf on the left held a lance bearing a pennant showing a strange rune. The sight of the blood-red symbol fluttering in the wind chilled Cooperstone to the core, though she could not have said why. Terror made not flesh, but fabric.

"Did you think the alarm was sounded for fun?" Rotha bit his lip. The tension was making him behave unfairly toward her. "Forgive . . ."

She smiled at him. It was a wavering smile. "You are forgiven, Burgomaster." Cooperstone watched the rest of the councilors take up position behind them. "I saw my last älf about . . ." she did calculations in her head ". . . fourteen cycles ago. When they introduced the new squadron commander."

"I wouldn't mind if it were something like that," grumbled Rotha, trying to identify the thirdling riding at the front. "But I don't think that's the reason. Their leader is still Hargorin Deathbringer." The faces of the älfar told him nothing; they were handsome, perfect, narrow, beardless—and cruel. Like all their kind.

The eye sockets seemed empty. That was the distinguishing feature when comparing them with their friendly relations, the elves. In daylight the whites of the eyes turned black as night. They couldn't conceal that.

He lifted his head and looked at the gate-watchmen. "None of you is to raise a weapon against the älfar," he called. "Or against the dwarves, either, whatever they do to me or the other councilors."

The soldiers saluted.

Cooperstone, still looking shocked, studied the burgo-master's face. "You think they want to harm *us*?"

"They'd be the first älfar ever to bring us anything good," he responded. The more the sweat dripped off his forehead or ran down under his clothing, the drier his mouth became. "Let them take us to task for whatever they think we've done wrong, as long as they spare the citizens."

"Very high-minded. But many think we should be fighting for the cause of freedom," the councilor said quietly, because the leader of the band was close now.

"Stop that. I've heard enough!" Rotha stared at her. "You know my views. We would have no chance at all against a hundred and fifty, and even if we did—what then?" He sighed and bowed his head to the rulers of East Idoslane. "They'd send out the next lot and Hangtower would never survive. Freedom isn't worth it. Those who won't serve should get out or commit suicide and not force their ideas of heroic death on others."

Cooperstone gritted her teeth and bowed to the thirdlings and the älfar, who had brought their night-mare mounts to a halt four paces away; in this position she could no longer see what was happening.

Leather creaked, harnesses clinked, the ponies snorted. Sometimes you could hear the rattle of chain mail under the warriors' black furs.

But neither the älfar nor Hargorin addressed the councilors. And until they did so, the latter were not allowed to raise their heads.

Rotha and Cooperstone heard someone dismount, landing heavily. There was the sound of crunching snow and then regular footsteps approached, announced by the rhythmic clink of metal.

The burgomaster saw iron-tipped boots the right size for a thirdling. And, anyway, everyone said the älfar made no noise when they walked and left no footprints. One of their many scary tricks. He was sweating even more heavily now; the silence was wearing him down and grating on his nerves more harshly than any yells or accusations.

A weapon was drawn slowly, then something swished through the air. To the right next to him there came a grinding sound followed by a gasp.

There was another swipe and blood poured down onto the fresh white snow. The head of Councilor Cooperstone rolled between his feet and Rotha cried out in horror. At the same moment the decapitated body of the woman crashed full length to the ground.

He could hold back no longer, he *had* to look up.

Hargorin Deathbringer, a dwarf of impressive stature, had thrown back his mantle to take better aim. In his right hand he held a long-handled hatchet whose blade was covered in blood. His chain-mail tunic with its metal discs was splashed now with red, and the tattooed visage and black-streaked tawny beard had blood spatters, too.

The reddish-brown eyebrows joined in a scowl as the dwarf noticed Rotha. "Who said you could raise your eyes?" he barked.

The burgomaster opened his mouth to speak, but words failed him. He saw that the saddles of the night-mares were empty. There were no footprints around where these brutal-ized former unicorns were standing. So it was true what they said! Meanwhile, the pennant with the cruel but fascinatingly beautiful runes flapped from the pole attached to the saddle.

"Let him off, Hargorin," said a soft voice next to his left

ear, and Rotha jumped. The breath that had wafted past his nose had smelled of nothing, nothing at all. "A weak human! Loss and fear have robbed him of his senses and are making him stupid."

Rotha was about to turn but his legs would not obey him. The älf had moved behind him soundlessly and the gods alone knew where the other two had got to.

Hargorin wiped his hatchet clean on the dead woman's clothes. "If you insist, Tirîgon," he said, crossing his arms. "He'll want to know why I took the councilor's life. You tell him. It was on your orders."

"She was guilty," the voice whispered into Rotha's ear. It sounded like it was a different speaker this time. "Cooperstone was in league with a condemned murderess and revolutionary. Stupidly, she was related to her as well. Foolish indeed!"

"A fairly far-flung family relationship, though," said one of the älfar, and this time Rotha thought it must be the third of them, speaking on his left side. "Did you not know, perhaps, wretched human?" Rotha croaked out a No and stared at Cooperstone's head. One eyelid hung down and the dead woman's final gaze seemed to be intended for him. He carefully covered it with snow. He couldn't bear the sight of his murdered friend.

Hargorin gruffly told the assembled Hangtower notables that they could lift their heads. "I see the tribute is ready. Good. We expect nothing less of Hangtower." He put the hatchet back in its holder on his back and then gave a sign; five dwarves dismounted and came to join him as he approached the wagon. They inspected the chests and sacks filled with coins and gold bars.

Rotha finally managed to stop himself shaking and turned

around. The älfar were standing in the gateway, talking. He saw they were two males and a female, but could not begin to guess their ages. If they had been humans, he'd have said not more than seventeen cycles, but they were certainly more mature than that.

What struck him was the similarity of their faces. The burgomaster assumed they were siblings. The female älf was robbed of any feminine attributes by her armor; your attention was drawn to her fascinatingly graceful, balanced features. Any male opponent would immediately be distracted by the sight of her—and would meet his death at her hands.

The älfar carried long slender swords on their backs. Rotha noted the solid parrying staves that stuck out, right and left; double-bladed daggers were fastened on their thighs. Their armor had a metal reinforcing band running the length of the spine. One of the men had a store of metal discs the size of the palm of a hand just above the buttocks; the woman had the same, attached to her upper arms. Perhaps for throwing?

The female älf came away from the group and approached him with a disarming smile that seemed reassuring—until he saw the black eye sockets. Any admiration for her beauty turned to fear.

"Firûsha is my name," she introduced herself in melodious tones. Rotha bowed to her again, as if she were a queen. If you thought about it, that's just what she was, for him. She decided who should live and who should die. She decided whether the town should perish or thrive. "There is a task. It is not aimed at Hangtower and its citizens but, all the same, if anyone should stand in our way, be he courageous or simply foolhardy, then the town will not survive to see the morrow." Firûsha's voice had remained friendly. "We wish to be taken to the family of the woman councilor, as quickly as possible. You will take us there, weak man."

Rotha gulped and choked. His throat was more constricted than the eye of a needle. "What—"

"No, burgomaster. Not *what*," she interrupted him kindly, and placed her gloved forefinger on his lips. "*Where*. Take us there. Hargorin and his soldiers will carry the tribute away now." She brushed the cap from off his head and stroked his brown hair. "You only need to be afraid if you don't follow my instructions."

Hargorin had swung himself up onto the driving seat and was driving the wagon out through the gate. One of the älfar mouthed something and the thirdling nodded. He left the town, the escort squadron stand surrounding him, and the dwarves moved slowly off.

The three night-mares stood snorting outside the gate, their red eyes fixed on the sentries. Now and then they would run their tongues across their muzzles, displaying vicious incisors.

The men drew back. No one wanted to risk being bitten or even torn to pieces. There were terrible stories about these älfar mounts. It was said they ate humans alive if they took the fancy. And that was one of the relatively harmless fates reported.

Meanwhile Rotha strode ahead, acting as guide for the älfar triplets. All the time he was thinking of how he could perhaps help the councilor's family without getting anyone into trouble. It was a decent family: A big one.

"She has three daughters and two sons," said Firûsha, as if she had read his thoughts. "Her mother lives with them. And her half-sister; that's right, isn't it?"

Distressed, Rotha nodded. There were no secrets. The only thing he could do was to stretch out the walk through the alleyways. He prayed to Palandiell that the news of the three merciless murderers would get round quickly enough for the family to have escaped.

"We won't let ourselves be taken for a ride, burgomaster," one of the älfar said, laying a sword blade on Rotha's shoulder. "Try it and we'll be coming knocking at your own door."

"No," stammered Rotha. "No, not that! I swear we'll reach the house any time now." Tears ran down his cheeks as he rounded the corner and pointed to the large house to which he was bringing death in threefold form. What else could he have done?

The älfar walked silently past him and he leaned against the wall, his legs unable to support him. Firûsha went first and her brothers followed her. One by one they pulled out their daggers and made for the entrance.

The älf woman knocked on the door, while one of the brothers disappeared up a side alley to reach the back of the house and the second launched himself upwards to land on the sill, vaulting on to reach the balcony, from where he made it onto the roof to enter the house via the chimney. At the same time, Firûsha kicked the door open.

Enslin Rotha sobbed when he heard the screams. He put his hands over his eyes. He couldn't bear to look.

Yet those awful screams of the dying, echoing round the narrow lanes, burned their way into his brain, forever reproaching him.

Hargorin guided the wagon away from the town; the Black Squadron surrounded their leader and the valuable tribute.

For today's orbit their destination was not far from Hangtower. They were due to go to Morningvale, a village in thirdling thrall. Hargorin had been granted possession by the älfar because of his loyalty and he had been grateful to receive it.

Here stood one of his strongholds, Vraccas-Spite.

It had taken fifty cycles to build it exactly to his specifications. It had no equal anywhere among the dwarf realms—or rather, in what remained now of the dwarf realms—for the strength and thickness of its walls. The älfar had been very impressed and surprised by his fortress, but he had explained to them that collecting the tribute tax wakened covetousness in others and the treasure had to be protected. There was no arguing with that.

When the squad turned east, rounding a small wood, the stronghold came into sight. At its highest point it was over thirty paces high, proudly displaying to travelers precisely who ruled this tract of land. And anyone who knew about dwarf-runes would be able to see that the incumbent hated all dwarves apart from the thirdling folk. From afar, the inscription on the castle wall promised all other dwarves death and destruction. Elsewhere the chiseled devices contained general vilifications. To the ignorant they might look like decoration, but any child of the Smith happening on these runes would be incensed and would attack immediately. Hargorin grinned in satisfaction as he admired his home.

Smoke billowed up from the chimneys of the houses and the shacks surrounding Vraccas-Spite. The human residents of Morningvale had sought the shelter and warmth of their own dwellings. He left them in peace. There was no urgent need for them to be doing the forced labor they owed him. He was distracted by the sound of cloth tearing on the cart behind him. He had heard it clearly even over the noise of the ponies' hooves.

Hargorin turned his head and looked at the sack that had torn because of the weight of its contents. He couldn't afford to lose a single coin. He would have to make good anything missing from the tribute and that went against the grain.

He was even more surprised to see a crossbow bolt sticking out of the sack.

"Keep going straight ahead into the wood," a woman's voice ordered.

Hargorin was certainly not going to do that. Instead, without warning, he hurled himself to the right. A whizzing brought a dull blow to his left shoulder. He only felt the pain a moment or two later.

The dwarf cowered down to get protection from the side of the wagon, but the horses, terrified by his swift movement and the sound of the arrow, whinnied wildly and bolted, leaving the reins trailing in the snow. They galloped up against the ponies in front of them, veering round to overtake them, the wagon swaying uncontrollably. Then they changed direction and headed for the trees, exactly the course the woman had demanded.

The thirdlings riding alongside watched in alarm and spurred their mounts to keep up with the runaway horses. The bloody shaft jutting out from Hargorin's back showed them that it was no accident that had sent him reeling from the driving seat.

"Rebels!" he shouted, pulling himself along the side of the

cart. "At least one of them." Despite the pain, he swung himself onto the open part of the cart, landing on a chest. He drew his long-handled hatchet and plunged its cutting edge into the sack where he thought the woman was hiding.

In the meantime two dwarves were trying to get their ponies in front of the horses so that they could grab their reins, but the petrified animals were going too fast. One by one the members of the Black Squadron fell back, leaving the speeding cart still heading toward the wood. Hargorin was on his own.

The hatchet blade had met something hard and there was a dull moan. The sack fell forward and, surrounded by fragments of wood and silver coins, a young woman tumbled to the floor. The dwarf presumed the rebels had put the wood in the sacks to create a space for the archer woman.

Hargorin recognized her immediately. "Mallenia," he snorted with satisfaction. "So the Black-Eyes were right to be suspicious of Hangtower. You *were* there." He took another swipe at her but she ducked to one side. The blade sank into the wood immediately next to her.

Mallenia, descendant of the famous hero Prince Mallen of Idoslane, aimed a kick at the thirdling and hit him in the chest. "The orbit will come when I will kill the älfar just like I'm going to kill you today, Hargorin!" she called out. "Freedom for Idoslane, Gauragar and Urgon!"

The dwarf fell back onto another sack, the crossbow bolt burying itself deeper into his flesh and emerging the other side, making a bump in the chain-mail shirt. He could feel that something had been severed in the shoulder joint; groaning, he let his arm hang down.

"The thirdlings and the älfar will be shown no mercy,"

she threatened passionately. "You've inflicted too much suffering on us all."

The chest Hargorin had been standing on opened up and a masked figure stepped out in a shower of coins. Holding a saber in one hand, he placed its blade at the thirdling's throat. "Stay where you are!" he commanded.

"You coward!" spat Hargorin. "At least have the courage to show your face like this murdering bitch."

"Fighting oppression and killing occupying forces puts us in the right, dwarf-scum!" muttered Mallenia. "It's you who are the murderers!"

Suddenly she spotted the Black Squadron galloping after them through the snow; they had not given up their pursuit by a long chalk. No thirdlings willingly resign themselves to failure, and this elite unit of the Desirers would be the last to think of doing so. In contrast to most other dwarf folk, they were excellent riders who had been perfecting their art for more than a hundred cycles. Because the other children of the Smith preferred not to use ponies, the thirdlings had the upper hand on the battlefield. This had been proved painfully time and again to the humans and dwarves who opposed them.

"We don't have much time left," she said to her companion and opened another of the chests to release another masked figure. The lock had jammed, preventing him from freeing himself from his hiding place.

The horses rushed along the narrow woodland path, clouds of snow rising in their wake. They had hardly reached the shelter of the trees before seven tree trunks came crashing down onto the path behind them to prevent pursuit. Anyone wishing to give chase would have to slash their way through dense undergrowth. This had all been prepared in advance and worked a treat.

The man got out of the wooden chest and went straight to the driving seat, fishing up the loose reins and taking control of the horses while the other man continued to hold his weapon at Hargorin's throat.

Mallenia clambered over to the thirdling and sat on the sack next to him. Her eyes scanned the wrinkled face of her captive; then she pulled a blanket over her shoulders. She was wearing only thin clothing instead of protective armor—a considerable risk, given her mission, but that could not be avoided. Otherwise she would not have been able to hide in the sack. Her long blond hair was gathered in a braid. Black knee-high laced boots each had long-handled daggers strapped to them, and she held a small crossbow, which she aimed at Hargorin.

"And now what?" asked the thirdling with contempt.

"Now we'll take the tribute somewhere safe to distribute to Idoslane's citizens at a later date. It belongs to them, after all. And not to you or your overlords," she retorted heatedly. "You're nothing but an occupying force here! You deserve death. You've no right to a single coin!"

It seemed Hargorin wanted to say something, but then thought better of it. He looked at the man with the saber, then dropped his voice. "Whatever you do, think first of your own family," he whispered to her suddenly.

A shudder of fear went through Mallenia. His words had not sounded icy or arrogant, but like an honest warning. Probably a thirdling trick to intimidate and confuse her. She laughed out loud to show she did not believe him.

He frowned. "So when you were inside that sack you won't have seen Councilor Cooperstone die?"

She shook her head, her fingers gripping the crossbow.

"I had to kill her on the orders of the älfar, and she won't be the only victim in your family. The älfar are out looking for them."

"The *älfar*?"

"And not just any älfar. The Dsôn Aklán came to Hangtower to wipe them out. Three siblings: Threefold viciousness and threefold cruelty." Hargorin's brown eyes were staring intently at her. "I'm not allowed to say, but they're out to kill anybody connected with Prince Mallen's line. It doesn't matter how far they have to travel to do it or where they have to go. But they claim it's *your* deeds, *your* insurgency, that is the cause for this persecution and slaughter. They want you to lose your support base among the people of Idoslane, Urgon and Gauragar. Your mission will fail and the land'll never be free. Not as long as the älfar are around."

Horrified, Mallenia stared at Hargorin's face in front of her. In her hiding place she had been unable to hear anything when her relative was killed other than dull murmurs, and she had likewise seen nothing through the slits in the sacking. She gulped. "I don't believe you," she said waveringly and aimed a kick at the shoulder where her crossbow bolt had struck him. "You thirdlings are all liars!"

Hargorin gritted his teeth to bite back a moan, then cursed out loud. "To Tion with you, you bitch! Don't believe me, then! I don't care."

"Watch him," she told the man with the saber while she went up to the front. "How far is it now?"

"We'll be out of the woods soon. Our people are waiting over there," he explained, pointing to the light area ahead that marked the way out of the dark trees; figures could be seen moving around.

"Excellent," she murmured, clapping him on the shoulder. But she was not able to enjoy her triumph over the Desirers, for Hargorin's words to her had fallen on fertile ground. Mallenia did not know what to do. Ride back to her family? Or go on ahead with the men?

The wagon soon left the shelter of the wood and the driver brought it to a halt near a group of two dozen riders.

They cheered Mallenia and started to unload the treasure. The Desirers would have to follow twenty-four different trails to retrieve the coins and gold bars. They would have no chance at all on their short-legged ponies, in spite of their riding prowess.

The tall woman was handed her padded armor with its engraved coat of arms of the family of Prince Mallen of Ido. As she put it on, her thoughts were on the heroic deeds of her ancestor, who had taken arms against Nôd'onn and the eoîl, risking his life more than once for the sake of Girdlegard. He had been a true and high-minded champion of justice, and she would continue his work until their people were free of the älfar and their cronies. She attached her short swords to her weapons belt, threw a hooded cloak around her shoulders and mounted her white steed.

Mallenia rode next to the cart on which the thirdling was being guarded. There was a pool of blood by his shoulder wound, dripping through the boards onto the snow.

"What shall we do with him?" the guard asked.

She considered the dwarf at length. "Kill him. Anyone who works with the älfar deserves to die," she said after careful thought. Then she spurred her horse to take her back to Hangtower. She wanted to help her family and prayed to the gods she might arrive in time. "We'll meet in four orbits' time in the usual place," she called, and disappeared behind a clump of trees at the edge of the forest.

The tribute money had been distributed and most of the messengers had left. Four of them were stowing the last of the sacks behind their saddles when the sound of approaching troops alerted them. The Black Squadron were coming up fast.

"Run for it!" the man guarding Hargorin shouted to his colleagues. "I'll take one of these horses . . ." But he was suddenly kicked and sent flying back against the lid of the box. As he fell, he drew his saber, swiping it from right to left in an attempt to slit the dwarf's throat, but the blade met resistance . . .

The dwarf had fended off the blade with his hand! Blood was gushing out of the cut and running down his beard, but Hargorin's eyes sparkled and he had a malicious grin on his face. He kicked the box and turned it over. Then, while his adversary was trying to regain his balance, he jumped up and punched the man in the face with his bloodied fist. The latter groaned and fell into the open chest, the lid banging shut on top of him.

"Ha!" The dwarf grabbed his long-handled hatchet, ran across the wagon and took a leap that landed him directly onto one of the four messengers. The hatchet blade struck the man's neck and his body fell into the snow, letting Hargorin take his place in the saddle. Without a moment's hesitation he turned the horse toward the next opponent and hit out with his weapon.

The man could not parry the powerful blow, and his sword

arm was severed between wrist and elbow. The heavy blade edge carried on its trajectory; fatally injured in the back of the neck, the dying man fell to the ground, spattering blood from the wound as if trying to write his own name in the snow.

The last two men made off but Hargorin took aim and hurled his ax after them with a wild shout. The weapon hummed through the air and split the spine of the messenger on the right. He fell at full gallop without a sound, somersaulting over and over.

"You shan't escape," the dwarf promised his last opponent and raced his pony after the man.

When he reached where the dead man lay with the hatchet in his back, Hargorin leaned down and picked up the weapon. Laughing, he tapped his horse's flank with the flat end of the hatchet; the horse surged forward.

Hargorin soon overtook the messenger, who was zigzagging his mount in an attempt to shake the pursuer off, but to no avail. The terrified man even tried cutting the ropes securing the money sacks, one by one, to lose weight and gain speed, but it was no use. After a skillful piece of deception and a nifty feint to the right, Hargorin came level with the man and landed a blow powerful enough to slice through reins, armor and clothing. With a scream the last of the messengers fell out of the saddle backwards and crashed onto the snow-covered earth.

The thirdling brought his mount to a halt and turned. He saw that the Black Squadron was approaching, some through the forest and others skirting the woods to the right and left. His injured shoulder was throbbing badly and his hand was hurting, but it did not matter as long as he could still move the fingers. The bones and tendons were untouched.

Hargorin let his snorting horse trot up to the man he'd just unseated, who was swaying on his feet, arms raised in surrender.

"What is that supposed to mean?" the dwarf exclaimed angrily. "You won't fight for your life?"

"I want to do a deal," he groaned.

"Is that so? What are you offering?"

"Spare my life and I'll tell you where our secret rendezvous is," he coughed, dropping his hand to press it against the wound in his belly.

"You'll betray your leader, the heroine of Idoslane, to save a life to be spent in shame and disgrace?" laughed Hargorin. "What makes your life worth so much more than hers?"

The man moaned and struggled. It was not an easy decision. "But I have a family," he mumbled in distress. "Four children and a wife—they all depend on me. I can't leave them on their own. Not in these times." He sank onto one knee as the dwarf came up closer to him. "Please spare my life and let me return to them!"

Hargorin looked down from his saddle and saw the honest concern and despair displayed on the man's face. "What is your name?"

"Tilman Berbusch," he answered.

"And is it a long journey back to where you live?"

He shook his head. "No. I should be able to get there in spite of the injury. I'm from Hillview." Tilman tried to catch his breath, but his injuries made it difficult. "The secret places are in . . ."

Hargorin lifted his hatchet and split the man's skull before he could finish his sentence. There was a crack, and blood poured out of the cut and out of his mouth and nose. When the thirdling pulled the blade out again, the lifeless corpse fell back.

"I shall look after your family, Tilman Berbusch from Hillview," Hargorin promised, all malice gone from his voice. He steered his horse round the body, back to the wagon and the Black Squadron. "Vraccas, forgive me. You alone know why I do this," he whispered, before rejoining his troop.

This orbit had cost him dear and his fortune would be plundered for it. The älfar always insisted on full payment, so he would have to make up the losses from his own coffers.

Hargorin raised his brown gaze westwards, where a dark cloud of smoke drifted up to the sky.

The Dsôn Aklán were finishing off their work in Hangtower, it seemed.

Mallenia took a look behind her and recognized a unit of the Black Squadron coming round the edge of the wood. She was far enough away from the dwarves. The Desirers no longer presented a danger.

But when she looked ahead, her heart sank. A huge cloud of smoke was billowing up from Hangtower; a sight that made deadly sense in light of those words of Hargorin Deathbringer.

She spurred her horse on to greater speed still, taking it back off open ground to the road to gain time.

The town gates stood wide open and several bodies—which, as she slowed her horse, she saw to be those of the sentries—lay out in the snow. A raging fire was crackling and hissing, a hubbub of voices reached her ears, and the horse snorted in fear.

The guards had been killed with precise stab wounds. The

decapitated body of a woman lay in the middle of the path. Mallenia could see it was Tilda Cooperstone. Her eyes filled with tears and she was overwhelmed with hatred and apprehension, prompting her to make her way hurriedly to her relative's house. Although she already knew she was too late.

The streets were filled with people shouting and lamenting, clutching their possessions; some were carrying their children while others were gathering what was most necessary or valuable, loading it onto horses, donkeys or oxen, and heading out of town.

Fire was out of control in the part of town where Cooperstone's house had stood. The building was in the middle of the inferno.

Mallenia stopped, while a stream of fleeing townspeople swept past her, some blindly bumping into her horse, which danced nervously on the spot. No one was fighting the flames—perhaps they had tried but been forced to give up the attempt. Without a miracle the whole of Hangtower would be razed to the ground.

Her thoughts were racing. She had not known Tilda well but had liked her open and generous spirit. They could not have met more than ten or so times altogether and Tilda would have had no inkling of the plan to steal the tribute. And she had been killed before the älfar could have known anything at all about the robbery. It was her ancestry alone that had sealed Tilda's fate.

The punishment that had been meted out to Tilda and Hangtower was unjustifiable. Totally unjustifiable.

Mallenia did not have any illusions that the älfar cared about justice. They were out to destroy all descendants of the house of Mallen and that was all. In that, at least, Hargorin had spoken the truth.

Somebody grabbed her right foot and the stirrup.

"It's you, Mallenia," said a man whose face she did not recognize at first under the soot and burn marks. His woolen coat and boots had been destroyed by the flames, as if he had been walking through the fire itself.

"Enslin?" she was about to dismount, but he stopped her with a gesture.

"Run! The Dsôn Aklán are still here," he cried, fear in his voice. "They're searching for you." He pulled at the horse's harness, turning the animal round to face the open gates. "You have to stay alive, Mallenia. Get away, keep up the resistance and never give up, do you hear? I was a fool not to support you all."

"I . . ." She ran her eyes over the picture of the fleeing masses, about to lose all they had in the world, everything they had built up over previous cycles. Her struggle seemed pointless to her now if it dragged innocent victims down with it.

Rotha patted her leg, his badly burned hand leaving a damp mark on her boot, and she thought she could feel the heat his body exuded. "The älfar and the thirdlings are the true enemies of our people, not you," he urged her to understand. "You are the only hope left to us. If you die, all is lost." He gave the stallion a slap on the rump and the horse lunged forward. However hard she tried to rein it in, Mallenia could not slow it down. The confusion and noise in the alleyways, the screaming, the smell of smoke and the crackling of the fire had overwhelmed the animal's senses.

Mallenia left Hangtower feeling more vulnerable and cast-down than ever, in spite of the success of the mission and her victory over the Desirers. Even the triumph she had scored over their leader. It was all fading fast.

III

The Outer Lands,
The Black Abyss,
Fortress Evildam,
Winter, 6491st Solar Cycle

Boïndil sat in the lamplight with a broad grin on his face, watching his friend stuffing himself with food. "So they didn't give you anything proper to eat on the other side?" he joked. "No one does rock-barley and gugul mince like Goda. Am I right, Scholar?"

They had withdrawn from the noisy company and were sitting in Boïndil's personal chambers. The walls were hung with weaponry and shields and one side of the room was covered with various maps of Girdlegard. The table they were sitting at had a detailed plan of the fortress displayed under a sheet of glass. The room spoke of attention to detail, strategy and combat readiness, such as befitted a general.

Tungdil had taken off his tionium armor and was wearing a dark beige garment decorated with runes and symbols; his brown beard was still trimmed short, as always, but now it was thicker and showed a distinctly silvery streak on the right side. His long brown hair was dressed close to the scalp with oil and hung down loose at the back. He stopped chewing. "You keep staring at me."

"Can you blame me?" laughed Ireheart, reaching for his tankard of beer. "I haven't seen you for two hundred and fifty cycles!"

"And now you want to know everything in a single evening by dint of staring yet more wrinkles into my face?" Tungdil countered with a smile. He took his own tankard to drink to Ireheart's health, then noticed what was in it. "Is that *water?*" he said in disgust, pushing the mug away. "Is there no brandy here for a warrior? Are all your soldiers drunkards, then? And why didn't they give me black beer like you?"

Boïndil put his drink down in surprise. "Last time we met you were being more careful with alcohol."

"More careful?" Tungdil looked confused, then his brow cleared. "Ah, I know what you mean." He took a long draft from his friend's tankard, not replacing it on the table until the last drop had been drained. He slammed it down on the table, wiped the foam from his lips and gave a resounding belch. "That's better." He grinned broadly.

Boïndil observed his friend, winked and broke into laughter. "That's the way! While we're at it, tell me: What do you think of my daughters and sons? Goda introduced you just now."

"The spitting image of their father. And that's meant as praise," Tungdil replied with a laugh. "No, seriously: You can be proud of them. I'm sorry I can't remember what they're all called, but one of each seems to have inherited their mother's magical gift. That's quite something! And the two sturdily built boys will be fine warriors. I saw them using a combat style that's a mixture of ubariu and dwarf fighting techniques. That makes them unique!"

He had the air of being uncomfortably affected as he continued. "Forgive me mentioning it, but the three others are not true to type . . . quite different . . ."

Ireheart was affronted. "What do you mean?"

Tungdil seemed to search for the right words. "I'm sorry to say so, but they're all . . ." and he frowned, ". . . they're *all* better craftsmen than you! Their stonework is excellent." Then he exploded with a mischievous gale of laughter.

Boïndil joined in, mightily relieved. "Yes, have your little jokes, go ahead." He looked happily at his friend. "I can't tell you how glad I am that you are back with us. I nearly didn't believe it was really you. You looked . . . so somber and dark, standing there in your armor at the head of the monsters' army. As if you were . . . one of them." He waited tensely to see how his friend would take that.

Tungdil looked down and touched his golden eye patch with his left hand. "A lot has happened, Ireheart," he answered, his voice deep, and altered now. The mirth had disappeared and shadows returned to his countenance. "Much has happened to me, and it has changed me." He regarded his one-time fighting companion. "I must ask you to make allowances for everything you may find strange in my behavior. You will have your doubts . . ."

"Me?" Boïndil laughed outright and called to one of the soldiers to bring a jug of beer. After a moment's thought he changed the command: He asked for a small barrel of beer and a bottle of the best brandy. The dwarves have a saying: Memories and worries need beer. "How could I . . ."

"You *will* doubt me, Ireheart," Tungdil whispered mysteriously. "And I *was* at the head of that army you saw me with."

Boïndil did not know what to say, so he just stared back at his companion.

Tungdil took a deep breath as if the memories were causing him physical pain.

They waited in silence until the door opened and the drink was served to them. Wordlessly, they each drained their next tankard, then Tungdil forced himself to speak.

"I have done deeds, Ireheart, that no one would believe. No one who knew the Tungdil I once was. But to survive in the places I have been, searching for a way out of the demonic world, I had to do these things." His voice was hoarse and he was staring straight through Boïndil, through to another world. "There are creatures, my friend, which can inflict the most terrible tortures on their victims. To get them subject to my will I had to be even worse." He touched the runes on his tunic. "Believe me, I *was* worse than them." He reached for the bottle.

Boïndil looked his friend over; he appeared strange, very strange. "Do you want to tell me about it?" he said finally, pouring himself a brandy. "Or . . ."

Tungdil shook his head. "In good time. I have lived too long in the darkness. Allow me to adjust to the light of your friendship." He cleared his throat. They drank a toast to each other. "So, what's new in Girdlegard?"

"Did you hear nothing on the other side?"

"No. There was no communication as long as the shield was in place." Tungdil started to drink more quickly now, and when he emptied the tankard he refilled it more generously each time. "You spoke of Lot-Ionan. Walking through the corridors here in the fortress I've picked up the odd snippet. Sounds worrying." He poured himself some more beer. "They spoke of a Dragon in the west, the kordrion in the north and the älfar taking over in the east. How much of this is true?"

"All of it, Scholar," sighed Boïndil. "Girdlegard is no longer a safe haven." He stood up and went over to a small table where more rolled-up maps lay. He selected one and spread it out in front of his friend. "Lot-Ionan has lost his reason. That's what they all say. He has overrun my homeland, the Blue Mountain Range, taking it from the secondlings. He's driven them out with his magic arts. Any refusing to leave were killed outright. He's collected famuli around himself and, if you ask me, he's preparing for war."

Tungdil stared at the lines on the map. "Against the kordrion?"

"No. Against the Dragon Lohasbrand, who has taken over in the Red Mountains, after driving out the firstlings. As far as we know there's only a handful of that tribe holding the pass in the west to fight off the monsters from outside." Boïndil pointed to Tabaîn and Weyurn. "They have to pay tribute to the Dragon. The Scaly One has found humans willing to be vassal-rulers under him. They call themselves Lohasbranders. They rule as if they are noblemen and have regiments of orcs doing their fighting." Boïndil pulled at his beard. "Yes, the pig-faces have got much smarter, or at least the ones the Dragon brought into Girdlegard. It doesn't make life any easier."

"By all that's infamous!" Tungdil exclaimed, thumping his fist down onto the table so violently that the bottle and tankards jumped.

Ireheart's eyes narrowed. "Infamous? How do you mean?"

Tungdil waved this aside. "Carry on," he said grimly.

"In the east the älfar have erected their towns again . . ."

"The *älfar* are *back*?"

Boïndil nodded. "But they're different ones. They came in through the High Pass after Lot-Ionan had banished the secondlings. They're led by an old acquaintance of ours: Aiphatòn. Do you remember him?"

"I do. And I'd never have thought he would imperil Girdlegard."

Ireheart nodded. "It took us all by surprise when he led the black-eyes back to their old haunts and waged war on the elves and the others who had helped the pointy-ears in the old days. Well, you can't really call it waging war. There were only about forty of the pointy-ears left at that stage."

"The Elves were wiped out . . . ?"

"No. *Most* of them were slaughtered, but the rest disappeared. Nobody knows where they went. There are various rumors about their end. I don't know all of the stories. But you won't see any elves in Girdlegard." Boïndil scratched his nose. "The thirdlings have made an alliance with Aiphatòn and they rule in the east over most of what used to be called Idoslane. The älfar hold sway in the former human kingdoms of Gauragar and Urgon in the north and east." He noticed that Tungdil's gaze seemed to go straight through the map. "Is this all too much for you?"

"Go on. I can take more pain than you think," his friend replied angrily.

"So it's just the north." Ireheart tapped the map. "Here, the Gray Range. Queen Balyndis . . . You know who she is?"

Tungdil nodded absently as though she were a matter of no concern to him.

Ireheart was surprised there was not more of a reaction to the name Balyndis, but he carried on with his report. "She holds the Stone Gate with her remaining fifthlings and takes arms against the kordrion and his brood. It's a long struggle, though, because the beast keeps reproducing. No one understands how that works, because there's only this one adult."

"Yes, well, that's something you wouldn't know: They don't need a female," Tungdil explained. "They can all lay eggs, so that makes them a real plague. On the other side, too. Unless you get them under your own control." He leaned back in his chair, his hands behind his head. His eye was focused on the ceiling. "It's incredible. I come home after two hundred and fifty cycles, exhausted from the constant battles I've had to fight. I'm desperate to find a quiet corner. But there's more turmoil here than there ever was on the other side of the magic shield." He kicked the underside of the table and this time the tankards and bottle toppled over. Boïndil tried to stop the spilled brandy affecting the lines drawn on the map. "So there's nobody in the whole of Girdlegard man enough? What about the long-uns? Does it have to be *me* again? Have I got to raise in anger the weapon I heartily wished to chuck into the depths of Weyurn's lakes?"

Ireheart gave an embarrassed little cough. "I forgot to mention that Weyurn isn't a land of lakes and islands anymore. When Lohasbrand came to Girdlegard he dug a massive passage and all the water escaped through the tunnels. The Dragon must have caused other leaks as well . . ."

With a wild roar Tungdil sprang up from his chair, grabbed hold of the corner of the heavy table and flung it, one-handed, across the room to hit a wall seven paces away. The solid wood broke as easily as if it had been rotten timber.

Boïndil watched his friend open-mouthed. No normal dwarf, however strong, would have been capable of that feat.

Tungdil gave a groan and put his head in his hands, sinking back down onto his seat and cursing in a language that

Boïndil did not understand. Runes on Tungdil's tunic started to glow softly.

The guards came rushing in at the clamor and turned to their general. He waved them back out. There would be talk.

"D'you see?" groaned Tungdil through his hands. "That's what I meant when I said there would be doubts. You're wondering how I managed to chuck a heavy table around like a sack of feathers."

"I suppose . . . you're right there, Scholar!" the dwarf agreed. You did it with *one* hand! That's quite something." He made an effort to appear jolly. "You wouldn't have been able to do that in the old days. That would have improved our chances with the pig-faces: Orc shot-put!"

Tungdil took his hands away from his face and looked at his friend. Round the golden eye patch thin black veins were disappearing into the skin. The word *älfar* came into Ireheart's head. "I can't explain," said Tungdil tiredly. "Not yet. I need you to trust me." He stretched out his hand. "Will you do that? I swear I will not abuse your trust and I shall not disappoint you; I swear it by all we have shared in the past!"

Boïndil took his hand after hesitating a moment. He assumed it would be the best way to help his one-time comrade-in-arms. If Tungdil could be sure he had a dwarf by his side whom he could trust he'd be certain to find his feet faster and soon be his old self again. *What happened to you?* "By all we have shared," he repeated the formula. "Ah, I'm sure Boëndal would be delighted to see you again."

"Boëndal?"

"My twin brother!" exclaimed Ireheart in surprise. First Balyndis, now Boëndal.

Tungdil hit himself on the forehead. "I'm sorry; my memory

is still swimming in the dark." He stood up, picking up the tankards that had survived their flight through the room. He filled them with black beer, handing one to Boïndil and keeping the other for himself. "When will I see him?"

"See who?" asked a baffled Ireheart.

"Boëndal, of course," he replied, happily. "Now that you mention him I can picture his face."

"Tungdil, my brother is long dead." Ireheart's lips narrowed. *What horrors have you gone through that you could have forgotten all that? How much has your mind suffered? Is it to do with that scar on your head?*

Tungdil stared at the floor. "Forgive me. It's . . ." He sighed.

"What about Sirka? Have you forgotten her as well?" Ireheart could see by the expression on his face that Tungdil had no idea who he was talking about. He took him by the shoulders. "Scholar, she was one of the undergroundlings! She was your great love! You mean to say you could forget something like that?" He stared in his friend's one eye, searching for an explanation, an excuse, an answer. The eyelid closed before the brown eye could divulge any secrets.

Tungdil turned his head away. "I am sorry," he repeated in a hoarse whisper. With a jerk he shook off his friend's hands and walked over toward the door. "We'll speak again in the morning, if that's all right. I need more time . . ." His boots crushed the fragments of the shattered table.

Ireheart got the impression that he was about to say more, but he opened the door and left without saying another word. "By Vraccas, what has happened to him?" he repeated under his breath, as he searched in the mess of splintered wood for the map of Girdlegard.

The map was useless, the brandy having destroyed the

painstaking work of the cartographer; names and contours were blurred and illegible.

Boïndil put his head on one side and looked at the heading: Girdlegard. The alcohol and the swelling of the paper had turned the word, with a bit of imagination, into Lostland.

"How true," he muttered, casting the map to the floor again. An opaque turquoise jewel caught his eye. He'd noticed it on his friend's belt buckle. It must have come off when he had pulled his table-throwing stunt.

Ireheart picked it up and started after Tungdil to hand it back. It was valuable. Gem cutting was not one of his strong points but he knew enough to be able to estimate the jewel's value. Smoke diamonds were extremely rare.

"I'm getting forgetful, too. I didn't tell him about the fourthlings. Or the freelings." Two more reasons to disturb his friend again before he went to sleep.

It all still seemed like a joke on the part of Vraccas that the realm of the fourthlings, smallest of the dwarves and presumably least well versed in the arts of fighting, should have managed to repel all invaders. The thirdlings had waged campaign after campaign against them but had been unsuccessful. The freelings had been able to resist conquest, too.

"He'll be surprised to hear that," he told himself as he pushed open the door to Tungdil's chamber after knocking several times. "Ho there, Scholar! I've got something of yours here. You've been throwing expensive diamonds around, did you know?"

Tungdil was standing with his back to the door and did not seem to have noticed him come in. He had removed his tunic, thus unintentionally giving Boïndil a full view of his bare back.

The skin was criss-crossed with scars.

Some were small puncture marks, others were long, reaching round to the front, narrow and broad, some of them jagged, some smooth, some caused by weapons, others made by teeth or claws. The scars had destroyed the tattooed runes and images.

Boïndil took a deep breath. His own body bore witness to sword fights and battles but what he saw here was uniquely terrible. He knew his friend to be a skilled fighter, so could not imagine what foe he must have faced to have these injuries. What would a warrior have to fear from combat with the kordrion?

Tungdil had still not noticed him. His head was bowed and he seemed to be staring down at his own chest. Then he threw a bloodied cloth into a bowl of water; he stifled a groan, and then a glow appeared before him.

Boïndil put the jewel soundlessly onto the chamber floor and withdrew swiftly from the scene.

He had disturbed his friend and witnessed something no one was intended to see. The dwarf left those quarters of the fortress and tried to combat the doubts in his mind by humming a tune. But he could not wave his qualms away, being particularly troubled by the appearance of those black veins around the missing eye. An insistent niggling suspicion made him want to lift that eye patch. What was it hiding?

Goda and Boïndil were sitting in the assembly room where the officers normally held their strategy meetings and discussed the guards' patrol rotas. A scale model of the Black Abyss and the fortress was displayed on the table; every detail was repeated here in miniature, enabling exact inspection routes to be specified.

"We shan't need that anymore." Ireheart touched the glass globe that had represented the barrier. He lifted it off and placed it aside. Then he carefully removed the model of the artifact as well. He stared at the rocks, deep in thought.

"You waiting for the kordrion to show up?" Goda teased him. "The model still matches reality in that respect: No sign of the monsters so far."

"I was wondering whether we can risk carrying out our old plan," he replied, running his hand over the edges of the Black Abyss. "We break off the edges here and fill it all up with low-grade iron and other metals. Then nothing else can get out to attack Girdlegard or the Outer Lands. A plug to keep in the evil." He glanced over to his wife. "What do you think? Would it be possible with your magic to get the abyss to cave in? But I know your famuli aren't ready yet to give the support you need."

Goda stroked Boïndil's back. "I might be able to do it, but it would take all the energy I have. I'd have no magic left. And the amount of molten metal we would need would be massive! Where would we get it all from?"

"The ubariu would supply it. They'd bring it from all the corners of their realm if it meant ridding themselves of the threat from the Black Abyss." Boïndil went over to the small table and poured out a cup of water for them both. "I'm afraid the monsters would dig through stone. They've waited more than two hundred and fifty cycles and they're confronting us with an army such as they had on the orbit when the barrier was first erected. Without the shield they would have overrun us."

Goda sat down. "You don't think your own fortress could withstand the hordes?"

"In the long run?" Boïndil shook his head. Tungdil's hints had sent shivers down his spine. "It doesn't bear thinking what will come crawling out of the abyss if we don't act soon. The kordrion would not be the worst of our worries."

"Who says the worst thing isn't already here among us?" she said in a low voice. She had not intended to speak the thought out loud, but her tongue was too quick. She looked down at the cup in her hand.

Ireheart had heard her words, of course. "You have suspicions about Tungdil?"

"I don't believe it's the *genuine* Tungdil we've welcomed here inside our walls," she responded firmly.

"It *is* him," Boïndil insisted resolutely, but he avoided her eyes.

"How do you know that? How can you be sure? Because you drank together yesterday?" Goda sighed. "I wish for your sake that it is our Tungdil and not an illusion sent by some dark power to trick us. But I think his behavior is so different . . ."

Boïndil gave a mirthless laugh. "He's spent many man-generations in a world devoid of anything except killing, pain and violence. Do you think he would come back to us with a broad grin on his face and cracking jokes all the time? *That* would have made me suspicious," he defended his friend. "If it had been me I'd probably have gone completely mad."

He looked at her. "Tungdil faced the kordrion all on his own! He did it for us!"

"It could have been agreed in advance," she objected.

"The beast lost an eye and its side was ripped open! It didn't look pleased!"

"But if there was a greater purpose? Like the conquest of Evildam? The kordrion has eyes enough to spare."

He snorted and waved his arms in the air. "Goda, you turn round everything I say with this . . . conspiracy phantom theory." Boïndil clucked his tongue, at a loss for words. "You are a maga. Why not cast one of your spells to check him out?" He stared at the model in fury and tried to organize his own thoughts. He was angry that Goda was, in effect, raking up his own doubts instead of calming his fears. And he had been so convinced about having his old friend back.

"I already did. When I introduced him to our children," she said, to his amazement. "And I . . ."

There was a knock at the door and a fully armored Tungdil appeared on the threshold. He saw at a glance they had been quarreling, however much they tried to hide the fact by their smiles.

"I'm too early, aren't I? Didn't we arrange to meet up?" he asked, entering the room. He took a seat on the other side of the table and looked at Goda, giving her a steely look, as though he had listened in to what she had been saying about him; then he turned to Ireheart, his voice warm. "Nice model," he said, praising the reproduction and winking. "Are there lots of little monsters in there, too?"

Boïndil laughed, relieved. "We've got a few pennants somewhere. But we'll have to find them first. Who'd have thought we'd be needing them so soon?" He gave his friend a quick run-through of the plan to seal up the ravine once and for all, so that nothing could ever escape again, large or small.

Goda kept out of the discussion and contented herself with observing Tungdil. She wanted to provoke him into betraying himself. In her view this was not the old celebrated hero but a piece of refined trickery, a clone of Tungdil. It was her responsibility to unmask the deception. But her steady gaze bounced back off him like a sword blade from a good suit of armor.

"The shafts and caves immediately below the abyss are deep and convoluted," Tungdil explained. "There's not enough metal in the whole of Girdlegard and the Outer Lands together to fill them up. But plugging the top of the ravine makes sense. That can't be attempted, however, until you've destroyed the army they've got lying in wait down there."

"The army you've led to us," Goda interrupted.

"I was its *leader*. It would have come to you anyway. *That's* different." Tungdil was remaining remarkably calm, Ireheart thought, remembering his violent reaction the night before. "I have spent cycle after cycle making a name for myself among the monsters of the abyss so that they would trust me and accept me as one of their own. That was the only way eventually to get to be their leader. A leader even the kordrion obeyed. For I knew full well the orbit would arrive when the barrier would fall and I wanted to be in the first ranks. As a thirdling, an ordinary child of the Smith, they would have torn me to shreds. And they nearly did at the beginning." With every phrase his words sounded darker and more threatening until he cleared his throat and removed the menace from his voice. "I let them believe I would lead them against you. It won't be long before they recover from their surprise and they'll be mounting another attack, more hate-filled than before."

"Evildam will be able to repel them," Ireheart said with all the conviction he could muster.

"It won't be enough, my friend. I know what's in store." Tungdil looked from Goda to Ireheart and back again. "You need an army, a huge army, able to swarm down into the upper chambers and tunnels, fighting the beasts in their lairs, while the preparations are in hand up here to fill in the ravine. And a magus. You'll need a powerful magus." He looked at Goda. "There's no other way."

She had noted the change in his tone. "So you're not going to help us?"

"What makes you assume that?" spluttered Boïndil. "Of course he will!"

"She's right," said Tungdil calmly, placing his gauntleted hands together as if in prayer, or as if he were keeping some tiny creature captive between his palms. "I've fought all my battles and have no further desire to be a warrior."

Ireheart's mouth dropped open. "You're joking, Scholar!" he exclaimed. "Don't take me for a fool! Don't joke about something like this! So many people have waited for you, putting all their hopes in you to drive injustice out of Girdlegard. Humans, elves—wherever they might be—and dwarves. Your own folk await you!"

"I know," Tungdil countered. "But I made no promises to anyone about returning to save them. I was able to thwart an initial attack on your fortress and have warned you about the extent of the threat you face. Now you know what you have to do. I shall do no more."

"It was a different story last night!" Ireheart was near despair. "You said yourself . . ."

". . . that I had returned home to find peace and quiet." Tungdil finished the phrase, resentment in his tone. "That was all. And I said I needed more time, to—"

"Which home did you mean, Tungdil Goldhand?" Goda intervened, ready with her next test. "Tell me: *Where* is your home? Back in the vaults of Lot-Ionan? That's long gone. Or do you long to return to the freelings in their underground realm, besieged by the thirdlings? Or do you want to go back to Balyndis, your first love? Or perhaps you feel like going to the undergroundlings to spend your twilight cycles?" She gestured toward the window. "Isn't it rather the case that you are at home in the land whose tunnels lead to the Black Abyss? By far the longest part of your life has been spent there. That fits the picture of a homeland best, don't you agree?" She stood up. "It would be all the same to me if you were just to disappear."

"Goda!" her husband bellowed, horrified, but she went on regardless.

"Perhaps you don't dare accept that you have doubts about him, Boïndil. But I am paying close attention to the doubts I have. What use to us is this Tungdil in his wonderful armor if he's not prepared to act?" she said aggressively. "By Vraccas, this can't be Tungdil!" Goda cast contemptuous looks at the one-eyed dwarf. "The Scholar would have done anything and everything in his power to put an end to the misery afflicting Girdlegard. If *those* had been your first words I would never have become suspicious." She leveled her index finger in his direction. "You are not Tungdil, so get back to the Black

Abyss where you came from before you undermine the morale of our troops. I'd rather have them thinking that you went away again in secret and that one orbit you will return a second time!"

She turned away, shaking Boïndil's hand off. Then she left the room.

Ireheart watched Tungdil, who appeared to be unmoved by the accusations. There were no protests, no objections. "Say something, Scholar!" he begged. "For the sake of our creator, the Divine Smith! Say something to dispute Goda's words—something to let me believe in you. To let us all believe in you! You have no idea what effect it will have on the remaining dwarves and humans if you withdraw in this way."

Tungdil got up, walked around the table and stood in front of his friend for three long moments, then placed his left hand on Boïndil's shoulder. Then he went out through the door to the corridor.

"That's not an answer!" Ireheart cried out angrily. "Come back here and give me an answer." He followed, rapidly catching up with Tungdil and grasping him by the shoulder, trying to force him to turn around. But he was not able to move the dwarf.

Boïndil felt his fingers tingling, and then a shock that knocked him off his feet, hurling him back against the wall. He fell to the stone floor with a groan.

Stars and sparks were dancing in front of his eyes, and he could make out his friend's face leaning over him in concern. "I'll fetch a healer," came the voice, distorted now. "You should not have done that, my hot-blooded friend. But never fear, you'll soon be fine again."

As that final sentence echoed in his ears, Boïndil lost consciousness.

Tungdil made his way to his chamber.

The upheaval caused by Boïndil's collapse had settled now. The healer who had been summoned assumed the commander of the fortress had suffered a simple fainting fit. Perhaps too much celebrating the night before.

Even if the odd person thought there was more to it than that, nobody saw any connection with Tungdil. Not openly, at least. And when he came round, Ireheart had not said anything that could throw suspicion on anyone in Evildam.

As he turned a corner, Tungdil came face to face with a dwarf-woman.

Judging from the slim young face she was not yet many cycles of age, though the skin was as tanned as that of a shepherd. She wore a beige tunic embroidered with thorn wreaths, the front only loosely fastened, showing the white shirt beneath decorated in a similar manner. Tungdil's gaze slid over the figure; he saw a shaved head and light blue eyes.

"You are Tungdil Goldhand?" she asked, unsure of herself.

"And you must be one of the undergroundlings," he said. "Taller than a dwarf-woman and smaller than a human."

She nodded and came a step closer. "I am Kiras." She lifted her face so that the light from the lamp illuminated it. "They say that I look very like a forebear of mine," she said, expectantly. Her eyes were fixed on Tungdil's eye. "I'm wearing a garment made to be like hers. For you."

Tungdil furrowed his brow. "What's that to me?"

"Can't you guess?" Kiras's hopeful expression changed. "I had been so looking forward to giving you a surprise. If you can't take *her* in your arms now you are back, I hoped I would be able to soothe your pain. I am one of Sirka's descendants." She gave him a radiant smile.

"That's all I need," muttered Tungdil bad-temperedly. "I don't want to hurt your feelings or to insult your bloodline, Kiras, but I can't remember her. I don't remember what she looked like and I don't remember loving her. Much of what I experienced in Girdlegard in the past has been wiped from my mind." He looked at her intently, as if the sight of her could bring back his memories. "No," he said finally. "No, I still can't see her even if I look at you."

Kiras gulped, her huge disappointment obvious. "Then let me still bid you welcome in her name, Tungdil," she said, moving to embrace him. "It doesn't matter whether you remember or not. I am her message to you. The love you shared . . ."

But the warrior drew back, evading her arms as if she carried a fatal contagion.

"No, Kiras, don't," he commanded darkly, his voice dimming the light in the corridor. "I don't want you to touch me."

The young undergroundling stood facing him, bewildered and shocked. She let her arms drop to her sides. "You are rejecting not only me, but Sirka herself in me!"

"Forget me. And pray to your god that you carry more of her in you. My inheritance is death." He stared at her, then walked round her to his rooms as if she were a piece of furniture in his way.

"But . . . I have a letter she wrote to you!" She reached to take a sealed parchment from her belt, holding it in an outstretched hand.

"Then burn it, or do whatever you like," he suggested, without turning round.

Kiras looked at him as he walked along the corridor. "This can't be happening," she whispered in disbelief. Slowly she lowered the hand holding the ancient letter. The lamps regained their former brilliance as he moved away into the distance.

"Didn't I warn you?" Goda had witnessed the incident from the shadows, the meeting between the undergroundling and the hero of the dwarves having been no coincidence. It was but one of many tests that would follow.

"How can he leave me like that?" Kiras asked angrily.

Goda watched the dwarf go, then put an arm around the undergroundling's shoulders to console her. *Because it is not the real Tungdil. Everyone will see that soon.*

Tungdil returned to his rooms, pulled off his gauntlets and placed them on a wooden chest. When he went to unfasten his armor, one of the runes, the one on his right breast, started to glow in warning.

"There's probably a very good reason why you didn't announce yourself when I came in," he said, facing forward. "You could make up for that mistake now. Because if you don't," and Tungdil laid his right hand on the grip of Bloodthirster, "I might assume you have come here with unfriendly intentions." He did not turn around, but just listened to the sounds and trusted in his armor.

There was a person standing behind him, likewise in armor. Metal clanked and a weapon was being drawn. "You are correct in your assumption," said the deep sonorous voice of an ubari. "But only if you refuse me answers to my questions."

This time Tungdil turned and looked at the warrior sitting next to the desk, waiting.

It was the ubariu's leader, who had escorted him, Boïndil and Goda back to the fortress from the artifact. Now he stood three paces from him, extra-long sword with its reinforced tip held diagonally in front of his body, the blade pointing down. His red eyes were focused on Tungdil attentively. He was nearly twice the height of the dwarf and the muscles in his upper arms were rippling with tension.

"What questions might an ubari have to put to me, Yagur?" Tungdil asked simply. "Or have you been told to put them under someone else's orders. *Her* orders, perhaps?"

Yagur did not respond to the insinuation. "I know the legends about you and the general, Tungdil Goldhand. Nothing is further from my mind than to insult you with a lack of respect on my part," he began carefully. "But I am not the only one who has doubts about you."

"And you thought if you hid in my room and threatened me with a sword that I'd be happy to tell you anything you wanted to know?" observed the dwarf, his one brown eye flashing with malice. "You're due a surprise there, Yagur." Slowly he lessened his grip on the weapon at his side. "What will you do if I stay silent? Try to bribe me? Beg me to talk?"

The ubari warrior lowered his head and took a step forward. "I can loosen tongues," he threatened.

"Believe me when I tell you that you won't get a chance to interrogate me against my will." Tungdil nodded toward the door. "Go and tell Goda whatever you like. I don't care if you lie to her. I won't tell on you." He opened the fastening on his weapons belt and laid it aside. Bloodthirster came to rest beside the gauntlets.

Yagur approached him. "If that's the way you want it," he said bitterly. His broad hand stretched out, pointing the sword at the dwarf's throat. "Don't try to resist. I'll take you somewhere we can talk without being disturbed."

"I don't think so." Tungdil did not move back, but allowed the ubari to clutch him by the collar. He suddenly placed his right hand on the warrior's hand, holding it fast. With his other hand he aimed a blow at the attacker's forearm. There was a crunching sound as the elbow fractured and the arm was ripped off. Blood poured out of the ugly stump.

Before Yagur could recover from the shock, Tungdil had dropped the limb, drawn the ubari's own dagger and plunged it into his neck. The huge fighter could do no more than utter a rattle, collapsing onto the flagstones and letting his sword fall.

"You'll have to speak more clearly, Yagur. I can't understand what you're saying." Tungdil stared pitilessly at the dying creature.

The door burst open and three more masked and heavily armed ubariu forced their way into the chamber.

The dwarf drew his head down into his shoulders, a cruel smile playing around his mouth. Thin black veins appeared from nowhere, radiating out from the eye patch and covering his whole face as if with a spider's web. "Let me guess: You are here to ask me questions," he said with malice. Two runes on his armor started to glow, throwing their golden light onto the attackers. "Let's hear them. But beware of my answers!"

The ubari stopped where they stood—then the alarm sounded. The trumpets gave the dreaded warning that signified the approach of monsters storming out of the Black Abyss to finish what the first wave had not achieved.

Tungdil straightened his shoulders, boundless arrogance in his expression. "You have a choice: Do you wish to die here in my chamber or out there on the battlefield?"

IV

Girdlegard,
Former Queendom of Weyurn,
Mifurdania,
Winter, 6491st Solar Cycle

Coïra scuttled from one shadow to the next. She chose the town's narrowest alleyways to avoid the orcs. The creatures never dared go down these lanes because they could only walk single file between the houses, so it was the perfect place to ambush hated enemies!

The guards seemed to have given up searching for her, convinced she must be back in her palace on the island known as Lakepride, but the Lohasbranders had got their heavily armed orcs to patrol the streets to intimidate the townspeople and bring home to them how powerful the Dragon was.

The situation in Mifurdania was extremely tense. The competition to select the most worthy person to follow in the footsteps of that fabulous actor of past renown, Rodario the Incredible, had attracted a large number of spectators, so the town was filled to bursting with visitors. And a popular freedom-fighter had been arrested after a number of the detested occupying forces had been killed. Even now calls were being made to the populace in leaflets issued from his very prison cell, encouraging them to resist and promising better times to come. A dangerous state of affairs.

There was talk in the taverns. It was said that liberation

was on its way. But none of the townsfolk spreading the news in low voices over beer and wine had any idea that Coïra was keen for rumor to turn into reality. The people's hero must not be allowed to die.

The young woman knew that freeing Rodario the Incomparable from his cell was not a purely selfless act on her part. At last she would have an opportunity to speak to the man she admired so much, not just for his poetry and courage, but also for his dazzling good looks, wit and charm. Thus her heart was beating faster than usual for several reasons. Apprehension about the coming attack on the prison was only one.

Coïra approached the eastern gate's high tower where the Dragon had ordered anyone infringing his laws to be incarcerated.

The number of prisoners had grown in recent cycles, so the tower had been extended upwards. This had led to the nickname *Reed Tower*, because the slender edifice would sway from side to side in a strong wind, losing the occasional stone from the battlements, which could come crashing down through the tiles of neighboring roofs below. If they put you in one of the top levels your life was more or less forfeit.

Coïra took a deep breath and looked up. Probably they would have put The Incomparable in one of the highest cells. She would have to fight her way up and make sure that no one was able to raise the alarm, or that would mean disaster for herself, too. Her magic arts would help in some measure, but she only ever had sufficient power for a few spells before she had to return to the source near the palace to renew her energy store. This made a maga like herself vulnerable.

"They should come up with an energy source you could

carry around with you," she said to herself, scurrying over to the tower's entrance.

Listening at the sturdy door she could hear nothing. She tried peering through the window grille but could only see a curtain. There was a light in the guardroom. That was all she could ascertain.

Coïra felt her blood pounding in her ears. So much was unknown and she had to confront it all. *How many orcs are sitting there?* she wondered. On normal orbits there would only be half a dozen guards, but now? Given the state of the town, perhaps three times that number.

She drew her sword from underneath her mantle, gathered her magic powers and prepared herself for a spell that would send the guards to sleep. She had tried it on humans often enough, but could not gauge how the green-skinned warders would react.

Pulling her shawl over mouth and nose, Coïra pressed down the door-catch and leaped into the room. "Don't move . . ." she cried, then fell silent.

The room was—empty.

Seven tankards stood on the table, all of them full. You could see the remains of a meal: Chewed chicken bones, crumbs and odd bits of vegetables were strewn on a large platter.

Coïra closed the door and crossed the room carefully. Perhaps the warders had gone up to bring the prisoners their food?

Her tortoiseshell eyes caught sight of a board next to the stairs with a row of hooks intended for bunches of keys, all of them empty.

More and more peculiar. The longer she stood there trying

to figure things out, the stronger her conviction became that someone had got there before her.

She ran up the steps to the first floor, weapon and spells at the ready.

Arriving at the first-floor landing she saw the cell doors hanging open. Did the Poet of Freedom have friends brave enough to free him despite the overwhelming numbers? She smiled at the thought. She continued running further up the stairs, finding cell after cell open and empty. Her disappointment at not being the one to liberate The Incomparable only lasted a second. What mattered was that he was free.

She hastened down the stairway again—and found herself face to face with Rodario the Seventh.

He was just as shocked as she was and even gave a little yelp of fright. His dagger clattered to the floor.

"What are you doing here?" asked the young woman.

Rodario looked bewildered and picked up his weapon, wiping it on his cloak and holding it ineffectually, then putting it away with an embarrassed air. She saw at once that he had no idea how to use it. "Probably the same as you," he stammered, seeing the sword she was carrying. He pushed the hair out of his eyes. "I'm here to free The Incomparable."

Coïra laughed. "All by yourself?"

The man frowned, looking hurt. "Of course. I wouldn't want to endanger anyone else." He glanced past her over to the steps. "Where is he?"

"We've both arrived too late. He's already free." She found it so touching that this skinny figure of a man, with no physical prowess, a contender fresh from humiliating defeat on stage, had turned out intent on fighting off the orc guards to free a rival, the favorite. This Rodario possessed none of the The Incomparable's charisma.

Rodario smiled all over his face. "Oh, thanks be to Samusin! All the better!" He seemed truly relieved. "Then the two of us can get away from here together, then." He watched her and obviously he liked what he saw. That was *all* she needed!

Suddenly they heard deep voices outside, the clank of armor and the stomp of heavy boots. It must be a guard unit back from patrol.

"There's only one exit to the tower," she whispered to Rodario, extinguishing the lamps. "Quick, hide!" He was about to run up the stairs to the first floor, but she grabbed his sleeve. "No, don't head for the cells. It'd be making things far too easy for the guards." She pushed him into a dark corner by the weapons stand, following him into the little niche, pressing herself against the wall where the shadows helped to conceal them. Maybe the guards would rush straight past.

The door burst open and an orc entered the room. Hardly three steps in, he was already bellowing out orders and pulling his sword out of its scabbard.

Eight of his soldiers stormed up the stairs with him, while four stayed down in the guardroom to secure the entrance. They lit the lamps.

Coïra knew a fight could not be avoided. And it would have to be won quickly before the other orcs came back down.

"I'll be needing you, Rodario the Seventh," she whispered in his ear. He was utterly transported as her breath played on his face.

"Anything you ask," he said eagerly. Unfortunately, not very quietly.

"Over there!" called one of the orcs excitedly. "In that corner!" He drew his sword; the other three followed suit and moved in to the attack.

"Didn't you do well?" Coïra said sarcastically under her breath as she prepared to use magic against the guards. Four yellow spheres the size of marbles flashed out of her left hand to hit the four attackers. As the spheres burst, the orcs' heads were enveloped in sparkling glitter.

Two of the creatures simply collapsed, but the others showed no effects.

"It's Coïra Weytana!" one of them yelled up the stairs. "The daughter of the maga is down here! Quick! Come and help us!"

"Go on, do it again!" said Rodario, brandishing his dagger. "Send them to their deaths!" He dashed up willy-nilly to the nearest orc and stabbed away.

Coïra was supremely conscious that The Seventh was neither good-looking nor articulate nor a trained fighter. His hurtling attack was so obvious that even a blind man would have seen it coming and could have taken action to avoid the blade. For a warrior, the clumsy assault did not constitute a challenge, merely an annoyance.

Accordingly the orc counterattacked with contempt. It reached for one of the tankards, stepped nimbly aside and walloped Rodario on the back of the skull as he stumbled through into thin air.

Groaning and losing his balance, the man tipped forward and spread his length on the table. The remaining tankards scattered, crashing to the floor, beer foaming in all directions . . .

Coïra drove her sword at the orc nearest her. He parried

at the last moment as the blade came close to his throat. Grunting, he pushed the sword away, launching a thrust of his own.

The young woman held her sword against his, but the strength behind his thrust nearly forced her to open her fingers. Her hand and forearm went numb. She would have to try a different sort of defense, even though she had wanted to avoid this.

She let off a lethal spell. Crackling red lightning bolts sizzled out of her eyes to hit the orc in the face. His skin boiled and blistered, his eyes melted and vaporized to tiny spots the size of a pea, and he plunged screaming to the ground.

The orc who had felled Rodario threw his knife at the maga. She used her skills to hold the whirling blade suspended in the air. A thought and a short formula were all it took, and the metal glowed red hot.

Coïra sent the glowing ball back to the thrower, who was unable to duck out of its way; it tracked his movements! The molten steel slapped against his neck and burrowed its way through the skin. The orc tried to wipe it away in his panic, burning his fingers to the bone. Intense pain made him pass out and fall to the floor.

Loud commands rang out and boots came clomping down the stairs.

Coïra ran to the table and grabbed the befuddled actor by the collar, pulling him upright. "Come on, you sorriest of all the sorry ones," she shouted, slapping his face to bring him round.

Rodario rolled his eyes and grinned at her vaguely. "Well done there, Princess."

"Yeah, can't say the same for you!" she ran to the door. "Out of here!" she ordered. "Or do you want to stay and fight the greenskins in further glorious battles?"

"But I don't know which way to go," he whimpered, holding a dagger in each hand. Two orcs came bounding down the stairs and stopped on the threshold.

Coïra sighed. She had suspected this would happen. "Come with me then. I'll keep you safe, even though it should really be the other way round. *You're* the man, after all."

"I know," he called glumly, making for the door. "The hero is supposed to rescue the princess, not vice versa."

"Right! Remember that for next time," she replied, running through the narrow lanes back to the place in the wall where she could slip through and where Loytan was waiting for her. With *two* horses. One had been intended for The Incomparable, but now Coïra found herself shepherding The Incomparable's pale imitation through Mifurdania. "This is simply not fair, gods," she murmured, turning her head to look at the actor.

He kept stumbling over his robe, then dropped his dagger and got down on hands and knees to look for it among the rubbish. Coïra had to pull him along.

They ran along in the shadow of the city walls without being pursued. The orcs were expecting her to be heading for the gates.

All of a sudden a form appeared out of one of the alleyways, holding a lantern in his left hand and obviously waiting for them.

Coïra recognized The Incomparable!

She ran up. He had a bloodied graze on his face and his right eye was swollen shut—evidence of orc and Lohasbrander attention. He held out his hand, first to the breathless man, then to the young woman. "I wanted to thank you both for what you were trying to do for me," he said quickly. "I shan't forget it."

"Come with us," responded Coïra, hoping he could not hear how loud her heart was beating. He had not let go of her hand. "We've got horses for you . . ."

The Incomparable shook his head. "I can't leave Mifurdania. There are so many people to whom my words may yet give hope. Now more than ever." He made as if to kiss her hand. "And I've still got to win my title." He nodded to Rodario and it seemed to Coïra that they were exchanging silent messages. "Take my friend with you. He's in more danger than I am. There's nobody in the town that would give him shelter and his face is very well known."

Rodario the Seventh gave an unhappy smile and played with the seam of his left sleeve.

Another wave of disappointment swamped Coïra, but she promised, "I will," conscious of her desire never to let The Incomparable go. Instead she must drag this idiot along with her while her dazzling champion stayed behind doing heroic deeds. Without her. *So unfair, gods!*

She bent forward and breathed a kiss onto The Incomparable's cheek, then went off, taking Rodario with her.

"What a man!" said the actor delightedly. "What wouldn't I give to be like him?"

"And what wouldn't I give if you were?" she added quietly, blushing. She was ashamed of herself for the mean remark, but Rodario didn't appear to have heard.

They reached the secret door in the town wall, an ancient

one from the days of the old Mifurdania, whence spies could have been dispatched during a siege to find out the enemy's plans. Few people knew of its existence but Coïra had been shown it by Loytan. The Lohasbranders did not know about it. And who would want to show it to them?

Coïra looked for the mechanism, while Rodario kept a lookout for any orcs.

"Oy! You down there!" The shout from above caught her by surprise and then an armored night-watchman leaned over the parapet to get a better look. "What are you up to?" He ran along till he came to the next set of steps, coming down with his pike raised, pointing down toward them, ready to stab.

Coïra took a step back and lifted her left arm to hold off the man with one of her sleep spells, but she had used up all her store of magic. A slight tingle and fluttering flames appeared on the ends of her fingers, but not enough to be effective. Harmless. A waste of effort.

The night-watchman cursed and put his bugle to his lips.

Then Rodario acted with, for him, great presence of mind. He hurled his second dagger upwards with great strength—but had omitted to take it out of its sheath first!

With a dull thud it collided with the warder's forehead. He gave a groan and disappeared behind the parapet; then they heard his body fall.

"I've lost my last knife!" complained Rodario. "Damn. It was expensive! It was made of . . ."

"Quiet!" Coïra pressed the opening mechanism and part of the wall could now be rolled to one side. "I'll buy you another one, but now, shift!" She hustled him out. "Even a blind chicken can find a grain of corn, they say."

"But I'm . . . not a chicken!" Rodario started to stammer.

Loytan was waiting on the other side and looked baffled when he recognized the actor. "You know you've got the wrong one, don't you, Princess?" he said to her accusingly, feeling duty-bound to point out her mistake.

Coïra sighed and swung herself up into the saddle. "Spare me," she hissed, watching how the actor managed to catch his foot in his robe while trying to get it into the stirrup. The horses moved quickly on and he was still hopping along next to them. "Not a word! I'll explain on the way," she added, seeing Loytan opening his mouth again.

At last The Seventh was in the saddle. "Right, we can escape now. I'm ready," he announced.

"I know who I want to escape from," she mouthed to Loytan, letting her mount gallop off.

The two men followed. "Where are we going?" called Rodario.

"To the palace," answered Coïra, looking back at the lights she had noticed. Riders with torches were on their trail and she could hear bloodhounds baying. The Lohasbranders were not going to let her get away so easily.

All the more reason to reach the source at Lakepride to stock up on energy.

Otherwise . . .

Girdlegard,
Protectorate of South Gauragar,
Winter, 6491st Solar Cycle

Hindrek steered the sledge piled high with logs toward the house in the snow-bound forest clearing.

He had prepared this store of timber a few cycles ago and now the time had come to bring the logs home ready to split them into firewood. The family's woodpile was running out. There had been barely enough to light the kitchen fire that morning.

Hindrek stopped the horses at the barn and called his sons to help with the unloading.

The door opened and two boys came running out, aged eleven and fourteen cycles. Like their father they were wearing coats and hats made of an odd mixture of patched furs ranging from rabbit to squirrel. It did not matter as long as they kept you warm. Their mother waved from the window, holding up a freshly skinned rabbit. It was to be their midday meal.

Hindrek stood on the back of the sledge handing the wood down to Cobert, the elder of the two boys. "So who caught the rabbit?"

"Me," said Ortram proudly. "It was in my trap."

"He always knows the places the smallest creatures go," laughed Cobert, grinning. "But I'm better with the bow, of course."

"But you haven't caught anything for ages," said his brother, sticking his tongue out. "I'm far better than you!"

"Yes, of course, we'd have starved to death without you, wouldn't we?" laughed Hindrek, passing him a large chunk of wood. "Go and chop this lot up. Do something for those muscles of yours, or you'll never be able to pull the bowstring back like your brother."

Now it was Cobert's turn to stick his tongue out. He went over to the block where the ax lay, his little brother following at his heels.

Hindrek watched them go, then raised his hand in greeting to his wife Qelda, who blew a kiss from the kitchen window. The man watched his two boys unload the sledge, squabbling about which of them was better at doing the heavy work.

Hindrek enjoyed his life as a forester, though he would have preferred not to be in the service of Duke Pawald, a vassal of the älfar. But they left him in peace as long as he carried out his tasks properly. He could only hope that his sons would one day live in freedom, unlike himself.

The wind turned and blew from the north, bringing wonderful music to their ears. Its tones moved them instantly, lifting the hairs on their arms and on the back of their necks.

The song was a sequence of meaningless syllables but the clarity of the woman's voice and the emotion with which she sang had them all entranced, rooting them to the spot and forcing them to stare into the forest from whence the sound came. But the melody grew ever fainter until finally silence returned.

Ortram turned to his father in ecstasy. "What was that?"

Hindrek shivered, filled with yearning, a longing to experience more of what he had just been granted. "I cannot tell. Perhaps a traveler passing the time on her journey by singing to herself."

Cobert threw his ax down onto the snow, heading straight for the trees. "I want to see what she looks like if she sings like that," he called, running off.

"Stay where you are!" his father ordered, leaping down from the sledge. "There's work to do." But he understood his son all too well. "Wait!" he called, pursuing his elder son as he disappeared among the trees. It was good that he had an excuse now to follow the song without having to face his wife's disapproval. "Ortram, you stay here. I'm going to get your brother."

He could see Cobert's patchwork coat flitting between the tree trunks in the distance. As if possessed, the boy forged onwards, drawing his father ever deeper into the forest after him. Soon the woodsman was perspiring under his heavy coat.

The shadows were darker here and it seemed the sun was becoming fainter the further he got from home. Hindrek grew uneasy.

"Cobert!" he called. "Don't go any further!" The father stopped, leaning on a Palandiell pine to get his breath back. "Something's not right. It must be the spirits of the forest playing tricks on us. Can't you hear me?" He listened hard.

There were those tones again.

All his cautiousness melted at the sound of that glass-clear singing voice. He knew only the desire to see the face of the singer. To admire her and hear her song. She must sing for him alone. No one else must have this pleasure!

Raging jealousy flamed up in his heart and, without realizing it, he pulled out his hunting knife. The heavy blade threw off a faint gleam.

Hindrek followed the melody; it was coming from close by now.

His swift steps turned into a run, a driven stumbling race forward, not stopping at any obstacle. The forester wanted to see the woman whose voice gave him such ecstasy of delights.

He fought his way through thickets, through snow, past banks of tearing thorns, over fallen trees, feeling no pain, his mouth set in a beatific smile, his eyes glinting feverishly. On, ever onward!

Then he stopped in his tracks, finding himself unexpectedly two paces away from his elder son. Bareheaded, Cobert was kneeling at the feet of a woman dressed in a black mantle decorated with silver thread. A song was issuing from her lips and the boy was listening spellbound. She had placed her right hand on his blond curls, stroking his head as if he were a lover.

Her countenance was full of grace; even the most beautiful woman Hindrek had ever met would have appeared ugly in comparison. In his mind nothing else existed except for this perfect figure. Her long black hair was moving gently in the breeze and framing her lovely face. On her brow a dark diadem made of tionium, silver and gold bore two large sparkling diamonds.

Hindrek felt a red-hot surge of jealousy that even the gentle song could not soften. It should be *him* there at her feet, not his son! Her delicate fingers should be stroking *his* head. What did the boy know of love and emotions?

His ill-will grew. When Cobert laid his cheek on the woman's hand and planted a kiss, Hindrek launched himself at his son's back with a roar and drove his hunting knife in through the ribs to the heart.

The singing stopped.

"Get away from her!" he screamed, hurling the corpse aside as if it were a sack of grain. "She is mine," he continued, his voice turning to a whisper. "I heard her first," and he sank onto his knees in the blood-soaked snow. He dropped his arms and gazed longingly at the silent, smiling woman. He waited for her to touch him as she had touched Cobert.

He raised his head and closed his eyes in anticipation. "Please, goddess, sing for me," he begged.

"What will you do for me, Hindrek?" she asked, reaching out to touch his cheek. "If I am to sing for you there is a price to pay."

"Anything," he answered at once through quivering lips. His body was racked with the pain of intense longing to hear those tones again, to hear them constantly until the end of his days. The voice must never stop. She must sing for him alone.

"Go back to your cabin and bring me the heads of your wife and child," said the beauty seductively. "Then I shall sing for you again." He opened his eyes and saw her bending over him. Her lips so nearly touched his own. "I shall sing you the song of lust."

Hindrek jumped up and ran off. He ran back the way he had come, hearing her voice, the sounds of her song, urging him ever faster, giving him untold energy; he raced home like the wind.

It had grown dark. Lamps were burning inside the cabin and smoke rose from the chimney. The horses had been unharnessed and there was a small pile of firewood by the chopping block.

The woodsman marched up to the house gasping for breath; with both hands he pulled the chopper out of the block. It would serve well to sever heads from shoulders. He did not want to make the singer, whose voice he heard in his head, wait any longer. The song of lust—he shivered in anticipation.

The door was pulled open and Ortram, on the threshold, called out in relief, "Mother, he's back. But where is Cobert?"

The boy's eyes grew wide as he noted the blood on his father's coat. "What's happened?"

Qelda appeared in the doorway, looking at her husband in concern. "Hindrek? What's wrong? Where is the boy?"

The familiar sound of her voice ruined the memory of the woman's song and the man stood there, his ax half raised. He blinked and saw the faces of his wife and son before him.

"I . . ." Try as he might he could not explain what had happened. "I was on the sledge . . ." Hindrek turned to the barn. "There was a voice, a song . . ." He attempted to hum the melody but in his mouth it sounded awful. "I followed her . . ."

Horror on her face, Qelda came up to him and gripped the handle of the ax. "Hindrek, where is Cobert? And whose is the blood on your coat?"

Her voice sounded discordant and shrill to his ears, so ugly in comparison with the enchanting singer's tones. It hurt. His face brightened. "The woman! In the forest . . . she sang for me."

"Mama," wept Ortram, running up and clasping his mother's waist. "What's wrong with father?"

Then they heard the strange melody again.

Silkily, it drifted out from the edges of the forest to their ears, taking their minds in thrall.

"Mama, there it is again!" the boy whispered.

"Be quiet!" shouted Hindrek, glaring at the boy in fury. "You sound like a rat squealing!"

His wife retreated in horror, pulling the boy with her. "Get back in the house," she said quickly, giving her husband a wide berth. There was only one explanation: "Your father is possessed by the forest spirits."

Hindrek's features darkened in distaste. "Silence! Stop that terrible screeching!" He lifted the ax, remembering the beauty's words to him. The promise of the song of lust. The price he had to pay.

Before Qelda could speak, he struck out.

The blade went through her neck; Hindrek was strong enough to sever it completely. The decapitated body fell at his side, the head landing in a snowdrift.

Ortram screamed out and stared at his mother's corpse, clutching himself, fists clenched, in shock and anger.

Without hesitation Hindrek stormed up to stop the terrible noise that was destroying the beautiful song. Four steps and he was in front of his son, wielding his ax, ready to strike. Soon, any moment now, he would be receiving his reward.

Something hit his right leg and he faltered. The ax blade whizzed harmlessly over the head of his son and the force of the follow-through made Hindrek overbalance. A crossbow bolt stuck out from his knee. He heard the sound of hooves. On the path that led to the village came four riders in brown leather armor and long light-colored surcoats. One of them held a crossbow that had just been fired.

"Get away from the child!" shouted the archer, reloading.

"The song of lust!" croaked Hindrek, using the ax as a crutch. He knew these men, Wislaf, Gerobert, Vlatin and Diederich, henchmen of Duke Pawald. They must have heard that divine singing as well and have come to deprive him of it!

As soon as he had struggled to his feet he hobbled over to the house where his son had taken refuge. "I want to hear the song of lust!" he raged, one hand on the wall for support while he smashed the ax blade into the door. From inside came the terrified screams of his son.

The riders came thundering up, yelling at the berserk woodsman as he attacked the door. He broke off and turned to them. "You want her for yourselves!" he shouted, his voice harsh. Then he hurled the ax in their direction. "You shall die!"

The ax hit Diederich's horse. It shied and reared up, throwing its rider into the snow.

"I'll start with you!" Hindrek drew his long dagger and hopped toward the man lying in the snow—and received another bolt in the chest. With a groan he pulled at the shaft, roughly a third of which still showed. He tipped forward and lay motionless.

Diederich, a man of about forty cycles, got up cursing; he dusted the snow off. "What, by all the hideous powers of Tion, has been happening here?"

Vlatin, the crossbow man, somewhat younger than Diederich, hooked his weapon onto his saddle and slipped down to the ground. Like his companions he sported a short beard. A cap made of sable protected him from the cold. "Loneliness gets to people. It can drive you mad, being isolated like this." He looked at the woman's body. "Can't think of any other explanation for what he's done."

Gerobert rode to the back of the cabin. "I'll have a look round here. Who knows what else we'll find."

Diederich, Vlatin and Wislaf—who, at twenty cycles of age, was the youngest of them—went gingerly to the door and kicked it in.

The interior of the cabin was clean and tidy. A pot simmered on the stove, it smelled like rabbit stew, and the table was laid. If it had not been for the dead bodies it was a peaceful enough scene.

Ortram was cowering next to the stove, a red-hot poker in his hand. His face was covered with tears and he was trembling all over.

"We're not going to hurt you," said Diederich gently, showing the boy that his hands were empty. "Your father can't harm you now."

But Ortram did not budge, wanting to keep his distance.

"There we were, off to buy furs, and we ran into a tragedy like this," said Wislaf quietly. "The things people do to each other . . ."

"How hypocritical, even if you do put it so well," chimed a harmonious voice at the door, its tone mocking. The men whirled round. Vlatin and Diederich drew their swords more out of surprise than fear.

An älf in a black cloak stepped over the threshold. He was so tall he had to duck his head to clear the doorway, and the weapon on his back made him appear taller still.

"We all know what you do to people when you feel like it." The second voice came from the fireplace behind them, and Wislaf spun round. A second älf, probably twin to the first judging from his face, showed in silhouette against the fire's glow. It was a mystery how the creature could emerge from flames like that without being scorched.

Diederich and Vlatin kept their swords at the ready. It seemed the new arrivals were trying to block their path.

Wislaf cleared his throat. "What are you doing here? Have you got anything to do with all this?"

"Us? Never. We wanted to pay a visit, that's all. The poor forester," said the älf at the door with a friendly smile. His white, even teeth shimmered like an animal's. "Call me Sisaroth and my brother Tirîgon," he said by way of an overdue introduction.

Wislaf responded. "We're Duke Pawald's men and vassals of the älf Môrslaron, to whom this Gauragar land belongs. You'll know that name, I'm sure," he added, in an attempt to ensure their safety. The älfar only respected their own kind, and if these strange siblings understood that he and his colleagues served another älf they would surely be left in peace.

To the men's relief Sisaroth nodded, without moving away from the door. "I know Môrslaron," he said, but it did not sound as if he were afraid of him. That, thought Wislaf, was not a good sign.

An älf woman appeared behind Sisaroth, pushing past him into the room. She, too, wore a black mantle; a diadem crowned her black hair, emphasizing her captivating beauty.

"Triplets," exclaimed Diederich.

"Well spotted," laughed the female älf. "Wouldn't it be appropriate to put your weapons away now? We're all on the same side, after all."

"Can we assist you?" asked Vlatin purposefully. He only had eyes for her.

The female exchanged glances with her brothers "If you would be so good: We are searching for a letter. Hindrek received it by mistake. When he read it he must have lost his mind. Älfar runes can have a lethal effect on humans sometimes. So I recommend utmost caution; see if you can find it but don't look at the content." With a curt gesture she set the men to search the cabin.

The älfar noticed the distraught child squatting by the

stove, and approached him on silent feet, the wooden floorboards not even giving a hint of a creak as she walked. It was as though she were a spirit rather than a living creature.

"You poor thing," she said, ignoring the poker he held, which was cooling rapidly but still giving off heat. She crouched down and touched his forehead. Ortram jerked away and stared at the hand in horror, but did not defend himself; her brothers stood motionless, watching Wislaf and the others as they searched the place.

"Here!" called Diederich, holding up an envelope. "This could be it, do you think?" He took great care not to cast his eyes over the writing.

Sisaroth beckoned him over and waited to be handed the letter. He skimmed the wording and gave Tirîgon a satisfied nod. "Perhaps the boy knows more," he said, turning to Ortram. "Sister, ask him what else the messenger gave his father."

The älf woman had not taken her eyes off the boy. "You heard?" she said gently. "What did your father talk about with the man who brought the letter?" Her black eyes poured terror into the boy; it seeped through his soul while she continued to smile graciously.

"About a town," he stammered, wanting to hit her, to poke out her terrible eyes with his fire-iron, to destroy her charming face and then run away. But he could not move; he was anchored by fear and forced to answer her.

"Tell me more, Ortram," she enticed, stroking his cheek.

"Topholiton," he whimpered. He thought he could see the blackness leaving her eye sockets and crawling over to him; dark threads hovered around his face. His breath came faster; he groaned.

"And who is in the town? Did the messenger say?"

The first traces of the black breath had nearly reached his right eye. Iciness radiated from it. "A woman called Mallenia," he shouted. "She's waiting there. I don't know anymore!" Ortram gulped. "Please, I don't know anything else!"

She ran her fingers through his hair. "I believe you."

"Mallenia?" said Vlatin in surprise. "The rebel? Didn't she recently attack the Black Squadron at Hangtower and steal the tribute money?"

Wislaf looked round. "Where has Gerobert got to? Didn't he say he'd join us when he'd taken a look around?"

"A big sturdy fellow with a beard and a dirty gray cloak?" inquired Tirîgon. "I saw him on a chestnut stallion."

"That's him," said Wislaf. "He rode off, you say?"

"No, that's not what I said." The älf pointed outside. "We met. Behind the cabin." He placed his right hand meaningfully on the handle of his double-edged dagger. "As I am standing before you, you may work out for yourself how our encounter went."

Diederich drew his sword. "Curse you! You devious creatures!" he spat. "Fine allies you are!"

Sisaroth laughed out loud. He said arrogantly to his brother, "How does he come to think that humans could be seen as our allies? They are vassals of Môrslaron, no more than that."

Tirîgon was amused. "And as Môrslaron is so far beneath us we can use anything that belongs to him as the fancy takes us." His voice turned deadly serious. "Use it or destroy it, as we please."

Wislaf and Vlatin both raised their swords. "I'm warning you," cried Wislaf.

"Sister, I think the men are getting rather hot-headed," called Sisaroth, making no attempt to defend himself with his daggers. "Would you like to perform something to calm them down?"

"You know how much that takes it out of me," she responded. "My voice suffers."

"No," groaned Ortram. "Please don't sing! Have pity . . ."

"But I can give it a try." The älf woman gave the boy a kiss on the cheek, took a deep breath and raised her voice in song.

V

The Outer Lands,
The Black Abyss,
Fortress Evildam,
Winter, 6491st Solar Cycle

Ireheart stood on the south tower watching the approach of the hideous and variegated monsters emerging from the chasm: A hotchpotch collection of horror about to swarm over the entire land.

Goda was at his side, a mantle draped around her shoulders. She was listening inside herself to her own remaining magic powers. The store of energy should be sufficient. *For now.*

Her hand slid to the little bag at her belt where she kept the fragments of the diamond she had retrieved from the site of the damaged artifact. These tiny shards still held residual energy and every minute particle would be needed.

Before the destruction of the artifact she had been able to draw down limitless force by placing her hands on the barrier. No longer.

The nearest magic source was only a few orbits' journey away, but lay in the region ruled by the älfar. Goda doubted she would reach it alive.

The other source was in Weyurn, much further away, and she could not think of traveling there when at any moment the Black Abyss could be spewing out rampaging hordes against Evildam. Rumor had it that the Dragon Lohasbrand was sitting on a further magic source in the Red Mountains—right in the middle of a dwarf realm, at that.

Goda sighed. All she had was a bag of diamond splinters with a fraction of the strength of the original artifact. The more of them she used up the worse the position of Evildam's defenders would be. She reckoned that, in the long run, the fortress catapults would not be able to repel Tion's evil creatures. They would have to find a new way to protect themselves.

"Where is Tungdil?" Ireheart asked the ubari next to him. "Have you sent a soldier to find him?"

"Yes, General." The warrior saluted. "His chamber was empty."

"He's probably left to go to Girdlegard," interjected Goda, arranging her mantle. "After all, he told us very clearly that he wanted nothing to do with fighting here. He'll be surprised to see what awaits him at home. If Girdlegard is his true home. Let us hope to Vraccas that we've not let the worst of the evils simply slip away like that!"

"I think we were pushing him too much," Ireheart ventured. "We all know what it's like to wage a war that lasts one, two or three cycles. But for over two hundred cycles he's done nothing else but fight battles." He glanced at his wife. "It may be late, perhaps too late, but I *do* understand his refusal."

"What is there to understand?" she replied dismissively. "I cannot . . ."

"No, Goda. Save your breath," he interrupted her. "Let Tungdil go off to Girdlegard and witness with his own eyes what has happened to the land and, you'll see, he'll be back to lead us against our tormentors. We can't talk him into it.

He has to want to do it." Ireheart gave the order to fire the catapults; the spear-slings sent their missiles flying to the targets. "He'll be back soon. Of his own free will," he said quietly, observing the beasts being killed by the sharp iron-tipped missiles. Their screams and groans came in a wave of sound that crashed against the walls of Evildam.

He had not wanted to tell Goda why he had collapsed in the corridor. No one else knew what had happened. But still he held fast to the conviction that it was indeed his friend, the Scholar, who had returned to them.

The armor, he told himself, might have been a gift from some magic being. Or perhaps there were metals used in its composition able to store protective magic for the wearer. That will have been why Goda's investigative spell had not worked. These metals would not notice the difference between a friendly touch and an attack. *If it wasn't Tungdil, why didn't he kill me? On the contrary, he went to fetch a healer for me.*

Ireheart sighed. All the same, his best friend seemed so alien to him. Different. Those cycles spent in the dark had wrought terrible changes in the Scholar. He had once driven out the demon alcohol successfully enough, but how do you rid the mind of what it has experienced?

"I'll get my old Tungdil back," he vowed, remembering how the three of them—his twin brother, himself and Tungdil—used to sit, beer in hand, laughing together, telling jokes and fooling around. He remembered how they had chased the orcs, how they'd sat under a tree to shelter from the rain, telling stories and making up things to tease each other with, how they had fought against the long-uns. How things used to be. "Vraccas and I will shake the darkness out of him."

The ubari raised his telescope to see how much damage the catapults were achieving. "They've dealt with the first wave of beasts, General," he reported. "But I can see that the next . . ." He stopped. "No. It's not monsters. It's something else," he said excitedly.

"The kordrion?" Ireheart took the wax ear plugs out of his pouch in readiness. All the soldiers had orders to use these to protect themselves from being paralyzed by the terrible roar of the winged monster. The catapults must not stop firing if the kordrion was threatening to emerge.

"No, more like . . ." The ubari passed him the telescope. "Have a look for yourself, General."

The dwarf squinted through the lens and tried to make out what was happening in the dark cleft of the abyss. "Some construction, long, narrow and tall," he reported for Goda's benefit. "It looks as if it's made out of bones. Or very light-colored wood. And they're keeping it behind the rock walls."

"An assault tower?" suggested the ubari. "Or a stack of storm ladders?"

"Probably," said Goda. "It would be the only way to conquer the fortress."

Ireheart adjusted the end of the telescope to improve the focus. If he were not mistaken, the construction was being bent back. "They're pulling it back . . . like a bow," he called out. "Tell the men on the catapults to aim for the middle of the abyss," he ordered the ubari. "I don't want that . . . thing shooting at us. Who knows what they're planning."

While his commands were being conveyed to the troops by bugle signals, the beasts on the other side were acting fast.

Ireheart saw the construction shoot forward like a young

tree held down under tension. Behind it, four long chains were thrown up into the air. White balls hung from them, each perhaps a full pace in diameter, and they had the appearance of spun cocoons. At the height of their trajectory the chains released them and the balls hurtled toward Evildam.

"Much too high," commented the ubari, grinning. "Stupid beasts! Too dumb to aim straight."

The nearer the strange spheres came the more obvious it was that they really were composed of spun threads.

"No, they intend them to go that high," countered Ireheart. "They'll come down behind the fortress! Tell the crews on the southwest ramparts to find out what happens when they come down. Maybe it's a diversionary tactic to keep us busy on both sides." He directed his gaze to Goda. "Can you stop them?"

She tilted her head and thought hard. "Wouldn't it be better to wait and see? It might just be a harmless distraction and then I'd have wasted my powers on something trivial."

Ireheart agreed and ordered the catapults to aim flaming arrows at the cocoons to send them up in a blaze. He watched what happened.

One of the shots was so true that it hit a ball in mid-flight. Flames consumed the sphere as if it had been soaked in petroleum; Ireheart heard the sizzling and crackling sound it made.

The casing turned to ash in the blink of an eye, releasing countless long-legged spider-like creatures the size of small dogs; they rained down, already fully aflame, crashing to the ground and causing a shower of sparks.

Most were destroyed by the fire, but three survived. They

raced toward the bastion on their hairy legs, their long mandibles clicking and clacking.

The remaining spheres landed and bounced a few times before bursting open to let more of the little beasts escape. The arrows fired at them found no hold on their chitin plating.

Boïndil cursed. "Use the spears . . ."

"General, they're reloading," shouted the ubari, prompting Ireheart to turn to the front again. The slender throwing device was being attached to the chains once more and pulled back toward the ground.

"Goda, destroy that thing," said Ireheart. "Or we'll never be able to cope with these animals. Who knows how many cocoons they have waiting to send out."

The dwarf-woman nodded and took the telescope to have a closer look at the sling mechanism. Otherwise she would not be able destroy it with her magic spell. With her other hand she groped in her bag for the diamond fragments and pulled one of them out. Before she exhausted her own store of energy it would be better to use the strength left in the splinters.

Goda sent out a destruction spell directed at the upper edge of the cliff wall of the ravine. Dazzling lightning shot from her hand and screamed into the stone, breaking off boulders to crash to the depths. Then came the sounds of things falling followed by cries of dismay from inside the ravine. The beasts had lost their new weapon and presumably some of their fighters as well.

Goda felt the splinter of diamond in her hand crumble into dust, which clung to her fingers.

"Well done," said Ireheart. He realized that Tungdil had

been correct. They would have to force the monsters away from the ravine mouth, and then bring the whole cliff down on top of them. Bringing down whole mountains—who could do that kind of thing better than his own folk?

Suddenly he heard the clank of weaponry.

Boïndil looked along the walkway to his left and saw that the spider creatures had climbed the fortress walls.

The ubariu, undergroundlings, humans and dwarves were fighting them with all their strength, but what he saw made Boïndil doubt that the creatures could be subdued easily. Only heavy weapons such as axes, cudgels and morning stars were having any effect on the hardened body cases. Swords were useless, ending up blunt and damaged.

"We need Vraccas to crush them with his hammer!" A glance to Goda was enough—she turned to the fight, her first since the building of the fortress.

She took another diamond fragment into her hand, preparing herself to hurl another spell, but suddenly a flash came from the right side of the Black Abyss. Where the steep slopes fell away almost vertically, a figure stood, casting a sulphur-yellow ball of pure magic in the dwarf-woman's direction.

The ubari had noticed the threatened danger and warned her with a shout.

She managed to form a barrier in front of the battlements so that the missile of magic crashed and exploded against it. A pressure wave whirled up the dust in front of the gate, obscuring their view of the Black Abyss, shields, helmets, flags and banners flying through the air as if in a hurricane. They would not be able to see a second wave of attackers approach.

"By the creator! Now evil has a magus on its side!" Ireheart coughed, pulling up his neck cloth to cover mouth and nose. "I call that a proper challenge!" He heard triumphant cheers resounding from the ramparts, and he peered through the veil of dust.

Tungdil was standing with the defenders, thrashing away at the spider creatures with Bloodthirster. His weapon smashed through the chitin armor plating of the insects, hurling their innards in all directions. Bluey-green blood spattered everywhere. Tungdil had taken off his helmet so that all the soldiers could see him.

The hero marched forward grimly, confronting the spider creatures, the inlay on his black armor flashing and glowing by turns. One of the beasts threw itself at him from behind, touching him with two of its legs, and instantly there was a loud bang, the creature exploding as if it had been detonated from within.

Boïndil gulped. Exactly that fate could have been his own end.

The warriors sprang back into combat with renewed vigor. Tungdil gave short commands and steered their counterattack better than any dwarf-king ever commanded his army. Ireheart had to hand it to him. He was already playing with the idea that he might pass command of the fortress to his friend—if he would accept it, of course.

The wavering veil of dirt and dust was starting to settle, allowing the fortress troops a view of the Black Abyss. Goda had a defense spell at the ready.

They were all astonished to find there was a new energy sphere in place over the abyss. It had an uneven reddish shimmer, seeming thicker here and there. But this time the edges reached nearly up to the four gates and the walls.

"Was that you?" Ireheart stared at Goda.

"No," she replied in surprise. She could still feel the fragment of diamond between her fingers. "It must be the enemy's magus."

Tungdil came up to them. He was accompanied by frenetic cheers and shouts and the thundering of weapons on shields. He was not remotely out of breath after his exertions.

Goda did not look at him, pretending instead that she had to keep her eyes on the Black Abyss. Ireheart stretched out his hand in welcome. "Excellent stuff, Scholar! Excellent! Like old times! Vraccas can be proud of you, just as I am!"

"Very flattering. In the old days I wasn't anything like as good," he responded with a curt smile, before turning to watch the pulsing red shield, his face draining of all color.

"Goda reckoned you'd gone straight off to Girdlegard and left us high and dry," Ireheart continued, moving to his friend's side. "Praise be to Vraccas that you stayed. Who knows how the orbit would have ended otherwise."

"The orbit isn't over yet. Let's see how useful I can be to Evildam." Tungdil ignored Goda totally and stepped forward to the parapet to observe the energy dome, turning to his friend. "It's worse than I thought," he confided. "We must travel to Girdlegard *at once*."

"I'm glad you've changed your mind about helping . . ." began Boïndil; then he paused, rubbing his silvery black beard. He didn't understand quite what Tungdil had meant. "Why do we have to go there? Here's where the threat is! And, by Vraccas, a threat indeed!"

"A threat you can do nothing about," replied Tungdil quietly. "Not you, not Goda and not me."

"But . . ." began Ireheart helplessly.

Tungdil beckoned him over and pointed to the ravine. "They will gather under the protection of the barrier, right up to its edges; no one will be able to stop them," he predicted. "They'll build towers and ladders at their leisure; they'll make battering rams and put them in position. The whole of the plain at all four points of the compass will be swarming with those cruel beasts. Then the dome will go and they'll attack." He placed his hand on Ireheart's shoulder. "You took immense trouble constructing Evildam, Boïndil, and it is a proud fortress, but it *will* fall." He stretched out the hand that held Bloodthirster. "They have someone on their side I thought was long dead. We need a magus to combat him. And, from what I hear, only Lot-Ionan could do that."

"But Lot-Ionan is evil," retorted Goda. "He no longer serves the cause of good."

"Exactly. *That's* why we need him," said Tungdil gently, looking at her; she dropped her gaze to hide her guilty conscience.

Ireheart had not noticed. "That won't work. He'll destroy us if we get close!! He has vowed to become the sole ruler of Girdlegard. He'll never help us voluntarily."

Tungdil replaced Bloodthirster in its sheath. "Then we will have to defeat him and *force* him to serve us." His smile was colder than frost.

"You've gone mad, Scholar!" the dwarf-twin exclaimed. "By Vraccas, you're talking about Lot-Ionan, the magus! Your foster-father! Do you remember what power he possessed when you left us? Can you imagine what he is capable of now?"

"We'll get a nice little army ready for him. An army of his enemies." Tungdil remained calm. "That would be, if I've understood you correctly: A dragon, a kordrion and Aiphatòn with his älfar," he said, counting on his fingers. "Perhaps we can get the thirdlings to join in as well. If they can dig up a magus or maga in Girdlegard that hates Lot-Ionan as much as your Goda does, then we're well away."

Boïndil gave a hollow laugh, fell silent, then he laughed again a couple of times, raising his arms in a gesture of mock despair. "We are lost. I have a madman here who believes in all seriousness that his ridiculous project will succeed," he cried, grabbing hold of his crow's beak. "Vraccas, you are cruel!"

"Stop complaining, Ireheart," Tungdil laughed at him. "Perhaps I'll have another idea, a better one. And anyway, it was *you* who always liked a challenge." He nodded to the dwarf-woman. "Goda and your children will stay here to help the soldiers should the beasts attack before we get back." He looked deep into his friend's eyes. "I need to meet with the remaining dwarf-rulers. And don't forget the freelings." He looked at the sun. "We'll leave at first light." Without waiting for an answer he returned to the battlement walkway, where the soldiers cheered him anew.

"Tell us who it is that's opposing us, and why you thought he was dead!" Goda called after him.

Tungdil looked back over his shoulder, revealing his golden eye patch, as though he could see with it. "His name wouldn't mean anything to you. And I thought he was dead because my sword ran him through and I took his armor." He walked on.

Goda followed him with her eyes. "I don't trust him," she said. "It could be a trick to get the worst of the magi together after we've wiped out all the other opponents in Girdlegard . . ."

Ireheart whirled round. "Stop it, Goda!" he snapped at her. "I'm going to Girdlegard with the Scholar and I'll do whatever he suggests. Because I," and he placed his right arm across his breast, "trust my heart."

He left her standing there and went after Tungdil to see to the soldiers who had been wounded in the fighting with the spider monsters. Beside them, the dead had been laid on their shields. One of them was Yagur. The injuries he had sustained were strange: His forearm had been pulled off and there was a stab wound to his throat. Not what you would expect if you were fighting a spider.

His astonishment grew.

Next to the ubari lay three of his closest friends, their armor pierced by something very sharp, judging by the smooth edges of the lacerations. They did not look like mandible bites.

The vague doubts within him were starting to turn into a mass chorus, fighting to be heard. They grew so loud that he decided, against his initial firm intention, to ask a few questions of the Scholar as they journeyed.

Girdlegard,
Former Queendom of Weyurn,
Lakepride,
Winter, 6491st Solar Cycle

Coïra had not thought it possible, but somehow she had managed to throw off her pursuers. She had acquired three extra horses, loaded them up with heavy weights, and led them alongside their own group for some time. After half an orbit's journey riding along the bed of a stream, she had let these three animals go free, while she herself rode on toward Lakepride. That had foxed whoever was following her. For now.

But her name was on the list of Weyurn folk with a high price on their heads, should anyone think of betraying her and taking hers to the Dragon. That had not made her journey an easy one.

She looked at Rodario riding beside her, bravely clinging on to the horse's back. They'd had to stop and wait four times already for him to remount after a fall.

"Not long now and we'll be safe," she said, to encourage him. "Can you see the island? It's one of the few proper islands left in my mother's realm. We'll have to go by boat."

A cry of dismay escaped his lips. "Deep water? I can't swim."

"In the old days every child in Weyurn could swim," tutted Loytan disapprovingly.

"That must have been a really long time ago. I'd say about a hundred cycles, at least? And anyway, I'm not from Weyurn," Rodario returned, sharply. "There was never any need for me to get to grip with the waves. A stream is quite sufficient for a good wash, and for rivers there are always bridges and ferries."

"This time we don't have a bridge to offer you," laughed Coïra. "It's only a short boat-ride. But, of course, if you can walk on water, please go ahead."

"Very funny, Princess," said Rodario, sounding hurt, though whether he really meant it or was just pretending it was impossible to tell.

They rode to the top of a sand dune, the sparse vegetation of which waved in the wind. There was hoarfrost on the grass stems, giving the appearance of glass; they rustled against each other, shimmering in the sunlight.

"Oh, how beautiful!" said Rodario, enchanted. "I wish I had pen and paper right now to write about it!"

Loytan groaned. "If you write stuff as bad as that act you did in the market square, give it a miss, for goodness' sake."

Coïra threw her companion a reproving look but said nothing.

Rodario's eyes narrowed. "One of these orbits you'll get a surprise when you see what I can do, Count Loytan," he prophesied. "And I bet you'll come running to apologize."

As he spoke, something in the actor's gaze brought Loytan up short. Was it a sudden manliness? Probably just imagination. "And you'll probably save my life and then marry the princess, I suppose?" He laughed, startling the seagulls.

"Why not?" The actor grinned at Coïra and rubbed his ungroomed beard. "Do you find me so ugly, or may I dream of a life at your side . . . ?"

She raised a finger in warning. "You are speaking out of turn, Rodario the Seventh! Consider who it is that you are addressing." She rode down the dune, heading for a narrow quay where a skiff lay moored, its small sail furled.

Rodario looked over to the island. It had to be a good mile from the shore.

But *island* was not really the expression to use. Ever since the water level in Weyurn's lakes had started to drop, cycle after cycle, many of the islands stood high above the surface, while others had been left completely isolated, far from the waterline. The inhabitants had installed pulley lifts and built flights of stairs to enable them to leave their islands. Fishermen had been forced to become farmers, turning the lakebed into agricultural land—not always very fertile land, at that.

The situation for Lakepride was not so critical. It seemed to float above the lake maybe sixty paces up, balanced on a stone pillar, resembling a tulip flower on its stem.

Rodario noted seven barges, three ships and eighteen smaller vessels moored at a landing stage below the island; the landing stage was secured by heavy chains and there was a precarious-looking spiral staircase leading up to where the people lived. He could see windlasses and pulleys among the equipment on the landing stage. The residents of Lakepride had made the best of their predicament.

"The island looks as if it might break off at any moment and come crashing down into the lake," said Rodario to Loytan, who nodded.

"Yes, you'd think so, but the pillar of stone it rests on is volcanic rock. Nothing can bring that down." He urged his horse onward down the side of the dune, more sliding than walking down. Rodario followed suit. "The people of Lakepride are lucky; at least they can still work as fisherfolk."

They waited by the low-slung sailing barge for the ferryman to emerge from his little hut. He wore a long dark-blue garment that did not disguise the strong shoulder muscles rippling beneath the fabric. Round his neck he wore the white kerchief of his guild, and his wrists were protected by leather supports to aid in the heavy work of propelling the boat. He recognized Coïra immediately and bowed low. "It will be an honor, Princess, to take you back to your palace," he said respectfully, inviting her onto his boat.

As always she attempted to pay for his services and as

always the payment was declined. She smiled at him. "If any orcs turn up looking for us . . ."

"I'll tell them I haven't seen you," said the man. "And if they want to cross I'll tell them the boat has sprung a leak."

Coïra stepped into the boat and patted her horse's neck. "Don't put yourself in danger on my account. Ferry them over if they insist, but I don't think they'll dare. The island is my undisputed realm. They know they can't harm me there."

Rodario and Loytan dismounted, as she had done, and held their animal's reins tightly while the ferryman hoisted the sail and started the crossing.

He had to tack against the wind, so they reached the landing stage in a wide arc. It brought huge rusty iron walls into view rising from the water below the island and a little to the east.

Rodario had noticed the structure and craned his neck to see more. "What is that? A groyne to protect the island?"

"No. It's a bulkhead." Coïra instructed the ferryman to change course so that they could inspect it.

"Bulkhead? What's that when it's at home?"

"It's to support the sides of a shaft. It's where we're heading first, so you'll have the chance to admire the dwarves' engineering skill," she explained. "The fifthlings built it at my great-grandmother's request."

"A shaft. In the middle of a lake. But . . . what for? And how deep does it go?" He was so excited that he walked forward to the bow. The breeze lifted his brown hair and played through his beard.

The ferry headed straight for the structure and Rodario could soon make out the dwarf-runes on the walls. A single iron plate was four paces wide and one pace thick. Ten of these placed side by side formed one wall, and hefty steel girders braced them diagonally. Algae and barnacles covered the outside and there was a metallic smell.

"But it's . . ." Rodario was at a loss for words to describe this impressive structure.

"It goes down two hundred paces below the keel of our boat," said Coïra, amused at the man's childlike enthusiasm. She took her scarf and tied it round her hair to keep it back. "That's how deep those metal walls go. At the bottom you can walk about without getting your feet wet, but I shan't take you with me when I go down, so you won't be able to see."

He turned to her. "Go down? You're going down there? What for?"

"Have a think and see if you can work it out for yourself." She raised her hand in greeting to a helmeted figure and called out three words that Rodario could not understand, an answer coming back in return. "I was giving the password. If they don't hear it the guards will sink any ship that approaches," she told him.

"So there's something down there that's very precious, very valuable to you . . ." He paused. "But of course! A magic source!"

"The last magic source in Girdlegard that can still be accessed," Loytan corrected. "Most of the others have dried up and only a few new ones have formed. There's one in the land of the älfar, and one in the Blue Mountains, of course, where Lot-Ionan has set up his realm and is training his famuli."

"As if I didn't know that," snapped Rodario.

Loytan grinned maliciously. "Obviously not. Or you wouldn't have had to ask."

The boat went round to the side of the shaft and moored at a floating landing stage where four guards stood waiting. They wore only light armor, in case they fell in and had to swim.

Coïra and her companions disembarked and climbed the iron steps to the narrow door at the top. Behind it was a walkway. Huts stood at the four corners of the shaft so that the guards could rest, or shelter in inclement weather.

Rodario could see a number of plaited wire ropes going from here to the top of the island, with cage-like gondolas attached. That would be how the guards, and their food and weapons, would be transported.

"There's a second level beneath the walkway," said Loytan, taking off his cap. "They've got catapults down there. No ship can withstand their fire."

"You're really prepared for anything." Rodario ventured closer to the inner parapet to take a look down. The wind tugged at his clothing, blowing it this way and that.

The shaft was a vast black hole down to nowhere. A damp moldy smell rose up from the depths, a bit like a cellar where metal had been stored.

"Not quite the type of accommodation for a princess, though, is it?" he said, holding tight to the edge. "Couldn't they have made it . . . a little more attractive?"

"That's never been a priority," laughed Coïra as she greeted the commander, who bowed to her. "Get the gondola ready to go down," she told him and the armored man hurried off. "It's kept over there in the eastern corner," she told Rodario. "You and Loytan will wait for me there."

"I'd love to see the magic wonder with my own eyes," he confessed. "Couldn't I watch?"

"It's quite unspectacular. Just a few sparks." Coïra went ahead. "Nothing worth seeing."

"You didn't tell him you bathe in the source naked," interjected Loytan, eyeing Rodario.

"Naked?" The actor blushed. "Oh, now I understand why I can't go with you. Though I envy whoever accompanies you."

"You don't know what is concealed under my clothes," she replied, embarrassed in her turn. "Your compliment is somewhat premature."

"It wasn't a compliment. I was talking about being able to see the source . . ." he went on, but noted that Coïra's expression had turned icy.

Loytan laughed out loud. "Oh, a true descendant of the Incredible Rodario. You certainly know how to charm a woman and wrap her round your little finger."

"Hold your tongues," she said sharply. "You're both making me very uncomfortable." She entered the little hut, where a gondola with a wire cage stood at the back. It was secured by two ropes through a loop at the top.

Coïra went over, stepped in and closed the door behind her, nodding to the guard. She moved a lever and the cabin dropped quickly down through a hole in the floor.

"Naked!" Rodario shook his head and sighed, going over to the hole and looking down. If he was not very much mistaken, the princess had already slipped out of her mantle and was unbuttoning her blouse. "I'd have been so glad to hold her clothes for her."

"You're not the only one, but there's only one man she

cares about: The unknown poet," said Loytan crossly, helping himself to tea. "Do you want a cup? To warm you up?"

Rodario looked down again and thought he could catch sight of shimmering skin. One's imagination could play such tricks . . . "Something to cool me down, rather," he replied, and his rejoinder was met with laughter.

"Good one!" the count laughed. He handed over a cup of hot tea regardless. "I think the unknown poet's days are numbered," he continued. "Now that we know who he is." Loytan's expression became thoughtful, the stubble giving him an older, manly look. "The Lohasbranders will wipe out his family and village."

"But they won't be able to destroy the dreams of freedom," Rodario replied as he sipped his tea, his eyes never shifting from the bottom of the shaft. "Impossible."

In the depths there came an azure shimmer, illuminating the bottom third of the shaft walls like blue jewels in the sun. He could see the silhouette of the young woman, and in his mind's eye he could imagine her naked. Unclothed and desirable.

He gave a deep sigh and turned away. "She will never love a man such as me," he murmured, downcast.

Loytan raised his cup in salute. "That makes two of us, my actor friend!"

He glanced at the nobleman. "But you are married!"

"Of course," he said awkwardly. "I just wanted you not to feel so alone." Loytan drank his tea. "As for being alone, what about your *own* family? You've been seen at the side of a notorious rebel—is there someone that needs to be protected from the Lohasbranders?"

Rodario shook his head. "No. My parents are long dead

and there's no one else. Apart from the descendants of the Incredible One, and I don't think the Dragon would go as far as to kill all of them."

"You never know." Loytan sat down. "You've been up for the contest eight times now and came last again. Why don't you give up?"

Rodario smiled sadly and fiddled with his beard. "I promised someone I'd keep entering until I won." He emptied his cup. "I know what you're going to say: An impossible endeavor. But one day, I swear . . ."

Loytan raised his hand. "You said that before and I still don't believe it. Especially now they're looking for you. You won't be able to return to Mifurdania and go on stage."

"Except maybe for my own execution," he joked. "And that *would* be a performance . . . Nobody could steal that show." He tossed his hair back theatrically.

"Hear, hear! Another flash of wit. And coming from you! Respect, friend. You're improving. I agree." Loytan placed his feet on the table, folded his hands and prepared for a nap. "It may be a long time before the princess gets back up." He closed his eyes. "Help yourself to more tea. And think up something appropriate to say in greeting to the rightful queen of Weyurn. Unlike her daughter, she's a stickler for etiquette."

Rodario drank his tea, placed the empty cup on the table and wandered over to the spy-hole again. The lighting effects in the shaft were still in full swing.

He looked over to Loytan, already snoring, then studied the ropes going down into the depths of the shaft. "You're a descendant of the Incredible Rodario," he told himself, screwing up his courage and pulling his gloves out of his belt and putting them on. He discarded the mantle; it would get in the way. "Here we go. Try something that would have impressed the Incredible One. You've made a fool of yourself often enough, even though it was in a good cause."

With one bound he reached up and grabbed the wire cables. Then, with more agility than he'd ever shown on stage, he went down the rope, hand over hand, letting himself down toward the bluish light.

In some places gaps between the iron plates were allowing trickles of water through; elsewhere, regular mini-fountains shot between corroded elements in the structure. However, the walls were holding solidly, despite the rust that had formed in thick layers. The structure had presumably not been intended for long-term use.

Rodario could not assess whether the Weyurn folk had the necessary skills for the upkeep of these iron walls. And the dwarves certainly had more pressing things on their minds than to come round and carry out repair work. They were battling away in the mountains, fighting for their very existence. Against dragons. Against the kordrion.

The bottom of the shaft was only about ten paces below him now. Planks had been laid across it so that the princess would not sink in the mud.

Rodario took a sharp breath and clung fast to the cable.

Loytan had told the truth: Coïra was indeed naked—apart from the leather gauntlet on her right arm.

She was floating in the middle of the shaft in the blue light, her long black hair drifting as if under water. The young woman had her eyes closed and was smiling. She was enjoying her energy bathe.

Rodario looked his fill, wondering when he was likely

ever to see such a perfectly formed female body naked again. But how strange that she had not removed her glove.

Suddenly he was overcome with shame. What he was doing just was not right.

I shall win her for myself, he vowed, and then looked away, embarrassed. He started the upward climb, inching his way up the wire rope.

The next time he saw Coïra without her clothes, he thought, she should be undressing for his eyes alone and doing so willingly. "Stand tall," he told himself. "Attitude is everything."

At that moment he heard someone shouting excitedly at the top of the shaft.

Hot and cold shivers ran down his spine. The guards had discovered him committing this inexcusable indiscretion!

VI

Down in the brick-built cellar four lamps shed a faint light over the score or so people gathered.

Most of them were glad not to be obviously recognizable. Simple clothing concealed social status or provenance, and they wore hoods to keep their faces in shadow.

They were meeting under the house of the sheriff, who was asleep two floors up, reluctant to know anything about what was going on here. His courage amounted only to leaving the iron-clad door to his cellar unlocked.

Mallenia, surrounded by her co-conspirators, could not believe what Frederik was telling her. "The thirdling is still alive?" She forced herself to take a deep breath. The air down here was stale and smelled of sweat and food. The group had been there for some time arguing and planning, as they sat among smoked hams, sauerkraut barrels, jars of jam and bottled fruit and tubs of salted meat.

Frederik nodded. He was a local butcher of good reputation and no one would have thought him likely to rebel against the vassal ruler and the älfar here in Topholiton. In his early thirties, he had a face that seemed much too nice for the butchery guild he belonged to; and certainly too nice for revolutions. "It is so, my lady. Hargorin heads the

Black Squadron once more and is riding out collecting the tribute. It is said his warriors are more brutal than ever." He took a folded paper out of his sleeve and handed it to her. "Read for yourself. The price on your life has been increased. Whoever brings your head to Hargorin may select what they like from his treasure store."

Mallenia looked at the sketch of herself on the crumpled paper and was dismayed how true to life it was; underneath the picture was the number 1,000. That was a great deal of gold. "They say that Hargorin's treasure hoard contains objects of breathtaking value," she said pensively.

Frederik looked enquiringly around the circle. He took off his cap, revealing short black hair. "My lady, I know you don't want to hear this but we think you should halt your activities. You have provoked the älfar and their henchmen to intolerable lengths and with rewards like this . . ."

"I shall go on provoking them," she interrupted without a moment's hesitation. "They will go on hounding me even if I crawl into some dark hole and hide for cycle after cycle." Mallenia surveyed the assembly.

Her fellow insurgents looked tired, fear and distress showing on many of the faces. They were frightened for their families. The death of friends, killed in the attack on the Black Squadron, had brought home to them that even the best-laid plans could go wrong.

Mallenia knew why Frederik was making this suggestion and she could not take it amiss. She smiled. "I thank you for what you have done in past cycles, but I am going to release you now," she said kindly, trying hard to show she harbored no resentment. "From now on I ride alone."

"My lady!" exclaimed Frederik in shock. "No! We don't want to give up . . ."

She put her hand on his arm. "It's all right, Frederik. I can't have you all taking these risks for the sake of my struggle."

"Gauragar is *our* homeland, my lady. We have the same duty as you to fight off the oppressors." He was not prepared to drop the subject. "We are glad to have you at our side. If the Urgon group were here, they would say the same."

Zedrik stood up. One of the sentries at Topholiton's gates, he was a rough man of rough appearance. He was only ever to be seen in armor, as if there were no life for him outside military service. "May the gods and yourself, my lady, forgive me, but I have been wondering about our cause for a long time—whether there's any point. We steal the tribute, kill a few thirdlings maybe, but does this make anything better for the people here in Gauragar?" Zedrik sounded disconsolate. "The people support us but they are the ones to suffer when the reprisals come."

"What do you suggest?" Frederik studied him. "Do you want to kowtow to the black-eyes forever and a day? Is that what you want for your children and their children? This oppression?"

"It's how it used to be, and we managed all right; it's not a bad life," replied Zedrik with a sigh. "We pay up and they leave us in peace."

Mallenia followed the dispute attentively, her decision now reinforced by what she'd heard. They must break up their organization. The butcher did not want to give up, as she had first thought, but some of the others did. Too many. Fear could lead to betrayal, just as a high reward might.

Frederik was disgusted. "Just how stupid are you, Zedrik? What happens when we've nothing left to pay them with? When they raze our villages to the ground because they want the land for their preposterous art projects; want to change everything to fit in with their mad ideas of aesthetics?" he cried, exasperated. "Does nobody remember what happened in Tareniaborn?"

Tareniaborn. Mallenia swallowed hard and the thought of the town with its forty thousand men, women and children, filled her with horror. Nothing like that had ever happened before.

It had been eleven cycles ago. One of the älfar princes had decided to turn the town into a work of art: Tareniaborn and all the land surrounding it.

To this day no one knew whether the älf had gone mad or whether each and every town in Idoslane could expect a similar fate.

"You were there, my lady. Think of how cruel our overlords were," Frederik demanded grimly. "And bear in mind, they're not going to shrink from violence on that scale if the fancy takes them again." All eyes in the cellar were on Mallenia.

"I can't say how it happened. I arrived when it was all over," she said. "I came on the town by accident when out riding with some volunteers. We were up on a hill and had a good view of the town and plain." She felt a fluttering in her stomach and started to feel sick. "We saw patterns in the snow round the walls, and the whole town glistened red. Everything, absolutely everything, was covered in a layer of frozen blood. Red ice, everywhere!" She saw in her mind's eye the ghastly lanes and alleys of Tareniaborn. "In the marketplace they'd strung up the hearts of the inhabitants, pierced with silver wire and silver rods, twisting them together to make a giant tree, the hearts of the adults on the trunk, those of the children on the twigs. And they'd hung the heads of newborn babes like fruit from the branches."

She could not go on. The tree and all its gory detail had swamped her imagination. The tiny bunches of different-colored hair, attached to look like leaves, making the whole work so horrendous . . .

Mallenia saw the disgust in the eyes of those around her. "Be glad you didn't see it." She continued softly, "In the fields round about they'd stripped and eviscerated the bodies, using the bones to form huge symbols on the ground, with the town at the center. Maybe it was all dedicated to one of their gods, who knows. But it was so incredibly awful that you actually *had* to look at it. A terrifying fascination. Bone laid next to bone as if there had never been another function for them apart from making those symbols on the ground." The young woman looked at Zedrik. "They'd placed the intestines in between the bones to give color. When we first saw it from the distance we didn't know what it was made of. Then we used our telescopes . . ."

The watchman ran outside, two others following him, not wanting to vomit over the feet of their friends.

Frederik had grown very pale, but kept his head. "And yet you think of giving up?" he confronted the others. "If the älfar decide to turn Topholiton into a *work of art*—you'll die with the knowledge that you were too cowardly to stand up and resist!" Anger had brought out the veins on his forehead.

"So what do we do?" called Zedrik from the doorway,

wiping his mouth. The tips of his boots were shiny and wet, bits of food still clinging to them. "Go to war? Against the thirdlings *and* the älfar? We'd have to kill our own families first so they're not executed by the enemy." He gave a choked laugh. "No one can save us from them, Frederik. Only the gods, perhaps, but they must have made up their minds to make us suffer for many cycles yet."

"The gods would come to our help if we dared to rebel against the vassal-rulers," replied the butcher fervently, but he was calmed by Mallenia's hand on his shoulder.

"I know how worried you all are but I do see that I should withdraw from the campaign for a time, as my good friend Frederik suggests," she announced, and a sigh of relief went round the room. "I shall let you know when we next ride out together but, until then, stay with your families and behave as if nothing were wrong. I need you alive." She stood up. "There will come a time when we will rise up against the älfar, but it will not be tomorrow and will not be in thirty orbits. We will know when an opportunity presents itself, and all three of the realms will be ready and waiting." She drew her sword and held it high. "For Gauragar, Urgon and Idoslane! For freedom for all!"

They all echoed her cry, cheering and applauding Mallenia, descendant of the famous prince.

Suddenly the lamps went out!

Somebody laughed nervously in the dark, others cried out in dismay, calling for light; Mallenia could hear that at least two of the conspirators had drawn their swords, fearing an attack—or was *this* an attack?

She ducked down and placed her left hand on her second sword, thinking through various possibilities of who could be attacking her here in the cellar: The thirdlings with Hargorin, some bounty hunters or the Dsôn Aklán älfar?

She realized there had not been a draft strong enough to extinguish all four lamps. Magic? A particular sort of magic. The hairs stood up on the back of her neck. *Have they found me?*

The cellar door banged open, dim light coming from the windows opposite.

A figure stood on the threshold, bending slightly forward, a long sword in his hand. The conspirators immediately recognized the sharply pointed ears and were terrified by the sight, because they knew what it meant for all those in the cellar: Death.

Behind the älf stood the sheriff, his face like wax in the light of a single ray of light.

"Well, well, what have we here? The rebels," said the älf in a velvety voice. "Well spotted, Sheriff. They have indeed broken into your cellar to steal supplies." The tone betrayed that he was protecting the sheriff and did not intend to connect him with the deeds of the rebels. The älf took a bag of gold from his belt and threw it over his shoulder, so that it fell in the snow in front of the sheriff. "Here—here's your reward."

"Have mercy, sire!" Zedrik was the first to whine. "Have mercy on our families! They knew nothing about what we've done." Sinking to his knees at the bottom of the steps, which were the only way out of the cellar, he stretched up his arms in supplication. "Spare their lives!"

The älf took two steps down in order to accommodate his full height. They could still only see his silhouette because the light was behind him. No one had dared try to relight the candles.

"So what exactly have you done? Let's have some confessions and then your families shall be allowed to continue to enjoy the light of day." He raised his sword arm and rested the weapon in the crook of his right arm as if he were holding a baby. "What do I hear?"

Zedrik sobbed. "We are guilty . . ."

". . . guilty of wanting freedom for Gauragar," interrupted Mallenia, standing up. "Of wanting to throw out our oppressors, the älfar, the thirdlings and the vassal-rulers, and bring them to justice!"

"No," shouted Zedrik. "Be quiet! You don't know . . ."

"Yes I do. I know full well. They are hunting down not only me but all who belong to the line of my forefather, Prince Mallen." She stared at the älf. "Look at him," she urged the conspirators. "He is playing a game and has no intention of sparing any of you. The only way to save your loved ones is to kill him before he learns your names and can pass them on." The young woman clenched her two swords tight in her fists and took up an attack stance.

The älf raised his head and looked at her. "Mallenia! I would be lying if I said I had not expected to find you here." He still kept his sword up against the crook of his arm, but let go of the hilt and drew something out from beneath his mantle. He tossed it to her. "I found this. Is it yours?"

An envelope fell at her feet. She recognized it at once. It contained a warning to Hindrek, a second cousin thrice removed. The fact the letter was here at her feet made it plain what had happened to him and his family. "Monsters, you are monsters. You deserve death a thousand times over," she hissed.

"Isn't it strange, then, that we bring thousandfold death

rather than receiving it?" He made a gesture and the lamps were relit. Then he put his hand back on the hilt of his weapon. "We bring death ourselves if we must. Or if we are in the mood. I was outside the cellar for some time, listening to what you said about Tareniaborn." His tone was conversational, as if he were chatting to friends or at some reception. The metal plates of his lamellar armor showed under his cloak. "I was moved by your words, proud of having had the pleasure of being the creator of the work of art you described. I, Tirîgon, designed the work you had admired in awe." He bowed in her direction. "It was both a pleasure and an honor to elevate the town in such a way and to release the inhabitants from their mortal concerns. All älfar remember Tareniaborn fondly. Humans, one finds, are at least good for one thing."

The horror experienced by the people in the cellar was palpable.

The älf was pleased to note it. "The vast gap between our race and yours is one that cannot be bridged," he said, breaking the silence. "On occasions such as this I notice it particularly: You are not prepared to take up your swords and kill for any other cause than to fight for freedom, or to gain riches or power. My race, however, can. Death and art form a unit. The transitory nature of life moves with grandeur and perfection." Tirîgon paused and looked at them all with regret. His eyes were steely blue, reflecting the lights. "I can see some very acceptable bone formations here in rather ugly bodies. They could be put to satisfactory aesthetic use."

Mallenia had heard enough of his self-glorification. She charged up to the älf, her swords in her hands.

Her opponent laughed with delight. "What bravery! What passion! Your bones will form an exquisite decoration. I do appreciate boldness and courage." He took his sword in both hands and held it out horizontally in front of him. The blade measured at least two arm-lengths and on a conventional battleground would bring its bearer enormous advantage of range—but between the barrels, tubs and shelves in the cellar the long sword imposed its own restrictions. This is what Mallenia was counting on.

Frederik followed her lead and swung his butcher's cleaver.

"Mind out!" she shouted to the men and women. "They are triplets. There will be two more somewhere." Then she had reached the älf and thrust his sword aside, ducking down and stabbing with her second weapon.

But the enemy had a devilish turn of speed and possessed skills she could not have dreamed of.

Tirîgon took off from the ground, leaping off the side wall and using the momentum to run several steps up toward the ceiling. After this acrobatic achievement, which he managed easily despite the weight of his armor, he landed behind Frederik and stabbed him in the back of the neck so that the sword emerged from his open mouth. From the front it looked as if the man were sticking out his tongue—a tongue made of pointed steel.

"Not a bad try, Mallenia," the älf mocked. "If the bold butcher hadn't been standing behind you, *you'd* be dead now." With a sudden jerk he twisted the blade and pulled it up vertically. The metal had been sharpened to such a degree that the head was cut in two halves. Blood, brains and liquid gushed out, splashing onto the floor of the cellar, then Frederik dropped forward where he stood, the butcher's cleaver crashing to the ground. The two halves of his head shifted, giving him a grotesque appearance.

Mallenia whirled round, one sword aimed at Tirîgon's head, the other at his belly. But now he was no longer standing behind her—or rather, yes, there he was, again.

The young woman felt the draft go through her blond hair, while her sword thrust met empty air. Then she was hit on the back, a blow that sent her flying against one of the stone sauerkraut vessels.

She landed against it, banging her hip, fell over it and came to rest lying by a tub of salted meat. She twisted on the floor and held her two blades up, crossed in front of her body for protection.

Not a moment too soon: Blades clashed and her arms took the force of the recoil. The älf had delivered a mighty blow. His weapon was a finger's breadth away from her nose.

With an angry roar she shoved his blade aside and kicked him in the middle. Even though the armor took much of the impact Tirîgon was forced backwards.

He laughed and circled his blade in the air, then gripped it again with both hands while Mallenia stood up and moved away from the stone tub.

She wanted a wall at her back. The enemy was too quick for her, and was superior in skill and strength. She did not think she stood a chance of leaving the cellar alive, being well aware that the älf was playing a game with her. Arrogance often came before a fall, however.

Her friends had moved back out of her way, following this uneven duel with fascination.

"Is this cellar full of cowards?" Tirîgon mocked. "There

are twenty of you . . . nineteen to one, if you so wish! Mallenia was right: If you don't kill me, your families will die—and yet still you are standing around like lemons, doing nothing?" He winked at Mallenia. "I owe your courage this mark of respect: You'll be the last one to die. Watch me and learn. You will need the knowledge to use against me." He took two swift steps, leaped on to the tub and launched himself into the air.

He landed feet first on the wall and ran up it diagonally to the ceiling and down the other side. As he ran he wielded his sword so nimbly against the conspirators gathered below him that the eye could not follow its movements. With every slash blood spurted high out of deep wounds. Screams echoed around.

He landed gracefully on a wine barrel and held his sword diagonally away from himself, surveying the scene with satisfaction at the speed of his attack. More than half of the rebels lay dead on the floor of the cellar. He left no wounded. "The art lies in avoiding the bones to save them for future use," he explained to the survivors, lifting the bloody blade. "As you know your fate now, are you ready to defend yourselves yet?"

Three women turned tail and made for the door.

But two more älfar were standing there, unmistakably the missing siblings Mallenia had warned them of. The Dsôn Aklán were all accounted for. They blocked the doorway with their mere presence and without drawing a weapon. Dark smiles were threat enough.

Tirîgon sprang down from the wine barrel to face the survivors, who now were determinedly drawing their swords and knives and surrounding him. "That was a long time coming," he observed maliciously. "My promise is this: If you can injure me—give me the slightest of scratches—your families shall live. Because you won't be able to *kill* me," said the älf complacently. He placed his sword in the scabbard he wore on his back. Presenting himself, unarmed, to the crowd, he stretched out his arms and turned on the spot. "What are we waiting for?"

Mallenia looked at the two älfar by the door. They had not moved. They were leaving their sibling to take his pleasure as he wished—then the älf woman turned to face Mallenia.

The haughty expression on the älf sister's countenance turned to curiosity. She was about to move forward, but her brother held her back. Her blue eyes stayed fixed on the Ido princess, as if she were studying the face of an old friend.

Mallenia had no idea why she was attracting such interest. Shaking off her sense of unease, she stepped over the dead bodies to reach the handful of her loyal followers about to enter the fray.

If she died, she wanted to die among her own people, fighting for Gauragar. Her movements were governed by an obsession to inflict a wound on the älf Tirîgon, thereby saving their families.

Tirîgon adjusted his tionium arm protectors and waited with a smile.

Uwo, a little man and the town's only fishmonger, thrust with his sword, making a quick move to one side.

The älf blocked the jab with his forearm and the blade broke into three from the impact. While the pieces were still in mid-air, Tirîgon grabbed one of them and hurled it at Uwo, hitting him in the chest. The man sank to the floor.

Already, Tirîgon had snatched the next piece of blade, which he threw at another attacker heading his way. The metal sliced through his throat and he fell, gurgling, hands clasping his neck, trying to close the gaping wound.

The courage of desperation drove the conspirators to a joint attack on the enemy, who was enjoying his sport, avoiding jabs and thrusts and deflecting blows in other directions, so that their blades hit their own friends.

By the end, only Mallenia and Arnfried the blacksmith were left to stand against the älf. The rest had fallen or were cowering on the earthen floor, fatally injured.

The smith, a strong man with a long beard and impressive muscles, was bleeding from a wound in his right shoulder, but he had his dagger gripped fast in his hand and was snorting with fury.

Tirîgon regarded the red splashes on his armor. "Regrettable," he said. "That should not have happened. The blood runs into the engraving and then clots."

Arnfried sprang abruptly forward to surprise the enemy. He feigned a stab with his knife and at the same time launched a punch to the face. Mallenia stormed in, taking advantage of the älf's defensive move.

The slim adversary avoided the blade and grabbed the blacksmith's balled fist with his left hand. But he had underestimated the man's strength and was forced backwards against a wine barrel.

Arnfried brought a knee up and rammed it into Tirîgon's ribs; the armor grated. Concerned, the female älf cried out in her own language.

Mallenia used her left-hand sword to jab at the älf, who stepped aside at the last moment. The tip of her sword went through wood, releasing a stream of white wine behind him that made the floor slippery.

"Respect," growled Tirîgon, addressing the smith and parrying his next attack with his other hand. There was a click and two metal discs shot out from the long outer side of his forearm bracers. Like lightning he drew them across the man's breast. Arnfried yelled out and jumped backwards, losing his balance on the wet floor. As he fell, the älf was directly above him and smashed a mighty blow into his solar plexus. Bones cracked and buried themselves in the lungs; the smith rolled in the mud in agony.

Without hesitation Mallenia threw herself at Tirîgon to pull him to the ground. He had noticed her coming at him out of the corner of his eye and leaped away—becoming a victim of the wet floor like the smith. His right foot slipped. Although he tried to steady himself he crashed against the tub of salted meat that Mallenia had earlier fallen foul of.

The female älf cried out.

Mallenia hurled both her swords at the enemy as he lay; one aimed at his head, the other at his groin. He would not, she hoped, be able to parry both strikes. But Tirîgon, acting on reflex, jerked up his plated arms: The first sword was deflected and flew off into a corner of the cellar, the second broke up on striking the tionium.

Nevertheless the älf emitted a groan.

Mallenia could not believe her eyes. A long thin splinter of blade had pierced the älf's cheek, nailing him to the barrel. Not a fatal wound by any means but certainly very painful. And, above all, it had destroyed the perfection of his countenance.

Behind her, Mallenia heard the sound of fast steps and metal scraping.

Meanwhile Tirîgon raised his hand and said something she did not understand; the injury to his face made the words sound terrible.

"You promised to spare our families," said Mallenia. She did not have to turn around to know that the älf woman was behind her with a drawn sword in her hand, ready to kill her. "Do you keep your word?"

The älf uttered a low "Yes."

"And I shall leave this cellar alive?"

"Never!" came a hiss at her back. But the defeated brother confirmed the agreement was to be honored.

"And you thought we couldn't kill you," Mallenia said carefully, her left hand on the handle of her knife. She bent down and cut off a lock of his black hair. "This will be a reminder of my triumph over you and your arrogance."

The murderous look in Tirîgon's eyes said all there was to say.

"Look after your luck, last of the Ido line," came the warning from the second älf at the door. "You will be able to leave the cellar. The conspirator families will be allowed to live. As far as we're concerned, that is. But what Emperor Aiphatòn does, when he hears about it, is another matter."

"He will certainly hear of it," said the älf sister gleefully.

Mallenia turned around angrily. The siblings were standing behind her, and the sister did indeed hold a sword in her hand. "I should have known you would find a loophole, a way of breaking the agreement!"

"It's not a loophole. It is an exact interpretation." The älf, identical to his wounded brother apart from the fact that his sword was different, bowed slightly. "If I were to interpret it even more minutely, I could say that, in reality, Tirîgon injured himself and it was not you who wrought a miracle." He pointed to his sister. "Firûsha would be happy were we to come to that view of things. As long as we are still deliberating how to construe the significance of your victory you will be able to reach the door unharmed." He took a deliberate step to the side to allow her to pass.

Mallenia did not hesitate, and hurried out of the room, with its awful stench of blood, guts, wine and salted meat.

As she left, she unfastened her hand-crossbow from under her cloak, cocked it and turned on the threshold. She pointed it at the wounded älf, aimed at his head and fired.

The bolt flew out and struck Tirîgon in the neck.

Mallenia cursed. She had been aiming at the head but her hand had been shaking. But if the gods—apart from Tion— were on her side she was now rid of this enemy.

She stepped out of the door in great haste, slamming it behind her. The key was on the outside, because the sheriff had forgotten to remove it. Thus she was able to lock the siblings in and make her escape. She would need the head start this gave her.

The älfar would be pursuing *her*, so the conspirators' families should be safe. For the moment. She could worry about everything else later.

Mallenia turned and saw the älfar mounts only five paces away. *Shall I?*

No one had ever dared ride one of the night-mares—or rather, nobody had lived to tell the tale.

She knew that taking one of these animals would give her the best chance of getting away. Conventional horses were hopelessly inferior to these tamed unicorns.

"Let's see if I can trick you," she murmured, approaching the beasts with the lock of Tirîgon's hair in her outstretched hand. She watched the nostrils of the night-mares attentively and thought she could identify which one was reacting to the smell of the tuft of hair.

She rubbed the lock of hair over her own face and arms, torso and legs. "Here, smell that? Tirîgon has said I can ride you," she said gently as she walked round the big black animal, its dreadful red eyes seeming to glow like molten lava. She put one foot in the stirrup and swung herself up into the saddle.

The night-mare reared up and whinnied; it sounded more like a screech. Then it stamped its hooves on the paving stones, striking white sparks that left scorch marks on the stone.

Mallenia grabbed hold of the animal's neck and made herself flat, so as to avoid being bitten, but she stayed on determinedly; then she dug her heels into the creature's flanks. "If you don't want to obey . . ." she threatened, and banged the handle of her dagger against the creature's forehead blaze.

The night-mare shot off and galloped through the dark streets. Sparks flew whenever its hooves struck the ground. As they rushed along, flashes lit up the walls like lightning in a storm.

Mallenia took hold of the reins and forced the night-mare to her will. This was like no horse she had ever ridden before. The skin round a normal horse's mouth would have torn or the neck vertebrae would have been damaged by the violence. But it seemed not to mind, and eventually obeyed her instructions. They raced toward the town gate; the attentive watchmen had already opened it for her. They must have thought she was one of the älfar.

Riding like the wind she left Topholiton and thundered along the road to the west.

The Outer Lands,
Seventy-four Miles Southwest of the Black Abyss,
Winter, 6491st Solar Cycle

Tungdil and Ireheart rode side by side, covering the miles to the fourthlings' stronghold through which they could gain access to Girdlegard. To their old home . . .

A meeting had been arranged with the remaining dwarf-rulers; messengers had been sent out in advance.

Boïndil had selected a white pony with brown markings; a second animal, heavily laden, was on a lead rein attached to his saddle. Tungdil rode a befún, after the habit of ubariu warriors.

The befún resembled a large gray-skinned orc on four legs with a short stumpy tail. The body was muscular and as broad as a horse, the nose flattened, which made the head quite short. Its squarish, three-fingered hands, covered with toughened skin, were adept at grasping things.

Ireheart knew that a befún would stand erect in battle, aiding its rider by the use of its claws as an extra weapon. A special saddle with a long, curved back support ensured the rider had the right posture and could not easily be dislodged.

The two dwarves made a strange pair. The companions were different in so many ways, not simply in their choice of mount.

Ireheart presented the classic dwarf-figure familiar throughout Girdlegard from ancient times, when the small-statured folk had campaigned heroically against Nôd'onn or the avatars or the creatures from the Black Abyss, described in so many heroic tales. Those grand days were long past; recent battles had ended in defeat: Against the älfar, against Lot-Ionan, against the Dragon . . . But the dwarves were still respected.

Ireheart sported an impressive braided beard and had a memorably wrinkled dwarf-face. He wore his reinforced chain-mail shirt under a light-colored fur coat with a hood. He had his crow's beak weapon fastened to his saddle, and was puffing away at his pipe while humming a tune.

Tungdil in his dark armor seemed more like a small squat älf. The fact that he rode a befún emphasized the spooky impression, and the weapon Bloodthirster at his side—the reforged älf sword he used—did not help to make him look like a friendly child of the Smith. Any dwarf of the thirdling tribe, the dwarf-haters, would have treated him with respect, assuming him to be one of their own.

It was thoughts such as these that occupied Boïndil constantly; he tried hard to push them out of his mind and not to think about the obvious changes in his friend.

Puffing blue smoke, he brought out his drinking flask. So that the water in it did not freeze, Ireheart carried the flask close to his body. "Well, do you remember the way?" he asked his friend, as he took a long draft from the flask. "I prefer to rely on my pony's memory. His head is bigger." He put the stopper back. "It must be a hundred and fifty cycles since I was last anywhere near here."

Tungdil laughed. "That makes two of us. But I can add a

further hundred cycles." He looked round. "No, try as I might, without the path I'd be completely lost. Or, at the very least, I'd take a very long time."

The companions fell silent again.

The clattering of hooves on stone was thrown back as an echo by the mountains; a light breeze chased the new-fallen snow and formed it into drifts in places, hazardous for the ponies.

"No questions at all, Tungdil?" Boïndil finally asked. He attempted a smoke ring.

Keeping his gaze solidly toward the front, Tungdil opened his mouth and said, "I'm still trying to come to terms with what you've told me. Lot-Ionan the Forbearing. What can have changed him so? Magic?" He was lost in thought for a time, then sighed deeply. "There are so many things I want to remember, to convince you that I really used to know them. To convince you that it's really me, your comrade-in-arms." He touched the scar on his brow. "It was this blow, I presume, that robbed me of my memories, both happy and sad. It was my master who delivered the blow and it nearly did for me. It didn't kill me but it wiped away images of my past. It's the only explanation I can come up with."

Ireheart studied the scar. "I've heard of that happening, someone losing their mind if they've been hit on the head in a fight. But losing your memory is the lesser evil, surely," he said, sounding relieved. "I should have realized . . ."

". . . except that all the people around you were telling you to fear the worst. They made you think I was not your old friend, the Scholar, who owes you so much." Tungdil fell silent again, lost in thought.

Ireheart let him be. He would ask him some other time about this *master* he had mentioned. But not now.

"I know! When I saw Lot-Ionan last he had a light blue robe and was wearing white gloves . . ." Tungdil seemed alarmed. "The gloves, Ireheart!" he cried excitedly. "I can see it clear as day; he needed gloves to cover the burns he sustained touching the artifact. The skin had healed but had stayed black."

"That's the idea, Scholar!" Ireheart greeted this successful recollection gladly. "The artifact treated the magus harshly. I had a bad feeling even then," he added angrily. "But I'm glad you can remember it. The artifact had denied him access because he was not pure in thought. At the time we thought it meant he had lost his purity through some trivial misdemeanor, but we've known for some time now that it must have been something much worse." Ireheart wished he had a whole band of pig-faced orcs at hand to take out his fury on. He had been blaming himself for several cycles for not having acted against Lot-Ionan; he had let Goda talk him round. "In part it is my fault. If we had stopped him then and there, or imprisoned him, the tribe of the secondlings would not have been practically eradicated."

"Goda was his apprentice?"

Ireheart nodded. "She was his famula for about ten cycles. The ubariu couldn't find anyone else to be their rune master. But then she noticed that the artifact was reacting differently from usual. When she touched the dome to refresh her magic, it was very painful. She thought her own purity of soul was in danger, but couldn't explain what the reason was. She had given birth to our firstborn quite a long time beforehand, so it wasn't that."

Tungdil adjusted the golden eye patch, and the polished metal flashed in the sunshine. "So the change was gradual?"

Ireheart looked at his friend and started wondering, despite himself. *Did he always wear the patch on the right side? Wasn't it the left eye that he'd lost?* He could not be sure, but the thought did nothing to put his mind at ease. He pulled himself together to reply.

"That's right. Until he tried to teach Goda some magic spells that she thought were just too cruel. When she refused to cooperate he fell in a rage and walked out. After that, a few letters came, asking her to go to him in Girdlegard so that they could talk it all through, but she did not want to leave the artifact unattended. The last letter was full of threats and said some dreadful things. We took it as confirmation that we'd made the right decision." Ireheart caught sight of a mountain hut on the road to the pass where travelers could shelter rather than spend the night out in the open. "Look! It'll be a bit basic, but much better than sleeping in the snow."

"And Girdlegard just sat back and *watched* him conquer the Blue Mountains?" objected Tungdil, unable to believe it.

"But what could they do against a magus, Scholar? After he'd been freed from petrification by bathing in the magic source his strength grew greater with each coming orbit. You would have thought he had the skills of two magi." Boïndil clenched his fists in helpless anger. "That was how he managed to wipe out nearly the whole of my tribe. He subjugated the very rocks to his commands. And with that power he defeated the dwarves."

"What do you mean? He made the tunnels fall in?"

"Exactly, Scholar. He sent one earthquake after another and our halls and strongholds collapsed. Passageways filled up with molten rock and water flooded the shafts. Thousands lost their lives, and then he lay in wait for the wave of refugees at the fortress Ogre's Death, and struck them down with magic spells."

Ireheart's eye filled with tears of anger and grief that rolled down his cheeks into his beard, where the freezing wind turned them to gems of ice. "There are hardly a hundred of them left. They took refuge with the freelings."

Tungdil grimaced. "That doesn't sound like the man who brought me up," he muttered. "I've no reason to doubt you, my friend. Something in the past must have contaminated him with evil. Perhaps the source that awakened him?"

Ireheart wiped the pearly tears away. They melted in his fingers. "No one knows. You're the only one who would dare take up arms against him. You, and maybe the Emperor Aiphatòn."

"The High Pass—is it open?"

"He closed it up after the black-eyes from the south marched through. He didn't want to let too many of Tion's monsters in, I suppose," said the dwarf dismissively. "Are we sticking to your plan, Scholar? Or have you thought of another way to defeat an adversary like him so that we can force him to serve us?"

Tungdil did not answer. He stared straight ahead at the hut. "Someone's expecting us," he said quietly. "I wonder why they haven't got a fire going."

Ireheart's eyes widened in anticipation. "Here we go! You think there are some footpads waiting to ambush us?" Secretly he was wondering how Tungdil could have spotted the enemy. The wind was blowing away from the hut, there were no tracks in the snow and he himself would have heard the tiniest of sounds in the stillness. He supposed it was down to the constant experience of battle sharpening his friend's senses. He got ready to wield his crow's beak, but Tungdil motioned him not to.

"I don't know how many they are. We'll act as though we haven't seen anything. That way he, or they, will think we're an easy target," he suggested.

"Because if they have crossbows they could shoot us out of our saddles. I get it," said Ireheart, pretending to be checking the buckles on the harness. "I hope the place is full of robbers," he said. "Ho, this'll be fun!"

"Not much fun for whoever's going to have to fight us." Tungdil patted his befún's neck. "Shall we have a bet?"

"No, not this time," said Ireheart with a grin.

VII

The oddly assorted dwarf-pair continued to ride toward the apparently deserted hut.

It was a mystery to Ireheart how Tungdil had sensed someone was lying in wait. He squinted over to his friend, looked ahead and shifted in the saddle.

They were thirty paces from the hut now and there was no sign of anyone.

"Are you sure, Scholar?" Ireheart enquired, laughing out loud as if they were telling each other jokes; that should fool anyone watching them. He saw that a couple of the runes on his friend's dark armor were glowing.

There was a smile on Tungdil's lips. "You'll see. Get ready."

"What if it's just some innocent travelers?"

"Sitting in the cold? Travelers who haven't stepped outside for orbits?" a disdainful Tungdil retorted.

"They . . ." Ireheart did not know what to say. Whatever he came up with made no sense at all.

Their animals halted some way off from the cabin and the dwarves dismounted.

"And now?" Boïndil wanted to know, slipping his pony's reins over a post. He didn't tie them in case they needed to leave in a hurry. "Do we storm in?"

"No," said Tungdil firmly, drawing Bloodthirster. "Go and

knock." He grinned and tapped on the head of Ireheart's crow's beak. "With that."

"Good idea! Off we go!" Ireheart laid his pipe on the ground near the door so that it wouldn't get damaged in the fighting. He took his faithful weapon and smashed it against the door. The lock splintered away from the wood and the door flew open so violently that the hinges broke off. It crashed to the floor.

Ireheart stormed in with a roar—and stared at the empty tables and benches; it was icy cold in the hut and there was no sign that anyone was or had recently been there.

"Well, then," he muttered, disappointedly. "Hey, Scholar! Did your senses fool you? Come and see!"

Behind him all was quiet.

Boïndil turned round, but Tungdil had disappeared. "What, by Vraccas, is happening now?" he thundered, catching a noise at his back. He whirled round, crow's beak raised high. "Scholar?"

He moved carefully into the room, one step at a time.

He checked the fireplace for ashes, the wooden floor for footprints. Not a single trace.

"It's the spirits of the mountain haunting us," he told himself silently. His gaze fell on a lonely dried sausage hanging above the stove. "Scholar? Tell me where you are? I don't want to clobber you by mistake."

Ireheart moved cautiously around the corner to the cooking stove. There was a thick layer of grease on it. No meals had been cooked there recently.

The string the sausage hung on, suspended from a rafter, made a rustling noise. The dwarf, surprised, noted there was no obvious draft in the cabin, but the string swung forward and backwards.

If he looked closely he could see the ceiling boards move slightly, and he grinned. *That's where the rat is hiding!* Whoever was waiting for them had crept up to the hayloft, to give the dwarves a false sense of security.

"Scholar?" he called again, before leaping onto the stove and hacking through the ceiling boards with his crow's beak. He jumped up and pulled at the handle with all his strength until the planks gave way.

Dried grass fell into the room, showering Boïndil; dust blurred his vision. But he thought he spied a movement in the hay. Certain that Tungdil would have made himself known if it were him, he struck out without mercy.

His blow was parried, metal hitting metal. Suddenly the crow's beak was wrenched aside and Ireheart needed all his strength to hang on to his weapon.

Surrounded by showers of drizzling hay and dust he tried another attack on his opponent, who still was only visible as a silhouette. Judging from the size it must be—a dwarf!

"Scholar, is it you?" he asked, to be on the safe side, holding back for a second.

A mistake.

A very narrow blade, more like a finger-slim iron rod, appeared in front of him and Boïndil was only just able to swivel his torso to the right to avoid being stabbed through the chest with the sharpened point. But it found its way through the material of his padded tunic, hitting his collarbone. Intense pain flashed through him.

Ireheart growled in rage, and the weapon was withdrawn. He felt his blood trickling warm from the wound, but realized the injury was relatively harmless. His shoulder and arm still worked and he could breathe without difficulty.

Angrily he grabbed the handle of his crow's beak again and jumped through the hay to attack. He circled round, waving the weapon; some time soon he was bound to hit something. "Don't hide, you coward!" he shouted, stepping out of the cloud of straw and dust. He coughed, his eyes streaming, then saw a figure by the door.

"Halt! Stay where you are!" He raced after it, following the unknown figure into the open air.

But once outside in the snow he saw that the attacker had completely vanished.

"How, by Tion's ghastly—" and then something struck him on the back of the head. His helmet took most of the force of the blow, but it was enough to make him giddy. "Yes, sneak up on me from behind; you can do that, can't you?" he raged, and a red veil laid itself over his already restricted sight. "Ho, stand and fight!" Battle-fury was about to overwhelm him.

The enemy was back at the door. He wore a close-fitting leather helmet with decorations of rivets and silver wire. His body was protected by dark leather armor with ornate tionium plates and his legs were concealed behind a skirt of iron discs. It looked like the kind of armor a thirdling would make.

"What do you know: A dwarf-hater! So what brings you here?" Boïndil wiped his eyes, then saw his pipe under the enemy's feet. Trampled and broken. "Look at that! You moron! How am I going to smoke now?" He clenched his teeth and snorted with fury. "It doesn't matter. I know who's going to smash you."

Tungdil appeared above them on the roof, Bloodthirster in his right hand. An impressive figure, Ireheart had to admit. "Something much more important," Tungdil called down. "How did he get through the Brown Mountains and past the fourthlings? We'll have to find out and stop the gap before others find it."

"Wait, Scholar. I'll put a few sharp questions to him!" Boïndil raised the crow's beak. "That's what this is for!" He dashed up to the dwarf, who bore a round shield in one hand and a weapon like a sword in the other. The base of the sword was thick to withstand heavy blows, then the blade thinned out to form a slender point, ideal for striking through gaps in an opponent's armor. "I'll break your rods in half!" he promised with a roar, turning inwards on the attack to make his strike impossible to parry.

The thirdling, however, was not going to place himself in the path of a crow's beak strike. He leaped to one side and lifted the arm that held the shield. Boïndil noticed far too late that something was being thrown at him.

A cloud of black powder exploded over him and he tumbled straight into it. His eyes smarted and streamed. It hurt to breathe now and he was coughing badly, unable to take in any air.

His battle-fury was inflamed now and he lashed about blindly, but his strength was dwindling and he soon collapsed, panting, into the snow.

The madness left him, and the snowy whiteness melted under the warmth of his body, washing the sting out of his eyes. When he lifted his head he could see again. He spat. The saliva was black, like the snow he was lying on.

Tungdil and the unknown fighter were locked in combat,

blades clashing repeatedly. The mountains sent the sound back as an echo as the two of them circled around in a lethal dance. Their whirling movements and maneuvers were nothing like those seen in conventional fighting. Ireheart had never seen anything of the kind before.

For Boïndil it was as if two brothers were fighting. In their black suits of armor they were so similar that it was only their weapons that distinguished them.

Tungdil's adversary had taken quite a beating. His shield was cut to shreds and the tip of the strange sword was missing. His armor hung open in places. Blood trickled out, red drops falling onto the snow.

Ireheart pushed himself up onto his feet. Gasping for breath and groaning, he raised the crow's beak. "Wait, Scholar! I'm coming!" he called, stumbling forward. "That skirt-wearer has got something coming to him from me!"

Tungdil took a strike on his armor, letting the blow slip past Bloodthirster. When the iron met the tionium there was a yellow flash of lightning and the enemy cried out. He had been forced to let go of his weapon; the sword fell and vanished, hissing, into the snow, sending up steam.

The unknown warrior withdrew three paces and lifted his left hand, uttering an unintelligible word—it sounded like the language of the älfar—from inside the helmet, and all the runes on Tungdil's armor lit up, bright as the sun! Boïndil's friend disappeared for a moment in a sea of dazzling rays.

Ireheart shielded his eyes with his hand and ran towards the enemy. "Let's be having you, you fiend!" But when he reached the place where his adversary had stood there was only a footprint leading away. *Has he jumped over the top?*

The tracks went over the edge of a steep slope, almost a sheer drop.

Far below he could make out a figure tumbling and somersaulting toward the valley before pulling out the damaged shield and sitting on it to sail down the mountainside at high speed on the icy snow. Round about him the drifts were starting to slide. An avalanche was going to accompany the thirdling to the valley floor.

"Ho! Skirt-wearer! Tion's not going to be on your side for much longer!" he shouted happily after the fleeing dwarf. "The White Death can have you, as far as I'm concerned!" Boïndil waited until he saw the snow swallow the figure up.

He turned back to Tungdil with a grin on his face. His friend was a few paces away. "Just a pity we didn't get to ask him a few sharp questions first. With this." He fingered his weapon. "Would you have let him live, Scholar?"

His friend said nothing and remained motionless.

Full of apprehension Ireheart hurried over to Tungdil and yanked his visor up using the end of his crow's beak. Tungdil's features were devoid of expression and his eyes looked through Ireheart into the distance. "Oh, by Vraccas! What's he done to you?" He tapped the armor. "Or was it this armor that did the damage? This black tin seems to have its drawbacks, too."

Ireheart picked up a handful of snow and threw it at his friend's face. At once the lids fluttered and the gaze returned to focus on him. "Aha, you can move again!" Ireheart sighed with relief.

"Not quite." Tungdil's face was red with exertion. "I've been trying, but the armor has me stuck fast!"

"What?" Ireheart put down his weapon, grabbed Tungdil's right arm and tried to push it up by force. The hinges stayed where they were, immobile, as if riveted in position. All he achieved was to set Tungdil rocking, such that he toppled backwards into the snow.

"Well done, Ireheart," he said sarcastically. "I'll freeze to death in here now."

"Might be better than being smothered in your own excrement?"

"I don't think that's funny, Ireheart!"

"Don't you worry. I'll look after you. We'll get your tin can open." Boïndil checked on the befún. "But not out here. The befún can pull you to the hut and the pony can tug you in through the door. I'll get you warmed up and then I'll have a think about what to do."

He was true to his word. After a bit of pulling and shoving Tungdil lay in his unwished-for, but secure, prison by the fire that Ireheart had lit. The door he had broken down earlier was now resting upright against the opening, jammed in place by a table to keep out the freshening wind. Boïndil prepared a simple but delicious meal from the provisions they had with them.

"Shall I feed you?" he offered, grinning. There was gloating pleasure in his tone, despite the worry that perhaps the armor would never release his friend: Maybe it would stay rigid forever. It had lost its somber and threatening nature, its aura of fear and awe. "Just a heap of expensive junk that doesn't work anymore," he muttered.

"No, I don't want you to feed me. Who knows where you'd drop the food," growled his bad-tempered companion, staring up at the dusty sausage still hanging from the rafters.

Ireheart ate with a healthy appetite. "Has this ever happened before, Scholar?" he asked, his mouth full.

"No. But I've never fought a thirdling before that speaks like an älf," he replied crossly.

Ireheart chewed and put his mind to the problem at hand. *If the armor was forced to go solid like that because the black-eye word was used, I wonder who created it in the first place. Who wore it before Tungdil?*

Before he had left them all and gone to the abyss, his friend would never in a million cycles have thought of using armor that was obviously of evil origin.

His brown eyes focused on the blade. Had he misjudged the hero? After all, Tungdil had once made himself a new weapon out of one belonging to an älf—*Bloodthirster*! Boïndil was pleased with the idea: Perhaps this very blade held the key to the change in Tungdil. He had become a dark and dangerous dwarf. Although, of course, present circumstances rendered him less than effective.

"Hope you don't want to make dwarf-water?"

"Not yet," said Tungdil impatiently.

"I could tip you over so that it runs out of your helmet?"

"You would, too."

"Of course." Ireheart laughed.

"By all that's infamous! If only I knew the counter-incantation."

Now Boïndil's jaw dropped open, showing the mouthful he had been chewing. "That thirdling put a spell on you? A dwarf-hater that can do magic?" He picked up his cup of tea. "Vraccas help us! It's getting more and more complicated."

"No, it wasn't magic. It was . . . a command," Tungdil said, attempting to explain the effect of the thirdling's words.

"Right. Like with a pony; I say *whoa* and it stands still." Ireheart pointed at the armor with his spoon. "Why would it do that?"

"So the wearer can be sure nobody else uses the armor," sighed the one-eyed dwarf. "It would take too long to go into it."

"Oh, I've got masses of time." He licked the spoon clean. "So've you, Scholar."

"I don't feel like explaining, dammit!"

"So, if I've understood correctly, it could happen again. For example, when you're having to deal with an orc. And that," Ireheart waved the spoon, "is something that's more than likely. Certainly in Girdlegard." He contemplated the runes. "You really should take it off as soon as it's working again. One of these orbits. Soon." He winked at Tungdil. "If I have to I'll drag you back all the way to Evildam. Back in my forge I've got all the tools I need to crack you open. I've got hammers this size!" He spread his arms wide.

"It wouldn't help." Tungdil watched the sausage swinging in the breeze. "It's enough to drive you mad!" he shouted, exasperated and trying with all his might to sit up. But the armor could not be moved. The joints did not even squeak.

"Do you think I could use you as a sledge?"

"You're enjoying this, aren't you? Taking the rise out of me?" said Tungdil accusingly. "Pity would be more appropriate than this teasing."

"I'm not being malicious. I'm just saying there are drawbacks to walking around in someone else's armor if it's as moody as a woman. I hope you see it that way, too." He took another mouthful and stood up. "I've got an idea," he mumbled, taking the crow's beak in one hand. Legs wide apart, he stood over Tungdil, about at the level of his friend's knees. "Perhaps it's the same as with a stubborn woman. If you want something from them you have to win them round." He shoved the last piece of bread in his mouth.

Tungdil stared at him in bewilderment. "What are you up to?"

"Winning it round. Properly." He took the measure of the blow he would land on the breastplate, using the flattened side of his war hammer. "It might hurt, Scholar. But it's in a good cause."

Tungdil's head bobbed up and down in the helmet; he was trying to break the armor's strength. "No, Ireheart! Wait! I . . . I'll remember, how . . ."

Ireheart raised his weapon. "Close your eyes. There's bound to be a flash," he warned cheerfully, and smashed the crow's beak down.

Girdlegard,
Former Queendom of Weyurn,
Lakepride,
Winter, 6491st Solar Cycle

Rodario cursed under his breath and tried to melt into the darkness of the shaft.

He was afraid the guards up on the walkway would shoot at him. How should they know that he was just a harmless, curious actor, not an adventurer or a bounty hunter after the money offered for Coïra's head?

He made himself as small as possible and waited to see what they would do. Calling out excuses would not be any use; any proclamations of innocence on his part would sound like unintelligible nonsense at this distance.

The shouts became louder, and a trumpet sounded a warning fanfare.

Rodario started to perspire. In other circumstances he would have felt honored should people make such a fuss on his account, but at present he could not enjoy the attention.

The bluish glow at the bottom of the lake was diminishing and Coïra drifted back down, twisting round to land on the planks where her clothes were.

Rodario was granted another full view, and was able to admire the princess in all her beauty, even though she was now covering herself. Utterly besotted, he gave a contented sigh.

Coïra fastened her belt, hurried to the gondola and moved the lever. The trip up to the surface began.

The actor ascended at the same time. Clinging to the cable, he was spared the exhausting business of having to pull himself up hand over hand, but the situation was not without danger: The wire rope attached to the winch at the top was coiling as the cage rose.

Rodario saw the square of light drawing closer and closer. The ropes were disappearing into it. Jets of water drenched his back as he was carried up. It was icy cold and he had to clench his teeth so as not to cry out. When he was pulled through the opening, he jumped aside and let go.

He landed safely on the floor and two stumbling extra steps absorbed the momentum. To his relief, there was no one waiting for him. The alarms and commotion had not been on his account.

Hardly had he regained his footing than the cage arrived, clanking and clattering. Coïra pushed aside the door and saw him. "What are you doing here?" she asked, fastening the top button of her blouse.

"I was waiting for you," he replied easily. *If you only knew what I have been watching all this time* . . . Rodario looked at her gloves. They were identical and did not have any runes or other decoration. Had she merely not had time to take off the second glove?

She noticed that a puddle was forming at his feet. "Don't tell me you're sweating in this weather."

"What do you mean . . . ?" He laughed in embarrassment. "Oh, that . . . I was soaked through by the ferry, coming over. All that spray . . ." Rodario turned toward her to show her where his shirt was wet.

"The spray? Well I never. Pretty specifically aimed, the spray, it seems. Never saw the like. I know the lake quite well." Coïra looked at him sternly. Her gaze wandered over him and she noted the dirt on his hands. "So you were waiting here the whole time, you say?"

Before he had to tell a lie the door opened and an excited Loytan stood facing them. "You must look at this, Your Highness!" he said, pointing outside. "There's a very strange race taking place."

Coïra looked Rodario keenly in the eyes once more, then ran out with Loytan. With a sigh of relief Rodario followed them out.

An icy storm wind had risen up and gray clouds hung over the lake. The waves splashing against the metal walls were noticeably higher than earlier; a fine mist covered cloaks, helmets and faces with tiny drops.

Loytan took them round to the west side, from where you could see past the island to the land. He handed her his telescope. "Have a look at the shore. Just now they were about half a mile from the ferryman's house."

The young woman lifted the glass to her eye. The shore was too distant for Rodario; he could just make out two black marks on two black spots chasing a white mark on a black spot.

"And? What is it?" he urged. One of the guards lent him a telescope. "Are those . . . night-mares?" he asked in a mixture of fright and surprise. The muscular black animals were galloping along the crest of the dunes. Under their hooves the sand seemed to be exploding, shooting up high, and there were flashes round the horses' feet. The black-clad riders on their backs were älfar.

Rodario turned to focus on the pitiable creature they were chasing and cried out in astonishment. "By Elria and Palandiell! What a sight! A human riding a night-mare!"

"I don't suppose you've even seen a night-mare before," countered Loytan.

"She must be a very brave woman, riding a mount like that one." Coïra saw the quarry's long blond hair flying in the wind.

"She must have killed an älf if she's riding a night-mare," Rodario interjected. He managed to get a clear view of the girl's face through the telescope. She was pretty and he saw no trace of fear in her features, just sheer determination. Her pursuers were not gaining on her. "It's amazing the animal is obeying her."

Loytan scratched his chin. "Lohasbrand won't like it if he hears the älfar have encroached on his territory."

"Am I correct in noting a certain satisfaction in your voice?" replied Coïra, looking at her faithful friend. "You think this might inflame the old enmity between the Dragon and the älfar if we go about things the right way?"

The young blond woman whom Rodario was observing was seeming increasingly familiar—and then it occurred to him where he had seen her face before. "By all the gods. It must be Mallenia!"

Coïra glanced over at him. "Mallenia? The freedom-fighter?"

Rodario nodded. He did not realize the princess was watching him. He continued to follow the progress onshore. "Yes! I know her face from the posters I saw on tour with the theater in Gauragar and Idoslane. The älfar and their vassal-rulers have put a huge price on her head."

"They seem to be taking the matter in hand personally now," Loytan remarked. "They're speeding up. It won't be long before they catch her."

Rodario lowered the telescope and moved toward Coïra. "Princess, even if it's nothing to do with us, I beg you: Help Mallenia of Idoslane," he implored. "I know how the people love her. If *she* dies the struggle against the oppressors in the east of Girdlegard will die, too."

Coïra raised her eyebrows.

Rodario took this as an invitation to say more to convince her.

"I beseech you, act to help her. You have the power to save her from the älfar and to keep Idoslane's hopes alive." He swallowed. "I would do it myself if I had your powers or a fast boat with enough men to confront the evil."

"And it wouldn't be good to have everyone know that Mallenia had been killed in Weyurn before your very eyes. Within sight of your mother's palace," Loytan observed, coming to his aid unexpectedly. "Conclusions might be drawn. It might be thought we were helping the älfar. Or that Mallenia was coming to us to organize a joint uprising, uniting resistance in Weyurn and Idoslane. One way or the other, when the Dragon hears about it, he'll be heading this way to investigate the rumors." The count fell silent for a moment. "The last time the Dragon came there were many deaths, if the reports are true."

Rodario did not warm to the man's reasoning, because it was based, it seemed, on personal fear rather than on any intent that good should prevail, but support was still support. "Your Highness, please!" He knelt at her feet. "I will be forever in your debt if you save Mallenia!"

Coïra *smiled* at him—smiled with a totally new expression in her eyes—and touched him on the shoulder. "Get up, Rodario the Seventh. You must not kneel before me. Someone with your noble attitude of mind certainly should not be kneeling." She climbed up the wall of the shaft—and jumped!

With a shocked cry Rodario rushed forward to stare into the raging water to look for Coïra.

Next moment he saw her racing at incredible speed, suspended above the storm-tossed waves, heading for the shore. A bluish light surrounded her and turquoise-colored lightning flashes carried her along.

"What a woman," he exclaimed in admiration, and he heard Loytan's spiteful laughter.

"Don't give yourself airs, actor!" he said. "Coïra may pay

you some attention now but she'll never respect you. You are beneath her dignity." His tone grew sharp.

"Listening to you one could presume you had intentions of your own that are not appropriate, sir. You are husband to another," Rodario said cuttingly as he pulled himself up to his full height. "Let's be frank: I don't much like you at the best of times, and that warning you've just given me is the last straw."

The count's expression lost all its superciliousness. "I see you have a sharp tongue when you need it."

"Sharp enough to have you in slices if you're looking to challenge me to a duel."

"I shan't need to do that. Coïra will always trust my word over yours. I'll make sure you leave us soon." Loytan bared his teeth. "When you've dried off, actor. Maybe. In those waters you can easily catch your death."

Rodario nonchalantly wiped a few drops off his arm. "A bit of spray doesn't bother me."

"Who's talking about a bit of spray?" Without warning Loytan gave Rodario a shove that sent him flying over the wall.

The actor's damp fingers could get no purchase on the metal. He tumbled down into the lake, crying out as he fell. The waters of the lake had been whipped up by the approaching storm.

He fell head first and the water felt like liquid ice. Every fiber of his being registered the bitter cold; he thought he could hear the blood freezing in his veins.

Underwater currents thrust him mercilessly against the metal wall of the shaft, scraping his face roughly. Then the life force in Rodario awoke. Whirling his arms about wildly, he fought his way up to the light where the surface must be.

Mallenia looked round again and saw only the älf woman, less than one hundred paces behind her, forcing her night-mare onwards with pitiless strokes of her riding crop.

"Faster!" the young woman screamed into the ear of her night-mare mount, drawing her knife and placing it at the animal's neck. "I swear you will die before me if they catch up."

Without warning, a black shadow appeared on her right; it had glowing red eyes and was charging down the sand dunes toward her. It collided with the night-mare she rode, hurling horse and rider to the ground. The second älf had overtaken her and thrown her off!

Mallenia and her stallion rolled in a confused heap down the slope of the dune to the shore. The night-mare made a shrill and furious shriek. She managed to keep out of the way of its thrashing legs, but the creature's vicious incisors grabbed her upper arm. A piece of flesh the size of a fist was gouged out of her, the animal's teeth grinding against bone as it clamped its jaws on the limb and hurled her toward the water.

Mallenia screamed and thought at first she had lost her arm completely. Blood poured out of the wound, splashing on the pebbles. Even if everything about her hurt she could not lie here. She sat up and was about to get to her feet to run, but her legs gave way beneath her.

Trampling hooves came ever nearer; the älf siblings rode up, closing the gap at their ease. Suddenly there was no longer any need for haste. The race was decided.

"There she is, the murderess and thief," said the female älf, full of hatred, leaping down from the saddle. She ran up to Mallenia and beat her with her riding stock.

The woman raised her uninjured arm to protect her head. Every blow cut into her skin. There were thorns plaited into the birch twigs that worked like the teeth of a saw. When she reached for her sword she was kicked in the head, landing backwards in the lake.

"Watch out, Firûsha, or she'll drown," said her brother in reproach. "We have so much planned for her. Tie up the wound in her arm or she'll bleed to death. The night-mare was obviously hungry."

Mallenia saw the älf leaning over her, then the gloved hands grabbed her by the collar, dragging her back to land. "She must not have a death as gentle as that." She punched the young woman on the chin to knock her out. When the girl's body went limp, the älf took Mallenia's belt and applied it tightly above the bite wound. The bleeding stopped at once. "What now, Sisaroth?"

The älf brother looked at the captive. "Get her back to Idoslane alive. The rebels' saint, their hope and inspiration, must be broken," he said. "We shall execute her in front of all of them. Then the uprising will be destroyed. The rebels will lose their cause. There is no one to take her place."

Firûsha looked up at her brother, still mounted on his night-mare. "Isn't there a big danger that a public execution will increase the risk of rebellion?"

Sisaroth smiled cruelly. "I certainly hope so. We'll put down the rebellion, killing all those involved in the resistance. They'll come, to try and free Mallenia, and they'll be met by death."

"A good plan." But Firûsha was still looking unconvinced.

"I see you have second thoughts," he enquired. "You think not?"

"No. I'm thinking what Aiphatòn will say."

The älf laughed out loud, throwing his head back. "Our ruler, the Unextinguishable Emperor, is much too busy keeping up the morale of his followers in the south." He dismounted and came up to her. "A weak fool, despite the power he has. He is afraid of a coup. What has become of him? In the past I would have died for him; now I would stand back and let him die first." The pebbles made no sound when he trod. "I had such great hopes of him, the descendant of the Unslayables, after he had defeated Lot-Ionan! He spoke as if he wanted to bring back the glorious reign of the first generation of älfar. Instead, he dragged a collection of second-rate älfar here to Girdlegard and he behaves like their servant! We never needed them in the first place. But this will all change. And soon."

Firûsha frowned. "You're keeping something from me, brother! Tell me what you know."

Sisaroth grinned. "I learned that they've made the Unextinguishable Emperor promise to march against the magus this very cycle."

Firûsha's eyes grew big. "That will be a hard war and will cost thousands of lives! Why would they do that?"

"To ensure access to the south is opened up again. Several of the inferior packs in the Outer Lands are waiting to be admitted. Aiphatòn doesn't realize that he's about to lose his power to foreign hands." Sisaroth stood by Mallenia and studied her face. "That's why it's important to calm the situation in Urgon, Idoslane and Gauragar. *Before* the war starts. Let them march south." He lowered his voice. "We agree, you and I, that we shan't let them into Dsôn Balsur, sister?"

"Agreed, as ever," came the instant answer. "Not into any of the three former elf realms. They belong to us, the Dsôn Aklán, not the foreigners." She emitted a high tone to summon the night-mare Mallenia had ridden. It trotted up, its head lowered, and came to a halt, snorting, in front of the älf woman. The girl's blood could be seen round its nostrils and mouth.

Firûsha drew her sword at lightning speed and cut off the creature's head with one mighty swipe. The night-mare and its severed head fell to the ground, blood drenching the captive girl from head to foot.

"Eat the traitor," Firûsha commanded the other night-mares. Greedily they began to gorge themselves on the creature's warm flesh. The long chase had made them hungry.

"What are two älfar doing here in Weyurn?" asked a woman's voice diagonally above them; their hands flew to the hilts of their swords as they whirled round simultaneously. "The Dragon won't like that."

Sisaroth and Firûsha saw a black-haired woman in fine raiment standing on the crest of the dunes; she carried no weapons. Her eyes shone brighter than those of a normal human—and much to the alarm of the älfar siblings.

"A maga," Sisaroth warned his sister in a whisper. He was aware of the invisible power the unknown figure wielded. She was full to overflowing with it. "And who are you?" he raised his voice to ask.

"That's no concern of yours," she replied harshly, with

obvious authority, gesturing toward the captive girl. "You will not harm her; you will get back on your night-mares and you will leave Weyurn. Get back to Idoslane or Gauragar or Urgon and do your evil deeds there."

Firûsha placed her right foot on Mallenia's breast. "No, she's going back to Idoslane, too."

"Just try to take her," the woman threatened, her expression amused. "The Dragon will be glad to hear of your attempt. He'd finally have an excuse to attack. The last war against the älfar was a long time ago. And I seem to remember your folk did not too well out of it."

"She is a wanted criminal—" Firûsha retorted, but the woman interrupted her fearlessly.

"Then you would have done better to catch her in Idoslane, not in Weyurn. Get out of here!" She raised her arms slightly. "This is your final warning."

Behind where the siblings stood the noise of the waves altered, and a man splashed up out of the water. His face was badly grazed and in his hand he held a dagger; he appeared resolute. As resolute as the figure of the woman on the dunes.

"Get away from her!" he commanded them. "Leave Mallenia be, or the maga will burn you to cinders!" He knelt down by the unconscious figure of Mallenia and pulled her away from the dangerous hooves of the grotesque night-mares. One of the animals kicked out at him with a hind leg; he avoided injury by a surprisingly adroit move.

"You are not of the Dragon's retinue," Sisaroth said confrontationally. "You wear no dragon-scale pendant at your neck. How is it that you threaten us with Lohasbrand as if you knew him well?"

The woman did not reply—at least not with her voice. Instead, she stretched out her right arm, palm upwards. A brilliant ball shone on her gloved hand and floated slowly toward the älfar, the light growing in intensity the nearer it came.

The night-mares snorted and hissed in fear, recoiling; the bearded young man threw himself over Mallenia to protect her from their hooves. Sisaroth and Firûsha grimaced as the rays hurt their eyes.

"At a word from me the sphere will burst open and blind you forever," the woman on the dunes told them. "If you can find the way home blind, then do as you wish. If not, I suggest strongly that you leave Weyurn. I shall tell the Dragon that the älfar have violated the agreement. I wonder how he will react."

Firûsha wanted to pull out her sword, but Sisaroth restrained her. Turning to his agitated night-mare he climbed into the saddle. Then he and his sister rode off east.

The sphere pursued them for a time, as if it were a full moon come down from the heavens. After ten miles or so the ball of light gradually dissolved into glittering dust that fell onto the snow, unnoticeable on the bright crystalline surface.

Immediately, Sisaroth halted the night-mare and Firûsha turned her own mount. The real moon illuminated their furious faces, on which spreading thin black lines were visible. Their tumultuous feelings could not be concealed. They would gladly have transformed their rage into murder, but they stood no chance against a maga. Not in open attack.

Looking over to the island, where numerous lights were burning now, they could make out the shape of the shaft's iron bulkhead in the middle of the lake.

"That's where we'll find what is due to us," said Sisaroth darkly, glancing at his sister. "Let us bring death to them over the water."

"I don't intend to leave without Mallenia," she agreed. "She is the key to our achieving power in the three kingdoms. I want revenge for Tirîgon!"

Sisaroth noticed a fishing village nearby and turned down the path towards it. "Let us enquire who lives on the Island of the Brave. And then we'll see if there are humans suitable for a work of art. I feel the need to create something important."

Firûsha said nothing. But she thought that the tall island would soon be called the Island of the Dead.

VIII

Mallenia opened her eyes to see an awning. It was mainly in orange and red, and had unfamiliar white and yellow embroidery; the air was damp and cool, as if the windows were wide open. The scent of beeswax candles gently pervaded the room, and the light flickered softly.

She turned her head and saw a black-haired woman of about her own age sitting at her bedside, wearing a bright red dress with a tight-fitting bodice that emphasized her figure; the skirt was full and elegant.

"Welcome." The woman smiled at Mallenia. "My name is Coïra and you are on the island Lakepride in Weyurn. In the palace here you should be safe from the älfar who were pursuing you, Mallenia of Ido," she said quietly. "We have been able to save your arm, but even with magic it will take some time to heal. The night-mare's bite took flesh and bone."

Mallenia looked at her upper arm, hidden under a thick bandage. She could still feel the bite. Clearing her throat, she said, "I owe my life to you. I will never be able to repay what you have done for me."

"There is no need," came the friendly response. "You are a freedom-fighter and have dared to do things I would never have the courage for."

"Don't be so modest, Princess," said a man's voice at the other side of the bed. "In Mifurdania you fought Lohasbrand's orcs. That makes you a defender of freedom." Before the Ido girl could turn her head, a man with an unkempt beard bent over her. "May I introduce myself? I am Rodario the Seventh," he said shyly.

"He protected you from the night-mares down on the shore," said Coïra, "while I was dealing with the älfar." She remembered that he had not explained yet why he had not drowned. Surely he had told her he could not swim?

"Then I am in your debt, also," Mallenia nodded.

"Oh, not really. We freedom-fighters must stick together," he said, playing down his involvement. "And *protected* is an exaggeration. I just made sure you weren't trampled by the animals' hooves, that's all."

Mallenia smiled at him, before looking at Coïra. "The älfar—you defeated them? Just *the two* of you?"

"Even if I am not the same kind of maga as my predecessors, I still have powers enough. It was lucky for you that the älfar turned up *after* I had refreshed my magic energy. If they had arrived earlier I wouldn't have been able to help." She poured Mallenia a glass of tea. "But I'm afraid I must disappoint you: The älfar are still alive; I drove them back to Idoslane."

Mallenia pressed her lips together so tightly that they turned white. "You don't know them."

"Brother and sister, aren't they?" asked Rodario. "They looked so alike."

"Triplets," corrected Mallenia, taking a sip of the tea to moisten her throat.

Coïra pushed back the strands of long black hair. "As we

met two of them and you were riding a night-mare, I think I know what must have happened."

"They caught me in Topholiton, in Gauragar. My comrades were all murdered; I managed to kill one of the siblings and I escaped. Then they overtook me," she reported. "And they *will* return to kill me. I heard them talking when they thought I was unconscious."

"You understand their speech?" Rodario sat down and studied the woman. He liked what he saw. He liked it very much. At least as much as he liked Coïra, although they were so different in build and coloring. He saw that the blond Mallenia was used to working out with weapons and exercise. "Respect! How did you learn the language? It's supposed to be extremely difficult."

Mallenia forced a smile to her lips, but it came out crooked. "When a land has been occupied for as many cycles as Idoslane has, you get to understand the words the oppressors use." She did not dare to touch the bandaged arm; the wound was itching and throbbing painfully as it started to heal. "How long will it take?"

"The bone was badly affected. Multiple splintering. My magic has been able to fuse the remaining pieces but it will be at least eight orbits before you can use the arm again." Coïra stood up. "In two orbits' time you can get up. Shall I send a messenger to tell your friends where you are?"

Mallenia gave a deep sigh. "There's nobody left. The Dsôn Aklán, as they call themselves, killed all who were close to me or who were descendants, like myself, of Prince Mallen."

Rodario sat up with interest. "What does that title mean?"

"Something like *gods of Dsôn*."

"Quite a title!" He rubbed his chin. "But tell me, what

was the reason for the slaughter? To stamp out rebellion once and for all? Or is there more to it?"

Mallenia was surprised. "What do you mean, *more*?"

"How should I know? You're from Idoslane and you know the old myths and sagas. Is there a prophecy, maybe, connecting the descendants of Mallen with the overthrow of a mighty enemy?"

Mallenia was suddenly touched with doubt. "That had never occurred to me," she confessed.

"The älfar are well known for mysticism. So people say," Rodario added. "It might be like them to hunt down yourself and the others to stop a prophecy coming true." He seemed no less excited by the idea than she was. "It sounds like a story that ought to be put on the stage, don't you think?"

"Your enthusiasm is all well and good, but which stage would you perform it on?" objected Coïra. She was afraid the injured girl would be upset by the man's wild speculations and not be able to get the rest she so sorely needed. "In Weyurn you have no spectators and in Idoslane you wouldn't manage more than two sentences if the älfar in the story don't come out the winners."

Rodario stroked his meager beard again, as if he were trying to encourage it to grow. "That's true," he said pensively. "I'll have to enquire." He looked at Mallenia. "We'll need to find out whether there's more than bloodthirstiness behind the killings that the black-eyes are carrying out."

She was about to answer, but there was a knock and a servant stuck his head round the door. "Princess, your mother wants you. A messenger has arrived. One of the Lohas-branders." She raised her hand in acknowledgment and the servant withdrew.

"Rest, now, Mallenia. We'll look in on you later," said Coïra as she left, motioning to Rodario to follow her. "The more sleep you can get, the quicker you'll recover."

The two left the room and walked side by side through the palace, which was built at the top of the island.

Rodario could not contain himself. "What do you think the Dragon wants?"

"I've been asking myself the same thing ever since I heard there was a message," said Coïra, deeply preoccupied. She reproached herself for having acted unwisely in Mifurdania in letting her identity be known. She had brought danger on herself and on her beloved mother. The Dragon did not forgive. Certainly he would not forgive the death of an ally or support given to a criminal.

"I could volunteer as a hostage if Lohasbrand demands one," he began, but she waved this suggestion aside.

"Nobody is volunteering. I thought we could try to divert the Dragon's attention to the two älfar, without letting on why they were here. The dead night-mare would be proof. Then maybe the little episode in Mifurdania would lose its significance," she said firmly, but she was not convinced by her own words. "Are you all right? Your face?"

Rodario touched his cheek. "It's nothing. The iron wall gave me a kiss."

"I don't understand how you managed to fall over the parapet. And to reach the shore. Didn't you tell me you couldn't swim?"

"Carelessness and a puddle on the slippery walkway. I think Samusin saved my life," he lied. He had decided not to say anything about Loytan's attack on him. He would settle the matter with the count man to man. And he'd make sure he never turned his back on him again. "It all makes sense. My clumsiness got me to the shore at just the right moment. You on your own facing those älfar—it doesn't bear thinking about."

Coïra laughed at how serious the actor sounded. As if he really believed that she would have been in difficulty without him. "Yes, you saved me, Rodario the Seventh," she said in friendly tones, taking his hand. "Who would have suspected this fighting spirit in you? Forgive my honesty but, personally, I would never have thought it of you. Not after your night-time adventure in Mifurdania."

"How should I take that?"

"The little yelp when I stood in front of you—it was quite sweet. Like a little girl."

"Bah!" he said, overacting again.

She had to laugh. "I'm glad your true nature has come to the fore." The maga looked into his brown eyes to add a teasing remark—but stopped, in confusion. The hesitant expression on Rodario's face had disappeared and given way momentarily to something decidedly masculine, an air of a victor.

The impression spread briefly to his whole figure, giving him a strikingly different aura; she stared at him—but then the boyish shyness returned.

Rodario smiled and pressed her hand. "I'm glad, too." He let go as they approached the passage and came in view of the servants. Coïra wondered what it was that had just happened.

They walked to the west wing together; this was the queen's residence, even if it was in reality her prison and had been so for some time.

The servant opened the door to the high tower and they stepped into the room with its big round many-paned window of leaded glass. Behind the window what was left of the lake's beauty spread out to the horizon. There were clouds over the glistening surface of the lake and individual islands stood high, like plates on pillars. Others had the form of spheres.

Wey the Eleventh, deposed queen of Weyurn, rested on a cushioned seat by the window. Round her sat, or stood, four heavily armed and armored Lohasbranders. Wey was wearing a silken wine-red dress and a cap of black lace.

What did not remotely go with her attire was the iron ring around her neck. Four chains were attached to it, each one leading to a guard. Rodario noticed a device on the ring that would cause it to close up tight if the chains were pulled. Death by suffocation. If all four men pulled at the same time, he imagined it would decapitate her.

Rodario admired Wey, who pretended to ignore the humiliating chains. He had heard that the guards never left her side, in order to prevent her having access to the magic source. The ruler was the most powerful maga in Girdlegard, people said, more powerful even than Lot-Ionan. Nobody knew how old she was.

The Dragon, Rodario remembered, had somehow managed to defeat her and had promised to spare her daughter, and her land, if she agreed to submit to this imprisonment. The Scaly One must have had only the narrowest of victories. Rodario wondered why nobody had killed the four Lohasbranders. Concern for the population?

Wey nodded to them and the chains clinked slightly. Coïra and the actor bowed and took their seats on chairs the servants brought.

A fifth Lohasbrander came out from behind a set of bookshelves with a heavy volume in his hands. Rodario thought he might be about fifty; he had short brown hair and a burn scar under his left eye. He was flanked by two orcs: Both of them tall, armed to the teeth and quite horrible. He noted the new arrivals, studied them in turn and sat down at the desk that really belonged to the queen.

"Wrong seat," Coïra said rudely to the man. "Unless you are in reality a woman under your armor and entitled to the crown of Weyurn."

The man laughed out loud. "The wildness of youth," he chuckled, opening the book to browse through its pages. "You are always so direct in your words. Considering what you have been up to your conduct might be described as audacious and unwise in the extreme."

Rodario viewed the scale of horn that the envoy wore on a chain round his neck. It was engraved with a design that showed the man to be one of the Dragon's privy councilors, meaning that his words would be command and law, as if he were speaking for the Scaly One himself. Rodario thought it was not a promising sign, and so he got up from his seat. "I admit everything; the guilt was mine alone."

"Guilt?" The man looked bewildered. "By Tion! Now I see: It's yet another of the would-be Rodarios." He groaned. "They should all be done away with. I can't stand that face." He leaned forward. "Let me see: Yours is too fat, the beard is ridiculous, you don't speak your lines properly; it's as if you had stuffed cotton wool in your cheeks. Quite the opposite of the one we executed in Mifurdania. I'm sure he would have won the contest."

Rodario and Coïra stiffened.

The man grinned at them. "Yes, and now you're not quite so full of yourselves, are you?" He pointed to the scale he wore. "Let's get back to the real reason for my visit. I am Präses Girín and I have been sent by Lohasbrand to investigate incidents that have occurred in Mifurdania. It is said," and he turned his attention to Coïra, "you were involved. Things happened which only a maga could have arranged." His left hand gestured toward Wey. "If your mother has not left the island, as the guards assure me, there remains only you. That is an infringement of the agreement!"

Rodario had not sat down again. "Präses, who did you execute?" he stammered.

Girín rolled his eyes. "There are so many of you. How should I know who everybody is? I think it was The *Incomparable* Rodario." He smirked. "The sword did for him in the end. He wasn't as elusive as he thought. So the rebellion has lost its head, in all senses of the word. All that nonsense about liberty and resistance has gone with the wind."

Coïra held her hand to her mouth. Rodario swayed on his feet. "Stand tall," he murmured, pulling himself together.

Girín looked at Coïra. "Let's get back to you . . ."

"You are accusing the wrong person," the actor interrupted, pulling himself to his full height. *Stand tall!* "It was me!"

"You?" Präses burst out laughing. "What's your game? You want me to die laughing?"

"As actors we have a few ways to trick our audiences. We can produce illusions with a little powder, we can turn out the lamps and we can call up demons, given a little time to prepare and the wherewithal," he explained. "You will be acquainted with the old stories of the wonderful magister technicus Furgas? I had time enough at my disposal to arrange the escape. A friend of mine disguised himself and the two of us stormed the tower to free The Incomparable One. The orcs were stupid enough to fall for it."

Girín stood up, then raised his left arm and beckoned. "Come here, actor."

Wey and Coïra exchanged horrified glances.

The princess found it touching how Rodario was trying to help her but was in a quandary. If the Lohasbrander came to the conclusion that she had overstepped the terms of the agreement, her mother's life would be in danger; but at the same time she did not want the actor to make this sacrifice. She was amazed at the bravery he was exhibiting. There was more man in Rodario than she had assumed on first meeting him.

The actor moved over to the desk and Girín studied him closely. "All right, show me how you did it," he challenged, leaning back in his chair. "Show me your fake magic."

"I . . . need time to prepare!" said Rodario, pushing up his sleeves. "Right then, for example, the ball of fire. Here you'd have a little device with special plant seeds. When I press the igniting trigger and the flint . . ."

Girín shook his head. "No, I don't want explanations. I want to see the real thing."

"I'd have to go back to Mifurdania to get my equipment." Rodario shrugged his shoulders. "Can't do it otherwise. Perhaps we'll get lucky and meet those älfar that are spying round here secretly in Weyurn."

"Of course," said Girín in superior tones. "Älfar. We see

them here all the time. Saw one the other day doing some fishing by the lake." The orcs grunted with laughter.

"Don't you believe me?" He turned to Coïra. "She had to take on three of them yesterday, or they'd have infiltrated Weyurn. Probably scouts. On the shore you'll see the remains of a night-mare carcass. They're probably still near at hand. Tell that to the Dragon. There's more than one who's not keeping to agreements, then."

Präses was sunk deep in thought. Then he sent one of the orcs over to the mainland.

Coïra had to suppress a smile. Rodario had cleverly diverted attention from himself. It was clear that Girín could not allow himself to be negligent in such a matter.

"But," said the Lohasbrander, facing Rodario again, "whatever the truth about the älfar story you've just fed me, it doesn't remove your guilt." He motioned to another orc and the creature approached the actor. "I will take you with me to Mifurdania and confront you with the guards that survived the attack. If they think it's possible that they confused Coïra with you in women's clothing, then the blame can be lifted from the Weyurn ruling family and nobody is harmed." Girín nodded to the queen. "For you, Rodario the Howevermanyeth, the journey is over, one way or the other. When you arrive the contest could be finished and you will learn the name of the winner before the executioner lays your head on the block."

The actor had gone pale; his hands were fastened behind his back with a chain the orc took from his belt. But Rodario was still standing tall, with his chin slightly raised.

Coïra looked over at her mother again and tried to read in her eyes what the queen was thinking.

"I was telling the truth, Präses," said Rodario. "But what if the orcs don't agree? How reliable are they?"

"If it turns out they are sure that it was indeed Coïra who was responsible for the attack on the prison, Wey will suffer the consequences." Girín sounded indifferent. "Those are the terms of the treaty you signed," he told the queen. "The Dragon insists the terms are strictly observed and does not want to be the only one to keep to the agreement. You can thank your own flesh and blood."

"No. She won't have to. Coïra had nothing to do with it," Rodario repeated. He was dragged to one side by the orc and forced to stand next to the desk.

"Mother, what do you say?" asked Coïra, her hands on her belt that lay loosely round her hips. "The älfar would not stop for Präses if they encountered him and he were to stand up to them?"

"Hardly," said the queen. "And we'd have to ask the Dragon for support immediately to help us get rid of the invaders who threaten our island."

"What are you talking about?" barked Girín, switching his gaze from mother to daughter and back. "There are no älfar here, and they certainly would not dare to attack an envoy of the mighty Lohasbrand. The consequences would be unthinkable."

Wey got up slowly from her chair, her hands folded in front of her, like Coïra's. "I have waited so long for the opportunity to be freed from these fetters, Präses," she announced with dignity, pride in her eyes. "The gods listened and sent them to me. On this *notable* orbit. Thanks to you and to the älfar."

Girín guessed what was coming and sprang up from his chair. "Quick! Kill them both!"

The orc drew a huge sword and was about to attack Coïra, while the four guards pulled at the chains holding the queen's collar. The circumference of the ring narrowed.

Rodario tripped up one of the orcs, but not sufficiently to bring the creature to the floor. It stumbled, though, and took a couple of moments to regain its balance.

Red lightning hit face and breast; the orc let out a shrill scream of pain and fell burning onto the marble flagstones. Even the dark blood issuing from its wounds was in flames. Rodario could not tear his eyes away.

White trails of energy laid themselves round the ring and prevented it being pulled any tighter. Then the flashes worked their way along the chains to the hands of the Lohasbrander guards. With a hiss their fingers caught fire, as if they were made of dry wood.

The flames traveled up with amazing speed, slipping under the armor. Smoke issued from the guards' collars. The soldiers dropped the chains and beat at their clothing trying to extinguish the flames. Seconds later they were on the floor, burned black.

The iron ring around Wey's neck burst open with a clang and fell, glowing, to her feet. The queen looked at Girín, who had drawn his sword and was standing by the great window, trembling all over. "Did you really think I had no more magic power, Lohasbrander?" she said angrily.

"The Dragon will come and annihilate you!" he said. "He will destroy the whole of Weyurn; it will be overwhelmed in a sea of fire and the lakes will boil away."

"The Dragon will learn nothing of this. But he will be told about you and the älfar who fought you. In the palace. You will be portrayed in a heroic light. You should be pleased about it." Coïra smiled and stepped over to Rodario. A quick flash and his bonds were released. "We shall implore him to seek out the älfar. Because, of course, we care about the future of Weyurn, just as he does, even if for different reasons. He will take up our offer, that much is certain."

"But before that," Wey went over to him, "you must die, to bring our story to a fitting end."

Girín struck the window with his sword, shattering some of the panes. A strong gust of wind swept in through the opening, blowing objects around. The curtains flapped, papers and cloths and empty glasses landed on the stone floor. The air was filled with noise. "Never!" he screamed and jumped out, knowing that though it was a considerable fall he would eventually hit the lake waters.

Rodario did not want to leave it to chance as to whether or not the man died. Surprisingly fast he bent over one of the dead guards, drew a dagger and hurled it at the falling figure.

The blade hit Präses in the back of the neck. His body went limp and the hand released the sword. Rodario was satisfied. The women rushed forward and watched the corpse fall. They saw Girín as a black dot flying to meet the waves.

"That must be . . . at least eighty paces down. The impact of the water would have broken his neck, anyway," said Rodario with enjoyment. "He just didn't think it through."

Coïra wondered if Rodario's good aim had been more luck than judgment. She could not decide. Together they saw how the Lohasbrander plunged into the waters of the lake and disappeared.

"Do we need his body?" Wey asked them.

"It would be as well. We've got enough corpses to convince the Dragon, but the cadaver of Präses would be most effective." Her eyes fixed on the boat nearing the shore. "There's the orc rowing over, the one he sent to find the night-mare."

Coïra had understood. "I will see to it he doesn't land, in case he saw who fell out of the window." She embraced her mother and held her tight for a long time. "How long I've waited for this!"

"It seemed like an eternity." Wey had closed her eyes and placed her arms around her daughter.

Rodario's heart was beating wildly. "What shall we do now?" he asked excitedly. "What's the plan? You do have a plan?"

"In part," replied Coïra, freeing herself from her mother's arms. "We let the Dragon think that the älfar killed his men. Then we'll see what happens. If we're lucky he'll wage war on them. While they wear each other down we can go about our other projects." She came up to him and embraced him. "You are welcome to contribute your ideas to our rebellion."

Rodario grew hot. In his imagination she was naked as he had seen her at the bottom of the shaft. "Gladly, princess," he breathed, lifting his arms awkwardly. Was he permitted to embrace her or not?

Before he could decide, Coïra let go. "You are a sweetie, Rodario the Seventh!"

"I do have a suggestion!" he hastened to say. "How would it be if we kept people thinking the unknown poet is still alive? I could take on his role—well, the rhyming, anyway."

Coïra nodded, although she was not over-enthusiastic.

"Do you think you'd be able to? Nothing against your poetry . . ."

"I am a quick learner. You'll see." He made a deep bow. "I promise you, you'll be surprised just *how* quick."

There was a glimpse, Coïra felt, an image of the other Rodario, the one who was manly and who could aim very straight when throwing a dagger. Suddenly she was keen to see his verses.

Wey was still standing at the window watching the lake. "See to the greenskin, Coïra," she commanded. "He's nearly at the shore." She turned to them. "I shall speak with our new poet in the meantime. There seems to be a hidden talent here."

Rodario bowed. "At your service, Majesty!"

The Outer Lands,
Seventy-six Miles Southwest of the Black Abyss,
Winter, 6491st Solar Cycle

The flattened head of the crow's beak hammer struck Tungdil's armored chest and the runes flared up once more on the tionium platings, as if issuing a challenge to the sun and stars.

The handle of the weapon flashed—and shot off diagonally to hit the ceiling. Then the crow's beak fell to the floor.

"Ha!" Boïndil was standing close to the feet of the recumbent dwarf. "This time I didn't get clobbered with a magic shock." He grinned and smoothed down his beard, realizing that the hairs were standing on end from the magic charge. "If I let go of the weapon at the last moment and jump out of the way, the energy can't get to me. Ho, Scholar, what do you say to that: Am I clever or am I clever?" He picked up the crow's beak and studied the metal head. "Hmm. It looks all right." Ireheart extended a hand to Tungdil. "How's it going? Can you move now?"

Tungdil blinked. "All I can see is bright lights in front of my eyes," he snapped, lifting his right arm. The friends clasped hands and soon the dwarf was on his feet next to Ireheart. "But it did help. Colossal shock and potentially self-destructive, but it did the trick."

Boïndil laughed. "Not really self-destructive." He looked at the huge hole the magic had torn in the ceiling, a hole the size of a cow. "Anyway, now I know what to do if you fall over again. You'll just have to make sure I'm always around. If you're not careful they might think you're a statue next time it happens and you'll end up on top of a pedestal."

Tungdil lifted his arms and legs, turned his head and twisted from side to side. The armor had regained its former flexibility and was behaving as if nothing untoward had occurred. "I'll try to remember that when I'm fighting our enemies," he replied, going over to the table to have something to eat at last. Ireheart did not seem to have left him much.

"I couldn't have known my treatment for broken armor would work so quickly," Ireheart apologized in response to the enquiringly raised eyebrow. "What exactly did you feel when I hit you?"

"I don't know. It should never have happened."

Boïndil laughed and caught the sausage to pull it down. "Hang on, I'll rub it clean in the snow. Should taste fine." He tapped it against Tungdil's armor. "When it's thawed out, I mean."

"I'll be all right with what I've got here," said Tungdil, stopping his friend leaving the hut. "And the thirdling? Where did he get to?"

"The White Death rode down to the valley and caught him. Vraccas was on our side." Ireheart thought hard, his brow furrowing. "I've never seen a skirt-wearer like that one before. In armor with those runes. I could swear they were älfish symbols. Very strange."

"What's strange about it? You said the thirdlings and the black-eyes had a pact." Tungdil took the last ladlefuls from the pot, tipped them onto a plate and sat down to eat.

"There's a big difference between making a pact and having weird runes and peculiar armor. What I've heard about the thirdlings didn't mention they were actually friends with the black-eyes, or that they'd give each other armory lessons." Ireheart could not help glancing at his friend's tionium covering.

Tungdil went on chewing and drank a mouthful of tea. "So you want to know what kind of being it was I robbed and killed," he said, interpreting Ireheart's questioning gaze.

"Exactly, Scholar. He must have been a swine of a fellow, I know. And he must have used bad magic to make the armor, just like the älfar do. That's obvious from what just happened." Ireheart looked at Tungdil. "What else should I know? For an emergency?"

Tungdil scraped up the last bit of food and licked the spoon clean. "That was very good," he said. "You didn't leave me much, but it was very good."

Boïndil frowned. "Is this a miserable attempt to avoid answering?" He hunted in his pocket and pulled out his substitute pipe. "Good thing I had a second one with me.

That idiot trampled on my favorite pipe. I'd smoked it in just right." He filled it with tobacco and lit it with a spill from the fire.

Tungdil paused, staring at the steam rising from his mug of tea. As it rose it mixed with the blue smoke Ireheart was puffing out.

"I met him one cycle after I arrived on the other side. At least I think it was a cycle. The light is different down there and you lose the sense of the length of an orbit. I was defending myself against a horde of orcs and was in trouble because of the injuries I'd received in the Black Abyss. I killed the first twenty orcs quickly, but more and more monsters kept emerging from the passageways, attracted by the screams of the dying. I had my back to the wall and was fighting for my life; I'd taken two crossbow bolts to the body and my arm was practically severed, so I sent my final prayer to Vraccas. Then he appeared." Tungdil's voice failed, as if he needed a drink of water. "He wore different armor from this set, but it was similar. It was the first suit he had forged." Tungdil leaned over to Boïndil. "I swear he had greater strength than any dwarf. Stronger than you, Boïndil. Take you and me and your brother together and you come close. He wields two weapons the weight of the crow's beak at the same time, and he's so fast on his feet you can't see his blows coming. He carries a third weapon in a harness on his back. He . . ."

"Has he got a name?" Ireheart was listening with rapt attention.

Tungdil's eye flickered and Boïndil was not sure if it was fear or anger at the interruption. "He has many names. One of them I can pronounce: Vraccas."

"*What?*" Ireheart sat bolt upright. "That's blasphemy! How does he dare to call himself that?"

"He is without doubt something special and until I turned up he was the only dwarf in the blackness of the other side." Tungdil shuddered. "If you could see him, Boïndil, you would understand why the name made sense to me. And he saved me from the orcs." He dropped his gaze and stared at the mug of tea. "He took me to his refuge, an old stronghold abandoned by Tion's hordes. He had reinforced its defenses as necessary and had installed a giant forge there. It was just the way I'd always imagined the creator's eternal smithy! He has forges hot enough to melt anything, Boïndil! Stone, ore, everything! I saw it with my own eye. Dragon's Breath is merely a warm breeze in comparison." Tungdil stood up, restless now. "He passed the time thinking up types of new armor and perfecting them. If you like, I was his apprentice."

Boïndil rubbed his beard. He did not like the sound of this. "And these runes? Did the false Vraccas think them up, too?"

Tungdil nodded. "He knew a lot about magic, I think. But it was a different art from that of the magae and magi in Girdlegard. On the one hand, spells are compressed into the runes and you can bring them to life by the use of particular words. On the other, sometimes they can function on their own."

"I remember," grumbled Ireheart. "The first time was enough for me." He glanced at the ceiling, where snowflakes were drifting through the hole in the roof before melting on the floor. *A hole in the roof is better than an arm torn off.* He leaned on his elbows and put his chin in his hands. "So he was your master?"

Tungdil was walking up and down. "He showed me forging techniques that were new, and I made my own armor using these new skills. It had not escaped my notice that he would be visited every so often by monsters, and that he was quite polite to them. Horrific creatures, Ireheart. They were messengers from the kordrion and other monsters who are worse still. They would order armor and weapons for their troops. And some of them wanted to get him to lead their own armies. They'd have given him whatever he asked. You know, there was constant war among the beasts, because by nature they were so violent and bloodthirsty and couldn't get out of the Black Abyss, so they would fight each other."

Ireheart's imagination was working overtime, creating terrifying images. He saw crudely hewn passages full of monsters, slaughtering each other and covering the walls and ceilings with blood and guts; enormous caverns filled with vicious fighting forces, roaring and rampaging and at each others' throats; black fortifications that they charged and rammed, the walls shaking from the impact and from the hail of missiles.

Boïndil felt Tungdil staring. His friend smiled knowingly.

"Nothing you can imagine is bad enough to describe what I saw," said the one-eyed dwarf softly, as he took his seat again. "What wouldn't I give for a good gulp of brandy and a barrel of black beer," he sighed.

"Me too," muttered Ireheart, in spite of himself. His friend's story had affected him deeply. "What happened to you after that?"

"My master, if we can call him that, never took up their offers. He did not wish to lead armies—why would he? They weren't his wars and they weren't his people."

"And where was he from?" Boïndil wanted to know.

Tungdil ignored the interruption. Perhaps on purpose? "He provided arms for all sides. He made everything they asked for, but never gave them armor as good as his own. After thirty cycles with him I had won his trust and complete confidence. He would send me as his agent to negotiate with the forces of evil. They started to make those same offers to me." He swallowed and looked down. "*I* didn't resist. Reason told me it was a good thing to send as many beasts as possible to their deaths and I could do that best by leading one lot against another. And I had to get to the Black Abyss—what better way to get there than at the head of an army?"

"A wise decision, Scholar," commented Boïndil.

"But it brought down the anger of my master on my head. I had always let him think that I was sticking to his own principles: Never take sides and make everyone pay." Tungdil was about to take another sip and saw his cup was empty. "A mercenary. For one hundred cycles I was no better than a mercenary, serving the rulers who offered the best wages. I had my own domain, Ireheart." He smiled, but it was a thoughtful smile and a cruel one. "Thousands followed my command, my two fortresses were impregnable. But that made the princes in the underworld mistrust me. The ones I served got together to try to defeat me."

"You had to escape?"

Tungdil laughed and the sound of his laughter sent shivers down Boïndil's spine. He noted the deep malice in the voice of his friend. "No. I defeated them all and seized their realms. My warriors were the best because I had trained them in the way of dwarves. They were able to cut great swathes through the lines of the enemy. My power lasted about thirty cycles and I was the undisputed overlord on the other side."

"And your former master had turned against you," Ireheart assumed. He could not banish the chill from his body. The shadows were making Tungdil's face harder, the furrows deepened and the scar on his brow darkened.

"Because there was no more money to be made. I had ruined trade for him." Tungdil took a deep breath. "Let me stop there for now, my friend. I am tired and pained by the memory of all those orbits in Girdlegard I had wanted to forget. They pain my heart and mind." Tungdil got up and walked to the beds. "Can you take first watch?"

"Of course, Scholar." Boïndil hid his disappointment as best he could. He had a thousand questions to bombard his friend with, but he took pity on his old comrade-in-arms, noting how stiff and tortured he seemed to be—like a dwarf of eight hundred cycles.

Ireheart got up, placing a few more small logs on the fire and in the stove so that they would not freeze. The vital heat they needed was escaping all too quickly through the gaping hole in the roof. When he turned round he saw that Tungdil had closed his eye and was already asleep.

The dwarf rubbed his beard. He stood in the middle of the room, at a loss. Time passed slowly.

Eventually he went over to where his friend lay.

He studied the familiar face closely. Slowly he stretched out his right hand, the fingers approaching the golden eye patch.

When his fingertips were a hair's breadth away, Ireheart hesitated. *It is not right*, he said to himself. He balled his fist and forced his arm away, turning around and making his way back to the table.

You'll regret this one day! That was an opportunity that won't come round again. The doubting voices in his mind were shouting and screaming at him, but Boïndil ignored them.

He stared up through the gap at the stars and prayed to Vraccas—to the true Vraccas—and this Vraccas did not live on the far side of the Black Abyss, among fiends and monsters.

IX

Girdlegard,
Northeast of the Brown Mountains,
In the Realm of the Fourthlings,
Winter, 6491st Solar Cycle

Ireheart and Tungdil made their way to the outlying fortress, Silverfast, built to protect Girdlegard against threats from the northeast.

The stronghold had been reinforced with basalt stone by the fourthlings two hundred and eleven cycles previously because it had to serve as the primary barrier should the beasts from the Black Abyss ever encroach on this territory.

The tall walls and watchtowers with their topping of snow blocked the view of the yet more imposing second line of defense: The fortress Goldfast. These two strongholds were intended to repel any invaders and deny them access to the Brown Range of mountains.

Looking at the blocks of stone, Ireheart could easily tell they had been cut by dwarf-hands, but the fourthlings had not been granted the same skill as masons that Vraccas had given to his own race. The fourthlings were masters in the art of working with precious metals.

The ponies and the befún curved round to face the glittering white plain—a plain that years earlier had been overrun first by orcs and then, immediately afterwards, by the acronta.

Ireheart was familiar with the epic stories about the battle but had not been there himself. "I can imagine how it happened. It must have been quite a fight; just my kind of thing!" he said. As he spoke, his breath formed a white cloud. "The pig-faced orcs, ogres and trolls would have hurled themselves at those walls and started to climb." He pointed to the right. "Over there the original watchtower collapsed under the constant catapult fire, killing hundreds of beasts." He sighed. "And then they got closer and closer, stormed up the ladders and were about to swarm through the gem-cutters' corridors, but . . ." he paused and looked at Tungdil, ". . . but then *they* appeared!"

Tungdil was listening but gave no sign that he knew how the story went.

"The monsters had nearly overwhelmed the fourthlings when the acronta rolled in over the plain and hunted down the orcs as if for sport, like a dog might chase a cat." He laughed and slapped his thigh. "What wouldn't I have given to have seen that and to have fought at their side!"

"Didn't the acronta eat the orcs afterwards?"

"Oh, yes, they did. Do you remember Djerûn, Andôkai's bodyguard—Andôkai the Tempestuous?" Boïndil looked at the walls, which had been repaired two hundred and fifty cycles ago, twice as thick as before, even though in truth the more dangerous enemies lay to the south of the dwarf realm. But in those times there had been no way of knowing that.

Two flags flew on the highest towers: One for the kingdom of the fourthlings and one for the union of all the dwarf realms. It was a nice fancy, because there was now no true community of dwarves as in the old times under the high king.

Tungdil patted the befún's neck. "No," he said honestly.

"There are large parts of my life I know hardly anything about." He touched the scar on his forehead and looked at Ireheart. "Tell me about this Djerůn character."

Ireheart gave a dismissive wave. "He's not important, Scholar. I just wanted to talk about the acronta and . . . it doesn't matter." He took his bugle, put it to his lips and sounded it. It was not long before an answering fanfare came from the walls. On hearing that he blew a different set of notes.

Slowly but surely, the gates of Silverfast were opened for them.

Tungdil and Ireheart rode up to the entrance in silence. A troop of dwarves stood in formation at the gate, pikestaffs in their hands.

The one-eyed dwarf noted that crossbow marksmen were manning the battlements. "We don't seem to be particularly welcome," he commented.

"They don't have anything against us personally. It's regulations," explained Boïndil. "Frandibar Gemholder of the Gold Beater clan adopted the procedure on my advice. Nobody gets through to the other side without undergoing a thorough check. Not even me." Ireheart was concerned about how the envoys of the dwarf-races would react to this folk hero, now so sadly changed.

They rode up to the guards.

"Not sure, Ireheart?" Tungdil's voice was devoid of bitterness or reproach. He smiled sadly. "There will be others to whom the notion of my being an impostor or a phantom will occur, when they see me. Especially when they hear my new suggestions for forcing Lot-Ionan to his knees. Because that's what we need to do: We have to bend him to our will, and *not* kill him. That, Ireheart, is going to be the most difficult thing, with a determined and desperate opponent."

"Desperate? Lot-Ionan is a magus; why should he be desperate?"

"The longer we fight against him, the more he will be overwhelmed with despair. Believe me." Again his features displayed a frightening mirth. The expression would have suited a demon. Ireheart would not have wanted to turn his back on Tungdil at that moment, but he returned his smile.

They had reached the sentries now: Heavily armed and grim-faced dwarves in thick coats. They held their pikes ready to be used instantaneously.

"State your names and your business," said the captain of the guard. Tungdil left the explanations to Boïndil.

Boïndil noticed that the guards' attention was focused on the Scholar. In his flamboyant armor and mounted as he was on a very unusual animal, he aroused curiosity and suspicion; that altered when they learned the somber dwarf's name.

"By Vraccas!" exclaimed the captain; he bowed to them both. "Can it be true that the two greatest dwarf-heroes have arrived to free Girdlegard? We did not expect you so soon. The delegates have not all come yet."

"Then we'll begin the strategy meeting without them," said Tungdil abruptly. "Can we pass?"

"Of course, Tungdil Goldhand," said the captain at once and gave a signal. The guards drew back to let them through.

"How do you know I am the real Tungdil Goldhand?" he asked darkly from atop his befún. "Do I look like a child of the Smith? In *this* armor? And what do the runes on the tionium signify? What if they meant death to observers?"

"Well . . . you're riding with Boïndil Doubleblade. He

identified himself with the bugle signal. I thought . . ." The dwarf-captain hesitated and looked at Ireheart. He had not expected to be blamed and criticized for the warm welcome he had given the new arrivals.

"Thank you. We'll find our own way in," said Boïndil in much friendlier tones. "Give us a soldier who can guide us swiftly and directly through the Brown Mountains to King Frandibar Gemholder. There is not an orbit to be lost. And the pressure of the crisis affects even such heroes as Tungdil Goldhand. Forgive the harshness of his manner." He spurred his pony on.

The captain saluted and called out a name; as soon as Ireheart and Tungdil had passed under the archway, an opening large enough to have admitted even a kordrion, a dwarf came riding after them to act as their guide. He kept his distance. The words of the somber hero had been noted.

"What was all that about, Scholar?" whispered an angry Boïndil. "Isn't it enough if they get suspicious gradually? Do you enjoy sowing doubts?"

"I thought there would be some kind of a check," he replied. "But they let us waltz in without asking us even to dismount. They should have searched our luggage at the very least." His right hand touched the breastplate and stroked one of the runes. "And with this armor, these runes, he just let me in. Did you see how they stared at me? As if I were a monster."

"At the moment that's just what you sound like, Scholar," Ireheart retorted, feeling insulted. "You're not happy, whatever people do. What advice would *you* have given him?"

"Go and tell the captain he must not admit a single dwarf after us," Tungdil said. "No matter who he is or who he claims to be. We saw one thirdling in the Outer Lands and I don't think he was the only one. They will try to break into the realm of the gem cutters from the north.

"A spy, then," Boïndil surmised. "Of course! They'll circumvent the Brown Range and check out the lie of the land and see where the defenses are weak before they attack."

Tungdil offered ironic applause. "Now you've understood. I hope you can see, then, why I acted as I did."

But Ireheart couldn't really, even though the explanation made some sense. Surely the Scholar could have spoken rationally and calmly to the captain. "I'll tell our leader. He'll pass it on to the Silverfast troops. They'll be more careful in future."

The main gate of Goldfast stood open in welcome for the heroes, and here again the dwarves were received with cheers of frenetic rejoicing, fanfares and drum rolls. All the guards had left their posts to greet the pair.

Waving and smiling to the crowd, Ireheart sneaked a look at Tungdil. The Scholar cast a stony gaze to right and left. He rested one hand on his thigh as he rode; the other held the reins of the befún. He entered the fortress like a grim, war-weary general: No hand raised in acknowledgment, no greeting, no smile. The only clues to his state of mind were the spark in his eye, his pride and his awareness of his own power.

They continued without delay and Tungdil urged their guide to make swift progress.

Ireheart was still thinking about the thirdling they had encountered at the mountain refuge. "It would mean," he blurted out while they were riding through a large cavern where the walls were covered in a film of water, "that the skirt-wearers have done more than merely form an alliance with the black-eyes."

Tungdil had shut his eye and was listening carefully to the falling drops of water in the wall niches.

"The armor carried älfar runes, didn't it?" Boïndil insisted, urging his pony to keep up with the befún. "I thought everything about the enemy dwarf was strange. That powder he strewed in my face, blinding me . . . where did he get that? The thirdlings usually rely on their military prowess and wouldn't use dirty tricks like that. And he moved in such an unusual way, not like a dwarf at all. He very nearly," he said, turning his face toward Tungdil, "made me think of Narmora. What do you think?"

Tungdil opened his eye and sighed. "So who is Narmora?"

"Who *was* Narmora, more like," growled Ireheart in exasperation. "By Vraccas! How am I expected to tell you what conclusions I've come to if you don't remember half the things we've been through together?"

"I, too, would prefer to be able to remember." Tungdil looked at his friend. "So was she an älf?"

"She was a half-älf. She was the companion of the crazy magister technicus . . ." He hesitated and waited tensely.

"Furgas," said Tungdil without hesitation. "I remember him very well. A true master, more than a genius. But then he was seduced by evil ideas and went mad. Narmora will have inherited . . . Was it her father or her mother that belonged to the älf folk?"

"The mother."

"So it goes like this," Tungdil summed up pensively. "You think the black-eyes have been training the thirdlings in their own dark arts. But how would that work? Our race has no talent for magic . . ."

"And what about Goda, then? And my children?" Ireheart objected, having to rein in his family pride. His life-companion *was* a maga. The only maga in the dwarf folk. "Goda belonged to the thirdlings once. Why should she be the only one?"

"If you follow that through, maybe the secret talent Vraccas gave to the thirdlings was the gift of magic," Tungdil mused. "A gift he never told them about, on purpose. He wanted them to find it out on their own, in good time."

Ireheart rubbed his beard and fiddled around arranging the braids. "Why would he do that? I think it's just a matter of chance." Even while he was speaking he was aware that his friend had spent many cycles in the vaults of a great magus. "Go on, Scholar, tell me. Did you ever have a go at spells yourself?"

"No."

That answer was so fast in coming that it made Boïndil's inner chorus of doubting voices wake up. He closed his eyes and demanded that they stop challenging his friend's identity, but however forcefully he pressed his eyelids shut the voices merely became hoarse, rather than going quiet; he waited in vain for them to be silent. *What evidence will allay these suspicions once and for all, Vraccas?*

After a long ride through the Brown Mountains and in through a vaulted arch, seven paces high and made of pure silver set with onyx stones, they reached an area of the dwarf realm set aside for official business.

On the walls of the corridors were depictions, more than life size, of events from the history of the fourthlings and of the other dwarf folk, displayed not in paint but in mosaic, using different-colored jewels. Shortly before they were told to dismount they saw a picture of the Black Abyss. The artist had placed a dwarf in heroic stance at the mouth of the ravine, the weapon Bloodthirster clearly recognizable in his hands.

Tungdil got down from the befún to inspect it. Slowly he raised his hand to touch his own image. "By all that's unholy," he mouthed, swallowing hard. "Such a long time. Such a long time ago."

Ireheart stood next to him and observed his expression. "Typical of the gem cutters. They could easily have done one of me as well," he complained jokingly, without taking his eyes off his friend's face.

"In truth, they could," said Tungdil absently, his armored gauntlet still resting on the mosaic. "I promise you'll be in the next one they do."

"Side by side, the two of us, Scholar."

Tungdil stared at the picture of the Black Abyss. "No. I shan't be on the next picture, Ireheart. I've already played my part. It is the turn of other heroes now." Tungdil turned abruptly to face his companion. "Heroes like you and your children. Heroic women like Goda." A tear rolled down his cheek and slid down into his beard to hide. "I shall merely be the one who brings things together, but the fighting and glorious deeds will be carried out without me." He took a deep breath and his expression became cold and hard again. "Let's get on."

Ireheart was too surprised to respond. He followed Tungdil, who was heading toward a huge door where the dwarf-leader stood; the door itself was covered in gold leaf, and runes picked out in diamonds shone brilliantly. They promised a haven of calm and safety to whoever passed through the doorway.

Four dwarf-sentries stood guard. It was obvious from their relatively slight stature that they were fourthlings; they saluted the new arrivals.

Tungdil and Ireheart stepped into the room one after the other. There was a hexagonal table in the middle, made of a bluish-gray ogre-eye stone. Each of the tribes had a place accorded them, and the freelings had also been included. The bitter enmity of the thirdlings had led to someone shattering the part of the table originally intended for them. Between the secondlings and thirdlings was a gaping hole.

This was not the only thing that struck the eye; only the representatives of the fifthlings and fourthlings were sitting at their places; there was food and drink arrayed on the table in front of them. The delegates of the various clans sat some distance off on stone benches.

Ireheart saw at once how few were gathered there. His courage started to ebb.

As the two of them entered the room, dwarves stood up and bowed their heads.

"Welcome," said one dwarf, wearing an ornamental silver cuirass with polished gold inlay. He made no secret of his wealth. It would have been difficult to conceal the brilliance of the dazzling jewels on his armor. He had long blond hair, his sideburns reached to his chest, while the beard on his chin curled down all the way to his belt; the remaining facial hair was smartly trimmed to a finger's length. "I am Frandibar Gemholder of the clan of the Gold Beaters and I am king of the fourthlings. I bid you both welcome, Tungdil Goldhand

and Boïndil Doubleblade, and am glad to be the first in Girdlegard to receive the heroes of our race. It is truly a great honor!" He approached them, stretching out his hand to Tungdil.

The one-eyed dwarf studied the king as if he were dealing with some leprous supplicant. He had to force himself to hold out his own hand, doing so slowly and reluctantly. Ireheart sighed, showing himself eager to greet the king in contrast, and giving a strong handshake.

Then a second dwarf came over from the table. His wavy dark-brown hair was worn in a plait, his beard was short and, in contrast to the ruler of the fourthlings, he wore combat dress that seemed to be a cross between chain mail and lamellar armor. On his weapons belt hung a two-headed morning star studded with spikes, and at his left side there was short-handled throwing ax.

His figure was impressively muscular. The fifthlings were a mixture of different dwarf-tribes and had accepted the heritage of the Gray Range. The original fifthlings, the defenders of the Stone Gate, had all died out, so Ireheart hazarded a guess that this dwarf's ancestors had been firstlings or secondlings.

"I am Balyndar Steelfinger of the clan of the Steel Fingers, son of Balyndis Steelfinger the First, queen of the tribe of the fifthlings," he said by way of introduction. "My mother sends her regrets, but she is needed at the Stone Gateway. We are not only dealing with Tion's monsters but are also having to cope with the ravages of a mysterious fever that has struck down many of the tribe. Her own health is fragile and she is not up to making the long and dangerous journey to the Brown Mountains." He bowed again. "I have come at her behest to find out what the hero of Girdlegard has to tell us. I must say straight off that my mother has her doubts: She does not believe Lot-Ionan can ever be defeated."

Ireheart looked at Tungdil, struck by the resemblance between his old friend and this young dwarf. The chin, mouth and nose were almost identical and their voices were so similar in intonation. *By Vraccas! If I didn't know better I'd take them for father and son.* A swift glance to Gemholder showed that the same thing had occurred to the king.

Tungdil watched the queen's son, opened his mouth to speak and shut it again. "I'm sorry," he said finally, sounding as if he had really intended to say something quite different. "We thought the sickness curse on the northern realm was banished for all time."

"Tion's power has grown. No surprise, considering what's been going on in Girdlegard," replied Balyndar. "But thank you for your sympathy." He nodded to the older dwarf.

Ireheart's eyes whizzed to and fro; he compared the dwarves as unobtrusively as possible and found his first impression confirmed.

Balyndis had been Tungdil's companion, but he had rejected her and selected an undergroundling as his mate: Sirka. Balyndis had gone to the fifthlings and been welcomed again by the king; soon she shared his throne and bore a son.

What an awful thought. The warrior screwed up his eyes. *The boy's age would be about right.*

"You will want to refresh yourselves . . ." Frandibar began.

But Tungdil shook his head. "We need to get down to business first," he interrupted, looking at the clan delegates.

"You may find yourselves amazed by what I say but don't laugh at my words or interrupt me. What I'm going to put to you is the only way to free Girdlegard from the repeated plagues and assaults it now suffers. From what our whole race now suffers." He walked round the table and reached the place where the table edge had been hacked away. "I am a thirdling and so I shall sit here," he announced. He held himself very upright, with neither fear nor awe in his expression. It was clear to all that he was accustomed to commanding and being instantly obeyed.

Boïndil was surprised to note that there was no resistance among the clans to what Tungdil had said. The hero was indeed an impressive presence. *Or does his appearance make them afraid, and that is why they are submitting?*

Gemholder got a servant to bring a chair for Tungdil and the dwarf took his place as if he were the king. As if he were still ruler over a realm and commander-in-chief of an army. "What about the office of high king?" he asked.

"After Ginsgar died and all the things that happened in Girdlegard there was no time to elect a high king to govern all the tribes," replied Balyndar. "We were all too busy fighting the attackers. And it's been like that right up until the present orbit, Tungdil."

"The secondlings have been wiped out, the thirdlings don't count. What about the firstlings? Have they crawled so deep into their tunnels for fear of the Dragon that they can't find the way out?" Tungdil looked first at Balyndar, then at Frandibar. "What's the last you heard from them?"

"There was a letter sent to my mother," said the fifthling. "A certain Xamtor Boldface was asking for support against the Dragon, but we had to tell him that we don't have enough soldiers to man an expedition. They would have had to fight their way past the kordrion and across Dragon-land to get to the Red Mountains." Balyndar's face went dark. "The Lohasbranders, it is said, kill any dwarf they set eyes on. Our deputation would never have reached the west alive."

"We thought the same," agreed the king of the fourthlings. "Queen Balyndis passed on the request to us, but we are having to defend ourselves against the thirdlings and the älfar. We need every weapon and warrior available."

Tungdil glanced over at the second unoccupied place at the table. "Where are the freelings?" Shoulders were shrugged. "Well, you've still got to put a coalition force together to fight for Girdlegard." Tungdil ran his gauntleted fingers over the broken edge of the table. "A fighting group composed of the best of the fourthlings and fifthlings. Like in the past when we were looking to forge Keenfire." He stopped. "Did Keenfire ever turn up again?" The dwarves shook their heads. Tungdil reached for his tankard and downed the contents in one; then he slammed it down and appeared to stare into the void.

Ireheart felt the unrest that was spreading through the gathering. *The clan chiefs had been expecting more than this.*

"Lot-Ionan," said Tungdil suddenly, and a jolt ran through the assembled company. His voice was deeper now and the sound of it struck fear in their hearts. "He is the last magus, and so, for our race, he is undefeatable. The tribes are in no position to be able to deal with our other adversaries; or, if they could, then only one at a time and with terrible losses. That would only give an advantage to remaining foes." He banged the table. "*If* you are mad enough to attack first. But if you let someone else do the spadework and wait with your attack until the enemy has been weakened, then victory is a possibility."

"What do you mean?" Balyndar wanted to know. He was drinking water, Ireheart noticed, and not touching any food that was heavy or greasy.

"We get the kordrion, the älfar, Lot-Ionan and the Dragon to wage war on each other," he explained, smiling darkly. "Whoever emerges as the victor will be annihilated by the children of the Smith."

Balyndar uttered a peculiar sound that turned into mocking laughter. "Simple as that? The four of them have split up our homeland among themselves for cycles now, but they'll attack each other at the drop of a hat just because the great Tungdil Goldhand turns up and asks them to?" He got up, looking furious. "My mother was right. You won't change anything. It's like being in a battle waiting for the veteran fighters to arrive, only for a feeble old man to turn up instead."

Hardly had he said that last word when he was hit so hard on the back that he fell forward onto the table. A shadow had grabbed him by the nape of the neck and was rubbing his face against the rune that stood for the realm of the fifthlings.

Ireheart blinked and then saw it was his friend. *How did he manage to move so quickly?*

"Balyndar Steelfinger! You may have inherited much from your mother, but not her iron will," said Tungdil angrily. "Take a look at the symbol for your tribe!" He increased the pressure. Balyndar tried to resist and turned to grab his attacker, but he could not. "Look at it, I said," shouted Tungdil. "The name Balyndis will be the last name of a sovereign in a whole line of queens and kings if we all follow your way of thinking. There'll be no one at all who can read about the exploits of the dwarves." He let Balyndar go and went back to his own seat.

Balyndar pushed himself upright and stared at the one-eyed dwarf in fury. On his right cheek and on his temple the rune had left an imprint that was gradually fading. "You dare to . . ."

"I dare, yes, *I do dare!*" Tungdil's voice drowned out the words of the younger dwarf. "I dare to tell you and the others what must be done. It is simple; all it takes is skill, courage and sharp blades. But *not* an army. Not at first." He pointed north. "Steal the kordrion's young and take them to Lot-Ionan. The beast will follow, looking for its offspring. You have to be ready with a small force to overthrow the victor. And the victor will definitely be Lot-Ionan. You need the magus to put a stop to what is being prepared in the Black Abyss."

Frandibar folded his arms. "What if the kordrion defeats the long-un? Then, according to you, we'd be helpless."

"He won't. A kordrion can't defend itself against magic. It might be able to destroy the wizard's famuli but it will be powerless faced with Lot-Ionan himself." Tungdil's fingers ran along the line of the Red Mountains on the map on the central table. "After that you take the best treasures from the Dragon's hoard and plant them on the älfar. Lohasbrand will set his humans and his orcs on the älfar in Dsôn Balsur, and because they won't be able to overrun the black-eyes on their own, he'll have to get over there himself." Tungdil's gaze swept over the assembled dwarves. "Again it will be the task of the children of the Smith to watch and wait. And then to attack the victor, who will be weakened by then, of course, from the battle. You should manage that. And there you are: Girdlegard is free of all tribulation."

"He's gone mad," came the voice of one of the clan leaders. "What kind of expedition would be able to do all that?"

"So do you not have any fresh heroes? Was it just a cheap excuse—let's do nothing at all until Tungdil comes back?" Tungdil whirled round. "I can see some strong arms and watchful eyes here in this room. Take Balyndar with you. He's an obvious choice." He pointed at Ireheart. "Don't forget my old comrade. He and his crow's beak will sort out enemy skulls and armor, no problem. Get yourself a skillful cross-bowman and send a handful of brave hearts along with them. When you've found them, offer prayers to your god, and send them on their way."

"And you won't be with them?" The king of the fourthlings was aghast.

"No." Tungdil sat down heavily in his chair. "After over two hundred cycles of constant war, battle and combat, enough is enough. I shall find myself a nice little place and shall watch from the sidelines as you eliminate evil. It's enough for me to know that I have given you the plan."

Balyndar had swallowed his anger and looked extremely disappointed. "So this is the great hero, whose deeds are so far out of our league. He looks like one of Tion's warriors and the speeches he makes demand the impossible of us. Then he sits down and takes his ease to watch us fail." He laughed joylessly. "Thank you, Tungdil Goldhand."

Ireheart heard the clan leaders talking quietly among themselves and observed that they were not following what was going on at the hexagonal table anymore. As for himself, he was still trying to think through the strategy his friend had outlined. *This meeting mustn't end in discord!* He took a deep breath, raised his voice and announced "The Scholar is right!"

Silence fell in the hall. All of them stared at him.

"He's right," Ireheart repeated, laying his hand on the map of Girdlegard. "We don't have massive armies to march in with. Our strongholds have been destroyed for the most part, and in those fortresses that still exist we sit waiting for death to take us. Either with älfar arrow, kordrion attack, fever, or dragon fire." He stood up. "Our only hope is to employ the tactics Tungdil has described." He placed his hand on his crow's beak. "I shall be of the party riding out to save our race. The fate of the dwarves must be decided by the dwarves themselves."

Frandibar studied him carefully, then looked at Tungdil. "There's certainly some truth in what we've heard," he said, speaking gravely. "And it will have an impact if we can say that Boïndil Doubleblade rides at the head of a band of daring warriors. But the one we really need is the most famous of us all." His eyes fixed on Tungdil. "I beseech you. Go with him. The time for rest is when Girdlegard is at peace once more."

Balyndar cast a contemptuous glance at Tungdil. "Otherwise we will have witnessed the most pointless return of a hero there has ever been in Girdlegard."

The one-eyed dwarf smiled maliciously. "Neither threat nor entreaty can move me. I have been through too much for that. I have lived through too much."

A thought flashed into Boïndil's mind that seemed perverse and monstrous enough to make some sort of sense. His friend could not be motivated by the offer of treasure or by appeals to altruism. He had been heaped with glory and wealth on the other side of the Black Abyss. *But there is one honor he is missing* . . . "And what if you were to lead us as high king of the dwarves, Scholar?" Ireheart spoke his thoughts out loud.

At once a clamor of voices broke out.

"Quiet!" demanded Frandibar, raising his arms. "Be quiet and let him finish."

Unruffled, Ireheart elucidated his idea. "This is not just a random suggestion. Think about it: With one of their own tribe at our head we have a chance to negotiate with the thirdlings. Imagine if we could do that . . . if Tungdil could do that—if he could convince them they'd be better off holding back while we fight the älfar, and waiting to see what happens. Or even supporting us in our fight."

No outcry ensued. The dwarf folk discussed the matter quietly among themselves, gesticulating and nodding or shaking their heads.

Ireheart and Tungdil exchanged glances. The smile had altered and now showed a mixture of amusement, disbelief and satisfaction.

Balyndar was frowning, his hand gripping his morning star. "I would have to vote in favor, even if he is not my first choice," he announced, turning to the assembly. "Boïndil Doubleblade's suggestion is not to be dismissed out of hand. We are in a position to elect Tungdil Goldhand as our high king. The generations coming after us can decide if we have acted sensibly in this crisis. We must not forget the effect it will have on Lot-Ionan when Tungdil appears. He was once his foster-father, after all." Balyndar turned to Tungdil. "But I have my doubts. I say this openly."

"Let it be a further reason to take part in the campaign yourself," said Ireheart, not able to quell his own growing misgivings when he saw Tungdil's smile. *Vraccas help us.*

Frandibar stayed silent for a time before getting to his feet. "Our race has never had to make a decision like this. Not until this orbit. It is important that every clan leader, man or woman, be asked his or her opinion." He pointed to the first dwarf of the fifthling tribe and recorded his approval of the plan.

It took a long time to ask each member of the assembly for their view.

But finally the decision was unanimous. All eyes rested on Tungdil when Frandibar opened his mouth to address the hero.

Ireheart came to Tungdil's chamber. A single candle still burned; tiny flames flickered in the fireplace, casting a dark-red glow over the room.

His friend was sitting by the fireplace in full armor, his back to the door. Although his chair was large, he only just fitted. His right hand lay on the pommel of Bloodthirster, while the tip of the weapon rested on the floor. The golden eye patch shimmered blood-red in the firelight and the inlaid patterns on the black tionium armor glowed as if they had come alive, warmed by the flames.

Ireheart saw that food on a plate next to Tungdil was untouched, but the beer jug lay empty on its side. "You're not happy with how the vote went, Scholar," he stated.

Tungdil did not answer.

"Scholar?" Ireheart came around the armchair to look at his friend's face. He was horrified.

The remaining brown eye had changed its color, taken over by green whirling patterns. Then dark-yellow spots appeared from the depths and suppressed the green. The black pupil looked glassy and dead.

Ireheart bent forward. "What's happening . . . ?"

Tungdil's gaze grew sharp again and once more his eye was brown. "I'm sorry, I was asleep," he said in greeting, rubbing his face as if he wanted to make sure everything was back in place. "What can I do for you?"

Boïndil pulled his head back, fighting down his astonishment and shock. "I wanted to know how you were feeling. If you were satisfied with how the vote went." He took a seat opposite Tungdil.

"Is that the real reason you came?" Tungdil was breathing heavily. "Or did you want to see what I get up to when I think no one is watching?"

"You're surely immune to being taken by surprise in that armor of yours." Ireheart attempted a light tone, his smile awry.

Tungdil looked at his friend and Ireheart was pleased to see the old familiar expression. He had no doubt about it; this was his true Scholar.

"I didn't ever ask you what you thought of my suggestion," Tungdil said. "About how we take on the enemy."

"Bit late for that now, surely? The decision is made."

"Yes, I should have taken you into my confidence earlier," replied Tungdil. "You were a wonderful advocate for me."

Boïndil smiled amiably. "I can't leave you to face those obstinate stubborn-heads all by yourself. What kind of comrade would that make me?" He rubbed his brow and put his fingertips together. "It will certainly be dangerous,

and undoubtedly there will be much loss of life. I have no
illusions on that score. But it could work, because none of
the enemies will be expecting a trick like we have planned.
We'll get them with their own weapons." He muttered into
his beard: "Well, at least the black-eyes."

"You're sure about this?"

Ireheart considered the matter. "There are many impon-
derables in your strategy that we can't influence. What if the
älfar kill the Dragon sooner than we intend them to? What
if the kordrion doesn't care about its brood like you assume
it does? What if Lot-Ionan only has to snap his fingers to
turn the beast to stone?" He folded his arms across his chest.
"But I think that's unlikely."

"Is that because you are sufficiently desperate to believe
anything or because it was me that suggested the plan?"

"I'm in favor because it's a good plan. Audacious, but
good," replied Ireheart thoughtfully. "I've been through so
much with you and we've made so many impossible things
happen, so I don't have doubts about this."

Tungdil nodded in silence and stretched out his hand for
the jug. Seeing it was empty he swept it from the table. "Do
you think the title of high king will suit me?"

That was a question Ireheart would have preferred not to
have to answer. "It was my idea, after all. If I hadn't been
convinced of that I wouldn't have put it to the assembly,"
he said, skirting around the difficulty.

"You *think* it was your idea. But what if my runes had
put a spell on you?" Tungdil suggested wearily. "If it was
me putting the idea into your head? So that I could get my
hands on the title at last, after all those cycles of wanting it.
Although I knew under normal circumstances it could never

happen? *It would never be allowed.*" The eyelid fluttered and the eyeball rolled back. He was practically asleep.

"I don't believe that, Scholar," said Ireheart quietly as he stood up. "If I don't want to do something I'm sure nobody else's thoughts can take hold of me." He looked around the chamber and found a blanket that he spread over Tungdil.

Ireheart's lips narrowed. "You will be the best high king the tribes have ever had," he whispered as he withdrew. "A high king born of crisis and one that will tower over all the previous incumbents. Perhaps the ruler who will finally be able to bring peace to the children of the Smith. Genuine peace and not just an armistice."

The warrior walked to the door and smiled at his sleeping comrade, then he left the sparsely furnished chamber, a room unworthy of a freshly elected high king.

X

Girdlegard,
Protectorate of Gauragar,
Eleven Miles East of the Entrance to the Gray Mountains,
Winter, 6491st/6492nd Solar Cycles

Ireheart's eyes were fixed on the chain of hills rising to the north. They were the foothills of the Gray Range, running across the horizon in a ribbon, and they promised the travelers a place of safety.

"I wish we were there already," he muttered into his mottled gray and white beard.

Tungdil was riding at his side, still preferring a befún to a pony. This made him taller in the saddle than the rest of the group, which consisted of the two of them and then Balyndar and his deputation of fifthlings. Frandibar had also given them his five best fourthling warriors, one of whom was a crossbow archer. "It never looked for a moment as if we were in any danger."

"That's what bothers me," said Balyndar, scanning the snowy expanse before them. "On the journey we narrowly escaped from a patrol of Duke Amtrin's men. He's in the service of the älfar."

"*Escaped!* Listen to that," snorted Ireheart. "I can't believe it! In the old days we'd have hunted them down instead of running away and hiding."

Balyndar assumed the words were intended as criticism of himself and his fifthling soldiers. "I don't blame you for talking like that, Doubleblade. You won't know that their patrols are always accompanied by two älfar archers with longbows. We can't compete with them."

"I know that," he growled. "My brother was nearly killed by their black arrows."

Tungdil sat up straight in the befún's saddle. "We're going to get a chance to prove the opposite," he said quietly, pointing to the southwest with Bloodthirster. "They've been following us for a while now. If I'm right, there are twenty of them. They could have overtaken us easily with those horses."

"They're waiting to see what we're doing. Which way we're heading." Balyndar let his pony drop back between Tungdil and Ireheart. "That's more than strange. The others always chased us."

"They'll be afraid." Boïndil gave a hearty laugh. "If they meet more than forty dwarves they start to sweat, no matter what the temperature is."

"I think," Tungdil took up his train of thought, "that they don't have any älfar with them. I can't make out any firebulls or night-mares. On snow like this it'd be easy to spot the animals."

"Or maybe they are circling round us to attack from the front. An ambush," Balyndar suggested in concern. He gave his fifthlings the order to have their shields at the ready.

Ireheart reckoned the enemy troop were a good two miles away, if not more. It was a miracle that Tungdil had been able to recognize anything at this distance, he thought. *When he lost that eye of his, did the vision in the other get sharper? Or what else could it be?*

The befún gave a warning snort and turned its head to

the right, where several large—up to seven paces high—dark gray boulders jutted out from the snow.

"Take cover!" Tungdil commanded, slipping out of the saddle. Ireheart did not hesitate and even Balyndar quickly followed suit.

The long black arrow aimed at the leader whirred through the air straight past his right ear and buried itself in the snow so deep that not even the fletching was visible above the white.

Immediately there followed a cry and one of the female dwarves fell back off her pony. An arrow had pierced the edge of her shield and gone straight through the protective helmet into her right temple.

Now all the dwarves had grasped that the archers attacking them were hidden behind the rocks. They dismounted quickly and used the bodies of their ponies as shields against the lethal arrows. Nobody panicked and nobody shouted out, as might have happened with humans in the same situation.

Another set of arrows hissed, and three dwarves fell. Hit in the heart or the head, none of them had any chance of surviving.

"Curse the black-eyes," raged Ireheart, crawling through the snow to Tungdil. "I'll shove a longbow up their arses and the arrows, too. Sideways!!"

"They're behind the second boulder from the front," said his friend calmly, spying out between the legs of his befún. "Can you see them? Their white cloaks make them nearly invisible against the snow."

Ireheart had to screw up his eyes to make out the figures, which bobbed up occasionally above the rocks they were hiding behind just long enough to fire their arrows before ducking down again. Again Ireheart was amazed by Tungdil's eyesight. "It's at least forty paces to that first rock," he calculated. "Time enough for them to finish us off with forty arrows." He turned to Balyndar. "Suggestions?"

One of the ponies collapsed with a whinny; an arrow had struck it in the eye. The älfar were changing their tactics and were going for the dwarves' cover. One small horse after another was killed, kicking out wildly, sometimes injuring their own riders with their hooves.

Ireheart grabbed a handful of snow and pressed it into a ball of ice. "Three shields on top of each other and we storm them? Scholar? We could make our way forwards like that."

"The patrol is galloping this way," called someone. "They're attacking!"

"This'll be getting crowded," muttered Ireheart.

A loud scream came from by the boulders.

Ireheart was quick enough turning his head to see one of the älfar swaying behind his rock, falling forward and plunging from his vantage point, his bow and arrows falling with him.

"What happened? Did his bowstring snap and strike him?" Ireheart noticed the snow had turned red where the älf lay.

"Didn't you hear the crossbow?" asked Tungdil.

A click and a second älf lay dead.

"Huzzah! It seems Frandibar has given us a damn good marksman." Boïndil laughed and jumped up, lifting his crow's beak and ordering the dwarf-warriors to form a protective wall with their shields to defend themselves against the riders' attack. "Now I feel better." He kept an eye out in the fray for the fourthling archer who had protected them from further losses. The marksman lay pressed close to the corpse of his pony and was calmly reloading his crossbow as the patrol came thundering up. The noise of their hooves grew louder and the group of dwarves prepared themselves for the full force of their attack.

The archer rested the stock of his crossbow on the saddle of his dead animal for support, lay down at full length on his stomach and focused his sights on the leader of the fast-approaching troops. From this distance he could easily see their insignia.

Another bolt whirred and the group's commander jerked backwards from the impact; his feet slipped out of the stirrups and he fell. The riders storming along in his wake were too late to swerve and he was swallowed up under flying hooves and a glistening whirling cloud of snow.

"Attack!" yelled Ireheart with a whoop of delight, rushing forward and circling his crow's beak overhead. The rage he would have directed against the älfar now needed a new target.

The troop followed him and raced toward the enemy with no thought of their own safety.

The cavalry group's riders fanned out, their attack formation disintegrating. So loud were the bloodcurdling cries of the dwarves that three of the attackers' number failed to hear the order to halt, instead continuing forward at full tilt while the rest of the mounted company fell back and prepared to retreat.

"Hey! Get over here so that I can run you through with the spike of my war hammer!" Ireheart ducked under the oncoming spear tip and struck the rider with the flat end of his weapon. The impact tore the man out of his saddle, leaving a large dent in his breastplate and blood pouring out of a gash.

Ireheart employed the remaining impetus to swing round in a circle, delivering a swipe with the spiked end to the next rider's thigh.

"Gotcha!" He took a strong wide-legged stance in the snow and held the handle of his crow's beak in both hands. "You're not going anywhere, long-un!"

At first the dwarf was pulled a few paces forward across the snow, but then he found stone underfoot. Now he could pull the man's leg sharply backwards, dislocating it at the hip-joint.

Balyndar propelled the third rider out of the saddle with a blow from his morning star. The spike-studded balls hit him on the neck and breast and the man fell gurgling to the snow.

Boïndil towered over his fallen prisoner, crow's beak in one hand as he pushed down on the man with his right foot. "How long have you been following us? What's your business?" he barked. "If you tell the truth you will live."

"We followed your tracks," the man groaned, pain distorting his voice and features alike. "We've been coming after you for two orbits. The älfar wanted you drawn into an ambush, so we could interrogate survivors to find out what you're up to. We were told not to attack you until they had opened fire."

Balyndar came over to join Ireheart. "Did you drop a messenger off first to send news of having found us?" he asked the captive, dangling the bloodied globe of his morning star above his face.

"No," he moaned. "We're the only ones who know about you being here."

Tungdil stomped over through the snow, his eye on the patrol retreating into the distance. "It makes no odds," he said darkly. "They'll be off to the nearest garrison to make a report. By that time we've got to be in the Gray Mountains. The älfar will be able to work out for themselves that a large dwarf-party will have something serious in mind that's not going to be good news. Those were the days, when we had the old tunnel system."

"What we need is the good old tunnel system," said Ireheart with regret.

"The tunnels are all flooded. I told you," said Balyndar. "We think that's where the water from Weyurn's dried-up lakes has ended up. It can't all have gone through to the Outer Lands."

Tungdil gave the order to remount and then placed Bloodthirster's tip at the nape of the captive's neck. "Anything else we should know?"

"I've told you everything!"

"Then you're no more use to us." His arm jerked forward, the blade he held slicing through skin, muscles and sinews; vertebrae cracked apart. "Right. Let's deal with the black-eyes," he said calmly to Balyndar and Ireheart.

"I promised I would spare his life!" Boïndil blurted out incredulously.

"If he told the truth. That's what you said," retorted Tungdil, going over to his befún, climbing into the saddle and heading over to the rocks where the dead älfar lay, sprawled in unnatural postures. "How would you know if he was lying to you?"

Balyndar watched the black-armored dwarf go, then turned his gaze to the corpse on the ground, the blood still welling.

"I'm not wasting any sympathy on the long-un," he said thoughtfully. "But I can't go along with Goldhand's action either. We could just have left him. The winter would have finished him off." He walked away to get his pony.

Ireheart pulled the end of his crow's beak out of the man's leg, cleaned it on the fellow's cloak and marched over to the rocks. *The old Tungdil would never have done that.* "Yes, he would," he muttered. "We had to do it. The Scholar was right. It wasn't nice, but it was necessary."

"Did you say something, General?" the dwarf with the crossbow turned to ask. "I didn't catch it."

Ireheart stopped and looked at the fourthling. Under an open mantle he was wearing light armor composed more of leather than of mail. The resultant lightness made for ease of movement; he wore a broad metal strip over the breast to protect heart and lungs. Shoulder-length brown hair was visible below the helmet; his beard, of the same color, was braided along the jaw line, with silver wire around the individual plaits. It gave him a dandyish air.

At his side hung a quiver with crossbow bolts and a device for anchoring the loading mechanism when he retightened the bow. The thick bowstring of the long-range weapon had to be cranked by hand. The firing force was immense, as the älfar and members of the mounted patrol had learned to their cost.

Boïndil examined the stock. "Actually," he said, "I've never liked crossbows and archery. They take all the fun out of fighting. But today I gave thanks to Vraccas that he let us have you by our side." He proffered his hand. "What is your name?"

"Goïmslin Fastdraw of the clan of the Sapphire Finders,

fourthling. But they call me Slîn," he said, fastening his crossbow to the saddle so that he was free to shake hands. "I know that all children of the Smith prefer the blade to the bolt. But if, like me, you're not so quick with the sword, then this is the only option." He pointed up to the rock formation. "When you go up to check on the älfar, have a look: I should have got both of them through the heart. If not, I owe you two gold coins."

"That exact?"

Slîn nodded. "I always aim for the heart. Whether it's women or my other victims." He winked and Ireheart had to laugh.

"I'll have a good look." He hurried off to join the others, who were already over by the rocks.

It was quite obvious how excellent Slîn's eye was. Both älfar lay in the snow with skewered hearts. The reinforced bolts had penetrated their armor and Boïndil found himself wondering if Tungdil's special armor would withstand such an impact.

"They've tethered their night-mares on the other side," Tungdil said in greeting.

Ireheart fingered the crow's beak. "They will follow their masters into death." He looked at the älfar archers' bodies and ordered them to be searched. Balyndar and his dwarves got to work.

Under the whitish gray mantles was the typical älfar lamellar armor; their swords lay unused in the scabbards, the two älfar having been given no opportunity to draw them against the dwarves. The dwarf-warriors were not interested in the food supplies the älfar had with them, but there was a fine dagger that one had carried in his belt.

Balyndar noticed it first. "By Vraccas!" he cried angrily,

pulling the knife out of its sheath. "That is the work of a dwarf-smith!" He turned the blade, held it to the sunlight, and ran his finger along it. "No question: This dagger was fashioned by a dwarf." He bent down to study the armor. "Unbelievable!" he exclaimed. "The thirdlings have been cooperating more closely with the älfar than I had ever feared."

Ireheart glanced over at Tungdil and thought of the dwarf-hater they had encountered in the Outer Lands. "The thirdlings made this armor?"

Balyndar looked up. "I'm absolutely sure of it."

"The thirdlings can expect no mercy from us when we've defeated the älfar," growled Boïndil. "Betraying the other tribes like that is unforgivable. They have given away the secrets of the forge."

"And yet you have a thirdling for your high king." Tungdil appeared very calm. He pushed the älfar body away from him with his boot. "Did the dwarf-armor help him any? As long as we have the better crossbow bolts the thirdlings can carry on making armor for them."

Balyndar turned the knife in his hands and ran his fingers over it. "There's something wrong." He started to unclothe the älfar bodies.

Tungdil called him back. "What are you doing?"

"I want to take the armor. To investigate it further. I think . . ."

"No time for that." The one-eyed dwarf beckoned the band to move off. "Go with Ireheart and help him deal with the night-mares. Then we leave. The patrol will soon reach another garrison belonging to the count and they'll be reporting what's happened here." Balyndar was about to respond but Tungdil raised his hand. "I'm *ordering* you." He stared at the fifthling, who shook his head but got up and made off, morning star in hand.

It had not escaped Boïndil's notice that, unseen by Tungdil, Balyndar had pocketed the knife. "Well, I'll be off," he said cheerily and followed Balyndar. But when he heard grinding sounds behind him he turned round. Tungdil was striking the bodies again and again, thrusting his weapon through their chests.

"What are you doing, Scholar?" he called in surprise.

"Making sure," replied Tungdil, wiping Bloodthirster on the snow and then getting back on his befún. "Hurry up. I want to get to the Gray Mountains." He let his mount move on so that he could take up the lead.

"He was destroying the runes," Balyndar said from behind. "Did you see them, too, Doubleblade?"

"Rune?" He came up to the fourthling, whose morning star was covered in blood. The night-mares were no longer alive. "I don't understand."

Balyndar drew a shape on the snow with the blood dripping from his weapon. "*That's* what I mean. If you look at the left side of your friend's armor, Doubleblade, you'll find that same symbol." He left Ireheart standing there and went back to his pony.

Girdlegard,
Dwarf Realm of the Fifthlings,
Gray Mountains,
Late Winter, 6491st/6492nd Solar Cycles

Access into the realm of the fifthlings had changed dramatically. A new stone building rose twenty paces high in front of the gate itself. There were many small apertures in the tower wall; the actual entrance was a relatively narrow door, just wide enough for a befún to pass through.

Ireheart guessed what the apertures were for. *If you tip molten pitch and hot coals down you could see off an army.*

The gate opened and a messenger and watchtower guards were waiting to greet them in the queen's name.

There was no rejoicing when they rode in, no fanfares sounded to announce their arrival in the Gray Mountains. The walls had not been adorned to celebrate their coming and there were no flags flying from the battlements. No dwarves had come to welcome them.

Ireheart was angry, but said nothing.

He knew that Balyndar had dispatched a warrior to announce their approach, but the reception was cool in the extreme. Dislike Tungdil's conduct and demeanor as one might, he was still the dwarves' high king. Respect for his high office should have made it automatic to show deference to the troops under his command, who would no doubt soon be expected to carry out heroic deeds.

"We're entering the realm of the fifthlings as if we are some third-rate undesirable merchants," said Slîn, nudging his pony up next to Boïndil's. His remark was loud enough for Balyndar and the messenger to hear. "Has the queen forgotten who it is she'll be receiving?"

"She has not," replied her son at the front of the train. "Unlike the fourthlings, our dwarves have been faced with an overwhelmingly tough task and are having to fight the kordrion as well as this deadly fever. Both adversaries have weakened us. We have better things to do than to stand in rows," he said disdainfully, "cheering and waving at heroes from the past. You will be given food and drink and, if you want singing and dancing, let me know. But it might be hard to make jolly hosts out of a tribe that's in mourning."

"No need to be so thin-skinned, Balyndar." Slîn bared his teeth. "I need hardly remind you that this welcome is not in accordance with the dignity of the high king you helped to elect."

Ireheart sent him a look that said to hold his tongue. "Let it go," he bade him quietly. "We don't need quarrels here. You'll be going into battle together, remember."

Slîn grinned. "But I shall, of course, be standing behind him," he said, placing a hand on the stock of his crossbow. "The prerogative of archers."

They rode through the passages in silence. The corridors were different now. Ireheart did not recognize anything, and they would have been hopelessly lost without their guide.

They were led to a hall, where they left their ponies and the befún and then continued on foot.

Their fifthling contingent peeled off from the troop one by one to return to their own clans, leaving the fourthlings, Tungdil and Ireheart alone with Balyndar.

"Feels a bit like a trap," whispered Slîn to his companions. He had his crossbow hanging on his back, and wore a nifty ax at his belt. "But, of course, we're among friends."

A second messenger joined them and said something quietly to Balyndar.

"My mother is looking forward to meeting the brave dwarves under the command of the High King Tungdil Goldhand," he announced, and gestured them toward a large simple iron gate guarded by two sentries with halberds.

"Wasn't the throne room on the other side?" asked Ireheart in surprise. "I know there've been a lot of changes . . ."

"You're right. This is not the *old* throne room we're coming to," Balyndar interrupted. "That was in the region of the Gray Mountains where the fever kept recurring. We don't go there anymore and won't make an exception to that rule, even for important visitors." He preceded them. "This is our new throne room." He signaled to the sentries to open the double doors.

Cool silvery light fell on them. The whole chamber was dressed out in polished steel. All the furniture shone cold in the lamp glow. Even the tall columns supporting the ceiling seemed to be made of burnished steel, so smooth that it reflected the surroundings perfectly.

Elaborate ornaments had been engraved and decorated to give emphasis to them. Confusing to the eye, the colored patterns seemed to move if you stared at them.

In another place the artist had chiseled likenesses of dwarf-rulers, decorating them with jewels or precious metals. It was obvious that the queen who used this room had once belonged to the tribe of the firstlings, talented smiths and metal-workers just as she was herself.

"It seems the mountain itself gave birth to this room," murmured one of the fourthlings. "Everything fits together so smoothly—no joins or sharp edges."

Balyndis Steelfinger was seated on the raised throne before them. Her long dark-brown hair was unbound under her sparkling steel helmet and her scaled armor, of the same material, was so bright that the visitors were forced to narrow their eyelids.

"Unthinkable what the effect would be if she were standing

in full sunshine," Slîn observed. "She'd dazzle anyone within ten paces."

Balyndis got to her feet and stepped down from her throne. "Enter and be seated at the fifthlings' table," she bade them. "I am glad you have come and was pleased to learn all the good news from your messenger. It seems Girdlegard will soon be freed from evil's oppression. Vraccas will surely be with us."

Ireheart did his best to watch Tungdil's face while the dwarf-queen approached them, hand outstretched. She had previously been Tungdil's companion for many cycles. They had lived together and she had borne him a son, lost in a terrible accident. This reunion should provide enough tension to set sparks flying. But search as he did for emotion in his friend's face, he noted none.

There was plenty of emotion, however, to be seen in the queen's features. "By Vraccas," Balyndis said with feeling, halting her steps as she came closer to the one-eyed dwarf. "It is true! Really true! You are alive and have come back from the dark!" Tears appeared in the corners of her eyes and trickled down her soft cheeks. The fluff on her face was more pronounced than on the younger females of her race. She stopped in front of Tungdil, visibly moved, her hand still held out toward him.

"Indeed. I have returned from the darkness. But I have brought the shadows with me," he answered. "I know who you are, Balyndis Steelfinger, queen of the fifthlings, but I do not remember anything of what once bound us together." In explanation he pointed to the scar on his forehead. "A blow to the head robbed me of much that was precious to me."

Balyndis swallowed and looked at him intently, as if thinking she could wreak a change in him and release those hidden memories. But when she saw that the expression in his brown eye did not alter, she let her arm drop, and knelt before him. "I greet you, High King Tungdil Goldhand," she said sadly, bowing her head. "May Vraccas bless you and all who follow you in your quest to save Girdlegard."

"I thank you, Queen Balyndis." He indicated to her by a touch on the shoulder that she should stand, and then made his way over to the laden table.

Many delicacies had been prepared and were displayed in dishes and on plates; the smell made Ireheart's mouth water as he realized how hungry he was.

"About time too," muttered Slîn at his side. "I was ready to start licking the furniture, my stomach was rumbling so."

They took their seats round the table. Dwarves served the food and ensured that neither plates nor jugs were ever empty. During the course of the meal Tungdil elucidated his mission again. Balyndis made no response apart from the occasional nod.

Ireheart got the impression that she was trying to read Tungdil's mind to fathom his feelings. *I wonder if she'll have any more luck than I've had.*

"Enough from me," his friend said eventually. "Tell me, the fever that broke out here: How long have you and the fifthlings been troubled by it?"

"Over a hundred cycles. It started slowly, so our healers didn't notice it at first," she explained, raising her tankard of black beer in a toast to the company. "But soon the incidence of illness increased and it reminded us of the plagues that struck the original fifthlings. We abandoned the tunnels and caves and had them sealed up. I could show you on the map which regions were affected."

"Did the outbreaks come randomly or is there a pattern to it?" asked Tungdil. He had hardly touched his food and Ireheart was sure he seemed much paler than usual. He studied the map they showed him, concentrating hard.

"We couldn't find any pattern to it," answered Balyndis. "We got the freelings to search the places where the highest mortality had occurred, to see if maybe the älfar were targeting us, but no traces were found. And those who were part of the freelings' expedition all fell ill a few orbits later. They died."

"How?" asked the one-eyed dwarf.

"They suffocated in their own blood. First they grew feverish and then their lungs filled with blood until they could not breathe." She shuddered. "An appalling death, Tungdil."

He pushed the map away and emptied his tankard—the seventh, if Ireheart had not lost count: A considerable amount for a dwarf who had not eaten anything much. Heroic achievement. "Did their limbs change color? Perhaps the tips of their fingers? What about their tongues?"

Balyndis and her son exchanged glances.

"I didn't tell him," said Balyndar. "Nobody knows."

Tungdil shot him a dangerous smile. "I don't need to be told. I worked it out for myself." He summoned a fresh tankard. "It's not a curse. It's an odorless gas."

Balyndar rolled his eyes. "No, it's not! We ruled that out."

"The methods for investigating the conventional humors exuded by the mountain are useless with this problem, Balyndar. It's the kordrion. In countless ways it's been responsible for the deaths in the Gray Range. It doesn't just eat those who confront it. Its excrement is lethal as well, causing the painful death Balyndis has just described as soon as it meets water." He took the map in his hand. "Ireheart told me that the kordrion is in the northern part of the Gray Mountains, near the Stone Gateway. That's your explanation: Rainwater washes the excrement down the slopes and it runs into the rivers that feed the canals, being washed down to the parts of the mountain where the so-called fever turns up."

"Even its shit is murderous?" exclaimed Ireheart in disbelief. "That's what I call a really devious monster! Good thing we're going to get rid of him."

"*We* aren't going to. It will be Lot-Ionan." He put the next full tankard to his lips and took a long draft. "I think it will take a cycle or two until the toxic effect fades away so that you can return to those regions." He saw that Balyndar did not believe him. "It is something to do with alchemy, Steelfinger," he explained. "I grew up in the house and laboratories of a magus. The composition of the kordrion's excrement is unique; if you like, a kind of dried acid. As soon as it comes into contact with water, the substances mix and a lethal gas is released. I used this several times on the other side of the Black Abyss if a siege wasn't going well." He finished his drink. "I don't give your sick dwarves much of a chance. The lungs won't recover from the acid burns. They're for the eternal smithy."

"I believe you," said Balyndis, pale now. She indicated where the kordrion was thought to have its eyrie. "Vraccas was good to us and we have always been able to destroy the soft eggs before they hatch. Our scouts report, though, that it's back in the nest and that the kordrion has learned to keep supplies. If we are out of luck it won't have to leave the clutch of eggs to get food. That was always our opportunity to make a move."

"We'll think up a suitable diversion," Ireheart said confidently. "Right, Scholar: We go to the nest, grab the eggs and run off through the Gray Range all the way to the entrance to Gauragar?"

"No. We must go over the summits, so that it can follow our tracks. I've worked out a route."

Balyndar's eyes widened. "In winter? Are you out of your mind?" After a pause he added, "High King."

Without hesitating, Tungdil recited the names of the summits they would have to cross, specifying places they would rest. "Does that still sound like madness to you," he asked cuttingly, "or more like a demanding but achievable journey?"

Balyndis nodded. "I'm amazed how much you still remember about my homeland, when there are so many other things you have forgotten." It was a snide remark, but one she couldn't resist making. "It seems your mind has concentrated on the scholarly side of your nature and eliminated all feeling. Is that how it is, High King?"

Tungdil turned his brown eye toward her. "That may indeed be so, Queen Balyndis. But it will help us and Girdlegard. I shan't be complaining."

"Nor me," announced Ireheart, still digesting the details of his friend's strategy. Throughout the whole of the journey so far he had not once seen Tungdil consult a map. His knowledge must be vast. "I suggest we set off as soon as possible before the wretched things hatch out."

"Tomorrow. As soon as the sun is up," said Tungdil, getting to his feet. "I would like to rest. Queen Balyndis, be good enough to have me shown to my chambers. And tomorrow my ponies must be fresh and ready. And we'll need provisions. Please arrange that."

She signaled to one of the dwarves to accompany the ruler of all the dwarf-tribes, and Tungdil left the throne room without even bidding farewell.

Slîn and the fourthlings withdrew, leaving Balyndis and her son alone with Boïndil.

They carried on eating in silence and later avoided any mention of Tungdil while they discussed such topics as the Black Abyss and the dangers facing Girdlegard. Ireheart, however, was well aware they couldn't skirt round the issue forever and, fed up with having constantly to defend the Scholar to others, he eventually took a quick draft of beer and broached the subject of his friend himself. "It may be that I'm mistaken, Balyndis, but there's a strong resemblance between Tungdil and your son."

He realized that the question was out of order, potentially problematic and possibly insulting. He was implying that she had deceived her husband, Glaïmbar Sharpax of the clan of the Iron Beaters and king of the fifthlings, passing off another's child as his son.

But Balyndis took his words with equanimity, relieved almost that it had been mentioned. "It is very obvious, isn't it?" she said softly. "It was a mistake to send Balyndar to the meeting in the Brown Mountains. All the clan leaders have seen him and his real father together, and will have put two and two together."

"Will this affect your regency, do you think?"

She shook her head. "No one is after my throne, now that Geroïn Leadenring is dead from the fever. He was the brother of Syndalis Leadenring, the king's second wife; she was rejected in favor of me. Geroïn and some of his clan never forgave me for that. I rule well though, and if the kordrion can be driven off, the tribe of the fifthlings will flourish." Balyndis started to cough.

"I had forgotten you are unwell," said Ireheart, in concern.

"It will get better. Now that we know what the cause of the fever and lung disease is."

"We have found the guilty party but we haven't found a cure." Ireheart tried to shut out from his mind the explanation the Scholar had given, in particular those words concerning the inevitable death of the sufferer. "But we're sure to find something to make it better," he hastened to say. He felt gloomy. *Pull yourself together. She's not dead yet.*

The queen sighed. "Glaïmbar knew."

"What? That Balyndar was not his son?"

"Yes. He never said so, but I could read his expression. He did not voice his suspicions or reject Balyndar; that was his greatness of heart. I loved him for that generosity." She gave a pained smile. "Balyndar will succeed to the fifthling throne after me, Ireheart. That's what Glaïmbar wanted, too, because he saw what a splendid ruler he will be one day."

"But he does not get on with his real father." Ireheart dusted a few crumbs off his beard, which had somehow trailed in his plate of food. "And he has a fair idea of who it is he's dealing with? I mean, he's not blind; he must have noticed the similarity."

"That could be the reason Balyndar doesn't like him. He doesn't want to be the son of Tungdil Goldhand, a complete stranger, rather than of Glaïmbar, whom he admired. Glaïmbar taught him to fight and I taught him the work of a smith. Tungdil didn't always come off particularly well when I told stories of him, if you take my meaning. After he ended our relationship in a letter, I was angry and disappointed in him for a long time. Age has made me milder." She closed her eyes. "But when I saw him standing in front of me again, Ireheart, all the old feelings came back."

"So you are convinced he really is Tungdil?" He bit his tongue: Too late.

To his surprise Balyndis smiled. "Don't be confused by the somber exterior. My heart"—here she placed her hand on her breast—"my heart recognized him at once. It has never misled me."

"It was the same for me," he replied. He lifted his tankard.

XI

Lakepride was easy to defend against attack, because the island rose high above the lake, meaning its soldiers needed no special equipment for hurling rocks. Simply rolling boulders over the edge would sink a ship. Structural improvements had been made to the shaft around the magic source, with men and materials carried on cables whizzing to and fro above the lake.

Mallenia and Rodario were observing the works from a vantage point on the watchtower battlements. Queen Wey and her daughter Coïra had ordered extensive preparations, anticipating an attack by the Dragon or his henchmen, the Lohasbranders.

"What you can see there is not the most powerful weapon against the Dragon," said Rodario.

"You mean the queen and her daughter." Mallenia looked down into the courtyard of the palace thirty paces below. The figures looked tiny. "You say they've both attained their full magic potency?"

"I've been told the queen has bathed in the magic source. The gods only know how she managed to preserve the remnants of her force for her escape, but as a result she's thought to be stronger than Lot-Ionan. I'm sure Lohasbrand will think twice before he attacks her." He stepped in front of Mallenia to look into her eyes. "And that's not to say he actually *will* attack. I think he'll swallow the bait about älfar spies in his realm. Dragons are paranoid and always suspicious someone is after their treasure."

Mallenia laughed. "So you're not just an actor, you're a dragon specialist?" She smiled and took his chin in her hand. "A man of many parts, Rodario the Seventh. If you had muscles as well, you'd be a real man."

He made a face and took his scrawny beard out of harm's way. But he did enjoy it when she teased him. "I take it as a sign of hidden affection when you insult me. You're sounding me out," he replied.

"Oh, so that's what you think?" She burst out laughing. "Sweet dreamer, dream on. My affection consists of wanting to protect you, like protecting a child. So vulnerable, so clumsy."

Like lightning he drew one of her own short swords. "You should be proud of yourself, Mallenia. Now you've managed to provoke me," he threatened. "En garde!"

She drew the other sword and went along with the joke. "Then attack me, Number Seven! Why don't you show this weak woman where her place is!" The muscles in her arm and chest rippled with the exertion; they were certainly stronger than his own.

Rodario made an obvious move to hit her and she caught his wrist to stay his hand. Then she gave him a kiss on the brow. "How funny," she mocked, pushing him back. "Try again, little man."

Apparently furious now, he hopped toward her, tripping over his mantle. He stumbled past her, heading for the parapet.

When Mallenia grabbed him to stop him plunging over the top—her fingers met thin air.

But her mouth met a kiss.

His lips were soft and pleasing on her own; there was a faint taste of the spiced tea he had drunk to warm him. Then he drew his head back and left her blushing.

"A hit!" he exulted, waving his weapon in the air. "That took you by surprise, didn't it, brave warrior woman? I won! The kiss is mightier than the sword!"

Mallenia swallowed hard. She was confused, still feeling the audacious embrace and not knowing how to react. It was an incredible invasion of her person, impudence that must be punished.

Rodario saw that she was visibly shaken. "Oh, I . . . didn't mean to embarrass you," he stuttered. "It was a game, and then you'd kissed me on the forehead, so . . ."

"A game indeed." She held her hand out, demanding her short sword, which he relinquished at once. "Let's forget it. You won and you won't get a second chance."

He cleared his throat. "Forgive me. I got carried away. I offer my sincere apologies. I should never have done that." He bowed. "Hit me if you want."

"So that you can dodge out of the way and kiss me again? No thanks, Rodario the Seventh," Mallenia said, stowing her weapons. "Let's leave it at that." She tried hard to treat the incident lightly but found it all very unsettling. It was a feeling she hated.

She marched off to the edge of the platform and stared out, admiring the beauty of the lake, but with her thoughts in turmoil. *It was only a stolen kiss*, she told herself. *A child's kiss. How can he make me feel like this?*

"Rodario? Mallenia? Are you up there?" Coïra's voice echoed up the stairwell.

"Yes, Princess. We're admiring the view and keeping watch for Weyurn's enemies," the actor answered. "What can we do for you?"

"Come down here," came a cheerful instruction. "I've got important news for Mallenia."

Rodario and the swordswoman hurried down the steps to join Coïra, who was coming up to meet them. "My mother received a message from one of the neighboring villages," she said. Her eyes fixed onto Mallenia's injured arm. "Remind me to check that bandage. We can take it off tomorrow. The wound should be healing well by now and will benefit from exposure to air and sunlight."

"Is it good news or bad?" Rodario urged.

"I don't know. My mother just sent for me. Let's go and find out."

They hastened through the palace, through high, sunlit corridors and anterooms, until they reached the place where they had first seen the monarch.

The window had been repaired and the view—of waves glittering in the sun, birds circling and colorful fishing boats bobbing on the water—had lost none of its fascination.

Queen Wey sat behind her desk. Her turquoise robe suited her splendidly and she looked well. But worry was etched on her features. "Sit down," she said to her guests. "There are things to report."

"Has something happened in Idoslane, ma'am?" asked Mallenia, taking her seat.

"No. In Soulham, a village near here. A fisherman tells me he saw two älfar locally," said the queen. "What troubles me is that he is the only one to have seen them. The other villagers are keeping silent. They are afraid. I'm sure the älfar are hiding there waiting for their chance." She looked at Mallenia. "The chance to get to Lakepride and kill you."

"Then let me follow it up, Mother," Coïra suggested at once. "They can't hurt me."

"You can't stop an assassin's arrow, my child," replied Wey. "You took them by surprise at the shore but now they know who their opponent is. The älfar will avoid showing themselves in the daytime." She looked at Mallenia. "I think we should give them an opportunity to find a way in. An opportunity that we control."

"In other words, a *trap*," said Rodario, delighted at the idea. "Your Majesty, that is an absolutely excellent plan."

"Why, thank you for your support, sir!" she retorted, highly amused. "The fisherman who came to speak to me about the älfar is going to spread a couple of rumors in the village to attract the attention of the black-eyes. They'll say that our guards are all stricken with the runs and can't leave their beds . . ."

"Who else knows you are now free of your chains, Your Majesty?" Mallenia was too alarmed to sit still. She had not yet escaped the shadow of death. "The älfar won't come if they think they'll have to contend with two magae in order to kill me."

"No one knows apart from my most loyal servants."

"And what will the Dragon say?" objected Rodario. "Is he coming? I thought I noticed a lot of activity on the battlements out by the magic source."

Wey looked at him steadily. "Do you know what, Rodario the Seventh? Sometimes you seem a bit strange," she said.

"We have an actor here who plays so many roles that he has forgotten where the real Rodario is."

Rodario went red. "I don't understand what you mean."

"I've been watching you. Sometimes you are very bold, my daughter tells me, then you're awkward, then swift and nimble; sometimes you have a way with words and at other times you stammer and stutter. You have good manners one moment and forget them the next. Like just now when you dared to interrupt a queen." She rubbed her temple as if she had a headache. "I don't think there is anything magic about you to explain this away. But your mind is—to put it mildly—confused. Am I right?"

Mallenia thought of the incident on the battlements and secretly felt she had to agree with the queen.

"I apologize, Your Majesty," he said contritely, making a deep bow in front of the queen. "Of course you are right. I should have waited."

"To return to your question, Rodario the Impatient," Queen Wey continued in a gentler tone of voice, "I must tell you that the Dragon has not yet sent an answer. And I am certain that he would be convinced by the night-mare cadaver and the corpses of his people." She turned to Mallenia. "But your concerns have priority. I don't like having the älfar near at hand. The Soulham fisherman will be returning to his village to spread those rumors. Then we will have to wait and pretend we are all ill with diarrhea. My guards have been told what's happening. Coïra will explain our plans. I have work to do." She glanced pointedly at the door.

The three needed no more explicit hint and left the room. The princess took them to her apartments, where they continued their discussion over tea and cake.

"It's simple," said Coïra. The älfar will find one of our guards and ask him about you, Mallenia. You wait in your chamber with me. When the älfar come I'll show them that it would be better if they left."

"You sound very confident." Rodario held a cup and a piece of cake in his hands. "Like your mother said: Don't you think they expect to find you?"

Coïra laughed. "What can they do, faced with a ball of pure magic?"

"Dodge?" he suggested, earning himself Mallenia's laughter. He was reveling in the proximity of these two young women. Such a shame he would have to split himself in two in order to continue enjoying the company of both. "Älfar are as quick as a bolt of lightning and agile as a cat. Had you thought of that?"

The princess made a sound to indicate her displeasure. "Stop complaining. It's a simple plan and therefore an excellent one."

Rodario bit into his cake and made a great show of chewing. "And what's plan B?" he mumbled through the crumbs. "What if brother and sister älf get past you? Who's going to save you?" He pointed to Coïra with the pastry. "Who'll save you when it all goes wrong?"

"You will," teased Mallenia. "At least, it sounds like you're volunteering."

"If my kisses have as paralyzing an effect on the älfar as they do on you, why not?" he countered. "But I'd only be dealing with the female älf. You'll have to tackle the brother." He slurped his tea noisily.

Coïra stared first at him and then at Mallenia, whose blushes showed that Rodario had not been lying. "You can have a try when the time comes," she said, without asking for further details.

"I would prefer it if we did not kill the älfar outright," hissed the Ido heroine venomously. "At least one of them should be alive for me to interrogate."

"That should be possible," Coïra allowed. "May I ask why?"

"I overheard them talking when they thought I was unconscious. I don't know if I understood aright. It is important for Girdlegard." Mallenia saw the keen curiosity in the others' faces. "I don't want to talk about it until I'm sure," she said firmly. "I don't want to make the horses shy unnecessarily, as they say."

"Well, that's an incentive to catch them alive!" exclaimed Rodario, stuffing the rest of the cake into his mouth. It was too late to apologize to Mallenia, anyway.

The full moon stood high over Girdlegard and thus over Lakepride.

It was a cloudless night; the lake glinted silver, leaving the few fishing boats out seeking eels and shrimps silhouetted like black shadows.

The boats headed for the island and sailed near the shaft. One of them approached dangerously close to the stone pillar on which the island was based—so close it nearly collided.

The helmsman wrenched the wheel round and skimmed past by a hair's-breadth.

At first sight there was nothing suspicious in this. The currents by the island could be tricky and even an experienced sailor could get into difficulties.

For Rodario, watching from his hiding place, it was proof enough that the älfar siblings, Sisaroth and Firûsha, had just set foot on land. He could not make them out yet, but that was hardly surprising.

"This is it," he murmured, climbing out of the wire observation basket and hurrying up the narrow steps to the top. He raced along the coastal path and ran to the palace entrance.

If Coïra and Mallenia had not thought out an emergency fall-back plan, but were relying totally on magic, then Rodario felt it his duty to have an alternative stratagem. His ideal scenario was for him to save both girls' lives. Heroic deeds always went down well when hearts were to be won. Or when hearts needed calming down.

Rodario was admitted by the sentries and raced through the dark palace as quickly as he could.

No one knew about his function as a secret reserve. Mallenia and Coïra were sitting in one room, Queen Wey was in the chamber opposite, ready to spring to her daughter's aid.

Rodario had to admit that it was impossible to subdue *both* magae. Even Sisaroth and Firûsha—the gods of Dsôn, whatever that meant—would be overcome. If Mallenia had managed to kill the third sibling with one shot from her little crossbow, what would the combined magic powers of two magae be able to achieve?

But perhaps Tion might be on his creatures' side that night . . . and then Rodario really would be needed.

Rodario had reached the curtained wall-niche where he had hidden his homemade contraptions. He quickly fastened the miniature bellows filled with flash powder to his forearms.

There was a flint he could activate, causing a spark to ignite the flying lycopodium seeds.

A magic fireball without using magic—or, at least, it would be a fireball good enough to impress theatergoers.

He had purchased the plan for the device for a considerable sum of money in Mifurdania's marketplace; it was said originally to have been invented by the legendary magister technicus, but Rodario did not believe that. He did not mind who had invented it though, as long as it worked. He had made two dry runs and they had both been successful.

"Let's see if I need you today." He pulled his sleeves down to hide the equipment, and then turned round.

Right in front of him Sisaroth appeared, smiling coldly at him.

Rodario had neither heard him approach nor felt any hint of a draft. "Ye gods!" the actor breathed. The älf executed a sudden movement. Something hard hit the actor on the head and a hot flash of lightning shot through his neck.

He collapsed onto the stone floor, while the älf stepped over his heavily bleeding body, making for Mallenia's chamber.

Mallenia was in full armor as she lay under the blanket, her face turned away from the door; the small mirror on her bedside table showed her what was happening at the entrance.

Pressed up close to the wardrobe, and invisible from the doorway, Coïra was waiting, her thoughts focused on her magic spells. She had to be in a position to cast one at a split second's notice if she was going to prevent the älfar killing Mallenia.

The two women were quiet, listening for any sounds coming from the hallway or outside the chamber windows.

They held their breath every time a footstep passed their door. So far there had been no sign of the siblings.

"Just so you understand: I didn't allow the actor to kiss me," Mallenia suddenly whispered. "He stole the kiss."

Coïra had to smile. "Of course. Typical," she replied quietly.

"He took me by surprise," she went on. "Next time I'll knock him down."

Coïra's curiosity about affairs of the heart was awoken. In spite of the circumstances. "I'm amazed he managed to do it. What happened? Were you distracted?"

"He tricked me," admitted Mallenia. "The weakling made a fool of me."

A faint squeak interrupted them: The catch on the door was moving slowly. They had put sand and salt in the mechanism.

Mallenia stared at the entrance. She could see no light under the door, so it could not be one of the servants checking that everything was all right. They had strict instructions to carry lamps when they came.

The catch stopped moving, then went slowly back into its original position.

"What shall we do?" asked Coïra in a muffled voice.

"We wait," Mallenia hissed. She thought it could well be Rodario on the other side. Did he want to apologize? Did he want something more of her? She sighed softly. The man was driving her crazy. As if he knew she had a thing about helpless types.

The time passed painfully slowly. Everything was quiet.

Whoever had been trying to enter the room must have changed their mind.

Then there was a scream!

"That was in Mother's room!" Coïra peeled herself out of the niche, ran to the door and pulled it open.

Sisaroth stood before her, waiting with two-handed sword raised ready to strike.

The maga did not think twice, but sent a destructive ball of pure energy at the älf—but he dodged the sphere that was shooting toward him, just as Rodario had joked he might.

The hurtling magic ball whizzed across the corridor, hitting the door three paces away on the other side of the passage. At that moment Queen Wey's door swung open and she stood on the threshold, face to face with her fate.

Coïra could see the fear in her mother's countenance. Horror-struck she watched her lips move in an attempt to form a counter-spell. Wey threw her arms up to protect herself, but Coïra felt only utter helplessness. And fear for her mother's life.

Girdlegard,
Dwarf Realm of the Fifthlings,
In the North of the Gray Mountains,
Late Winter, 6491st/6492nd Solar Cycles

"This is where the kordrion was last cycle." Balyndar studied the steep cliffs intently, searching for signs of a certain distinctive shadow. "It flies around looking for prey. If it turns up, stand tight against the rock face."

The dwarf-group got into pairs: The narrow ravine only allowed them to go two abreast.

The dark gray rock walls were rough as a whetstone and contact with anything metal caused ridges and scratches. Ireheart made use of the chance to sharpen the tip of his spike. The others took care not to scrape along the abrasive walls by accident. It would do no favors to armor, clothing or skin.

Apart from Balyndar, Tungdil, Slîn and Boïndil, the expedition had the three warriors from the fourthling tribe with them. Balyndis had sent along five of her fifthlings, all of them excellent in combat; they pulled their equipment behind them on the sledges they intended to use for transporting the kordrion's young.

Tungdil stopped in the middle of the path and lifted his head, breathing in the clear, icy air.

"The nest," Balyndar went on, "will be on the southern side of the Dragon's Tongue. It always lays its eggs in the south. The monster digs a hole into the rock; we'll see it from quite a distance. It's like a large cave, so huge the entrance can't be concealed. After leaving the ravine it'll take us another half-orbit to get to it. We'll need another full orbit for the ascent."

"What are you doing, Scholar?" Ireheart wanted to know.

"Smelling," he said bluntly. "We need to hurry." He speeded up, making for the end of the ravine.

Balyndar glanced at Ireheart, who shrugged in response. "Can you be a bit more specific?" Ireheart asked his friend. "I don't object to running but I want to know why I'm having to."

"The eggs are nearly ready to hatch!" Tungdil called back over his shoulder.

Ireheart's own deliberately loud sniff echoed back from

the walls. "Can't smell a thing." He trotted up to his friend.

"That's because you don't know what to expect. Did you notice the mossy odor?"

"Yes, of course . . ." Boïndil fell silent. Then, after a moment's thought, he exclaimed, "By Vraccas! It didn't mean anything to me. I should have noticed that everything green here is covered in snow and anything containing water frozen solid. The moss should be the same."

"There you are, you see. If I give you a tiny clue you can work it out for yourself."

Tungdil emerged out into the light. A veil of mist was slowly rising in the warmth of the sun. "Excellent cover for our climb!" he said, signaling to the group to move faster. "We could be up there by nightfall."

"Hardly. It's a difficult climb," Balyndar contradicted him. "The next stretch is notorious for snowdrifts. And we'll need to conserve energy. We've got an exhausting dash ahead of us with the kordrion breathing down our necks."

Tungdil had not slackened his pace and was a considerable distance ahead. Ireheart assumed this was his way of showing that he did not intend to discuss his commands with anyone. *This mission is definitely going to be loads of fun.*

"He's going to get us all killed," Balyndar protested, starting to run. The rest followed suit.

"Ah, many's the time we thought that in the past, but the Scholar always found a way out," Boïndil reassured him. "And anyway, he's the high king. He's allowed to." He showed his teeth in a smile to show it had been a joke.

"And how many never returned?" asked Slîn. But when

he saw Boïndil's face he did not persist. "Charming," he murmured, panting a little from the weight of his crossbow. "Vraccas, let me be one of those who make it back home again," muttered Slîn. "In *one* piece." As he ran he grabbed a drink of water. "So what does the kordrion do all day in the Gray Mountains? It's a pretty lonely, dead-end sort of place it rules over here."

"It doesn't *rule* over anywhere," snarled Balyndar who felt this was addressed to him. "It's a verminous pest infesting the area." He pointed south toward Girdlegard. "From what we hear, it flies off to the long-uns. After it's wiped out a few villages, the humans voluntarily put gifts of food out on the fields to keep it off their backs. The areas it's been targeting are in the former Gauragar and in Urgon and Tabaîn. So it affects the Dragon Lohasbrand as much as the älfar and their vassals. But none of them dares brave the mountains to get to the eyrie."

Slîn sniffed contemptuously. "Real heroes, then."

"It's easier for everyone to wait and see when the fifthlings will finish it off," Ireheart added cynically. "I should be angrier, but since their cowardice may be a help to us, my fury has almost faded away. But only *almost*."

The fourthling saw no sign of the beast. "Maybe Lohasbrand has made a deal with the kordrion?"

"No," contradicted Tungdil at the head of the column. "A kordrion wants total dominance; it's just like a dragon, though with less mental capacity. Its size doesn't give it any advantage over a dragon because the scaled beasts are cleverer. The kordrion has ordered its realm and feels at ease, otherwise it wouldn't be nesting. It's content to eat without having to hunt. Lohasbrand, on the other hand, functions precisely like a typical dragon: Reigns like a king, exacting tribute from his subjects, and so on."

"Nice. Charming," said Slîn peevishly. "But it's not right that all the monsters should end up coming to us from all over the shop, just to enjoy an easy life."

Ireheart laughed. "I would love to see them all killed, and to celebrate I'd sing an old song the drunkard Bavragor taught me."

"Bavragor?" asked Balyndar. "The name rings a bell . . ."

"He was one of those who accompanied me and never came back," said Tungdil darkly, speaking over his shoulder. "Is that enough of an answer?"

The fifthling, caught out, nodded.

Tungdil's grim expression was enough to spur the group on. He rarely said a word and when he did it was a command.

Under cover of the mist they began their ascent to the kordrion's cave and by nightfall they had reached it. A hole in the cliff, ten paces wide, yawned at them, an overwhelming smell of fresh, damp moss emanating from within.

Ireheart held his crow's beak in his right hand and stared at the entrance. "You're sure it's not at home, Scholar?"

"I wouldn't have urged you to hurry if it was. Whatever Balyndar thinks of me, I wouldn't throw us all to the beast as a sacrifice." The stars were faintly reflected in the gold of his eye patch.

"Hang on! I've seen you fighting a kordrion! And if you'd kept on you'd have had him down!" Ireheart butted in.

Tungdil took another deep breath. "This one's different; I could tell from the way he's built his eyrie. Sometimes they just drop their eggs and leave the young to their fate. It's unusual to have an eyrie and a nest. And as for my little victory over a kordrion: I can't surprise this one, it doesn't trust me. And it's been out of captivity for too long, living in the wild. We'd need a dozen or so of me if we wanted to beat this foe."

"A *dozen* Scholars? No wonder Balyndis has had no luck." Ireheart lowered his weapon and helped the others to haul their equipment up onto the narrow ledge. The sledges, cords, cables and hooks, together with their provisions, were suspended on ropes they had anchored to the rock every few paces of their climb.

"We won't find a better opponent for Lot-Ionan," Tungdil agreed. He waited until the other dwarves had heaved up and secured their gear, then he spoke. "Eat now, then sleep till I wake you. After that, prepare to be on the run for orbits at a time. You'll get no more sleep until we've got a long way away from the monster. An enraged kordrion can fly very fast." He drew Bloodthirster. "I'll take first watch."

The dwarves looked at one another and went off to the sledges to shut their eyes for a while; with warm rugs of cat fur over them and bearded faces wrapped in scarves, they lay down to rest. They trusted their high king.

Ireheart was unsure what to do. His legs were painful and as heavy as ten sacks of lead shot, but on the other hand he did not want to leave his friend—who had made the same exhausting climb in his peculiar armor—alone on watch.

His eyes were tired and smarting and he could hear his stomach rumbling. "I need something to eat first, Vraccas, or my insides will be louder than a thunderstorm." He went over to the sledge that held their food supplies. "Then, perhaps, a little smoke, to aid digestion, and the world will look a whole lot better," he muttered to himself.

When he opened the first layer of leather to get at the bread something caught his eye on the edge of the rock they had pulled themselves up over. He was surprised to see a metal retaining hook, shiny and without rust. There was a dusting of snow on it . . . Hoar frost would have made sense, but snow?

"What does it mean?" He leaned over and brushed the snow aside. One glimpse was enough to tell him the hook was not one of their own. "Well, I'll be squashed flat with a hammer . . ." he cursed, rushing over to tell Tungdil what he had found.

The one-eyed dwarf didn't want to come and inspect it. Instead he turned on his heel and stormed into the cave. Ireheart followed him.

The smell of moss grew stronger and became over-whelming, making it difficult to breathe.

Ireheart lit a torch, intent on carefully examining what they found. What he saw caused him great concern.

The kordrion's brood had consisted of pale cocoons each the size of a human—until unidentified intruders had turned up and slashed them to ribbons. Opaque sticky liquid covered the floor ankle deep, almost frozen solid near the mouth of the cave; dead and dismembered embryonic kordrions lay among the mess.

"So that's put paid to our great plan." Ireheart squatted down to look at the corpses. They reminded him a little of flying fish, but they had more eyes and were ten times as large. "What can have done it?"

"They were either mad or desperate, the same as us." Tungdil stomped about the cave, bending over to examine individual body parts. "I should say there were ten of them with very sharp weapons—you can tell from the cuts," he imparted to his friend. "And the prints say: Dwarves."

"Balyndis would never have kept it from us if she'd sent people out," said Ireheart, moving through the carnage. "Despite all this slaughter the overriding smell is still the moss. It could have been worse; anyone who's been covered head to foot with the stinking guts from an orc's slit belly will know what I mean." As he walked across to Tungdil he surveyed the scene.

The one-eyed dwarf yelled a warning at him, "No, don't!"

"Don't *what*?"

"Too late. You've trodden in it."

"Oh, it doesn't matter." Ireheart gestured dismissively. "It's only moss. Perhaps Goda will like the smell."

"It's not just her that will like it. The thing is, that smell will stick to your clothes. And to you. The kordrion will assume you killed his young," Tungdil explained.

Ireheart stared open-mouthed in distress. "Just me? What about you, Scholar?"

"I didn't touch anything and, anyway, nothing sticks to tionium. I can wash off any splashes," he replied. He examined the cave floor minutely. "There was an extra cocoon just here. They've taken it with them." He rubbed his nose. "I wonder why."

Ireheart laughed. "Not the same reason as us, surely?"

"We'll have to find them to stop them doing something stupid." He pointed to the entrance. "Wake the others and tell them. I'll check outside for tracks." He kicked one of the mutilated dead. "When they're grown they're ten times the weight of a warrior in full armor. If our thieves haven't taken to the skies we'll find them and confront them."

They left the cave together, Tungdil to the right, Ireheart to the left.

Boïndil woke the troops and explained. As he was summing up Tungdil came over.

"I've found their tracks. They've climbed down on the other side of the mountain," he informed them calmly. "We'll follow them and get the last of the kordrion's offspring. They can give it to us voluntarily or we can force them to hand it over. That cocoon is our only chance for a long, long time. The kordrion needs at least three cycles before it's ready to lay again." He looked at their faces. "It's vital nothing injures the outer casing. It would mean death for the young, and the parent would smell that at once. There'd be no more point in its following us."

Except to pursue and slaughter its offspring's killers, thought Ireheart.

Slîn scowled. "Any idea who's stolen a march on us? It's almost as if our plans had been overheard. But who's behind this? And what's he planning to do with the cocoon?"

"I hadn't told them yet that we've found dwarf-bootprints," said Ireheart.

"Children of the Smith?" Balyndar gave a short mirthless laugh. "Or small humans? Or gnomes and cobolds with stolen footwear playing a trick?"

"Courageous cobolds?" Ireheart dismissed the idea. "Cobolds would never put themselves within ten miles of a kordrion."

"We'll soon see who we have to thank for this disaster." Tungdil indicated they should break camp and stow their gear. "Boïndil, you stay close to me from now on," came the quiet instruction.

"I don't need a nursemaid."

"You'll need protection from the kordrion. Even if he's stronger than I am I can fight him off for long enough to give us a chance to escape. I'm going to need you on this mission." Tungdil was serious and honestly concerned for his friend's safety. "It is only the *first* of many. But all of our plans must work if we are to free Girdlegard and save it from the army gathering in the Black Abyss."

Ireheart swallowed hard. The inner chorus of doubting voices that had previously troubled him fell silent, not a single one able to protest now against his conviction that his friend could be trusted. He nodded to Tungdil and followed him to the other side of the eyrie, where a broad set of tracks led to the steep slope.

Tungdil surveyed the path the thieves must have taken. "What do you make of that?" he asked.

"I don't see the marks of any runners. So, have they used their shields to slide the cocoon down the mountain?" Ireheart raised his eyebrows. "Madness. They haven't abseiled, they've just slipped and slithered down!" He thought of the dwarf-hater they had seen careering down the mountainside in the Outer Lands. *Could the thirdling skirt-wearers be behind this?*

Tungdil looked at the other dwarves, who were catching up with them now: Bearded faces with crystals of ice around noses and mouths, eyes sparkling with determination. "Do you lot think we're brave enough to do what those thieves have done?" His manner indicated, once more, that his questions were not questions, but commands. He took one of the sledges, pushing it off and jumping on board. Speeding over the edge, it was more a fall than a ride across the snow as he shot down toward the valley.

"How many usually die on his little missions?" muttered Slîn, taking the leather band of his crossbow firmly in his hand. He shoved his own sledge downhill.

Ireheart was ahead of him, launching himself into the wild ride with a triumphant cry, "Vraccas!"

After a few paces, picking up speed all the time and with the strong icy wind bringing tears to his eyes, every bone in his body juddering and jarring, he knew one thing for certain: A lightning journey by tunnel car through the depths of the mountains was a princesses' tea-party compared to this.

XII

Girdlegard,
Dwarf Realm of the Fifthlings,
In the North of the Gray Range of Mountains,
Late Winter, 6491st/6492nd Solar Cycles

Tungdil stood at the edge of a snowy stretch of ground between two mountain slopes, completely at a loss. The tracks made by the cocoon-thieves ended abruptly at the tips of his own boots. The prints disappeared at the edge of a precipice. "They've climbed straight down the cliff." He bent forward to spy into the depths. It was impossible to see the foot of the cliff. "Must be at least three hundred paces to the bottom. Can't make head or tail of it."

Balyndar and Ireheart were waiting at his side. "Or perhaps they can fly, after all," said the fifthling, checking overhead. "I can't make anything out on the rocks above us, either."

Ireheart searched around in the snow until he found solid rock. "And there's no secret passage. I'd be able to hear it." He noticed the funny looks the others were giving him. "So? I just wanted to make sure."

Tungdil went a couple of paces to one side on the virgin snow of the plain. "Not a bad idea." He bent down and carefully brushed off the thin top layer of freshly fallen snow. In the older ice crystals underneath there were clear marks of something being dragged. "Clever of them," he acknowledged. "They've put a load of snow on one of the sledges and they're using it to conceal their tracks. To make us think they've abseiled down the cliff. But in reality they've gone this way." With a grin he gave the signal for them to march on.

"It's a good thing I'm here," joked Ireheart. "If I hadn't checked for underground passages we'd all have had to shin down that precipice on a bit of string. I'm a brainy dwarf, of course."

"If you say so. They're heading east," stated Balyndar. A thin layer of ice had formed on his mantle; every time he moved there was a rustling sound. "If they keep on in this direction they'll come to the Red Mountains. The path dates from old times, when the fast tunnels had been forgotten. The track hasn't been maintained properly by the tribes and it's sure to be hard going. More a climb than a walk."

Ireheart had another new idea. "If they're planning to take the kordrion's young off to Lohasbrand . . . perhaps it's a bunch of mini orcs we're on the trail of? The Dragon's bred them specially small so they can use our tunnels and narrow mountain paths? The long-uns, of course, used to breed tiny dogs for going down badger setts and foxholes. Why shouldn't it work with orcs?"

"It's worrying, the things you come up with sometimes," said Balyndar, surveying the plain. "What would the Dragon want with the cocoons?"

"How should I know? To break the kordrion's will and enforce his loyalty?"

The fifthling tutted, not even bothering to respond to that. "If we head out across the plain the enemy will be able to see us coming. Shall we hug the cliffs?"

"We've not a grain in the hour-glass to lose. Straight across," ordered Tungdil, setting off.

Ireheart followed him at once. "What about my theory, Scholar?" he urged, with the eagerness of a young child. "Seems obvious to me."

"Possible but not probable," replied Tungdil. "Perhaps the firstlings had the same idea as us and sent out a scouting party."

"Playing the monsters off against each other to free themselves from the Dragon's clutches and destroy the kordrion, who'll have been weakened from the fighting?" Ireheart had a good long think. "Could be. But it's pretty odd they're putting the idea into practice at the same time as us." The more he considered it, the less he liked his own theory. "Nonsense. They would have gone to see Balyndis and asked for permission and support for the expedition. That's what you do if you're on someone else's territory."

Suddenly Tungdil stood stock still. "Ireheart, Balyndar, Slîn," he whispered. "Come with me. The rest of you keep going to the other side of the plain and wait for our signal." He hurried off, bent low, going toward a cleft in the rocks that Ireheart and the others hadn't noticed.

"It's a bit of a miracle the way he finds things," said Slîn. "I wouldn't have seen that till I'd walked into it."

"Vraccas has a soft spot for our Scholar," laughed Boïndil. "It's always been like that as long as I've known him." *Nothing's changed.*

The little band stepped cautiously into the cleft in the rock; it was dark but the air smelled fresh, not stale.

"A tunnel," whispered Boïndil.

"They probably won't have come upon it purely by chance. Whoever destroyed the nest and stole the cocoons— it's been a long time in the planning." Tungdil led them along a sloping passage. They found crudely hewn steps leading further down.

From below they heard muffled voices.

"We've got them," whispered Ireheart, full of anticipation. "Let me go in first, Scholar! I'll finish them all off! No one will escape me in these narrow . . ."

"Pull yourself together," hissed Tungdil.

"Go on, let him," said Slîn softly. "It's fine with me . . ."

At that very moment the kordrion's screeching roar was heard outside! Wind shot through the tunnel, leaving them standing in whirling snowflakes.

Boïndil shuddered and remained motionless for a second before coming to his senses. He thought at once of the others in his party, who would be left facing the kordrion on the plain. "May Vraccas be with them!" he prayed. "Let them find shelter before it gets to them. We need every man jack of them if we are to free Girdlegard." He was about to put in his wax earplugs and go over to Tungdil, but his friend was already heading down the steps. There was no time to give support or employ caution. The kordrion young had priority.

The steps were old, crumbling away in places under their feet. Slîn lost his balance and was only saved by Balyndar's presence of mind; otherwise he would have tumbled head first down the stairs.

"Shouldn't we go back to help the others," asked the fifthling. "They'll be killed . . ."

"And so will we if we move out into the open without the cocoon," interjected Tungdil. "And anyway, to the kordrion Ireheart smells like his offspring's murderer. We're no use if we fall in battle—the only ones to benefit would be our enemies. They will have to look to their own devices."

Finally they reached the ground level and the passage became wider. They fanned out, with Tungdil and Ireheart in the first row, followed by Balyndar and Slîn.

"This leads due east," said Ireheart. "Our forefathers will have made the tunnel because they knew the high passes would not always be free."

Tungdil stopped abruptly and Slîn cannoned into him.

A loud and furious laugh swept through the passage. "They're sending out their heroes as if they had dozens more where they come from," came a deep voice. "The dwarf world will be hit hard by the loss. What will the tribes do without their figureheads and famous icons of bravery? Will the others emigrate? Commit suicide?"

Slîn bent and quickly lit two torches he had taken from his rucksack; he kept one and handed the other to Balyndar.

"Come out of the dark and I'll clobber your big mouth for you," Ireheart bellowed in rage. "Are you a coward?"

"No. I am someone who likes the dark and knows it is his ally," the speaker replied. "Why should I step into the light? You come over here!"

"Is there something wrong with your voice? You sound like a girl," shouted Ireheart. He tried to challenge the stranger. "Did a gugul bite off your manhood?" An insult like that and his own combat fire would certainly have flared up.

"Why are you following us? Are the dwarves now worshippers of the kordrion and want to return his offspring to him?"

"We demand you give us the cocoon you stole," answered Tungdil, motioning Boïndil to desist from his next vocal onslaught. *But I'd just made up such a good new insult*, thought the latter, ruefully. *Ah well, I'll just have to save it for another occasion.*

"Too late," said the voice in the darkness. "We've got it, we need it and we won't give it up."

"Then we'll come and take it!" Tungdil drew Bloodthirster. "There's only ten of you. And even though your footprints tell me you belong to our race we shall not spare you."

Silence ensued.

"We're not dwarves," said another voice just behind them, a voice out of the dark as deep as the grave. "Not anymore."

Why can't I see them? Boïndil stared intently into the blackness until he thought he could make out a shape. Then, as if from nowhere, appeared the form of a warrior; he was the size of a dwarf, in the same armor as the dwarf-hater they had come across in the Outer Lands. It was as if the passage itself had given birth to him; his helmet was closed and in his right hand he held a tionium spear with a long, pointed end.

"That's an älf's weapon," growled Ireheart, pushing in front of Slîn. "It goes with the runes on your armor, you traitor! The thirdlings have gone too far. They can't be allowed to rule."

The dwarf came to a halt two paces away.

Slîn was aiming the crossbow at him, Balyndar covered the rest of the passage, and Tungdil rested his own weapon against his shoulder. Nothing in Tungdil's demeanor showed he felt fear, although both he and his companions knew themselves to be surrounded.

"You didn't listen to what I said, Boïndil Doubleblade," said the stranger, lifting his visor. "We're no longer dwarves."

Ireheart inhaled sharply. At first he thought the dwarf had no face, but then he realized the blackness was the dye used for his beard. "You still look like one to me," he responded. "Right, are you going to hand over the cocoon?"

The stranger laughed, pleasantly now. "I've stepped into your light, so you should reciprocate and come into the dark." He lifted his left hand and clenched his fist.

The torchlight suddenly went out, leaving only a dull red glow.

"Älfar tricks," Ireheart spat out, caught by surprise. "Vraccas, strike them with your hammer. The skirt-wearers have betrayed your creation."

There was a loud click when Slîn fired the crossbow. The sound of splintering wood told them his bolt had missed its target.

"We can see you as clearly as if you stood in the full light of day," the dwarf said to them. "When your torches light up again, don't move, or we'll kill you."

The torches flared up.

Ireheart cursed. He was flanked by two dwarves in black armor and the blade of a curved dagger was at his throat; another knife hovered by his eye. Again, he had neither heard his adversaries approach nor noticed a current of air. "May Vraccas toss you in his furnace and burn your treacherous souls," he said contemptuously. He couldn't see what effect his words had; the visor was still shut.

Tungdil was surrounded by three of the armored foe and saw spears aiming at him. No one was trying to get very close.

"I'll ask you again: What do you want the embryo for?" Their leader had not moved.

"To stuff it up your arse," was Ireheart's venomous reply. "Leave me enough room for my crow's beak and I'll make you a bigger hole."

"Truth would be appropriate at this stage," said Tungdil surprisingly. "Because I hope we can come to an agreement. Meeting dwarves—beings like yourselves here and with the booty that was to be ours—makes me hopeful that the gods intended this." He looked at the spear points that threatened his face, throat and groin. "We wanted to steal the offspring of the kordrion and bring them to Lot-Ionan, to provoke the monster to attack the magus. Then a dwarf-army would have set out to destroy the sorcerer, who would have been weakened by then." He studied the leader. "You are heading east. I don't see any Dragon emblems on you, so you don't belong to Lohasbrand. I expect you had a similar plan to our own. You wanted to drive the kordrion to attack the Dragon and then to take on the victor in battle. Am I right?"

Their leader gave a smile of acknowledgment and nodded. "You are indeed, Tungdil Goldhand."

"Who are you working for? For the älfar? Do they want to take over the west and north of Girdlegard like they did in the east?" Tungdil remained as calm as a rock, as if it were he who had the upper hand.

"That's none of your business. But I have a suggestion to make to you."

"Keep your suggestions," growled Ireheart, wondering in which order he should attack his guards. He worked out a strategy that would free him. *By Vraccas! You traitors will see what a warrior like me is made of.*

"Go ahead. Anything that prevents unnecessary bloodshed will be accepted gladly," replied Tungdil.

Astonished and indignant, Ireheart heard his friend giving in. "But not by me, Scholar!" he contradicted. "These are our deadly enemies! Murderers and traitors because they're with the älfar . . ."

Tungdil's gaze silenced him. He looked round at the others, but Slîn was shuffling his feet and Balyndar was chewing his own cheek. Nobody spoke up in support.

The spears were withdrawn and Tungdil went a few paces further into the passage to discuss things. Away from his party.

Ireheart caught the words of the first few sentences the two exchanged but did not understand the content. The sound was familiar but it took him some time before his mind registered what his heart had rejected as a possibility. They were speaking the älfar tongue! *The very last thing you'd expect.*

"Charming," said Slîn, annoyed. "Our high king goes over to talk to dwarves who don't want to be dwarves, thinking instead that they are really vertically challenged älfar." He turned to look at his captors. "Might we learn what you call yourselves?" No answer was forthcoming.

Balyndar uttered a curse. "What shall we do, Boïndil?"

"How should I know? I'm a warrior, not a thinker." Ireheart's muscles tensed almost imperceptibly—but the blade at his throat was pressed closer. His guards were on the ball. "Yes, all right, all right. I won't move," he said to appease them. He watched Tungdil and the other dwarf talking.

After a long time—to Ireheart it seemed endless—Tungdil and the leader returned.

At a signal from the stranger the guards lowered their

weapons and moved behind their commander; Tungdil came to Ireheart's side.

"We have won ourselves some new friends," he announced, as if it were the most normal thing in the world. "If you would care to introduce yourself to my companions?" he suggested, replacing Bloodthirster in its sheath.

The dwarf nodded. "I am Barskalín, the sytràp of the Zhadár. The Zhadár is an älfar word that means *The Invisible Ones*. Sytràp just means *commander*." His left arm described a semicircle. "These are my ten best Zhadár and the rest are waiting at a secret place for our return. To explain why we're here, I'll need to go into more detail."

"There's no time for that! What about our companions out there on the plain?" said Ireheart sharply. "We have to help them against the kordrion!" With an angry glance at Tungdil he added, "Maybe our new friends could give us a hand and show us what they're worth."

Barskalín shook his head. "They are dead, Boïndil. The kordrion wiped them out. One of my invisible Zhadár placed at the cave entrance told me that before I showed myself to you. It was wise of you to follow us into the tunnel."

Balyndar gasped. "Dead?"

"The kordrion caught them on the plain. How could they have escaped his white fire?" Barskalín nodded down the passage. "We should talk about it later and put a few miles between us and the beast for now. It will follow our scent."

Ireheart looked first at Slîn and Balyndar, and then at Tungdil. "And where do we go now?"

He had been thinking the Scholar would answer, but it was the sytràp who said, "To the south, to the Red Mountains."

How did the Scholar do that? Ireheart had not expected this, and to judge by the astounded faces of Slîn and Balyndar, they had not reckoned with it either. But he felt no relief.

Nor was he relieved when they were shown something he assumed to be the cocoon, which the Zhadár had hidden under a thick pile of warm furs and dragged along the passage on a shield on rollers.

Girdlegard,
Dwarf Realm of the Fifthlings,
In the North of the Gray Range of Mountains,
Late Winter, 6491st/6492nd Solar Cycles

Indistinguishable one from another and vaguely ominous in their identical armor, the Zhadár marched swiftly in the company of the surviving members of the fourthling and fifthling band. They had fastened the cocoon and their equipment and provisions onto a shield and were pulling it along.

"How did you talk them into cooperating, Scholar?" asked Boïndil as they went.

"We'll have to keep an eye on them," Balyndar chipped in. "And more important still—what do they want in exchange?"

Slîn looked round. "I shan't be able to sleep, I can feel it in my bones. Not one of them has shown us his face. Except for Barskalín."

"You'll be told next time we stop. It's better if you hear it from him," Tungdil placated them, then moved on quickly to catch up with the commander.

"They're chatting again. Like old friends." Slîn nudged Balyndar and pointed toward Tungdil's back, indicating a particular rune. "The Zhadár have got the same one on their armor," he mouthed. "You know what? I bet it's no coincidence that we've teamed up. The plan about the nest was Tungdil's—perhaps these are his warriors and are just pretending to be . . . Zhadár?"

"Maybe you're right," said the fifthling pensively.

"Stop that nonsense!" commanded Ireheart in the uncomfortable knowledge that he could not tell them what to do.

Balyndar looked at him disapprovingly. "You keep changing your ideas, Boïndil Doubleblade. One minute you're on his side, then you start to wobble, then you change your mind again." He stuck his hands in his belt. "You'll have to come to a decision. When it's all over."

Ireheart was angry. "We've got a job to do and we'll do it, and it doesn't matter who helps us as long as it serves Girdlegard," he said, avoiding the issue. "There have been losses. Now we have new soldiers and we have the kordrion's young."

"He's right," said Slîn. "We're better off like this than being a pile of ash out on the plain. Or devoured by the monster." He fell silent.

When they came to a cave with a water source, Tungdil signaled to the company to halt and Barskalín complied.

"It's pretty clear which of them gives the orders," commented Ireheart, bursting with curiosity. He, Slîn and Balyndar settled down away from the Zhadár to eat. *I want to know what the story is with these Zhadár. Vraccas can't be giving his blessing to this.* He glanced at his friend, who was talking to the sytràp. They were studying a map that they had unrolled and spread out, each running their fingers over the lines. Eventually they seemed to have finished and came over.

Barskalín sat down on a boulder. "I owe you an explanation about myself and the Zhadár," he began. He released his helmet strap, revealing a shaved skull dyed black. "As I was saying: We *used* to be thirdlings. Each of us is more than four hundred cycles old and we're all excellent warriors. When Aiphatòn and his southern älfar marched in and it became clear no one could stop them, our king suggested a pact. To our astonishment they agreed." His gaze wandered over the dwarf-faces. "After about twenty cycles the Dsôn Aklán made us an offer: They were looking for volunteers to train up and learn certain crafts. In exchange it was arranged that this particular unit would eliminate all the dwarf-tribes of Girdlegard."

"May Vraccas shove a red-hot hammer through their stupid ears!" Ireheart took a swig from his flask.

"They wanted Girdlegard naked, without a single defender." Balyndar's expression darkened. "It would have meant the end."

"The älfar from the south are different from those in the sagas?" Slîn wondered.

Barskalín confirmed this with a nod. "They are wilder, more cruel . . ."

Ireheart laughed. "Am I hearing aright? More cruel? How could that be?"

"It can be, Boïndil," answered a subdued Tungdil. "Believe me, it can."

"They aren't the only ones. A few hundred älfar from the north have somehow managed to enter Girdlegard without

Aiphatòn's help. He's known as emperor among the southern älfar." Barskalín continued his report. "It was the Dsôn Aklán who aided the northerners."

Boïndil turned to Balyndar. "How did they get past you?"

"They didn't!" insisted the fifthling. "We keep the Stone Gate and nothing got through. It's nonsense!"

Barskalín threw him a disapproving glance. "They got into Girdlegard without your knowledge. The dwarves couldn't have stopped them. The älfar rediscovered an old passage they had used many cycles ago to invade the elf realm Lesinteïl."

"By Vraccas! Then we must find the entrance and close it up." Slîn looked at Ireheart. "There's no point in keeping up the fortresses, otherwise."

"The passage no longer exists. It collapsed and it's under-water now." The sytràp folded his hands. "In any case, there's conflict now among the älfar. The Dsôn Aklán and their followers consider themselves to be the rightful successors to the Unslayables and, as such, morally and in every way superior to their cousins from the south. The northerners were the ones we had an alliance with." The sytràp grinned maliciously. "I'm sure they would have sent us to fight the southern älfar sooner or later. I'd bet anything."

"Well, well." Ireheart stroked his beard. "That's useful to know. So the black-eyes don't like each other either."

"The southerners are in the majority and they've taken over Dsôn Balsur and the former elf realm of Âlandur. The northern älfar have rebuilt the city of Dsôn in an artificial crater in the former elf realm of Lesinteïl, now renamed Dsôn Bhará—the true Dsôn. Yours, Tungdil Goldhand, is a name they pronounce with hatred. They haven't forgotten that it was you who sent the city of the Unslayables up in flames." Barskalín looked round at the others. "They taught us everything and trained us in their arts and skills."

"How? Dwarves and magic? What's more, magic originating from our oldest and most terrible foes?" Balyndar cut himself a piece of ham.

"It was a long and painful process involving many gruesome rituals," Barskalín explained, seeming distressed. "It felt as if they had burned out the very souls that Vraccas endowed us with. What you see is the outer shell, filled with something that would make you shudder with fear if you ever caught sight of it."

Boïndil glanced at Tungdil and remembered the vicious scars covering his torso. Perhaps he had also undergone that transformation? Is that why his face had the fine black älfarlike lines?

Barskalín cleared his throat. His voice had gone and he needed something to drink before he could continue his story. "After one hundred cycles in their service the Dsôn Aklán considered us to be loyal followers." He looked at Slîn. "We spied on your strongholds and killed anyone in our path. I could find my way through Goldfast and Silverfast blindfold. There are no secrets. If we wanted to," he lowered his voice, "we could lead the älfar or the thirdlings straight into the fourthling realm. You wouldn't be able to stop us."

The fourthling gulped. "That's . . . impossible."

Barskalín pointed to Tungdil and Boïndil. "Ask them. They came across one of my Zhadár in the Outer Lands. He had been traveling through the Brown Mountains, on a reconnaissance mission through your territory. Then he was going to spy out Evildam and follow up the rumors about the return of the greatest dwarf-hero." He laughed. "He reported the rumors had been correct. He only just managed to escape from you."

Ireheart spluttered and spat out his drink. "He survived the White Death?"

"We're tough." Barskalín smiled mysteriously.

"And they sent you to steal the cocoons?" Balyndar had not taken his eyes off the sytràp.

"Yes. The älfar . . . the Dsôn Aklán, want to stir up a war in the west to further their own plans. A diversion only. That's purely my interpretation, of course." Barskalín looked at Ireheart. "Emperor Aiphatòn is preparing for a campaign against Lot-Ionan. He intends to march to the south to overthrow the magus and his famuli. Then he will open the High Pass to allow more älfar through."

"That's good news!" Slîn filled his pipe. "We don't need to start any wars! Let the two of them sort things out between them and we'll hang around and see who wins. Let's kill the kordrion's young and bide our time."

Balyndar placed his fingertips together thoughtfully. "I thought our own plan was . . . better." He addressed Barskalín. "I want to know the reason you and I are sitting peaceably next to each other instead of fighting. You are working for our enemies but you're still ready to help us take the cocoon to Lot-Ionan?"

"Treachery," Tungdil said calmly. "The Zhadár never obeyed wholeheartedly, but have been waiting for an opportunity to change sides."

"That's right." Barskalín nodded. "Tungdil Goldhand is a thirdling. A lot has changed in the thirdlings' way of thinking and the dwarf laughed at for many cycles has become our greatest hero. He stood alone to fight against immense odds. And now he is the high king of all the dwarf-tribes—who else could we follow with both our head and our heart? We have been waiting for so many cycles to eliminate the älfar. To destroy them with their own weapons and arts."

"That was what you planned when you volunteered?" Ireheart stared at the sytràp, finding it hard to grasp the immensity of what they had taken on. "By Vraccas, quite a sacrifice!"

"*If* what he says is true." Balyndar sounded less than convinced.

"I believe him." Slîn nodded and chewed on the stem of his pipe.

Barskalín smiled, a row of white teeth shining in the dark face. "To follow Tungdil Goldhand and help to free Girdlegard. That was always our intention. And now we have the opportunity, we'll be able to carry out that plan." He indicated his nine companions. "Altogether there are twenty-three of us . . ."

Balyndar's laughter was ironic. "That's plenty to make the älfar run off, tails between their legs."

Now, for the first time, the commander of the Zhadár showed impatience. "Each one of us can deal with twenty opponents without exertion. In *conventional* combat. But if we use our special powers we can confound a small army, let me tell you, Balyndar Steelfinger of the clan of the Steel Fingers! If you thought the only thing our älfar skills are good for is to put the lights out you've got another think coming." He scowled. "I've walked past you five dozen times during the course of your life and you never knew. I stood at your cradle, I stood at your bed while you slept. The Gray

Mountains hold no secrets for me or my Zhadár." His hand lay on the handle of his curved dagger. "You have me to thank for the fact I didn't lead the thirdlings into your mother's kingdom. The strongholds would have fallen as well." He stood up and came over to the fifthling to speak low into his ear. "I know all your secrets, heir apparent to the fifthling crown," he whispered, then straightened up. "So you are in the best of hands. It is an honor for us to be able to serve the high king."

Balyndar sat thunderstruck; he had turned as pale as a linen shirt.

Tungdil shook hands with Barskalín, who returned to his Zhadár troops; the two groups of warriors bedded down for the night in separate corners of the cave.

Ireheart could not understand why Balyndar was suddenly monosyllabic, but he was still mulling over what the sytràp had reported. "Vraccas, now I'm positive that it was your work: Letting us meet the Zhadár warrior in the mountains. I thank you," he prayed quietly. "Now grant victory to the Invisibles and ourselves. I would give anything to hear dwarves and humans able to laugh again."

"Would you give your life?" Slîn asked, having overheard. "Would you die for the cause?" He turned over and put his hands behind his head, his pipe clamped in the corner of his mouth. "I would. But only if at least one of us survives to report our heroic deeds. Otherwise even the most glorious of deaths is a waste of time."

Ireheart wanted to reply but his throat had gone dry. Perhaps it was better not to answer.

He might have said the wrong thing.

* * *

Girdlegard,
Protectorate of Gauragar,
Twenty Miles South of the Gray Mountains,
Late Winter, 6491st/6492nd Solar Cycles

Ireheart was feeling uneasy.

They had taken off his chain mail and any clothing that had been in contact with the cocoon and had tied it to a horse bought for the purpose, in order to duplicate the scent trails and keep the kordrion busy. As soon as the beast found the horse and consumed it, iron rings, shirt, hose and all, it would know it should have followed the other track; Ireheart was wearing random cast-offs that his companions could spare.

"I feel like some ragged peddler," he said, down in the dumps.

"And what is wrong with my trousers?" asked their crossbow specialist with a grin. "If you burst the seams with your fat arse, you'll have to buy me some new ones."

"It's not fat, it's all muscle. You fourthlings don't have any. Your trousers would just about fit our children." Ireheart looked back at Balyndar, who was holding the älfar dagger they had taken off the dead archer. He turned the weapon, running his fingers over the blade, and then struck it at a certain angle against his forearm protectors.

It was not a strong blow—but the blade sang out and snapped in two.

"As I thought," muttered the fifthling, discarding the useless weapon.

"What did you think?" asked Ireheart, and Balyndar gave a jerk. He had not known he was being observed. "That the dagger was faulty?"

"Yes. Something was wrong, but I didn't know what." He tried to explain. "We firstlings have a good eye for metalcraft. I knew a dwarf had made it, but something wasn't right. The smith had included a fine layer of a hard, brittle metal. It hadn't fused to the steel and I could see that, if subjected to stress—for example in combat—the blade would break off." Balyndar looked at Ireheart. "It was constructed *deliberately* as an inferior piece of work. It wasn't a mistake."

"So the thirdlings are sabotaging the black-eyes' plans, too, like the Zhadár," noted Boïndil with satisfaction.

"Well, I wouldn't go that far. It could be a single dwarf with a conscience." The fifthling dampened Ireheart's enthusiasm. "If there were a lot of this treachery going on, even the älfar would notice and there'd be consequences for the thirdlings. Fatal consequences." He looked at Tungdil, who was up front at the Zhadár commander's side, climbing the next slope. "The thirdlings may be good warriors, better than all of us. But they can't win against the älfar. The black-eyes have far superior numbers."

"It's a bit early to be seeing them as allies on the strength of one faulty dagger," Ireheart agreed. He looked up, surprised at the swift approach of a cloud.

When Slîn followed his gaze, his arm shot up into the air. "Kordrion! To the north!"

Ireheart was angry with himself that he had not seen it. "I think I must be getting old."

They dived for cover among the rocks, while Ireheart raced off to tell Tungdil. "What do we do, Scholar?"

The one-eyed dwarf stood straight and unruffled, his right hand shielding his brow as he scanned the sky. "It's closer than we'd want. Our trick with the false trail isn't working anymore."

Boïndil was sulking. "So I lost my clothes and armor for nothing?"

"It's given us a good head start. But that seems to be over." Tungdil spotted the kordrion between the clouds. "He's keeping a lookout. It won't take him long to spot us."

"That means we'll never make it to Lot-Ionan, Scholar?"

"Precisely." Tungdil looked back over his shoulder. "But we can take our gift to someone else. We've got to use the opportunity to cause our enemies maximum damage."

Ireheart recognized where they were heading. "Dsôn Bahrá."

"It would be the safest. The path will be downhill most of the way and our sledges will help. And there'll be caves we can hide in when the kordrion gets too close." Tungdil looked at Barskalín, who nodded in agreement.

"That sounds like fun: slipping in unnoticed among the black-eyes. What a challenge!" Ireheart signaled to Slîn and Balyndar to come over; the Invisibles left their hiding places and began pushing the sledges uphill.

"I don't intend to slip in unnoticed," said Tungdil. "It wouldn't work, anyway. I'll introduce myself as a transformed Tungdil whose greatest wish is to wipe out dwarfdom completely. I'll offer the älfar my assistance. We'll offload the baby kordrion secretly and wait to see what happens. We'll have an alternative plan ready." He looked at his friend. "Ireheart, you, Balyndar and Slîn will have to wear Zhadár armor."

"Charming," was the unhappy fourthling's comment.

"Don't worry. They'll have something in your size," joked Ireheart. "One of their women's outfits."

Balyndar put his hands on his hips. "I don't like it."

"You don't have to like it. I am your high king so you'll do what I say." Tungdil sounded extraordinarily calm and determined. "The kordrion is too fast for us and you can't argue with me on that score. If there's a chance to deploy the embryo against the enemy, we'll do it." He swung himself onto one of the sledges. "We'll be in Dsôn Bahrá in a couple of orbits. Follow me!" He pushed off and sailed down the slope.

The Zhadár followed him one by one, racing downhill; Slîn and Ireheart prepared to do likewise.

But Balyndar was standing next to his sledge staring at the others. "I don't know if we're doing the right thing here, Boïndil Doubleblade," he said broodingly.

"The stories they write about us will show whether it was right or not, Balyndar," Ireheart said in consolation. "I don't know the answer, and I'm sure the Scholar doesn't know either yet. Our plan is up the spout and we've got to make the best of things. With the help of Vraccas perhaps we will achieve more than we think." He patted him on the shoulder. "Trust your father." The words had already left his lips before Ireheart realized what he had said.

Balyndar slowly turned to face him. "What idiocy are you babbling?"

Boïndil gave a forced laugh. "A joke, to cheer you up a bit."

"Then it didn't work. Not with that joke." To Ireheart's great relief the fifthling went off to his sledge and started to push it. "Don't you know a better one?"

"What about the one where an orc asks a dwarf the way?"

Balyndar made a dismissive gesture. "Boring. Every dwarf knows that one."

"But not my version," Ireheart replied proudly and took a deep breath. "An orc comes along and sees a dwarf and he wants to know . . ."

"Horsemen!" Slîn called excitedly. "Down there, to the right of the sledges in the little valley. They're heading straight for the Zhadár!"

Why does he always see the danger before I do? Ireheart looked where Slîn had pointed.

Balyndar tried to calculate how many riders there were. "The Black Squadron," he exclaimed in consternation, launching himself onto his sledge on his stomach. "Quick, we've got to catch the others up and warn them!" He raced off.

Slîn did not wait to be told twice. He zoomed down the slope in the same daring pose.

"Hey! Hey! Wait for me!" Ireheart pushed his sledge off, ran alongside it a few paces and then jumped on. "By Vraccas! How am I ever supposed to tell a joke properly?"

XIII

Girdlegard,
Black Abyss,
Fortress Evildam,
Late Winter, 6491st/ 6492nd Solar Cycles

Goda contemplated the pulsating edges of the flickering red dome close to the walls of Evildam. The sight reminded her of waves lapping and she knew that, as with the sea, terrible monsters were lying in wait under the surface. She knew why the dwarf-race feared deep water.

Troubled, the maga pulled her cloak tighter round her shoulders. The energy sphere now reached all the way to their stone walls—but she was powerless to affect its growth.

Kiras, in breastplate and limb protectors over thick clothing, was at her side. Using a telescope she watched the enemy's newly erected protective barrier. "The walls haven't been damaged. I can't see any cracks or bulges. The red glow doesn't seem to be harming the stone. The warriors feared the force might bring down Evildam, but that's not happening."

"But the monsters can come directly up to our fortress walls. That is bad. I'll need something to shrink the sphere down again." Goda's right hand played with the diamond splinters in her pocket. *But what?*

"He killed them," said Kiras firmly, addressing the maga.

Goda knew exactly what the undergroundling was referring to. "I know. Ireheart saw the injuries on the ubariu, too," she replied after a while.

When the two women stood side by side it was obvious how different their respective dwarf-races were. Kiras, taller and slimmer in stature, was almost like a small human; Goda, in contrast, was one of Girdlegard's archetypal thickset dwarves. Kiras did not have the darkish fluff on the cheeks that was noticeable on Goda's round face.

"But Boïndil said nothing." Kiras could discern monsters behind the red screen running across the plain round the Black Abyss and marking certain places out with flags.

"And he never will. Unless the dwarf pretending to be Tungdil Goldhand finally admits that he is an impostor." Their attempt to force his hand had failed. Goda looked both ways along the battlements. They were manned at all times, the catapult teams at their stations, ready to take immediate action if the fiends attacked.

"That'll never happen. Those dead soldiers we found are evidence that he's pursuing his own ends with every conceivable means." Kiras lowered the telescope to look at Goda. A flash caught her eye and when she turned in its direction she saw that it came from the eastern battlements. One of the guards had polished his shield so well that it was dazzling her. She thought she could even feel the heat of the reflection it sent. "Is it true they've made him high king?"

The maga nodded. "And I thank Vraccas that I'm here in Evildam! This way I'm not subject to his commands."

The undergroundling leaned against the parapet. "I wonder what happened to the real Tungdil: Dead, captive or has he become something even worse than this thing, this fraud calling himself the hero?"

Goda sighed. "There's no way of knowing."

Kiras suddenly brightened up and looked across at the red

sphere. "What if we captured one of the monsters for interrogation? Can't you make a hole in the screen big enough
for me and a few ubariu?"

Goda found the idea ridiculous at first but, on reflection
. . . "Why didn't I think of that?"

"Because you've got too much to think about. You have
to command the fortress and be our maga, constantly on
guard against sorcery." Kiras offered this excuse with a smile,
grasping Goda's hands. "I don't tell you this often enough:
You are like a mother to me. I can never thank you enough
for what you have done for me."

"That's why I shan't find it easy to send you in there. Not
only because of the monsters—there's a magus over there as
well. And who knows how long I'll be able to hold the
opening for you?" Goda shook her head. "No, we'll drop
that idea."

A fanfare sounded, drawing their attention to the scene.
The women picked up their telescopes.

A variety of creatures were running around, busy as ants,
dragging stones to the places marked with pennants and
building protective walls. Judging from the speed they were
working at they had to be trying to get things completed by
nightfall.

Elsewhere, large fat creatures with broad long-taloned
paws were digging furiously. As soon as the holes had reached
a certain depth they motioned over other workers to bring
tubs of molten metal to tip in. Then long iron spikes were
set at angles into the cooling substance.

"They're making fixtures for siege machines." Kiras
surveyed the scene through her telescope.

"Catapults, I'd say. Like the one I destroyed that they were using down in the ravine." Goda summoned one of the ubariu and asked his opinion; he agreed with her.

While they spoke, other beasts raced up behind the screen, dozens of them dragging huge long timbers. One of the fat monsters supervised their orderly construction and, bit by bit, the confused heap of wood became a siege tower.

"You were right," said the maga to Kiras. "And over there they're making an undercarriage for a battering ram." She called for two of her children, Sanda and Bandaál, who she had been training up in magic skills. "We can't wait any longer. The magic sphere must be held back before those machines can reach our walls."

Kiras stared. "What are they doing?"

Goda looked down.

The monsters had half erected the first four siege towers, and then switched to the task of carrying stone blocks over and placing them on the wooden platforms; other workers brought long coils of rope, one end of which dangled back down into the ravine.

"Weights," decided the undergroundling. "I don't know what they're for yet, but they look like counterweights."

"They'll be putting up a bigger catapult in the ravine itself, I suppose," said the ubari soldier, screwing up his pink eyes to see better. "One of the beasts has got a white flag. He's coming up to the gate."

Goda assumed it was a herald come to negotiate. If it had not been for the barrier and the enemy magus she would have nailed the creature to the ground with a rain of arrows, then buried it under a rock the size of a house so that the brood of Tion could see what the dwarves had in store for all of them. But in the present situation this seemed unwise.

Negotiations, even if Goda did not intend to put the results into practice, would take time. And treasure chests full of time were what she needed, waiting for Ireheart to return with enough allied soldiers to confront the enemy magus.

It would not be easy. Her husband and the one-eyed dwarf calling himself Tungdil had a daunting task; everyone knew that. Unlike the soldiers defending Evildam, Goda was not optimistic about being able to face down Lot-Ionan and force him to his knees.

The creature heading for the gate was walking more slowly now. It stopped three paces away and called out in a quavering voice. The guards passed on the message.

"Has it brought a list of demands?" Goda asked the others. "I wonder."

The three of them hurried down. Goda, Kiras and the ubari went to the lift along corridors and past battlements and catapults. The open cabin took them down to ground level for the main gate. A soldier came up, a roll of parchment in his hands. "It was posted through the barrier into the spy-hole, Maga," he explained.

"Put it down," Goda instructed him. "Carefully."

The guard looked surprised. "It's only parchment."

"Do what you are told!" snapped Kiras. "Who knows what spell they might have put on it. It could be a trick."

The soldier did as he was ordered.

Goda approached the roll and spoke a security incantation to check whether the enemy magus had impregnated the parchment with a spell that would start to work when it was unrolled. She relaxed when the green flickering cloud did not change color—a sure indication that all was in order.

She picked it up, unrolled it and read:

Defenders,

I, Bearer of Many Names on this side of the Abyss and beyond, demand that you surrender the fortress with immediate effect. Open the gates and withdraw!

Further, I demand the entire hinterland be instantly subjected to my rule. I am inclined to be merciful if this happens without delay. If not, pity will be shown neither to soldiers nor citizens and I shall instruct my warriors that everything is to be destroyed.

I, Bearer of Many Names, am in possession of power beyond anything your own magus can compete with. Your magus should surrender to me voluntarily. If, on the other hand, I am forced to, I shall use my might to sweep him aside, and then shall have my troops wreak greater havoc still on the land.

The reply to this announcement must be received within seven sun courses, no more.

If the reply is not forthcoming within the set period I shall consider my demands to have been rejected and I shall know how to proceed to achieve my justified claims.

Nothing and no one can save you from my anger if you challenge me.

Goda handed the parchment to Kiras. "Insolent is too harmless a word for this fanatical rubbish!"

"Arrogant," judged the undergroundling on skimming the content. "Arrogant and stupid. Someone's getting rather big for his boots today."

The maga went to the gate and had the sentry open the spy-hole. Directly in front of her she saw the red shimmer of the sphere the foe had erected, providing cover for war engines to be moved in close. You would not make demands like that unless you had great power, there was no disputing that. "Maybe he really is that powerful." She clutched one of the diamond splinters and prepared a spell to attack the red sphere.

A narrow bolt of lightning sped through the spy-hole from the tip of her middle finger; it hit the barrier.

There was a humming sound like in a beehive and then a dark coloring spread where the spell had struck. Red turned to orange and then finally to dazzling yellow.

"Close up the spy-hole!" Goda commanded, stepping away from the gate.

Kiras and the guards could no longer see what was happening on the other side but they heard a loud explosion.

The fortress gate, although reinforced with iron plates, bolts and rods, shuddered under the impact. The hinges shrieked and flakes of rust flew off the metal. The blast was so strong that the entrance opened up a little as some of the metal fastenings fractured, flying in splinters around the heads of the defenders. The ubari standing at Goda's side was struck and fell to the ground groaning; the undergroundling cried out and grasped her head. Shrapnel had torn off half her ear.

Goda, attending to the needs of the wounded, vowed never to try an experiment like that again. *It doesn't bear thinking about what would have occurred if I'd used a really strong spell.*

She knew now that the barrier would return any attack with tenfold magic firepower.

Girdlegard,
Protectorate of Gauragar,
Twenty Miles South of the Entrance to the Gray Mountains,
Late Winter, 6491st/6492nd Solar Cycles

Ireheart watched the vanguard of the Black Squadron—whatever that might be—come riding out of the little valley to arrive ten paces away from where Tungdil was standing in a dip in the landscape. He could do nothing to prevent this. He could make out ponies and dwarves with dark armor remarkably similar to that of the Invisibles.

As soon as the squadron noticed the sledges they fanned out, covering the entire breadth of the hollow; there was no way through.

Tungdil halted his sledge and the Zhadár, one by one, slowed down, then dismounted, forming a circle, using their shield-sledges as protection to create a mini fortification with Tungdil and Barskalín in the center. Slîn and Balyndar came up and joined them.

Damn and blast. This is not going to go well. Ireheart doubted he could reach them before the Black Squadron tightened their ring round the Zhadár. *Oh, what the blazes . . . I'll barge my way through.* "Nothing on this mission is going as planned. Not even when we haven't got a plan!" he cursed under his breath and made himself as small as possible so as to offer the wind less resistance.

In an audaciously dangerous maneuver he swerved past the pony legs, headed for the last gap in the squadron's ranks and crashed his sledge full tilt against a Zhadár shield.

Ireheart was hurled up into the air, then he slammed into the protective wall and slid into the snow, springing back on his feet immediately, his weapon at the ready. "Get back!" he yelled at the rider in front of him, but he could hardly see what he was doing, what with the melting snow dripping into his eyes. "I swear I'll get you with my crow's beak where it'll really hurt."

A chorus of loud laughter broke out.

"There are not many children of the Smith who carry a weapon such as yours and who are as old as you," someone scoffed, but still with a trace of respect in the voice. The dwarf sprang down from the saddle, chains clinking.

Boïndil swiftly wiped the snow off his face. Now he could see the dwarf-warrior clearly: He bore a long-handled ax in his right hand. A thick mantle was worn over reinforced chain mail and the bright red beard had black streaks in it. Green eyes surveyed Ireheart; the body was tensed and the warrior was watching out for a surprise attack born of desperation.

"It would be a pleasure to try my strength against yours," said the unknown dwarf. "Boïndil Doubleblade." Then he turned to the Zhadár. "What's this about, Barskalîn? Since when are you afraid of me and my soldiers?"

"I'm not afraid of them or of you. But I was not sure you were still their leader, Hargorin Deathbringer." On his command all the shields were lowered and then Barskalîn approached his friend. "I wasn't expecting to meet you and the Desirers on my travels."

Ireheart's gaze went from one to the other. "What—by the Smith—is happening here?" He looked at the riders' dark armor. "Desirers?"

"They collect tribute for the älfar from what was once

Idoslane." Balyndar spoke with hearty disdain. "Robbers and murderers, nothing more."

"Don't be so hasty." Barskalín held out his hand to Hargorin and introduced Slîn, Balyndar and Ireheart. "Now bend the knee before the new high king of the dwarflands," he announced dramatically. "For he is one of your own, a thirdling. Tungdil Goldhand!"

Hargorin took a step back in surprise and stared at the one-eyed dwarf emerging from the ranks of the Zhadár; then his gaze took in the armor, and Bloodthirster, and finally the hard facial features. He saw the insignia of a high king. "Well, I'll be . . ." His voice trailed off in disbelief, then he sank onto one knee and bowed his head, proffering Tungdil his ax.

The Black Squadron dismounted and one hundred and fifty warriors, male and female, all made their reverences to the ruler of all dwarves.

Ireheart looked around with a grin. "If this happens every ten miles or so all the way to Dsôn Bhará, we'll soon have a decent army to put the wind up the älfar and chuck them out of Girdlegard," he laughed. "Scholar, will you take a look at this! Thirdlings showing you respect!"

Tungdil commanded Hargorin and his squadron to stand. "If I understand Barskalín and yourself correctly may I assume you share the same views on the älfar?"

Hargorin glanced at the sytràp, who nodded permission to continue. "Lord, many of us have been waiting for you to return to lead your tribe against all the enemies." As he spoke he seemed radiant with delight. "You don't know it but our folk recount legends about your fame."

Tungdil looked at Barskalín, who shrugged and said, "I haven't had time to tell you."

This will make a good story for the campfire. Ireheart gave a broad grin. "So, my Scholar . . . A fairy-tale hero fêted by the thirdlings now."

"If he's so popular with the thirdlings, this gives us untold opportunities," remarked Slîn.

"Not all revere him," Hargorin was quick to point out. "But very, very many do." He beamed at Tungdil. "One of the legends describes your heroic deeds on the far side of the Black Abyss. When I see you wearing this armor it feels like it was a prophecy. The story describes you exactly like this."

Barskalîn gave two of his Zhadár orders to watch the sky for any signs of the kordrion's approach. "We need to find ourselves somewhere nice and quiet where we can talk properly," he suggested. "Have you got a place near here, old friend?"

Hargorin nodded. "Half an orbit's ride away. It's one of my fortresses. Let's harness our ponies to your sledges and make for the stronghold."

"Is it strong enough to withstand a kordrion attack?"

Hargorin's expression did not change. "It can hold up for a good while, at least. And if the tower were to collapse we can still escape through the tunnels." He looked at Barskalín. "What have you been up to? Why is the beast after you?"

The sytràp laughed. "We'll tell you later. Take the high king to your home and look after us well. Then we'll have time to talk." He became serious. "You will have to come to a decision about whom to serve," he said, suddenly formal.

"I did that many cycles ago." The thirdling bowed to

Tungdil. "Whatever leads you to the land of the älfar, from now on I and the Black Squadron shall serve only you, Sire. You will bring us glory. As our legends promise."

Balyndar rolled his eyes. But a happy Slîn on the other hand appeared gratified. "Absolutely charming."

"Charming sounds . . . feminine. But I certainly find it all . . . extraordinary." Ireheart was pleased that instead of the battle he had been fearing they were now celebrating with their new brothers-in-arms. But he could not shrug off his disquiet at the amount of black there was around him. It was like a weather front of gathering thunderclouds; would it discharge itself into a terrible storm? If so, it was clear that at its very eye would be standing none other than his friend Tungdil.

"It will suck us all in," he said under his breath, remembering that he too would soon be donning the dark armor of the Zhadár. "Vraccas, don't let me turn into one of them just because I have to wear their black plating."

Again it was Slîn who overheard. This fourthling had highly developed hearing. "You're afraid you might become like them? Boïndil, it's only black steel we're going to be putting on." He tapped himself on the chest, then touched his head. "Our hearts and minds will still belong to us. Look on it as a harmless disguise." He threw one end of a rope to one of the riders; the other was tied to his sledge. "If you like, I'll look after you, my poor little dwarf."

Ireheart laughed. "You're right to make fun of my childish thoughts." He got his sledge ready.

Pulled swiftly across the snow, they soon learned the disadvantages of this mode of travel: The ponies' hooves kicked up the snow and whirled icy clouds into their faces such that, before long, they'd all taken on the appearance of small, grim, bearded snowmen.

Through the snow Ireheart saw the twenty-pace-high curtain wall loom up in front; he also saw blasphemous insults daubed on it that would make any decent dwarf shudder in his boots.

This was nothing less than pure hatred of Vraccas in the form of runes. The symbols swore total annihilation of all the tribes. Shameful slogans daubed on many of the blocks of stone: Vraccas the Cripple, Vraccas the Powerless, Vraccas the Impotent . . .

Ireheart was not the only one to notice.

"I'm not setting foot in there," cried Slîn, and Balyndar nodded in agreement. "This is appalling. Vraccas would be enraged if we accepted hospitality from Hargorin Deathbringer. And I can't help feeling we're definitely going to need the Creator-God on our side in the next few orbits."

Ireheart agreed. "We'll find ourselves somewhere else to stay—in one of the village houses."

They shouted to the squadron to stop but, not hearing them, the band rode on through the settlement, heading for the main gate of Vraccas-Spite. Finally, the three dwarves cut through the ropes and got off their sledges. Hargorin and Barskalín turned round, and Tungdil ordered a halt.

"What's going on, Ireheart?" The one-eyed dwarf was surprised. "Why don't you want the safety of the stronghold?"

"It may not bother you, Scholar." He pointed to the inscriptions. "*But it bothers me!* I worship Vraccas and that's why I won't enter this fortress, where his name is insulted and his words are dragged through the mud." He got up and brushed the snow off his mantle. "We'll find a bed with the villagers."

"You know that the kordrion will hunt you down as the murderer of its young because of the scent on you of the cocoon?" Tungdil warned. "You won't have much protection in one of those flimsy huts. You won't even have woken up before the white fire gets you."

Boïndil indicated the Invisibles. "The Zhadár walked through the same blood and smashed eggs."

Barskalín looked a bit shamefaced when he said, "But our armor is made of tionium."

"Blasted bloody orcshit! That would have to happen to me!" He raised his eyebrows. "I don't care. Vraccas will protect me, because I shan't go in there," he said, pointing to the door. "Not under any circumstances." Slîn and Balyndar stood at his right and left.

Boïndil was aware that the group had formed into two distinct fronts. On the one side was the Black Squadron with Barskalín and on the other was him and two dwarves he did not know very well, but one of whom, at least, he found tolerable enough.

And it seemed to him that Tungdil would be going over to the dark ones' side and not to his own.

Hargorin, with Tungdil's permission, ordered his squad to enter the fortress. The Zhadár followed them in. Deathbringer came slowly over to the three adamant dwarves. "I understand you full well, Boïndil. But trust me when I tell you that the appearance of my house is purely a front." He pulled out a pendant from under his chain mail: a vraccasium hammer with the sign of the Smith. "I am his," he whispered.

"The whole squadron is his. But we had to disguise our intentions, like the Zhadár, so the älfar wouldn't suspect us. That has meant we can move around freely all over the lands where the black-eyes are in power. We know a lot about Idoslane and about the resistance movement. Even if the humans consider us unspeakable, we are really on their side. One orbit we shall need this knowledge in order to break the oppressive rule of evil." Hargorin smiled. "Believe me, Boïndil. For every stone bearing an insult to Vraccas I have begged the creator's forgiveness and I know that I will receive mercy when I reach the eternal forge. The deception has been essential. These have not been the times for open warfare." He looked over his shoulder. "But with Goldhand's return the fight has begun."

Ireheart looked at Balyndar, then at Slîn. They seemed not to want to be convinced. "I shall be staying out here in the village," he repeated, a little less aggressively this time. "Blasphemy is blasphemy. Can you recommend somewhere we can stay?"

"Perhaps one of the cheaper ones. Our war coffers are not overflowing," added Slîn.

Hargorin gave up. "Say that I sent you and you won't be charged anything. When we meet to arrange the rest of the journey we'll come to the house you choose. Just let me know where you're staying." He turned away and exchanged a few words with Tungdil and Barskalín.

The one-eyed dwarf lifted his hand. "We'll be there when the kordrion comes to get you," he called. "Sleep well." Then he disappeared into the fortress with the others; the door closed with a dull clang, robbing the three dwarves of the sight of the high king.

"Three against three," remarked Slîn.

"What?" flashed Balyndar.

The fourthling pointed to the little gap through which they could just see glimpses of tionium armor. "Us three against those three. I'll take Hargorin. He's a good target. Ireheart should fight Tungdil and Balyndar can challenge Barskalín."

"I'll have Tungdil," said the fifthling.

"What are you blethering about? You're splitting the hairs in my beard," Ireheart thundered. "We will not be fighting each other."

"It was just a thought. Forgive me. I got carried away." Slîn stared at the tips of his boots and was really embarrassed. "It won't happen again, Boïndil."

Ireheart thought that Balyndar's tone of voice showed he shared the same thoughts. Serious thoughts. "Let's find somewhere to stay. Any preferences?"

Slîn swiveled round to look at the little stone and half-timbered houses ringing the walls of Vraccas-Spite. "They all look the same. I can't decide."

"Then let's go for the one that's furthest away from the blasphemous inscriptions." Balyndar went off, dragging his sledge behind him, going back the way they had come.

They reached a farmhouse with a large barn and knocked. It was not long before someone opened the door.

A young woman stood on the threshold studying them from head to foot. "You're not one of Deathbringer's people?" she said in surprise. She popped her head out to look toward the stronghold. "Quick, come in, before they see you! They'll kill you if they see you!"

Ireheart found her solicitude for three total stranger

dwarves quite touching. "Good woman, do not concern your-self . . ."

Balyndar pushed past him. "May Vraccas bless you! Thank you for the warning." Unobserved, he winked at Ireheart. He was obviously planning to pretend he was a newcomer and nothing to do with the thirdling leader. He told her their names. "We thought it was a dwarf-fortress holding out against the älfar, but when we saw the runes we knew we were wrong. But we're too tired to travel on."

Slîn had grasped the idea and pretended he was afraid. "Blasted dwarf-haters!"

Ireheart was still hovering in the doorway; it did not seem right to deceive these humans. On the other hand, they could learn things about Hargorin Deathbringer that he would not be vouchsafing to his guests. "Again, our thanks," he said and entered the house. "May Vraccas always keep your hearth warm to reward you for your bravery and generosity."

Ireheart, Slîn and Balyndar were led to a large kitchen where the rest of the family was gathered. Ireheart counted eleven, ranging from ancient to newborn, round the table. The food smelled of cooked cereal of some kind and hearty smoked bacon.

"Grolf and Lirf! Go and put their sledges in the barn, then hide their tracks," the young woman ordered. Two young fellows jumped up. "We have guests," she said, introducing the dwarves. "True children of the Smith and not thirdlings."

"By Palandiell, you've chosen the worst place to stop in the whole of Gauragar," called the old man, whose mouth showed only two teeth. His laugh was as hollow as an empty tin.

"They're going to spend the night here. We can think about how to get them away in the morning without being seen. The thirdling lord won't let them live if he finds them." The young woman put her hand to her brow. "By the gods! I have forgotten to tell you who I am. I am Rilde, and this is my farm." Then she went round the table doing the introductions.

"Boïndil Doubleblade?" An older woman, called Mila, was staring at him. "*The* Boïndil, who fought so many battles for Girdlegard?"

Ireheart felt himself grow taller with pride.

"Then he's come to kill Hargorin," whooped the girl called Xara.

"Be quiet!" Lombrecht hushed her. He was the toothless old farmer to whom the farm had once belonged. "Hargorin is a good overlord. Who knows who would succeed him?"

Ireheart saw that Lombrecht had a pendant depicting Sitalia. "A human who worships the elf goddess?" he said, while a bench was being dragged over for them. "That's a rarity."

"And brave." Slîn nodded to the window to show that the thirdlings disliked the elves even more than they hated the dwarf-tribes.

"Someone has to keep their memory alive," answered the elderly farmer, while Rilde filled wooden bowls for them. "They were always a part of Girdlegard and must not be forgotten."

The three dwarves exchanged surprised glances.

"I thought all the elves had fled to a secret hiding place," Ireheart said, eating his first spoonful. It wasn't bad, though not a patch on Goda's minced gugul. "They're in a grove somewhere, waiting for the children of the Smith to pull the diamond out of the fire again before they get burned. Isn't that so?"

Rilde sat next to them and Xara brought them three cups and a jug of light beer. "It would be nice if that were the case," she sighed. "But the legends of my people tell a different story."

"I think I should spend more time with the long-uns," Slîn whispered to Balyndar, as he tamed his hunger. "This is where to get the latest news."

Ireheart looked at Rilde. "Tell us what you know. Where are the last of the elves?"

"I'll tell you the story of how the älfar came back to Girdlegard and destroyed the last of the elves." Lombrecht cleared his throat. "It was over two hundred cycles past. A pair of elf lovers met at a pond, the Moon Pond, over where the old elf realm of Lesinteïl used to be. Their names were Fanaríl and Alysante . . ."

The children were wide-eyed; the dwarves listened, rapt, to the old man's words and were soon so drawn in that they forgot where they were. They saw the tale unfold in their imagination.

"My life shall be your life. Now and forever," whispered the elf-girl, bowing her head to kiss her darling. Water streamed out of her wet hair onto his naked chest, dripping down his skin and into the soft grass.

Fanaríl laughed and returned her caresses. "You look like a water nymph—a mermaid, not an elf," he teased, sitting up.

Alysante squatted naked before him; the last rays of

sun shone through the trees, making her face glow and adding to her beauty.

The elf took her hand and kissed it gently, first on the back, then on the palm. "My life for your life," he vowed. "I cannot exist without you."

Alysante embraced him tenderly. With the warmth of their young bodies, passion arose; they made love on the bank of the dream-touched pond.

Afterwards they ran hand in hand to the ice-cold waters to refresh themselves, diving energetically head first into the lake.

The splashing made waves, causing the blue and white water lilies to bob up and down on the surface and the pond to overflow, lapping onto the banks up to the rich green grass.

"See how they dance, Fanaríl!" she laughed and swam over to her heart's darling, putting her arms around his neck and kissing him. "They're dancing for us."

"But they only flower for your sake," he answered, stroking her face tenderly as he broke away. "I'll gather some for you." Fanaríl swam off.

"No!" Alysante tried to prevent him. "There's an undertow! Be careful or it'll pull you down."

The elf-girl trod water, keeping her eyes on her companion, but the sun's last rays reflected on the wavelets so strongly that she had to look away. She could hear the slap of his arms in the water and the splash that his feet made . . .

Suddenly these regular sounds stopped.

"Fanaríl!" she cried, frightened for him. Her voice echoed over the pond but there was no answer.

Alysante quickly swam back to land and clambered onto a rock to get a better view.

Three water lilies were missing, but she could not see the elf.

Her fear increased.

The clear waters of the Moon Pond, which the rest of the elves in their village tended to shun, was suddenly as dark as ink. The beauty of the place disappeared with the last rays of the setting sun and shadows made the dreamy surroundings appear somber and forbidding. The deep waters, in which they had bathed so gaily, could suddenly be housing some gruesome monster. Alysante had always been warned by her father that the pond became evil at nightfall. Now they were to pay the price for their disobedience.

The fine blond hairs rose on the back of her neck. The elf-girl did not dare approach the bank. She ran to where she had left her clothes and dressed quickly. One last look at the surface of the pond and then she was going to run to get help—but a body shot up through the water three paces away from her and launched itself on her with a roar.

Alysante stumbled back with a scream, her hand on the handle of her knife. She stabbed at the creature attacking her.

"No! Stop!" the creature begged, holding out three water lilies. "It's me: Fanaríl!"

Her fear subsided and her vision cleared so that she could recognize her beloved, who was now bleeding from a knife wound on his chest. "By Sitalia! Forgive me!" she exclaimed in horror. "I thought . . ."

Fanaríl inspected the shallow wound. "It's just a scratch," he reassured her, handing her the bunch of flowers. "It's my own fault. I should not have given you a fright like that."

In her relief, Alysante pressed a kiss onto his lips before bringing him his clothes in exchange for his gift. "Never do that again," she begged. "You know what they say about the pond, however beautiful it is here." She was shaking as she put away her dagger. "I thought a beast must have caught hold of you under the water and it wanted to eat me before I could go for help."

Fanaríl burst out laughing. "It's only a pond the old folk tell stories about. But they're not true. That's all it is." Suddenly he stared at the waves, his eyes wide. "There!" he shouted. "Look there! What's that?"

The elf-girl whirled round. "Where?"

Upon which, her lover pushed her straight into the water!

"There's a mermaid!" laughed Fanaríl, as she sank in the dark waters.

The water lilies bobbed up and down on the surface. Alysante did not reappear.

"I know what you're up to," grinned the elf. "But you can't scare me."

He stepped nearer and scanned the murky depths for sight of her.

He could just make out a pale oval. A face, coming closer.

"I can see you!"

Fanaríl got ready to grab her by the shoulders and push her under again.

She burst up through the surface with a splash. Fanaríl greeted her with laughter so that she would know her attempt to frighten him had not worked.

But his hands did not meet her naked shoulders. They met hard leather!

For the space of one long breath he gazed into the beautiful but cold face of an unknown elf-woman, then a bolt of lightning shot through his stomach and warmth spread over him. Fanaríl saw the long sword she had rammed through his body. He collapsed, mortally wounded.

The elf-woman rose up out of the Moon Pond and with her left hand pushed a lock of black hair out of her face. She looked round her and disappeared silently into the nearby wood.

At the same moment Alysante jumped out of the water. Her pitiful attempt to emulate the roar of a beast turned into a gale of laughter. "It's no good," she spluttered, rubbing the water out of her eyes. "Did I make my darling boy die of fright?" she giggled when she saw Fanaríl lying there.

Only when she saw the red stain and cut on his robe did Alysante understand that he was not play-acting.

She sank down beside him on her knees and examined his wound, looking round to check for attackers. "Sitalia, save him! Fanaríl, open your eyes! You must stay awake . . ."

Drops splashing onto her back warned the girl before a broad shadow fell over her. A horse snorted.

Alysante looked over her shoulder and her hand flew to her dagger for the second time that evening.

Two huge black stallions with dark saddles stood behind her with angry red eyes full of hate. In the middle of their foreheads she could see the sawn-off stump of a horn and, as the night-mares stepped up out of the water, their hooves sent out lightning flashes, lighting up the water.

Alysante knew what she was facing.

Black-haired twin älfar sat on the backs of the night-mares, each in elaborate dark armor, and one of them held a mighty sword in his right hand. He brought the weapon down so fast that she missed its movement. The long sword's tip was planted on her back. Moisture ran off the blade onto her wet bodice; now she was cold with fear.

"Say who you are, elf-woman," he demanded roughly. Trembling, she said her name. "Is your village far from here?" Now she stayed silent and promptly the blade dug into her ribs. Warm blood trickled out of the narrow wound, coloring her dress red. "Answer!"

Alysante turned away from the sword and ran off toward the trees. She must warn her friends!

Sobbing with desperation and fear she raced through the thicket. Her thoughts were in turmoil. In her mind's eye she saw her dead lover and felt his lifeblood still sticky on her fingers. She couldn't understand where the älfar had come from. Had they been asleep at the bottom of the Moon Pond? Had Tion hurled them in past the mountains of the dwarves?

She was panting hard, her mind in a whirl—then she realized she was leading them directly to the very last of her people!

Alysante climbed up the nearest tree to continue her flight overhead from branch to branch, leaving no prints to follow.

At long last, fighting for breath and with aching arms, she reached the edge of the settlement. She saw the glow of lanterns illuminating the delicate houses and ancient Palandiell beech trees. They promised safety.

She climbed down the tree in relief and was about to go over to the buildings when a strong hand grabbed her from behind, hurling her to the ground. A boot was placed on the nape of her neck, pressing her into the forest floor without mercy.

"You were asked by Tirîgon whether your village was far from the pond," whispered a female voice in her ear. "I shall take him your answer, elf-woman." A knife scraped coming out of its scabbard. "Now I shall send you to your lover. Be sure the rest of your relatives will be joining you this very night."

Alysante tried to utter a final warning cry, but the double blade rushed down and took her to the land where Fanaríl sat waiting, tear-drenched in his despair.

There was total stillness in the kitchen.

Ireheart was amazed how good a storyteller Lombrecht had been, given his lack of teeth.

"And that," Lombrecht summed up," is how the älfar came back into Girdlegard.

"Didn't Emperor Aiphatòn bring them in from the south?" Slîn asked, indicating to the other two dwarves that he was sounding these simple humans out as to the extent of their knowledge.

Ireheart was letting the implications of the story sink in. Barskalín had hinted that the älfar had entered from the north. Lombrecht had told the story of their return. A kernel of truth, then.

Lombrecht replied, "*It's said* they came out of the south. But I know this story and I like it. Aiphatòn will have made up the other story to make himself more glorious. We all know the magus cannot be beaten."

"Does your tale have an explanation for how the black-eyes got out of the water so easily, as if they could breathe underwater like the fishes?" The mere thought of a black pond made him extremely uneasy.

"My grandfather used to tell me there was an underground river that rose in a grotto in the Outer Lands and emerged into the Moon Pond. It brought evil with it and made people frightened if they found the water and wanted to bathe. That must be why it's got the bad aura and why there are so many legends about it." Lombrecht used his spoon to scratch a sketch map on the table. "The älfar will have followed the course of the underground river, underneath the Gray Mountains and the fifthlings, and then they got out of the water. Later on they rebuilt Dsôn Bhará and called themselves Dsôn Aklán."

Ireheart pushed away his empty plate. "But Girdlegard must be overflowing with älfar if that's the case. That route must still be open."

"No, the tunnel collapsed. That's what we think, because the Moon Pond dried up completely. It's just a rocky hollow now where nothing grows. It's where the älfar put their town. But there's no tunnel, it's said," said Rilde, relief in her voice.

"We still have too many of them anyway," said Lombrecht,

getting Xara to bring him a jug of beer, which he emptied at one draft. A loud belch ensued.

Slîn applauded. "Well done, old man. Nice quality. Now I know how he lost his teeth," he chuckled to Ireheart. "We could make him an honorary dwarf, don't you think?"

Balyndar shook his head. "We should get to bed. We don't know what we'll have to do tomorrow." He got up.

Rilde stood up. "Of course. You can sleep in the barn. Or in the cowshed loft. It'll be warmer there."

"The loft for me," said the fifthling at once. "I'd rather smell of cows and be warm."

They went to their quarters and Grolf and Lirf brought them a stack of old horse blankets to keep out the cold.

The warmth and smell of cattle came up through the floorboards and Ireheart soon started to doze off, exhausted.

His last thought was that they had forgotten to inform Hargorin where they were staying. That meant they would have to rise early and knock at the door of the fortress. He did not want Rilde or her family to know. They should not connect the honest dwarves of Girdlegard with either the Black Squadron or the Zhadár.

Ireheart, Slîn and Balyndar managed to pack their things and leave the farm without being observed.

They walked along at the edge of the settlement and approached the second gate of the fortress, where they knocked. Even though the guard recognized them at once and, in Hargorin Deathbringer's name, invited them in, they refused to enter the courtyard. The sentry sent someone to tell the thirdling leader.

It was not long before he reappeared. Behind him came

three servants carrying a bench and a table laid with a meal for them.

"You can eat outside if you prefer," they were told. "But be quick. The troop is about to head for Dsôn Bhará."

The three dwarves looked at one another and started to eat in silence outside the gates of the fortress. This conflicted with Ireheart's plan to keep their presence secret. The sun was not yet fully risen, but word would soon get around.

"We should have used false names," said Balyndar, sipping his hot tea. "Now they'll think we're with the dishonorable ones."

"That won't go down well in songs about us," sighed Slîn, nodding toward the courtyard where the servants were bringing out stands bearing black armor. "Those'll be for us."

"Well, I'm not going to put that stuff on in full view." Ireheart desperately looked around for somewhere to withdraw to. There was no way though that he would step inside Vraccas-Spite.

They used their cloaks as curtains to help each other robe up and put on armor and weapons.

Ireheart thought Balyndar looked more and more like his father now. It was obvious whose son he really was.

Slîn, on the other hand, did not look right in his borrowed get-up. Several of the pieces were too loose for the crossbowman. He fiddled with his armor unhappily and the metal squeaked. "You two at least have the air of warriors," he said to Ireheart and Balyndar.

"You look a bit like a gnome in disguise," teased Boïndil.

The Black Squadron were assembling in the courtyard, with Tungdil, Hargorin and Barskalín in cavalry armor riding in front. It was an impressive and worrying picture. Stable hands hurried over with ponies for the three dwarves waiting outside.

"Good morning," Tungdil greeted them. "We missed you."

"Was there a reason you didn't let us know where you spent the night?" Hargorin's query sounded harmless but Ireheart thought he was suspicious.

"Didn't ask their names," he said quickly, before Slîn could answer.

The fortress commander was not satisfied with that. "Which house was it, then?"

I shan't betray them. Ireheart swung himself up into the saddle and moved up to be next to Tungdil. Hargorin had to move aside. "No idea. Some house where all the furniture was too big for me." He gave an innocent grin.

Slîn laughed out loud and Balyndar joined in. They mounted up and the band of riders set off.

Ireheart looked around: They were now a group of over a hundred and fifty. "I assume the Zhadár and the Black Squadron have mingled?"

"Indeed, Ireheart." Tungdil's response was not ironic. "The Dsôn Aklán are to think they are still busy trying to steal kordrion eggs."

"What about the strategy meeting, Scholar?" asked Ireheart, pushing down his visor. "Where are we holding that?"

"We've already had it. We brought it forward." Tungdil looked at him amicably and reprovingly at one and the same time. "We didn't know where to send the messenger to tell you."

Ireheart saw the sense in that. "Then tell me what's been decided."

The one-eyed dwarf turned to the front and raised his arm in a signal to the company. Behind him a standard was hoisted high, displaying the unfamiliar rune that seemed a mixture of dwarf and älfar script. "There's time enough to tell you on the way." He lowered his head slightly. "What do you say to my coat of arms, Ireheart? Isn't it fine?"

Boïndil nodded. But it wasn't fine. Not fine at all.

XIV

Wey's mouth moved, her hands jerked into the air, forming signs to avert approaching doom—but the spell her daughter had invoked came too fast. She closed her eyes and held her breath.

"Mother!" Coïra exclaimed at the sight of the flames.

Sisaroth had provoked her into using her magic without thinking and now a disaster had occurred. The magic fire burned like glowing coals.

Coïra had attempted a counter-spell but could only watch the flames imprison her mother. The young woman shook and her lips went numb.

The älf had not left. He had ducked away under the ball of magic and was crouching on the floor. From there he could attack with his two-hander; the blade tip was close to Coïra's throat.

"Watch out!" Mallenia saw the maga was paralyzed with horror, and pulled her out of the way. The knife blade missed her narrowly.

Sisaroth followed through but was held back by the swords of the Ido warrior maid. The two-hander clanged as it crashed into her blades. "Aha! Our rebel!" He gave an evil laugh and kicked sharply in her direction. "This time you won't get away."

Mallenia dodged the flying boot and dropped back onto the bed. "Coïra! Do something!" The älf leaped toward her. She had to admire the incredible elegance of his movements, but she was poised either to parry or to dodge his next attack. "Coïra! For goodness' sake!"

The flickering light in the corridor died and there was the sound of a body falling to the floor.

Mallenia glanced past Sisaroth. Queen Wey the Eleventh lay on the marble floor slabs, a smoking blackened bundle; her wide-open eyes were the only touch of white in the scorched face. Her skin hung off her in shreds and her hair had been burned away. But—did the eyes not just move? She looked more closely. "Coïra! Your mother is alive!"

The älf laughed. "Death has not forgotten her." He threw his two-hander at the Ido, striking her on the upper arm just where the night-mare had bitten her. His blade cut through her flesh as if it were soft butter, nailing Mallenia through the bone to the wardrobe.

Groaning, she dropped one of her own swords, but pointed the second at her enemy's face. "By the gods, Princess. Hurry! Or we are done for!"

Coïra took two paces and held fast to the doorframe, looking wildly around her, still in deep shock.

Sisaroth watched the maga before turning back to deal with Mallenia. He sat down on the bed in front of her. "The last of Prince Mallen's line," he said. "You have caused us much trouble, but the hunt has been enjoyable. Now the chase is over." He looked over to the corridor and gave a signal to someone outside. "You will die in your own land in full view of all, Mallenia of Ido. On the executioner's block. Your blond hair will fall into your own blood. This is the punishment for rebellion, conspiracy and murder."

"I know your plans," she answered in the language of the älfar. "You can't fool me."

Sisaroth scowled in pain. "What excruciating pronunciation! Who taught you that? Tell me his name, so I can kill him."

"So I've found out how to torture you?" She laughed.

The älf hardly moved, it was more a jerk; he punched her in the face. Her knees gave way. As she sank down the two-handed sword cut deeper into her arm. Another metallic clang: She had dropped her second sword.

"Use our language again and I will tear out your tongue." Sisaroth opened the cupboard door Mallenia was fastened to. He moved the door so that she should see what was happening in the passage: The älf woman was bent over Wey, sticking the point of her two-handed sword into the queen's back. "The name of her death is Firûsha," he said in a low, dark voice.

"No!" cried the Ido woman in despair. "Kill me but let her live. What use is her death to you?"

"We will gain the Dragon's gratitude. We have done what he does not dare to do himself." Sisaroth raised his hand, his sister nodded.

"She sent a message to Lohasbrand," Mallenia gasped. "The Dragon will guess that you killed not only her but also the orcs and Präses. He will wage war on Idoslane and the älfar regions. Everywhere! Your plan will fail." She looked down at the injured monarch. "Only she can keep you safe."

Sisaroth's face lost its superior expression.

His sister looked at him. "If she speaks true then we should let her live."

"Why? So she can tell Lohasbrand more lies? Or so she can go back to her magic source for fresh energy and launch a campaign against us in revenge?" Sisaroth's decision had been made. "It was the will of Tion and Samusin that brought us to Lakepride. Now it's time changes were wrought among the mighty of Girdlegard. Why not start in Weyurn and shoot the first arrow here?"

"Is that the right choice?" wondered Firûsha.

"Yes." He stood up, drew his dagger and went out to the corridor. "A shame not to be able to take the bones with us. What a waste." The älf knelt down and stabbed the maga at the base of the neck. He quickly decapitated her and discarded the head to ensure no healing magic could ever reunite skull and torso. He raised his eyes and looked at Coïra. "The daughter must follow. You shall be her death, sister."

Mallenia gritted her teeth and let herself drop. The blade she was pinioned by severed flesh and bone, and blood streamed out—but she was free. Her fingers closed around the sword handle and she ran to the defenseless young maga to protect her from Sisaroth. A final act of defiance.

Firûsha sprang to intercept her and struck a blow that shattered the Ido's blade. "These human weapons are worth nothing." She laughed and grabbed hold of Mallenia's wound, pressing hard, then she tossed her back onto the bed. "Good blood," she said over her shoulder to her brother. "We should collect it when we execute her. Who knows what we could create with that." Then she looked at Coïra. "Sweet maga blood. That will add a certain something to any work of art." Then she gave a sigh of regret. "But we have nothing to save it in."

She dimly heard voices out in the corridor. The guards must be coming.

"Help! We've been attacked!" shouted Mallenia.

Firûsha and Sisaroth laughed. They were not going to be put to flight by the soldiers charging up to them. The palace would soon have more dead to mourn.

The älf came up to Coïra, bloody knife in hand. Watching the countenance of the distraught young woman in order to follow her death throes, he made to thrust the dagger in.

At the same moment he was hit on the head by a helmet and Sisaroth's strike missed its target. The blade met wood and broke off. The helmet bounced, rattling across the floor.

The älf whirled around, drawing his second double-bladed knife but was engulfed in a wave of fire!

"Cowardly murderer!" someone shouted. "You can't kill a descendant of the Incredible Rodario that easily!" The next wave of flame shot out with a hiss but Sisaroth dodged this one.

Mallenia recognized Rodario's voice. "Fetch help!" she called, assuming the man would be unable to hold the älfar off for long.

Firûsha struck her on the head with the blade's broadside; the Ido girl fell, half concussed, to the cushions. The female älf sprang to her brother's aid . . .

. . . but was met by a bright yellow flash that struck her in the breast. A hole the size of a man's hand was punched through her body and she was thrown across the room and out through the window. The impact shattered the glass and the panes melted in the magic force. Firûsha had not uttered more than an agonized gasp.

Mallenia turned quickly and saw Coïra's clear eyes and outstretched arms. "Thanks be to the gods," she croaked.

"Thanks? For what? For the death of my mother?" the maga replied bitterly, hurrying out in the direction of the noise of fighting.

The Ido girl was too weak to stand. She saw the reflection of flashes; they were followed by crackling noises like those of a great fire, then shrieks and the clash of weapons. The fight against the remaining älfar sibling was in full swing. She felt her spark of life was dwindling. She had lost too much blood.

Her eyelids fluttered; they seemed heavier than an anvil. The pain had faded. She struggled against the overwhelming desire to give up, to sleep and sleep and sleep . . .

Girdlegard,
Dsôn Bhará,
Twelve Miles North of Dsôn,
Late Winter, 6491st/6492nd Solar Cycles

The winter had already lost much of its strength and snow was now melting in the hills and on the meadows. From all sides there came the sound of running water, and small streams swelled to raging torrents as, drop by drop, the last of the ice disappeared.

Tungdil's group with the Zhadár and the Desirers was riding through boggy terrain, clothes soaked through and armor suffering from the frequent showers.

Nevertheless they were making steady progress toward

their first destination: Dsôn, the second city of that name, and home to the northern älfar.

"No sign of the kordrion," Ireheart said. "I wonder if he's given up the chase?"

"As long as his young is alive he will keep searching," Tungdil reassured him.

Ireheart sighed and reflected that it had been a reasonably quick journey under the circumstances. It was down to Hargorin Deathbringer that they had been able to approach the älfar capital without being stopped by any of the patrols; everyone knew the Black Squadron and its leader.

Ireheart noticed a band of riders: Älfar, long lances in their hands, mounted on firebulls. *I was counting my chickens before they hatched.* He grinned. *Maybe there* will *be work to do.*

Tungdil glanced at Hargorin. "Let me speak to them. They'll be wanting to know the meaning of the standard."

The älfar brought their bulls to a halt and their leader gave a curt order to his soldiers to lower their pikes, while he urged his own snorting bull a few paces forward. "We understood you rode alone, Hargorin Deathbringer. But we are told you have a dwarf with you who bears an unusual device on his coat of arms." As he looked at Tungdil the eyes took in every detail and every rune on the armor.

Ireheart watched the älf, whose long blond hair was visible below the tionium helmet, forming a collar round neck and shoulders. His face was like all the others: Handsome, cruel and with black eye sockets. *I'd love, just once, to see a fat älf. A fat, clumsy älf, uglier than the mate of the ugliest pig-faced orc. And with crooked teeth.* The dwarf grinned to himself behind his closed visor. Like Slîn, Balyndar and the twenty-three Zhadár, he managed to merge unobtrusively with the mass of the squadron's soldiers. Their disguise must not be noticed. It was vital for the success of their mission.

"Greetings, Ùtsintas," said Tungdil in a deep voice that commanded respect, a voice Ireheart had never heard his friend use before. Hargorin had told him the name of the älf leader. "I am Tungdil Goldhand, high king of the dwarf-tribes in Girdlegard, and a member of the thirdling folk."

Ùtsintas opened his mouth. "It's not as easy . . ."

But Tungdil carried on regardless. "Take me to the Dsôn Aklán. I have a bargain to strike. Now."

Ùtsintas closed his mouth again. This prompted another hidden grin from Ireheart. *That black-eyes has never been spoken to like this before.*

Tungdil leaned forward on his pony. "Did you hear me, Ùtsintas? Or perhaps you do not know my name? Are you so young that you have never been told about the dwarf who razed the original city of Dsôn to the ground?"

"Of course I know the name . . ." The älf was unsure of himself and looked at the standard. "What does the flag mean? It's written neither in älfar nor in dwarf-language. It seems to be a mixture of the two . . ."

"It means that I am commander and king at the same time. In the land beyond the Black Abyss." Tungdil had his pony move to the front, right up close. With the dwarf on its back even the small pony seemed superior to the firebull, showing no fear of the massive bulk and threatening horns.

"You claim to be Tungdil Goldhand and to have returned from that place? How would that have been possible?" Ùtsintas was gradually regaining his composure.

"The barrier fell for a few moments. That's how I managed

to get back." Tungdil's face darkened. "Now I have to speak to the Dsôn Aklán. Do you wish me to ride past you or will you accompany me and Hargorin Deathbringer?"

Ireheart felt like laughing out loud. *My Scholar is treating the älf like his messenger boy.*

"Other creatures are not permitted to set foot in the holy crater."

Tungdil's laugh was unpleasant. "I was in the real city of Dsôn long before you, Ùtsintas." The Black Squadron sniggered, joined in the fun, humiliating the älf even more. "Be the one who crowns the pact between the thirdlings and your own folk." He touched the hilt of Bloodthirster, as if by accident. "I am on my way to Dsôn. With or without you."

Ùtsintas stared at Tungdil and then nodded. "I shall take you." And, indicating Hargorin, "He can wait here with your people."

"No. I am entitled to an escort," Tungdil contradicted. "Thirty men at the very least. Do not attempt to argue."

The älf paused. "Thirty. No more than that."

Tungdil signaled to the Zhadár, Ireheart, Slîn and Balyndar to join him. "These are Hargorin's best men. They instantly swore allegiance to me and they shall be rewarded with the sight of Dsôn."

Ùtsintas sent them a warning glance. "You are to follow me, not taking any other path. Anyone contravening this order will be killed. This holds for you as well, Tungdil Goldhand." He turned his firebull's head and led the way.

Tungdil's smile was full of malice. "*You* would not be able to kill me."

The chosen band of dwarves followed him; Hargorin fell back to wait for them.

Ireheart had to restrain himself from talking to Slîn. He thought Tungdil's acting was superb.

The last few miles through the crater toward the new Dsôn they rode in silence. Gruesome sculptures and monuments were to be seen as they passed; they had a certain aesthetic quality to them but were hideously cruel in concept, formed as they were from bones wired together with gold, tionium and other precious metals; dead trees had been adorned with skulls, and elsewhere there was a structure reminding Ireheart of a large windmill moving in the breeze. He got the distinct impression that those sails were made of skin. He did not wish to learn what sort of skin had been used.

The nearer they got to the deep crater, the more numerous the works of art became until there was hardly any space between the sculptures. They appeared like a nightmarish forest. It all stemmed from the älfar obsession with the transience of nature; they imitated death in all its forms. It did not do much for morale.

Ireheart was finding it hard to hold his tongue. The grim statues made him talkative. He wanted to speak to the Scholar about what he could see, and wanted to ask Balyndar and Slîn their impressions. But it had been agreed in advance that strict silence would be observed.

The Zhadár had been given their orders: They were to get the sledge with the kordrion's young unobtrusively into the center of the city and leave it hidden there; perhaps they could even take it into the palace itself.

I wonder if the älfar rulers have rebuilt the Tower of Bones? The old tower in Dsôn Balsur had been constructed out of the skeletons of slain enemies, but would two hundred cycles have been long enough to amass sufficient quantities to build anew? Ireheart stretched up in his saddle for a better view but could not see any tall buildings rising up out of the vast hole the city occupied.

Noticing a particular artwork he had to overcome the impulse to attack Ùtsintas and the other älfar with his crow's beak; from Slîn's helmet, too, emerged a groan of horror. Walls specially erected for the purpose had been decorated with carved reliefs, showing the älfar defeating their foes. But where the älfar were shown life size and worked in silver and tionium, the artist had used real bodies for their enemies. Ireheart was having to look at the rotting corpses of fellow dwarves.

"There must be a hundred at least," exclaimed Balyndar, unable to control his disgust. "Such an end is an insult to any child of the Smith!" he went on, in a lower voice this time. "To decay and disintegrate like worthless orcs and all for the enjoyment of the black-eyes—we can't accept this. They need proper burial . . ."

"Quiet!" Tungdil ordered. "Be quiet or your lust for revenge will endanger a much more important mission."

Ùtsintas turned round. "One hundred?" he repeated in amusement; he seemed not to have heard the rest of the exchange. "The artist needs to replace them every quarter-cycle. The bodies keep better in the winter of course. New humans are relatively easy to supply. Dwarves are difficult to get hold of. We harvest them mostly from the fourthlings. They're the easiest ones."

"*Harvest?*" exclaimed Ireheart.

Ùtsintas grinned. This time he had heard. "I'm surprised that a Desirer should be such a sensitive soul. You're the ones that bring us the material."

"Don't mind him. He got out of bed on the wrong side," said Tungdil. "I have to put up with his moodiness all the time."

"If you wish to be rid of him . . ." The älf gestured toward the wall relief.

"Ho! I could cut you down to size so you fit, yourself, black-eyes!" Ireheart retorted. He would have been delighted to drive the arrogance out of this uppity älf.

"Enough!" snarled Tungdil peremptorily. "Or I shall take up the offer Ùtsintas just made."

Ireheart noted with distress that Tungdil's words had not sounded remotely like acting.

They soon reached the sharply winding path that led down into the heart of the crater.

Boïndil uttered a gasp of surprise at the sight. At first glance he had realized that the walls of the crater had been dug vertically; the diameter had to be about twelve miles and the depth of the vast hole nearly three.

The floor of the crater was black; the älfar had covered the ground with some material that made it look deeper still. Around two hundred strangely shaped houses had been positioned in a specific pattern round the central mountain. A contrasting mixture of white and black wood had been used to great effect for the buildings. In some cases the roof was pointed, in others it took the form of a gentle diagonal slope with balconies; other houses had hexagonal towers, and sharp corners were a feature used throughout.

I'd like to take a closer look, thought Ireheart. *I wonder how their furniture is constructed. The black-eyes who live there must have to keep their helmets on all the time so as not to bang their heads on the sharp bits.*

Sculptures had been erected in the open spaces between the houses.

Ireheart reckoned the mountain itself must be a mile high, and two miles wide. A rectangular building of dark gray marble had been built, crowned with a shimmering, sparkling dome of black glass. A massive tower rose at the back of the mountain, easily twenty paces by twenty, and a hundred paces high. Wires ran from the tip of the tower, criss-crossing the city and reaching the edges of the crater.

What is all that for? wondered Ireheart. He would need to get closer to study the detail.

"It's not like the Dsôn I used to know. You have made many changes," Tungdil said to Ùtsintas. "The houses look lonely and isolated there in the crater."

"It's a beginning," said the älf. "There will be more of when we've got rid of all the fifthlings."

"But then you'd still have the kordrion sitting in the Gray Mountains. It eats everything it finds," Tungdil pointed out.

"We won't have a problem there. We'll let it deal with those troublesome rock-diggers first. That saves us the bother." Ùtsintas pointed to the marble building. "That's the Dsôn Akláns' palace."

"In the old city the mountain was taller, and the crater has changed as well. Why is that?"

"You'll have to ask the Dsôn Aklán. He will decide if it is any of your business to be told." The älf turned the firebull to take the broad path downhill.

Ireheart noted that it grew darker all the time as they made their way down, hairpin bend by hairpin bend. The somber gloom that the city exuded infiltrated his very soul.

The blackness of the crater floor came from a surface

layer of tiny stones. He assumed they had removed part of the top of the mountain and ground up the resulting rock. That would have obviated the need to transport the residue up the difficult winding paths of the crater sides.

They continued straight on toward the mountain and its palace.

Ireheart was burning to ask his friend how the Zhadár were going to be able to deposit and hide the kordrion cocoon. They were all being carefully watched. The dark mood was robbing him of courage and any sense of optimism.

As he raised his head, the sky seemed so very far away. *Vraccas, you know I don't mind being under the earth, but this is different. I feel so ill at ease here. I want to be back in the sun*, he prayed.

They rode past more artworks dedicated to the honor of Tion and the Unslayables and to the memory of those who had lived in the city before the Star of Judgment fell and destroyed it.

As if obeying a soundless command, Útsintas and his men bowed their heads. "Show respect," the älf told Tungdil and the dwarves. "Bow your heads."

"To dead älfar?" Tungdil nearly laughed.

"To their spirits," replied Útsintas quietly. "They remain here to guard the Moon Pond against the elves. When the Dsôn Aklán returned, the spirits appeared to them and demanded everything you see here as payment for their protection."

To Ireheart's surprise the Scholar did indeed bow his head, so the rest of the band felt duty-bound to follow suit, pretending to offer respect.

"I remember I felt I was never alone when I came into the old city of Dsôn, to burn it down," Tungdil said to the älf. "I thought what I could hear was the sound of the wind."

"It was the spirits," Ùtsintas repeated, urging his firebull forward. "Let us make haste. He will not receive us after sundown."

They rode to the foot of the mountain. A mighty staircase led upwards. This was also constructed of gray marble; to the right and left there flowed streams of crimson, going down in steps, with fountains every thirty paces spurting red water.

The firebulls and ponies took the steps one at a time until they had covered a third of the way. From there the party dismounted and went on foot.

Ireheart found the stair-climbing quite strenuous, as the height of each step was designed for an älf's stride and not for dwarf-legs. He could not help admiring the masonry work. It seemed to have been perfectly executed, as far as he could judge. Perfect, as always, for älfar.

To add sparkle to the stairs every third step had been highly polished and decorated with jewels. Some of the steps were made of transparent crystal, allowing a view of the red water that flowed beneath.

"They've taken a lot of trouble," said Tungdil. "Though I miss the ivory tower."

"The Dsôn Aklán did not wish to invite comparison with the Unslayables. Only the Emperor Aiphatòn would be entitled to do that. He lives elsewhere." Ùtsintas took the last stair and reached the plateau in front of the palace.

Tungdil followed him, then came Ireheart and the rest. They were now forty paces from the mighty marble façade.

Boïndil doubted that a crossbow bolt could reach the height of the roof where the dark dome shimmered and shone.

"And what kind of palace has the emperor built for himself?" Tungdil wanted to know.

"As far as I know he does not have one. I have never had the chance of visiting him." Ùtsintas led them to the door at the end of a row of giant columns supporting the entrance canopy.

Ireheart grinned again. *You won't be allowed to because the black-eyes from the south won't let you in*, he thought. He suddenly realized that the älfar patrols in Dsôn Bhará were not for quelling Gauragar resistance but for keeping their own unwelcome relatives off their backs. *I'll take any bets no southern älf has ever been in this crater.*

The älfar had not lost their love of working with all types of bone. The dwarves saw bones of all shapes and sizes fixed to the walls as adornment, arranged to make fascinating patterns, leading the beholder's gaze along to the entrance itself. The portal, which was seven paces high and four wide, was decorated with slices of bone arranged with studious accuracy; skulls filled the gaps. The head shapes of all the races in Girdlegard were represented here. Except for the älfar.

Four sentries guarded the entrance and opened the door for the visitors. Beyond the portal was a high dark corridor, its walls covered in carmine red fabric. No gruesome pictures, no bonework, nothing to upset or horrify you.

Hmm, not as I thought at all. Ireheart was slightly puzzled as he followed Tungdil and Ùtsintas along winding passageways. The company halted in front of a black door.

"I will tell the Dsôn Aklán you are here and what you

want." Their leader knocked on the door and an älf wearing a long robe let him in.

Outside, Ireheart could not contain himself. He pushed up his visor. "I can't believe it!" he said quietly, wiping the sweat off his face. The climb had made him quite hot. "I'm right in the middle of the black-eyes' realm!"

Tungdil quickly snapped his friend's visor shut. "Don't say a word. They may be watching us."

Ireheart pushed it up again. "But my tongue is on fire. I need . . ."

"Will you be quiet?" snarled Balyndar, giving him a shove. The visor clanged shut once more. "He'll be the death of us if he can't stop talking."

"Push me around again, fifthling, and . . ."

Ùtsintas reappeared and led them through a second, dark-red door. Here they were received by seven älfar in long black robes. They did not seem concerned that they would be significantly outnumbered should it come to a fight. They ushered Tungdil and his escort into the presence of the ruler of Dsôn.

The dwarves entered the black-painted hall. Blue flames flickered in shallow braziers. Dark red lengths of fabric hung from the ceiling and there was a smell of smoldering spices.

They walked toward an elevated throne covered in a white velvet throw, which contrasted effectively with the dark-haired älf in full armor who sat there. He held a white fan in one hand to shield his face from their inquiring eyes.

I could try numbering them so I don't mix them up, thought Ireheart, smiling to himself behind his visor.

Tungdil halted and sketched a bow. "I am . . ."

"I know who you are," the älf interrupted. "Even if you do use a different name."

Ireheart was taken aback. A feeling of unease made the hairs on his arms stand up. He checked the exit and gripped his crow's beak.

The älf rose, elegance itself, and strode down the four steps. "I did not think I should ever see you again."

Tungdil's eyes narrowed. Boïndil saw that he was struggling with his memory.

"How long has it been? Two hundred cycles?" The älf lowered his fan and gave the one-eyed dwarf a friendly smile of welcome. On his neck there was a narrow wound caused by a crossbow bolt and his cheek also bore a scar.

"Tirîgon!" Tungdil beamed and opened his arms wide.

Then something happened that was, from Ireheart's point of view, quite appalling: The älf bent down and hugged the Scholar as if greeting a very close friend. Both of them were laughing. "Can I call you Balodil or shall we leave it at Tungdil?"

The dwarf behind Ireheart gave a sob of exasperation and turned away in distress. Presumably one of the Zhadár, thought Boïndil, given a theatrical and emotional performance like that. "Keep quiet, can't you?" he whispered, lifting his visor to be heard. "The Scholar knows what he's doing." But while the words were leaving his mouth he was himself beset with uncertainty. The familiarity with which the älf and Tungdil had greeted each other, the way those two dark figures fitted in to the world of evil, all this served to stir the doubts Boïndil had so recently succeeded in putting aside.

The Zhadár swallowed another sob and fell silent, nodding.

Ireheart turned to the front and watched as Tungdil and the älf clasped hands again, now deep in discussion. They must know each other from their time in the Black Abyss.

He was trying to work out how the black-eyes had been able to cross the barrier before Tungdil. Suddenly he felt sick. He remembered exactly when it was he had last heard the name Tirîgon: They were standing in the presence of the perverted and legendary älf who had wiped out the last of the elves of Girdlegard. *What will he do if one of our company drops his disguise?*

XV

"Who would have thought we would meet here in Dsôn Bhará, of all places?" Tirîgon gazed at Tungdil in delighted surprise.

Ireheart saw that the two had enjoyed more than mere acquaintance; it did nothing to reassure him. His Scholar together with one of the worst älfar of the past two hundred cycles, the one who had eliminated the last of the elves of Girdlegard. *This feels like trouble.* He was itching to join in their conversation but knew he must not try. Now less than ever.

Tungdil laughed darkly. "You know that dwarves hate water as much you hate elves. I would never have been able to swim through the Moon Pond. The curse of Elria would have seen me drowned."

"You had to wait so long to return." The älf looked at the escort and Ireheart found the blue-eyed gaze very unpleasant when it rested on him. "But I see you have taken over our Desirers."

"They follow me because I am the high king." He smiled. "You have no need to fear me, Tirîgon. I have come to make you and the Dsôn Aklán an offer."

"I am delighted to hear it. I am only sorry that my brother

and sister are not with me. They are in Gauragar, hunting down the woman who caused this." He pointed at the injury to his face.

"You leave your revenge up to them?"

"I was at death's door, Balo . . . Tungdil. It was Mallenia of Ido. The cowardly bitch shot at me with a crossbow and sent a bolt through my neck long after our duel was over."

Ireheart noted that the älf was omitting to mention which of them had won the duel. *So it won't have been you, Scarface.*

Tirîgon signaled for chairs and refreshments to be brought. They sat down at a table in front of the throne. "And anyway, one of us had to look after Dsôn Bhará. What do you think of the city?"

"It is very different from the true Dsôn." Tungdil frowned. "They tell us my name is spoken here with hatred."

"Only by those who do not know you from the other side. Do not be concerned." Tirîgon gestured to one of the human slaves to pour their drink. The slave woman served the älf first and Ireheart last.

Ireheart guessed her beauty was perfection to human eyes, but for himself he preferred something with a little more substance, like his own Goda. This one looked more like an älf than a human: Slender, slim-faced and with graceful movements.

"Seeing you here I must assume you are still kindly disposed to us." Tirîgon sounded curious. "We once worked hand in hand and with great success."

"That's the way it should still be." Tungdil drank his wine. "The dwarves have elected me their high king and the tribe of the thirdlings will serve me as their supreme ruler. My reputation with the thirdlings is now very different, Hargorin tells me."

"You have considerable authority with them as a warrior." The älf had understood the implication. "Thus it will be with you we negotiate when we need thirdling support to police the three kingdoms. I am pleased to hear it." Tirîgon raised his goblet. "To the old times!"

"The very old times!" Tungdil returned the toast. "Of course I am on your side. I hear there have been disputes with your relations from the south."

Ireheart had interpreted Tungdil's words as a message: The *very* old times. The good times.

Tirîgon's serenity faded. He drained his cup and called for more. "There is no evidence that they are actually related to us," he snapped. "But it is true: We don't like them and they don't like us."

Tungdil licked a droplet of wine from the rim of his goblet. "But they have superiority of numbers."

Again, another hidden message.

"We shall be glad of your help. My siblings will be pleased." Tirîgon lifted his cup in salute. "Since I am aware that you never act without due thought and intent, tell me what you want in return."

"All the dwarf kingdoms." The response came swift as a bolt from a crossbow.

Tirîgon lowered his head. "Tungdil, I would happily promise you that, but it is not within my gift."

"But when our campaign is over, you will have that power."

Ireheart saw the älf registering growing surprise but no doubt. *He must trust Tungdil to the hilt.*

"I have a plan . . ."

Tirîgon laughed out loud. "That cunning dwarf-mind! You always had a clever plan over on the other side. Your plans always worked, so I've no reason to doubt you now." He sat back in his chair. "Tell me about it."

Tungdil outlined the scheme to play the Dragon off against Lot-Ionan; the kordrion and the tribe of fifthlings would be destroyed together, by the thirdling army. "The route is already secure. You and your älfar will be ready to attack the southern älfar . . ."

Tirîgon raised his hand. "No. They will be fighting Lot-Ionan under that fool, the Emperor Aiphatòn. They're off to the Blue Mountains with everything they've got."

"All the better." Tungdil pretended he had not known about the attack. "So the Dragon can launch himself on the victor. You bring your forces up secretly, and we join you as soon as we've got rid of the kordrion and the fifthlings. After that, Girdlegard will be yours." He leaned forward. "That's if you leave the dwarf realms to me."

"Here am I, making a pact with a dwarf against my own emperor, the last of the descendants of the Unslayables," Tirîgon said thoughtfully. "That is mad enough to work. I trust you and your bright ideas, Balodil." He frowned in annoyance. "I mean Tungdil."

By Vraccas! When he was with the monsters he called himself by the name of his own son! Ireheart's wavering conviction that this was indeed the true Tungdil and not an impostor started to gain firmer footing. How else could he have known that name? And, he thought, Tungdil's approach was excellent, although fate was playing a hand in it, too.

"Your siblings will follow your lead, or do I have to fight

the three of you when I've polished off the enemies in the north and south?" Tungdil's question had a trace of mirth but its core was serious.

Tirîgon helped himself to some of the food, putting small slices slowly into his mouth. "They will approve of our pact." He closed his eyes in pleasure. "That was the first time I've been able to enjoy my food since being wounded." He invited his guest to eat. "We shall inform you when Aiphatòn and his false followers leave to attack Lot-Ionan. Where do we send the message?"

"To Hargorin's estate in the north. That's probably the best place to find me while we're preparing for the campaign. And if I'm not there someone will know how to contact me." Tungdil tried some of the meat.

Let it have been an animal, Vraccas, and not anything else. Not anything they didn't have a use for in their art, prayed Ireheart. The sight of pink roast flesh made him hungry. It smelled good, even if he had never wanted to sink his teeth into black-eye food.

"I'll get over to Aiphatòn as quickly as possible and pay him a call," stated Tungdil, helping himself to more of the wine. "The emperor must not think I'm against him. My last meeting went peacefully, and I want to tell him, for form's sake, that we can continue the alliance."

"So you'll be offering him the same pact?"

"Yes. But for the campaign against Lot-Ionan, my atrocious foster-father." Tungdil grinned. "Then I shall withdraw and promise to return with a huge army of troops."

"He will have the surprise of his life." Tirîgon laid his cutlery aside. "But can't I tempt you to stay?"

Sacred forge! Don't let us spend a single night in Dsôn!

Ireheart hoped fervently that Tungdil would turn down the offer of hospitality.

"I'm afraid not, old friend. We'll have to move swiftly if we want to meet up with the emperor, I should think?"

"Yes. You should find him in the former Âlandur. He has given the realm to his friends from the south." The älf spoke with open dislike.

"And what about Dsôn Balsur? Has it been rebuilt?"

Tirîgon shrugged. "It's all one to me, while they're living there. It will take us some time to remove their unwholesome influence in the place. They have no appreciation of art at all, or beauty, poetry, painting or other aesthetic concepts." He shuddered. "It is impossible that Tion created them."

"Unless he was drunk?" suggested Ireheart, over-hastily.

Tirîgon and Tungdil turned their heads slowly in his direction. "So you have people in your escort who enjoy a pleasantry," the älf noted with amusement.

"He never usually has a good joke to tell." Tungdil tutted and shook his head. "Perhaps a rare spark of inspiration."

"Don't let him tell that one to the emperor. It could be his best and final joke." The älf rose. One of the robed älfar approached with a whispered message. "I won't detain you any longer, Tungdil Goldhand." They embraced. "Our pact is settled. You shall have the dwarf realms and we shall have Girdlegard." His laughter was cold. "The land is in desperate need of our art. It will be a pleasure for me to reform it to our taste."

"Even two hundred cycles ago your reputation as an artist was brilliant. I am keen to see what you are capable of now." Tungdil clasped the älf's right hand and beamed at him. "In three cycles at the outside it will be us in charge and no one else! Give my greetings to your siblings." He turned and went to the door. His escort of Invisibles surrounded him and Ireheart was at his side.

"Tungdil," called Tirîgon, as they reached the door. They stopped and the one-eyed dwarf turned to face the älf. "What about the barrier? Is it holding again?"

"Yes," lied Tungdil, cold as ice.

"That's good. It would be bad if your master were to turn up here to demand the return of his armor." Tirîgon paused. "Or did you kill him in the end, perhaps?"

"I tried to. It didn't work. That's why I want the dwarf realms: No one shall be allowed through the gate." Tungdil turned and marched off. "Tion is with us, Tirîgon. Be sure of that."

They left the hall and the seven silent älfar led them out through the palace to the open air.

"At last!" Ireheart took a deep breath and pushed his visor up. "I couldn't have stood it in there much longer. I don't know what it was I was eating but it doesn't smell nice when it comes up again."

Slîn laughed and opened his own visor as well. "Onions and preserved gugul mince? I saw you had a jar of that in your pack. Goda send you off with that, then?"

"You never gave us any." Tungdil gave him a disapproving look. "How mean of you." Then he grinned. It was obvious that he was relieved to have got in and out of the palace safely. And with such success. "Ireheart, you must curb your tongue in future. We were in luck. It was a good thing Tirîgon found your remark funny." After a short pause he added. "So did I, by the way."

Darkness had fallen. But when Ireheart looked up at the

sky he saw no stars! "By Vraccas!" he exclaimed, horrified. "What have the älfar done?"

All the dwarves looked up and stared.

"The constellations have all disappeared!" Balyndar whispered, fearfully.

"The stars must be refusing to shine on an älfar city," suggested Slîn.

Ireheart conquered his incredulity and turned to the tower with its cables spreading out in all directions. "It's to do with that tower."

Tungdil followed his gaze and thought. "Let's get on or we'll be arousing suspicion. And pull your visors down in case we meet anyone."

They went down the steps to where their ponies were waiting. Overhead they caught a slight rustling sound.

"I don't believe it," said Slîn in amazement as he looked up at the sky.

A starry firmament had appeared above their heads but it was different from the one the dwarves were familiar with. The heavenly bodies they saw now were not as they knew them. And there were shimmering moons, three or four times the size of Girdlegard's own.

"I don't know how they've done it, but the city must have moved to another place entirely." Boïndil could not get his fill of the splendid sight.

Balyndar snorted. "What do you mean?"

"Perhaps you never stick your head out of the caves but I've traveled a lot in Girdlegard. Wherever I went, the stars were always the same."

"There's a deep insight for you," mocked Slîn. "Only here they're not. But we're still in Girdlegard."

"Exactly. That's why I said they've moved the city *out* of Girdlegard. I admit it doesn't sound very likely."

"So how do we get back?" Slîn mounted and turned to look at the winding cliffside path. "Who knows where we'll end up?"

"Over to you, Scholar."

Tungdil looked up. "Canvasses."

"Canvasses." At first Ireheart did not understand. "Oh, I see, like curtains, but . . . sideways?" He looked up again. "They pull them across the crater on those ropes to give the älfar down here an artificial night sky to admire—is that what you mean?"

"Exactly, Ireheart. That's what I mean. I expect they cover the city on especially bright days, or when it's very hot. A protective screen."

"That's an amazing amount of trouble to go to." Balyndar seemed relieved at the explanation.

"But it's also beautiful. You'll have to give them that." Tungdil rode ahead, followed by the Zhadár and the rest of the company.

Ireheart was pleased to note they were not escorted. Tirîgon must trust his dwarf-friend completely if he was letting them wander the streets unaccompanied. *Trust and black-eyes: That's a weird combination. That Tirîgon must have something up his sleeve.* At the bottom of the winding climb he thought he could make out Útsintas and the älfar on their firebulls. *I'm not going to let anyone entice me into a trap.*

"This is the ideal chance to get rid of the kordrion young," he mouthed to Tungdil.

"Already done," answered one of the Zhadár. "We left the cocoon on the stairway up to the palace behind one of the pillars. They won't find it—unless they've got a nose like a kordrion."

Ireheart was impressed. "And now?"

"Let's ride off to the Dragon as fast as we can. Then we plunder his treasure hoard," said Tungdil, putting his plan to them. "Isn't that a messenger over there with Ùtsintas?"

"If you say so. I can only see some scrawny black-eyes and overweight fighting cows." Ireheart had given up being surprised about the Scholar's unnaturally good vision.

Tungdil had been correct. When they reached the älf and their escort, an imperial messenger was waiting with an invitation to visit Âlandur, now known as Phôseon Dwhamant. This came from the Emperor Aiphatòn himself. They could not decline it.

And so the lie Tungdil had told came true after all.

Tirîgon was on his throne watching the slave woman clear the table. Such lowly occupations were beneath the dignity of any älf. She fulfilled her function well enough and was not so ugly as to offend the eye. It had taken some time to find a halfway acceptable slave for the palace.

"Tell me, why are most of your kind just so revolting to look at?" he mused, as he sipped from his glass of wine.

The slave looked round at him in fright. He had used his own language and she was not sure she had understood an instruction aright. Anyone in the service of an älf knew what the punishment would be.

"Don't worry," he said, this time in the tongue spoken in Gauragar. "Get on with your work."

One of the robe-wearers came over to him. "Dsôn Aklán,

it is as you suspected." He knelt before the throne. "They had the kordrion's young with them."

"Those confounded Zhadár! Did they really think I would not recognize them in the armor of the Desirers? Nobody deceives me! They are our creatures and we are their masters! We created them," he raged, hurling his wineglass across the room. "Deserters like Hargorin Deathbringer. They shall die!" He took a deep breath. "Do you have the cocoon now?"

The älf nodded. "We had to search for ages, but we found it in the end."

"Then pack it up well, disguise it as provisions and send a messenger with it to accompany Goldhand to Phôseon Dwhamant. A splendid gift for an emperor," he commanded. "Has the kordrion been sighted again?"

"Yes, Dsôn Aklán. Not four miles from here. It is following the scent of its young."

Tirîgon nodded in satisfaction. "Good. Does Goldhand suspect anything? Did he accept the messenger as genuine?"

"He thinks he's genuine. They are making their way southwest."

"Then make sure they get my *provisions*." Tirîgon waved the slave girl over to give him more wine. "And instruct the patrols that any Zhadár found on Dsôn Bhará territory are to be put to death immediately. That's if any of them survive the kordrion's attack." He sat down again. Everything reverted to the normal state of affairs.

"Yes, Dsôn Aklán." The älf hurried out.

Tirîgon gave a sigh of satisfaction. Aiphatòn, most of his retinue and Tungdil with the treacherous Zhadár had thus all been catered for. He had known them at first glance by how they held themselves, whatever kind of armor they might have been sporting. And to his knowledge no Desirer ever carried a crow's beak at his side.

"The good thing is that everyone will think it was a trap set by Tungdil Goldhand to get rid of the emperor of the älfar," he told the slave girl, who, once more, understood not a word he was saying.

She indicated the wine jug and a fresh goblet enquiringly; he motioned her to come over.

"And if Aiphatòn survives and wants revenge, he can direct his anger to the thirdlings. If he dies, I'll be happy to take his place." He looked along the woman's bare arm, focusing particularly on the elbow. "You have attractive bones, my dear. Did you know that?" He touched her forearm lightly. "Incredibly beautiful bones for a human." He smiled at her. "I suppose I'll have to look for a new slave woman now. You are destined for higher things. Art will elevate you."

The girl shivered and smiled shyly in response.

Girdlegard,
Phôseon Dwhamant (Formerly the Elf Realm of Âlandur),
Phôseon,
Late Winter, 6491st/6492nd Solar Cycles

"We could have killed the messenger and ridden off to the Red Mountains," murmured Slîn. "We could have pretended we'd been attacked on the way. By the resistance movement."

"What kind of idiots would be attacking the Black Squadron? Especially if it's accompanied by a troop of älfar?" hissed Balyndar disbelievingly. "Not even I would have believed you."

Ireheart had been listening in on the argument these

dwarves had been engaged in ever since leaving Dsôn. The fourthling would find reasons for not going to visit Aiphatòn, and the fifthling would find one objection after another to his arguments. *Unbearable!* "Why don't the two of you shut up? You're lucky you're in the middle of our party so that the row you're making is drowned out by the sound of hooves. If the älfar catch wind of what you're saying . . ." He hoped this hint would be enough.

It would be a lie to claim he felt no unease about going from one älfar realm to another. And he knew nothing about these southern älfar at all. He had no idea what Aiphatòn wanted from them.

On the one hand Ireheart loved being on the march again, with that old sense of adventure he had delighted in as a young dwarf. But, on the other hand, part of him was pining for the Outer Lands, where Goda and the children were. He was worried for their safety and concerned about the fortress. The enemy magus was hugely powerful, it seemed from the hints Tirîgon had given.

They rode through Phôseon Dwhamant, known as Âlandur until usurped by the älf regime. *And who could possibly have opposed them?*

The älfar from the south shared the northerners' love of the obscure and transient. The elf groves had been burned down, as Ireheart could see as they passed through the plain. Trouble had been taken to ensure no trees would ever grow again. Whichever way he looked he saw only bald hillsides where the snow was now melting. Not even a bush to be seen.

"If your eyesight's good you can see all the way from one end of the älf realms to the other," said Slîn. "*Good territory for me and my crossbow.*"

"There's something over there!" called Balyndar. "It looks like a brown block that's just fallen from the sky."

They all looked. The first thought that occurred to Ireheart was that it resembled a beehive, only it was square rather than a semi-oval basket shape. He reckoned the dimensions to be around nine hundred paces wide and three hundred high. He could not see how far back it went. It had small towers like chimneys and on top of the structure there were flags on tall poles. Ireheart could count thirty levels overall, of varying heights. Some of the walls were solid, others were in the form of arcaded galleries with high rooms and painted ceilings; the next floor up consisted of a row of smaller windows reflecting the sun.

"What is that?" asked Slîn.

"A city," replied Balyndar. "An artificial mountain with an artificial town."

"That's Phôseon," said Ùtsintas, who was riding up at the front with Tungdil. "There are about ten thousand living here. The southern älfar like this kind of community."

Tungdil looked at the block. "What's it like inside?"

"Difficult to describe. I only know it from people's reports because I've never been allowed in." There was no regret in the älf's voice. "There will be vertical ravines, long shafts and hanging gardens reached by bridges. Apparently they sway in the wind that blows through the artificial canyons."

"It sounds a little like a dwarf realm," Slîn remarked quietly to Ireheart.

"Is your brain tangled round your own bowstrings?" he retorted. "There's absolutely nothing dwarflike about all that!"

"Hanging gardens?" asked the warrior in surprise. "Our

vegetables grow in the earth and that's just the way it should be."

They were still a mile away from the city when the gates opened and mounted troops poured out.

The messenger exchanged a few swift words with Ùtsintas and rode off toward the älfar. They met up halfway and entered into a discussion; then the messenger gave a hand signal.

Ùtsintas turned to Tungdil. "You should ride on alone now. My mission ends here." He gave his escort a command and turned the firebull around. The älfar thundered off back to Dsôn Bhará.

Tungdil scanned the façade. "Looks like it's going to be an interesting visit that we'll be paying the emperor," he told Ireheart, then ordered: "We'll ride in as a group. No use of weapons—neither by the Zhadár nor by the Desirers. Here, we are the guests of the Emperor Aiphatòn and shall behave accordingly." He spurred his pony on and the company followed him.

Ireheart tried to look for distinguishing characteristics in the Phôseon älfar on their night-mares. *I should have known. They look like all the others.*

They had the familiar black tionium armor, although the runes were a little different this time. But he was no scholar, so he might have been mistaken.

The messenger was talking to Tungdil. "We may enter. The emperor is expecting us, I'm told," the Scholar said, interpreting for the dwarves. "Remember my orders." Then he cantered off after the älfar.

Ireheart could not deny that this building, city, fortress, or whatever the block was supposed to be, was absolutely fascinating. Not that he would have wanted to live in it, of course, but he was curious. His native dwarf blood made him eager to see more. Secondlings were expert masons and thus his spirit of enquiry was understandable. As the walls had been plastered he could not see what the building material had been, and he wondered how they had been able to make the foundations stable enough to carry the weight of the edifice.

The archway was seven paces high and only five wide. Ireheart noted the sharp ends of the metal grille suspended above their heads as they went through; this portcullis could be lowered at will for defense.

"They seem to set less store on pomp and decoration," Slîn whispered. "It is . . . sober and unadorned. Apart from the chiseled reliefs in the walls."

"They've been marked into the plasterwork," he said. "But have a look at the great variety of patterns. You'd need a steady hand for that work."

Arriving in a generous interior courtyard they surveyed the high galleries, windows and stonework. Inquisitive älfar were looking down at them or were talking to each other, or eating; the various levels were connected either by external stairways or lifts on cables. Way above their heads the clouds raced past.

"Well, when all's said and done, I must admit the black-eyes have put up something really impressive." Ireheart patted his pony's neck. When he looked around he saw the metal grilles lowering one after the other as the main gate was shut. "I've never seen the like."

"They're not so keen on nature—unless they can control it, like in their gardens," Slîn suggested. "Have you noticed?

They've turned the entire elf realm into a desert. Nothing but flat, bare earth."

"You can see your enemies all the sooner, you're not leaving them any material to attack you with in a siege and you're not giving them anywhere to hide from your spears and arrows," said Balyndar. "It all makes sense . . . it looks as if they live well here."

"The emperor awaits Tungdil Goldhand in the audience chamber," said the messenger. "Only five guards may accompany you. The rest must remain in the courtyard."

Tungdil chose Slîn, Ireheart, Balyndar and two Zhadár. "Whatever happens, you are not to kill a single älf," he warned Hargorin and Barskalín.

A different älf led them this time and the messenger stayed to supervise the dwarves. They were transported to an upper storey in a lift that was operated by means of a lever.

Kordrion dung! But it's a bit like our own constructions, thought Ireheart.

At the end of the ascent they stepped out into a hallway of columns that were maybe ten paces high. The walls were painted in matt white and decorated with black shapes reminiscent of silhouette figures, depicting battles, cityscapes or erotic scenes.

However much Ireheart looked around him as they approached the throne he noted none of the morbid aesthetic that held sway among the northern älfar.

Aiphatòn was seated on the throne.

He hasn't grown any older! Ireheart recognized the child of the Unslayables at once. His appearance was unique: Chest, abdomen, lower body, shoulders and upper arms were all covered in armor directly fused to his shimmering white flesh.

The head was shaved, emphasizing the shape of the long, sharp ears; his hands lay in heavy gauntlets. He had draped his lower body in a kind of wraparound skirt revealing his naked toes beneath the hem. In his right hand Aiphatòn gripped a spear with a slender blade sporting greenish glowing runes.

"Tungdil Goldhand is high king of the dwarf-tribes," Aiphatòn called across the hall, staring at them. At least, Ireheart suspected he was staring at them; you could not see what he was looking at because the black eye sockets were unfathomable. "So both of us have risen to supreme power over our two peoples." He waited until the dwarves were standing before him, then bowed his head. "Welcome to Phôseon."

"My thanks, emperor." Tungdil sketched a bow.

"I often think of our talk onboard ship. I told you why I had chosen my name."

"The life-star of the elves, you said," Tungdil responded. "It has disappeared now from the night sky."

"Yes. On their return the Dsôn Aklán were extremely thorough."

"That does not surprise me." The one-eyed dwarf met the emperor's gaze steadily. "But when I heard what path you took, I was surprised indeed. You had intended to join the elves. Then, on the ship, you told me that you had no wish to be an älf like your parents." He raised his hands, indicating the walls. "Now I find you here within these walls, emperor of the älfar and ruler over a mighty realm!"

"And you advised me to hide away from humans, dwarves and elves. Because none would be able to look on me without fear or hatred." Aiphatòn smiled. "And then you said I should avoid Girdlegard. Your exact words were: Look for your own kind." He ran his left hand over the metal plates. "I thought about it for a long time but did not know where I would find anything like myself. But I followed your words of advice and left Girdlegard for the south. I hoped that I would meet other älfar whose nature was more similar to that of the elves. I was a creature with no home and who had only enemies in this world." His voice grew lower and lower.

Ireheart was astonished. *So it was the Scholar's advice that sent Aiphatòn back to the älfar!*

"When you said goodbye you told me you would find a place for yourself." Tungdil tilted his head. "Was this what you planned? Conquering Girdlegard by force?"

To Ireheart's eyes Aiphatòn appeared tired. Tired and depressed, as if a great burden rested on his soul. It was impossible to gauge his state of mind from his dark eye sockets, but the lines on his countenance betrayed him. It was the way the Scholar had looked on his return from the Black Abyss.

"What brings you to me, Tungdil Goldhand?" he asked, a jolt running through his body. He sat upright and proud upon his throne. There was no trace now of low spirits. "What could the high king of the children of the Smith have to propose to me? Do you come with threats, or requests, or to suggest an alliance?"

Tungdil frowned, puzzled. "We came to Phôseon at your invitation."

Aiphatòn shook his head. "No. I've only just heard that you had returned to Girdlegard. They told me you wanted to negotiate with me."

"Your messenger brought us here," insisted Tungdil.

Aiphatòn's face again showed surprise. "As I did not send a messenger, let us ask him to whom I owe the pleasure of your visit." He called the guard over and gave instructions. "Where did you meet the älf?"

"He came to Dsôn Bhará, when we were being received by the Dsôn Aklán. I'd thought we would find you there." Tungdil answered with a half-truth.

"Charming," murmured Slîn. "Absolutely charming! We've been tricked."

"Blast that Tirîgon!" Ireheart exploded.

A loud melodious ringing was heard. It was repeated quickly.

"Alarm?" Boïndil looked to the right and left at the älfar guards. "Get ready," he gave the cue. "If the black-eye moves, mow it down!"

Aiphatòn rose from his throne and looked at the window. "We are being attacked," he stated, incredulous. He looked at Tungdil enquiringly. "Someone has been foolish enough to attack us now, after one hundred and eighty cycles!"

"It's nothing to do with me," Tungdil said calmly. "Probably . . ."

Then they heard a bloodcurdling scream and a great shadow filled the window.

Ireheart swallowed hard and instinctively wiped his hands over his armor as if to remove the traces of the smell of the kordrion's young. *The kordrion has followed me instead of the cocoon!*

XVI

The kordrion's earth-shattering cry resounded for a second time, but by now Ireheart and the others had inserted their wax earplugs, muffling the monster's terrible roar so that it could no longer root them to the spot.

Tungdil drew Bloodthirster. "We are all victims of Tirîgon's treachery, Aiphatòn. He's the only one who can have put the kordrion on our trail. When we're finished here we can both ask him what the blazes he meant by it," he barked. "My men and I will fight to defend you, to show that the guilt is not ours."

That's another clever move from the Scholar, thought Ireheart.

The emperor had grabbed hold of his spear and was aiming it at Tungdil. "I can see from your armor that you must have been very close to the älfar in recent cycles. Perhaps closer than you wanted to be," he replied. "What proof do I have that you are not working with Tirîgon in this? You could be wanting to take advantage of the confusion in order to kill me." Aiphatòn was keeping his eyes firmly trained on all the dwarves—or at least, that is how it seemed. *You can't really tell, of course.* Ireheart certainly felt he was being watched.

"Remember how we talked onboard ship. Isn't that evidence enough that my intentions are honorable?"

The doors flew open and armored älfar stormed in. They held their traditional long narrow-bladed spears pointed at the dwarves.

Aiphatòn stood motionless as a statue. "We have both changed since then, Tungdil Goldhand."

"Not as much as it may seem." Tungdil gestured to the window with his weapon. "Permit me to stand at your side in the battle. You will see the truth of what I say."

The älf lowered his spear, and under his helmet Ireheart heaved a sigh of relief. "You may." Aiphatòn turned and left the hall with Tungdil at his heels, leaving Ireheart, Slîn, Balyndar and the Zhadár alone in the throne room.

Slîn lifted his visor. "What, by Vraccas, do we do now?" He took his crossbow in his hands and loaded it in readiness.

"We shan't have to help those two," said Balyndar, going over to the window to check on the kordrion's whereabouts. Its shadow passed over Phôseon and a vertical sheet of white flame shot down in front of the embrasure. Screams rang out and stinking black smoke drifted up. "It got the black-eyes two floors down from us," he reported.

"I don't suppose they will have anything to counter an attack like this." Slîn touched his weapon. "The crossbow makes me feel a little more confident."

Ireheart was trying to work out a plan. "Right, everyone off to the lift. I want to get up onto the roof of this weird place. I can't see enough here."

"Charming! I'll be able to get a better aim at the kordrion up there." The fourthling ran along at Boïndil's side, with Balyndar and the Zhadár following less enthusiastically.

The lift whizzed them up to the top and soon they were standing on the city's gently sloping roof. From up there the city looked like a smooth plateau surrounded by unnaturally straight ravines. Dotted about were small square towers with vertical slits. Air blew through the spaces, causing a soft noise. *Chimneys?* Black sails made of linen had been strung up for food to dry. In other areas the älfar had stored huge leather sacks, also in black.

Ireheart presumed they were to let water be warmed by the sun. His jaw dropped when he took in just how big Phôseon was. "It must be a good . . . two miles long!"

Slîn pointed out the firing towers on wheeled ramps ready to be maneuvered to the corners of the roof.

But those responsible for constructing this city had not reckoned with an enemy with the advantages of flight. Three of the domes were already manned and were hurling missiles at the monster. Too slow! If there had been a besieging army at the foot of the walls this hail of arrows and spears would have been an unbeatable defense system, with the projectiles traveling many hundreds of paces before hitting their targets. But with an attacker like the kordrion, although a few hits were landed, they were ineffective.

Slîn regarded his crossbow. "My bolt is a bit on the small side," he sighed.

"I expect your women say that all the time," one of the Zhadár said, his comrades laughing in response.

The fourthling turned in fury, his crossbow raised. "It'll be big enough for you and your filthy mouth!"

"What do you think he means?" joked the Zhadár. "Keep it. I don't want it."

"Shut up, you idiot gnome-brains! What on earth do you

think you're doing, winding each other up at a time like this?" Ireheart reprimanded them angrily, adjusting his helmet and fastening the chin strap until it was uncomfortably tight, but secure. "So, the kordrion is after me? Then it will be risking its life. I'm going to entice it over to the firing towers." He instructed the Zhadár to inform the älfar manning the towers of his strategy.

"Brave," said the fourthling. "But dangerous."

"Oh, that's nothing! I like a challenge." Ireheart dismissed the objection and took firm hold of his crow's beak. He bared his teeth. "Come on if you're hard enough, you filthy creature! You want the murderer of your young?"

The Zhadár hastened between the firing towers. When they had passed the dwarf's message to seven of them, it was time.

"It's heading back," warned Balyndar. "Heading straight for us!"

"That's the way!" Boïndil set off for a section of the extensive roof area that could be covered by fire from all seven towers. The kordrion's wings swished and whistled in the air, giving Ireheart an impression of the speed of its approach—but it was not coming in his direction!

He stopped, gasping for breath and turned around. "Hey! You ugly bug-eyed monster!" He brandished his weapon to draw attention to himself. "Ho there! I'm the one who destroyed your nestlings! Are you blind?"

He watched in amazement as the huge, gray-skinned kordrion landed on the roof and slipped head first into one of the artificial ravines. Four feet like canine paws carried the weight of the hefty body. The ones in front were more like arms, with strong flexible claws. The barrage from the catapults did not seem to trouble it at all and the few spears and arrows that struck it were not inflicting serious injuries. The monster's claws scrabbled for a hold on the stonework, leaving deep marks.

"No, no, no!" yelled Ireheart. "Come back here!" *Stupid animal!*

Slîn and Balyndar came over to him.

"What's it doing?" groaned the fourthling, watching the tip of the monster's tail disappear.

Balyndar was holding his side in pain and gasped. "It's crawling in like a bear into a beehive."

They both looked accusingly at Ireheart. "Wasn't it supposed to be attacking *you*?"

"Well, yes." Boïndil wiped the sweat from his forehead using the end of one his braids. "There must be something in Phôseon that's more interesting than me." Then he laughed. "Let's go! We'll do for it. If Vraccas is on our side the beast will get stuck down there and we'll be able to cut it into tiny slices."

He ran over to the edge of the ravine and saw that the kordrion was pushing its way past the hanging gardens, looking for a horizontal passage wide enough for its massive bulk.

"Follow me!" Ireheart leaped.

His flight was a short one. He landed in a blossom hedge that covered him from head to foot in white pollen dust. *Now I look like a fairy*, he thought, and grinned. *A pretty little bearded fairy.* He fought his way free of the hedge, sneezing, and made for the bridge that led to the level the kordrion was attempting to gain forcible entry to. *What, by Tion . . .*

Balyndar and Slîn landed next to him, their fall broken by the dense black-leaved foliage of some small trees. They both crawled out of the tangle of branches, cursing, bits of leaf and twigs stuck in the gaps on their armor. No time to get rid of all that. They pursued the kordrion with utmost haste.

Ireheart had nearly caught up with the monster and could see it clearly.

The wings were folded close to its muscular body, with no room to extend them in these narrow corridors. One was a little shorter than the other, as if it had regrown after an injury, perhaps. It was using its sharp claws to move its long, gray, wrinkled body, measuring twenty paces high and sixty in length. It dragged itself along through Phôseon, pushing forward with its legs.

It had crouched down as flat as it could, like a cat stalking a bird. Its back scraped against the ceiling of the arcaded corridor, damaging the stonework and causing large cracks. The floor was also suffering under a weight load it had never been designed to bear.

Ireheart had reached the tip of the tail and was unsure how to proceed. *Shall I overtake it and attack from below? Shall I hack at the tail tip and attack when it turns round?*

Before he could come to a decision, the kordrion suddenly slipped into the next vertical shaft and disappeared.

"What are you looking for, Bug-Eyes?" Ireheart was now at the edge and could see the monster several levels beneath him, creeping back into the building. "You're looking for something, that's for sure." He turned and found a long flag hanging from the wall. Pulling it away, he wrapped one end round a column and used it to climb down to the floor that the kordrion had selected. When he landed he took out his crow's beak again. "You're not getting away from me that easily."

Slîn and Balyndar slid down the flag to arrive behind Ireheart. They were breathless from the effort as the three of them pursued the monster.

The kordrion encountered no resistance. The älfar had never reckoned with a creature like this breaking into their city. The dwarves passed bitten-off limbs and pools of blood or smashed and mutilated bodies; these were the simple inhabitants of the town, as could be seen by the clothing they had worn. They had neither weapons nor armor at their disposal.

"It's gone off to the right!" called Balyndar. "Over there in the wide passage."

"I can see for myself," growled Ireheart, who had grown tired of all this chasing about. He wanted a proper fight and was not interested in completing an endurance test.

They rounded the corner and were confronted with a broad gap in the walls, forming a path through to the gate they had entered by.

And that was where the kordrion was heading, still crouching low against the ground. Its back scraped some of the hanging gardens, making them sway and come away from their anchorages so that soil and plants rained down. Its claws hurled any älfar aside who had not sought cover; some of them the creature gobbled up or chewed to get at their blood, spitting out the remnants.

"Ho!" shouted Ireheart, hurrying onwards as fast as his legs could carry him. "Ho! You with the ugly face! Stand still for a change!"

"What's it want at the gate?" Balyndar did not seem so bothered by all the running. "So it's not you it's trying to follow, Doubleblade."

Slîn dropped behind. "Don't wait for me," he panted. "I'll catch up. This armor is so heavy . . ."

Ireheart grabbed him by his forearm protectors. "You are a child of the Smith! Make a bit of an effort; you need to win your share in the glory of killing the kordrion. When will a fourthling ever get a chance like this again?" Secretly he was wondering where on earth Tungdil and Aiphatòn had got to.

He stepped over the debris and piles of sand from the hanging gardens; they kept having to make detours round broken lumps of masonry that had fallen from the façade. The vibrations caused by the kordrion's progress, together with the violent swinging of its powerful tail, were destroying Phôseon.

"It's . . . got . . . to the . . . gate." Slîn could hardly speak, he was so out of breath. They were a hundred paces behind their quarry. "I'm . . . done for." He stopped and rested his crossbow on a tree trunk. "I'll cover you . . . from here."

Ireheart and Balyndar hurried on.

"Have you got a plan?" asked the fifthling.

"Yes. To kill it," replied Ireheart. "The simplest plans are always the best ones."

They reached the open square in front of the gate.

The kordrion turned and twisted as if possessed, crouching down and arching its back and seizing the Black Squadron's ponies. The animals neighed loudly in terror and bolted, running chaotically about, but they could not escape the predator's claws. A slaughter ensued and there was an overwhelming stink of fresh blood, with red smears and spatters on the walls. The sandy floor was soaked.

The dwarves had withdrawn to hide in the arcades and were bombarding the monster from under cover. A few of the älfar soldiers were helping out, loosing their arrows or casting their lances or spears from the upper galleries.

"So it doesn't like ponies?" Ireheart was surprised. "Is that why it's not bothering with the murderer of its own young?"

Balyndar had been looking around and had found a pack-horse that was attracting the kordrion's attention. "Look over there. It's not attacking that one."

"Maybe it likes horses?" Ireheart attempted a joke, but grew serious. "I know what you mean. That's the one Tirîgon sent with us. Did the älf get our provisions confused with kordrion feed? Let's have a look and see what's really in there." Balyndar followed him.

In the meantime three of the firing towers on the roof had rolled forward to the edge. The barrage was now becoming dangerous for the mighty beast; more and more älfar were in the courtyard and soon the kordrion was losing blood from countless wounds. It gave a maddened scream, thrashing with its tail and causing untold damage.

But it's not trying to escape, although it must know that every minute spent here brings it closer to death. Ireheart was quite near to it now.

One of the talons touched the packhorse, but very cautiously.

Ireheart had caught up. With a vicious swipe of the crow's beak he attacked the long investigating finger. "That stays here!!" he yelled furiously, yanking the handle of his weapon.

With a loud tearing sound the blade ripped through the pale gray skin. "That's our horse!"

Balyndar leaped in, smashing his morning star down onto the claw so that blood gushed out.

With a screech the kordrion pushed forward and tried to spread its wings, but the surrounding walls made this impossible. However, the very attempt caused further destruction.

"Look out!" Ireheart pulled Balyndar aside as a large lump of heavy plasterwork threatened to fall straight on top of him. "Even the best of helmets won't save you from that kind of thing."

The kordrion snapped at them and the dwarves ducked to avoid its ugly mouth.

Ireheart used the opportunity to strike one of its lower eyes. The eye immediately burst open and the creature bellowed with pain.

The spike had buried itself in a bone. Ireheart did not release his hold on the weapon and was dragged upwards as the creature raised its head. The swift movement made him giddy and drove the air out of his lungs, leaving him gasping like a landed carp—but he didn't let go. "I won't be shaken off!" he called. "Is that all you can do? A bit further, you hideous freak! You won't scare me! I can take the altitude!"

Then an arrow got him in the left foot.

"Cursed black-eyes!" he yelled. "Can't you aim straight like your northern relatives?" His arms grew heavy and his own weight, together with that of the armor, dragged at him. But to let go would be instant death.

Then he saw Aiphatòn leap out of a window seven floors up above the kordrion's back, his spear tip targeting the creature's neck.

With that thing? Ireheart could not believe it. "Oh, Vraccas! He's got a little needle! He's going to prick it with a little needle!"

The monster ducked and shook its head. The crow's beak spike came loose and the dwarf flew off to the right through the air like a missile four paces above the ground, landing in a heap of butchered ponies, whose steaming intestines cushioned his fall.

He struggled up in a rage, broke off the arrow under the sole of his foot and stood. "Now you've really made me mad!" The red mask of battle-fury was setting in. Only the kordrion was unmoved. "I'll give you such a battering—I'll have you in pieces!"

Aiphatòn had leaped onto the creature's back and was stabbing away through the spinal column, finding the spaces between the huge vertebrae.

The kordrion arched up with a screech—and Tungdil jumped down onto it from one of the lower galleries, ramming Bloodthirster into a different place on the backbone, paralyzing the creature's right leg. It fell to its knees and lurched against the east façade, breaking the wall down. The building above it collapsed, covering the kordrion with a hail of heavy masonry.

Aiphatòn and Tungdil had taken refuge just in time and were waiting on a balcony on the western side.

But the beast was nowhere near the end of its strength.

Thrashing its tail it destroyed the gate and stonework above, killing dozens of älfar, who fell with the collapsing wall, to be crushed by falling chunks of masonry, while others were hit by the tail and hurled through the air to fall, broken, to the ground.

The beast rose from the debris with a cry; it staggered and crashed head first into a wall.

Ireheart had reached the kordrion again. "You'll be quiet soon enough!" He swung his arm back and whacked his crow's beak into the area of the soft underbelly where he supposed the genitals to be. The skin ripped open and the monster uttered a shrill cry. "Ha! That's what I like to hear," Ireheart bellowed merrily. "Let's have another!" He repeated his winning strike. "Sing it for me again!"

Aiphatòn and Tungdil moved in to help the sturdy warrior finish the beast off. They had to keep dodging the wildly flailing taloned limbs; its vast wings opened and closed convulsively, causing yet more damage to the fabric of Phôseon.

"Stop! Now!" Ireheart clambered boldly up the creature's long neck and brought the spike of his weapon forcefully down through the kordrion's skull. "Let's have you dead, you wretched fiend!"

And now, indeed, the vast body of the kordrion slumped. With a last groan it thrashed its tail for a final time, then fell over, destroying more of the buildings. Clouds of dust rose up.

Ireheart used his plait to wipe away the sweat and other unpleasant liquids from his forehead and beard, but there was too much of it. He was merely smearing it over his face as if he had been using a paint brush. There would have to be a bath. A shallow one, though.

"By Vraccas, the dwarves done good!" he crowed, lifting his weapon so that the kordrion blood dripped off it. Close by he saw his one-eyed friend nodding approvingly. Aiphatòn was back down on the ground staring up at the bulk of the huge beast.

There were still occasional bumps, bangs and crashes as more of the plaster and brickwork came down; the distress of any surviving ponies could be also heard, mixed with the moans of the wounded.

Then there was a single cry of relief, taken up by more and more of the älfar as they realized the creature had been slain. The call echoed in chorus through the alleys and ravines of the city.

Ireheart clambered over the neck and onto the belly to join Tungdil. "I don't get what they're saying but it sounds as if they like us," he said brightly, lowering the crow's beak and putting both hands on the shaft. He looked extremely pleased with himself. "At last—my kind of adversary. There won't be many dwarves who can outdo my deeds today." He looked around and through the settling dust saw the faces of the älfar rejoicing.

Tungdil slapped him on the shoulder. "Well done, Ireheart. They are saying . . ."

"Don't tell me, Scholar," he interrupted. "That way I can imagine the black-eyes are adoring me instead of wanting to kill me." He looked down at his injured foot, where the feathered arrow shaft still stuck up through the boot. "Perhaps that was one of them trying it on just now."

Tungdil laughed and started to climb down. "Come on. I want to find out what Aiphatòn has to say about our help."

At sunset Tungdil, Ireheart, Slîn, Balyndar, Hargorin and Barskalín assembled in the emperor's throne room; five of the Zhadár came along as well.

They were invited to sit at a table where goblets and jugs of wine stood ready. Nothing was poured out yet. Beforehand,

Aiphatòn had arranged for them to be shown to chambers where they could rest from their exertions.

They met up in the room they had first seen on arrival. The paintings on the walls had changed. The black and white silhouette designs were now full-color floor-to-ceiling landscapes of absurd beauty and if you looked carefully, the shrubs and trees were not depictions of real plants but were made up of tiny painted corpses, with wounds and cut throats.

"Just as barmy as their relations," said Ireheart in disgust. "But that ointment they gave us really works. I can hardly feel the hole in my foot."

"Who knows what it's made of," muttered Slîn. "But I'm not complaining. They treated me like a king."

"Apart from the bath," murmured Ireheart. "I had to get rid of most of the water before I got in. It was nearly up to my knees!"

"You mean because of Elria and her water curse?" Slîn's face bore a broad grin. "I've never heard of a dwarf drowning in a bath."

"And I didn't want to be the first!" He lifted his hand to show the amount of water for a proper bath. "From my fingertips to my wrist, that's all it needs."

Slîn burst out laughing. "That's only about enough to wet your manliness."

"I understand the fourthlings are smaller in all areas than the other tribes," Balyndar threw in.

"My bolt always reaches the target. I can always hear it hit home," said Slîn, pointing to the morning star. "But you will be built like your weapons: Too much force in the balls and only a little spike."

Ireheart roared with laughter.

Aiphatòn's entrance put a swift end to the dwarves' banter. He shook everyone's hands—except for those of the Zhadár—then took his seat at the head of the table. Two älfar came up to pour out a variety of wines.

The emperor studied his visitors closely, his eye sockets black as night.

So he does not wish to put aside the blemish—or perhaps he can't? Ireheart wondered.

"You and your friends have amply demonstrated that you are not among Phôseon's enemies." Aiphatòn's voice was calm and steady as he raised his cup in salute. "For this and your support in our hour of need I thank you." He drank a toast to them.

"The kordrion young we found on the packhorse had been smuggled into our train," replied Tungdil. "In my view Tirîgon is the only one who could have done this. And that means that at least one of the Dsôn Aklán is against you." He looked at the emperor expectantly.

Aiphatòn slowly replaced his goblet. "Your tone suggests to me that you know more, Tungdil." He gestured to his älfar to leave the chamber, then ran his eyes over the dwarf-faces. "Before we go on, I should like to ask that only those permitted to hear all the truth remain in the room with us."

Tungdil nodded, but continued, "As some of them still do not trust me because I returned after two hundred and fifty cycles of forced exile and they doubt my integrity, I shall not ask anyone to leave the room. I want all of them to hear what the emperor of the älfar and the high king of the dwarf-tribes have to say to each other."

Ireheart breathed a sigh of relief. He had feared that only

he would be allowed to stay. *That would have meant yet more bad blood.*

"Our original plan was different," Tungdil began, after taking a swig of wine. He explained to the älf leader what they had first intended to do with the kordrion's young. He described what was waiting in the Black Abyss and told him they needed Lot-Ionan and what they planned to do with the Dragon and his treasure: To get the Dragon to the magus and provoke a war between them.

Aiphatòn listened with no sign of emotion.

"Things have happened differently," Tungdil summed up. "And a good thing too, because I think the southern älfar will be better as our allies than as our foes when we march against Lot-Ionan. That was what you were planning, yourselves."

"To march against a magus is pure suicide," answered Aiphatòn soberly. "That is why I gave in to what my subjects from the south have been urging." He poured himself more wine and smiled. "I see you are surprised?"

Ireheart looked around. Nobody spoke, so he said, "I thought you meant to go to your own death?"

Aiphatòn leaned slightly forward, chin on his hand. "I never wished to be like my father. I always said that. And yet I have become like him. It would be too easy to find excuses for what I have done to Girdlegard, but I admit it all. That is why I shall lead them to the south to ensure their eradication in battle with Lot-Ionan."

"Hurrah! That's the right attitude!" Ireheart applauded in spite of himself, and then coughed to cover his embarrassment.

"I have been dazzled for too many cycles, inebriated by

my own power. I have made conquests, taken lives and broken the will of the people. Not because I had to but because I could. Because I was stronger," the emperor explained. "That terrible intoxication has passed now, but the memory of my guilt remains. With every new day I see the suffering I inflicted on Idoslane, Urgon and Gauragar. It has to end. And *I* shall end it."

"The Dsôn Aklán and northern älfar won't follow you," Tungdil pointed out.

"That is why I shall return alone from the Blue Mountains and destroy Dsôn Bhará with my own hands. There are only a few hundred älfar who gained entry to Girdlegard through the secret passageway under the Moon Pond. I shall deal with them on my own." As if to prove his intentions the runes on his armor started to glow. "Your arrival and plan, Tungdil, have strengthened my resolve. Once the Dragon is dead, nothing stands in the way of Girdlegard's liberation." He closed his eyes and a red tear emerged from under the lid and made its way down his cheek. "I never wanted to be like the Unslayables. My words shall at last be matched by my deeds."

Ireheart tried to catch Tungdil's attention. The Scholar returned his gaze. "It could not have worked out better," was the silent message.

"Would you be prepared to support us against the enemies from the Black Abyss?" Tungdil asked. "A warrior such as yourself . . ."

Aiphatòn shook his bald head. "When I have wiped out my own race, my debt of guilt to Girdlegard will have been settled. I led the älfar into Girdlegard and I shall free the humans from that yoke again. Without the oppression they have suffered the humans will be prepared to follow you in battle to the Outer Lands to defend their new-won freedom." He opened his eyes again. "I suggest that I announce to the älfar that we have signed a peace treaty with all the dwarf-tribes, and not only with the thirdlings. You must swear to me that nothing of what I have said will get out."

"Of course, for our own sakes," promised Ireheart, speaking for them all. "If the black-eyes got wind of your plan and opted to stay here instead of going to fight the magus, we'd have a much tougher task to get rid of them." He grinned and gave thanks to Vraccas. This was all turning out so much better than he could have assumed when the journey started.

Balyndar stared at Aiphatòn. "What about you? When all the älfar are dead, what will you do?"

He drew a deep breath. "I shall go away. To the east, to see what I shall find. I swear that I shall never return to Girdlegard—unless, of course, I am invited." He smiled at Tungdil. "For whatever reasons. And with the help of your gods and mine," he raised his goblet in a toast, "the last remaining northern älfar and I shall die together."

Tungdil bowed to him. "My respect for your courage, Aiphatòn. I see that I was not mistaken in you." He stood up. "With your permission we shall now withdraw. On the morrow we shall head for the Red Mountains to test the waters with the Dragon. For him and his orcs we shall lay a trail he can't ignore."

"By the time he arrives I should be in the Blue Mountains with the army. Lot-Ionan and his famuli won't find my troops easy to contend with, but they will be victorious. Then the Dragon and the orcs will arrive just in time to take on the magi." Aiphatòn also got to his feet. "But have a care that Lohasbrand does not turn Lot-Ionan into a glowing torch. The Scaly One is very powerful. He managed to subjugate Queen Wey the Eleventh, a mighty ruler with the reputation of being a great maga. If Lot-Ionan is killed you will be faced with the problem of cleansing the Black Abyss on your own."

Tungdil's eye narrowed. "Is she still alive?"

"Queen Wey? Yes. As far as I know. And she has a daughter said to be good at magic." The älf had understood the reason behind the question. "They would make excellent allies once the Dragon has been vanquished. If Lot-Ionan were to die she would be my first choice to aid us against the monsters in the Outer Lands." He shook hands with the dwarves once more. "May Vraccas be with you. If fate wills it we shall meet again." Aiphatòn left the throne room.

Onwards and upwards! Vraccas, we shall do heroic deeds! Ireheart helped himself to water, drank and belched, patting himself on the belly. "Bed now, Scholar? We'll have an early start in the morning, off to relieve the Dragon of his treasure. And to pay our respects to a lady sorceress, I understand?"

Tungdil laughed. "Off to bed."

Girdlegard,
Former Queendom of Weyurn,
Lakepride,
Late Winter, 6491st/6492nd Solar Cycles

By the large round window in her mother's study Coïra sat staring out at the lake. The white mourning veil on her hair and the black of her high-necked dress made her look older, Rodario thought.

He was sitting next to her, fidgeting with a quill pen. Mallenia was pacing up and down with her hands clasped behind her back. The carpet muffled the sound of her steps but the regular click-clack of her boot heels could still be heard.

The actor laid the feather quill aside and attempted to look the young maga in the eyes, but noted her fresh tears. He had a thin bandage round his neck, chiefly for decoration and as a souvenir of the wound Sisaroth had inflicted on him. The blade had slipped on the antique pendant he wore and this had taken the force of the blow. "Princess, it was not your fault. The älfar set a trap for you," said Rodario gently. "If you had been a swordswoman something similar could have happened with your weapon. The älfar know how to deceive and trick. You could not have prevented it."

"That," she said, with a sob in her voice, "is your fifth attempt to convince me that my mother did not die as a result of my incompetence. But again you fail to get me to change my opinion of events." She stared at her hands. "These are what I killed her with. These hands and the wretched magic she taught me herself."

"You were trying to kill the älf . . ." he began, but she whirled round.

"But who is it lying in the crypt next to my father? The älf?" she cried in despair. "I must never use magic again."

"But you saved Mallenia's life with your magic spell," he protested, trying a different tack. "And who will protect your subjects against the Dragon if he turns up here? Don't abandon your skills, Princess!"

"Yes, I must," she whispered, her anger fading now. She looked out at the lake again. "To be doubly sure, I should destroy the source. Before Lot-Ionan or the älfar can use it."

"You want to demolish the shaft?" Mallenia had stopped pacing and her eyes were flashing. "I know you are grieving. I, too, have lost many relatives but I'm not using that as an excuse to crawl away and hide and bewail my fate."

Coïra did not even look at her. "Go back to Idoslane, Mallenia," she advised her in a flat voice. "It was when you arrived here that everything started to go wrong in Lakepride. If only I had not listened to this third-rate actor, the älfar would have caught and killed you. Then everything would have been different."

"It's a waste of time going over it again and again," Rodario said, throwing Mallenia a warning glance to discourage her from making a sharp retort. "You are Weyurn's new queen . . ."

"It's Lohasbrand who is the ruler, in case you had forgotten," she interrupted coldly. "All I am is an incompetent maga sitting on a rock in the middle of a shrinking lake, having extinguished the life of my own mother."

Rodario sighed. "It was the *älf* who decapitated her."

"But it was me who injured her so badly that she could not defend herself. Can't you understand?"

"Where did the älfar go? Is there any trace?" Mallenia asked. "I've missed a lot. It's taken me a long time to recover."

"Sisaroth has left the island. At least *he* won't be coming back to try to kill us. And where his sister is, only the waters know." Rodario sounded impatient. He was keen to be raising Coïra's spirits, not making reports for Mallenia. Coïra was Girdlegard's last maga and must not be permitted to cast her powers aside in this way. But she was so grief-ridden that no one could expect her to listen to reason. Since the death of her mother she had not bathed in the magic source and her inner reservoir must be practically exhausted by now after the combat with the älfar and the effort of saving Mallenia.

He dared to come closer to her. "Princess, how do you think I feel?"

"Did *you* bring about your mother's death through your own stupidity?"

"No . . ."

"Then you have no idea what I'm going through," she said, her voice wavering. "I can hear her screams when it's quiet. And when I look in the mirror I can see her face on fire. If someone lays a fire and I smell the smoke it makes me vomit." She closed her eyes and held her hands in front of her face. "The älf should have killed me in her place," Coïra sobbed.

Rodario cared not a fig for the difference in status between them. He took her in his arms and pulled her to him, pressing her head against his chest. She threw her arms around him and sobbed her heart out.

Mallenia sat near the door and said nothing. She knew the value of such comfort—but to her surprise she suddenly felt jealous.

For some reason she had become besotted by this weakling of an actor. Probably because he was so gloriously un-macho and so different from every man she had ever known. The kiss he had stolen from her had only confirmed what her soul had long known.

She watched Rodario rocking the princess in his arms. *I*

can't ever tell him. Everyone would laugh at us, she thought unhappily. *Look, here comes the warrior maiden with her lapdog rhymester. Anyone her swords cannot conquer he bores to death with the power of his tongue.* Despite her unhappiness the very thought made her grin.

She tried to distract herself by thinking about the älfar twins. Mallenia had the corpse of the älfar woman in her mind's eye. They had found it floating in the lake, but before they could reach it, it had sunk. She had clearly seen that Firûsha's breast and belly had been split open. She had initially survived the extremely serious injuries the maga had inflicted on her, and had died from the impact when she fell.

Probably Sisaroth had gone off to search for his sister, or for her body. Perhaps there was a special älfar ritual he was following; this delay could give them a much-needed respite from attack. And no one knew how the Dragon was going to react. He had not yet sent an answer.

There came a knock at the door: Loytan entered without waiting, and was already in the room before freezing at the sight of Rodario and the princess locked in an embrace. "How dare you, you jumped-up little actor?" he exclaimed, his voice husky with indignation. "Get your hands off the queen this instant! Come outside if you are man enough and I'll show you how to behave."

Mallenia coughed to announce her presence. "You've chosen the wrong moment for insisting on social niceties, Count Loytan," she told him. "Calm down." She saw the letter in his hand. "Is that Lohasbrand's reply?"

"And what is that to you?"

She frowned impatiently. "When you have collected yourself and can think, you may remember that I am from the high-born race of the Ido, *count*," she retorted boldly. "I am entitled to be addressed as the Regent of Idoslane. If you are as keen on etiquette and the proprieties as you would have us believe, then you will greet me with a sweeping bow every time you come into my presence, and you will call me *Your Highness*." She saw him grow red. "Is that the way you want it, *count*?"

He was stony-faced with anger. "I have not opened the letter," he responded. "And yes, it is from Lohasbrand." He went over to put the missive on the desk.

Coïra freed herself from Rodario's arms and wiped the tears from her face. "Thank you," she said and opened the envelope. Her eyes quickly scanned the lines and a fragment of dragon scale fell out onto the wooden desk. This was proof that the letter contained authentic instructions from Lohasbrand.

"And?" Rodario tried to glimpse the contents over her shoulder in a manner inappropriate for a man of his class. Loytan shot him a murderous glance and clenched his fists.

"He commands me to search for the älf and to take him prisoner. To this end he is sending one hundred orcs for my use," she summarized. "And he insists on my taking an oath of allegiance."

"That would mean being constrained with a collar like your mother," said Rodario, horrified. "Surrounded by four guards? Abjuring magic completely?"

"I don't care. That way I shall never be tempted to get back down to the lakebed to reinforce my powers," she answered dully.

"Majesty, you mustn't!" Mallenia was beside herself. "You are the last of all the maga . . ."

Coïra's countenance darkened. "So what?"

Rodario cursed under his breath. Mallenia had done the one thing he had been trying to avert—and he saw that the queen now would not be persuaded to change her mind. "It has been a difficult day and we are all over-excited. Let's get some sleep. We can discuss this tomorrow."

"Who are you to talk to Her Majesty like that?" raged Loytan. "You'll not be discussing anything with anyone." Then he glanced at Mallenia, fearing a reproof.

"Rodario is right." Coïra dried her tears. "I am exhausted and need to rest. Let us meet in the morning to talk about what the future holds. All of us," she repeated emphatically, passing close by the actor as she left the room.

He heard her whispered "thank you" and then she was gone, followed by Loytan.

Rodario stared out of the window for some time before setting off for his own chamber, taking a detour via the open arcaded walk. He loved the freshness that came from the lake waters.

He would never have believed himself capable of driving the älf away with his fire-seeds trick. He thought it more likely that the black-eye had retreated in private sorrow over the sister's death. Sisaroth had killed eighteen grown men before making off. *May Firûsha rot at the bottom of the lake*, he wished.

Lost in thought, he had not noticed someone stepping out of the shadows. Only when the new arrival coughed did Rodario pay any attention. "Loytan. I didn't expect to find you here," he lied, brightly. "Is it time for that beating now?"

Count Loytan came nearer. "When I chucked you into the lake I should have shackled you first, stage scum!" He pointed down at the water. "This time that won't be necessary. A fall of eighty paces should be sufficient to break your neck. Then there's an end to your play-acting! You will not be missed."

"You took me by surprise last time, count. Do you think you could do the same thing now?"

Loytan laughed in his face. "Without your theater tricks you're nothing. Nothing at all," he taunted, fitting knuckle-dusters over his hands.

Rodario grinned. "But you don't seem to be relying on hitting me unaided. Do you think my chin is that hard?"

"I don't want to have to touch vermin like you more than once, that's all," the count retorted.

"And how have I made you so jealous? I was only comforting Coïra. Does your lady countess know about your private passion for Weyurn's new queen?" Rodario was enjoying pouring oil onto the fire. It was always easier to fight an adversary who was beside himself with anger. "I'd be happy to inform her."

"There'll be nothing left of you able to utter a single word." Loytan moved swiftly, but the actor stepped backwards.

"Stay where you are!" ordered the count.

"If you insist." Rodario sighed. "But I warn you: If you attack me now no one will ever see you again. Not even your lady wife."

"Dream on, idiot! And anyway, she already hates me." Loytan launched a blow—and his fist met thin air!

"On stage you have to be agile and move quickly." Rodario had simply done a forward roll between his attacker's legs and had sprung upright. He kicked the count on the behind, making him stagger. "What's the matter? Was that all you had in mind?"

Loytan struck out again.

"Saw that coming a mile off." Rodario blocked the charging fist and his arm did not even quiver as he pushed his elbow into his attacker's face. Grabbing the man's hair, he dragged him down; at the same time he propelled his knee at Loytan's nose; there was a crunch as the bone broke. Then he released his hold on Loytan and kicked him in the belly.

The count fell groaning to his knees. "I'll kill you for that," he croaked.

"Weren't you going to do that anyway?" Rodario put on a look of surprise. "And anyway, it's my turn to have a crack at murder now, not yours. For what you did out there at the shaft." He watched Loytan toss away the knuckledusters and draw a knife.

Rodario dodged two attacks, ducked under a third before showering a concerted hail of blows on his opponent, so that blood started pouring out of the cuts on his face. Loytan collapsed, fighting for breath. "You know," Rodario explained to his injured rival, "when you're an actor you need many talents. In order to portray a valiant warrior, for example, it's not enough simply to put on some armor; I have to actually be like a warrior. To fight like him, do you understand? I won't deny that it sometimes comes in very useful."

Loytan dragged himself up on the wall, coughing and spluttering. "That took more than a few hours to learn," he mumbled. Three teeth lay on the floor.

Rodario made a bow. "Thank you for your kind words. You should see me fence. I'm a real master with the rapier." He laughed. "Another time, perhaps. When you feel like a duel again and have recovered from your injuries." He thought for a moment. "Now what was it that you were wanting to ask me?"

Loytan reached under his coat and threw a lump of cotton wool to the floor. "I found this in your room."

"Ah yes, my stage props. What a discovery."

"You have your face padded out all the time, don't you? And that beard and mustache are only stuck on," Loytan went on, wiping the blood off his mouth. "Who are you really? Why do you keep up this masquerade from dawn to dusk?"

The expression in Rodario's eyes altered and became deadly serious. "Curiosity has killed more than just a cat, my friend." He took a sudden step forward, grabbing the count by belt and collar. "So you'll be in good company." He lifted the thin man and pushed him over the wall.

There was no scream.

Maybe I didn't push him far enough out? Rodario leaned over the balustrade and saw Loytan four paces down hanging by one hand from a drain pipe. "Your excellent reflexes won't get you very far, except downwards." He ran to a nearby brazier, the coals in it cold now, and started to drag it over to the wall.

The count was still attempting to climb up the pipe.

"Wait! I'll throw you something to hold on to." Grinning, he rolled the wrought iron container over the side. "Here! Catch! It'll take you quickly and safely to the bottom."

Rodario saw how the brazier smashed the pipe, plunging Loytan down toward the water. The iron basket followed at speed. No splash was audible from up here. "Give my regards to the älf woman," he called down.

Then he made sure that his actions had not been observed.

The windows on that side were dark and the chambers unoccupied. Rodario allowed himself a broader grin as he picked up the cotton wool and stowed it under his coat. He preferred people to go on underestimating him.

He was about to turn on his heel and continue on his way when he saw a vague outline against the evening sky. It looked at first sight like a bird.

The nearer the shape came, the larger it grew and the closer it came to the magic source, the surer Rodario became that this was no bird, but . . .

"Lohasbrand," he yelled and ran off. "To arms! To arms! The Dragon is coming!"

XVII

Girdlegard,
Former Queendom of Weyurn,
Eight Miles from Lakepride,
Late Winter, 6491st/6492nd Solar Cycles

The kordrion's assault had cost Tungdil twenty-one Black Squadron dwarves and three Zhadár. They burned the bodies of the dead warriors and took their ashes to be buried back in the Red Mountains with all ceremony. Dwarf-remains belonged in the mountains, not in a desert and certainly not in an älfar realm.

But they had also lost the majority of the ponies. There was nothing for it but to cover the initial miles to the north-west border of Phôseon Dwhamant on foot before buying in more stock bit by bit from the farmers of the former kingdom of Tabaîn.

It was inevitable that a marching column such as theirs would attract attention. Tungdil urged them on. Orbit for orbit they marched on through the dried-up lakebed, now covered with ice and frozen fog which crackled underfoot.

They passed islands towering high on stalks, reminding Ireheart of huge stone mushrooms. There were also many small islands that had collapsed without the buoyancy provided by surrounding water. They had toppled over and broken apart.

It looks unreal. As if the gods were planning to make a new country. Particularly fascinating were the places where reefs had been. They soared up like sharpened mountains, sometimes a good hundred paces high. The travelers came upon stranded wrecks of ships and the remains of mighty fish. The dwarves guided their ponies through the arched bones, which they could ride through without banging their heads, such was the size of the skeletons.

I know now why I have always avoided deep water like the plague. Ireheart looked at the fish and at the thick skulls with their incisor-lined jaws. No prey would escape those sharp teeth.

"You'd think our high king was trying to avoid any conflict with the Lohasbranders and the orc contingents," Slîn remarked as they rode along.

"Yes, indeed," Ireheart agreed. "But it's not a question of being frightened of battle," he stressed. "It's about making swift progress. Our priority is to reach the Red Mountains and the Dragon's hoard to relieve him of the most valuable pieces of treasure, so that he'll attack Lot-Ionan in revenge."

"So why the diversion to see Queen Wey the Eleventh in Lakepride?" Slîn asked.

"Could it be that you weren't paying attention? Because the Scholar wants to suggest we wage a joint campaign against Lot-Ionan as soon as the Dragon and his orcs have left for the south," replied Ireheart. "On the way back, when we're nicely loaded up with the Dragon's valuables, we can come and collect her answer." He looked around at the landscape. "This is the kind of lake I like," he said with satisfaction. "Back home they'll be astonished when I tell them I've been walking around on the bottom of a lake and Elria can't get me!"

"Unless it rains," Slîn pointed out.

Ireheart gave him a suspicious glance. "What do you mean?"

"If it rains hard the water won't soak in. It will collect on this hardened surface like in a dish. If we happened to be at the deepest part of the dish at the time we'd end up having to swim." Slîn enjoyed catastrophizing. "And we all know the dwarf-race is none too good at swimming."

Ireheart checked the sky. It was growing steadily darker. "Vraccas, send us anything, send us molten rock—anything but Elria's rain. Don't let her water us like a crop of peas."

Tungdil pointed. "We need to get back to the bank and head south. We should end up directly opposite Lakepride. From there it's only a short boat-ride to the maga's island."

Ireheart's good mood was now thoroughly dispersed. The thought of those fish skeletons came back to him. "Curses! So I shall have to set foot on a boat, after all."

"It's been fine so far," Slîn attempted to cheer him up. "And so what if we do fall in? I like a good bath."

"That's because you're a pansy fourthling," came the mocking response from under a helmet. It was a Zhadár laughing at him.

Ireheart remembered that coarse voice. It was the same warrior who had tried to provoke Slîn with remarks about bolt length when they were up on the roof. He fell back to come level with the armored voice. "Was that you just now?"

"Was that me what?"

It was not the right voice. "No, it wasn't you. But you know who I mean: The one who's trying to stir things up—the troublemaker." Ireheart pushed the man's visor up. A blackened face with a short beard. As a dwarf Ireheart was finding it extremely difficult to tell one of these Invisibles from another. The dye gave them all the same appearance. It was really a kind of protection to stop them being identified; no one would be able to describe an attacker. "Whichever helmet you're hiding under," he called out, "hold your tongue. I won't have this sort of thing." He guided his pony to the front of the column again.

Tungdil had already changed direction and was riding with Barskalín, heading for the dunes. The remnants of the lake must lie behind them.

Ireheart urged his mount up. Its hooves sank in the loose dune sand. Then they reached the top and could see the edge of the lake. There was an island some four miles out, resting on a basalt stone pillar. To the left of it iron walls could be seen rising out of the water.

"That's Lakepride over there," said Tungdil. "We've arrived." He pointed to the iron building. "The source is underwater so I suppose that's a mineshaft of some sort."

"Yes," said Balyndar. "My mother sent her fifthlings as a favor to help one of Weyurn's queens with the construction."

"A masterpiece!" Ireheart was extravagant in his praise. "The pressure on the walls must be enormous."

Balyndar did not conceal his pride in his tribe's achievement. "Our engineers put in the wall supports to keep the water out. If it were a marine environment, like in the Outer Lands, where there are tides to cope with, it wouldn't have worked."

"That's the advantage held by the fifthlings. They took in the best of all the tribes and so they're way ahead with all the special skills the dwarves have, "Slîn said generously. "I'd be interested in taking a look at that shaft. I can't really imagine what it must be like."

Barskalín pointed out a village about half a mile away. The upturned boats and fishing nets drying on the sand looked promising. "We'll get ourselves a little fleet to take us over to the island."

Tungdil turned his pony's head toward the village. "Or one boat that can take ten of us. I don't want to arrive with the Black Squadron. You can get somewhere to stay in the village. We shan't be spending long with the queen."

They galloped off to the village.

Ireheart was not surprised to hear a tinny alarm bell greeting them; it sounded as if the bell itself was frightened. "Not quite the joyful fanfare of welcome we're used to, is it, Scholar?" he said, watching what the humans were up to. "They're running to the lake."

"They're launching the boats." Slîn pointed to those who were making a break for it.

"I bet they think we've been sent by the älfar." Balyndar touched his own black armor. "We don't really look like friendly visitors. The last time any dwarves were here will have been ages ago when they were building the shaft."

Hargorin laughed. "They seem to know my Black Squadron."

"Send a couple of men over quickly to tell them we come in peace," Tungdil ordered. "You're right, Balyndar, I should have thought of that . . . We're spreading fear even when we don't want to. Back where I've come from that would have been a good thing. But not here. I'm sorry."

Ireheart sent his friend an encouraging look. *He really seems bothered about it.*

Two of the Black Squadron rode ahead, calling out as they went.

Ireheart looked up at the glowing evening sky before it disappeared into the gloom of night—and he made out the shape of a flying monster making for Lakepride from the east. He could not say exactly what it was but it was moving fast. And it looked pretty determined. He called out to Tungdil. "You know more about monsters than I do: *What is that?*"

The dwarves watched as the creature approached the island and royal palace.

"I don't know," said the one-eyed dwarf. "But I don't think it's bringing Her Majesty a nice present."

"Then we're here right on time." Slîn was getting excited. "We can help her and then she'll be in our debt. We won't even have to ask her to come with us. She'll do it anyway because it will be the decent thing."

"That's how I see it, too." Tungdil got the squadron to stop on the bank where the villagers were standing by the boats listening suspiciously to their messengers. "Let's get ourselves over to the island."

Ireheart studied the water in apprehension as the waves lapped against the bank. "I hope Elria didn't hear me just now," he muttered into his beard, "and that all the fish bigger than my little finger are now dead."

Rodario ran back into the palace and was relieved to note his warnings had been acted upon. Shouts came from all sides and alarm gongs sounded. Heavy boots thudded along the corridors. It was not only the fortress out at the shaft that was preparing for an attack—the defense positions here at the palace were also being manned.

He reached Mallenia's quarters, where he found her in the

doorway, already in half her armor, buckling the leather straps. "Do you know what's happening?"

"That alarm is being sounded for me," he said proudly.

"You? But you're not dangerous." Mallenia drew her sword and laughed. "No, seriously. Do you know what all the commotion is about?"

"I saw something flying toward the shaft. I thought it would be wise to alert the palace so they can greet the attacker properly . . ." He stopped, noticing that she was only half listening and was looking past him over his shoulder.

Mallenia lifted her arm. "Queen Coïra. Are you looking for us?"

He turned to find the young maga hurrying toward them, surrounded by guards. She was wearing a black robe embroidered in white, her hair covered by the white veil. "It's the Dragon," she cried. "Lohasbrand has arrived."

"To attack us or to discuss what you wrote?" Mallenia sketched a curtsey. Rodario forgot to bow.

"I don't know. Wasn't he going to send me a hundred orcs to help capture the älf?" She ran on and waved them to follow her.

"Where are you off to?" Rodario asked. "Is there a safe room at the bottom of the island's base where you can wait to see what happens?"

"I need to get to the magic source."

"Don't make the mistake of destroying it without thinking carefully . . ."

"Nonsense," she interrupted. "I don't want to demolish the shaft. I haven't got enough magic in reserve to defend us against the Scaly One."

Rodario and the Ido girl exchanged relieved glances. "We're pleased to hear you've made your decision."

"And it is down to the two of you that I am able to do this. I have thought a great deal about what you both said and I agree that I must face up to my responsibilities. My mother will not have trained me in vain." She gave them a brisk smile. "But it won't be easy. I'm not a fighter at heart."

She reached the platform from where the cable gondola could take her to the shaft. Coïra was about to get in to the car but Rodario held her back. "Wouldn't it be better to take the stairs? Our lives might hang from a rope."

"It'll be fine." The queen got into the gondola. "Trust me."

"I trust the construction but not that dragon that's circling round the island." He looked for the creature but it was not visible. "Where has it got to?"

"It's underneath the island!" Mallenia shouted, coming over. "Let's pray to Elria and Palandiell that we can get to the shaft in one piece."

"Count Loytan will cover us with his catapult fire." Coïra ordered four of the guards to join her, and the last of them shut the door after her as the steep downward trip began.

"Count Loytan is not at the fort, Highness," said one of the men. "We met him up on the palace walls but no one has seen him since."

Rodario was glad he had turned his face away: No one could read his expression. He considered himself a gifted enough actor to conceal his grin, but better safe than sorry.

The gondola swayed in the evening breeze and Mallenia went very pale. The rocking movement was not too severe, however, as the anchoring bolts were all secure.

It was all too slow for Coïra's liking, and she told the guards to release the brakes a little further.

"But Your Highness, that'll mean we'll be too fast to stop at the landing stage." The man risked an objection. "It's not safe to go any quicker."

The gondola had already dropped further away from the island when Rodario spied the creature again. "There it is! It's hanging underneath the rock!"

Mallenia, Coïra and the soldiers leaned out for a better view.

It was like a lizard with the wings of a grasshopper. The scaled body was ten paces long, the mouth large enough to swallow a whole cow, and the black skin was shimmering damply in the last of the evening light: Rodario could pick out yellow and blue markings. It was wearing an iron chain around its neck, bearing an onyx pendant the size of a handcart.

"Why aren't the catapults on the fortress firing?" He was worried now.

The stony eyes had the gondola in their sights.

Mallenia looked down at the arrow slings, which seemed to be aimed straight at them. "It's because of us. We're in the line of fire so we're giving the creature cover."

"It can't be the Dragon—no, it's certainly not Lohasbrand." Coïra stated.

"Perhaps a small friend of his? Has he been sent out as an advance messenger?" Rodario could not make head or tail of the creature's appearance. He had never met the like in any of the sagas he was conversant with. "It's staring at me," he said, moving away from the window. "As if it really likes actors."

"I'm sure it only eats good ones," Mallenia teased him, aware once more that she was behaving like a silly girl in love—and that this was a highly unsuitable time for such behavior.

"It's staring at all of us," said Coïra.

"To be honest, that's not much of a comfort . . ." Rodario turned to the queen. "Can't you send some magic his way? Zap him on the ugly bonce!"

She refused. "We don't know yet what it wants. Perhaps it's a peace-loving creature."

"In Girdlegard? Looking like that?" He watched, shuddering, as the creature dangled a blue tongue. "There! Do you see? It's getting up an appetite."

Their gondola was two-thirds of the way across.

The creature dropped down and spun round as it fell, spreading its horny wings to come gliding over to the gondola. It opened its mouth and showed a row of very sharp teeth.

"I think it's making abundantly clear what it wants." Rodario sank down in front of Coïra to beg. "Save us!"

The queen did not need his plea. She collected the last remnants of her magic powers and sent a red lightning bolt through the window toward the swiftly approaching creature.

Her attack hit home!

The magic energy shattered the creature's face and part of its neck, and its flight ended in a series of erratic swoops as it entangled itself in the cables holding the gondola aloft. Now the fortress soldiers could use their long-range ballistic weaponry.

The cabin was suddenly jerked upwards with a clank and

then came the sound of ripping and tearing. Next moment, they were falling toward the lake.

"Stop!" Rodario yelled, petrified, trying to grab hold of one of the supports. "Coïra! Do something! Brakes! We're falling!"

The cable car turned and Rodario caught sight of the injured creature following them, its talons at the ready.

"Forget what I just said: Make it go quicker. Quicker! Now!" Rodario shouted, falling against Mallenia and yelling in her ear. "The beast is nearly on us!"

Tungdil was on the first fishing boat with Slîn, Balyndar, Ireheart and ten of the Zhadár, heading for Lakepride with all sails set. They witnessed exactly what was happening four miles away.

Slîn looked back at the small fleet of boats carrying the Black Squadron and the rest of the Zhadár. The villagers had agreed to take the dwarves over to the island when they heard the names Tungdil and Boïndil, and when the monster turned up they put on an extra burst of speed. "Coïra won't have any experience yet as a maga."

"But I'm glad we've got a maga we can even consult," responded Balyndar. "I was shocked to hear of the queen's death."

Boïndil hopped impatiently from one foot to the other. He felt extremely uneasy being on the lake and had no wish to know how deep it was—only the thinnest of planks separated him from the water. He wanted to start fighting, but how could he do that stuck on this barge? He had not the faintest idea what kind of creature it was that was attacking the cable car. "What on earth is it? It's not a dragon," he said to Tungdil.

"I'm trying to work out whether it's good or bad." Tungdil stared fixedly ahead and saw the red flash aimed at the creature; the dying monster was tangled in the cables. "Lohasbrand won't have sent him. Dragons don't tolerate other monsters in their kingdom. He would have killed this creature himself if it had turned up in the Red Mountains."

When the cable snapped and the car started to fall to the lake, Ireheart cursed out loud. "Now we've lost that maga, too. It's enough to drive you mad!" The fortress in the lake was shooting tiny black clouds of arrows and spears.

"She should be able to save herself. If she can't do that she'd be no use to us against Lot-Ionan either." Tungdil sounded detached.

The flying beast had tugged the cables away on both sides as it flapped its wings helplessly, cutting itself on the ropes. It screamed and reeled after the cabin, as if it wanted to tear it apart.

"Maybe the queen should start doing something?" Ireheart sounded doubtful. "They're about to crash."

At that moment the monster completed a final erratic lurch through the air and disappeared head first into the open shaft, streaming with blood and spattering red on the walls.

"Ugh, that's what I call an unlucky turn of events." Ireheart could see that the gondola had stopped, mid-fall, and was now swaying like a pendulum, swinging toward then away from the pillar that supported Lakepride island. "Look, one of the ropes has held firm!"

Tungdil grimaced. "I'd also prefer it if the maga actually did something. I'm not convinced of her competence."

Ireheart was about to say something when a mighty explosion occurred.

A bright green column of fire erupted out of the shaft, blowing the whole construction up to the skies. The dwarves thought they could make out shapes of people, remnants of catapults, parts of the roof, some wooden beams and other bits and pieces hurtling through the air, driven by the force of the blast. The spectacle was accompanied by a whistling screech, the walls of the shaft glowed first red then white from the extreme heat, and then the waters around the area began to boil and steam rose up in clouds.

Another blast. The flames died down, only to be replaced by a ball of light directly over the opening to the shaft.

Below, far down on the bottom of the lake, there was a silvery flash and a circle of shimmering fire spread out. The dwarves could see right down through it as it raced across the lakebed. Ireheart thought he could feel a slight tingling when it went under their boat. The runes on Tungdil's armor shone out.

Immediately afterwards there was a sound like a volcanic eruption. The lake surface started to shake. Waves swept against the keels of the boats, making them bob erratically.

A third detonation shattered the walls of the shaft as if they had been made of brittle glass and not the toughest of steel.

The lake waters streamed in, creating an undertow that dragged the fishing boats toward the island. The hole filled up, bubbling and raging, and then a column of water shot up as high as the palace itself before sinking again.

"Hold tight," was all that Tungdil said, as a powerful wave

hurtled their way. He grabbed hold of the mast and hunched down, bracing himself.

"I hate Elria," growled Ireheart, finding a rope to cling to. "She always finds a way to ruin things for me when I go on a journey."

The rump of the boat rose up, surrounded by spray, and a huge breaker covered the dwarves with ice-cold lake water. Then they pitched down again. Their vessel shook and shuddered, but did not overturn.

Slîn looked back over his shoulder. Not all of their party had fared so well. Two of the boats had foundered. "May Vraccas preserve them from Elria's wrath," he prayed briefly, then set his gaze ahead.

Steam still rose where the steel walls had been. A loud rumbling filled the air. The pillar on which the island rested was starting to crumble at one side. The basalt stone was breaking apart and the island's equilibrium was lost.

As the island toppled slowly to the left-hand side, the supporting column of rock snapped completely and Lakepride hit the water. A second massive wave rolled toward the boats. The fishermen were beside themselves with terror. Their little ship surged upwards once more on the crest of the wave.

Tungdil stood at the mast, a picture of calm, as he scanned the tormented surface of the lake.

"Well, Scholar?" called Ireheart. He steadied himself on the planks and leaned forward to counteract the movement of the boat. "Do you think there's any hope of survivors?"

This second wave was much stronger than the first, Ireheart noted from the angle the boat took and the length of time it seemed suspended. *I'll never, ever go on a lake again. Never*

ever! He was dreading the pitching crash when the wave finally sent them plunging down again.

They were briefly horizontal before the bows pitched forward and they hurtled down the back of the wave. They were not far from where the shaft, until very recently, had been, and where the island had stood.

"Dwarf overboard!" came a shout behind him. Balyndar stood at the low railing and pointed to starboard. "Slîn's been hit by the breaker and dragged under!"

Tungdil did not even turn round. "We have to look for the maga," he answered. "We've enough dwarves. There's only one maga."

Ireheart stared at his friend, baffled by this cold-hearted attitude. *He's reverting to the Tungdil who came back to us from the Outer Lands with a reputation for horrific deeds of cruelty.* He saw some buoys on deck that the fishermen used to mark the location of their nets. They were made of pigs' bladders filled with air, cork tree branches or glass balls encased in string.

Ireheart grabbed four of them and ran over to Balyndar. "Where is he?"

Together they stared out at the waves until the fifthling located the missing dwarf. "There! Cast it now!"

Ireheart hurled the floats out, putting all his strength behind the throw so that they carried all the way to him.

A spluttering, paddling Slîn grabbed hold of the rope tied to one of the floats and pulled it over, but he continued to sink due to the weight of his armor. He was fighting for his life, they could see. It was only when he managed to pull the other three floats over that he was able to keep his head above water. It was enough to enable him to breathe.

Ireheart was relieved and went back to join Tungdil in the bows. "We've saved him. One of the other boats will pick him up."

"Good." He stretched up to see more distinctly something he had caught sight of through the spray.

"You might just as well have said 'I couldn't care less,' Scholar," Ireheart said reproachfully. "That's what your tone of voice was saying."

Tungdil turned round suddenly and, for a blink of an eye, looked as if he were going to hit Boïndil. His face was full of fury. "If I need a crossbowman, I'll find a new one. If I need a maga, what do I do then?" he countered the rebuke. "It's good that Slîn is safe. No more than that. Without Coïra our chances of prevailing against Lot-Ionan are diminished. It'll make no difference not having Slîn with us. He won't have the kind of weapon that can kill a magus outright." He looked at the fisherman and directed, "Hard to port."

Ireheart did not know what to say. *This was a real blow.*

The boat slipped round and headed for some of the floating rubble.

It was still rocking about and the lake had not yet settled. The fisherman reefed the sails to decrease their speed; he did not want to hole the boat. There were constant bumps and clanks as driftwood and flotsam collided with the hull.

Tungdil had a boathook in his hand, held like a harpoon. "Look out for survivors. If you see a woman tell me at once. The others can pick up the men."

Ireheart lifted a net and stared out at the water. "A woman!" he called, pointing to a blonde girl in leather armor, motionless, face up, floating next to an empty barrel.

Tungdil used the hook to pull her nearer and the Zhadár

heaved her up over the side. "Is that the maga?" he asked the fisherman.

"No, sir, the queen has black hair," was the reply.

Ireheart laid the girl down by the mast and quickly covered her with a blanket before Tungdil could think of chucking her overboard again; her lips were blue and quivering. "That's good," he said reassuringly. "You're alive." She looked pretty tall and strong for a human. *A warrior-girl, then.*

One of the Zhadár whistled and pointed to starboard.

They changed course to head for what he had seen. Tungdil fished the next woman out of the lake. She was wearing a black robe and had long dark hair. She, too, was unconscious. And she wasn't breathing!

"That's her," whispered the frightened fisherman. "That's the queen! Elria, be merciful!"

"Elria? I'll show Elria!" Ireheart turned her over and trod on her back with his boots till the water gushed out of her mouth and she started to cough. "There! Hurrah! I am a born healer!" He helped the maga to turn over and wrapped her in a new blanket. "You owe your life to Vraccas," he told her kindly.

"It felt more like the sole of a boot," she groaned.

Tungdil came over and looked down at her. "Welcome back to the land of the living, Coïra Weytana, queen of Weyurn."

She coughed again and gave him a grateful nod.

"This is High King Tungdil Goldhand," said Ireheart, introducing his friend first, then himself and then the others on board. "We arrived just in time."

There was a splash next to the boat and a man's hand was seen clamped to the railing; then the second hand appeared and a torso pulled itself up over the side. Brown hair was slapped tight to his head and his aristocratic face was beardless. "I assume I am allowed on board?" He looked at the assembled crowd in astonishment. "Well I never. A sailing barge full of dwarves!"

"By all the spirits of the dead!" Ireheart's eyebrows were raised in amazement, because he thought he was seeing the ghost of a man who had long since died. The clean-shaven ghost of a man. "Rodario?"

XVIII

Girdlegard,
Former Queendom of Weyurn,
Lakeside,
Late Winter, 6491st/6492nd Solar Cycles

Nobody in the quiet hamlet of Lakeside could have dreamed that they might one day have the privilege of offering hospitality not only to their queen, but also to those illustrious dwarf-heroes of cycles long past, Tungdil Goldhand and Boïndil Doubleblade, the celebrated Mallenia of Ido, and a descendant of the fabled Rodario the Incredible. Not even the best storyteller in the village could have imagined such a company in their midst.

The eminent visitors were gathered in the taproom of the harborside inn, drinking hot tea, mulled wine or spiced beer. The villagers had withdrawn out of respect and were pushing and shoving each other at the window and the doorway, trying to get a glimpse of the high personages. They sent in a few of their number to convey their best wishes or make presentations of gifts, but without a specific invitation none of them dared to approach closer than four paces.

"You're positive the magic source has been destroyed?" Tungdil addressed Coïra, who was now wearing the simple garb of a fisherwoman and had wrapped herself in a blanket.

"I realized straightaway," she answered despondently. "All the energy was released and I managed to absorb some of it, but . . . now . . . it is dead. There is nothing left at all where the source used to be."

Ireheart thought back to the fizzing sensation and how the runes on Tungdil's armor had started to glow. That must have been the reason: Magic had been set free into the air! Personally, he could have done without that experience, but the loss of the magic source would be of terrible significance for them all!

Coïra smiled at her subjects even if she found it hard. None of this was their fault and she did not want to disappoint anyone. She gestured to a little girl with a basket of gifts, accepted the presents graciously and stroked the girl's blond hair. "Thank you very much." Curtseying prettily, the young girl hurried back to the others waiting outside.

"I simply can't think what kind of creature was responsible for Lakepride's collapse and the destruction of the magic source," said Tungdil.

The maga shook her head and gave her attention to the gifts she had been brought: There was a brooch made of fish bone with an image of the island engraved on it. Sighing, she clasped it in her hand.

"I think it must have been Lot-Ionan." Rodario the Seventh looked round the circle. "The magus must have created that monster and sent it here, either to kill the maga or to destroy her source of magic. Once it knew that it was dying it threw itself down the shaft to carry out its mission." He touched his throat. "I saw quite clearly that it was wearing a chain with an onyx pendant. Perhaps that was the cause of the explosion?"

"Possibly." Coïra nodded thoughtfully. "Perhaps he put a

spell in the stone. It must have been some very powerful sorcery to have an effect like that."

"This brings us to a vital issue. Are you prepared to help us fight the magus?" Tungdil looked at her searchingly. "More to the point: Are you capable of helping us?"

"So you want to pursue the Dragon first and then go off to the south," she summarized. "If we accept Rodario's idea, Lot-Ionan won't have attacked me and the source for no reason. Sooner or later he will attempt to conquer Girdlegard, and this act will have been the opening gambit for a takeover of Weyurn. He knows I need the source to be able to put up any lasting resistance."

"How much magic power were you able to absorb?" Tungdil wanted to know.

"Enough for now." Coïra sat up straight in her chair. "I'd need more if I were to campaign against Lot-Ionan. That will be what you were asking, Tungdil Goldhand."

"To be frank, I doubt you would be powerful enough to do anything to stop him."

Ireheart listened as his friend deliberately provoked the young maga. *Any minute now he'll be needing his armor!* But to his surprise she responded with a friendly smile.

"I know what you think of me: A young woman, hardly out of training, and one who's managed to bungle things so badly as to kill her own mother. But I assure you that I am spurred on by these drawbacks. Perhaps a warrior heart will be bestowed on me yet." She paused. "I shall accompany you to the Red Mountains."

"Your Majesty!" objected Rodario. "To wage war on the Dragon is . . ."

". . . is an excellent decision," interjected Tungdil. "I know why you wish to come with us: I've heard the rumors that there may be a further magic source in the firstlings' realm."

The same idea had just occurred to Ireheart. Goda had occasionally mentioned that merchants traveling from the west to trade with the fourthlings had spoken of mysterious lights in the Red Mountains. She had deduced the lights might have a connection with magic. However, it had been no more than rumors and vague speculation.

"Exactly. I will come with you and will collect as much magic power as I can; then I can help you against the magus."

Rodario raised his hand. "Permit me to speak. What assurance do we have that Lot-Ionan hasn't sent more of these creatures up into the mountains or over to where the älfar are?"

"There's no guarantee. But Lohasbrand can deal with them as easy as pie. I don't suppose the älfar would be able to do the same, unless they've got Aiphatòn at their side," Tungdil replied.

Mallenia had kept quiet throughout this exchange, limiting herself to furious glances at Hargorin Deathbringer. But she had held her tongue for the sake of peace. Ireheart could tell she was finding it difficult. In her opinion the Deathbringer had committed too many crimes in the name of the älfar. Ireheart had to admit she had a point. "I don't like the pact we've entered into with the black-eyes. They've oppressed my people for so many cycles now and suddenly it's all sweetness and light with Aiphatòn and he's planning to lead the älfar to their deaths and to destroy their empires?" Her mouth narrowed to a very thin line. "I don't believe it."

"Who says the thirdlings are going to join us?" Rodario asked them to consider. "Right, one of their number has become high king—but don't they still despise the other dwarf-tribes?" He glanced at Hargorin and Barskalín. "How can you remove my doubts for me?"

"Your doubts?" asked Hargorin in astonishment. "You're an actor. You're only sitting at this same table because you invited yourself. You have no part in decisions concerning the future existence of Girdlegard. You can't even fight. But I suppose we can take you along as a mascot." Barskalín laughed in agreement.

Now a smile, dangerous enough to rival Tungdil's best, crept onto the actor's visage. "Try to strike me and you'll have to take back those words."

Coïra leaned over to speak to Mallenia. "If I'm not mistaken, his face is looking much thinner."

The Ido girl agreed. "And the lake has torn off a few beard hairs, I see." Looking more closely she noted a distinct dark shadow round his chin, throat and cheeks. "But they'll be growing back with a vengeance, stronger than ever, I expect." The two girls exchanged glances, each reading the other's suspicions.

In the meantime Hargorin had got up from his seat and had planted himself in front of Rodario. "You don't know what you've taken on."

"Yes, I do," he said confidently. "But it is not nice to fight in the presence of ladies. It would not be fitting to smear the place with your blood and guts while they are watching. And at the moment we have a more pressing task."

"Stop it! Both of you!" Tungdil called impatiently.

"But I'm not being taken seriously merely because I appear on the stage. I can't accept that. My question was not stupid: I was wondering about the loyalty of the thirdlings," Rodario returned. "What if they decide to help the älfar? They've served them for over two hundred cycles. If there's a shift in the balance of power they'll suffer great losses—never mind that, they'll be exposed to the rage of the humans in Urgon, Idoslane, and Gauragar. They'd be definitely better off if there's no change at the top."

"It's worth considering," Mallenia agreed. In gratitude Rodario sent her a long, warm look.

Rodario placed his hands on the table. "Can you understand why I'm hesitating here? What if the dwarf-haters were to attack the fourthlings and fifthlings while they're marching south? We'd never manage a campaign against Lot-Ionan after that."

"We follow Tungdil Goldhand," smoldered Hargorin.

"We—do you mean all the thirdlings or a substantial majority?" Rodario tried to pin him down to specifics. "It would be interesting to learn what the minority might get up to? And what about the freelings? Where are they?"

Barskalín broke in: "They've dug themselves in in the last of their cities and are fighting off the thirdlings . . ."

"Aha!" said Rodario. "There you are, you see! The thirdlings are still attacking the other tribes." He folded his arms belligerently. "I don't see, with all due respect, any change in their attitude."

"That will be because I haven't issued any commands to them to stop what they are doing." All heads swiveled round to Tungdil. "If the thirdlings suddenly changed their tune the älfar would smell a rat. Then Aiphatòn's plan would be jeopardized and the northern älfar would be suspicious, too. That's why I haven't told them to stop their attacks. I can't do that before Aiphatòn has set out with his army. The freelings will just have to bide their time and hold them off."

Nobody dared to respond.

Finally, Ireheart cleared his throat. "So, tomorrow we'll set off to Lohasbrand's hideout. We'll pinch his best bits of treasure and then hie ourselves off to the magus. As soon as we hear from the emperor of the black-eyes, we'll send off some riders to order the thirdlings and the other dwarf-tribes to get to the south to capture a weakened Lot-Ionan." He looked at the queen. "With your help."

"Neatly summed up," commented Rodario. "I'm with you."

"Me too," said Mallenia. "Idoslane will do its bit to free Girdlegard just as it did under my ancestor. We can't provide an army, but I can fight for you. The rest of my resistance fighters will deal with any älfar still at large. I'll write to them straightaway. They will watch for a suitable opportunity."

"Good." Tungdil seemed satisfied.

Rodario put up his hand again. "How would it be if we were to announce to the *people*, and not just to the resistance, that Girdlegard is about to be liberated? If we have supporters who have sniffed the wind of freedom and want to rise up against the Lohasbrander and the last vassals of the älfar, they'll be unstoppable."

"Girdlegard's too big for that," Tungdil contradicted him.

"Somebody shove something in that actor's mouth. Preferably something sharp," murmured Hargorin.

Rodario pointed to his throat. "If I had an ugly beard like yours I'd be more careful who I insulted."

Ireheart grimaced. Dwarves normally enjoyed a joke, even quite earthy ones, but you could not ridicule a dwarf's beard with impunity. Mockery and fire were the worst enemies of a beard. "Stop that now if you want to get out of here with your life and fine features intact," he called to him quietly. "Apologize to him . . ."

Hargorin had sprung up to confront the actor. "You're just desperate for a beating, aren't you?" he yelled, waving his fists.

"Forgive me," said Rodario nicely to the two ladies, then he shot out his foot, fished out the tip of the long beard in question, grabbed it with his right hand and yanked. His left arm flew up and his elbow crashed against the dwarf's forehead, making him gasp.

Rodario slipped out of his seat without letting go of the beard, pulling Hargorin after him. He pushed his feet against the dwarf's stomach and overturned him so that he landed on his back on the wooden floor.

The actor did a backwards somersault and ended up sitting on the dwarf's barrel chest, still holding the beard, which he pulled sharply to one side. Once he had anchored it under his foot the dwarf was completely helpless.

Ireheart had been taken as much by surprise as all the others in the room.

From somewhere or other Rodario had pulled out a knife and was holding it at the dwarf's exposed neck. "I think it's a real shame that one is considered a true man only if one can either fight or go round grabbing all the women in sight," he breathed, but his eyes were hard and were watching for any movement his opponent might attempt. "I've convinced you now, haven't I, Hargorin Deathbringer?"

Mallenia's picture of the helpless failed actor disappeared in a puff of smoke and Coïra saw him in a totally new light.

The women stared at him wondering how this change could have been so sudden. It could only have been that the previous incarnation had been a deceit.

Cool as a cucumber, Rodario let go of the beard, stood up and offered Hargorin his hand.

The thirdling got up without accepting any help. The shame had been too deeply felt and his beard had suffered, too.

Ireheart knew that the leader of the Black Squadron was never likely to forgive Rodario for this. *Blood will be spilt.*

"A charming interlude indeed," commented Slîn happily.

"Tell us how an actor learns to fight like that," Tungdil challenged Rodario.

"And why you took so much trouble *not* to look like your forefather," added Coïra. "If I think of you with a beard and mustache you're the spitting image of him."

"That's just what *I* said," mumbled Ireheart. "As soon as I saw him clamber on board."

Rodario returned to his seat and bowed to the ladies. "I must apologize to both of you, because I have been playing a part up till now. But now it is time to remove the veil from the secret of the unknown poet."

"You? You say that was you?" Coïra exclaimed, laughing in disbelief. She looked at him full of curiosity. "You're having us on."

"Impossible," said Mallenia at once. "You . . ." She stopped, in confusion.

Rodario bowed as if facing an adoring audience of theatergoers. "But, yes, indeed, I am the unknown poet," he answered. "Who would ever have suspected me—me who resembled fabulous forefather Rodario so little—of being the freedom-fighter and rabble-rouser, slayer of Lohasbranders and their orcs? Deception provides the best protection, as always."

Ireheart could not stop himself looking across at Tungdil when he heard these words—and he noted a sly smile playing round his friend's lips. *Only coincidence*, he fervently hoped.

Rodario stroked his prominent chin. "I noticed very soon how similar my looks were to those of my famous ancestor. On stage in Idoslane, Tabaîn and Gauragar I never wore make-up, but when the performances were over I would put on my disguise," he laughed, sitting down. "I made myself act the fool and lost the competitions on purpose, wanting to make sure nobody credited me with any intelligence."

Coïra pictured him that night when they had met in the tower in Mifurdania. "I really did have you down as a clumsy loser and clown," she said in surprise. "And I bet you *do* know how to ride?"

"Well, yes, I do, Your Majesty," he replied. "It was a role I was playing. And of course I do know how to swim or I would never have survived the fall from the walls of the shaft."

"A real hero," said Mallenia with a grin. "There we were, thinking the poor man was needing help, when all along he's a trained fighter. And a good one, at that, as I've just seen."

Rodario winked at her. "Thank you . . . must I say 'Your Highness' to you?" She dismissed the thought with a gesture. "But that is only part of the truth. Because there is not just *the one* unknown poet."

"What are you going on about?" Ireheart frowned. "You just told us . . ."

"There isn't just *the one*." Rodario raised his forefinger, smiling as he did so. "The competition in Mifurdania is a brilliant front for us all. The descendants of the Incredible Rodario have been working for freedom ever since the Dragon took over. Whether male or female, we have dedicated ourselves to the fight for liberty and have been working against the occupying powers wherever we go with our traveling theaters. We hang our poems on doors and walls and keep the thought of freedom alive in people's hearts. We can travel everywhere in Lohasbrand's conquered lands and we fight the Dragon with our own means." He took a gulp of wine. "The competition serves the purpose of letting us exchange news, write new lines, make new plans. We are always ready to support the people against the vassals of the Scaly One as soon as the gods grant us an opportunity. We know their weaknesses, their habits, their secret camps— everything!" He lifted his glass in salute and toasted Tungdil. "Thanks to you, Tungdil Goldhand, the opportunity has now arrived. The gods have sent you to us." He drank to Tungdil's health and the assembled company joined in the toast.

Coïra looked hard at him, eager questions on her lips. "Tell me: What really happened that evening at the tower?"

Rodario laughed. "We freed The Incomparable but we forgot to take his valuables with us. There were a few very rare pieces and I dared to return for them. When you found me I had already collected them. And I handed them back to The Incomparable Rodario in the alleyway without your seeing what I was up to." He beamed at her and struck a pose.

"Just like the Incredible Rodario," Ireheart acknowledged. "Add a little beard and I'd be convinced he had survived the last two hundred and fifty cycles, just like me."

The queen nodded.

"The death of this friend pained me very much, but luckily it escaped your notice," he went on. "I knew the cause would continue to exist. Today I can see the fight was worth it."

"And why did you accompany Coïra when she escaped?" Mallenia wanted to know. "Did I get that bit right?"

"Well, there was a sudden opportunity to get to know the maga slightly better and to find out whether or not she could be won over to our cause, namely to prepare for a rebellion. If I had got the impression that she was a devout little woman, I would have pushed off, sharpish." Rodario bowed again. "But I quickly realized that you were anything but submissive. So I stayed and observed you and how you acted. Increasingly I realized that things would work out." He looked at the Ido girl. "When you and the älf turned up, Mallenia, the scales fell from my eyes: Girdlegard was heading for freedom. Or for ruin. The first option I wanted to support; the second to prevent."

"I see freedom coming," replied Coïra warmly. "Who would be able to resist this alliance of determined groups?"

He smiled at her.

Ireheart rubbed his hands in glee. "Excellent! We've got everything we need. If Rodario contacts his friends and Mallenia gets in touch with hers, the storm can break. So we can concentrate entirely on the south, now, Scholar, can't we?"

Tungdil rubbed his forehead and touched the scar. His brown eye stared rigidly into space; he did not seem to have been listening.

"What about Sisaroth?" Barskalín wanted to know. "I know him. Among other things he trained the Zhadár, and he won't give up until he has avenged the death of his sister. If he realizes the queen and Mallenia are still alive, we'll have a dangerous älf on our tails, ready to pick us off one by one."

"Hmm. I'm sure he's more likely to hold back and wait for the Dragon to attack," Hargorin said, disagreeing with him. "I've known the Dsôn Aklán for a very long time. They would do anything to preserve their city in Dsôn Bhará from harm. We understand they intend to found a new älfar empire there. Sisaroth must think that Lohasbrand will be sending at least a scouting party out into the älfar regions to investigate what has been happening on his own territory."

Barskalín thought about it. "That could be so."

"And if Elria's having a good day, the black-eyes could just have drowned in the tidal wave," Ireheart chipped in cheerfully. "That's if he was anywhere near just now."

Suddenly, Tungdil's body convulsed. He sank with a moan onto the table, holding his head. Blood oozed out between his fingers.

The dwarves sprang up and pulled out their weapons, thinking there had been an attack, but Ireheart saw that the old scar on his friend's forehead had opened up. "Come on, give me a hand, let's get him up to his room," he told Hargorin and Barskalín.

"Shall I?" Coïra had risen. "A healing spell . . ."

"No, no magic!" Boïndil was emphatic on that score, not knowing how the armor would react. "It's an old wound. He must have hit his head back there on the ship and the scar has come open. I'll put in some stitches. We leave at sun-up." He left the company and he and Hargorin and Barskalín carried Tungdil to bed through the taproom and up to the guestroom at the back, where they laid him on the bed.

"Thanks." Ireheart sent the dwarves away and waited until they had left the room.

The door closed just in time.

Tungdil opened his eye suddenly and Ireheart saw once more the mysterious vortex of colors round the black of the pupil.

The open wound closed itself with a slight plop, and the facial bones moved gratingly, giving the dwarf a thinner countenance that reminded the horrified Ireheart much more of the way an älf would look.

"By Vraccas!" he groaned, staggering back two paces and grabbing the handle of his crow's beak. It looked as if his friend were changing shape.

Fine black lines appeared from under the golden eye patch, seeming to cut the face into segments. Drops of blood dripped out—then all the runes on the armor glowed, forcing Boïndil to shut his eyes.

When he could see again, his friend looked as he had done before he had swooned. There were no more wounds on his face, the scar had healed and the black lines had gone; the familiar visage of old.

Ireheart approached the bed carefully. "What shall I do with you, Scholar?" he whispered, swallowing hard. "Whenever I think I can trust you something happens to feed my suspicions." He pulled a stool over and decided it would be better if he kept watch in the room that night.

And he could not even say for sure whether it was to protect Tungdil, or to protect their group from his influence.

Girdlegard,
Former Queendom of Weyurn,
Entrance to the Red Mountains,
Spring, 6492nd Solar Cycle

Ireheart rode behind Tungdil with his eyes on the slopes of the Red Mountains. Even though he gave the impression of studying the landscape, he was thinking about that night when Tungdil had, for a time, undergone a short-lived change. A frightening change . . .

They had never spoken about it and their company believed the fairy story about his having fainted. *What is wrong with him? Is it a demon inside him? Is it a curse he's under?* The chorus of doubters in Ireheart's head was singing fit to bust.

On Tungdil's orders they had taken the old path leading to a narrow valley that wound its way to a dark-red mountain.

Older memories rose up in Ireheart's mind as they approached the entrance.

There were five bends in the valley and in the old days the firstlings had erected strongholds here, thick defensive ramparts with gates secured by dwarf-runes to keep their enemies out. The two of them had once fled here to escape from the älfar Sinthoras and Caphalor when they were looking for a firstling smith, and had found one in the shape of a dwarf-woman: Balyndis Steelfinger, now the fifthlings' queen.

The old buildings had gone. Today there were wooden palisades instead of walls. Behind the pointed stakes he could see the glint of helmets and spears; judging by their size, these would be orcs.

"Up there," Tungdil pointed at the Red Mountains, "is where the entrance used to be."

"Not anymore. It disappeared when the stronghold went. The Dragon demolished everything that smacked of the first-lings." Rodario pointed to one side. "Behind that heap of stones there's said to be a huge cavern. It's a passage the Scaly One made for himself and the Lohasbranders use it to get into the dwarves' cave system."

"That will be the old emergency exit gate," Ireheart supposed. He was occupied in trying to count the helmets he could see. "I think they've only got about twenty guards. Pig-faces."

"Why would they put any more here?" said Slîn, his eyes glued on the sky. "Who would want to enter the lair of a dragon?"

"Dwarves," replied Ireheart briskly. "Our ancestors drove off the dragons and we'll be doing it again." He looked at Tungdil. "You want us to ride into the valley in broad daylight?"

"No. The Zhadár can show us what they've learned from the älfar," he said, looking at Barskalín. "You take on the gates one after another. Don't open them until all the guards are dead. Find out how we can get inside without the Dragon knowing."

"If we want to empty his treasure hoard wouldn't it be better if we slipped in without killing the guards? It will only draw attention to ourselves if we attack them," Rodario pointed out. "Lohasbrand will act more swiftly then than we would like."

"The orcs will die silently. It will be some time before their deaths are noticed." Tungdil pointed to Hargorin.

"We've been discussing the matter en route and feel that we should split up as soon as we've plundered the hoard. The Zhadár will go with us and Hargorin will lead the Black Squadron. They'll take a different route to the south and some of them will go off to the dwarf realms as messengers to request they send their armies so that we can proceed against Lot-Ionan. Others will ride to Aiphatòn." He indicated Rodario. "And they'll take his letters to the descendants of the fabulous Rodario the Incredible."

It's a good thing we met up. We wouldn't have been able to scrape that many messengers together from our original numbers. I suppose they'll be reliable. Ireheart was not upset to learn they would be losing the Desirers. "We'll rendezvous by the Blue Mountains, I suppose," he said.

"Preparations should be finished by the middle of spring. Ours and the emperor's. We can start then." Tungdil glanced up at the imposing mountain glowing red in the light.

"I still don't understand how we get away from Lohasbrand if, as they say, he can smell you from miles away." Rodario was not satisfied yet. "And don't tell me I'm just an actor with no idea about warfare." Mallenia and Coïra gave him silent support on this.

"But that's what you are," said Hargorin contemptuously.

"The Dragon won't know at first what's happening. He'll think it's rebels and he'll leave it to the orcs to put the insurgency down—that is, until he notices what's missing," explained Tungdil. "By that time we'll be halfway to Lot-Ionan. *At least!* We'll have to ride all day and change horses when they tire. Without that head start we'll never make it. If he catches us, then . . ." he glanced over at Coïra ". . . we'll have to kill Lohasbrand. But if that happens we lose a vital element in our strategy to weaken Lot-Ionan. If he gets too close, we'll attempt to drive him off."

"You're putting a whole lot of responsibility my way," said the queen, looking doubtful.

"I am. Because I have to. It's in battle we get our warrior hearts, not when we sit listening to tales about war." He fixed his eye on her. "Come right out and say if you're too scared. Then I'll change the plan."

Coïra's maga-pride was hurt. "Of course we'll manage to defeat the Dragon, and the magus, too. By the time we arrive, Lot-Ionan will be weak enough, so I, too, assume our strategy will succeed."

The sun disappeared behind the clouds and the first raindrops fell noisily onto their metal armor.

Tungdil turned his pony and rode away from the valley entrance. "There are caves over there. We'll make camp till the Zhadár return and report the outcome of their mission."

They found shelter before the rain got heavier. Soon it was streaming down over the cave entrance. It washed away the last of the snow and removed any trace of the company's tracks.

Dwarves and humans settled in the large cavern to rest before the attack they would be launching on the Lohasbranders and the orcs. Ireheart saw to his pony and wandered around, observing the Desirers. Hargorin was selecting his messengers so that they could leave at first light to take the news to Aiphatòn, the resistance fighters and the dwarf-tribes. *There's no stopping it now.*

Then he went over to the Invisibles to see how the preparations were going for their night's work.

They were sitting talking quietly with Barskalín. They had

short beards all, were black from head to foot and were heavily armed. *I really can't tell them apart. Do I dare to talk to them?* he wondered. *Who knows how many of them will return?*

This thought did not arrive unprompted. The doubters in his head were demanding to know how many would return. Whoever knew the sign for controlling the Scholar's armor and making it freeze would know more about the runes generally. It was important. He'd already decided how he would approach the subject.

He waited until the Zhadár had stopped talking, then went slowly nearer, taking care to ensure Barskalín was looking the other way, because he would be sure not to want his people talking to a secondling. *Talking? Being interrogated, more like.*

"Might I have a closer look at your weaponry?" Ireheart asked the nearest of the warriors, who was sitting on the ground sharpening his dagger. He smiled and squatted down. That way he would not attract attention.

The Zhadár turned and looked up, puzzled. "Of course," he said, handing Ireheart the weapon.

"Do you lot like jokes? My favorite's the one about the orc and the dwarf."

"Really? I've never really got that one," replied the Zhadár. "Why would an orc ask one of us the way?"

Ireheart was at a loss there. "But that's what makes it so funny."

"Funny? I just think it's . . . unlikely. Any greenskin knows that a dwarf would cut his head off." He laughed. "And then there's the punch line! What the dwarf says and does . . . Very strange. But not funny."

"Ah," said Ireheart, confused. "Tastes differ, it seems." He decided to change his tactics, away from the topic of jokes. He turned the dagger in his hands and admired the runes and the strength of the blade in order to flatter the Zhadár. "What do these symbols mean?"

The other dwarf explained patiently that the runes promised death to the enemy.

"Just like us," Ireheart said, a little clumsily. "I mean to say, you used to be like us . . ." He stopped short and handed the knife back.

Now it was the Zhadár's turn to grin. "What is it you want to know, Doubleblade?"

"Is it so obvious?"

"Yes. You're an excellent warrior but a terrible spy."

"It's not really my thing. I like to do things more directly." Ireheart laughed and sat down; he heard and felt his flask slip off his belt onto the cave floor. He drew a symbol on the floor similar to the rune that Tungdil bore on his armor.

The Zhadár said, "You've seen it on the high king's armor. Frak told us he'd given Goldhand quite a shock."

"Frak?"

"The Zhadár you came across in the Outer Lands."

"So do you know the secret of the armor?"

"Is there one? Because it's magic?"

Ireheart nodded. "Yes."

"It's not a secret. Any magus or maga and anyone that knows a bit about magic will see it straightaway on the high king. Or was it a particular sort of magic?" The Zhadár went back to sharpening his dagger. "I'm not allowed to talk about it."

"But I *must* know. If an älf casts a spell at Tungdil and

locks him into the armor again, I've got to be able to unfreeze him without taking my crow's beak to him every time." He found the black, almost empty eye sockets of his opposite number unsettling. It was hard to have a proper conversation with a dwarf whose eyes you could not read.

"You used your weapon to release him from the armor?" The dwarf laughed. "It's a miracle your hands didn't explode."

"I was careful." Ireheart was getting quite excited. He seemed to be close to solving a few puzzles. He glanced over at Barskalín and Tungdil. Both were busy. "Tell me, please! The high king's life may depend on it."

"It probably will." The Zhadár put down his whetstone. "Remember these words." He uttered some sounds that Ireheart was not able to copy.

Hurt, Boïndil regarded the other dwarf, suddenly convinced that he was talking to the one he called the Trouble Maker. His sounded like the joker's voice. "I can't say that."

"Then practice. For the high king's sake." He chortled, then stopped and swore, grimacing. The whole thing took only a couple of seconds, but it was enough to scare Ireheart into taking hold of his weapon. But the Zhadár had calmed down. "What else?"

"So they are really älf runes?"

"Yes. The ones on our armor are pure älf but there are some on the high king's armor that I can't read," the Zhadár admitted. "It's obvious. But they've got something älf-like about them. And dwarflike." He saw Barskalín had just turned round, and frowned. "There's something I've got to do," he said, getting up.

"Hey, hang on! Wait a moment. I knew all that. The explanation?" Ireheart was disappointed but realized he was not going to get any more secrets out of the Zhadár. But he'd been told the words needed to release the paralysis of the armor.

He wondered how many commands there were to make his friend's armor perform other tricks, whether the wearer wanted to or otherwise. *He really ought to take it off when we meet Lot-Ionan in battle. I shall have to sell him the idea somehow*, he decided.

He reached for his flask and opened it without looking, while continuing to watch the Zhadár company. They were working quietly, sharpening their weapons and exchanging the armor of the Black Squadron for their own. They kept stopping, closing their eyes and seeming to pray before carrying on.

Ireheart's lips were on the neck of the flask and liquid sloshed into his mouth; he swallowed without paying attention.

Then he noticed the foul taste—not a bit like the herbal tea he had filled his flask with. He spat the second mouthful onto the sandy floor of the cave. The liquid was a dull blackish red, viscous and slow to disperse.

"What's that?" Ireheart looked at the flask. *That's not mine!* His own still lay on the ground where it had fallen.

Revolted by the taste he spat again, then grabbed his own bottle and rinsed his mouth out. The metallic taste reminded him of blood and strong alcohol and it stayed heavy on his tongue, like pitch.

"Whose is this?" he called out, holding up the flask after he had screwed the top back on.

The Zhadár he had been talking to came running up. "It's mine," he said, annoyed. "I must have dropped it." He grabbed hold of it as eagerly as if it contained one of Girdlegard's prime wines.

"What's it got in it?"

The Zhadár looked shocked. "Why? You didn't drink any, did you?"

Something in his voice warned Ireheart not to admit he had. Instead he pointed to the damp patch in the sand. "No, but it can't have been closed properly and the stuff that's leaked looks odd and smells peculiar," he lied, hoping Vraccas would not make him blush. "Is it herb brandy?" He grinned. "Maybe that's where you get your special powers! A magic drink, eh?"

The dark dwarf leaned forward. "It's distilled elf blood," he muttered to Ireheart. "It's been modified with terrible älfar magic, then distilled, boiled up and diluted with brandy." Then the Zhadár pulled a face again, and gave four weird laughs before looking normal once more.

Ireheart felt sick. "Elf blood," he repeated. "What's it good for?"

"Our magic," sang the Zhadár. "Our magic." Then he turned and went back to his comrades.

"O Vraccas! What have I done that you punish me like this?" Ireheart murmured in distress, placing his hand on his stomach. "Who knows what that stuff will do to me?"

So long as he did not notice any change, he decided, he would keep his misfortune to himself. Maybe the crazy Zhadár had just been having him on and it was, perhaps, merely a harmless liqueur.

XIX

When darkness fell the Zhadár set off out from the cave in the pouring rain and disappeared into the murk after only a few paces, lost to Ireheart's view. Having glided out into the night, they seemed to become part of it.

"Odd fellows." Rodario nodded at the women. "I wonder what Boïndil has learned from that Zhadár." He went over to Ireheart.

Rodario's continued transformation had not escaped Coïra. She noted he now wore chain mail and carried a sword at his side. Having not shaved since his involuntary unmasking, he now sported a short beard on his square-jawed face. This and his manly bearing meant he had nothing in common with the figure everyone was familiar with: The eternal failure in the Mifurdania competitions.

Mallenia, on the other hand, was watching the maga, her rival, while at the same time berating herself for having fallen for a man who had never existed. Her heart had been captivated by a stage character, a seemingly vulnerable, clumsy man who had suddenly turned out to be brave and bold. The former incarnation had appealed to Mallenia more because she was a born protectress. But still . . .

Coïra sighed. "Who would have thought it?"

"That he's a real man?" Mallenia gave a bitter laugh and cut herself a slice of bread to spread with seed oil. "I'm as surprised as you."

The maga reached for her flask and took a drink. She looked at the Ido girl. "How does he kiss?" she demanded directly.

"What?" Mallenia nearly choked.

Coïra's eyes shone; she clasped her knees to her as she sat. "He stole a kiss, didn't he? What was it like? Tell me, do!"

"Are you in love with him?"

"Maybe," she answered daringly. "He'll think I'm a love-sick young girl if he finds out. But I don't care."

"Isn't he a bit too old for you? He's more my age, about thirty cycles, and you've surely only seen twenty?" Mallenia realized that her tone was unfriendly.

Coïra noticed it as well and looked at the Ido girl in puzzlement. "Is that a touch of jealousy?"

"No," she snapped—and next moment she was furious with herself. That had been as good as an acknowledgment. She had little experience in affairs of the heart. The struggle for freedom had left no room for that kind of thing. There had been only two short outings into the realm of physical passion.

"It seems to me his kiss has done more than you want to admit," said the maga, putting her leather drinking pouch back on the floor. She pushed back her dark hair and tied it at the nape. She could not help grinning. "So there we are, in the middle of a great adventure, just about to launch an attack on the Dragon, and we find we both fancy the same man. The gods have a strange sense of humor."

At first Mallenia wanted to deny everything, but she dismissed that idea. Why should she not own up to her feelings? "It's much harder for me, Coïra," she said. "I actually preferred him when he was Rodario the Clumsy."

"Then be glad you never saw him the way I did. You would have run a mile! We'll get him to play the helpless clown and audacious hero on alternate orbits." She handed the other girl her flask. "Let us vow never to fall out over him."

"Fall out?" Mallenia was not aware of any pact of friendship. She stared indecisively at the flask.

"Look! You'll soon be on the throne of Idoslane and I shall be taking over from my mother in Weyurn. How nice it would be if, as two future rulers, we were to get on well and not start fighting and feuding over some man. Otherwise we may end up with a war between our two countries." Even if it was clear from her smile that she did not mean these words seriously, there was a grain of truth in them.

So Mallenia accepted the flask, unscrewed the top and drank to sisterhood. Coïra then did the same. "He kisses in the most masculine way," the Ido girl confessed. "I was puzzled at the time but did not worry about it. My suspicions were overcome by his acting talents." She continued eating. "Are you going to tell him how you feel?"

"Tell him I love him?" The maga sighed. "I don't know. It would be . . . it would be so humiliating if I told him and he laughed at me. Or if he turned me down for another." She looked Mallenia in the eye. "It was you he stole the kiss from, not me. My jealousy is bound to be stronger than yours."

Mallenia hesitated. "Well, if you say so . . . But I think

he saw it as a sort of game. It wasn't serious. He has no idea how I feel about him."

They smiled at each other and both turned to look at Rodario, who seemed to sense their eyes on him. He swiveled round to meet the double gaze, and waved before turning back to his discussion with Ireheart.

"Men." Mallenia drew out her sword and proceeded to sharpen it.

Coïra cut herself a slice of ham. "You're better off than me."

"How do you mean?" asked Mallenia.

"You're good with weapons. I need magic to defend myself. And without a magic source my inner reserves are quickly exhausted." The maga chewed on the tasty meat. "And I'm not terribly brave. I've never needed to be."

"You're joking! You stood up to the älfar!"

"But I had lots of magic power in me then. No bravery required."

"You said you got some energy from the source in Lakepride when it was released in the explosion." Mallenia raised her head. "So you've got enough to cast some spells?"

"Of course. But it's not nearly as much as I would have absorbed on my normal long exposure." She spoke hesitantly. "I'm pinning my hopes on finding another source in the Red Mountains."

Now the Ido girl was paying close attention. She picked up the flask again. "If this pouch represents your potential reservoir, how much would you say you had at the moment?"

Coïra unscrewed the top and let the contents pour out in a thin stream until there was only a third left. Wordlessly, she put the lid back on and handed it back.

"Is that all?"

The maga shook her head. "That's it. But it'll be enough to deal with the orcs. The new source will give me back all my previous strength."

"And it won't be difficult to locate?"

"I have a feel for such things. There is a spell for detecting the presence of magic. That'll help a lot."

Mallenia gave her attention to her second sword. "You were right. I'd rather rely on cold steel for my defense."

Rodario came over to them. "And here we have the most enchanting ladies in all Girdlegard," he greeted them cheerily. "And the most powerful."

"He's overdoing it," Mallenia said to Coïra. "And anyway, *enchanting* would only apply to the maga." She picked up her sword and pointed it at Rodario. "I, on the other hand, am as *sharp* as steel and have *winning* ways, Rodario the Seventh." She flashed her eyes at him maliciously, while the dark-haired girl put her hand quickly over her mouth to stifle her giggles.

A bewildered Rodario turned from one to the other. "I get the impression that something has been cooked up in my absence. I feel I am the focus of a conspiracy."

"No. Don't worry. We wouldn't concern ourselves with trivial things," the maga returned, with a wink, helping herself to more food.

A Zhadár came back into camp with the news that the five gates were now open. At once the dwarves, together with the remains of the decimated Black Squadron, set off to join the Invisibles.

"They've not been gone long," Slîn said to Balyndar,

loading his crossbow as he walked. They left the cave together and ran down to the valley through the rain.

"I'd have liked to have seen it all, but they wouldn't let me go with them." Ireheart was curious about the Invisibles' special skills.

"It was probably better this way." Tungdil pulled out Bloodthirster. "It wouldn't have been your sort of fight, Ireheart. You're not silent when you attack orcs: You normally brandish your crow's beak, yell and swear a lot, and smash up their armor. It gets quite loud."

A Zhadár stood waiting for them at the first of the wooden gates, now open.

As they hurried through they saw a couple of dozen orcs lying in the mud, with their throats cut. Others had received dents and slashes to their armor and some had their heads entirely missing.

This image was regularly repeated. A Zhadár stood at each of the gates with massacred guards behind him in the mire.

Ireheart was impressed. "Well, fry me an elf!" he murmured.

At last they arrived at the pass that led to the Red Mountains. The orcs had erected a further wooden palisade; this time it was Barskalín who was waiting for them.

"We killed the sentries like you said," he reported to Tungdil. "No alarm was sounded."

"I would have expected nothing less and am very pleased," Tungdil praised him. "How many orcs so far?"

"We killed a hundred and fourteen of them and two Lohasbranders who were in the guardroom. They were acting as officers," the sytràp explained. "We took a third one prisoner because we thought you'd want to interrogate him."

"Excellent." Tungdil followed him inside; Ireheart and the rest joined them.

The cave was high-ceilinged, stark and bare. The orcs and Lohasbranders had not troubled to make it homely. On closer examination faint remains of dwarf-runes and masonry carvings could still be seen. At the front of the cave, right next to the palisade fence, there were two wooden barrack buildings where the orc crews would have been quartered; nearby were two smaller sheds. Barskalín explained one was a storeroom and the other was a jail cell whose two orc occupants they also slaughtered.

Ireheart listened in surprise. *These Zhadár are as dangerous as the black-eyes!*

Hargorin told his soldiers to guard the cave and to spread out over the four passageways. None of the tunnels was large enough to admit a full-grown dragon, they were relieved to note. Lohasbrand would not be able to attack them in here.

On the way into the first of the barrack buildings, where the Zhadár were holding the captive Lohasbrander, Ireheart inspected the corpses. "It's a mystery how the Invisibles managed to do all that without the pig-faces putting up any resistance," he remarked to Slîn, so astonished that he could not help commenting.

"They've learned a frightening amount from the älfar," the fourthling agreed. "I keep thinking about how well they know my native land. They could easily do the same thing in the Brown Mountains." He looked at Balyndar. "Or with the fifthlings. Or the freelings. Just imagine what might have happened had the älfar trained up some thirdlings keen to kill the other dwarves! We'd have been wiped out ages ago."

"They wouldn't have found it this easy," Balyndar observed, looking at one of the dead orcs, whose throat had been cut.

"But the losses would have been terrible," Ireheart replied, as he went inside the building.

Tungdil was standing with Barskalín in front of the captured Lohasbrander, who they had forced to his knees and chained to a wooden pillar. He wore black lamellar armor and had light fair hair sticking up all over his head. In stature he was podgy yet strongly built, and the fair beard on his broad face was stained red with the blood oozing from a cut on his left cheek.

"That's Wielgar!" cried Coïra. "He's one of the Lohasbranders who were in Mifurdania recently. He's the one who had The Incomparable Rodario executed."

"Well, well, the little maga," he groaned. "That attempt at rebellion will cost you dear. The Dragon will reduce your land to rubble and ashes!"

"We've things planned for Lohasbrand. He won't have time to get up to any such tricks." Tungdil planted himself in front of the man. "Where will we find the magic source and the Dragon's treasure?" Wielgar started to laugh. Tungdil went on, "Before you do that, think hard. I am a past master in administering pain." He drew up a small bench, released the man's right arm and forced it down onto the wood. "We'll start with the fingers, bit by bit. I'll hammer each segment flat as a pancake." He bound up the upper arm so that the blood loss would not prove fatal. "Then I'll make my way up the limb, cutting it into slices. I'll let you see them before I shove them in your mouth to keep your strength up. Then we'll have a go with the other arm."

Wielgar seemed worried. "I am an admirer of the Dragon and one of his highest officers . . ."

"I couldn't care less." The flat side of Bloodthirster's blade flashed down and the tip of one finger was transformed into a mushy mess; the nail fell off and blood flowed.

Wielgar yelled. "You shall all die!" he vowed. "Give up now."

Tungdil reminded him, "You know what my questions are. Do we have any answers yet?"

"There is no magic source," he moaned. And, as the sword was lifted again, he screamed, "There is no magic source! Believe me! We know the rumors but we've never found anything."

"How would you? You're not magi," Coïra remarked.

"The Dragon told us," he countered, one eye on Bloodthirster, which was hovering over his hand. "I swear by Samusin that there's no magic at all in the Red Range. Except for the maga."

Coïra looked at Mallenia and implored her silently not to think of mentioning her present weakened state. "That's all right," she said, feigning indifference. "I've got enough magic to kill ten dragons. But I shall use a spell to check whether or not he's telling the truth; if his next answer is a lie, his head will burst open." She moved her fingers, closed her eyes and touched his brow with her left index finger. "Is there a magic source?"

"No!" Wielgar cried out, beside himself with terror. "No, by all . . ."

"And the treasure?" Tungdil reminded the Lohasbrander and took aim for a further blow.

"Miles away, seventy miles to the west," he said straightaway. "He had everything moved there, all the tribute collected in his name."

Ireheart could not restrain himself anymore. "How many pig-faces does he have under his command?"

Wielgar shrugged. "Thousands. We counted them."

"Right, right. Thousands, then." Tungdil slammed the weapon down and shattered the little finger completely. "Try again. Or do you want the maga to do another spell, to make your head . . ."

"Not more than seven thousand," Wielgar shouted. "They live in the caves and we call them up when we need them. Then there's another thousand traveling around with the governors in Weyurn." He stared at the dwarf in rage. "They'll be here any time now and they'll wipe you out. A report has gone out about this attack."

"It has certainly not," Barskalín contradicted. "Apart from him no one was left alive, Tungdil. Nobody escaped."

"You missed one." Wielgar gave a sly grin. "A second lookout position, in the rocks above the entrance. The guards will be on their way."

"We should get out of here," said Coïra uneasily.

"Without nicking a single thing from the treasure hoard? Why should Lohasbrand bother coming after us?"

"We need something to make the Dragon follow us," Tungdil said.

"How about this guy?" suggested Rodario, pointing at Wielgar. "If he's really as important as he claims to be, Lohasbrand is sure to want to have him back."

Wielgar laughed again. "Another of those stupid Rodarios. They get absolutely everywhere. But he's just right for this farce."

A loud hissing roar echoed around the cave; excited shouts came through from outside, and steps approached the barracks.

"Lohasbrand!" Mallenia looked at everyone. "He's found us!"

"He can't get in through the passages. We're safe from him." Ireheart looked at the doorway, where one of the Black Squadron came rushing through. "But he's not safe from us!"

"The Dragon is coming, sir," the squadron soldier reported to Tungdil. "We heard his roar through the second passageway. Hargorin wants to know what your instructions are."

Wielgar laughed triumphantly. "If you ask me, you should run for your lives. Perhaps you'll find a little hole outside— somewhere to hide in."

Tungdil studied the Lohasbrander at length, making his confident merriment ebb quickly away. "We attack," he announced. "Then I'll come back and cut your head off." He ran out.

"Huzzah! We're off to get the Dragon!" Ireheart raised his crow's beak. "I still need to cross him off my list of monsters." He followed his friend.

Slîn sighed as he looked at his crossbow. "I've got the wrong weapon again. What use am I against dragon scales?"

"Shoot him in the eye?" came Rodario's helpful suggestion. "If I were a dragon I'm sure that would annoy me terribly." He looked at the women. "It'll be a tough battle, but we have an excellent maga on our side. I'll cover you but you'll have to kill Lohasbrand for me."

Coïra attempted a smile, and failed. Mallenia put her hand on the queen's shoulder to encourage her. Together they ran off after the dwarves, who had raced out like a black cloud toward the second passageway.

Again came the Dragon's deafening roar, and hot stinking steam entered the corridor. Surely a prelude to worse to come.

Ireheart did not move from Tungdil's side; they reached a further cave.

Without warning, a burst of flame shot down on them!

The Zhadár and the Black Squadron raised their shields to defend themselves against the fire.

Ireheart could feel the heat swarming over them, but the shields had protected them from severe burns. *Isn't that a bit on the harmless side? We should have been incinerated! There's nothing hotter than a dragon's breath!* "Overhead," he called. "He must have climbed up on the ceiling, the coward!"

But, however hard he looked, there was no dragon to be seen clinging to the ceiling. When he looked at his shield he noticed there was only a little soot on it. The fifthlings' forge had once been set alight by the breath of a dragon. Lohasbrand, in contrast, seemed to have no really dangerous flames at his disposal.

But the Scaly One's roar erupted again, from the back of the cave.

Now they could see the dark-green dragon-head perched on top of a long neck. The elongated skull was visible over the top of a boulder and smoke was rising from the nostrils at the end of its narrow snout. It was a threat, to force them to leave the cave.

Ireheart took a firmer grip on his weapon. "How did it get there so fast?"

Soldiers appeared from behind the stone and took up their positions. Ireheart reckoned there were about eighty warriors, all wearing lamellar plated armor and emerald green cloaks: On their heads they wore familiar helmets in the shape of a dragon, and they carried spears and shields.

"The mighty Dragon Lohasbrand commands you to leave here immediately," one of their number called out. "Or he will kill you and all your families."

"That's exactly why we are here," said Coïra, stepping forward. "To stop this. We have put up with him and you for far too long." She was relying on support from Tungdil Goldhand and the dwarves. *Should a warrior heart be beating quite so fast?* "Weyurn demands the return of its freedom!"

One of the Lohasbranders lowered the tip of his spear to aim it at her. "The Dragon laughs at your crazy attempt to seize power. If you disappear, now, he is prepared to forget what you have planned."

Ireheart thought this conduct on the part of the man, and particularly on the part of the Dragon, was very strange. It ought to have been easy for such a monster to intimidate them all by sheer size and strength. *They say the Dragon is fifty paces long and ten paces broad.* A glance at Tungdil assured him that his friend was thinking along the same lines—or had he already worked out what was happening? Had he missed some clue from Wielgar's interrogation?

He studied the block of stone above which the dragon-head rose up. "*That little rock* is never going to be big enough to hide Lohasbrand," he murmured, and waved to Slîn to join him. "Shoot the dragon in the eye."

"Did Tungdil say to?"

"No, we don't need him."

"Charming . . ."

He shoved him. "Come on. Hurry up!"

Slîn hesitated. "You want to provoke an attack?"

"Get on with it!" snarled Ireheart. "Nothing will happen." He stood so that the archer could aim at the target without being seen by the Lohasbranders.

Slîn took a deep breath and held it while he drew back the trigger mechanism. A click, and the bolt whizzed through the air, hitting the creature in the middle of the right pupil.

"You never missed?" asked Ireheart accusingly.

"No, of course not!" Slîn was furious. "I couldn't miss a target like that even after a jug of brandy and a barrel of black beer!" He loaded the weapon again to prove his point and a second projectile landed up touching the first. "Charming, indeed! It doesn't feel any pain!"

Nobody had spotted what they were up to.

The rationale behind this extraordinary phenomenon suddenly occurred to Ireheart. He looked at Slîn excitedly. "At this rate we might stud him all over with bolts and he wouldn't notice at all."

"True." The fourthling shuddered. "An immortal dragon? By Vraccas . . ."

"No." Ireheart laughed out loud. "*That's it!* That's why he's not coming out from behind the rock."

"What?" called Slîn. "Why not?" He did not get an answer.

Ireheart went over to Tungdil and whispered his idea.

The Scholar smiled and clapped him on the shoulder. "Well done! If you carry on like this, Girdlegard won't need me at all. Splendid, Ireheart! I could sense something wasn't right. That explains everything. You've taken away the Dragon's power." He lifted Bloodthirster and looked along the ranks. All the dwarves were awaiting his orders. "Maga Coïra, you and Mallenia and Rodario keep back behind our lines. If the Dragon attacks you then go into action. We'll do the rest." Then he lowered his sword and stormed forward.

The Zhadár and Black Squadron were close on his heels, yelling fit to bust and brandishing their weapons.

They may have looked like a random horde but these warriors were well trained and adopted a distinct formation. Hargorin's soldiers went in as the first wave, to carve out gaps in the enemy lines. The Zhadár would then push through these breaks to attack like shadows from behind to confuse the foe.

Ireheart threw himself into the fray with passion. "Hey there, Lohasbranders! Let's have your shields out of the way!" he bellowed enthusiastically, smashing the first one with a crow's beak broadside. He ducked under a darting spear tip, took a step to the left and hacked his metal spike into the opponent's ribcage; there was a gratifying scream.

Ireheart sprang through into the gap, pushing away the Zhadár trying to follow him. "Get off! This is my place!" he snarled, yanking the metal spur out of the dead body to thrust it into the living body of the next foe careless enough to leave himself undefended.

The iron hook tore the lamellar garb apart and sliced through the flesh beneath it. The Lohasbrander fell groaning to the floor.

"One less!" cheered the dwarf, delivering a sharp kick to another's shield, making the holder fall backwards. Ireheart jumped onto the shield, crushing the man underneath. "It's always going to be dark for you now, dragon friend," he growled, whacking the flat side of the crow's beak into the man's face.

Behind his stone the Dragon was roaring and raging—but he wasn't coming out.

Ireheart had fought his way through the ranks of men, clearing a path the Zhadár were making use of. They, Tungdil and he sneaked round behind the boulder to launch themselves on Lohasbrand with loud oaths.

What they saw made them stop in mid-attack.

A dozen men and women were operating the dragon-head and neck on long poles, which they were raising and lowering to give the impression the creature was moving. Others were making the snout open and close; directly adjacent five more of them were banging away on boxes and drums and metal sheets to create the dragon's roaring voice. They had constructed a sort of funnel arrangement to increase the volume of noise.

"Puppeteers! Will you look at that! Just what I thought!" Ireheart grinned. "You can't trick a dwarf that easily, you idiot play actors!" He sprang into their midst, whirling his crow's beak in circles; the Zhadár and the squadron followed suit.

The wooden poles that were wielded against them soon fell, smashed by powerful blows; Ireheart's battle-fury kicked in, sending a red mask of rage over his face.

Yelling and cheering he dealt out shattering blows with his weapon, feeling blood spurting, and hearing the cries and groans of the wounded and dying—until his friend's voice reached him. With immense difficulty he forced back the tide of fever, the fire in his veins, the bloodlust that had taken him over. He rubbed his eyes and surveyed the carnage.

Human remains lay scattered around.

They had not put up much of a fight and Ireheart had been disappointed at the lack of resistance. Catching his breath, he aimed a kick at the stuffed dragon-head. Sweat was pouring off him. "Ha! Dead!" He cleaned off his weapon in a foul temper. "What a let-down. I still can't cross off killing a dragon on my list."

Hargorin came round the rock with a troop of his men expecting to help Ireheart fight the Dragon. He halted the soldiers and came over to inspect what was left of the enemy soldiers and the monster. "Wielgar has a lot of explaining to do," was his only comment. Coïra, Mallenia and Rodario also arrived and stared in astonishment at the bloodbath and the dragon cadaver.

"I don't need Wielgar." Boïndil looked at Tungdil. "The Dragon must have died some time back and the Lohasbranders kept quiet about it so that the people would carry on obeying them. And the pig-faces, too, I suppose." The one-eyed dwarf nodded.

The maga clenched her fists. "To Tion with the lot of the bastards! They deserve their deaths three times over. How long have they been pulling the wool over our eyes?" She almost did not want to know the answer so that she would not have to reproach herself with anything. Had they not been terrified of reprisals from the Dragon they would surely have driven out the occupying forces from their island realm and her mother would have been able to free herself much sooner from her shackles. Then she would never have been slain in battle with the älfar . . .

Hatred flamed up in her heart on a scale she had never experienced before. She wanted every last one of the enemy to know her feelings.

Coïra whirled round on her heel and hurried back to the barracks to confront Wielgar.

"Follow her." Tungdil ran after her and left it up to Hargorin and Barskalín to finish off the wounded and guard the cave entrance.

They reached the hut in time to see the maga slicing off the struggling, shrieking Wielgar's ears and hurling them disdainfully at him. She swung her sword arm in preparation for a blow to his heart, but Tungdil restrained her and pushed her aside.

"No, Your Majesty! First he has to answer some questions, then you shall have your revenge," he said to calm her. Rodario and Mallenia held Coïra back, and stopped her lunging at the prisoner, knife in hand.

Tungdil confronted Wielgar, whose shoulders were now drenched in the blood that was streaming down left and right. "We have defeated your friends, Lohasbrander. How long have you been playing this trick on the people of Weyurn?"

"All is lost. It's all over." The man sobbed and let himself hang drooping in his chains.

Ireheart threw some water over him. "Talk, longlegs. Or I'll get salt to rub in your wounds."

"Forty cycles," he whimpered.

"Forty?" yelled Coïra, quite beside herself. You've oppressed us for forty years without reason, letting us live in fear, just so you could live in luxury?" She lunged forward again. If it had not been for Rodario and Mallenia, she would have killed him there and then. "I curse you, Wielgar! I curse you and all your band!"

The Lohasbrander sobbed. "We found the Dragon one morning dead in a ravine and we knew our reign would be over if anyone found out. So we brought his body back and stuffed it so we could trick the orcs and ensure they would go on serving us."

"Just what I said," Ireheart remarked, glad to have his theory confirmed. He folded his arms across his broad dwarf-chest.

"Old Clever Clogs," replied Slîn.

"For once," added Balyndar spitefully.

Tungdil kicked Wielgar. "How many orcs have you got?"

"The ones you killed and one thousand in Weyurn. That's all," the man howled. "The dwarves have blocked the western approaches and aren't letting any more orcs through."

Ireheart stood up tall and proud. "Balyndis will be pleased to hear that. Her tribe has done good work there. Vraccas has blessed them with an iron will." He turned to the human and asked, "What happened to the treasure?"

Wielgar sniffed. Saliva and mucus ran down his face. "We spent it all ages ago. There's nothing left. That's why we raised the tribute rate, so we could start getting some more money in."

Coïra spat at him. "You are worse than the orcs, worse than the lowest scum," she hissed. "To oppress and deceive your own people out of pure greed!"

Wielgar let his head sink down and whimpered to himself.

Tungdil came over to the queen. "Majesty, your realm has achieved freedom quicker than we thought possible. The squadron's messengers can spread the news throughout the land and we'll send them out with parts of the Dragon's head as evidence." He looked at her sharply. "You will still accompany me to the south to fight Lot-Ionan."

"I . . ." She was struggling to reply.

"Your help is more sorely needed than ever. If Lohasbrand no longer exists as an adversary to keep Lot-Ionan in check, we will need your magic powers or Girdlegard cannot survive." The brown in his single eye seemed to grow darker. "If we don't succeed in defeating the magus, evil will pour out of the Black Abyss unchecked. Not even the eoîl and avatars were as bad or as powerful a scourge as what will befall us all if that happens."

Coïra gulped and looked at Mallenia. "Yes. Of course I shall follow you, high king," she replied meekly. "Without you and your bold plan I would never have come to the Red Mountains and my people would not be free. I am in your debt. My whole land is in your debt."

He nodded to her and smiled. Like the old Tungdil, thought Ireheart. "Thank you. We shall rest for the length of one orbit and then we shall set out for the Blue Mountains. We'll leave messages here for the firstlings. They will find them sooner or later. We don't have time to send an expedition out west to look for them." He left the barracks to inform Hargorin and Barskalín.

Now Rodario and Mallenia could release the maga.

"Go outside," said Coïra quietly. "I want to be alone with this scum." Her eyes were brimming with tears of rage. They left the room, and as Ireheart pulled the door to behind him they heard Wielgar's first scream.

"I wouldn't have thought her capable of that," commented Rodario. "She looked so gentle. So kind."

"Just think what the Lohasbranders have done to her." Mallenia could certainly understand the queen's attitude. She wanted to get all the älfar in her clutches one by one to pay them back for the terror they had inflicted for so very many cycles on her land.

Wielgar cried out again, loud and shrill. Full of the fear of death.

"Will you be dealing in similar vein with the vassal-rulers?" The actor studied her face intently.

"They will be tried in the courts. We'll take them prisoner, subject them to judgment and punish them according to the verdicts." The Ido girl looked at Hargorin. "He is the best example of how easily one can be deceived."

"I could employ him in my theater troupe." Rodario nodded. "He tricked the älfar for such a long time in order to be ready when the opportunity arose. If he had courted their enmity it would have served him and the thirdlings ill indeed."

They went into the neighboring building, where they found the orcs' quarters. It was surprisingly clean and did not even smell strongly.

"What about the thirdlings in älfar service who oppressed the population in whole swathes of the land?" Rodario and Mallenia sat down on a bench by the window, from where they could keep an eye on events in the cave.

"It will be difficult to get Urgon, Idoslane and Gauragar to understand that the thirdlings were only acting a role. I'll ask the high king how we should proceed. If the thirdlings were to withdraw into the mountains, no one will pursue them." Mallenia tried to work out how much truth she could confide in Rodario as to the present state of Coïra's magic powers.

She looked him in the eyes and her heart started to race. Even now, when he had shrugged off the mantle of helplessness, she could not take her eyes off him. *Where will it all end?* "The journey in the next few orbits will take us right across Rân Ribastur and Sangpur," she said, to take her mind off things. And she wanted to hear his point of view. "What do you know about the queendoms?"

He held her eyes, searching to read her expression until she dropped her gaze. "Well, Rân Ribastur is covered in trees and Sangpur is covered in sand," he said, amused by her reaction.

"That's not what I meant." Mallenia was furious with herself for blushing, and for feeling light-headed, too. Next time she would show him that she could not be unsettled so easily. "It's all under Lot-Ionan now."

"Aha! You wanted to know what to expect when we get there?" He leaned back and thought she looked rather lovely when she blushed. She was obviously pretty inexperienced with men and affairs of the heart. "Rumor has it that he has shared out the land to his famuli, who are doing their magic experiments there and generally bothering the residents. He guards his magic source jealously and only lets his famuli have access one by one and at set times, so that he can keep an eye on them. He seems to have developed a kind of persecution mania. If we are to believe the stories, he has six or seven separate phobias. He must be making a collection."

"Don't the rumors say how many famuli there are? I ask because of Queen Coïra. She'll have to put them all out of action." Mallenia tapped her sword hilt. "You can't always use one of these to deal with a magician."

"I see things just the same as you." He pulled a face. "People come up with different versions. Some say he only has two famuli and that they hate each other. Others claim he has ten, each one more powerful than the last." His expression now became conspiratorial. "But they are said to be at war with each other as well. They all want Lot-Ionan's good opinion, hoping to inherit from him. If one of them wins access to the magic source they'll have control over all the other famuli. They have created magic creatures and use them to get at each other. Particularly in Rân Ribastur I expect we'll be under constant attack from these strange figures who derive their being from magic. But we'll be fine. We have our maga with us."

Mallenia swore under her breath. She was wondering how much energy Coïra still had; she would have to preserve it in order to be able to face down the magus. There was simply no time to travel to the land of the älfar to let Coïra bathe in that magic source. Tungdil Goldhand must be told the truth, or, in spite of having the Zhadár with them, their whole company might be wiped out fast.

Rodario was sitting with his chin supported on his hands, staring at Mallenia's face, trying to read her thoughts. "I have heard of one beast more terrible than all others. Do you want to know its name?"

Mallenia was not really listening, but she lifted her hand to indicate that she did want to know the name.

"Xolototh," he said in a dread and somber tone. "It hunts down humans, especially pretty blonde females."

"What does it do with them? Take them prisoner?"

"Oh no, nothing like that. It does this." He leaned forward quick as a flash and gave her a swift kiss.

Or rather, he had *intended* to give her a quick kiss.

But when he pulled his head back he felt her hand at the nape of his neck, pulling his mouth toward hers again. She smiled at him and closed her eyes to sink into the embrace. Attack was the best form of defense in these circumstances. And certainly the sweetest.

XX

Winter was gone and with it the ice and snow from round the fortress—the magic red barrier, on the other hand, was still in place.

Goda watched it at dawn, and at mid-orbit, and at orbit's end, and late at night, as if her steady gaze could somehow make it dissolve so that the stronghold's catapults might be put into action against their foe.

But this did not happen. The glowing red screen, not unlike a thin gauze curtain in appearance, was resistant to all Goda's wishes, prayers and spells.

Kiras came up to bring her an early-morning cup of tea. Together they observed the plain around the ravine. It had been transformed into a vast military encampment.

"Have you any idea what it means?" The tall undergroundling was surveying the scene before her.

Goda understood what she was referring to. The monsters had been making strange marks on the rock; viewed from above they formed a pattern. She guessed that they represented magic preparations rather than indications of where the monsters should be deployed in battle. There were several hundred troops by the Black Abyss, but nothing pointed to any immediate plans for attack. They were waiting, with all their war equipment around them. Waiting, just waiting.

"No," she said slowly. "It could be a series of runes, but I can't read them."

"Then that's even more worrying." Kiras leaned against the battlements. "I've been asking around and nobody has an explanation for these strange marks on the ground."

"They're from a foreign land. They'll not be able to understand our language either."

"The thing that calls itself Tungdil—I bet it'd be able to read them." Kiras looked at Goda.

"But it's not here. We must manage without it. And anyway, it'd tell us nothing but lies." The dwarf took out a sheet of paper on which she had previously made an exact copy of the runes she had noted. Comparing the two patterns, she realized that changes had been made. She placed the paper on the parapet and took a quill and pot of ink out of her reticule. She entered the new marks and tried, again in vain, to make sense of the drawing.

"What are you getting the guards to do with those mirrors? Whenever the sun is out they're out there, practicing."

"It's just a wild idea. I need to do more research."

An ubari brought in some news and a dwarf in black armor. He waited two paces behind the ubari messenger, not seeming particularly anxious. Goda and Kiras quickly exchanged glances. "Lady, he says that he comes from Tungdil Goldhand."

The dwarf bowed. "I am Jarkalín Blackfist, one of the Black Squadron riding south with the high king against Lot-Ionan."

Kiras looked him up and down. "Are all of Goldhand's

troops dressing in black nowadays? He seems to attract evil."

"Tell me how you met up with him," Goda demanded, holding out her hand for the message. Jarkalín gave her two leather rolls, and to the ubari he handed a sealed piece of waxed cloth with a letter enclosed in it; the symbol on one of the leather rolls was unfamiliar.

Jarkalín bowed. "This is from Aiphatòn, emperor of the älfar."

Kiras and Goda stared at him in disbelief as if he had turned into a sharp-fanged rabbit before their very eyes.

Jarkalín gave a concise report of events. ". . . then the high king's company set off for the south. I was sent out with twenty others to bring the news," he concluded. "On the way back to the fortress I received Aiphatòn's letter for you." He bowed. "I shall wait for your answer to the high king." Jarkalín withdrew three paces so that the queen could read the letter.

"Aiphatòn has turned into an ally, it seems." Goda was puzzled by the turn of events. "Maybe Vraccas is on Tungdil's side, after all."

"Or perhaps it's another god completely, out to trick us," Kiras said sharply, her visage darkening.

Goda opened Ireheart's letter, which told in few words the same story as Jarkalín's spoken report. Aiphatòn wrote that the älfar were on the march and had started their campaign against Lot-Ionan.

"The emperor does not think the war will be over before the summer ends. The abyss must be contained at least till then," she told Kiras as her gaze swept over the red globe that covered the area round the ravine. "I have

a feeling our enemies will not wait that long. It's decep-
tively quiet out there, a charade to lull us into a false
sense of security." She was struck by the difference between
the älf's script and her husband's hand: The one curved
and graceful, the other characterized by short straight
lines, a steady pressure on the pen nib and several blots
on the paper where the dwarf had been careless.

"Do we risk a sortie?" suggested Kiras.

Goda sighed. She had often played through this scenario
in her head.

It would be enough if they could destroy the enemy's
equipment. The monsters had taken an age to assemble it all
and they would need a long time to replace it. "I'd have to
drop the barrier. That will take a lot of my energy and I can't
say how long I can hold it open." She opened the next letter.

It was from the freelings, to say they were sending a
contingent to join Tungdil. The siege the älfar and the
thirdlings had subjected them to was now over—this had
been effected by the negotiations or commands of the high
king.

"They are glad the hero has returned to unite and lead
the dwarf-tribes," she relayed to Kiras, who grimaced. "In
their eyes Tungdil Goldhand is the greatest dwarf-leader ever
and has united the factions and will bring them all lasting
peace following the promised defeat of Lot-Ionan."

"Why do I feel so angry and so helpless?" the undergroundling exclaimed desperately, addressing the skies.
"Shouldn't I be rejoicing at all this good news?"

Goda embraced her. "I feel the same. We are the only ones
who believe the one who returned from the abyss is a being
sent by the darkness."

"And he is uniting all the forces of evil under his banner. No one else can see it." Kiras ground her teeth. "I'd swear that Tungdil's pact with Aiphatòn is of a completely different nature than it's purported to be." Her eyes flashed. "Of course! It's the other way around!"

Goda did not follow. "Explain."

Kiras pointed to the screen. "Tungdil is gathering these horrors to form an army: Aiphatòn, Lot-Ionan, himself and these beasts from the Black Abyss with their sorcerer-commander. He won't destroy them, he'll consolidate them. An army nobody can stop." She passed her hand over her face. "By Ubar! Do not let my terrible conviction prove true!"

Goda opened another letter. She lowered it in surprise. "It is from Rognor Mortalblow, king of the thirdlings . . . He says he's pulling his troops out of the Brown Mountains and the freelings' caves to march against Lot-Ionan." She emptied her beaker. "You see me totally at a loss, Kiras. I don't know what to think!"

"All the demons and evil spirits are with Goldhand," she hissed, smiting the battlements with her hand in exasperation. "He must have put a spell on Mortalblow to soften his mind and bend his will."

"You can't do that with a spell."

"There are no such spells that *you* know of, Goda." The undergroundling was close to tears—tears of anger. "No one else can see what we can see," she whispered in despair. "They're all running after him. Running to their destruction." She buried her face in her hands. "That's what he'll bring them: Destruction," she mumbled.

The maga skimmed the letters again to be sure she had understood everything correctly, then she called the ubari over. "Summon the officers. Tell them to gather in the conference chamber. We'll be making a sortie."

Kiras straightened up and wiped away a tear. "I'll come, too," she announced. "I want to see with my own eyes exactly what's been going on."

Goda gave her an anxious glance.

Rattling and groaning, the mechanism to open the great southern gate slowly started to move. Four hundred soldiers waited, poised to sally forth.

At the head of the force stood a hundred dwarves, then came two hundred combined ubariu and undergroundlings; the rear was brought up by one hundred humans, archers and crossbowmen, to provide covering fire for the warriors and to check enemy attacks at source.

Goda looked at her daughter Sanda and her son Bandaál, both standing by Kiras among the dwarves at the front. These two children of hers had inherited her magic gifts and knew their way around spells and incantations. They waved at their mother.

The maga was including them in this force so that they could, if necessary, recite spells to protect them from enemy sorcery. She was uneasy sending her own flesh and blood to the other side, but there was no other way. She would have her hands full, holding the gap in the screen open for them; her children would not be capable of doing that.

And there was another of her offspring among the company of brave hearts. He had not brooked any attempt to hand over command to anyone else: Boëndalin Powerthrust, her oldest son, an excellent warrior, taking after his father. He stood proudly in the first row, holding a shield and his two-bladed ax. He greeted his mother with a nod, his eyes flashing with battle-lust. He controlled his hot blood better than his father could, which was why the command was safe in his hands. His skill with weapons made him the best warrior in Evildam.

Between the double gates of the fortress a slit was visible now, letting in a reddish shimmering light.

"May Vraccas be with you," called Goda. "You have your orders: Destroy as much as you can and come back quickly if the opposition is strong. We don't need heroic sacrifices today. Save them for another time."

Kiras raised her hand. She was wearing leather armor and carrying a sword-ax, a weapon the undergroundlings had developed in the last eighty cycles. On one side you had a blade, and at the end there was a narrow ax head that could be employed against shields and helmets.

Sanda and Bandaál had the traditional dwarf chain-mail shirt, helmet and shield; they carried axes in their belts. Their priority would be to counteract any magic attack. Goda had also given them each ten splinters of diamond. They were to use up this external energy first before having recourse to their own inner powers.

Goda raised her arm and concentrated. She did not want to repeat her mistake of trying to break the screen by force. Instead she wanted to chip away at it gently with magic, to scrape and abrade it until a weak spot developed. A weak spot large enough for all these warriors.

Her lips moved and she assayed a combination of formulae. She was not entirely sure what would work, but had a few ideas.

Pulsating white magic left her fingertips and snaked toward

the barrier, smoothing itself around, like a cat encircling the legs of a human.

No resistance was encountered.

Goda sighed with relief and increased the area covered, so that it would be large enough for the ubariu to walk through.

Sparks appeared and this part of the screen turned a lighter color, going pale pink and then disappearing completely until only the white could be seen.

"Off you go," Goda commanded, holding her magic firmly to support the rest of the barrier. Where red and white met, there was hissing and crackling and occasional sparks, which, if they touched anything, left a black scorch mark.

The troops stormed out without any battle cries and fanned out to form a long line, while the archers remained behind preparing to shoot their arrows and crossbow bolts. The attack began.

The first of the tents and buildings fell to the warriors without a sound. Only when the flames shot up, leaping from one length of canvas to the next, to spread to the whole encampment, did the horrified howls of the monsters ring out. Trumpets gave the alarm. Drum rolls called them to arms.

Goda kept her arm outstretched and fed further magic into her spell in order to be able to maintain it. She was afraid she might not be able to open the gap again if she allowed the first beam to fail.

"May Vraccas be with you," she repeated quietly. *And with my own children, above all things.*

Kiras followed close on Boëndalin's heels.

They ran forward, passing through the gap in the barrier.

The undergroundling felt pain for a fleeting moment as they did so.

"Take out the big machines by the walls first, and the tents," Boëndalin ordered, telling the archers to prepare their fire arrows. While the unit moved over to the right, their burning missiles shot in the opposite direction to keep the monsters occupied extinguishing the flames. Then they confronted their first opponents.

Kiras was struck by the ease with which they were able to rampage unopposed. They had caught their foes unawares at their midday meal—indeed, how could they have possibly guessed that Goda was going to open the barrier?

In the course of all the turmoil created by the attack more fires broke out as cooking stoves were kicked over in the general confusion.

Before long all the machines by the gates had been destroyed; the largest ones now were three hundred paces away. From the direction of the gates impressive numbers of strangely diverse monsters came surging toward the dwarves.

"Archers! Fire!" Boëndalin ordered the rest of the company to continue advancing. Arrows skimmed overhead from behind, targeting the monster horde, bringing some of them dead or injured to the ground. "And now have at them! Down with them all! Over there, get to the catapult!" the dwarf shouted as he rammed the sharpened edge of his shield into an opponent's neck. Slicing through leather protection the metal opened the monster's throat all the way to the spine. The beast went flying, as good as decapitated.

The commando troops slashed and bashed their way through the enemy. Kiras, dispatching many opponents herself, had to admire Boëndalin's skill, whether in giving orders or fighting. She would appreciate a partner like that at her side, but a sense of tradition made it an unsuitable match. Undergroundlings and dwarves did not mix. Not for long, anyway.

They had reached the tall catapult towers. Two-thirds of her group gave covering fire while the others hacked at the guy ropes, smashed the supports and inflicted so much damage on the device that there was a loud crash as the construction shuddered and fell.

"Get out of here!" Boëndalin commanded. Like Kiras, he had seen that the enemy was regrouping. "We'll withdraw back to the gate. We have done well!"

The undergroundling looked at one of the odd poles that stood apparently isolated on the plain, a taut chain leading back from it down the Black Abyss. It was only a couple of hundred paces away. "What about that, Boëndalin?" Kiras called out. "Can't we get that one, too?" Success had gone to her head. "We can do it!"

The dwarf looked at the beasts. Behind a furrowed brow his brain was working furiously. They still had not found out what the masts were for, and there were about four dozen of them planted round the entrance to the ravine.

"It's not far," she said, enticingly. "Whatever they're for, we can easily get rid of them. And we haven't seen hide nor hair of their magus yet."

Boëndalin glanced at his siblings, who both indicated their approval.

One of the ubariu protested, wary of the long distance back to safety; their retreat could be cut off. Their armor had grown no lighter in all that fighting and running was getting more difficult now. For all of them.

"Let's attack," was Boëndalin's decision finally. He charged off. "Archers, fire to the left and right! Undergroundlings, bring up the rear!"

In this formation they reached the first of the mysterious metal poles. The foundations, made of solid lumps of cast iron, were almost impossible to dislodge.

"Get the ubariu to bend the poles back toward the chasm— they are already under tensile stress." Boëndalin gave the command and reconfigured his troops.

Kiras was following the action out of the corner of her eye, watching the powerful warriors thronging around the pole, some pushing, the others pulling.

The metal creaked and gave way. The huge chain, which had the diameter of a tree trunk, suddenly went slack and dropped to the ground. Two of the ubariu failed to leap to safety swiftly enough and were crushed to death in their armor, squashed like insects by the heavy links.

"Come on! Let's get the next one!" Boëndalin pointed over to the right.

This time the ubari expressed his objections forcefully. "Your mother said we were not to cross a line that's over three hundred paces behind us now. Sir!" His pink eyes were full of reproach. "And there are over forty of these masts to be dealt with. We'll never do it." He pointed to the left, where a wall of beasts was advancing on them. These had shields for protection against arrows and crossbow fire; no comparison with the random rabble they had previously faced. They were still three hundred paces away. "We need to retreat, sir!"

Boëndalin exchanged glances with Sanda and Bandaál. "Keep that lot off our backs," he told them. "We'll bring down another dozen of the masts, and then," he said, looking angrily at the ubari, "I'll be the one to order the retreat. No one else."

The dwarf-famuli took up position and raised their hands. Their fingers described runes in the air, and their diamond splinters shone out dazzlingly bright, surrendering the last of their magic to empower the formulae.

A dark-blue beam shot out from the palm of Sanda's hand, forging a path through the attackers from the front of the wave right through to the last man. Everything the beam of light touched was immediately vaporized to a stinking black cloud, with only molten clumps of metal remaining of armor and weapons.

"What do you say to that, brother of mine?" she said, panting heavily, and flashing a challenge with her eyes.

Bandaál formed a half-globe with his hands, the open side directed toward the beasts. He blew gently through his fingers and his breath became a tornado to rout the enemy.

Half of them were swept off their feet, banners went flying and even creatures the size of an ubari were blown about like puppets of straw. Arrows that had been on their way toward the dwarves were forced back on the ranks of monsters.

Bandaál lowered his arms, grinning at his sister. "I think my spell was eminently superior."

"It's not a game!" Kiras had been watching them and waved them on to join the others who were charging off toward the next pole. "Come on! We've got to stick together!" She looked back at the southern gate, which now seemed a very long way off. The undergroundling was shocked to see the white shimmer they had come through now appeared rather pink. "I think Goda is having trouble holding open the gap!"

The famuli looked at the opening, and thus missed seeing the horde of monsters split in two to reveal a small-statured warrior striding to the front.

Kiras took her telescope off her belt to get a closer look.

A dwarf in glorious red-gold vraccassium armor with deep black tionium inlay was stomping toward the apprentice magicians; in his hands he carried two war hammers with silver and gold heads studded with jewels reflecting the light. He did not look anywhere near as dangerous as Tungdil Goldhand. Perhaps it was the color of his armor plates.

His visor was open—and she felt suddenly nauseous. The dwarf had no lower jaw!

Through the focused lenses she saw the long-healed injury in all its terrifying detail. A blow must have cost him jawbone and teeth. A healer had simply sewn up the loose flesh and tightened it so that the dwarf could take in food and continue to live, and had left him a narrow slit below the upper jaw through which presumably the food could be pushed in. But he would not be able to speak or chew, Kiras thought. Long black beard hair reached down from his cheeks to his chest. No hair at all grew where the scars were.

Some of the nose was missing, too. Cartilage had been cut away and the hole was protected by a silver plate. Two vertical slits allowed air to be taken in. The very appearance, like a skull, would be enough to root any enemy to the spot. The brown eyes burned with hatred and pain.

"By all the . . ." Kiras put her telescope down swiftly as

an icy shudder ran through her body. *This must be the master that had been spoken of.* She told the famuli about this new danger, Boëndalin and the troops not having noticed, being busy with the attempt to demolish the next metal pole.

"Let me," Bandaál said. "I'm older than you." He prepared his magic spell, took out a further diamond splinter and clasped it determinedly in his hand to make use of its energy. He murmured a banning spell and a column of gray light the size of a human rose up before them. At the final word of the incantation if shot off in a straight line toward the dwarf, transforming itself in mid-flight.

It broadened out and developed spikes like fingers. It was clear to Kiras that nothing would survive contact with this phenomenon.

The dwarf stopped, twirled his weapons and abruptly laid the hammers crosswise together.

A loud bang ensued and a second column appeared—but this one was as high as one of the catapults. It surged off, spreading in the same way as the first, developing spikes the length of spears. The two shapes sped toward each other between the two armies. Bandaál's collapsed with a crash and the other dwarf's deadly wall of light continued on its path.

Boëndalin had turned round now and had seen what was happening. He screamed out commands, ordering an immediate retreat. The discipline among his troops was incredible and no one broke ranks or shouted, but they all raced faster than they had ever run before to leave the battlefield.

"By Vraccas!" Sanda cast a green lightning flash against

the encroaching wall but it melted away harmlessly on contact.

"It'll have us any second!" Kiras looked at Boëndalin, who was gesturing to them. It was impossible to avoid the magic pillar—it was moving too fast.

Sanda took hold of her remaining eight diamond splinters and told her brother to do the same. "Quick, a sphere," she panted, grabbing his hand. Both of them knelt down.

"Get down," Bandaál told the undergroundling, "or you'll lose your head."

Kiras threw herself onto the ground behind the siblings. The pillar hummed close. A milky hemisphere had enclosed them and, at the next moment, the pillar of light crashed into it.

One by one its spikes broke off and lightning bolts flashed hither and thither, but the three of them were unharmed. Kiras had a sense that every piece of metal near her, even the smallest rivet on her armor, was growing hot, and she felt her whole body being pinched and jabbed.

Then the attack was over.

"We've destroyed it," gasped Sanda in relief. The sphere collapsed and she felt the wind that the wall of light had stirred up gust past her. Dust whirled up, getting between their teeth.

The undergroundling turned her head. "No!" she groaned. Before the wave of dirt hid the scene from view she saw the wall of light heading directly for Boëndalin and his troops. Then the dust cloud became too dense for her to see anything more.

Bandaál and Sanda pulled Kiras to her feet and, holding each other's hands so that they would not get lost in the gray veil of dust, they stumbled on toward the safety of the southern gate.

All of a sudden the wind changed and they could see looming up through the dirt, less than ten paces ahead, the form of the unknown dwarf. He was holding his hammers right and left of him, arms spread out, the heads pointing down.

Sanda screamed when she saw him, clapping her hand to her mouth. Bandaál took a deep breath.

Kiras, on the other hand, looked past him to where Boëndalin's unit had been standing.

The men and women had been caught mid-flight by the magic. Their bodies lay scattered on the ground, and Kiras scanned the carpet of limbs and torsos in vain for any signs of movement. She was suffused with guilt. If she had never pointed out the masts to Boëndalin, they would all have been safely back in the Evildam fortress by now.

The dwarf's head was held low. A black lock of hair fell over his brow and blew about in the light breeze. Without a word from him, black flames emerged from the hammer-heads and he slowly raised his arms.

Kiras stepped in front of the siblings and gripped her sword-ax. "Try to get to the gate," she told them. She was more afraid than she had ever been, but was not going to leave Bandaál and Sanda here alone. "Go on!" the under-groundling urged. "You are more useful than I am."

Brother and sister raced off and the dwarf let them pass. His brown eyes held Kiras in their gaze. His face was expressionless, or was that an attempt at a smile on his cheeks?

Kiras forced saliva down her dry throat. It ran slow as

treacle down her gullet. "You'll have to attack if you want me dead!" she called to the dwarf, pointing her weapon at him. "You will be . . ."

She spoke no more.

The dwarf moved too swiftly for her to be able to follow. He was suddenly right in front of her and struck her in the chest with his burning hammer. Her armor burst into flames, even though it was not made of any flammable material.

The second hammer hit her on the back of the head and she collapsed, swooning. She could hear the crackle of flames at her ear. The metal of her helmet did not seem to care that it *could not* burn. Flames flickered at the holes made by the hammers.

As she fell she pushed her helmet off and rolled onto her belly to extinguish the fire on her breast.

A foot turned her over onto her back and the terrible face of her enemy was directly above her own. He was staring at her as he raised his hammer again. The black fire around him had died away but its heat was still overwhelming. He pressed the hammer head against her brow and the metal ate into her flesh.

Kiras gave a scream and lost consciousness.

Goda saw the glowing wall of light approach the fleeing figures and forgot all her previous intentions. Three of her children were in mortal danger. If she did nothing neither she nor Ireheart would ever find forgiveness.

She leaped through the gap and let fall the spell that had been holding the opening against the company's return. She hurried forward to protect Boëndalin and his troop from the magic forces attacking them.

Goda racked her brain to find some incantation she could use against the wall of light. The enemy magus possessed enormous power. This shimmering wall of spikes was rushing up behind the troops, who turned to face it when Boëndalin gave the command. They crouched down behind their shields.

The maga panted; there were still three hundred paces to cover before she could reach her eldest son. She had grasped the fact that she would never manage to protect all the warriors from the wall's onslaught. In her left hand she had two dozen splinters of the magic diamond. They would be no help now.

"Take them softly to the eternal smithy," Goda prayed, weaving a protective spell which she placed only around Boëndalin. He disappeared in a flickering cloud.

Then the wall of light hit the troop.

It was painful for her to witness the deaths of so many fine fighting souls. The spikes pierced shields and armor, bodies and heads, and speared the dead onto the living until they all lay heaped up like sand on a shovel; finally the wind fell and the corpses rolled apart to scatter on the ground, the momentum still driving them.

"Boëndalin!" she screamed, running on. She could see him, surrounded by the shimmering. He was standing in front of the pile of slaughtered warriors, unable to understand how he had been spared and the others had not. "This way," called Goda. Between her fingers the diamond splinters crumbled and were blown away.

Thick veils of dust took away her vision. Fearful of a further attack, she put her hand back into her pocket, calculating how many splinters remained. She noted that she was down to half the original stock. Again she called her son's name.

"I'm here, mother," he gasped, coming toward her through the fog of swirling dirt. He was holding his arm across mouth and nose and had screwed up his eyes against the dust storm. "What happened?"

"The magus has . . ." As the clouds of dirt thinned out, Goda could see Bandaál and Sanda with Kiras standing before a dwarf in reddish-gold armor. His back was turned to her as if he had nothing to fear from her. Or had he not seen her? "Is that him?"

Boëndalin's glance flew between his siblings and the corpses on the ground. "Why didn't you save all of us?" he asked, his voice hoarse.

The hammer heads started to emit black fire.

"He's attacking them!" Goda hastily prepared a spell.

Bandaál and Sanda ran past the unknown figure, while the undergroundling confronted the dwarf in combat.

Boëndalin wanted to charge off to help her, but Goda restrained him. "You cannot help her against this enemy. Only my powers can effect anything." She chose an assault spell that would bombard the dwarf with multiple lightning strikes. But before she had finished speaking the charm, the foe had felled Kiras with a double blow, finally forcing his hammer onto her face; the undergroundling lay motionless.

Goda released the energies.

Lightning flashes shot out from the tips of her fingers, aimed at the dwarf, who straightened up, crossed his hammers over each other and held them up, arms outstretched.

Bandaál and Sanda had now reached their mother and saw what was unfolding.

The glowing flashes crossed the distance in zigzag lines, overtaking each other in a race to see which would reach the adversary first.

The first lightning bolt hit the hammer head, and discharged its power. Brighter than the flash itself, the symbols on the metal shone out. Then came the next strike.

The dwarf was forced back by the impact, his heels dragging great gouges through the dusty ground surface—but he did not go up in smoke, or fall! When the last bolt had hit him, he turned his upper body slightly and spread his arms again. It was a pose of consummate superiority.

Then he turned away and strode back to his beasts. He left Kiras lying there.

Abruptly he circled round again, his hammers crossed against the maga. Two of the armor runes shone out and seemed to be feeding light to a jewel that was placed above his solar plexus. The gem glowed and released an ochre-colored thick beam, for which the weapon heads formed a lateral boundary; the dwarf seemed to be steering it by manipulating the hammers.

Giving a deep dangerous roar he flew over to Goda and her children; the earth beneath him was scorched black.

Goda put her hand back into her pocket and created a hasty counter-spell, which crashed into the enemy magic with a crackling, hissing sound, shattering it like porcelain. The heat they were showered with took away their breath and singed beards and eyebrows and rebellious locks of hair. They had to shut their eyes against the blast to prevent them drying out.

When they looked up once more the dwarf had gone. The

monsters were waiting four hundred paces away at the entrance to the abyss, watching them.

"Go and fetch Kiras," Goda commanded quietly. The magus had made himself invisible.

Boëndalin sped off, threw the undergroundling over his shoulder and returned with her.

Then the monsters roared and charged.

They reached the barrier in the nick of time, and behind it lay the saving grace of the southern gate. Goda collected the last remnants of concentration and, with extreme difficulty, forced the red screen open for a second time.

She was the last of the group to re-enter the fortress. But when the gate closed behind her she still did not feel safe. The power of the disfigured dwarf had been far greater than she had feared.

Boëndalin laid Kiras on a stretcher. "See what you can do for her, mother," he asked, as he dampened the girl's face with water.

The soldiers around them and up on the battlements sent sympathetic glances to the returnees; one or two were angry, critical because of the disastrous outcome of the sortie and the death of so many warriors. Boëndalin gave a deep sigh.

Goda checked the undergroundling's heartbeat. "She'll be all right," she comforted Boëndalin and her other two children, both of whom stood at her side, quite distraught. "Apart from the burn on her face she doesn't seem to have sustained serious injury."

The maga did not recognize the symbol that the enemy magus had imprinted on the undergroundling's forehead. Was it intended as a branding mark of humiliation? Why had he spared her life? Because she had been so stupidly brave?

"It's all my fault," said Boëndalin to Goda. He sounded more than downcast. "We should have retreated after destroying the catapults. It was only because I insisted on leading the troops to the masts. That's why they all died." He lifted his head. "It was my fault," he called up to the silent soldiers guarding the walls.

"Nonsense. This is war, and war kills. It kills humans, dwarves, ubariu and undergroundlings." Goda contradicted him. "All of them knew that it was a really dangerous mission. They all volunteered to go with you."

Boëndalin was past consolation. "I should be lying out there with them." He lowered his voice. "It is only thanks to your art that I am still alive. It wasn't my strong arms or my skills as a commander that saved me. The name of each of the fallen will remind me that I must be a better leader." He was about to go.

Goda touched him on the shoulder. "And yet the mission did succeed. The camp has been burned down and the catapults have been destroyed. They have not sacrificed their lives for nothing."

"They would not have lost their lives at all if I hadn't given those commands." He left them and walked to his quarters.

Sanda and Bandaál came over and, in long tearful embraces, thanked her for saving their lives. Goda sent them off to rest.

She stepped into the lift to go up to the tower to survey the scene of conflict. She had not lied to them. The mission had won the defenders valuable time and the knowledge that, without outside support, they would never be able to vanquish their opponents' magus.

Her gaze swept over the barrier, now obscured under clouds of smoke. In spite of all their losses she remained convinced that they had scored a victory over the monsters; albeit a two-edged victory.

We shall have to wait until the summer, Vraccas, she said in prayer. Her hand felt for the diamond fragments and found only four, together with a great deal of dust. The last ones . . .

XXI

Girdlegard,
Former Queendom of Rân Ribastur,
Former Northwestern Border,
Spring, 6492nd Solar Cycle

The air was cool and fresh but the sun was doing its best to warm the travelers. The tender golden rays shimmered through the canopy of dense foliage above their heads. There was a scent of nature reawakening and the first flowers were in bloom.

They were not riding particularly fast, not wanting to arrive in the Blue Mountains before Aiphatòn and his älfar. Tungdil and Ireheart were at the head of the column, then some of the Zhadár and Barskalín, and, in the middle, Slîn and Balyndar, with the remainder of the Invisibles bringing up the rear.

"Our messages will all have been delivered by now." Ireheart blinked in the sunlight. "I wonder what Goda thinks? What will she say to our successes?"

"It won't make any difference," Tungdil hazarded. "She'll still have her doubts about me? Unlike you. And I can't blame her. In her place I'd be even more suspicious now. The victories only prove to her how evil I must be," he laughed. "The älfar and myself, then the Black Squadron and the Zhadár as my new allies—a whole collection of bad lads." This sounded like the old Scholar now.

If you only knew what I was thinking about. Ireheart

hoped that his friend was not able to read his mind, because such thoughts had been exactly what had been going through it. Add to that those black lines on Tungdil's face and the inexplicable changes in his eye. He had to force himself to join in the laughter. "Yes, it's a troop Nôd'onn would have given his eye-teeth for. In the old days."

"A very long time ago." Tungdil cast a quick look back over his shoulder. "Everything's going our way, and some things were just handed to us on a silver plate."

"I wonder if we'll catch sight of the firstlings. May Vraccas make sure they find our message quickly." Ireheart relaxed his grip on his pony's reins and it trotted contentedly along. "The points are set now, like for the old mountain tunnel trains. I'd be a whole lot happier traveling in one of them, too."

"That would be fine, perfect if you're good at breathing underwater!"

"Elria could hardly have thought up a better way to punish us dwarves, could she? To get all of Weyurn's lakes to drain down into our tunnel complex." Ireheart looked ahead to where their road left the woods and led through the meadows. "We've still not seen a single human. Or anything else, for that matter."

"Did you hear the stories Rodario was telling us about Rân Ribastur?" Tungdil grinned and, as always at such moments, Ireheart felt so happy to be at his side. As it had been in the old, old orbits . . . the feeling was comforting. "Magic animals, which the famuli set upon each other; a spell put on great swathes of the land; and nature drawing the traveler to his doom." Tungdil tapped his armor for good luck. "I'm all right as long as I've got my armor."

Has he ever taken it off? At any time during the whole

journey? Ireheart tried to remember when he had seen Tungdil without his coat of armor. Certainly not during the journey to Lot-Ionan. But he didn't seem to stink, he didn't complain, he—didn't sleep?

Hoofbeats approached and the fair-haired Ido girl came up to Tungdil's side. "Excuse me for interrupting but I must tell you this," she said directly. "I must speak to you, Goldhand."

"Whatever you have to say to me Ireheart can hear, too," said the one-eyed dwarf, and Boïndil took it as further confirmation that they were dealing with the genuine Tungdil Goldhand.

Mallenia nodded. "It's about the queen. You should know that she has hardly any magic power left."

Aha. It was all going so nicely till now. Ireheart's eyebrows were raised so high they nearly touched his hairline, but he kept quiet.

"How do you know?" Tungdil asked.

"She told me so herself." Mallenia put her hand on her sword. "I had to tell you."

"Why didn't she tell us herself?" Ireheart blurted out. "What use is it if we think she's on an equal footing with Lot-Ionan only to find, the first time we meet him, that instead of an inferno we have a miserable little flicker emerging from her fingertips?"

"I don't know. She had hoped to be able to renew her powers in a source in the Red Mountains, but that did not happen." Mallenia's expression was apologetic. "I would have wished to bring you better news than this."

"Blessed hammers!" Ireheart went on cursing for a while, then growled angrily. "So what now?"

Tungdil rubbed his short brown beard. "We'll have to make sure the maga doesn't use up any of the energy she still has, whether to defend herself or us, until we've got her to Lot-Ionan. Then we'll have to find a way to take her to the source so she can refresh her magic," he said after some thought. He did not seem particularly concerned that their most important weapon was going to be far less effective than they had assumed. "We won't tell the others. They should go on believing the maga is in full possession of her magic faculties. I'll have a word with her when the opportunity arises." He ordered the company to halt at the edge of the forest. "It shall remain our secret for now. Leave the others their illusion."

"And how are you going to . . ." Ireheart could not go on, because Tungdil had turned his pony round and was sitting up tall in the saddle.

"Listen to me," he called to the group. "We are now in the territory of Rân Ribastur, and some of you are aware of the possible dangers that may await us here." He pointed to Coïra. "She will not use her magic here. The queen is accompanying us to Lot-Ionan and is not here to protect us against robbers or mythical beasts. We are dwarves and should be able to defend ourselves!" A muffled roar of approval was heard. "So, do not depend on the queen's magic powers. She will not be employing them, not even if one of us is in mortal danger. On the contrary, we pledge our lives to protect her and get her safely to the Blue Mountains without her using any of her own spells. Be on your guard and report anything you hear." He lifted Bloodthirster. "Our steel can cope with any danger!"

In renewed confirmation the dwarves and Zhadár banged their shields, then dismounted and made camp.

Ireheart grinned at his friend. His announcement covered everything nicely. *Clever as ever.*

Rodario, who now sported a neat beard and thin mustache, and was thus the spitting image of his ancestor, arranged his blanket under the canvas protection from sun or rain.

He had chosen a green lavender bush, stable enough to tie the canvas to. When he looked at Queen Coïra he saw she was having difficulties with putting up her tent. He crawled over. "Let me help you, Your Majesty."

"Oh, there's no need for that," she said, smiling gratefully.

"I'd be happy to help."

"I meant there's no need to call me *Your Majesty.* I thought I'd told you that before. We've been through too much together and so I should like to grant you this privilege."

Rodario returned the friendly gesture and smoothed out her blanket for her, rolling her extra clothing into a pillow. "There you are. Your royal bedstead now awaits."

She laughed and lay down, sliding this way and that. "It's not quite like home comforts but I'm sure I'll sleep well in this fresh air. Though I shall miss the cries of the seagulls."

"Ah, you'll see. We'll patch up the lakebed and fill the Bath again, as I used to call your people's realm." He winked. "Not far from our camp there is a little stream with a waterfall." He slipped off his armor and outer clothing. "I don't know how you're feeling, but I'm longing for a swim . . . or at least to get rid of some of this dirt." He stretched out his hand to her. "Would you like to come with me?"

She laughed. "Are you trying to seduce me?"

"Of course not. I'll keep watch on the river bank while you bathe, and then you can do the same for me."

Coïra's laughter subsided and she appeared uneasy and dejected. "No, I'd rather stay where I am safe in the dwarves' protection. You were telling the story about that thing that lies in wait for travelers, and even if I'm not blond . . ."

"Did Mallenia tell you about Xolototh?" Rodario looked over to the Ido girl who was arranging her bedding not far away.

"And that there was another kiss, yes. But this time, maybe, she took *you* by surprise." Coïra could not resist this little dig. "I know I don't have to be afraid of the Xolototh but I have a healthy respect for the enchanted creatures and plants in Rân Ribastur." She sat down on her blanket. "You'd better go on your own, Rodario."

He nodded and looked disappointed. Then he disappeared off through the bushes.

Coïra sighed with relief. She had not been sure whether she had managed to conceal her own feelings. An actor like him would surely notice when someone was pretending.

What Rodario could not know was that she had longed to accompany him. And she would have bathed with him in the water.

Coïra looked over at Mallenia, who was the exact opposite of herself in stature, coloring, and very nature. Yet the two of them shared an obsession with Rodario the Seventh, she was sure of that.

What can it lead to? she asked herself for the one hundred and twenty-seventh time. She lay down and closed her eyes.

But sleep was a long time coming. She kept seeing the man in her mind's eye. Eventually, she got up with a sigh and surveyed the camp. All was quiet. Nobody was paying her any attention, so she slipped through the undergrowth, following the sound of water.

The splashing turned into a rushing sound and a fine spray covered the leaves with drops of moisture.

Coïra peered through the greenery and spotted a small waterfall, not more than seven paces high, and a pool of water perhaps eight paces in diameter at the base of a gray rock wall. Creepers overhung the stone and flowers on the bank quivered incessantly as they were sprinkled with the water droplets.

The actor's clothing lay in a heap on the bank, far enough away from the spray to stay dry. With his back to her, Rodario stood naked in the pool in a theatrical pose before the cascade, waving his arms. He walked up and down, showing his profile. His mouth was opening and closing as though rehearsing for some grand role.

Coïra had to grin. She allowed her gaze to slip down from his hips, but did not look directly at his manhood. Not that she was uninterested to see what he had to offer in that area, but decency forbade her to be inquisitive. Perhaps the orbit would come when she might see it in different circumstances.

"And? What do you think of him?"

Coïra was startled, hearing a woman's voice behind her. Looking over her shoulder she saw Mallenia. "I was worried . . ." she sought an excuse.

"Of course you were, my queen. Same as me. The Zhadár that are guarding our camp are certainly not able to protect us properly," she smiled. "If anyone had told me that I would find myself standing next to the ruler of Weyurn watching a naked man bathe in a forest stream I think I would have slapped their face for the effrontery." She bent one of the branches aside to get a better look. "Take a look at that! He has a very fine physique. Those padded clothes he was wearing hid his real shape." She noticed that Coïra was not really watching. "Don't you find him attractive? I thought you liked proper heroes and well-built men."

"I . . . don't want to see everything," she said, avoiding a direct answer.

The Ido girl laughed quietly and looked at the black-haired queen. "What shall we do? Shall we share him or do we have to compete for his affections? Or shall we fight over him and be enemies forever? Idoslane and Weyurn can wage war about it."

"We could just kill him, of course. That would be the simplest solution." Coïra sighed.

Mallenia's eyes flashed in amusement. "True enough. But I wouldn't want so drastic a course of action. It's hardly his fault that both of us have fallen for him."

"He could have paid court to just the one of us, instead of both," the maga objected. "And, if I think about it, you're already at an advantage. You've had two kisses."

"The first one didn't count." Mallenia put her hand on the queen's shoulder. "We should not risk our friendship for his sake. You saved my life and I shall never forget that." She became serious. "Do you want me to stand back and leave him to you? If you tell me to I shall respect your wishes."

Coïra shook her head. "That would not be fair."

Mallenia smiled at her. "I respect you all the more for

that." She gestured toward the little pool. "Off you go. Go and help him bathe."

No!" she exclaimed. "I can't do that!"

"That's the only way to find out what he wants and how he feels about you. Don't hesitate. I did, for too long." Mallenia gave the maga a little shove which sent her tumbling out of the bushes.

She stumbled through the undergrowth toward the stream before regaining her balance. Before she could hide again Rodario had seen her.

Coïra could not hear what he called out. From the bushes Mallenia urged her to go on to the waterfall, and then withdrew. *Well then*, the maga said to herself, and stepped toward the cascade, which sprayed her with a fine mist and wetted her face, her hair and her clothing.

"I thought I would take you up on your offer," she called out, standing in such a way as not to see all of him. Or his little Rodario.

"Very nice of you," he said quietly, walking past her and bending over, so that she saw his taut buttocks. She turned swiftly away. "I'm finished here now. But I'll keep watch for you. He pulled on his long shirt and hid his nakedness. "May I help you undress? You must be used to having assistance, you being a princess and all."

"Only from my maid. Never from someone I don't know." She indicated he should turn round while she took off her clothes, layer by layer. Until she got to the gloves. The air was cool and she was shivering. She stepped quickly into the water, which was surprisingly warm. "You can turn round again now."

Rodario sat down on the bank and watched the maga

with an impenetrable smile. "Strange bathing practices," he said, pointing at the gloves. "Why is that?"

"They . . . there's a spell on them. I never take them off."

"A spell?" he dangled his feet in the water and observed her. "What sort of spell? Are your fingers so ugly that you have to hide them? Or do you have dirt under your fingernails from all the alchemy experiments you do?"

She splashed him, taking care to keep her upper body under water and out of sight. Coïra had surprised herself. What did she think he would do? That he might be bold enough to come into the pool to join her? That he would not behave as a man of honor should? How did heroes behave when they weren't campaigning against injustice and oppression? "You are making fun of me."

"Never!" Suddenly his gaze traveled past her, to the pool itself. "Do you know the story of the Moon Pond? Old Boïndil told me the tale . . . he's not much of a connoisseur about elf romances but he certainly enjoyed the killing sequences in the story. I prefer to concentrate on other parts." He retold the story and Coïra listened, spellbound, as she swam in the pool. "What do you think? Do you think there may be more passageways like the one in the story?" Again, he was staring at the water.

"Now I understand!" She laughed. "You're trying to frighten me."

"No, I'm not. But we are in Rân Ribastur—the enchanted land, if you like. It doesn't have to be an älf that comes riding out of the waves, but there could be something lying in wait for you," he said simply, paddling his feet in the water. "Perhaps I should wake it up. It won't have been seen very often by a woman of your beauty."

She was going to call out a response—but then she felt a movement by her right foot. She could not hold back the scream. Rodario stopped splashing. "There's something there!"

"Now you're trying to trick me," he said with a mischievous smile.

"No, I . . ." Something thin and long wrapped itself around her right leg, tightening its grip. Coïra stared under the water in horror but could not make anything out. There were too many bubbles. Then she was pulled downwards. She held out her arms to Rodario. "Pull me out! Quick!" She was frightened now.

Rodario could see from her expression that she was not joking. He grabbed her fingers and pulled. He was getting nowhere. He tugged again.

"Wait!" He got a foothold against the rock. Now he had a strong enough hold to heave the maga out of the water. At that moment he had no eyes for her breasts and her slender body. He saw something clinging to her leg that looked like a white tentacle. It let go of its victim and Coïra shot out of the water as Rodario pulled her hard.

Rodario fell over backwards and the maga landed full length on top of him. She had dark-red lines along her leg but no injuries. She was furious and resentful. "That was all your fault! You made that thing grab me!"

"It was your own idea," he said defensively. "How was I to know the pool would have the power to make your thoughts come true?" In one hand he held something made of leather.

"You said the land was enchanted! You could have worked it out for yourself!" Coïra had talked herself into a fury, even if some of it was put on for his benefit. Because she was naked she felt she ought to stay where she was, so as not to show him even more of herself. Even more than he had already seen. "What if it comes out?"

"But you can detect magic, can't you?"

Coïra opened her mouth to give some sharp retort. Then their eyes met. And melted. Their bodies exchanged warmth and fanned the inner fires that poets and bards have so often sung about. Neither was able to resist a surge of passion as their lips touched, and they kissed tenderly.

And again.

And once more.

"Your glove, my queen," said Rodario croakily, his feelings getting the better of him. He held the leather item out to her. "It came off your arm when I pulled you out of the water."

Without thinking she snatched for it—and Rodario caught sight of her right forearm. The daze of happiness on his face was wiped away as if he'd been given a smack in the face. From the elbow down the arm was transparent and glassy in places, while other parts were raw flesh, showing muscles and tendons and veins, under a see-through layer of skin. "Oh, ye gods!" he stammered. "What a ghastly . . ."

Coïra sprang up with a sob, grabbed her clothes and ran off.

Ireheart sat next to Tungdil at the campfire, where they were cooking meat, bread and vegetables on little spits. "What a shame we've got no more cheese," he said.

"I can still remember the stink of it!" retorted Tungdil, who had taken off his helmet, gauntlets and greaves. "Very well indeed. Trying to forget." He tasted the meat, which had been hopping through the fields half an hour earlier in the form of a rabbit. "I prefer this."

Ireheart was giving his ration a more critical inspection.

Tungdil finished chewing. "What's the matter? Doesn't it smell bad enough?"

He turned and twiddled the spit as if looking for something wrong with it.

"Do you think it might have absorbed some of the magic?"

"What magic?"

"How should I know?" Ireheart snapped. "If it ate a . . . flower that one of the famuli had modified?"

"Are you starting to believe your own fairy tales? Or is this some myth put about by our young Rodario?" Tungdil went on eating, unconcerned.

"It's just what they're all saying." He looked around. "Where's he got to, anyway?"

"He'll be wherever Coïra's disappeared to." Tungdil pointed over to the bushes.

"Aha!" was Ireheart's grinned, rather than spoken, comment.

"Gone for a swim. Not to have it off. The Zhadár are keeping an eye on them, Barskalín tells me. They'll be safe enough from attack."

Ireheart put the piece of roast rabbit down. "So it's true."

Tungdil sighed. "What do you mean—*so it's true?*"

"Magic!"

"No, not magic, by all that's unholy!" Tungdil said. "I said *attacks*! Wild animals or unfriendly forest-dwellers." He slammed his hand down on the ground. "There isn't any magic here. And there aren't any famuli here either. Never have been. The land is safe and the rabbits are especially safe."

"The rabbits weren't safe from us, though, were they?" Ireheart glanced at the runes on Tungdil's armor and grew deadly serious. "Those runes: They'd light up, wouldn't they, if the food was going to harm you?"

Slowly, very slowly, Tungdil put his food down. "Yes, they would," he grunted in reply. His patience was coming to an end. "Give me your rabbit. I'll eat it."

"Right you are, Scholar." Ireheart handed his meat over. "But just take a bite."

"*What?*"

"Take a bite. I just want to see if my rabbit is as safe as yours was." He pointed to the decorative inlay. "If it starts to glow I'll know not to eat the rest." He folded his arms across his chest. "Come on, hurry up. I'm hungry."

Tungdil stared at him in exasperation, then burst out laughing. "That's the kind of thing I really missed on the other side, Ireheart," he gasped, when he had calmed down. "There was nobody there like you." He bit into the meat and, when his runes stayed dark, he handed the food back to his friend. "I'll be glad to live in peace and quiet somewhere after these next battles," he went on, retrieving some vegetables from the edge of the fire. "I only hope I'll be able to adapt."

Ireheart was chomping his way through his meal with renewed appetite. "I managed to. Well, there was always some skirmish or other, out at Evildam, and we'd talk a lot about what battles might occur, but we weren't immersed in war all the time like you were. To live with the possibility is a sight different from actually having to fight day in, day out." He pointed his meat spit at Slîn and Balyndar. "In case you decide you'd rather be fighting, you could go back with the fifthlings. I've heard there's always trouble at the Stone Gate. Now the kordrion's gone, the first of the smaller monsters will be along soon."

"With my son? No thanks."

Ireheart coughed and looked at Tungdil, who was gnawing at some half-cooked vegetable and putting some spice on it made from dried rato herbs and salt. "So you know?"

"Of course."

"How?"

"You talk in your sleep, Ireheart." Tungdil shot him a smile over the top of the parsnip he was eating.

And once more the warrior-twin realized he was being taken for a ride. "You're taking the piss."

"Yup. I just felt like it." Tungdil chucked the empty stick into the fire. "I managed to hang on to one eye so I'm not completely blind. If everyone else can see it, why not me? He's exactly like me. It must be Tion's own work if Balyndar is not my flesh and blood. He hasn't said anything to me so I'll not broach the subject with him. I can understand it. It makes sense for him to reject me." He leaned back against a tree trunk and took out his flask. "It'll be easier for him if he continues to regard the king as his father. However this particular adventure turns out it'll be better for him if our two names are not mentioned in the same breath." He opened the flask and drank.

"I wish you sounded a bit more confident, my learned leader and high king," Ireheart muttered. He contemplated the bare bones left in his hands sadly. "There was hardly any meat on one of them. All fiddly little gristly bits. Not like a gugul. I'd give anything for one of them as my main course now." He looked at his friend. "Well? How does it make you feel, knowing you and Balyndis have a son?"

Tungdil stared into the fire. "I don't feel anything. For me he's just one of the dwarves like all the rest," he said dully, his eye unfocused.

Ireheart pulled a baked root out of the fire, shaved off the skin and added seasoning. "That's really sad, Scholar. I love my children, and there's no better feeling, you know. They make you furious at times but you get to be awfully proud of them as well." He nodded in Balyndar's direction. "He'd be one to be proud of. Looks fantastic, very good soldier and he'll make a splendid king for the fifthlings one day. Balyndis has brought him up well."

"Yes indeed, I would be proud of him," Tungdil repeated, lost in thought. "I will ensure he gets back unharmed to his mother," he vowed to the flames, closing his eye. "You take the first watch, Ireheart. Wake me when you get too tired."

Boïndil bit into the vegetable, which cracked open in his teeth like a juicy apple. "Before you seek the refuge of sleep," he said, "tell me one thing: Who are the unholy ones?"

"Gods in the land of the Black Abyss." Tungdil did not take the trouble to lift his eyelid.

"Ho, that's not a lot to go on. What kind of gods?"

"Cruel gods, Ireheart. Let me rest."

"And go on waiting?" He chucked the empty spit at Tungdil—it did not occur to him until afterwards what a risk he was taking. He screwed his eyes shut to be on the safe side and lifted his hand to shield his face.

The wooden spit hit the armor and fell to the ground.

There were no flashes or any other magic effects. Tungdil did not seem to have noticed.

Ireheart was about to say something but thought better of it. The soft voice of the last of his doubters demanded it. Who knows what this knowledge might be good for, it whispered in his ear, warning him not to betray himself. "Scholar! Tell me about these unholy ones? You know I like a good story," he urged his friend.

"The unholy ones," Tungdil began in a deep voice, "are ghostly beings. They show themselves in the blood of those who are sacrificed to them. This lifeblood can give them shape and form. A terrifying form that only the priests may behold without losing their minds."

"And were you one of them?"

"No. But I was able to look on them and keep my wits."

"Maybe that's why your mind has holes in it now."

"Firstly, my mind does not have holes in it. My memory does. And secondly, I've had enough of telling horror stories now."

Ireheart hugged his knees and wiggled his toes. "How many unholy ones are there? What do they do to be worshipped like that? Do they help in warfare?" He looked at Tungdil, who was already asleep. "Oy, Scholar! Give me a chance to learn something!" Should he dare to throw another piece of wood? "How do you know Tirîgon so well? I mean, what did the two of you get up to over there? And why on earth did you take the name of your dead . . . ?"

"That's enough!" The eye shot open and Ireheart was greeted with a stare that delivered physical pain. The brown iris was penetrating as an arrow, then it disappeared to be replaced by a greenish pulsating light, which transmuted into a pale blue.

One last flicker and the brown returned. "I want to sleep, Ireheart. There are many orbits ahead of us on our ride to the Blue Mountains and I will tell you more each time we make camp for the night. But not now!" He spoke with emphasis, regal and sharp, annihilating any objection. Then he shut his eye and arranged himself in a more comfortable position.

"Hmm," said Ireheart, kicking up the dust. *That was the false Tungdil again.* Without thinking, he picked up a branch and started whittling away at the end. His movements gradually became slower; his gaze rested on the sleeping dwarf.

"Then I'll sing a song to stave off boredom," he decided, and began a tune that Bavragor had taught him. He tapped out the rhythm on his leg armor.

But Tungdil did not react. Annoyingly.

At that moment Rodario came tearing through the bushes, his clothes awry, as if he had dressed in a hurry. "The queen has gone!" he called out in agitation.

"Disappeared off the face of the earth or has she run away because you were importunate?" Ireheart grinned. "Thought you were having a bathe. Not likely!"

Rodario came up to him. "She was scared . . . and ran away."

"Scared of your one-eyed trouser snake, I suppose."

"Listen to me!" He grabbed the dwarf by his broad shoulders. "She's run off into the undergrowth."

"You still haven't said what scared her, but never mind." He called Barskalín to ask which way the queen had gone.

But the Zhadárs' leader did not know. "My men were following her. We were watching the surrounding area, we weren't watching her and the actor," he explained to Ireheart.

"You were spying on us?" fumed Rodario.

"No. Or this would never have happened," muttered

Boïndil bad-temperedly, turning to Tungdil. "Scholar, wake up. We've got to find the maga and catch her. The nervous little filly has been shocked by a trouser snake and has run off into the undergrowth somewhere."

A very sleepy Tungdil opened his eye reluctantly. The glance he shot at Rodario promised him a long, unpleasant death.

They raced through the thickets downstream in a long line.

They could not take the ponies with them so the Zhadár and dwarves had to go on foot to pick up the queen's tracks.

The Invisibles easily found her trail but the maga had a head start. Their short legs put them at a disadvantage, but they could not let Rodario or Mallenia run off ahead under their own steam, for neither had the skills needed to follow the faint marks left by the maga's feet.

The part of the forest they were in now was not welcoming. There must have been a forest fire there about a quarter of a cycle ago, one that had left ruined tree trunks behind. Scorched and shriveled and dead, these hulks stood eerily on the black empty ground.

Men and dwarves ran through the ash, their feet disturbing it so that it rose in clouds to clog mouths and noses, and make eyes smart. Half-burned branches crumbled under their feet, and their boots and clothing turned gray.

Then they came to the ruins of an old building. The fire must have taken hold of a little forest hamlet. Ireheart could see skeletons. *Why did the people not flee from the flames— perhaps they were not able to run?* The thought of magic occurred to him at once . . .

"Over there!" called Tungdil, pointing to the right. "I can see someone running."

Ireheart could not see a thing. "I think . . ."

"Yes," agreed Barskalín. "It's a human."

Mallenia nodded to Rodario to put on a spurt of speed. "We'll catch up with her," the latter told the dwarves, as he followed Mallenia.

Strange emotions were swirling within him. On the one hand he was reproaching himself, but on the other he was not sure why: Coïra had taken flight because of his cry of horror, which she had misunderstood. But there was no time now to put things right. First of all they would have to catch up with her.

Mallenia had shot ahead, but he would not be shaken off. The group of dwarves were now some way behind.

The forest was changing again. The trunks now seemed to have been bent and twisted by the force of the fire, taking on the strangest of shapes. It was already growing darker here, so that the trees appeared terrifying, and the deathly hush that surrounded them made Rodario deeply uneasy. He was glad he had his sword at his side. And Mallenia, who was definitely a better warrior than he was.

"Coïra, stop!" he called out after her as she ran through the trees. She was extremely agile. "We are really worried about you!"

But the fugitive was not listening.

"Come on, call yourself a hero? Get a move on," said Mallenia, increasing her speed. "I don't like it. Everything here is dead. This forest is scary."

He silently agreed with her. There was nothing here, however, that could harm them: The fire was long gone, having consumed everything living and turned it all to ash.

The queen had changed course and was heading off to the right.

Between the scorched tree trunks they spied the outline of a fortified house, a defended barn or similar. Judging from the marks left by the flames it seemed the fire must have broken out in this building and then spread to the forest.

The queen ran through the small gate and disappeared inside the ruin.

"What's she doing?" panted Rodario. "Is she trying to hide from us?"

"That's just stupid. Childish and stupid." Mallenia left the forest and headed for the entrance. "Queen Coïra! Come out of there before you fall down some hole or get buried by falling masonry!" She went into the courtyard with Rodario at her heels.

They waited, listening out and watching the broken window panes, which stared back at them like empty eye sockets.

"Coïra?" Rodario called, very worried now. "You misunderstood me back there at the pool. If you come out I can explain."

"So it is your fault." Mallenia seized on this possibility. "I bet you said the wrong thing."

Rodario had decided not to speak about the ghastly discovery he had made. He wanted to speak to Coïra first. "Something like that." When he saw a face by one of the downstairs windows he raced off. "Coïra! Wait for me!" He grabbed hold of the crumbling wooden supports and peered into the dark room.

He was staring at a pair of light-colored eyes that were watching him fearfully—they were the eyes of a man!

XXII

Rodario sprang back and turned to Mallenia. "It's a *man* in there!"

"Are you sure?"

He leaned further in over the wooden frame and surveyed the stranger's face. "Absolutely sure. The stubble is a strong clue."

"Indeed, then it won't be the queen. Unless she has metamorphosed." Mallenia came over to the window to see for herself.

She guessed the man to be in his late thirties; once upon a time the garb he clutched about his body must have been a luxurious robe the color of malachite. Now it was a shabby tattered rag: Thorns had torn holes, and the forest floor had stained it. The man was wearing a greasy leather cap on his dark blond hair.

"What is your name?" she demanded.

The man cringed and crawled further back inside the room. As he did so, ash and charcoal crunched under his hands and feet.

Rodario caught sight of four costly rings on his fingers. "He's no beggar, that's for sure."

"Perhaps he managed to escape the fire but lost his mind?"

Mallenia kicked the wall sharply. "Where is the queen?" At the gate Tungdil was arriving with the other dwarves; she told him quickly what they had found.

Rodario climbed in through the window and slowly went up to the man. "Don't be afraid. We won't hurt you."

"Says who?" came Ireheart's voice from the open window. "If he's a villain, then we will."

"But you aren't a villain, are you?" Rodario crouched down by the man. "You're some rich man who has lost his way? Perhaps you were robbed? Or have magic plants been your downfall? Have you caught sight of a woman with long dark hair? In a dark-blue dress?" Behind him there came a crash and metallic clang, and gray dust rose up, settling on the sweaty face of this unknown figure.

It was Tungdil, who had just jumped in at the window. The man whimpered and cowered, his arms round his head for protection.

Tungdil grasped the man's right hand and pulled it hard, then brushed the dirt off the man's sleeve to reveal an embroidered symbol. He frowned and his face grew dark. "You are one of Nudin's followers," he challenged the man, grabbing him by the throat. "You have the effrontery to copy his style of dress and even his rings!"

Rodario stood up and placed a hand on his sword hilt. "One of Lot-Ionan's famuli?"

"Ha!" said Ireheart, triumphantly. "What a good thing I didn't agree we wouldn't harm him."

"He looks like one." Tungdil dragged the man over to the window and hurled him out into the courtyard. "We'll find out what he was doing here. And how much magic he still has." He instructed the Zhadár to increase their vigilance, then climbed back out. "Did he tell you his name?"

"No." Rodario followed the two of them outside and stood by Mallenia. "I wanted to try the gentle approach first. He seemed very distressed so I thought rough and loud treatment wouldn't prove helpful."

Tungdil drew Bloodthirster, placing the weapon's tip at the man's throat. "Talk!"

"Franek," he stammered. "My name is Franek."

Ireheart grinned. Occasionally there was something to be said for the dwarf-technique of interrogation.

"What brought you here? Why are you dressed like Nudin?" Tungdil gave him a kick that had him over on his back. "I don't have time to waste. We're looking for a woman . . ."

"I saw her!" Franek said quickly, raising his hands. "Please don't! I saw her! I know which way she went."

Ireheart had his crow's beak ready. "He could have been sent by Lot-Ionan to lead us into a trap."

"But how would he know we were coming?" Rodario studied Franek. "Shouldn't we hear his story first?"

"For me the queen is more important," interjected Mallenia. "And the same should go for all of us, surely?" She addressed the putative famulus. "Tell us! Where did she go?"

He slowly lifted his arm and pointed east. "To the Votons. She'll be dead by now."

"Who are the Votons?" Tungdil did not remove Bloodthirster from the man's throat.

"Hideous beings. Chimera, the result of Vot's experiments. He was one of Lot-Ionan's famuli," he explained, breathless with fear. "They used to be humans but he equipped them with the limbs of animals. They broke out of his laboratories and fled here."

Tungdil gave orders to Barskalín in a language they did not understand and the Zhadár raced off; then he turned to Rodario. "You stay and keep an eye on our friend here. He'll have a few more questions to answer when we get back with the queen."

Ireheart shook his head doubtfully. "We're setting an actor to guard a famulus?"

"If he could still do magic he probably wouldn't look like a dog that's been beaten half to death." The one-eyed dwarf indicated the quiescent runes on his armor as evidence there was no magic activity present. "Slîn can keep you company. The rest of you—come with me." He charged after the Invisibles, leaving the three of them alone in the courtyard.

Slîn closed the gate and lit a fire. Rodario handed Franek something to drink and brought over a few old timbers to sit on.

The fourthling laid his loaded crossbow on his knee. He scanned their surroundings carefully, on watch.

"Right, then, Franek. How about you help us to while away the time by telling us what made you want to carry on Nudin's work?" Rodario sliced some bread and ham. He gave some to Slîn, and the rest he passed to the famulus. "So you were apprenticed to Lot-Ionan?"

Franek looked at the actor. "A group of dwarves in black armor, an actor and a blond woman, all looking for a queen— that all seems very odd."

"Don't try to turn things around, my friend. You are going to report first," said Rodario. "Or I take your food away."

"I'll shoot it out of his mouth for him," Slîn offered, lifting the bow. "The food and bolt will fly out together through the back of his neck."

Franek stretched out his hands to the warmth of the flames. Out of the sun it quickly grew cool; spring had not yet transformed the winter nights. "All right. I'll tell you." He took a deep breath.

"I'll know if you're spinning a yarn," the fourthling warned him before he began. "Then my finger will jerk on the crossbow and you know what will happen next."

Rodario looked at him, tight-lipped. Franek began his story.

"Ingratitude. That's all I ever got from the magus. A girl friend and I fetched him out of a cellar in Porista when he was imprisoned there as a statue. We escaped from the guards, but the statue was stolen by other famuli. I nearly died. When I had recovered, I tried to enter Lot-Ionan's service. I wanted to become a magus, and that's how I was granted my longevity." He asked for, and was given, more water. "I was always there when he needed me. Together we conquered the Blue Mountains and annihilated the dwarves . . ."

"Charming. Tell us something different," growled Slîn, waving the crossbow. "My finger gets itchy when I hear stuff like that."

"As I was saying. We closed the gate to the south. And I supported him when he was nearly killed by the leader of the black-eyes. And how did he repay me?" He indicated his apparel. "Threw me out, he did."

"Not without reason, I expect?" Rodario listened carefully, trying to see if Franek was lying. He hadn't noticed anything yet.

"For a stupid reason."

"What was it?" Slîn's fingers caressed the crossbow. "I want to know."

Franek sighed. "The magic source. No one is allowed near it to refresh their powers without his permission."

"But you went there anyway?"

"What choice did I have? He was asleep and I had to . . ." He stopped. "Anyway. One of the other famuli woke Lot-Ionan and told on me. So he drove me out of the caves and allowed all the other famuli to hunt me down and try to kill me. Traitors had to be punished, he said."

"He's right there," muttered Slîn with a grin.

"If it hadn't been for me he'd still have been lying in a cellar in Porista, the old fool!" Franek did not follow up Slîn's remark. "I escaped through the deserts of Sangpur. Finally there was only one of them on my tail, and I threw him off the scent near where the Votons hang out." He looked at Rodario. "I thought you were him, that's why I ran away."

"How many pupils does the magus still have?"

"Four. Two of them are not much use, but he hasn't noticed that yet. Vot and Bumina are his best ones, apart from me, of course." Franek shrugged. "There's really nothing else to tell."

Slîn looked at Rodario. "Didn't he just say he'd shaken off his pursuer near the Votons?"

The actor had been watching Franek's features so closely for signs of dissembling that he had missed this detail. "By Palandiell! We must warn the others!"

Slîn looked doubtful. "How would you find them in the dark? My sight is sharper than yours, but I can't run so fast." Without warning, he shot Franek in the thigh. The man collapsed with an agonized cry. "Serves you right, you treacherous long-un. For every one of our lot that gets hurt there'll be another crossbow bolt for you. Three if anyone's killed. Luckily, you're long enough to have room for several shots." He reloaded.

"Stop it, Slîn!" Rodario called out. He could understand his comrade's anger. Franek had purposely kept them in the dark about the danger.

Rodario helped the victim to extract the bolt from his flesh and bandaged the injury with a strip of material they cut out of his robe.

"I forgot about Droman," whimpered the famulus, clutching his leg. The bandage was already soaked through with blood. "I swear by Samusin that I didn't send your friends off to danger on purpose."

"Well," said Slîn, "pain's good for making you remember." He did not regret having shot the man.

Rodario got up and went to the gate, opening it a crack. He looked at the crippled, charred trees.

There were particularly tall ones by the barn, stretching up into the night sky, and they cast long shadows. He could neither see nor hear anything of the Ido girl or the dwarves.

"How strong is Droman?" he called back into the yard.

"His sorcery, you mean?" Franek groaned, tearing off a second bandage from his clothing to stop the bleeding. "He's not as good as me if my magic is working properly. But my magic powers are exhausted. I can't even heal myself." He looked at Slîn. "So I'd be as vulnerable as you or this mole fellow here."

Rodario saw a shadow in the woods. It was bent double and making its way over to the barn, dodging from tree to tree. "Not nice," he murmured, both in reply to Franek's words and in response to the sight.

The worrying thing was that the longer he stared, the more shadows he thought he could see. The silhouettes did not look human.

He quickly locked the gate and returned to the fire, throwing more logs on. "Votons," he explained. I hope they're afraid of fire. Now would be a good time to show off your skills, Slîn."

"Charming!" The dwarf took his bolts and stood up. "As long as there are no more than fifty of them we should be all right. After that I run out of ammunition."

Rodario did not answer. He thought there might be more.

They were running through the twilight, with two Zhadár at the front. The size of more footprints they had found indicated they were probably made by Coïra.

But they had also found a number of different tracks that were not so easy to identify. Without what they had heard from the famulus about the Votons they would probably have thought them made by a herd of cattle, but the creatures responsible for these seemed to have both human and animal feet. Barskalín identified cattle prints alongside the human first, but there were also the pad marks of bears and other wild animals.

"I know why I don't like magic," said Ireheart grimly. "Unnatural animals! They may have legs like cows, but you won't be able to cut them up and roast them on a spit to eat."

"Isn't your wife a maga? And two of your children, too?" Tungdil jumped over a fallen tree with ease, as if the armor didn't represent any additional weight.

Ireheart took a little longer to get over the obstacle. "That's a different sort of magic," he corrected. "Dwarf-magic. It's never hurt me, not in two hundred cycles. Never harmed me or anyone else."

"But if Goda had remained with Lot-Ionan, who do you think we would have been campaigning against now?" Tungdil's voice sounded like a chief negotiator picking holes in the argument of the other side. "And perhaps it would have been *you* wearing my sort of armor."

"Never," Boïndil blurted out. "I mean, Goda would never have allied herself to evil . . ."

"Fair enough. I was only putting an idea out there."

Tungdil swung to the left at a signal from the Zhadár. The trees were thinning out and they found the queen face down on the scorched earth.

"Vraccas, don't let her be dead," Ireheart prayed, leaping forward and waving his crow's beak threateningly. "Ho, you mad magus-inspired creatures! Stay in your hiding places!" He lowered his head. "Or, better still, come out and let me rearrange your limbs for you!"

Tungdil knelt down next to the girl and turned her over; the Zhadár surrounded them, keeping a sharp lookout over the surrounding area. "She's still breathing," he said to Ireheart. "I can't see any injuries. Perhaps she's just overcome with exhaustion."

Coïra's eyelids flickered. "Take care," she whispered weakly. "They have set a trap for you . . . a famulus . . ."

A bright stream of magic shot out from behind the trees and struck one of the Zhadár full in the face. His head vaporized and his torso tumbled convulsing to the ground, as if the body was trying to carry out avoidance tactics. Blood came spurting out of the stump, splashing everyone.

"Get under cover!" Tungdil leaped forward, trying to locate the famulus in the shadows.

Ireheart certainly was not going to be seeking shelter. "He's mine!" He ran four paces at Tungdil's side to face the perfidious attacker. "I'll beat you to a pulp, Franek!" he vowed, utterly convinced the famulus they had found must have overpowered the actor and fourthling and followed them to attack from behind! "You won't get away with this!" he shouted angrily.

He was all the more bemused, then, to see a man appear before him in a pale gray hooded tunic and knee-high boots and with a broad sword hanging from his weapons belt. He was wearing light brown gloves and had his arms half raised. Presumably this unknown figure was in the middle of casting another spell.

"How many more of you are there in this accursed forest?" yelled Ireheart, launching an attack. "You're worse than mushrooms!" Then he realized he had misjudged the distance between himself and his foe.

Before he could reach his adversary he saw the left hand release three lilac-colored rays that fused into one, heading his way!

Just before the ray touched him, a black wall sprang up to protect him and then Ireheart saw a number of runes glowing brightly in front of his face as a wave of heat passed over him.

The dazzling light affected his eyes. No matter which way he turned his head, he could only register the afterimages of those symbols, making it well-nigh impossible to attack the famulus. "Scholar?" he called, listening for a response.

There was a hissing sound and again it grew as bright as day.

"Blast! Things were just getting better!" Ireheart complained. He could hear the clank of metal on metal, then there was a roar, and brightness and dark alternated swiftly—until there was a loud shout and a body fell onto the ash-strewn forest floor.

"Tungdil!" At least Ireheart was now able to recognize outlines. The squat black shape in front of him must be his friend. A human lay dead on the ground. "Thanks be to Vraccas," he said, relieved and disappointed at one and the same time. He had badly wanted to be the one to fell the enemy. "This hocus pocus is getting on my nerves. How did he get here?" He rubbed his eyes until he could see clearly again.

Tungdil had sliced the magician right through, and then finished him off with stabs to the heart. "These are Lot-Ionan's personal signature runes on his tunic," he mused.

"Was it him and Franek together, do you think, setting up that ambush? Or is he here by coincidence?" Ireheart went over to join Tungdil. The two of them looked at the young man's corpse.

Tungdil rammed Bloodthirster into the ground and searched the body and the rucksack. Apart from a bag of coins he found two keys, some provisions, and maps of Sangpur and Rân Ribastur. "Not very much there."

"No. Not very much." Ireheart leaned on his weapon. "Let's get back to the barn. Franek can tell us who this fellow is."

Tungdil ordered two of the Zhadár to carry the corpse. Mallenia supported the half-conscious Coïra. She was too weak to be able to speak much but hinted that the famulus had ambushed her and struck her down with a spell.

"Oh, my blessed forge," Ireheart murmured, stroking his beard. "If she can't stand up to a poxy famulus, how is she ever supposed to cope against Lot-Ionan?"

"Victoriously," was Balyndar's reply. "*I* don't doubt her abilities. If you get an arrow in the back what earthly use are your crow's beak and all your courage?"

Ireheart had to admit the young dwarf was right. But he was not happy about it and for some time went on searching for what would have been the perfect riposte.

Slîn had climbed up to the hayloft and opened the loading hatch above the gate. Lying flat on his stomach, he held the crossbow in front of him, his bolts stacked at one side.

As he watched the scorched forest, he made out several figures approaching the ruined building. His dwarf-eyes enabled him to detect the enemies in the twilight.

Whatever the famulus Vot had done in his experiments, merging humans and animals, these creatures were horrific!

Slîn saw a massive man's body which bore an ox head; where flesh met fur a stream of pus was oozing out. A pair of arms had been exchanged for the paws of a bear; on another monster he saw the hind legs of a horse, and yet others had tentacles instead of arms.

Some of the experiments were even worse: Vot had given human limbs and heads to animals. In three cases the chimerae had extra heads.

The clothes of these former human beings hung in shreds;

some of the monsters were completely naked, while others wore blood-soaked rags.

Slîn was more deeply disturbed by the sight of these abused and mutilated bodies than he would have been by a host of Tion's own monsters. Knowing that these had once been ordinary humans, not evil beasts, affected him greatly.

Even as he aimed at the heart of the first approaching enemy, his conscience told him he should spare the creatures and try to help cure them. *Perhaps Coïra can do something* was his first thought. But it was no good. She would have to conserve her magic powers in order to prevail against Lot-Ionan.

It's no use putting things off. Slîn doubted the horde of chimerae would be persuaded to stop on the strength of a vague promise or two. He had no choice. "Vraccas, you know this is the only way." He fired the bolt.

The shot pierced the naked breast of the bull-headed man, who stumbled and measured his length on the ash-covered floor. Clouds of dust rose up.

Slîn reloaded. The chimerae were a good three hundred paces away. *It's impossible to shoot all of them. I haven't got the ammunition or the time.* He yelled down to the others to hide and to keep their weapons at the ready. "I shan't be able to hold them all off."

His next victim was a woman with the legs of a horse. She was quicker on her feet than the others. She fell to the ground with a scream, losing her sword.

Two wolf-based chimerae were coming through the trees; they had human heads, but Vot had grafted on animal snouts, which gave them a grotesque appearance.

Slîn managed to shoot one of them, but the second had already reached the gate.

"Watch out! There's one at the gate!" he warned Rodario and Franek, reaching for his bugle. He desperately needed the support of the Zhadár, otherwise his mission to find fame and adventure in the burned-out forests of Rân Ribastur would be meeting an untimely end.

He let out a blast on the bugle and the chimerae reacted with shock to the sudden booming noise. Then he concentrated on doing away with the biggest and most dangerous-looking of the monsters. In some cases he shot them through the heart, but they only seemed to die after he had sent several bolts through their heads. Magic had made them almost invulnerable. *Or perhaps their hearts are not in the normal place?*

The selection he made led to some of the smaller chimerae getting through to the gate. They set up a cacophony of roars, shrieks and barks, sending shivers up the dwarf's spine.

Suddenly there was a crash and the creatures' noise was now coming from the inner courtyard.

Where else am I expected to be, all at the same time? Slîn turned round and aimed at the first thing he saw.

Rodario and Franek had not sought hiding places. Instead they had lit an enormous fire in the middle of the yard and armed themselves with burning planks.

"Charming. The long-uns are keen to do the hero thing," Slîn mumbled into his beard, shooting one of the wolf figures, which had been about to spring at the actor. In contrast to normal animals, these beasts did not seem worried by the heat and flames.

Something whipped through the air behind him and there

was a tight feeling round his ankle, as a tentacle trapped his leg. He turned, reloading as he did so.

A chimera man with tentacle arms had pulled himself up the wall and was halfway through the hatch; one arm was wrapped around Slîn's leg and with the other he was hanging from a beam. "Come over here to me, dwarf!" he growled. The tentacles tightened.

"I'd rather send you something over!" Slîn fired, but because his leg was being tugged from under him, he lost his footing and the bolt went astray, piercing not the creature's heart but its shoulder.

The chimera man screamed and pulled Slîn over, while climbing further up through the hatch. The second tentacle grabbed a beam and broke a piece off to use as a club. The makeshift weapon thundered down but the dwarf had seen it coming and was able to dodge. Holding the crossbow steady with both hands, he swung it like a pick-ax against the massive tentacle, but it was not enough to sever it.

Now he was at the feet of the chimera man. The enemy pressed his boot into Slîn's face; the tentacle round the leg slackened, and then was placed round his throat.

The dwarf employed the second mechanism on his crossbow, making a hidden dagger shoot out. He sliced through the tentacle and his adversary hopped backwards.

"I don't need the bolts!" Slîn shouted as he followed through, stabbing again and again.

But his adversary had been paying attention. He swerved and the stump of his tentacle swept the crossbow aside. The second long snake-like arm was going for Slîn's head.

Slîn ducked and pulled a hatchet out of his belt. He limped over to the right to put a support pillar between himself and the monster. The leg that had been mangled felt swollen. He was struggling to avoid further attacks.

Two more hybrids swung up through the trap door; they also had tentacles instead of arms. Vot had given the woman the head of a boar; the man had the skull of a bear on his shoulders.

The three of them united to hunt Slîn down, sending out their whip-like arms time and again to block off any escape.

Slîn was at his wits' end. "You asked for it," he told the chimera, brandishing his hatchet. "I'll do for you all!" With a loud war cry he launched himself at the creatures. A second tentacle dropped, severed, to the floor, where it executed a macabre spiraling dance.

But then four tentacles surged forward and swarmed round to encompass his upper body, legs and throat.

Slîn felt himself lifted up, then the pressure became pain and his head swam. He wanted to call out, but the bonds round his throat were too tight and he failed to utter a single sound.

Rodario dodged the attacking bear claws and smashed the burning plank against the chimera's head. Red and yellow sparks flew up and the head snapped round; the neck broke with an audible crack and the chimera fell dead.

"Another over by you, Franek!" he warned the famulus.

The man avoided the fangs from the wolf's head and hit back with both the planks he was holding, crushing bone between the two pieces of wood.

Rodario glanced over at the open gate where the monsters were flooding in. Slîn had already sounded a bugle call for assistance, but if Tungdil and the Zhadár did not arrive soon, help would be too late arriving. "Why doesn't he shoot?"

Suddenly the dwarf appeared in the loft opening, took aim and dispatched a wolf chimera with a single shot; then he disappeared.

"What's Beardy doing up there?" Franek was thrashing about with the planks but the attackers kept returning for more. They had smelled blood and were not going to give up or be frightened off.

Rodario exchanged one of the planks for his sword. Fire was not working for them, so it would have to be steel. "And all this just because Coïra got the wrong end of the stick," he muttered, as he stabbed a horse-headed woman. Her claw-like fingers failed to grab him and she careered past into the flames. "I could be lying by the pond with her doing all sorts of nice things."

"The pond?" Franek was running a creature through, half-dog, half-man. "Not the one by the waterfall?"

"Yes, that one."

"Then you were lucky. There's a monster at the bottom of that pool. Vot created that one, too." Franek was having to step back to avoid a man who had giant crab's pincers instead of hands. "Sometimes it comes out and eats everything it can grab."

Rodario groaned. *I might easily have had Coïra's death on my conscience.* "It sounds like you've been around these parts some time?"

"I had no choice." The famulus leaped through the flames to escape the clutches of a monster, which promptly turned its attentions on the actor.

Rodario struck out, but the crab claw caught the blade

and snapped it off! "Oh Samusin and Palandiell! Can one of you gods spare a second and come down and help us here?" He hurled the remains of the shattered weapon, injuring the chimera on the head. But he was not able to kill it.

The foe sprang forward, pincers agape.

Ireheart suddenly appeared and hit out with his crow's beak. The flat side smashed the armor and the claws were broken into tiny pieces. Blood sprayed out of a wound. "Ho, a fish-man!" Ireheart rammed the spike through the creature's throat and dragged it to the flames. A quick flick of the wrist and the sharp end of the crow's beak slid out of the creature's flesh and the creature stumbled into the fire. "Mmm, that smells good! A little bit of mayonnaise on the crab and supper is ready!" He laughed out loud.

Rodario saw the Zhadár attacking the monsters from the rear. The chimerae had no idea what was happening to them. They didn't have a chance. Only Ireheart had been too proud to be one of a crowd. He had stormed all the way to the front of the throng to get first choice of the enemy. It had been the saving of Rodario.

"Slîn's up there!" he called, pointing to the loft. "He's not alone."

"He'll be all right," said Ireheart, hurrying to get to one of the last of the hybrids before a Zhadár did.

"They are huge beasts up there fighting him. Bigger than all these," Rodario shouted.

Boïndil turned and looked toward the hayloft above the gate. "Then I'll go and check. Fourthlings aren't known for their stamina in battle." He grinned and made his way over, felling a lynx-chimera as he went which Barskalín had had his eye on. "Ha! I got there first!"

Rodario was impressed by the speed and precision with which the Invisibles had moved in. The battle in the courtyard was over before he knew it. Surrounded by the dead bodies of that intimidating horde of rampaging monsters, he was struck also by how quiet everything suddenly was.

Tungdil had taken no part in the general slaughter. He was talking to Mallenia, who was still supporting Coïra. Balyndar stood guard over Franek.

"My queen!" Rodario hurried over to the young woman. She looked exhausted.

Lifting her eyes hesitantly, she instinctively hugged her right arm closer to her body. "I'm all right. The famulus tried but he couldn't kill me."

"Franek didn't warn us until it was too late. Maybe he forgot on purpose." He looked at the famulus, then at Tungdil. "I'd advise you to have a word or two with him. He seemed more eager to talk when you were being persuasive. Maybe his memory has improved a bit."

A loud dwarf-laugh rang out from up in the hayloft, then came the sound of steel on flesh. And then a scream.

"What's happening?" Tungdil looked at the hatch.

"I sent Boïndil to do some tidying up," Rodario explained. "I think Slîn was having trouble and it seems to be giving your friend a great deal of pleasure to help him out."

They heard Ireheart laughing again, and then angry voices, curses and noise of the crow's beak smashing home.

Balyndar gave a command to the Zhadár, but Tungdil interrupted with a gesture. "No, let him do it on his own. Why shouldn't he have a bit of fun?" He stomped over to Lot-Ionan's former pupil.

Rodario asked Mallenia to leave him and the maga alone

for a few moments. After a swift exchange of glances with the queen, the Ido girl followed Tungdil.

Coïra looked up shyly, "Did you . . . ?"

"No, I haven't told anyone what I saw. And I shan't." Rodario took her left hand. "Back there at the pond you misunderstood me."

"What was there to misunderstand?" she flashed, hurt. "You said, *How ghastly!*" Her anger vanished and her shoulders drooped. "But you were right. Let me explain what you saw."

"But first I want you to know what I was really trying to say: 'What a ghastly injury, Coïra.' That's what I was saying."

"Is that all?" She sought his eyes.

"That's all. You are far too beautiful and kind and sweet-natured for anyone to say anything unpleasant about. I think you know what feelings I have for you." Rodario smiled at her and took her hand in his. "Will you tell me about it now?"

A muffled cry rang out and a chimera came flying through the hayloft hatch; he landed directly at the feet of two Zhadár, with blood spurting from the many injuries to his chest. For a split second Ireheart was visible in the opening, long enough for a wave and for them to know he was unharmed. Then he raised his weapon and leaped off to the right with a war cry.

"He lives only to fight," was Coïra's comment.

"It's battle-frenzy. Hot blood. They always used to say that about him—and rightly so," the actor said with a grin. Crashes and thumps echoed down from the hayloft. "He's having the time of his life, egging them on."

The maga slipped her hand under his arm. "Thank you,"

she whispered. "Thank you for keeping silent, and for not despising me on account of my arm." It seemed to be difficult for her to speak about the disfiguring blemish. "It happened while I was doing magic once. A spell exploded in my hand and damaged it badly. You would not understand the technicalities because you are not a magus, but take my word for it: Some parts of the magic spell remain lodged in my flesh. That's why I can't heal the wound permanently; it can only be hidden if I've enough magic power in me to suppress it. The less power I'm left with, the more the injury opens up and festers. A long-lasting spell contains the sensitive area inside a kind of glass covering. That's what you saw. No one notices; I always wear gloves."

Rodario felt enormous sympathy for the young woman. "And what happens when your magic runs out *completely*?"

"My arm will be destroyed." Coïra gave a brave smile. "I shall lose it."

"From the state of your arm I can guess you have very little magic left. Am I right?" He checked how close the dwarves were standing, to see if they would have been able to overhear.

A second chimera came flying through the loft opening, landing next to the first. Its skull had been smashed and there was a gash on the right-hand side of its head.

"One more to go!" they heard Ireheart crowing. "One more, then I'm done! Huzzah! They're a whole lot tougher than orcs!"

The Zhadár laughed.

Coïra took a deep breath. "It's true. That's why I had set my hopes on the source that was supposed to be in the Red Mountains."

Rodario felt he must have turned pale. "So are you in any way capable of facing Lot-Ionan?"

"Now I've done it!" They all heard Boïndil's voice, as a third defeated chimera plunged to the ground from the hayloft. The victorious dwarf appeared, supporting Slîn and wearing a grin wider than his own face. "That was just my type of battle," he exulted. "Decisive victory, killing marauding beasts, saving a comrade's life—what more could I want?" He nudged Slîn, who moaned in response. "Ho fourthling, show your teeth and smile for us! You're still alive! These beasts aren't!" he said, indicating the three slaughtered tentacle-creatures. He brought the dwarf over to the fire and set him down next to Balyndar and Franek. "I could murder a whole barrel of dwarf-beer." He gave a deep sigh.

Rodario applauded and put on a cheerful face. Then he turned back to Coïra. "Tell me, honestly: Can you defeat Lot-Ionan? Or not?"

XXIII

The Outer Lands,
The Black Abyss,
Fortress Evildam,
Spring, 6492nd Solar Cycle

Goda leaped up, awakened from deepest sleep. *Alarm trumpets?*

The door burst open and Boëndalin called her to come out onto the battlements. "The barrier! It's gone! The beasts are trying to get through the North Gate!"

The maga sprang out of bed, throwing her robe over her night attire; she slipped her boots on and followed her son. It must still be the middle of the night—it felt, at least, as though she had only just dropped off. She grabbed her coat and the reticule that contained the last four splinters of diamond.

She had not vouchsafed to a soul the current state of the magic defenses—not even to her children.

Their recent sortie was deemed a victory despite the heavy losses and they had celebrated in order to honor the sacrifice of the fallen warriors. The monsters of the Black Abyss were beginning to rebuild their war machinery, it was true, but they were working more slowly this time. They seemed exhausted. And that had been enough to give the defenders a ray of hope.

But appearances have been deceptive, Goda thought, as she and Boëndalin traveled up in the lift to reach the tower. *They've tricked us and lulled us into being negligent.*

The battlement walkways and tower over the gateway were starkly illuminated, with all the torches lit. Streams of boiling pitch were being tipped out of the special gullies and glowing coals hurled down onto the beasts laying siege to the fortress; arrows and spears shot out from the catapults. Burning sacks of petroleum were dropped over the edge to burst on landing, turning monsters into living torches. Fire arrows whizzed to and fro between the defenders and besiegers, piercing the black clouds. It was an impressive picture.

But the monsters were not dismayed by the strength of the bombardment.

Small mobile battering rams were at hand and already being used, as Goda could hear from the repeated thuds. The screams of monsters in the distance sounded only as a monotonous low murmur, like the babbling of a brook.

The magic screen had disappeared, and none of the smaller beasts were on the plain anymore. They were all heading for the North Gate, taking their half-completed siege towers with them.

"I don't get it," Goda said to herself. *Why on earth the North Gate? Are they trying to draw our attention away from the South Gate?* She leaned over and looked down.

"We thought it was a trick at first, too," Boëndalin said. "But the other towers report no activity. The beasts are attacking in the north in a mad frenzy and the gate guards are in trouble. I've given orders for all the soldiers and ammunition to be sent over."

"I want to see for myself." Goda watched the Black Abyss

closely as she ran with her son, past the western gate and on to the northern defenses. It was a very long way.

The ravine was in darkness and the paths leading out of it were empty and abandoned. Every single one of the monsters had assembled at the northern gateway.

"Either their reinforcements are hiding, waiting to see what the outcome will be, or else they haven't got any extra forces," Boëndalin told her when he saw her enquiring glance. "So the northern gate is not a bad choice for them. It's the last place we would have expected them to attack."

"But they must know we can move in extra troops fast along the battlements and through the inside corridors," she objected. "It's a false attack, I'm convinced. They're trying to distract us." She watched the fighting, which was growing more violent now. "Where is their magus?"

"No sign of him," replied Boëndalin. "Do you think . . . ?"

"They are carrying out the attack *for him*," said Goda. "He's planning something. He wants to tie up all our efforts on that one side." She looked over at the south tower and stopped. "I'm going to hurry back. You get to the north tower and take command. As soon as you spot the magus, send me a message." She embraced him swiftly and departed at speed.

Boëndalin charged off in the opposite direction.

Bandaál tied his boots, threw on his chain-mail shirt, grabbed his ax and hurried into the corridor. Even if no one had given them the call to arms, the young famulus wanted to be part of this. The fortress might be in need of every bit of available help.

"Wait!" The door to Sanda's chamber was open and his

sister came out. She was also wearing armor and carrying an ax. They were both gifted in magic but this did not prevent them using conventional weapons sometimes. Not being the same standard as their mother, they could not rely solely on their magic.

"Didn't they wake you, either?" Bandaál adjusted her helmet.

She thanked him by correcting the lacing on his chain-mail tunic. "No. Mother wanted to let us sleep."

He looked at her. "Or do you think it's because of the failure of the mission?"

"It wasn't a failure," she retorted. "We killed lots of the beasts and destroyed masses of their equipment."

He sighed. "You know what I mean." He ran off, his sister at his heels.

"You reckon they think more highly of our warlike siblings and brother Boëndalin? That may be so." Sanda held her ax in her hand; it got in the way in her belt. "That's why it's important we are seen."

They hurried along the corridor that housed their family's rooms. This was where the dwarves rested, and where they shared their community life. Evildam was nothing but an artificial symmetrical mountain with a system of tunnels and chambers.

They crossed the communal living area where the Doubleblades often met up and sat together in the evenings to discuss the events of the orbit, on past the kitchen, and then they reached the lift shaft that went all the way from the foundations to the highest battlement tower. The lift was a tremendous boon.

Bandaál touched the lever to move the weights and call

the lift cage down to their level. "I wonder what the monsters are up to?"

"It must be pretty bad if they sounded the alarm for the whole fortress," said Sanda, thoughtfully.

"Apart from where we were." Bandaál decided that, after the attack—or whatever it was—he would have a serious talk with his mother. Even if she did not want any of her famuli near her, he and his sister needed to be told of any danger. How did it look if the fortress commander's own children slept on in comfort while the defenders on the walls were fighting for their lives?

The lift cabin turned up and they pushed the grille aside and got in.

To their surprise the lift traveled down, not up, as the young magician had directed the machine.

"Is it broken?" Bandaál moved the handle a few times and the cage's descent slowed.

"Perhaps there's someone else wanting to use it?" Sanda counted the marks on the shaft wall as they passed; they had reached the ground floor. The lift jerked to a halt—but there was no one standing waiting.

"Where are we?"

"By the entrance." Sanda looked out. "Hey? Anybody there? Did someone want to come up top with us?"

Then the cabin was jolted. One of the transmission chains had broken, slamming onto the roof of the cage and unreeling noisily. The whole cage structure creaked and bent under the extra weight and the cabin started to crumple.

"Get out!" Bandaál ordered, giving his sister a push. Before he could follow her, the second chain broke and the lift shot down into the darkness.

Sanda stumbled forward into the corridor, heard the infernal crash behind her and whirled round. She saw the second chain flying past and heard the bang and clank of the impact; the chains were still unreeling and burying the lift and her brother with it. He was right down at the bottom of the fortress lift shaft.

"Bandaál!" she shrieked in alarm and went over to the shaft, where the ends of the chain were snaking past. One last clank and then quiet. Far below her she could make out the steel-gray shimmer of the broken cabin and the chain links. "Bandaál!"

The dwarf-girl turned and was about to head for the stairs—but someone called her name. The voice came from the shaft.

She turned quickly, leaned over and used her hands as a loud hailer. "Bandaál! Hang on!"

A beige shimmer of light coming from above made her lift her head. She froze with terror and could not turn away.

Five paces overhead the leader of the monsters hovered in mid-air. Countless fingers of light shot out from his vraccassium armor to meet the walls of the shaft, as he sank gently down. He had his hammers stuck in his belt; his right armored gauntlet was glowing and held a torn length of glowing chain links. The lift's collapse had not been an accident.

Still held aloft by the beams, he gradually reached Sanda's level and walked toward her. The soles of his boots met stone with a metallic clank. He crouched down by the dwarf-girl.

His left hand took hold of Sanda's chin, forcing her head round so that she was staring her adversary directly in the disfigured face. She noticed a turquoise smoke diamond in the palm of the gauntlet. Horror was starkly obvious in her eyes but she was unable to make a sound.

The dwarf's face moved, and folds developed around his eyes in semblance of a smile, although any real expression was impossible because of the mutilation. He tossed the length of chain down the shaft, then ran the back of his gauntleted hand through her hair, along her neck, across her breast, down to her waist. Then he stood up without letting go of her chin, pulling her upright.

Sanda could do nothing to defend herself. The very sight of him, the smell of stale sweat and festering wounds and the slight pulsating throbbing that went through her from his touch, all left her unable to move. His magic power, she registered subconsciously, was greater than anything she had ever felt before. Not even the artifact could outdo this.

The dwarf made a moaning sound, then looked down the shaft and stretched out his free hand. He released a rust-brown beam from the smoke diamond completely destroying what was left of the lift. The metal melted in the magic onslaught, bending and oozing to the ground in molten droplets.

"No!" shouted Sanda, terrified for her brother.

The dwarf let go of her chin and hit her across the face so that she fell against the wall and slid to the ground. At the same time he raised the other arm without interrupting the ray of light. This blasted out great chunks of the shaft wall, until the entire edifice shook.

He grabbed Sanda by the nape of the neck and set her on her feet, pushing her along ahead of himself. As soon as she made any slight movement of defiance he gave her a shock that flooded every organ in her body with pain.

The famula sobbed as blood ran down from the cut on her head, dripping down to the floor. She did not know what the dwarf intended to do with her. Why didn't he just kill her? Or did he . . . could he . . . surely not . . . ?

When he pushed her into a side corridor and tugged at her robe, her worst fears proved true.

Goda had reached the south tower when the building shook under her feet—it was only a slight vibration and a human would not have noticed it at all, but dwarves are sensitive.

"I knew it!" She ran to the lift and found only an empty shaft. No matter how she turned the levers, nothing happened. When she looked over to the rollers round which the chains would normally be wound, there was only bare stone.

A dwarf came running up the stairs. "My lady, the lift has crashed!" he said, fighting for breath. "Both chains have broken."

"Impossible! They can withstand a greater load than would ever fit in the cabin." She took a jewel in her hand. "Call the guards. They must search the place floor by floor. "I'll start down in the foundations."

The soldier asked, "What are we searching for?"

"Intruders."

"The gate is bolted and barred and no one . . ."

"Do what I say!" she snapped and flew down the stairs. It would take forever to get down to the basement like this.

To construct a fortress by simply building onto sand or earth would be criminally stupid, because its weight would make it subside, jeopardizing the whole edifice. For this reason Evildam's foundations were made from huge blocks brought in by dwarf-muscle effort and complicated technology. The foundations were reinforced on the side nearest the Black Abyss in case of an incursion. Bottles of poison, acid and gas; false walls that would collapse; all this and more had been put in place to greet any subterranean invader. No one could undermine a dwarf-stronghold.

Despite falling down seven steps, Goda arrived at the bottom in one piece. She had not noticed the coating of blood on the floor. She stopped and listened attentively.

She heard someone whimpering. It was her daughter's voice!

The maga slipped quietly through the corridor and the sounds grew louder, coming from one of the side passages.

She looked carefully round the corner and saw the opposing magus about to strip her daughter naked.

Goda pressed the diamond splinter in her hand so hard that she drew blood. She must not let her fear gain the upper hand. Too much was at stake. *Vraccas, you hold in your hands your own fate and that of my daughter!* She leaped round the corner and hurled a spell against the enemy dwarf.

He noticed too late to invoke a counter-spell. Instead, he threw Sanda into the corridor, pulled back his arms and offered his armored chest to the incoming beams of lava-red light.

The magic hit home and the dwarf's armor glowed like fiery coals fanned by bellows. The vraccassium changed color to a flaming yellow, sucking the magic in, while the runes turned black as night.

"Kill him, Sanda!" yelled Goda. She had nothing but dust in her hand. She swiftly took out the next diamond splinter to add to her spell or to respond to an attack. But what she had just seen stole any last hope. She would never be able to overcome this dwarf with magic.

The glow vanished and Goda saw Sanda behind the enemy, ax raised. She thrust its blade down, hitting the dwarf in the tiny gap between the side of the neck and the edge of his helmet. But the blow was deflected by a protective layer of chain mail; the dwarf swayed slightly, making a frightful gurgling sound.

"Save Bandaál!" cried Sanda, "He's at the bottom of the shaft . . ."

The dwarf hit out behind him and his gauntlet caught Sanda on the temple; she crumpled up.

Goda did not hesitate for a single eye-blink. Her daughter was not now in immediate danger and so she could risk using one of her strongest spells. It was the one she had originally employed to blast away the mountain above the Black Abyss, so it ought to suffice for this dwarf. It would *have* to!

She concentrated hard and sent out a lightning flash beam toward her adversary.

The dwarf hunched down and stretched out his arms as if appealing for clemency. But the energy streamed into the smoke diamond in his armored fist, turning it into a sparkling turquoise star. As the magic heated the metal there was a smell of burning flesh and the dwarf cried out in a voice more bloodcurdling than anything Goda had heard before in her whole life. But, determined to absorb the magic energy, he still did not lower his arm.

Yet again she felt a diamond splinter turn to useless powder between her fingers. The powerful beam failed. "I'm not letting you leave Evildam alive," she threatened, reaching into her bag. But she found nothing—except a hole. "No!" *When I fell on the stairs!*

The enemy magus groaned; smoke issued from the joints of his gauntlet, but he had survived the magic blast. His powers of resistance were incredible!

Goda now had nothing to fall back on but her own innate magic. "I shall defeat you!" she growled, lifting her arms. "We don't need a false Tungdil and we don't need a Lot-Ionan to be rid . . ."

The dwarf laid his smoldering hand on Sanda's breast, and fixed Goda with hate-filled eyes. He touched one of the runes on his breastplate with his left hand and a transparent dark-yellow sphere enveloped the two of them. Another blink of an eye later and they had disappeared, together with the magic ball!

"Vraccas, no!" Goda whispered in horror and ran to where the magus had just been standing. Her daughter's blood, her ax, shreds of her tattered undergarments and some charred pieces of material—nothing else. "How did he do that?" She ran back into the passage, back to the main corridor, back to the shaft—nothing!

Footsteps rang out and a unit of dwarf-warriors charged up the steps. "My lady, what has happened?"

"Find my daughter," she told them, stammering with anxiety; then she remembered what Sanda had said. "No! Go down to the basement and find my son, Bandaál, at the bottom of the shaft! Quick!" she screamed, distraught, and raced up the staircase. She tried the place where she had slipped on the steps, and picked up one of the lost splinters; she had no time to look for the others. If need be she would get some soldiers to do a thorough search later on.

Holding the diamond fragment she raced downstairs to where the soldiers were trawling through the debris of the cabin at the bottom of the shaft. The cage walls had mostly fused with the metal chains when they had melted; on top of the ruined cage were piles of huge sections of collapsed masonry.

"Let me through!" Her voice broke with emotion. In a frenzy of desperate anxiety for her son she labored at the wreckage, burning her hands on hot metal, but not stopping for a second, until she glimpsed a bloodied hand. "Bandaál!" She pulled at the blackened debris which had, by some miracle, buried but not smothered him in molten metal.

More of the dwarves and ubariu sprang to assist her, bringing crowbars, poles and rope.

Together they managed to hack out a niche in the mix of metal and stone. Goda peered in, candle in hand.

"He is still alive!" she sobbed in utter relief. "I can see that he's breathing!"

A loud crash came from above their heads; dust and small stones rained down. The damaged lift shaft was threatening to collapse.

"We must get out, my lady!" A ubari's hand shook her shoulder.

But she snapped back at him not to touch her. "We must free my son first."

"Look out, below!" called a voice. "The supports are about to give way!"

Goda looked at the diamond splinter. *I have no choice.*

He is nearly a magus. And he is my son. She closed her eyes and chanted a spell.

As if moved by spirit hands the great lumps of broken stone levitated, revealing Bandaál's body. Three of the dwarves pulled the badly injured famulus out of the shaft and took him to safety on a stretcher. Goda withdrew as well, before letting the spell drop.

A grinding grumbling sound above them preceded a rock-fall that could not be stopped by the debris floating in the air. It all crashed down, some of the rocks rolling out of the shaft right to the feet of the dwarves.

Grayish clouds of dust shot along the corridors as the shaft walls collapsed. The soldiers and maga were covered from head to foot in a thick layer of dirty white particles.

Goda opened her hand and let the remains of the crumbled diamond drift down onto the rest of the dust. It made no difference now. Then she set off after the stretcher, not knowing which child to worry about first: Bandaál or Sanda?

Girdlegard,
The Former Queendom of Rân Ribastur,
Northwest,
Spring, 6492nd Solar Cycle

Coïra cast her eyes down. "Not unless Aiphatòn and the älfar have managed to deplete Lot-Ionan's strength significantly," she whispered. "I have prayed to the gods to let me find an undiscovered source of magic somewhere on the way! Perhaps they will have pity on us and there will be a miracle."

Rodario unobtrusively indicated Franek, who, surrounded by

dwarves, was talking to Tungdil and Ireheart. He looked intimidated and was defending himself with upraised hands against harsh rebukes. "Perhaps he is our miracle." The two of them sat down and he told her what the exiled famulus had reported.

"It was this Droman character that I met," she said, leaning against Rodario's shoulder, glad to have sorted out their difficulties and misunderstandings. "He chased me with a tranquillizer spell and dragged me off to a clearing when he saw I was not on my own. But they defeated him."

"It didn't go well for him, as I hear." He put his arm around her shoulders to comfort her.

Coïra nodded. "That's right." She was enjoying his presence but her eyes were wary, watching for Mallenia, who was over with the dwarves. She had a guilty conscience because Rodario was spending time looking after her, and she was aware of her friend's feelings. He must be told the truth and made to understand how embarrassing the situation was for the two girls. "Rodario, there's something I've got to tell you," she began, but just then Tungdil turned round and waved them over.

"Keep it for later," said Rodario. "Our leader wants us now." He helped her up and they walked past the fire and over to the dwarves.

Tungdil made room for them at the campfire. "Franek regrets that he forgot to tell us about the famulus who had been chasing him."

"He regrets it so much that he wants to lead the way," Ireheart added merrily. "Not that we thoroughly trust the little wizardling. If he takes us into a trap he will die before any of us do." He thumped Franek on the back. "Ho! I'm right there, aren't I?"

"Yes," the famulus coughed out his answer. "I will do everything I can to make Lot-Ionan pay for his betrayal and his ingratitude toward me." He looked at them all. "I know nobody here will trust my words if I swear an oath, so I shan't bother. Suffice it to say, hatred unites us. That is stronger than anything else."

"Hatred?" Rodario was baffled. "Was our mission . . . ?"

"Hatred of my foster-father for letting himself become such an evil person and for inflicting such damage on my native land," said Tungdil. "I have sworn he shall die; remember, actor. Against your will."

Rodario hit himself on the back of the head, noting the comedy that was being played out for the benefit of the famulus. "I keep forgetting that you insist on killing him," he announced. "You have, of course, every justification for doing so."

Franek appeared to swallow this, or else he was keeping his suspicions to himself. "And we've agreed I shall be allowed to bathe in the magic source?"

"Not before Coïra has used it, little wizard," Ireheart stressed threateningly. "You will wait your turn nicely."

"I don't mind that. The source has enough energy for thousands of us." Franek scratched his stubbly chin. "It will be a great feeling. After such a long time."

"Get some sleep. We'll be leaving first thing." Tungdil assigned one of the Zhadár to guard duty, then moved off with Ireheart, Rodario, Barskalín, Mallenia and Coïra to find a place to sit at a suitable distance from the famulus.

"Providence has sent him to us."

Mallenia folded her hands and found a stone to sit on; the whole group settled down to talk. "You don't think it could just be a very clever trick on the part of the magus?"

"No. He's got no idea we're coming," Tungdil insisted. "If he did, he'd have sent out all his magic apprentices, not just the one."

"Droman. That was his name?" Coïra placed a hand on her back where the man's magic had hit her. She thought she could still feel warmth on that spot. "He wasn't a bad magus."

"But he wasn't good enough," said Ireheart. "The Scholar took him apart." He remembered that he had not actually seen how the famulus had died. Because his eyes had been dazzled.

"I talked to Franek and his story sounded credible. He was one of those young people who smuggled Lot-Ionan's statue out of the former palace in Porista. We never met him at the time, however," Tungdil explained. "We dealt with the other ones: Risava, Dergard and Lomostin."

Ireheart was amazed at Tungdil's precise memory of the names. How was it that he was able to remember such insignificant details? He knew the story, himself, of course, but though he remembered how the statue had been hunted down, and could also recall the long-legged frog-figure that had turned up to steal it back, for the life of him and for all the gold in Girdlegard he would not have been able to come up with the names of the statue's abductors.

Tungdil stared at the tips of his fingers. "I asked him if he could give us some explanation of the change in Lot-Ionan. When he told me how the magus dresses, how he conducts himself and speaks, I was forced to think of Nôd'onn."

"Not him again! We did away with that evil. The daemon

cannot have returned." Ireheart pretended to be swinging an ax. "You took Keenfire and split the fog down the middle . . . you know, that cloud-creature."

"Do you remember how we all wondered who had drilled a hole in Lot-Ionan's statue?"

"Someone trying . . . to kill him? To gain access to his magic powers?" Ireheart's eyes grew huge. "No, someone *was inserting something into him*. By Vraccas! They put the seed of evil into him when he was defenseless and when we woke him up again the seed started to sprout!"

Tungdil nodded. "Franek says that Risava nearly killed him when he objected to her plan. It was her who wanted Lot-Ionan to turn evil after his release."

Boïndil's face became thoughtful. "I'm trying to imagine what you stick into someone to make them evil. It sounds so . . . simple? But I'm sure it's not."

Coïra nodded. "I can't imagine it, either."

"Don't trouble your heads. You'd never work it out." Tungdil picked up a stone. "Risava had picked up a splinter of the malachite crystal that used to belong to Nôd'onn. She kept it. When Franek brought her the petrified statue of Lot-Ionan, she knew how she could try to use it. She drilled a hole and put the last fragment of evil into him. Lot-Ionan never had a chance to protect himself."

Ireheart scraped his foot along the ash-strewn ground. "That would mean that Lot-Ionan is actually innocent. He can't help what he has done. Because he . . . is possessed." *How infuriating. So we can't just do away with him.*

"I suppose we could have expected no less from Nudin, when the demon changed him into Nôd'onn," Mallenia interjected. "It doesn't free us from the duty of pursuing him."

"We have to. At all costs. We need him to defeat Vraccas," Tungdil said emphatically.

"To defeat your master, Scholar, not Vraccas. The god Vraccas is my creator, but the dwarf we want to kill is no divinity." Ireheart studied his friend. "I've been thinking: Can't we take the splinter out of Lot-Ionan? And make him good?"

"We need an evil magus to help us against my former master," Tungdil argued. "I would also have preferred to free him from the evil curse first."

Coïra wiped her nose with a handkerchief. "I hope we manage it. To free him from the malachite splinter."

"I know exactly where it lies. It will be painful for Lot-Ionan but he will survive. With Goda and yourself, Your Majesty, we have two magae who can apply healing remedies to ensure his recovery after the operation." Tungdil looked round. "Not a word of our plan to Franek. He has to think that we want to kill Lot-Ionan in order to liberate Girdlegard. If we deprive him of this goal, he may decide he doesn't want to help us."

Ireheart frowned. "All well and good, but we won't let Franek enter the magic source, will we, Scholar? Who knows what deceitful tricks he has up his sleeve? He could easily have been the one who shoved that malachite into Lot-Ionan's body. You can't trust the word of a traitor."

"I'm against it, too," said Rodario, and Mallenia agreed with him. "We should overpower him and tie him up as soon as we arrive. Then the secondlings can decide his fate. He was involved in the destruction of their homeland and has that guilt to bear." He looked at Ireheart. "I don't suppose you want to let him get off scot-free."

"Ho! I certainly do not!" Ireheart tapped his crow's beak. "An eye for an eye."

Tungdil studied his friend. "You watch him, Ireheart. Franek trusts us as little as we trust him. I'm sure he'll want to cancel our forced alliance before we do. If he tries to escape, you'll know what to do." He looked at Coïra. "And the same as before goes for you now. Don't go using your magic. You've seen we can manage to keep the enemy off without it."

She nodded. He was obviously not intending to blab out her secret. To make sure Rodario did not, either, she took his hand and pressed it. He looked surprised, but said nothing.

Tungdil pointed to the house behind them, while calling over one of the Zhadár to bring him the rucksack the dead famulus had been carrying. "You all get some rest. We'll move on in the morning. Unfortunately the incident with Droman means we'll have to speed up. Lot-Ionan will be wondering where his famulus has got to and he'll be sending out scouts to find him. We know full well, ever since Lakepride, that he's capable of causing serious trouble." He unrolled the maps on his knee and called Barskalín. "Let's find the quickest route."

Mallenia got up. "What if we get there before the älfar?"

Tungdil was poring over the sketch map. "We'll still head for Lot-Ionan's realm. Time is running out."

"So suddenly?" queried Rodario.

"So suddenly." The one-eyed dwarf said nothing more on the subject and busied himself with the maps. The group retired, bewildered, to the gate house.

Coïra found Mallenia, who had sorted herself out a corner of the attic and was spreading her blanket to lie on. "I wanted to thank you for coming to find me."

"You would have done the same for me." The Ido girl sat down and got comfortable, then spread her long mantle over herself. She looked at the maga for a long time. "You didn't think I'd abandon you because of our rivalry for Rodario's affections?"

Coïra attempted a smile.

"Look," Mallenia raised herself up on her elbows. "You've got an advantage over me when it comes to winning his heart. I saw you take his hand just now. He didn't object." Her eyes fixed the maga. "When I said at the pool that we should share him, I meant it. It's up to you."

"And up to Rodario," Coïra corrected.

"He's a man. He's bound to like the idea of having two women," retorted Mallenia with a grin, settling down on her hard bed. "I'm not worried about the choice he'll make." She clasped her hands behind her head. "There are regions in Tabaîn where it's considered quite normal for a man to have as many wives as he likes, as long as he's able to feed and clothe them. There's nothing shameful about a set-up like that. Or do you disagree? Nobody would be forcing us into it."

Coïra did not know what to reply. Of course they had heard in Weyurn about the practices in neighboring Tabaîn, but she had always been troubled by the idea of this kind of communal living. And she was not yet clear in her own mind how she felt about Rodario. Youthful infatuation or the love of her life? If he was the love of her life, would she be prepared to share him with another—and why should she?

"I didn't get the impression that Rodario finds you attractive. Not enough to stay with you for long, anyway," she said, puzzled to hear this sharpness in her own voice. Jealousy.

Mallenia, who had been amiable up to now, made a face. "I get it. You want to put it to the test and see which of us he's more strongly attracted to."

Coïra sighed. "What do we do if he doesn't fancy either of us?"

"The man does not exist who would turn down the offer of a princess *and* a queen for his mistress. And it's us that are sharing him. We made the agreement first. We'll continue to let him think he's managing to wind us round his little finger." Mallenia looked at Rodario, who was talking to Slîn. "So, is it all right if I kiss him again and see how things develop? It might turn out in your favor."

"And if he tells you he only loves me, will you stop pursuing him?"

"If he tells me that of his own free will and is prepared to swear it, then I'll leave you both to it." The Ido girl nodded and held out her right hand. "Is it a deal?"

The maga hesitated. "Won't there be a strained feeling between the two of us, if one has to leave the field, defeated?"

"No."

"And we won't fall out?"

"No, Your Majesty," said Mallenia, smiling. "We'll complete our mission successfully and then relationships between our two realms will be more amicable than ever. I swear it on the soul of my ancestor, Prince Mallen of Ido." She proffered her hand once more.

"And Rodario shan't learn of our bargain?"

The Ido princess laughed. "Of course not. May the gods forbid! He'd feel his manhood was being impugned."

At last Coïra felt able to seal the deal by shaking hands. "So be it." The two women embraced and wished each other a good night.

Rodario cast a glance their way. "What's happening over there?" he wondered.

Slîn cranked the crossbow mechanism and leaned the weapon up against the wall, close at hand if needed. All he would have to do was insert a bolt ready to fire. "Women, eh? They're always scheming. And it's us men on the receiving end." He grinned and offered Rodario a flask of brandy.

"It's a very wise dwarf you are, Slîn," said the actor, taking a drink.

XXIV

The Outer Lands,
The Black Abyss,
Fortress Evildam,
Spring, 6492nd Solar Cycle

Goda prayed to Vraccas longer than was her wont.

As soon as the sun rose she was on her knees by her little shrine, begging her creator to come to the aid of her daughter Sanda, who she presumed was now in the beasts' lair, in the clutches of the terrible dwarf.

"Annihilate him," she whispered, tears flowing through the down on her cheeks. "Smash him to pieces, Vraccas, with your great hammer, cast him into the forge and incinerate his soul. He has turned his back on you and has the worst of all evil plans in store." She stood up. "You know that Ireheart and I have been defending the humans and all the other peoples in your name. Do not allow us to be repaid in this way." She bowed before the tiny Vraccas figurine, crafted from pure vraccasium, then left her chamber.

Out in the corridor a messenger hurried to meet her. "My lady, they have sent a negotiator," he announced. "He's at the southern gate."

Her heart began to race. Hastening after the messenger, she soon reached the half-open gate and stepped through, right up to the edge of the red screen.

On the other side stood a monster with features similar

to a human but it was considerably taller and very muscular. It had three arms—one on each side and one in the middle of the chest—and held two long shields and a huge pike. The beast had not been equipped with armor, but the body had several layers of leather clothing; the odor coming through the barrier was revolting.

"The one who bears many names and who is our master," it said in a rough voice, showing sharp teeth as broad as a dwarf's finger, "sends his instructions to you, sorceress; you are to surrender the fortress immediately. Otherwise the one who bears many names and who is our master will kill your own flesh and blood. After he has violated her many times, and then sent you, orbit by orbit, a further slice of her body: The fingers first, then the forearms, and so on. With his magic powers he will ensure that she continues to live right up until the end and experiences pain fully . . ."

Goda raised her hand. "Enough. Go back to him and tell him that I cannot do that. There is more at stake than my own daughter. But I shall kill him with my own hands if he harms her. And tell him that *my* magic power is also great. I am not afraid of him." She nearly choked, but controlled herself, determined not to show fear.

"If your powers were really great the barrier would have been destroyed and you would already have launched your attack," the monster replied. "As the one who bears many names and who is our master thought you might respond like that, he has a proposal that he thinks you will find you can accept in exchange for the life of your daughter."

"I am not prepared to bargain." Goda turned away. "No matter what the stakes."

"Her life in exchange for that of Balodil," it called after her.

"I know of no Balodil." She stopped, a cold shiver running down her spine.

"The one who bears many names and who is our master says you know the one about whom I speak." It made several strange noises, a cross between a belch and a growl. "He has taken your daughter to a place you will never find. Even if it came to a battle and you penetrated the ravine, your daughter would not be there. You will only get her back if the one who bears many names and who is our master receives Balodil's corpse and the armor he stole."

Goda turned to the messenger, who was holding his two shields closer now, in order to be able to hide behind them if necessary. "I am a dwarf and would never betray one of my own kind," she said, her voice quivering. "Tell your master he may expect nothing of me. Apart from a painful death if he touches my daughter." She strode off abruptly and gave the sentries a sign to close the gate.

"He who bears many names and who is our master accords you three orbits in which to make up your mind. After that time has elapsed you will receive the fingers of your daughter's right hand," Goda heard the creature say before the gates thudded shut.

Much as the dwarf-woman tried not to waste further thought on the offer, she could not forget it. "What harm if I were to kill the deceiver?" she said to herself once she had returned to her own chamber. She knelt again at the shrine and prayed to Vraccas. "You know he is not really Tungdil. To exchange his life for Sanda's would not be a crime, but a doubly good deed." She shut her eyes and saw her daughter's countenance before her. She wept.

Girdlegard,
Former Queendom of Rân Ribastur,
In the Southeast,
Spring, 6492nd Solar Cycle

Tungdil had decided not to take the most direct route, which would have involved a long march through the Sangpur deserts, and so their company had set off for the southern part of Rân Ribastur; they would head east later on, to make straight for the Blue Mountains.

They had seen very few humans. Tungdil, using the maps carefully, had led them through the forests, which grew so thick in places that they had to walk in single file, with the head of the column slashing at the undergrowth to carve out a path. They had abandoned the ponies.

They purchased provisions from the smallholdings they passed on the way. Rodario and Mallenia were in charge of buying stores; that way, no one got to see the dwarves.

And things were astonishingly quiet.

There were no wild animal attacks and the legendary enchanted creatures and magic plants left them in peace as well. But they were given dire warnings about not leaving the path and not traveling through the forest by night.

Making a final stop on the territory of the former queendom, they rested one late afternoon in the shadow of towering trees, whose foliage let through hardly any light; the canopy of leaves would give them protection from the heat waiting to hit them a few miles further to the east when they emerged from the forest.

Slîn used his telescope to scan the dunes about four miles away. "The light is shimmering as if it were water."

"And I'm very glad to know that it's not," said Ireheart, who was sitting on the ground, his back against a tree trunk. "I can't wait to get away from all these creepy creepers but I'm not too keen on burning hot sand, either."

"Or the icy nights of the desert." Balyndar filled his drinking pouch with water from the little stream. "Dwarves are mountain people. I don't mind the cold if I'm where I belong."

"I couldn't agree more, fifthling." Slîn nodded and swung his telescope. "Nothing for miles. No long-uns, no trees, no shade." He lowered the glass. "It'll be the first time for me, going into the desert."

"It's said to be very beautiful," said Rodario, trying to see the bright side of what was probably going to be the toughest part of their journey. "A desert isn't only sand. There'll be rocks aplenty. That'll cheer you up, friend Slîn." He altered his voice and took on the persona of a storyteller. "In the old days the queendom was a mountain region, one peak higher than the next. People say the wind in Sangpur is so fierce that it eroded the mountains into sand inside of seven times seven cycles. Now, this is all that remains."

"You can tell that to your grandmother," growled Ireheart. Rodario beamed. "I did. She believed me."

"Well it's nonsense! The only mountains in Girdlegard are our own. The only *genuine* mountains."

"Isn't it amazing what they can find to quarrel about?" Coïra remarked to Mallenia, passing her the salami. "About *mountains.*"

"I know men who'll start a fight about the dimensions of their own little man," replied the girl from Ido, and the other woman laughed.

"You see? They're laughing at us," Slîn complained to Rodario. "There's some kind of conspiracy going on. It started that night we were in the burned-out farmhouse."

The actor stroked his chin in thought. "Yes, you're right. The fine ladies choose to make us the butt of their jokes." He winked at Coïra, who smiled back before glancing quickly at Mallenia. The Ido girl nodded to her, which Rodario found surprising. He was pretty sure he had missed something.

"What else do you know about the desert?" Balyndar urged. "I don't want fairy tales. I want the truth."

"Then you'd better ask the Scholar," said Ireheart. "He always used to know that kind of stuff."

"And we've got Franek." Coïra waved the famulus over. "We were just talking about the desert; what can we expect, apart from heat and sandstorms?" she asked him. "You must have crossed the desert when you escaped from Lot-Ionan?"

He sat down on the green moss and scooped up some water from the stream to drink and to cool his face. "May Samusin be by our sides . . ."

"May *Vraccas* continue to stand by us," Ireheart corrected sharply. "I want nothing to do with that other god. And I certainly don't want to owe him any favors." Slîn and Balyndar were of the same opinion. Ireheart filled his pipe indignantly. *That'll be the day . . .*

Franek started again. "Whoever is protecting us we're going to need his help on the final miles through to the Blue Mountains. Bumina has gone to ground in the desert. She always planned to give eternal life to dead things."

"Hey, undeads! We know all about them, don't we?" Ireheart called to Tungdil, who was sitting talking to Barskalín. "I'm not afraid of them. In the time of the Perished Land we cut them down, whole ranks of them, one, two, three, fast as you like!" He accompanied his words with appropriate arm movements, losing odd bits of tobacco.

"That's not what I meant . . ." replied Franek.

"Then you weren't expressing yourself clearly," Slîn interjected, grinning. He enjoyed being able to play out his distrust of the famulus. "Why don't you come to the point?" Humans and dwarves laughed in response.

Franek didn't rise to their bait. Rodario admired his cool. "Bumina found places in the desert where she released some magic and she sealed it in," he explained slowly. "She wanted the magic to find itself something to embody, to incorporate itself. At first the experiments failed and the magic capacities dissipated. But, with time, she discovered the formula to enforce her will on the magic to do what she wanted by employing runes. She was assiduous and persevered until circumstances conspired . . ."

Ireheart thumped his crow's beak handle on the ground. "Tell it properly, wizardling. Say it so we can understand." The audience laughed again.

Now Franek grew impatient. "So it's not just your stature that's diminutive. Your brain must be the same," he hissed venomously.

"Ooh, a hit!" Rodario commented.

Ireheart's chest and arm muscles jerked dangerously. "Have a care, little wizardling. Or my hand will slip and I'm not sure my tiny brain will be able to hold me back." He pointed to Coïra. "We already have a maga and we can find the way without you."

Franek made an obscene gesture—and in a flash Ireheart was beside him, grabbing his little finger and snapping the top joint; it cracked and the famulus shrieked with pain.

"Sorry, it's the fault of my tiny brain," said the dwarf in a dangerously quiet voice. "If I were brighter, of course, I'm sure I wouldn't have done that. And just think what else I might be stupid enough to do to you?" He played with the crow's beak. "Having a hole in your foot is probably quite painful, my little sorcerer's apprentice."

"Stop it, Ireheart," Tungdil ordered, looking up from his study of the maps. "Leave him be. He is on our side."

"But he insulted me!" the old warrior fumed, pointing with his pipe. "It was him that started it!"

"Then that's an end to it now. Sit down and let me get on with my work." Tungdil pored over the map again.

Franek clutched his damaged finger and showered his assailant with ferocious looks. Ireheart was sitting now next to Slîn. "Well at least he can't do any magic now, even if he gets to bathe in the source," he whispered to the fourthling, who burst out laughing.

"I hope the sand creatures gobble you up," the famulus spat out between clenched teeth.

"Ah," said Balyndar. "So that's what the magic does. It makes creatures of sand."

"Sand creatures. Beings made of stone, made of . . . made of everything that is dead and that is in the magic places," Franek summed up, staring at his hand. He did not dare straighten the fractured finger.

"How can we best deal with them?" Rodario did not relish the idea of having to contend with a wall of stone or rubble.

"Us? We can't do anything." Franek pointed to Coïra. "This is a test for her. Only counter-magic can destroy these fiends. Conventional weapons will be worse than useless."

"We'll see about that." Ireheart tested his crow's beak for sharpness and puffed away furiously at his pipe until his head disappeared behind a cloud of smoke. Neither he, Balyndar, Slîn or Franek saw how pale Coïra had gone.

Tungdil gave the order for them to set off. "The sun is low enough now. We can make a start. It's better if we can adapt slowly to the changes in temperature." He got the Zhadár to put white cloaks over their dark armor, to deflect the sun's rays. This should help them avoid heatstroke; Tungdil and the others protected themselves in a similar way, putting on wide white tunics.

"I look like an icicle," joked Slîn.

"An icicle with a beard?" Rodario grinned.

Barskalín and Tungdil took the lead, then came several Zhadár, then the dwarves and the humans; the rest of the Invisibles brought up the rear.

Even a march of four miles, after coming out of the shelter of the trees and heading toward the dunes, had them breaking out in a sweat, in spite of the spring weather and the advanced hour. When they climbed up the soft sand, walking became much more onerous.

Their heavy armor quickly caused the dwarves to get out of breath, however grateful they normally were for its reliable protection in a fight—Tungdil was the only one who seemed to have no difficulty in coping with the heat. He stomped off ahead as if he were a machine and not a creature made of flesh and blood.

Neither Ireheart nor the other dwarves wanted to show they were struggling. Not until the night stars shone above their heads and it had grown extremely cold did Tungdil tell them to settle down, in sight of a rock formation. But he was not going to let them rest for long, it seemed. Slîn sank down onto the sand and took off his helmet; he was exhausted.

"We have crossed the first belt of sand," their leader announced. "We'll camp over there by the rocks. They'll afford enough shelter if a storm comes up."

"That's another three miles," Slîn said. It was obvious he was not willing to take one more step. "It's just as good here."

Tungdil shot him a look. "We march. If you can't take it, sit and wait for dawn. We'll collect you when the horizon is pale blue." Without giving the rebellious dwarf another thought, he set off.

"Come on, fourthling." Surprisingly, it was Balyndar who spoke. "Let's show our high king what you are made of."

"The crossbow is so heavy," he complained. "The weight is making my legs tired."

"Hand it to me. Let's go." Balyndar stretched out a hand to haul him up. "Three miles is nothing."

Slîn looked at the fifthling. "How did I get to earn your sympathy?"

"We are all in this together, Slîn, whether we like it or not. We know you're good with the crossbow. We need you."

Balyndar shouldered the weapon. "And it really is heavy."

"I don't suppose he could have kept going for as long as you did, fourthling," Ireheart added with a wink.

Slîn looked from one to the other. "You're taking the piss!"

"No, we're not. I swear by Vraccas."

"It's just, it's late. I want to get some rest. And you're stopping me if we leave you here," said Balyndar, deadly serious, then he smiled.

Slîn turned to Rodario. "They've both got a touch of the sun. That'll be it."

The actor put on a sympathetic face. "Yes, it's said the sun can easily have that effect. The juices the brain swims in—they dry up and, hey presto, there you are, turned into a nicer person, whether you want to be or not."

"So maybe we should put Lot-Ionan out in the sunshine for a bit, what do you say?" Coïra chimed in, laughing. "Sounds simple enough."

"But you can see that it works, if you look at these two stubborn, bad-tempered dwarves here," said Rodario, bowing to Ireheart and Balyndar as an apology for the teasing.

After a considerable amount of fooling and joking they reached the rock, which rose twenty paces high and was eight paces by eight in ground area. Tungdil chose the eastern side for their camp and instructed the guards to wake them at first light.

They were too tired to prepare a meal and, one by one, they fell asleep. Even hunger would not keep them from the realm of dreams tonight.

Ireheart glanced at Tungdil, who was resting sitting upright, his back to the rock. In the starlight his bearded face appeared older than ever; his eye was open and fixed on the dark skies. His lips moved. Then the runes on his tionium armor began to glow. Only then did he shut his eye.

Ireheart dozed off.

The Outer Lands,
The Black Abyss,
Fortress Evildam,
Spring, 6492nd Solar Cycle

Goda stared at the parcel packed in waxed paper. It had been found at dawn by sentries at the western gate.

Even though she had been prewarned about what the monsters' leader was going to do, she did not want to have to see her daughter's severed fingers.

Her hands worked of their own accord, opening the knots in the string, unfolding the paper and lifting off the lid of the unadorned box.

Goda looked away as the smell of blood hit her nostrils.

She bent slowly forward; her very eyes seemed afraid of what was in the container.

"Vraccas," she groaned. Her fear grew stronger. The next parcel would contain Sanda's forearm. And the orbit after that she would receive the upper arm. Then the fingers of the other hand. Bit by bit.

Her cruelly fertile imagination saw her mutilated daughter; soon there would be only a bloody torso and a head. Goda could hear her screams, her pleas, her sobs—because her mother was refusing to kill a dwarf she did not even believe to be the real Tungdil . . .

"I can't," she sobbed, throwing herself onto her knees before the shrine. "I can't sacrifice my daughter like that, Vraccas. Not for the sake of some charlatan whose lies everyone else has fallen for." She stared at the little statue. "I shall have to strike a deal with this enemy. I have no other choice . . ."

There was a loud knock at the door. "My lady! My lady! Come quick! A miracle!" came a soldier's voice.

Goda wiped the tears from her face and opened the door.

"My lady, your daughter! She has come back and is waiting for you at the gate!" he enthused.

"My . . . daughter?" She looked at the table where the little box with the fingers lay. Then she hurried out, her head spinning, reeling from joy and shock. When she reached the southern gate at last, there was Sanda!

She was still wearing the chain-mail shirt, but it hung down on her limply and badly laced; her face showed severe bruising and the right sleeve was blood-soaked. Her dark hair hung lank and greasy. But Sanda was smiling.

"My daughter!" Goda took her in her arms and pressed her to her breast, her eyes shut. They remained in that tight embrace for several moments. "What has he done to you?" Goda stared anxiously into her daughter's brown eyes.

Sanda avoided her gaze and her pupils flickered. "He beat me and humiliated me. It was a place just like Tungdil said the Black Abyss was," she whispered and began to shake, hugging herself. "I never want to go there again," she said out loud, looking at her mother. "I'd rather die."

Goda was about to answer, when her eyes fell on the right arm. She was looking for the wound, but saw—a healthy arm with no fingers missing!

She forgot what she had been intending to say and snatched up the girl's hand. "How is that possible, Sanda?" The digits were pink and tender as those of a newborn baby.

"He who bears many names cut them off," she said in a faltering voice. "He grew me new ones in their place. It was dreadfully painful but not as painful as the other things he did to me." She looked at her hand. "As the other things he did . . ." she repeated quietly, swaying on her feet.

Goda supported her. "Why did he let you go?"

"He didn't let me go. I escaped," said Sanda, her knees buckling under her. Goda sat her down on a bench and sent for water. "I escaped and I ran and ran, Mother. I ran and then I got lost but somehow I got away." She looked at her hand. "Quick, give me a knife!" she cried, holding her hand outstretched. "Those are not my fingers! They are *his*! He made them grow there! They will obey his will!"

"Hush, my child." Goda took her in her arms and rocked her as she had done with the infant Sanda. "You are back with us now."

Sanda coughed. "They are *his* fingers. I touched the barrier and it opened up for me," she said abstractedly. "Why else would the screen do that?" Then she gave a long shrill scream. "The evil is now part of me!" With untold strength she tore herself out of her mother's embrace, grabbed an ax from a startled sentry and had chopped off the fingers before Goda could stop her. "There! I've done it!" Sanda trampled on the severed digits, while blood spurted out of the stumps on her hand.

"Vraccas, restore her mind!" cried a horrified Goda,

holding her fast. The sentries helped her. They bandaged up the bleeding hand so that Sanda would not die from blood loss and carried the fainting girl up to her chamber. There, her mother undressed her and bathed her.

Sanda's body showed that she had been tortured. Goda wept tears of fury and hate. "For this I shall put him to death so slowly that it takes him a whole cycle to die," she vowed. "What he deals out to others he shall suffer himself." As she dried her daughter's arms—she was brought up short. There was a mark on the inside of the left upper arm. She had never noticed it before. It was not a result of the torture she had endured. It was the size of a fingernail, red. It looked as if it had grown there.

Instinctively Goda recoiled and studied the dwarf-girl with different eyes. She started to doubt that it was really her own daughter. Had their enemy sent a copy, a clone? The same as he had done with Tungdil?

"Vraccas, rid me of my suspicions," she prayed in sudden despair. "I'm sure she will always have had this mark but please let me remember having seen it before." Still holding the towel she rested her hands in her lap and watched her daughter closely. She noted other peculiarities. Was the chin always so soft? Were the cheekbones not normally a little higher? And what about the nose? Even the shape of the eyebrows seemed suspect.

"No," she said. "It is my daughter! It really is!" Goda dried Sanda's shoulders and covered them with the sheet. "It is her. I'm not going to succumb to a trick. The enemy is trying to make me doubt her, wanting to sow distrust." She took a deep breath and stood up to go to the guards to hear what had been happening in the plain by the Black Ravine.

She had to force herself to place a farewell kiss on her daughter's brow.

Girdlegard,
Former Queendom of Sangpur,
Southwest,
Spring, 6492nd Solar Cycle

Ireheart woke up and opened his eyes.

Above him the stars glinted; around him he could hear quiet snores, and then the crunch of sand. This came from Slîn's boots; the fourthling was on watch, striding up and down. The two Zhadár who shared the guard duty made no sound when they walked.

Apart from that the camp was silent.

What woke me? Ireheart was surprised. While he was pondering, the stars appeared to be growing brighter. Now they were as bright as the sun by day, but they gave off no warmth. *What's . . . ?* He sat up.

Day seemed to have dawned.

Their surroundings showed up clear and distinct; he could even see Slîn relieving himself over at the rock; he was writing his name in the sand with dwarf-water. That was easy enough if you had a short name, of course, but it didn't ever work with Ireheart's. And if you wanted to put the family name as well, you'd have to drink an awful lot.

He rubbed his eyes but it was still bright, even though the sun had not yet risen. When he looked at his hands he saw a black liquid on his fingertips! It had come from rubbing his eyes.

He was suddenly frightened. *What is happening? Is this place cursed?*

He got up and Slîn looked over at him at once. Ireheart acknowledged him with a gesture and went over to ask if he had noticed anything strange.

He could see the fourthling clearly. He could discern every single ripple in the sand at his feet and could hear the slightest of noises, even the very grains of sand as they were shifted by the breeze. But Ireheart knew perfectly well that his hearing was not good. All that noisy clanging and battering in battles had taken their toll and in recent cycles he had been having trouble with the higher-pitched tones.

But tonight it was different.

After two paces he was overcome with thirst; the need was so strong that it could not wait until after he had talked to Slîn. So he turned on his heel and went back to where he had been lying, to collect his flask.

Ireheart drank and drank and drank, but the thirst could not be slaked. Water seemed to increase his need rather than quench it!

Out of breath from drinking so fast, he tossed the flask aside and took hold of Balyndar's. There was not enough coming out for his liking, so he took his knife to the pouch, forcing the last drop down his burning gullet.

In a fury he chucked the empty leather to the ground. *Vraccas, what is wrong with me?* He was already stretching his hand out for the next soldier's drinking vessel. As he lifted his hand he felt a sharp pain in his wrist.

A scorpion had been hiding under the flask and had defended itself with its sting. Ireheart stamped on the insect and drew out his knife to open the wound and suck out the poison.

But when he looked at his arm he saw the wound was glowing yellow! There was a shimmer surrounding the sting; he could feel the heat coursing up his arm, and then the glow died away.

Ireheart sat down on the sand. *Have I just healed myself from the poison? Or was that a miracle sent by Vraccas?*

Thirst flamed up once more, torturing him. He clutched at his throat with both hands to try to soothe his discomfort. Then he stuffed a handful of sand in his mouth to stop the burning sensation. It did not work.

He swayed and tipped sideways as the stars above his head swirled and circled.

Then the agony began.

Ireheart was well acquainted with the pain of burns; he had suffered sword injuries or arrow wounds; he knew how it felt to have a dislocated shoulder or a sprained ankle; he had known toothache and fever. If he put all those tortures together and multiplied them tenfold he was getting close to what he was now suddenly subjected to.

His breathing stopped and he could not move a muscle. His mind was drawn upwards to the stars and he felt he was floating like a layer of gold leaf in the warm air of the forge.

Then he tasted blood in his mouth and all around abruptly went dark.

Blinking, he saw the stars once more as tiny specks of light against the black firmament; next to him he saw a Zhadár stowing away his flask and smiling at him.

It's that confounded crazy troublemaker! "It would have to be you," muttered Ireheart, before he spat out a mouthful. He knew this taste well. It was that stuff that was apparently distilled elf water. "Did you just give me that Tion water?"

The crazy Zhadár bared his teeth and nodded. "It's the only

thing that helps when you've got the bad thirst," he piped, in a high voice like a castrato. "It's the only thing! One drop and the fire dies down." He chuckled and laid his finger to his black lips. "Shhhh! We must not tell anyone that I gave you some of that. Barskalín would be furious. We haven't got much of it and it's the most precious thing we have."

Ireheart waited. His thirst had actually gone. Sand scrunched between his teeth, but there was no more water left to rinse his mouth out with.

"It'll keep you going for a few orbits. Then the thirst will return," the Zhadár mouthed, giggling. "Do you notice how wonderful it makes life? The most obscure secrets of the universe make sense and it makes you as strong as a giant!" He stood up and made an exaggerated bow. "Ireheart, Ireheart. Soon you'll be one of us. A little bit like us. Your soul has changed color and is starting to become as black as ours," he fluted in his high-pitched tones, then adding in a bass note: "Soon!" He stepped back silently and rejoined his comrades, lying down on his blanket.

Ireheart found it impossible to get back to sleep.

He had been shown clearly that the liquid was not merely a herbal distillation, as he had at first hoped. Until now he had completely forgotten that he had helped himself from another's flask. What did it all mean? And why, by Vraccas, had it taken so long to show the effects?

Tossing and turning on his blanket helped not a jot. He got up and went over to the Zhadár. "Oy, wake up," he said, shaking him by the shoulder. "Tell me what's happening to me."

The Invisible's eyes opened and a grin appeared on his face. "Come with me." He bounded up, grabbed the dwarf by the sleeve and tugged him over to a gap in the rocks.

"Nobody must see us," he whispered. "It is forbidden to reveal our secrets." He crouched down, pulling Ireheart down, too. "Elf blood, distilled and . . ."

"You told me that already . . . but is it the truth?" Ireheart interrupted angrily. "What is it doing to me and how does it change the color of my soul? Will I ever get to the eternal forge now? Will Vraccas admit me?"

"Perhaps not all of your soul," the Zhadár conceded regretfully. "Vraccas may have to burn out the affected part and let the rest of you enter. If he is kindly disposed to you."

"Listen . . . have you got a name?"

"Balodil," said the Zhadár, the answer shooting out like an arrow.

"That's nonsense. That's the name the Scholar took when he went into the beasts' realm of eternal terrors."

"But it was mine first," came the sulky response.

Ireheart's eyes narrowed. "Is that so? Then tell me who gave you that name."

Balodil said nothing but pointed silently at Tungdil as he slept.

"Of course," groaned Ireheart. "Vraccas, what else do you have in store for me? A crazy Zhadár who pretends to be the Scholar's son."

"He dropped me into the river when we were crossing on the bridge," said Balodil resentfully. "I can remember how the current took hold of me and dragged me under. I couldn't breathe. Some time later I woke up. I was with some humans. They fed me and made me work for them but then they sold me and I escaped when the älfar invaded." He told his story quickly and without a pause. "I ran all the way to the caves of Toboribor. I lived there for many, many cycles. That's all.

I survived from orbit to orbit by stealing from the outlying farms. Until Barskalín found me and took me off to join the Zhadár." He grinned, raising his arms and flexing his muscles. "I'm the strongest of all of them." Balodil pointed back to Tungdil. "It was him that dropped me in the water. Even if he used to look different. I recognized him straightaway."

Ireheart could hardly believe what he was hearing. A chilling story; abstruse enough to be true? It could all be a pack of lies. *Did Tungdil maybe tell him about losing his son?*

He shook his head. Very few people knew the story of Tungdil and Balyndis's first child: The effect on Tungdil of the child's loss had nearly driven him mad with alcohol and grief. And after all the cycles that had passed in the meantime. There were so many other tales that could be told.

Ireheart looked at Balodil and tried to spot similarities between him and Tungdil or, indeed, Balyndis. He saw no resemblance and was angry with himself for giving any credence to the words of a crazy Zhadár. "Whatever . . . Balodil: Just tell me what I can do about all this."

The Zhadár glanced furtively back over his shoulder. "You have the curse of the elves on you now."

"You don't mean to say you used their blood for this revolting stuff?"

"Yes, we did. We found the last of the elves and took them prisoner . . ."

"I thought the älfar had eliminated all the pointy-ears?"

"No, they didn't get all of them. We finished the task off. All except two. They cursed us all and anyone who would partake of the drink. If anyone can free you from the stain on your soul it will be one of the two elves still alive." Balodil cocked an ear. "I must get back to the others. Barskalín has woken up. If I'm away too long he'll think something's wrong." He put his hands on Ireheart's shoulders. "Swear you'll not betray me. Nobody must know that we spared the lives of two of the elves. Not until all the älfar have been wiped out." The grip on his shoulders was painful.

"All right, I swear, for Vraccas's sake."

Balodil released him and disappeared into the shadows.

"What do I do when the thirst comes back?" Ireheart asked in a muffled whisper.

"I'll be there and I'll help you slake your thirst," came the answer out of the dark.

He sighed. "Vraccas, whenever I think it can't get any worse, you have a surprise in store for me," he grumbled. "My soul is besmirched, I have an elf curse on me and the only pointy-ears who might be able to help me—well, no one knows where they are or if they're even still around." He fiddled with his trousers, preparing to give some dwarf-water to the desert. "Oh, and let's not forget the monsters of the Black Abyss. And Lot-Ionan, who we have to defeat but mustn't kill. All the usual suspects for a dwarf like me to contend with. Anyone would think it was some marketplace bard coming up with this tale. Perhaps you've got a pet storyteller, Vraccas, giving you ideas." He directed his dwarf-water to describe at least the first letter of his name in the sand.

He was not surprised in the slightest to note that his stream ran black as ink before it trickled away between the grains of sand.

XXV

They left the belt of sand behind them, marched through fields of boulders, traversed valleys and skirted ravines in which, numberless cycles earlier, vast rivers had run. Now they were met only with dust, stones and the occasional bleached skeleton.

This stretch of the Sangpur desert appealed to Ireheart because it resembled his old habitat with its soaring rock walls, its chasms, its echoes, its subterranean passages, here cut by racing water and not by dwarf-hand. The landscape had something primeval to it. *I could almost start to like it here if it weren't hotter than the inside of a maniac's forge.*

Today they were making their way through a labyrinth of sunken walkways in which Franek, at the head of the company with Tungdil and Barskalín, kept getting lost. It was only thanks to the dwarves that they ever found their way out again. One of the Zhadár climbed up high to get a better view and pointed them in the right direction for the east.

"Our water supplies are running out. We should have got to the village you told us about three orbits ago," said Tungdil. "If we don't reach it tomorrow, you're for the chop, famulus, for having tricked us. I think you're taking us round in circles hoping we die of thirst."

The man gasped. "Oh sure, and I'm taking myself round in those same circles to die with you? Not a good move."

"Who says you don't have a secret reservoir near here?" Ireheart moved up to the head of the column. "What kind of a village did you say it was?"

"A desert market; a trading station. We'll get everything we need. They used to sell dwarf-made goods there, weapons particularly. Even today you can get some quite rare items." Franek looked down at the clothes he was wearing, marked over and over with salt rings. "They know me there."

"Is that a good or a bad thing?" Ireheart laughed. "I like to be prepared. I'd like to know whether they'll greet us at spear-point because we have you with us."

"We'll be safe enough. The town belongs to me." He drew in a hot lungful of air. "Well, it *was* mine until Lot-Ionan chucked me out."

"What was your research area? I don't remember—or maybe you never said?" Ireheart looked at Balyndar, who carried the slit water pouch at his belt. He had assumed the damage must have been an accident. Perhaps he had dreamed that the pouch was the head of an orc rising up out of the sand to attack him. Then he must have slashed at it with his knife. After hearing this, none of the others cared to sleep in his immediate vicinity.

Behind Balyndar came the Zhadár who called himself Balodil. Ireheart had stopped believing that he might really be the Scholar's own son. The age did not seem right. Barskalín told them that only old dwarves were taken into the ranks of the Zhadár. The real Balodil would not have been old. At least, not old for a dwarf.

"I was studying how to maximize size in animals. And in things," answered Franek.

"Aha," grinned Ireheart. "That will have made you popular with the ladies, I'll be bound?"

"It's not what you think, beard-face," the famulus retorted. "You, of course, could do with a bit of growth. If you were a few hands taller you'd be able to breathe the same air as I do."

"I could easily bring you down to size, long-un! I've got an iron-clad winner of a spell. I'd only have to let it circle." Ireheart lifted the crow's beak, but lowered it when he caught Tungdil's disapproving eye. "Just wait," he grumbled.

"Did you have any luck?" the one-eyed dwarf enquired.

"The experiments with plants worked all right. Same thing with simple animal life. Insects were good, as well."

"Hey! How about a giant gugul!" bellowed Ireheart. "First a wonderful fight with the beast and then a magnificent feast." He gave Franek a playful shove. "See? Tell us, how much did you get things to grow?"

"The body of the giant scorpion that I magicked must have measured seven paces from tail to tip," Franek said, putting on a self-important face. "My experiments consisted of getting grasshoppers to grow large enough for us to ride on. They would be splendid mounts for the desert. But there was a high turnover rate. They kept dying on us."

"Are we far enough away from the place you practiced your spells? I don't like scorpions, and I certainly don't like them when they're that big." Ireheart was remembering a particular example they had met the night before. The pincers of a giant scorpion would surely grab a warrior and slice him in two, complete with his armor, and the huge sting would stab right through instead of poisoning him. No, he really did not want to meet one of those.

"This is exactly where I conducted my experiments." Franek laughed. "But there's nothing left of them now. I didn't want them to take over and destroy the town. Of course, I may have overlooked some of their young."

"Charming," said Slîn, taking his crossbow in his hands.

The Zhadár, watching their progress from on high as he leaped like a rock-ape from one stone to the next, reported that he could see a settlement at the end of the ravine they were marching through. He came back down to join them. The company followed his instructions and took one more turn in this confusing maze of intersecting clefts.

There was no question: In front of them lay a town.

But part of it was under a huge sand dune and stood empty and abandoned. The low, flat-roofed buildings, painted white against the sun, all looked intact but there was no sign of life in the streets.

Franek turned to Tungdil, flabbergasted. "Less than forty cycles ago there were forty thousand people living here! I swear!"

"Lot-Ionan is not just out to get you but plans death for everyone connected to you, I expect," said Ireheart. "Vicious old man—he's working out his grievance."

"What a fool!" Franek's display of anger did not seem simulated. "They weren't to blame!"

"Does the town have a well?" Tungdil asked, indifferent to Franek's fury.

"Yes . . ."

"Then let's get there." Tungdil set off, the group in his wake. "Be prepared for absolutely anything. Lot-Ionan, or whoever has done this, will be expecting Franek to turn up sooner or later." As he walked he drew his weapon, Bloodthirster, and his lips moved in silent prayer.

Ireheart felt the familiar, enjoyable tension creeping up his spine. With his crow's beak in his left hand he kept constant watch on their surroundings. *Please, no giant scorpions.* Together with the humans he kept to the edge of the road, while the watchful Zhadár whooshed past, using the house roofs and side streets, on the lookout for any ambush or trap.

Franek led them through the alleyways to a small square measuring ten paces by ten; the houses roundabouts were tiny. The remnants of old market stalls lay tumbled on the flagstones, many of which were cracked or broken. Others showed deep ruts. Ireheart observed the scene. *Something massive crashed down here.*

Slîn bent down and picked up a golden bracelet. "Will you look at that?" he said, showing it to the others. "It was just lying there!" He examined the piece with expert eyes. "This is a splendid example of a goldsmith's craft. I would say it's worth about four hundred gold coins."

"This used to be the jewelers' market," said Franek, going over to the fountain in the middle of the square. He tasted the water that came splashing out of a stone pillar to collect in a basin. "It's safe. The source of this water can't be got at to poison it. At least, it would be terribly difficult. It comes from a very long way down underground."

"Could probably be done by magic, though?" Ireheart continued to scan the windows of the houses.

Franek filled his drinking pouch. "No, I would have noticed."

"And how would you have done that, clever clogs?" Ireheart was not going to be fobbed off so easily.

"I'm a magus, so I have an instinct." He indicated Coïra. "Get her to check it out if you don't believe me."

The maga, who like Rodario and Mallenia was suffering from bad sunburn, came closer and pretended to pronounce a spell. She had to rely on the judgment of the famulus, because she did not want to waste the last of her magic on apparently trivial matters. Her already limited powers were waning further, at any rate, evaporating like water in the heat of the sun. She was desperate to reach the magic source in the Blue Mountains and steep herself in it before her deformed arm rotted away. Looking at her, Rodario was aware she was keeping up a pretence, deceiving the dwarves as to her state of health. "There is no magic contamination," she announced.

Franek looked triumphant and superior, Ireheart gave in and everyone started to fill their flasks.

Tungdil told Slîn to put the bracelet back. "It's not yours. Perhaps the townspeople will come back and they'd call you a thief."

One of the Zhadár up on the roof called out a warning. Barskalín turned to the one-eyed dwarf and interpreted. "They've spotted some bodies. He says they look as if a butcher has been at them. The flesh has been scraped off and the bones smashed. Judging from the state of the cadavers they think it must have happened about ten orbits ago."

Franek went and sat down in the shade, joining the other humans. "Lot-Ionan has no army. It could perhaps have been bandits that did this, but my feeling is that Lot-Ionan, or maybe Bumina, sent a magic creature to kill them or drive them all out of the town." He turned to Coïra. "You'll have to be more on your guard. Do us a discovery spell, so that we'll know if we're safe."

"Yes. Do that," Tungdil urged her. "I don't want to walk into an ambush so close now to our goal. You'll be able to see more than the Zhadár can."

Coïra was about to object, but her curiosity got the better of her. Tungdil knew very well that she had practically no magic left at her disposal—why was he making such a demand? Did he have no idea at all how much effort casting such a spell would involve? "I'll do it from up there," she said, nodding to Rodario to accompany her into the nearest large house.

They climbed the steps, going up two floors to stand on the whitewashed roof of a building that gave them a good view of the whole settlement.

"Are you really going to do it?" the actor asked her.

"Yes," she lied. "It's to protect all of us." She waved her arms about, closed her eyes once, then opened them and turned round three times on the spot. "I don't feel anything. We're safe, but nevertheless we should hurry. I'm uneasy. I'll tell Tungdil so, before he decides we should camp here."

Rodario took her hand. "I'm glad to see your hand is still in its rightful place."

"For a while, at least. But I shan't be able to do much more." She smiled at him and they returned to the others so that the maga could make her report to the high king. She made no secret of her feelings of disquiet about the place. "Have you noticed the vultures are missing? It's unnatural.

They only come down to feast if they know they won't be disturbed." That alone, she argued, was reason enough for departing swiftly from the town.

"That may be so. But it's you, maga, in particular I'm thinking of when I order a rest stop." Tungdil, over by the fountain, commanded the Zhadár to investigate the neighboring houses, and to move in if they found no danger. "The day is too hot for us to march on and, anyway, we are close now to the Blue Mountains. I've agreed with Barskalín that we should travel at night and rest by day. That way we should avoid being seen." He collected water in his open hand and washed his face; a droplet hanging from the eye patch shimmered gold in the light. "As there are no magic traps there's no reason we shouldn't remain here for a time. Right?"

Coïra hesitated, then nodded. "No reason not to." She went back into the house with Rodario, her conscience pricking her. Her right arm was burning and throbbing: Not a good sign.

Curiosity got the better of Ireheart, Slîn and Balyndar, overcoming their professed intentions and their common sense.

They wandered round the streets, ready for combat, searching abandoned houses for signs of recent occupation. The Zhadár were protecting the group at the jewelers' market and the three dwarves felt strong enough to see off any attacks by robbers or wild animals.

Slîn held his crossbow against his shoulder. "We should make less noise," he said.

Balyndar laughed at him. "That's because you're the one with a weapon that always has to be reloaded."

Ireheart grinned. "Come on, let's find where they traded dwarf-goods," he suggested, turning down one of the side streets, where he saw two crossed hammers on a sign over a shop doorway. That was a good enough clue for him. It might be a blacksmith's; he would feel at home there. He wiped the sweat off his forehead. "I hope they'll have some oil for my chain mail. I'm nearly out of it."

"What shall we do if we find things our own folk have made?" Slîn wanted to know. "Can we take them with us?"

"That's what I was thinking. I don't envy the long-uns their wealth, but if the town is going to disappear under yet more sand, I'd like to salvage things made by our own tribes." Ireheart stepped into the shop, where he found tools of every sort, ranging from nail clippers to quarry drills.

Two of them sifted through the items on show while the third kept watch outside. They worked their way from shop to shop until they reached the edge of the immense dune. A number of booths had already been half swamped by the encroaching sands, and it proved to be these that were advertising dwarf-wares.

The trio hesitated at the buildings, whose facades were cracked. They knew that the sand represented an enormous weight, even if the individual grains were so light.

"Looks dangerous to me," said Slîn.

"But it might be worth the risk." Balyndar gestured with the morning star toward a sign reading *Weapons made by the Children of Vraccas*. The door had already been broken open, and swords, spears and axes lay scattered around. "Someone's already done their shopping, it seems, without asking the owner."

Ireheart rubbed his cheeks, tossed his black plait out of

the way and strode in. It was obvious that he had made his decision. "Slîn, you stand guard," he ordered. "If the roof falls in, at least one of us will survive."

"That's a nice thought," the fourthling beamed. He stayed outside under the porch while Ireheart and Balyndar stepped carefully over a heap of daggers, knives and axes.

It was clear at once that they had stumbled on a small treasure trove—but it had already been pillaged. The display cases were empty, the glass fronts shattered. Only the normal run of weapons—still, however, of excellent quality— remained hanging on the walls or from the ceiling.

"What a shame," said Balyndar as he stepped over the mess.

"This stuff on the floor isn't dwarf-manufacture," muttered Ireheart, crouching down. "They're forgeries," he snorted. "The robbers could obviously tell the difference between quality stuff and fake."

"By Vraccas," Balyndar called out excitedly. Ireheart hurried over. "Do you see what I see?"

The warrior saw a cabinet with a broken pane of glass. Inside was a velvet cushion and below that was a piece of parchment with wording in human language: "The legendary Keenfire—the original weapon." Next to it lay a little booklet and a certificate verifying authenticity, issued by the shop- keeper, one Esuo Wopkat, and vouchsafing the return of the purchase price should the weapon prove to be a forgery.

Ireheart laughed outright. "Yet another of them!"

"I know, they were a real hit with the souvenir shops," said Balyndar, reaching into the vitrine to retrieve the booklet. "This says how it was found."

"Let me guess," called Ireheart, enthusiastic as a young

child with a riddle. "Hmm, let's see . . . it was found this time on the top of the Dragon's Tongue? Or in the caves of Toboribor? No, wait . . . In the lost vaults of Lot-Ionan?"

"No, none of those." Balyndar cleared his throat and began to read:

Esteemed customers, collectors and experts,

The ax you hold in your hands is made from the purest, most durable of steel; the claws at the end are of stone, the handle is made of sigurdacia wood, the inlays and runes are from all the rare metals to be found in the mountains; the blade, however, is edged in diamonds.

The weapon was forged in the hottest furnace possible. The name of the item is Keenfire.

Forget everything you have heard from the charlatans.

This one is the only true Keenfire. It was found on the dried-up floor of Weyurn's lakes and was smuggled out of the land under the greatest of perils for the finder.

The location was near the hole from which Lohasbrand emerged. I am not able to say how this occurred.

A fisherman's son brought the ax to me, saying his cousin had found it. He had shown it to a dwarf, who recognized its true value and killed the man. However, while fleeing, the dwarf needed to cross a river and drowned, when justice and the curse of Elria triumphed.

The fisherman wanted nothing to do with the ax because he feared the dwarves would attack him for it, so he sent his son to me with it. I made him a very good offer and so was able to take possession of Keenfire.

I know it is the legendary ax with which Tungdil Goldhand performed so many valiant deeds for Girdlegard. I was intending to keep it safely against his return, but without him it has no power, so I've decided to part with it. For gold.

Should the hero ever return, give him this ax. I am certain he will amply reward you.

Sincerely,
Esuo Wopkat

Ireheart whistled. "That's the best story so far. At least the facts seem to match up nicely."

"How do you mean?"

"It sounds genuine. If I remember rightly, the last Unslayable ran off with Keenfire and threw it away en route when we were pursuing him." Ireheart beamed. "He will have thought a lake would be the last place a dwarf would want to search for it. So he tossed it into the water before he went down the shaft."

"You don't really believe it, do you?" Balyndar shut the little book and chucked it back into the broken cabinet. "And anyway, the thing's been stolen. It could be anywhere by now."

"Hey there!" said Slîn, at the entrance, holding up a dusty ax. "Look what I found outside in the dirt. It was smack in front of my boots."

Ireheart and Balyndar looked at each other.

The fourthling blew the encrusted sand off. "I don't know what kind it is, but I'll have a better idea when I've given it a bit of a wash." He inspected the blade. "Are those diamonds? Who do . . . ?" He noticed the other two were staring at him, then he fell silent, swallowing hard. "By Vraccas!" he croaked in awe, kneeling down and placing the ax reverently on the ground in front of him.

"By Vraccas," said Balyndar and Ireheart simultaneously, coming over to the doorway and crouching down to look at the weapon.

Ireheart took his drinking flask from his belt and poured some water onto the ax head to reveal some of the fine detail. "I . . ." His voice died away.

"Charming!" Slîn heard a chinking sound behind the two dwarves and raised his crossbow. He saw a dagger slip forward in the cabinet, fall off the shelf and drop on to the counter. He was just drawing breath again in relief when he noticed a sword releasing itself from its fastenings and sailing down to the counter as well. "Something weird is happening here," he told his companions, who were intent on examining the runes and inlays. "We must warn the others."

"Just shoot the silly mouse if you're scared of it," Balyndar said briskly, misinterpreting the sounds.

"Yes, before Franek's spell makes it grow the size of an ox," added Ireheart, completing the thought as he ran his fingers carefully along the ax blade. "Well, I'll be damned!"

Slîn had leaped up, not wanting to believe his eyes: Shields, lances, daggers, swords and other weapons were zooming together from all corners of the room to make a monster with human form. A deadly creation, born from magic.

"Absolutely charming! I fear the maga wasn't using the right spell when she checked this place out for safety," he said, speaking very fast.

"Oh, so it is a giant mouse?" the fifthling mocked.

"Turn round and look, you idiots!" snapped Slîn, aiming

his bow at the creature—well aware this would not help. Franek had told them that only magic itself could overcome one of these creatures.

"Mind yourself, gem-cutter. You can't talk to me like that just because we let you travel with us. It doesn't mean I like you. And I won't be spoken to like that."

Ireheart was about to tear his eyes away from the newfound ax when it picked itself up and whirled past their noses; an unseen power dragged his crow's beak from his grasp and Balyndar lost his morning star. "What . . . ?"

At last they turned round and saw their enemy. An enemy they now faced unarmed.

The creature had formed a massive hand composed of knives; it was holding Keenfire up and the handle of the crow's beak pointing down. The being clattered its way over toward the dwarf-trio.

Ireheart realized now where the marks on the flagstones at the jewelers' market had come from, and he knew also who had stripped the meat off the bones of the corpses they'd found. He grabbed Balyndar by the sleeve, pulled him up and they walked backwards, very slowly.

"Why didn't you warn us, fourthling?" the fifthling growled.

Slîn laughed mirthlessly. "Good joke. You were both immersed in ax-worship." He pointed with his crossbow at the creature. "It's over there if you still want it."

"I certainly do!" Ireheart nodded, frowning and lowering his head between his shoulders aggressively. "I don't mind the blades. No one is going to threaten me with my own weapon!" He lifted up a wooden strut from a broken cabinet and whacked the enemy with it.

There was a click and the arm made of spears and lances whirred, rotating like a drill, crashing into the wood.

Ireheart was showered with sawdust and found his hands were empty. "Confounded . . ." He turned in dismay. "Let's get out of here." He ran off, with Slîn and Balyndar at his heels. They charged down the street side by side.

"Which way?" asked the fifthling, glancing round at the artificial monster, which was just emerging, doubled-up, from the shop doorway. The weapons that had been lying in a heap in front of the shop rushed up to fuse with all the others.

That was not all.

Clicking and scraping, the steel-and-magic creature changed shape, giving itself three extra pairs of legs and thinning down its core so that it turned into a spider, setting off after them.

"We've got to lure Keenfire back to Tungdil. He'll be able to take it for himself," panted Ireheart as he ran. "I'm incensed that I'm having to run away from my own weapon."

They rounded the corner into an alleyway too narrow for the spider creature to fit through.

But when they heard the rattling and clattering come closer nobody had to turn and look in order to know the thing pursuing them had transformed itself again. It was chasing them through the streets as if it were herding stampeding guguls.

Rodario was sitting in front of the house in the shade with a few sheets of paper, noting down his thoughts with a quill pen. He had composed some lines on liberty and adventure.

Mallenia brought him out a glass of water. As she passed

it to him her fingers touched his hand. As if by accident. They looked at each other.

"How is Coïra?" he asked, his eyes returning to the page.

"Quite weak now from the long march. If you grow up in a land where water is the dominant element you have a tough time in the desert." Mallenia dropped her voice. "You know she's hardly got any magic left."

He looked at her in surprise. "How do you . . . ?"

"She told me. She says she's only got about a third of the magic energy she would normally have. The amount grows smaller orbit by orbit. We must get her to the source as quickly as possible." She drank some water. "We can only hope the gods preserve us from any magic attacks."

Rodario went on writing and asked, "What else did she tell you?"

"*What else?*" Mallenia's tone of voice indicated sharp attention. "Is there something else?"

"No." He tried to change the subject. "I mean, I don't know. You women seem to like having secrets. So I thought I might learn something new. Who else knows about her difficulties?"

"Tungdil and Boïndil. That's all. That's the way it has to stay." She glanced at his notes. "What are you doing there?"

"I'm writing. For what's about to happen."

"Not the fight against Lot-Ionan?"

"No. For after that. It's just ideas. The descendants of the Incredible Rodario will take them to the people of Girdlegard as soon as the battle for the future has been won. The unknown poet has done his duty as a freedom-fighter, but our work as actors and bards is not over." He was unusually serious, almost statesmanlike. "We must establish order quickly before greedy despots emerge to usurp powers they are not entitled to." Rodario offered her a seat next to him. "I should like to ensure it is you and no one else that sits on the throne of Idoslane."

"That's good of you." The Ido girl sat down by him and stared at the fountain. "Were you offended by the kiss I gave you?"

"No." He put his pen down.

"I got the impression you were no longer interested in me." She sipped her drink, then turned her head. "Stupidly enough I am still keen on you, even if I can hardly wait for the return of my old, shy Rodario."

"He's still around, deep inside," he replied with a smile. Then he took a deep breath. "Women don't like sharing their men. So I think it's only fair to say I ought to release you and concentrate my attentions on Coïra."

"You may laugh, but the maga and I have already discussed this." Mallenia smiled. "The latest state of play is that we don't mind sharing you."

Now Rodario had to put the paper and quill pen aside. "You've done what?"

"We did what men always want us to do: We came to an agreement," she repeated, and raised her hand to stroke his cheek. "So you don't have to decide between us, Rodario, and we won't be scratching each other's eyes out or declaring war on each other's realms." She smiled and was delighted by his reaction. Suddenly he looked vulnerable again; the helpless Rodario she found so attractive was back. "There's one condition, however: You will never share a bed with both of us at the same time."

"I don't believe what I'm hearing," he laughed, half in

amusement, half in astonishment. "And I really don't know . . ." He got up and paced up and down across the square. ". . . I really don't know if I like this idea."

"Aha. So it bothers your manly nature to hear that two women have set the rules this time."

"No," he said at once. "Or perhaps, yes?" He scratched his head, then his beard. "This has never ever happened to me before," he muttered. He came to a standstill and put his hands on his hips, staring at the blond warrior-girl. "Who do you think you are?" he burst out indignantly.

"Who? Me?" Mallenia pointed to herself.

"No. Both of you. Coïra and you! You've sworn sister-hood, you want to make me your . . . slave, but you never . . ." he said, wagging his forefinger, "thought to let me in on the secret!" He kicked the ground. "I feel . . . humiliated and abused!"

She was speechless. "Here I am, telling you that two girls are in love with you and that you can have both of them, and you throw a tantrum like a jealous child?" She put her head back and laughed out loud. "How very, very sweet! Ah, this is the other Rodario you're showing me, just to please me. How kind of you."

"What?" He waved his arms about in exasperation. "Ye gods! What is the world coming to?"

Mallenia stood up, a grin on her face.

"Stop!" he called as she approached him. "Stay where you are! Before I know it you'll be wanting to kiss me because you think I'm so sweet . . ."

"Exactly."

". . . and adorable."

"True." She was nearly upon him, but he dodged and

banged his hip on the stone fountain. "What do we have to do to rid you of your bad mood? Perhaps we should let you think you have seduced us both?" Mallenia's tone was mocking and she was amused to see him blush. It was hard to see how the calm, eloquent Rodario, who had been philosophizing about Girdlegard's future, and this infuriated man could be one and the same person. At least she knew now how to make her pet Rodario put in an appearance.

The actor raised his hands to push her away. "Don't come too close. I'll have to give the matter a lot of thought before I kiss either one of you ever again."

"Yes, you will," she said, laughing and turning away. "You'll find me with Coïra."

Rodario perched on the edge of the fountain, reached into the water and cooled his face. "Women!" he murmured. "Sharing me out! Me! The very nerve of it!"

The water ran down to the tip of his nose, over his cheeks and mouth into his smart little beard. He felt a little calmer.

Of course he was attracted to the Ido girl, and the thought of having both women really was not to be sneezed at—but actually he felt insulted. His masculine pride was hurt. His Rodario pride. How could this be happening to a descendant of the Incredible Rodario? He should be conquering hearts, not being haggled over and shared out like a sack of grain.

"To make a pact like that! What a nerve!" he muttered, feeling the cool dampness dripping onto his shoulder as the water soaked through his shirt. The fountain was splashing more loudly now.

It was so hot that he did not find this unwelcome, but he could not explain why the jet of water had changed direction.

Rodario turned his head—and froze. Towering four paces high behind him was a being similar to a human, but formed entirely of water. It had a broad head and a snoutlike face with long teeth. Teeth made of solid water . . .

Turning round again he pretended he had not noticed anything untoward as he peeled himself away from the stone surround of the fountain and walked over to the house entrance. He must call Coïra to come and see this phenomenon and tell him what it was. It was really not the normal way for a fountain to conduct itself!

The splashing grew louder, then he heard the Zhadár calling down from the rooftops, and felt a wave swirl round his legs. In an instant it had pulled him off his feet and he disappeared into the water, spluttering madly.

Coïra opened her eyes, having felt something cold on her forehead. Mallenia was sitting next to her, wiping her face with a damp cloth. "This time you're looking after me," she said, weakly.

"You have heatstroke," replied the Ido girl. "Rodario should have been taking better care of you."

"You had a talk with him, I heard."

Mallenia passed her something to drink. "I told him that we had agreed to share him."

The maga felt giddy. "But he was not to be told anything at all!" she protested. "You've broken our agreement on purpose."

"It didn't make sense otherwise. One of these days he was going to work out for himself that we women had made common cause and that we were in charge, not him. He can take out his anger on me. It's not your fault."

Coïra sighed and emptied her glass. "So that's why he was shouting."

"He looked so cute," the Ido girl said dreamily. "He was as helpless as a young child again. You would have given him to me straightaway if you'd seen him like that." Out of the corner of her eye she saw something move in the shadows in a corner where a pile of bricks was stacked. Hadn't they moved too? They seemed to have formed a little tower. She furrowed her brow. "It's this confounded heat," she said. "I can't take the heat."

"What did Rodario say?"

"He said he'd have to think about it."

"I knew it! Now he'll reject both of us!" Coïra sat up where she had been lying. "That really wasn't very bright."

"Keep calm," Mallenia told her, clasping her hand. "He has a head on his shoulders and will soon realize what he is being offered. What we have offered him. If he throws this opportunity away, he's too stupid to be companion to either of us."

The maga thought hard, then smiled shyly. "Maybe. I don't fancy stupid men."

Mallenia caught another movement in the same corner.

The bricks were actually moving closer together. She stared at the place intently.

The bricks were forming stacks and piling up wildly. They shaped a leg, but then the supply ran out, so square bricks broke out of the wall as if following some silent command.

Coïra's attention was caught by this movement, too. The brick creature was growing taller by the minute and, at the same time, the fabric of the walls was becoming steadily more damaged, until they started to cave in. Outside, the Zhadár were shouting.

Mallenia dragged the maga up, seeing giant cracks appear in the roof above their heads. "Let's get out! Quick! The building's going to collapse!"

The two girls ran to the door—but they were met by a wall of water with Rodario swimming within it, trying to get out.

The rear of the building crashed down.

"Get out through the window at the back," the Ido ordered, tugging Coïra along. "Didn't you say there was no magic here?"

The maga had no answer. The shock was overwhelming, as was the realization that she must bear the responsibility and guilt for allowing their party to walk into a trap.

XXVI

"Is it still tailing us?" Ireheart turned left and found himself in a wider lane that seemed unfamiliar. *How did that happen?* They appeared to have got lost trying to escape. "This confounded maze!"

"No," Slîn called out, bringing up the rear. "I can't see it anymore."

"I know why," barked Balyndar, stopping in his tracks and grabbing Ireheart by the collar. "It's in front of us!"

The creature made of shields, spears, daggers, knives, swords and countless other weapons rounded the corner. It had taken on a shape vaguely like a scorpion with six sets of pincers snapping open and shut.

"Charming," said Slîn, pointing to the right. "Get in here. The alley will be too narrow for it."

"Then it'll just turn itself into a snake," Ireheart replied in a fury. "It can pursue us wherever we go. Running away is no use at all."

"Yes it is. It means we stay alive until we've thought of a way to outwit it," wheezed the fourthling.

"Shoot it with your crossbow," Balyndar snapped. "You're never able to keep up with us, anyway."

Ireheart was racking his brains. Only magic would get

them out of this spot, but if they could not find their way back to the queen they were wasting their time. All this running was tiring them out and the steel creature would fall on them and scrape the flesh off their bones. He caught sight of his own crow's beak dangling at the end of the poisonous sting. Balyndar's morning star was next to it. "What works with iron?" he mused wildly, getting nowhere.

"Rust?" suggested Balyndar sarcastically.

"An enormous magnet," said Slîn.

"What a great idea! And where do you propose we get one of those? Can you find us a pulling-stone big enough to attract and immobilize four hundred sackfuls of iron and steel?" the fifthling mocked.

"And what about the rust idea? Where'd you get that all of a sudden?" Slîn snarled back.

The creature was drawing close, so they had to charge on.

Ireheart thought the pulling-stone idea was not to be discounted. Such magnets were fashioned from a mineral that made most metals, including iron, stick to it. Only gold, silver and other precious metals were unaffected. *But to stop this enemy we'd need a whole mountain of magnets. It's a waste of time just hanging around waiting for a miracle. Time is one thing we don't have.*

"We split up," he commanded.

"Won't the creature just do the same?" whimpered Slîn.

"You're the only one of us with a weapon. All we can do is chuck stones at it." Balyndar sounded as angry as Ireheart felt.

Then Slîn did something unexpected. He stopped, got down on one knee and lifted his crossbow. "Anybody know where a scorpion keeps its heart?" he asked, his voice determined, as he took aim at the creature, which was twirling its various weapons in the air and approaching fast. Its sword-legs scraped and clicked their way over the flagstones.

"Forget it: It's hopeless. Come with us." Ireheart was about to grab hold of him, but the fourthling shook his hand off.

"Just tell me where its heart will be."

Balyndar picked up a rock and threw it at the creature. "It's made of iron and magic! It can't be shot down."

They saw how the stone, shortly before hitting its target, was grabbed by the metal pincers and crushed.

"Ho, that's my crow's beak! You'll ruin it if you use it on stone!" shouted Ireheart.

Slîn had made his decision. He pointed the device down slightly, aimed, concentrated and fired.

The bolt whizzed off.

The shot was too fast for their foe's reflexes. It whirred in between the edges of two shields and buried itself in the body. There was a clatter, and the whole creature fell and disintegrated.

But the various parts—swords, daggers, spears and other blades—had not lost their momentum. A whole arsenal was flying directly at the three dwarves. The weapons' combined weight alone would have been lethal.

"Move aside!" yelled Ireheart, throwing himself through a closed door, which burst open at the first impact. Surrounded by bits of wood he found himself in a hallway. He could feel something on his foot but no pain.

He quickly rolled onto his back to check on his companions. He sighed with relief when he saw they had dodged the hail of weapons by diving for cover under a courtyard arch. The alley they had all been standing in was littered with steel weapons that had buried themselves in the flagstones.

"I'll never criticize a crossbow again. Or Slîn, for that matter," Ireheart mumbled. He stood up, dusted himself off and stepped out into the sun. Now he could see the extent of the damage: Flying weapons had sunk into the very walls.

"I don't believe it," said Balyndar, looking at Slîn, who was grinning as he reloaded his crossbow. "What are those bolts made of? Let's use them against Lot-Ionan!"

Coïra and Mallenia suddenly stood before them. It was obvious who they really had to thank for their deliverance. Slîn made a face, and the fifthling laughed.

They retrieved their own weapons from the tumble of iron and steel, not forgetting Keenfire, before hurrying to join the ladies.

"We were just in time," said Mallenia, staring at the alleyway that bristled with weapons. "We met similar creatures back where we were resting."

Vraccas—I've a bone to pick with her! Ireheart planted himself squarely in front of the maga. "Didn't you tell us there was no magic here? Perhaps you're not as good at your job as you profess to be," he complained, until Rodario interrupted.

"Not now! We have to get back to protect the others from the water-creature. There was a stone creature following us as well, but Coïra dealt with that one." Mallenia supported her friend, who had gone very pale in spite of the sunburn. Ireheart feared she might have next to no magic powers still at her disposal. "Follow us."

The dwarves checked behind and then the five of them

clambered over bricks and broken roof tiles to reach the jewelry market. Mallenia explained to them that the debris represented the remnants of the disintegrated stone monster that had been chasing the girls.

"Will there be enough for one more spell?" the Ido girl whispered to her as they walked.

"There will, but I can only do weak spells now. It'll be enough to break up a shape formed from magic, but it won't be powerful enough to eradicate it completely. We must leave town," she urged breathlessly. "The magic fields are tied to this place. We'll be safer out in the desert."

Mallenia cursed Bumina and the trap she had set, which had been intended for Franek and not for them.

They reached the square and found puddles everywhere. Rodario lay on the ground coughing and spluttering, trying to collect up his papers but then discarding them in disgust. Tungdil's armor was steaming gently and his hair hung down wet, as if he had just taken a bath.

"What happened, Scholar?" Ireheart helped Rodario up.

"The magic cannot withstand my armor. The water-shape left as soon as it tried to swallow me," he said grimly, turning to Coïra. "And your advice is?"

"To leave. We cannot destroy the magic, but it cannot get away from here," she said, holding her side. Her right forearm felt as if it were made of raw flesh—which was in fact the case when magic was not sustaining it. It would not be long before she lost the limb.

"Right, then we'll do that before the next . . ." Tungdil stopped, fascinated by the ax Ireheart bore in his left hand. The ax head was glowing, the inlays and the diamonds shining out dazzling as any star. "What, by all that's infamous . . . ?"

Ireheart likewise noted the way Keenfire was glowing. "It wasn't doing that just now," he said, taken aback. He saw Barskalín come out of a shop doorway. "Ah, that explains it. The ax doesn't like the Zhadár." He lifted it up and studied it carefully. "By Vraccas! It must be the real Keenfire!" he exclaimed, when he realized what was happening. "Scholar, your old weapon has made its way back to you!!" He went over to the one-eyed dwarf and held out the ax. "Take it. It is back with its rightful master—a fit weapon for a high king."

Tungdil looked at it and Boïndil thought he saw fear in Tungdil's eyes. "Give it to Balyndar," he ordered after a while. "My weapon is Bloodthirster."

"Scholar!" exclaimed Ireheart, horrified. *Three steps backwards!*

"Bloodthirster has been with me for hundreds of cycles and we know each other now." He pointed to the fifthling. "He is the son of the valiant dwarf-woman who was there when Keenfire was forged. The ax will be aware of the connection and will serve him now as well as it ever served me." He called Barskalín over and gave orders to set off immediately.

Ireheart pressed Keenfire into Balyndar's hand. The ax head was still shimmering, and would presumably continue to do so as long as the Zhadár were in the vicinity. *Or Tungdil, of course*, added a little doubting voice. "Take good care of it," was all he said.

Balyndar was touched and awed to have been given this weapon, as was obvious from the way he received it. "Vraccas, I vow I shall destroy your enemies and those of my own folk, whenever there is need," he vowed simply. He discarded his own morning star, not dignifying Tungdil with a single glance or bestowing on him a word of thanks for the more-than-generous gesture.

The company proceeded swiftly toward the east, escaping from the town and its magic ambushes. Going east was the shortest way out. Dwarves, humans and Zhadár all kept their eyes peeled, wary for danger.

The ground beneath Coïra's feet seemed to sway and rock. She held on to Rodario's arm and was about to say something but her strength abandoned her. He carried her and marched on.

The desert loomed up ahead of them. It was less than forty paces to the gate of the settlement.

"We're almost out of the town now," Ireheart said happily. "Our maga can rest now. Ho, that . . ."

An old friend in new garb confronted them. Knives, shields, swords and lances had turned themselves into a form four paces high, on legs and with a squat little body. Stretched out toward them were four arms with rotating blades going so fast that they appeared as a metallic shimmer, whistling and humming as the wind blew up the dust on the road behind them.

"There's no time to wake the maga," ordered Tungdil, indicating the next alleyway. "Split up. We've got to get past this beast. As soon as we're in the desert we'll be safe."

"Mind your weapons," warned Ireheart, grasping the crow's beak with all his might. "You're not skipping away from me again," he muttered to the weapon. "And if you do, then take me with you and we'll have this magic monster in little pieces."

Their flight began in earnest.

The group sprang apart, each finding their own way past their adversary. Ireheart, Slîn and Balyndar had decided to go with Rodario. In spite of all his heroic bravado they did not trust the actor to be able to get past the creature fast enough carrying the maga.

Ireheart looked at the enemy, which had selected itself an easier target. Its whirling blades had sliced two Zhadár to ribbons. Several of the blades broke off during this exercise, and some of the spears fell off as well, but new items from the arsenal replaced them; guts and odd bits of flesh from the victims flew through the air.

"Whatever happens, don't let it get you," Ireheart urged his companions.

Somehow they reached the safety of the desert, Rodario not stopping until he was twenty paces into the deep sand. He was exhausted. Sinking to his knees he let Coïra slip to the ground. Then he turned and looked back at the town.

He and the three dwarves looked on helplessly as the blade monster continually changed shape to insinuate itself into the narrowest of alleyways, taking out one Zhadár after another. The Invisibles seemed to be its favorite targets.

Eventually, Tungdil, Franek and Mallenia emerged to join them, but they waited in vain for Barskalín and his troops. As if the iron creature had not been danger enough, now a being the size of a house and composed entirely of sand was stomping through the streets.

"Our Troublemaker," called Ireheart, seeing three Zhadár come running out of a courtyard and race toward them.

More did not survive.

The Outer Lands,
The Black Abyss,

Fortress Evildam,
Late Spring, 6492nd Solar Cycle

Goda sat in her chamber sorting through the latest messages from Girdlegard.

Had she been asked to summarize them, she would have said that everywhere else things were going better than they were in Evildam.

Rebellion against the Lohasbranders had broken out in Weyurn and Tabaîn, and it was clear that neither a dragon nor any additional orc reinforcements had turned up there to quash it. The freedom-storm let loose by Rodario's descendants could not now be contained.

There had been deaths and injuries but the humans in the oppressed regions had driven the pig-faces back into the Red Mountains. The Lohasbranders and their vassals had been tried and then, mostly, executed. Goda was amazed that after two hundred cycles of despotic rule, the newly liberated humans were bothering to use the courts to apportion blame and decide punishment.

The Red Mountains were back in the hands of the children of the Smith. That was where the next message was from: Xamtor, king of the firstlings, had written to say that all the orcs who had fled there from the revenge of the humans in Weyurn and Tabaîn had been killed.

Goda consulted a map of Girdlegard and ran her hand down the western edge. The chains of oppression had been smashed. "Vraccas, don't take away your protection," she prayed. There was a knock at the door. "Come in!"

Kiras stepped into the room. She was wearing a headband to cover the burn on her forehead. "You were asking for me?"

"Yes." She indicated a chair. "How are my poor children? I expect you were with them?"

The undergroundling sat down. "Yes, but the guard told me you visited them this morning."

"That was this morning."

Kiras placed her hand on Goda's. "Your son seems better and Sanda's mind is clearing after the torture she was put through. She'll soon be herself again. Apart from the fingers she chopped off when she was so disturbed."

Both of them knew things would never be the same as before.

"There is news. *Good* news." Goda showed her the letters and opened up another message, scanning the content. "Oh, excellent. The fire of freedom has crossed the border into Gauragar. The thirdlings have left their garrison and retreated into the Black Mountains, so as not to have to fight against the humans. According to these reports," she said, handing the letter over to Kiras, "the southern älfar are already at the Ogre's Death fortress."

"We haven't received any news from Ireheart, though."

"That's right. I'm very concerned." Goda listened to her heart, trying to gauge by instinct whether her partner was alive or dead. She felt no premonition that he might be ill or dead, so supposed his group must be approaching their target: Lot-Ionan. "I know they will prevail."

"That's good. We need the help of a magus . . ." Kiras looked at Goda.

The dwarf-woman tried to smile. "I know what you mean."

Kiras smiled back. "The guards report that everything is quiet at the barrier. The monsters have not attempted to set up new camps. It seems their attack on the northeastern gate left them with a bloody enough nose to discourage them from attempting a repeat performance."

Goda was relieved to hear it. There was only one more splinter of diamond—the one she must have dropped on the stairs when she fell—and no matter how many of her servants had searched on their hands and knees, she'd been unable to locate it. Nobody knew about the unfortunate state of affairs with the magic reservoir. "I wonder how seriously I managed to injure the dwarf. Maybe that is the reason they haven't attacked again?"

"He has seen what power you possess. He presumably thought it would be easy to overcome our defenses. But now he knows better." The undergroundling adjusted her headband.

Goda looked at the girl's bald head. "Does it hurt?"

"No. Just a feeling of heat and pressure from the wound." Kiras made light of her discomfort. "What bothers me is the thought that I'm carrying around some sort of symbol and I don't know what it means." She looked at the maga. "So I will go to a healer later on and have it cut out. I'd hate to think the dwarf has branded me in order to take possession of me whenever he wants to. I won't have that."

"I don't think it's anything magic, but I understand you want to be on the safe side." She smiled. "I want you to tell the officers about our news at the briefing. That's why I summoned you."

"Won't you be there? What shall I say when they ask where you are?"

"Tell them I'm investigating something." Goda could see the undergroundling was keen to know what she was hinting at, but did not want to go into details.

When she was alone again, Goda wrapped material around her knees, and padded her hands in the same way, leaving her fingers free. Then she went back to the stairs to search for the splinter again.

She was more than ever reliant on its power. It must be found.

The dwarf-woman was convinced she would be able to find it, even if it took her several orbits of searching. In the next battle that very splinter would be crucial.

But as she strode through her rooms an unpleasant thought occurred to her: Perhaps someone had already found it and was keeping it. Without reporting it to her. *And Sanda had been on those stairs.*

Girdlegard,
Former Queendom of Sangpur,
Southwest,
Late Spring, 6492nd Solar Cycle

The Blue Range was no longer merely a dark line on the horizon with an almost invisible promise of lofty peaks, but a discernible chain of mountains rising from the desert, like a life-saving island in the middle of an ocean.

"What do you say, Scholar? Eighty miles to the fortress?" Ireheart felt his chain-mail shirt was a little looser now. They had all lost weight; their food had been scant and the journey strenuous.

"About that. But we're not heading for Ogre's Death." He called Franek over. "You were saying we should go a different way?"

The famulus nodded. "Bumina always took a certain path

when she wanted to leave the tunnels and escape from Lot-Ionan's surveillance in order to conduct her experiments in the desert."

Ireheart made a face. "Oh, that would be the same Bumina that set all those traps for us in the desert trading station because she knew you'd be coming back?"

"She didn't realize I knew her secret," Franek replied. "It's not dangerous."

"In this land there's absolutely nothing that's not dangerous," said Ireheart crossly, kicking at the sand. "Even the grains of sand are waiting to kill you."

"But times are coming soon when everything will be peaceful again." Tungdil set off, letting the famulus lead the way.

Their little group was sadly reduced in strength, meaning their confidence had also dwindled, or so it seemed to Ireheart. The only one who clung steadfastly to his belief in the success of their mission was the one who at first had refused to join them, and who could not be fully trusted: Tungdil Goldhand.

Of the three Zhadár who had survived, now only two remained: Ireheart had named them Troublemaker, Gasper and Growler. Gasper, however, had been found dead at the fireside one morning, an empty Zhadár drinking flask clutched in his hands.

Tungdil had assumed the Invisible had died of thirst, but Ireheart knew better. Unfortunately. He expected the same fate awaited him, but so far the deadly thirst had been staved off. For now.

"What a bunch of heroes," he muttered. The totally exhausted maga had, by now, to be half carried; they would have to drag her to the magic source. *Let's hope we don't run into that Bumina. Or friend Vot.*

They continued marching, sweeping southwards at nightfall, and hugging the foothills on all subsequent orbits. At last they saw the Ogre's Death fortress not ten miles away.

And saw it was already under siege!

Aiphatòn had led his troops south in a forced march. Ireheart and Tungdil observed the army camp carefully. It had been pitched at a considerable distance from the fortress and they could see that some of the älfar had set up tents on the slopes to the left and right of the fortress walls.

"They've got no siege towers with them," noted Ireheart in surprise. "Do they reckon Lot-Ionan is just going to open the front door?"

"Aiphatòn has defeated the magus once before. So Lot-Ionan won't want open combat. He'll send the älfar into the tunnels to attack the emperor," Tungdil guessed. "Lot-Ionan's famuli will have to play gatekeeper while he waits to see what happens."

"How many black-eyes do you think there are?" Balyndar was fastening the string on a sack where he was keeping Keenfire. The ax kept glowing all day long and seemed very disconcerted by the presence of the Zhadár. He had concealed it in the sack so that, to the ax in the darkness, they would not be so conspicuous.

"Difficult to say. But I'd reckon at least fifty thousand." Ireheart handed him the telescope. "They won't wait long before they attack for, in the desert, they'd soon run out of water and provisions with an army that size."

"One up to Lot-Ionan, then," said Mallenia. "He can sit back and wait for them. And for Aiphatòn it's even better.

If he really wants to get rid of all the southern älfar all he has to do is poison their food."

"You're a dangerous ally, Princess."

"I fought for the resistance. We weren't choosy about how we killed our enemies," she replied.

Franek showed Tungdil roughly where the path was. "We should get there today. After a few hundred paces it opens up into a cavern. We can rest there and won't be seen."

They moved on in single file, so as not to leave incriminating tracks. The älfar would be bound to have their spies and scouts roaming around.

Slîn was humming his favorite dwarf-tune. He had learned it from Ireheart a long while ago. "It'll be the luck of Tion if we don't succeed," he said suddenly to Balyndar with utter conviction. "We've got heroes, we've got weapons and we've got Vraccas on our side. We can't fail."

Ireheart suspected the fourthling was only saying this to drum up the necessary courage for himself and the rest. Lesser warriors would have turned tail after the losses their group had sustained. "Of course," he chimed in, "but let's keep quiet now. The pointy-ears have good hearing and they're downwind from us."

Without further discussion they ventured out into the stony landscape and found the path by moonlight, with Franek guiding them. After a short march he took them through a passage and indicated where they would be spending the night. The cave was practically round, measuring seven paces in diameter, and the roof was just high enough to allow the famulus to stand upright.

"Charming! It's as if it has been designed especially for

us," said Slîn, as he touched the cave walls. "It's nice and warm in here."

They settled down for the night and lit themselves two torches.

Tungdil set up a guard duty rota to be shared out between the Zhadár, himself and Ireheart. The exhausted humans were to get some rest to restore themselves for the journey on the morrow. Franek and Tungdil studied the map and discussed their route: A straight line toward the Blue Mountains.

Ireheart came over and looked at the map. "That road is new," he said. "It must have been laid out after I left for the Outer Lands to help with the construction of Evildam." He pointed to the tunnel-system entrance. "Our folk would never have allowed such a vulnerable point in the defenses. You can tell straight off that the long-uns have no instinct for this sort of thing."

"It wasn't Bumina who built the road," said Franek. "Lot-Ionan would have noticed if quarrying had been going on."

"Then it must have been Aiphatòn that time he defeated the magus," said Ireheart, stubbornly refusing to acknowledge the possibility of any dwarf-input in constructing this new road. "I say again: The secondlings would never have built a road that leads, if not directly to the heart, to the very body of the realm! Never!" He folded his arms and his eyebrows seemed to be glued to the bridge of his nose.

"I couldn't care less," said Tungdil. "The path is there and we'll use it. Tomorrow."

He sent the Zhadár out to stand guard. His next glance was toward the humans in their company. They were huddled up by the cave wall, Rodario in the middle, Coïra on his left and Mallenia on his right. "We have Keenfire," he said softly. "If we had known earlier what luck we would have, there would have been no need to endanger the queen like we have. Balyndar has it. You couldn't ask for a better weapon with which to confront Lot-Ionan."

"But the wrong dwarf is wielding it," Ireheart blurted out.

"I've told you why." The one-eyed dwarf rose to his feet. "And I'm sticking to that. Keenfire is in safe hands." He went over to the opposite wall, sat on his blanket and closed his eyelid. This was his way of showing he wanted to be alone.

It won't end well. You should be using Keenfire, not that älfar implement you've got now. Ireheart ran his hands over his chain-mail shirt and returned to Slîn and Balyndar.

"Now the Zhadár have gone I can have a look at it without us all getting dazzled," said the fifthling, removing the cover from the ax head.

But the inlaid markings were still shining.

The three of them all looked at the sleeping figure of Tungdil.

Slîn spoke what was on his mind. "Is the ax trying to warn us about him?" He frowned. "How could he be an enemy to our folk?"

"I knew it," growled Balyndar, packing Keenfire away again. "I never trusted that dwarf. Just because he claims to be Tungdil Goldhand . . ."

"Stop it, the lot of you! Brains like a load of gnomes!" Ireheart interrupted. "The blade might be worried about the famulus." *Or me*, he added to himself. He did not want them suspecting anything about himself or his friend. "I wouldn't trust him as much as I trust my Scholar."

"Hmm," said Slîn, uncertain now.

The three of them had something to eat and shared out the water rations, while each of them examined his own thoughts.

Ireheart looked over at Tungdil as he slept: The face, the deep lines, the golden eye patch and the long brown hair. *I'm not going to lose my trust in you. Keenfire is warning us of a different danger. It can't mean you.*

A slim silhouette appeared at the cave entrance, a spear in his left hand.

"Black-eyes," yelled Ireheart, leaping to his feet and brandishing his crow's beak. "The Zhadár sentry must have gone blind! I'll . . ."

"Slow down, Boïndil Doubleblade," the älf said, striding forward into the light of the campfire. The armor incorporated into his body was unique: Aiphatòn! "I am not here to cause you any harm but to inform you what is about to take place."

Tungdil was on his feet, but looking relaxed. "I have been expecting you, emperor."

"Oh, you have, have you?" grumbled Ireheart, thumping his crow's beak down at his feet. "So how did he find us?"

Aiphatòn pointed to the entrance. "My scouts reported a small group approaching the Blue Mountains from the west. I guessed it would be you, so I followed your tracks." He swept his gaze over the assembled company. "Is this all you are?"

"Yes. We lost many Zhadár in battle and the Black Squadron did not join us," answered Tungdil. "Have you heard anything from Hargorin Deathbringer?"

"No. He's not with us." Aiphatòn turned his slender älf face to Tungdil. "The attack starts tomorrow. Word has got round that the rebellions in the west of Girdlegard have spread to Gauragar and to my other possessions. It's said that the thirdlings have left their positions and have withdrawn to their strongholds in the Black Mountains. The älfar want to open the gates to allow reinforcements in, to get the situation under control before the uprising turns into a prolonged civil war." He sat down, because the low ceiling was making it uncomfortable to stand. "Is it true that Lohasbrand is dead?"

"Yes. And has been for a long time." Tungdil gave a concise account of their recent experiences, not hiding the fact that they had killed one of the Dsôn Aklán.

"But there are still two of the triplets alive." Aiphatòn looked at Mallenia, who was cursing under her breath. "Tirîgon survived the shot and has been convalescing back in Dsôn Bhará. I shall kill him for you, Princess. It will be on my way . . ." he said amiably. "But I have heard nothing more of Firûsha. She is apparently at the bottom of the lake."

"May Elria ensure she sinks further down than the heaviest of stones, to be eaten up by fishes," murmured Ireheart. "Oh yes, and may Lakepride crash down on her while we're at it."

Aiphatòn went into detail about his planned attack. It sounded worryingly simple. "We storm them. From three sides at once."

"He's got two famuli left for his defense. We killed one of his other two and another is on our side. They'll bombard you with spells." Tungdil took a seat opposite the älf. "You've got fifty thousand with you?"

Aiphatòn nodded. "And if we get only ten thousand of them into the tunnel system, that's all right with me, as you know. I shall be leading the attack," he said, his left hand against his armor. "And the spells they cast on me I shall catch and send back, as I did before when fighting Lot-Ionan."

"They are more likely to send their magic against your warriors." Tungdil looked at him. "Won't they take flight when they see the attack is bound to fail?"

"I have told them we must act swiftly if we want to escape death. And älfar can be extremely fast," said Aiphatòn calmly.

"No wonder, with those long legs." Ireheart played with his beard. "Anyone could run fast with legs like that. But you'll bang your heads in those low-ceilinged tunnels!"

The emperor grinned at Ireheart. "Still the old Boïndil!"

Tungdil had come up with a new concern. "Your soldiers are sufficiently fired up to get into the tunnels. But then you'll have no control over them. What if they find Lot-Ionan and kill him? You know we need the magus alive."

"I've told them we need him alive to open the gate for us. That's incentive enough."

Ireheart cleared his throat. "What if the incentive is so great that they actually do it? How are we going to get the magus out of the clutches of ten thousand älfar?" He stroked his crow's beak. "Now, don't think I'm a coward, emperor of the black-eyes. I like a challenge and I like to have a good few opponents. But does it have to be that many? And ones with those . . . skills?"

"I've just been thinking about that," Tungdil admitted, tapping his left forefinger against his eye patch with an audible clink.

"I've made arrangements to ensure that the majority of them will not survive the fighting. There are substances toxic enough to poison a whole lake with one drop." The älf looked at Tungdil. "The water supplies for my warriors have been treated with this poison. They will all die after two orbits, either in the desert or in the Blue Mountains. That will be the ideal moment for you to get the magus from me."

"That's good news!" Ireheart was relieved. Clearly, Aiphatòn had had the same idea as Mallenia. "And then you'll be off to Dsôn Bhará on your own to eradicate the northern älfar before disappearing forever?"

Aiphatòn was amused by the way the dwarves reacted to his plan. He was not offended by the question. "Yes, Boïndil Doubleblade. That is what I shall do. I shall leave, taking an evil away from Girdlegard."

"That's going to be quite an orbit." Ireheart rubbed his hands, looking forward to it. "Then, after all that, off to the north!"

The älf stood up and nodded to them. "I shall go back and tell my soldiers that I have encountered and killed some traveling merchants. That way you won't be pursued by my forces." He raised his hand in leave-taking before going out of the cave.

"Mallenia scored a bull's eye with her idea about poison." Ireheart was glad that the älf had gone. "We'll get Lot-Ionan sooner or later, Scholar."

Tungdil nodded. "Indeed." He put his hand on his friend's back, his brown eye warm. "Get some rest, my friend. You need your sleep just as much as Rodario and his two women."

There's absolutely no trace of eye-swirl or sparks. Ireheart suppressed a yawn. "Yes. But don't forget to wake me. Putting the Zhadár on watch together is not a good idea. We've just seen how they let the most dangerous long-ears in the whole of Girdlegard walk in," he said, exaggerating wildly. "The legendary Zhadár! Ha! We've got two of them left. And what did for the others? Magic creatures."

"The only things able to defeat the Invisibles," guessed Tungdil. He considered his options. "I think we should keep them both safely out of the action."

"What? I can't be hearing right, Scholar!"

"Troublemaker and Growler, as you call them, know all the secrets of the Dsôn Aklán," he said with emphasis. "If Aiphatòn were to fail, their knowledge would be vitally important in helping us to defeat the black-eyes. Only then will Girdlegard find peace."

Ireheart looked dismayed. "Does that mean it's my job to look after Troublemaker and Growler, and not the other way around?"

Tungdil made as if to applaud and then slipped back down onto his blanket.

"If we go on like this, I'll be drinking from an älf flask of my own free will." Ireheart stuck his finger in his ear crossly and stomped off to tell Balyndar and Slîn the outcome of their strategy discussion.

XXVII

Girdlegard,
Blue Mountains,
Realm of the Secondlings,
Late Spring, 6492nd Solar Cycle

Ireheart was overwhelmed by his impressions.

He was back in the homeland he had left so long ago; because of Lot-Ionan it had been impossible since for him even to make visits. He took a deep breath and recognized the unique smell of the Blue Mountains, remembering these same tunnels from the old days. He was dismayed by the dilapidation.

Vaults, passageways, caverns, halls and chambers—every-where was in need of attention. A mountain is not dead, as humans tend to assume. Things there are always on the move. Rocks shift as the mountain grows, shudders and sways. Places die away, and the inhabitants of the mountain have to adjust accordingly. Supports have to be put in, rubble cleared, new chambers hewn. Since Lot-Ionan's takeover, none of the maintenance had been carried out.

"Cracks, roof falls, leaks," he noted with distress. "What a disgrace! For that alone the hocus-pocus wizard deserves a good beating!"

"Quite apart from the wanton destruction," added Slîn.

"That'll have been the experiments he and the famuli carried out," said Franek, who was at the head of the company alongside Tungdil.

"Then you deserve the same beating," growled Ireheart, giving him a shove. "A mountain will be resentful. I hope it doesn't take it out on us, when my folk move in again."

"I'm sure it will be glad to have you back," said Slîn. "It must be totally sick of magic by now."

The humans followed the dwarves, with the Zhadár bringing up the rear. In the temperate cool of the mountain they had regained their strength; they had located an underground stream and drunk fresh courage with every gulp of water. Now they were on their way to a second, vital, source. Franek did not seem to have trouble recalling which tunnel to take.

Ireheart was being more cautious than usual. *As soon as the little wizard shows the slightest indication of trying to trick us, I'll split his skull with my crow's beak spike and give his brain some fresh air.*

"The älfar attack should already be underway," Rodario told Mallenia. They had taken Coïra between them and were helping her along. To be on the safe side. "Nobody will be in our way."

"Apart from Lot-Ionan," interjected Mallenia.

Rodario dismissed the idea. "What are the chances of encountering the magus in this enormous underground realm?"

"He could be at the magic source, guarding it. Then things would be difficult for us." She spoke quietly, not wanting the dwarves or Zhadár to overhear.

"There it is," said Franek, indicating an oval door inside a palandium arch that had runes chiseled into the lintel. "The source is behind that door."

"What do the symbols mean?" asked Tungdil as he headed for the entrance.

"It's a formula. It has to be pronounced to make the door open. That way Lot-Ionan knows somebody's going in. He's got a bracelet that starts to glow when the incantation is spoken," the famulus explained.

Tungdil considered the entrance. "How did *you* get in? You knew about the security arrangements."

"I tried a counter-incantation I thought was foolproof." Franek looked down, humiliated. "It cost me my position."

"We could just break the door down, Scholar." Ireheart looked at Balyndar. "Keenfire can make a nice little hole in it and overcome any magic device."

"But Lot-Ionan would still know," warned Franek. "He can turn up very quickly, before the queen and I have had a chance to refresh our own stores of magic. He won't be weakened yet."

"So we're practically at our destination but we can't go in," said Balyndar impatiently. "If the magus finds us now we've got no chance."

"You and Tungdil will survive," Ireheart ventured. "You're both immune to magic."

Tungdil pursed his lips and lifted Bloodthirster. "Balyndar is right. We'll go in and let Queen Coïra bathe in the pool; Balyndar and I will stand guard and make sure Lot-Ionan can't surprise us." He turned to the maga. "How long would you need?"

"It depends on the strength of the source," she said, uncertainly.

"It's enormously powerful," Franek said. "It never took me longer than a few moments."

"We can hold him off that long," said the fifthling

determinedly, nodding at Tungdil. The one-eyed dwarf barged the door.

A loud hissing sound ensued as the runes above the entrance flared, showering Tungdil with sparks, but his tionium armor absorbed the spell as if it had been harmless rays of light. The wood splintered and the door burst open.

Tungdil stood on the threshold with his weapon raised above his head, checking in all directions to see if it was safe. "There's no one here," he called back.

The others hurried over and Balyndar remained at the doorway, facing out, Keenfire in his hands.

It was a small chamber, really more like a sauna. Steps led to a vertical shaft protected with a grille; the walls were decorated with a mosaic portrait of Lot-Ionan's face.

The magus has changed a lot, thought Ireheart. Compared with how he used to look he had gone bald, and he had three reddish-silver tufts of hair on his chin. The eyebrows were bushier, too. His features had become crueler and more demonic, as if the bones had been rearranged. But it was unmistakably the face of the Scholar's one-time foster-father.

"Coïra needs to stand over the shaft," said Franek. "Her weight will cause the grating to sink five paces down, bringing her directly to the magic force field. She'll need to use a spell to bring herself up again."

Slîn and Balyndar were at the door. "Why don't the steps go right down into the source?"

"Lot-Ionan wanted it like this. I don't know what his motives were." He saw Ireheart's suspicious expression. "Well, let me go first if you think it's a trap."

"Oh, I can see you'd like that," Ireheart laughed. "Scholar, what do we do here?"

Tungdil gestured to Coïra to come over to the shaft. "If anything happens to her, kill Franek," was the only instruction he gave.

"That's easy. I can do that," Boïndil replied.

The queen was taken down the steps by Rodario and Mallenia and, as they withdrew, she sank down, the grating lowering itself with a click.

"I shan't bother to remove my clothing this time," she said. "You will have other opportunities to admire me naked."

"I can hear something being wound tight," said Slîn, listening to the mechanism.

"Take care!" Rodario called to Mallenia. "I don't like it. How do we get her up again?"

The Ido girl took off her belt and asked for Rodario's as well. She swiftly tied them together and tested the knot. "If Coïra jumps she can reach this and we can pull her up." She knelt and looked down. "Dark as the grave," she said quietly.

"Horrid thing to say." Rodario knelt also. The clicking still continued indicating that the grating had not reached the bottom. "Has it started yet?"

A blue shimmering light surrounding the maga showed that the source was bestowing its power.

They waited in silence. The tension in the chamber had them all sweating, except for Tungdil, who was the very embodiment of calm, as if he were in possession of a secret certainty that they would all leave the Blue Mountains alive with Lot-Ionan their captive.

Ireheart kept switching his attention between the source and the door. "I hate this," he grunted, wiping his sweating hands yet again on his undershirt. "Oh, how I hate this. I'd rather be in a battle for a whole orbit."

In the corridor all was quiet. Not a sound, no shouts, and no Lot-Ionan.

"Where do we go to find him?" Tungdil demanded of Franek.

The famulus shrugged. "He could be anywhere, but I reckon he won't be far. I'm surprised he hasn't turned up yet to see what's . . ."

"Quiet," ordered Balyndar. "Someone's coming!"

Rodario could see that Coïra was undergoing contortions in the blue light, as if in intense pain. She crouched down, cowering and holding tight to the walls, swaying and moaning. This was not at all how he remembered events at the source near Lakepride. "Coïra, are you all right?"

No answer.

"We ought to get her out of there," he decided, letting the end of the improvised rope down. "Catch!"

Ireheart stood behind Balyndar and Tungdil, taking care not to touch his friend's armor as he peered out between them.

A young woman in a dark-blue figure-hugging dress raced toward the chamber, her long dark hair streaming out behind her.

Terrified, she glanced over her shoulder; she had not seen the dwarves at the chamber entrance. An arrow jutted out of her shoulder. A greeting from the älfar archers.

"The little sorceress is injured. Good!" murmured Boïndil. *So she must have used up all her magic at the first encounter, and needs to get it recharged.* She would be an easy victim. "Will you let me have her?" he asked Tungdil and Balyndar.

Bumina saw them and stopped short. "Dwarves? By Samusin, how did you get in here?"

Franek came up behind the dwarves and addressed Bumina. "You didn't expect this, did you?" he said with malicious glee. "Oh dear, did the älfar hurt you?" He pulled out his dagger. "That's nothing to what I'm going to do to you! You destroyed my town! The trap had your signature all over it."

"Lot-Ionan made me do it." Bumina studied the dwarves and tried to gauge what they would do. She raised her arms. "Get out of the way and let me into the source."

Tungdil and Balyndar both raised their weapons at the same time.

Rodario called down the shaft, but there was still no answer from the queen. Uttering a curse, he jumped down, directing his fall as best he could by bracing hands and feet against the walls. He landed by Coïra, who had collapsed; he, too, was covered in a white light, but he felt nothing.

"What is it?" he said, helping her up.

"The source is incredibly . . . powerful," she groaned. "I'm not used to it and it really hurts! It's drenching me with power, more than I've ever known." Her next sentence was a muffled groan and her fingers clutched at Rodario's collar. "I can't concentrate on finding the right spell to get out of here," she stammered. "Help me . . ." Her body became rigid and then repeatedly convulsed unnaturally.

Rodario took her girdle and told Mallenia to throw down the improvised rope. He tied the belts together, fastened them to Coïra's hands and threw the other end back up. "Pull her up!" he shouted, crouching down to lift her onto his shoulders. "I'll support her from below."

The rope tightened and soon the young woman was being pulled gradually out of the sphere of magic influence.

The clicking ceased, and the grille slid sideways under Rodario's feet!

The dwarves up at the doorway knew nothing of this.

Franek was still laughing at Bumina. "If you really had any magic power you would have cast a spell at us."

"You haven't used magic either, so I can only assume your reservoir is as empty as mine."

Ireheart looked over his shoulder. Coïra was being heaved up out of the shaft by Mallenia. The queen thanked her, gasping for air, and then stood up. She no longer looked as drained as she had done and there was a new spark in her eyes. "But now we have a maga strong enough to magic the two of you into the ground."

Tungdil turned quickly round and nodded at Franek, who could hardly wait to get down into the source. "Your turn now." Without warning he plunged Bloodthirster twice into the stomach of the famulus. "Go to Samusin or to whichever god you want."

Franek collapsed onto the stone flags, gurgling horribly, still moving his lips inaudibly. His fingernails scratched at his killer's tionium shin protectors. By the time his head hit the floor he was dead.

Ireheart was not distressed but he was surprised. *Another deed the old Tungdil would not have carried out.*

"He told us about your secret path," Tungdil said to Bumina. "That's how we got in." He lifted Bloodthirster, red and dripping. "Where is Lot-Ionan? Don't even think about running away."

The famula recoiled. She turned and started to run, but

Tungdil hurled his weapon at her with a furious roar. It hit her on the back, exactly where the arrow had struck. Screaming, she fell to the ground, felled by the impact.

With one bound Tungdil was by her side, brutally tearing Bloodthirster out of her flesh; he used his boot to turn her over, then placed the weapon's sharp tip at her throat. "I'll count to three and if I don't get told where to find him you will die," he snarled. The deep voice sent shivers up Ireheart's spine. "*One . . . !*"

"Die and lose your soul!" Bumina whimpered.

"It's no good trying to protect your master. You'll be harming yourself, not him. *Two!*" He increased the pressure he was exerting, and the blade penetrated her flesh.

"Gone! He's gone!!"

"*Three!*" Without showing any emotion Tungdil pushed Bloodthirster through her throat. The famula attempted to gasp for air, coughing and spluttering, her hands grasping the deadly weapon instinctively, but the arm of the dwarf was like steel. Bumina fought death—and lost. Her eyes went dull and her life left her.

"We'll look for him ourselves," Tungdil announced. "He can't be far away."

"Nor can the black-eyes," said Ireheart, unable to take in what his friend had just done. These humans had deserved to die. But the way he had done it: That was extraordinary. Thorough.

"Help!" they heard Mallenia's voice. "I need your strong arms!"

Ireheart was about to turn round and help the Ido girl but at that moment he saw älfar charging round the corner. He reckoned there must be about seventeen of them, all wearing black leather armor, with iron plates over the breast. Their weapons were of various kinds, but similar to swords. His battle-lust flared up on the spot. "I'll be with you in a tick," he called. "I've just got a few black-eyes to flatten!" He raised up his crow's beak and hurled himself at the enemy with a mighty war cry to Vraccas.

A black shadow overtook him.

"Oh no! Scholar, don't spoil my fun," he complained. "You go and help Mallenia! Leave them . . ."

To me is what he had intended to say, but Bloodthirster crashed horizontally into the side of the first älf, slicing into him as easily as if he had been made of wax. While that enemy was still falling to the ground, Tungdil was already striking the next one, making a hole in his chest before yanking out the dripping steel spike to plunge it into the neck of a third älf. Blood was everywhere.

Ireheart stared at his friend in astonishment. He had never seen him fighting so brutally.

The swiftness of his movements was such that he was faster than the black-eyes he was fighting; the älfar did not know what had hit them. They had never fought dwarves before and had certainly never met an adversary like this. Black blood was raining all around, severed limbs fell, weapons and armor shattered at each of Bloodthirster's strikes.

Tungdil was screaming like a mad dog on each attack he launched. He mowed his way through the ranks of the älfar, cutting a path. The fallen were blocking Ireheart's view. When the last of the enemies was slain, he saw Tungdil standing with his back to him at the far end of the corridor. He had blood all over him, dripping from his armor and helmet.

"Vraccas help us!" he heard Balyndar say.

Turning round he saw a very pale fifthling at his right hand. Balyndar had also followed the course of the combat. To be more exact, it had not been combat but slaughter. *Faced with Tungdil those älfar were like drunken orcs.* And yet Ireheart knew that he himself would never have been able to fight his way from one end of the passage to the other like that. Not nowadays and not without taking some injury.

Coïra had been too busy to watch. She was staring into the darkness of the shaft. In order to be able to get Rodario out with magic she first had to be able to see him.

She lifted her hand and a torch flew into her outstretched fingers. She trained its light down into the dark shaft until she could see the actor. He was clinging to the open grille with both hands, poised perilously above the abyss.

But the grille was moving again, coming up. This would mean Rodario's fingers would be crushed and he would fall.

This time the maga had no problem finding the right magic formula. Now that she was outside the source she no longer felt confused and overcome with the ecstasy that had robbed her of the power of clear thought.

Invisible powers took hold of the actor and lifted him, pulling him through the narrow gap between wall and grille and floating him up out of the shaft to land between the two women.

Hardly was he back on his feet than Coïra rushed into his arms to embrace him. But she released him at once. "I must see what's happening outside," she said, excusing herself.

"A hero," said Mallenia, giving him a kiss on the cheek.

"But you did need a bit of help. I like that." She grinned and followed the maga out to where the dwarves were.

Rodario rubbed his painful hands, checking the cuts on his palms. "Samusin, god of justice, I thank you," he prayed. Then he noticed Franek's dead body and the black blood coating the threshold. Next to him there was a loud click and the grille was back in place.

"Huzzah! May Vraccas be praised! More black-eyes!" Rodario could hear Ireheart's happy voice. "Scholar, these ones are mine, got it? I can't let you have all . . . Scholar! SCHOLAR!" There ensued loud shouts and the clash of weapons. "He's only gone and done it again!"

Rodario put his hands on his hips, took a deep breath and drew his sword. It was sometimes nice not to be a hero. Unfortunately he considered himself to be one now and heroes had to fight.

He followed the Zhadár; Mallenia, Coïra and Slîn were ahead of him, with Balyndar and Ireheart racing in front. He could not see Tungdil anywhere but he could hear the continuous barrage of battle and screams coming from another passage.

"Why won't anyone tell me what's happening?" he complained in his best stage manner, hurrying so as not to miss the finale.

They trotted along through the tunnels of the dwarf realm, always on the lookout in case they encountered Lot-Ionan, the älfar or Vot, the last famulus. Ireheart reckoned they had been doing this for around three orbits now.

However, they had met nothing and nobody.

The älfar slaughtered by Tungdil in his solo assault had

not been part of the main force; they seemed to have belonged to a scouting party who had entered the cave system by skirting Vot and Bumina. *They were probably trying to kill Bumina before she got to the magic source to replenish her reserves, and they ran straight into our arms.* Boïndil grinned. *Nice one!*

But Ireheart was still mad at Tungdil for having taken on and killed over twenty-five warriors at lightning speed. It had not seemed to cost the other dwarf any noticeable effort, nor had the missing eye limited his performance in any way. Ireheart found himself having to admit that Tungdil was superior to him in combat skills, flexibility and speed. In the old days they had been about equal but after this orbit he was painfully aware that he could no longer compete.

"Off to the right," he instructed, leading the group into the former throne room.

The pomp and splendor of this hall had long passed, the famuli having conducted experiments that had caused the cave walls and several of the high pillars to collapse. There were holes and burns in the battle scenes showing historical victories of the dwarves; upturned braziers and fallen lamps lay scattered on the ground.

The table for the use of the dwarf-kings and the carved stone dais for the clan leaders had been smashed; the impressive marble throne on which Gundrabur Whitecrown had once sat now lay shattered after some spell had been let loose. A symbol for the loss of dwarf-power.

Ireheart had been hoping to find Lot-Ionan hiding here.

"This isn't working," said Rodario, noting the dwarf's drooping shoulders. "We could be wandering around in these mountains for ages without ever coming across the magus."

"But what else can we do?" Slîn asked Coïra. "Didn't you say you had a special spell?"

"To locate him?" She shook her head.

Mallenia sat down on a section of fallen pillar. She made no attempt to conceal her dissatisfaction. "We need a new plan. Who knows what's happening back at the Black Abyss or in my country?"

"You don't have to worry about the älfar. The poison must have worked by now. There won't be more than a few of them still alive," Tungdil reassured her. "Any survivors won't be a danger to us and Aiphatòn will dispatch them all soon."

"We should have stayed by the source," complained Balyndar. "Sooner or later Lot-Ionan would have come along."

"There's nothing to say we can't go back there." Ireheart stretched and heard a crack as the vertebrae altered position. "I'm getting old," he noted with astonishment. "Anyone would think my bones were made of wood."

"Back to the source," ordered Tungdil. "We'll need to find provisions on the way. Our stomachs are rumbling so loudly that we don't stand a chance of creeping up on the enemy."

The group turned, about to leave the throne chamber, but then heard footsteps from the other side of the room.

A young man of not more than thirty cycles entered the hall and spotted the Zhadár, who brought up the rear of their party. He lifted his right arm and sent a dazzling lilac-colored magic beam shooting their way.

Troublemaker and Growler had the presence of mind to dodge behind a stone pillar.

"Thanks, Vraccas," cheered Ireheart, wheeling around on his heel. "We've found Vot!"

"Charming! But actually, he found us," said Slîn, going down on one knee and lifting his crossbow ready to fire, all in one smooth movement. Before anyone could stop him he had sent a bolt flying at the famulus. "And *this* is my magic!"

Vot had not seen what was coming and had his arms raised to conjure up a new spell. The missile went straight to his heart but a glowing light showed that he was already starting to heal himself with magic.

Tungdil raised Bloodthirster to attack him and Coïra sent out a shimmering chaining spell to tie his hands and bind up his eyes. Now he was as good as harmless, because he could no longer see his target and thus could not cast any spells.

"We want your master: Lot-Ionan," said Tungdil. "We asked Bumina his whereabouts a few orbits ago but she didn't want to tell us, so her corpse now rots at the entrance to the source. It's up to you what fate you choose."

Vot had not yet lost his arrogance. "Who do you think you are? How dare you . . . ?"

The dark-clad dwarf cut along his throat with the tip of his blade so that the wound bled profusely without endangering his life. "The next strike will have more power behind it."

"Lot-Ionan is not here," said Vot through clenched teeth. He had understood that it was not his place to ask any of the questions.

Ireheart kicked his shin. "You are about to meet your death if you lie to us again, my lad."

"I'm telling the truth," said the terrified famulus. "The magus has left."

Tungdil moved the tip of Bloodthirster and pressed it into the young man's chest. "Where's he gone? Tell me or let's see how quickly you can heal yourself this time."

Vot lay still, not daring to move. "He's gone north," came his quiet voice. "He's going north to punish the älfar for their attack. He knew about their plans and left us in charge of guarding the source. On their return to their lands they were to find only ruins."

"That's a lie!" exclaimed Ireheart. "Franek told us he never lets his famuli use the pool without supervision."

Vot sighed. "Circumstances forced him."

"I don't believe you." Tungdil inserted his blade in a different place.

"It's the truth! He let us have three visits. After that a destruction spell will be set off in the chamber," Vot said quickly.

"What is he going to do exactly in the north?"

"Lay waste to the älfar realm for attacking him. What else?"

"Yes, and what else?" Ireheart imitated the famulus. "I do that every orbit: I get up, I shovel stuff, then I fill in the Black Abyss with my bare hands and then I do a little bit of destruction just to keep my hand in."

Vot snorted with derision. "Lot-Ionan is powerful enough to turn whole swathes of land to desert. He has learned to take up enormous amounts of magic energy. The älfar will soon be feeling the results."

"There's another magic source there," Ireheart told Tungdil. "It seems Lot-Ionan wants to spread out his sphere of influence to the other side of Girdlegard."

"He will see that neither the kordrion nor the Dragon exist. The älfar have been wiped out—and he can take over as undisputed ruler of Girdlegard," Tungdil continued the line of thought.

"So we might just as well have waited in comfort with Aiphatòn," sighed Slîn. "He would have come to us."

"Then we wouldn't have found the ax." Balyndar lifted Keenfire. "It will serve us well."

"Off to the north, then." Rodario studied his worn-out boots. "But this time let's get some horses so we don't have to do the whole thing on foot."

Troublemaker shouted a warning and drew his weapon.

The group sprang away from the entrance, abandoning Vot to his pool of blood.

"Confound it!" Ireheart saw an approaching horde of älfar stumble into the throne room from the side entrance they had been intending to leave by. Congealing black blood dripped out of their mouths and noses and many of them were swaying as they walked; when they raised their weapons to confront the group of humans and dwarves they gave the impression of being extremely weak. The poison had not killed them yet but it was winning.

Älfar were streaming in through the second door as well, and leading them—was Aiphatòn. As he passed he stabbed Vot with his spear, hoisted the corpse up for all to see and made a short speech.

Mallenia interpreted. "He says the sorcerer that put the curse on them has now been killed and that they will soon recover. To get free of the spell they need to find Lot-Ionan. The . . ." she searched for the right word ". . . dwarves— that's you—aren't worth expending any time and effort on.

The magus must be found; that is the most important thing."

One of the älfar stepped forward to speak to Aiphatòn.

"He thinks they ought to kill us first. He recognized Keenfire and is afraid we will make trouble. He thinks we probably know how to activate hidden traps from the old dwarf-times, installed to deter invaders." Mallenia continued to pay attention. "If I've got this right, the älfar we see here are the last of the whole contingent."

Hmm, difficult. Ireheart was already doing some rough calculations in his head and arrived at three hundred adversaries in total. In normal circumstances he would hardly have thought they had a chance. But their maga was newly refreshed with magic, Tungdil was a dangerous force to be reckoned with, and Balyndar had Keenfire, so the battle might be more of a competition to see which of them killed the highest number. He was the one with the worst outlook. "I'll take Aiphatòn," he whispered to Tungdil.

"You will wait." Tungdil told Coïra to hold a defense spell in readiness in case a shower of arrows came their way.

Mallenia insisted they let her listen. "The emperor is rejecting the suggestion. He says they can take us on after the gate has been opened. First of all they need to search for the magus."

"He's obviously trying to protect us," said a relieved Rodario. Like Mallenia, he too had drawn his sword.

"I don't think he will succeed. And he doesn't need to." Tungdil sprang up the steps to the ruined throne, brandished Bloodthirster and called out.

"Do I want to know what he's saying?" Rodario sighed.

"Well, I do." Ireheart grinned in joyful anticipation. "He'll finish off the black-eyes! They'll be eliminated from the mountains, as is only right. We'll do it, us dwarves!" He smiled grimly. "Vraccas, what a glorious orbit this will be!"

"Tungdil's telling them it was him who brought the curse down on them and that they must take his life if they want to break the spell."

A roar went through the älfar and the first of them charged forward to hurl themselves on the one-eyed dwarf.

He spread his arms and held Bloodthirster out. One rune after the other flared up on the black tionium, and the more runes that joined in, the more dazzling their light.

"Why do I get the feeling I'm not going to get anywhere this time either," muttered Ireheart.

As the wave of älfar crashed up against the steps leading to the stage, Tungdil leaped over their heads into the very midst of his attackers and disappeared from his friends' sight. But the sounds of metal striking metal, the shrieks of pain and the spraying blood coming over to drench them told more than any direct view could have done.

"They're actually not touching any of us!" Rodario was astonished.

"I'm not letting this happen! I want some of this!" Ireheart began his own attack.

Balyndar followed suit with Keenfire, whose diamonds and inlaid patterns were blazing out. With each stroke the ax head left a fiery trail in the air and the blade severed everything it touched. They fought their way through the mass of älfar side by side. At first the enemy did not notice them, but soon they turned their attention to the new threat presented by the dwarves.

Now they had a battle after Ireheart's own heart! "Bring

me your lives, you long-legged land-plagues!" he bellowed enthusiastically, smashing heads indiscriminately "You'll regret ever having set foot in my native land! Oh *and how* you will regret it!"

Ireheart fought one grisly fight after another, taking his share of cuts and stab wounds, but this did not deter him. He was too deeply immersed in battle-rage and saw a red mist over the whole scene. His blood was coursing faster, hotter and more vitally through his veins, and though he had lost sight of Balyndar, this did not worry him. He forgot everything in his merciless killing spree.

The ranks of the enemy grew ever thinner. Ireheart felled another älf by hooking the spike of the crow's beak around his foot; then he whacked the flat side of the weapon into the face of the struggling warrior. Looking round, he realized that his latest victim was the last of the enemy. "Ho, are we done already?" he yelled.

Tungdil was sitting on the steps with Bloodthirster on his knee. He was staring blankly ahead. Rodario, Coïra and Mallenia were standing together, looking as if they had not had to use their swords at all; dead älfar all around them had been burned beyond recognition. Such was the power of magic.

Slîn wandered among the dead recovering the bolts he had shot. Balyndar knelt in front of a stone statue, his hands on the shaft of Keenfire, and his eyes closed. He was doubtless praying to Vraccas and offering thanks for the victory.

The corpses of the älfar surrounded them, blood forming a giant pool like ink on the flagstones. The Blue Mountains were refusing to let the black liquid drain away.

"Scholar?"

"He is lost in his memories," said a soft voice behind him.

Still half intoxicated by the battle, Ireheart whirled round and struck out. The crow's beak crashed against a slender spear. It was Aiphatòn standing there. "Lucky escape," he sniffed.

"Too slow," the emperor corrected him amicably. "You must be tired. Otherwise I'm sure you would have got me and killed me like all the rest, Boïndil Doubleblade."

The dwarf narrowed his eyes. "I can tell when I'm being mocked."

"That wasn't my intention."

"You didn't intend to mock me or you didn't intend I should be able to tell?"

"I didn't intend to mock you." Aiphatòn inclined his head to Ireheart. "Forgive me."

The dwarf made a dismissive gesture, feeling a bit stupid standing next to an älf whose armor showed no bloodstains. "You weren't fighting?"

"These are your mountains. I considered it more appropriate to leave their cleansing to you," answered Aiphatòn. "My contribution was to poison them. That made it possible for you to defeat them. Otherwise I would probably have stepped into the fray on your side." He surveyed the heaped bodies. "I was never one of them, even if I believed it for a time. It was a mistake that I have now corrected." He looked at Ireheart. "The southern gate has not been touched and the few who escaped the magic spells of Vot and Bumina have now died in the tunnels." He pointed to Tungdil. "He ought to take the armor off. Or it will take possession of him more and more."

"Possession?"

"Didn't you know?"

Ireheart grabbed his water flask and moistened his dry throat. "I suspected it," he replied quietly. "How much do you know about it?"

"Nothing at all. But I can read the symbols. It indicates a pact between the armor and the one who wears it that each will protect the other and that they will never part. Then the day will come when the wearer will never want to take it off at all. Not even to sleep. Not even when he eats. Not even when he defecates. His flesh will be rubbed raw by it, gangrene will set in and Tungdil will die in his own excrement." Aiphatòn saw the horror in the dwarf's face. "Make him take it off." He strode past, toward the door. "I am going to Dsôn Bhará, to finish my mission."

"Perhaps it won't be necessary." Ireheart explained what Vot had vouchsafed to them.

The älf considered the implications. "Then I shall see what the magus has left. If he and I encounter each other I shall overpower him and leave him bound and tethered for you to find." He winked at Ireheart. "Look after your friend if his life is dear to you." With these words he left the hall.

The dwarf followed him with his eyes, then looked at Tungdil, who was still seated on the remains of the throne, staring at the wall, one hand stroking his thigh guards, lost in thought.

XXVIII

Girdlegard,
Former Queendom of Sangpur,
At the border with Gauragar,
Late Spring, 6492nd Solar Cycle

The desert was safely behind them now—their journey had been speeded up by the horses they had acquired at an oasis.

If they maintained present progress they would soon be in the central region of the älfar realm and thus near Lot-Ionan. Only short rests were accorded, enough to refresh the horses. Dwarves and humans ate while they rode.

During one of these evening pauses Rodario was sitting opposite the two women, his face indicating that he had an important announcement to make. "I accept," he stated.

Coïra and Mallenia exchanged glances.

"The clause about not sharing a bed with the two of you at the same time: I accept," he repeated. "I don't want to have to do without either one of you. The last few orbits have brought this home to me. And if two such charming ladies make me an offer of the kind you've made, I would be mad to turn it down."

Coïra leaned forward, beaming, to give him a resounding kiss on the left cheek, while Mallenia did the same on the right. A dutiful little gesture to seal an unusual pre-liaison agreement.

Ireheart had been watching the three of them and shook

his head. "I'll never understand these long-uns," he told Tungdil. "Would you take a look at that constellation over there?"

"If they're fond of each other and are happy with the relationship, what's wrong with that?" Tungdil put a large branch on the fire over which their supper was roasting: Slîn had shot them four rabbits. "I'd be the last person to criticize their arrangements." He put his hand on his back to ease it.

"Shall I help you take the armor off? It must be uncomfortable." Ireheart stretched out his hand to undo the buckles but his friend evaded him.

"Our mission is dangerous. Anything could occur. I won't want to lose vital minutes putting my armor on and I can't risk being injured through only having my normal leather jerkin on just because it's more comfortable," said Tungdil, rejecting his offer of assistance.

"When was the last time you took it off?"

"A long time ago."

"Indeed it was, Scholar." Ireheart passed him a rabbit thigh. The meat was piping hot and smelled delicious. "Here, eat this. It'll make you big and strong so that you can continue doing those great deeds we saw in the Blue Mountains." He started eating the other thigh. "I don't know how you do it: All that energy and stamina. Even at my wildest I don't come near."

"I've had a deal more practice than you, my friend," Tungdil replied. He ate his food but displayed little appetite.

Ireheart pretended to have seen something on the back of the tionium armor. "There you are! There's dirt on it. And here's a big dent. How did that happen? We should give it a thorough clean. Or it might get fractious and stop protecting you. It might even go all hard again, like a steel girder, and then I'll have to bash away at it as though I'm ringing a bell, just to get you out of it!" He attempted levity.

Tungdil turned to him curiously. "Why on earth do you want me to take it off?"

"Me?"

"You're a rotten actor, Ireheart. You always were." He chewed and swallowed the meat. "What have you got against it?"

Ireheart had no idea how he could get out of answering that mercilessly direct question, so he went on the offensive: "I've heard some stories about suits of armor like that and they can take over whoever wears them. The poor sods end horribly, stuck in their metal casing, and I wouldn't want that to happen to you," he blurted out, gesturing with the rabbit bone. "All I know is, you haven't taken it off for thirty orbits and I've seen you stroking the leg protectors as if they are made of the skin of a virgin dwarf!"

Tungdil was about to reply but then fell silent. "You're quite right," he said quietly, chucking the remains of his rabbit piece in the fire. "It would be very difficult for me to leave it off. Very difficult."

"Then take it off now. At least for tonight. I'll keep watch twice as thoroughly as usual," Ireheart made an effort to encourage him.

But straightaway the runes lit up, shining like the eyes of a wild animal. "No," his friend said, refusing to comply. "It doesn't feel right."

"Then tell me when you do intend to take it off."

"When it's all over," Tungdil replied tiredly. "Let's not

argue about it, Ireheart. I swear I'll take it off when the Black Abyss is closed up and we've defeated my former master." He held out his hand. "Will that do?"

"Yes, Scholar!" Ireheart shook hands, and then the warrior turned back to the rabbits. "Grub up!" he shouted, so loud that the dwarves and humans all jumped. That made him grin. He could not see the Zhadár anywhere; they must be sitting in the shade somewhere keeping a weather eye out.

"So then, what do you think of me now?" Tungdil took his drinking flask, which he had filled with palm brandy. He took out the stopper and swallowed a deep draft of the strong liquor.

"Because you won't take the suit of armor off?"

"No. What do you think of me?" He wiped some of the strong-smelling fruity liquid out of his beard. "Do you think I am the genuine Tungdil?"

Ireheart smiled. "I've thought that for a long time. Sometimes there's a little gnome at the back of my mind that makes me notice minor things about you that you never used to have. But we all change, don't we?" he answered, truthfully. "I'm positive you're you, Scholar, and not a doppelganger or an illusion or anything evil sent by the powers of the Black Abyss."

Tungdil waited until everyone had gathered around the fire, had their food and gone away again. Slîn had his toolkit spread out and was working on his crossbow, and Balyndar was looking at Keenfire, which still was refusing to quieten down.

"Only a minority elected me to the office of high king," Tungdil started cautiously. "The fourthlings and fifthlings. What if the firstlings and secondlings speak out against me? What then?"

"You have the thirdlings' support."

"Yes, but the thirdlings don't count. Not in this." Tungdil contemplated Balyndar. "He'd be a much better high king. Or his mother could be high queen. The other three tribes would be happy with that."

Ireheart took the proffered palm brandy and swallowed some, choking and spluttering. "I'm used to a lot of things," he croaked, "but this is rough enough to eat your eyeballs up! And you've only got the one!" Tungdil laughed. "It sounds as if you want to give the title up! And to think I had to use it as bait to get you to join us, Scholar!"

"I only wanted it to force the dwarves to follow my orders," he admitted. "The word of a high king has more weight than the word of Tungdil Goldhand, especially if lots of people are saying he's not even the real one. Do you get me?" He gave a faint smile. "Most of them will be surprised when I hand the title back when our mission is over."

"*Hand it back?*" Ireheart slapped his thigh. "Ho! Only our very own genuine Scholar could come up with something like that! A doppelganger would have been enjoying his power and would abuse it." He laughed. "Yes, it will take them by surprise." He nodded over at Balyndar. "Why don't you tell him now?"

"Why would I?"

"So he changes his attitude toward you."

Tungdil took another slug of the palm brandy. "I don't want him to. It's better if things stay as they are. If he makes it to king of the fifthlings the blemish on his pedigree should not be public knowledge. It's better if he's seen to have a different father. He can keep his secret."

"Well, he could, but for the resemblance . . ."

"Coincidence, no more than that. I shall never refer to him as my son." He gave Ireheart a steady stare. "And neither will you."

"Of course not, Scholar. That's a matter between yourself, Balyndis and Balyndar." His throat still felt dry in spite of what he had drunk. He was aware what this signified and did not care for it at all. *Shall I ever manage to resist this thirst?* He was stubborn enough to be able to, surely. "Do you know who you would suggest as the next high king?"

"No. I shall keep out of things. I want to retire to somewhere in Girdlegard where I won't have to deal with any of our tribes. That's what I'm working toward." Tungdil's hard face lost its hostility. "If anyone wants to come visiting, that's fine. But I won't live with dwarves anymore."

"Have you grown to hate your own folk while you were in exile?"

"No, it's the other way around." He played with his fingers. "Some of them cheer when they see me, but the others no longer understand me. The changes wrought by two hundred and fifty cycles of war, evil and violence cannot be undone. I'd rather live at peace and be lonely than live in the midst of crowds and have people hate me. That way I can make sure that only the ones who trust me will come to visit." His single brown eye glinted warmly. "I'd be glad, Ireheart, if you would be one of that number."

The warrior was touched. "Have I ever deserted you, Scholar?" His speech was beginning to slur. The thirst he had on him was burning through his whole body; he would not have been surprised to see little black clouds coming out of his mouth. He stood up. "I want to stretch my legs and go for a dwarf-water break. I'll go and see what Troublemaker and Growler have to say for themselves." He moved away quickly, leaving the campfire, off past the humans and into the half-light.

Panting, he ran to the small wood. "Troublemaker?"

Ireheart listened out, choking, as his gullet stung and bubbled. His throat was burning ever hotter and there was a whistling sound when he breathed in. He felt as dizzy as if he had just drunk the last of ten tankards of black beer.

"Troublemaker!" he coughed, sinking down on his knees, gasping, and wondering if he would feel better if he swallowed a knife to make his throat wider.

Out of the corner of his eye he saw a black hand proffering a drinking flask.

Greedily Ireheart snatched the flask and took one or two sips before it was wrenched back out of his fingers; the burning sensation ceased abruptly and his breathing normalized.

He turned his head and saw the Zhadár circling round and squatting in front of him. "Thank you."

Balodil threw the drinking pouch back over. "Take it. It belonged to the Zhadár we lost in the desert. There's hardly any left, but it should be enough for you. If I die you'll have my flask, too."

"But . . . it's no good," said Ireheart in despair, with the taste of blood still in his mouth. "I'm turning into a half-Zhadár!"

Balodil sat down and leaned against a tree trunk. "There's a way for you to escape that fate and save your soul. I told you before." He gave a stupid little chuckle, sang the beginning strain of a dwarf-song and sneezed. "Barskalín was utterly convinced that one of the elves we spared would be able to free us from the curse. Because our intentions had been good."

"And how would the pointy-ears manage that?"

"I don't know. It's up to you. But the elf will be able to break the spell that's on you, because you never wanted to become one of us," the Zhadár breathed, rocking his upper body in time to some melody that only he could hear. "First find your elf and ask him what to do," he hummed in a singsong tone. "You won't have much more time before you change permanently."

"I haven't changed!" Ireheart said sullenly.

"Oh, yes, you have. I can smell that you have." Balodil laughed. "I don't know how the elf will do it but he will have heard your name and will know you are considered one of the good ones who took the side of the elves in the old days, so I don't expect the pointy-ears will let you die."

"Did I just hear the word *die*?"

Balodil made a face as if he were thinking hard to recall what word he had just said, then he whistled like a bird. "Yes, die. If you run out of this stuff for slaking your thirst, you will die." Clucking quietly like a hen he got up and marched off back to the camp.

"That'll be better than going mad like you," muttered Ireheart, forcing himself upright. He stowed the nearly empty flask under his chain-mail shirt. "So I have to place my hopes on some pointy-ears taking pity on me. And first of all I've got to find him. But how?" he grumbled, as he followed Balodil.

In his mind's eye he saw an elf-trap composed of a cage with a plate of salad as bait. Ireheart couldn't stop himself grinning.

Girdlegard,
Former Kingdom of Gauragar,

Near Dsôn Balsur,
Late Spring, 6492nd Solar Cycle

Wherever the group galloped past on their horses the freedom-fighters had been there before them.

In some places they saw castles burning or estates in ruins, elsewhere they saw bodies dangling at crossroads or bordering their route. The corpses had been stripped and presumably tortured before being hanged; some bore signs listing their crimes.

"The courts of the simple folk work quickly here in Gauragar," was Rodario's comment.

"I can't blame them," said Mallenia.

"It won't just be here this is happening," Coïra assumed. "This prairie fire of public anger will be burning in Idoslane and in my own realm."

Tungdil did not waste a single glance at the cadavers. He probably did not even find it particularly shocking. "A prairie fire purifies, but it must not be allowed to get out of control or there'll be utter chaos. The rule of law must be quickly re-established."

"We're almost there," shouted Ireheart, laughing. "Catch Lot-Ionan, fill in the Black Abyss and we're finished. You'll see. In sixty orbits it'll all be done and dusted. If not sooner." Slîn and Balyndar grinned and the humans all laughed. The Zhadár were as quiet as ever.

With frequent changes of mount when the horses tired they raced onward, even if the dwarves did not look especially elegant bouncing up and down. The horses were certainly faster than the ponies they normally used. But all of them, except Tungdil, vowed never to sit on a horse ever again once their mission was over.

They could tell from the environment that they were now in Dsôn Balsur, the oldest part of the älfar territory. It was from here that the älfar had spread their influence to the south.

They passed hideous sculptures made of bone, dead plants and other objects that were oddly fascinating but morbid in the extreme, repelling dwarves and humans alike. It was, however, impossible to deny that the älfar were perfectionists.

Of course it was Tungdil who saw the cloud of smoke first. "Dsôn is on fire," he announced, pointing to the north.

Now the others could see it, too.

"I thought it was a thunder cloud," said Rodario.

"Lot-Ionan is already at work destroying the city." Ireheart looked at the distant crater in which the city lay. "How many black-eyes has he bumped off so far, I wonder?"

"Let's hope he's wiped them all out." Rodario felt the fear rising in him. Nobody knew exactly how they were going to confront the magus. There was no set plan, just a vague idea: Tungdil and Balyndar would distract his attention and Coïra was then going to overwhelm him somehow. The rest of the group would hold itself in readiness to move in where needed. The rest: That was him and Mallenia. The Zhadár were under Tungdil's command and presumably they would be willing to attack the magus directly. They were not afraid of death.

"What do you think we will be allowed to do?" Rodario asked the Ido girl, who rode at his side as deep in thought as he was himself.

"That depends whether Vraccas and Samusin are with us," she replied. The wind was whipping her hair around her face, although she had gathered it in with a ribbon. "Our leader has condemned us to inaction, though I'm finding it hard to agree with him on this: You and me, Rodario, are as useless in a struggle against a magus of Lot-Ionan's stature as a two-handed sword to fight a fly."

The actor made a face. "It doesn't look as if Aiphatòn has defeated the magus."

Mallenia looked at the edge of the crater about a mile and a half away. Nobody was stopping them and there were no älfar in sight. "No, seemingly not. Maybe he's been killed in battle."

Tungdil pointed. "We ride to the edge and see what's up in Dsôn," he called out to the rest of the group.

They cantered over, halting their horses at the edge of the canyon.

Ireheart thought he had seen this all before. In Dsôn Bhará.

But the construction of Dsôn was different from the more northern älfar city. The ivory tower that had once risen on that hill had been replaced by a tower of somber basalt. The building glittered from inlaid strips of gold, silver and other precious metals, like veins of ore in a rock face soaking evil up out of the shady ground to supply the building.

And it was the only building still standing.

"By Vraccas! Someone's been busy!" Ireheart looked down on the burning houses, blazing away with bright yellow fire. The flames encompassed the whole of the crater.

He drew a telescope out of his luggage to inspect the inferno. "It will be impossible to enter," he said, bringing home to the others what a terrible state the city was in. "The flames are leaping up several paces high and the ground is covered in molten bubbling metal. It will be many orbits before we can go there without ending up like roast chicken."

The wind turned and drove the clouds of smoke toward them—but before they lost sight of everything Ireheart made out a figure on the plateau by the tower: A figure in a black and white robe, holding an onyx-headed staff in his left hand. "Lot-Ionan!" he exclaimed, pointing excitedly.

He saw the magus send out a black lightning ray from his jewel, felling an älf who had come storming out of the tower at him. The magic beam caught him in the throat, which exploded, sending the head shooting off two paces into the air before it tumbled to the ground to roll down the dark steps. The torso fell, convulsing.

"Did you see that, Scholar?" asked Ireheart. He was feeling distinctly uneasy.

"What's that?" asked Rodario in alarm.

"Lot-Ionan just blasted an älf's head off with magic," Tungdil said simply.

Ireheart looked back at the sea of flames. "*He* might be able to fly to escape the fire, but how are we going to catch him?"

Tungdil looked at Coïra, who nodded back at him. "Balyndar comes with us. You all wait here," he ordered. "Magic created the fire. Magic can put it out." He steered his horse down the steep path and the fifthling and the maga followed at once. Everybody knew there was no other choice.

Through driving clouds of smoke they watched the three make their way down the hairpin bends to reach the valley floor to the tower.

"I don't like this," murmured Slîn.

"Nor do I," said Rodario, worried about the girl. "Has anyone got a suggestion what we do to while away the time?"

Mallenia grinned, opened her mouth to make a proposal, but started coughing. Blood seeped over her lips and she tipped forward out of the saddle, crashing to the ground. The black shaft of an älf arrow stuck out of her back!

"Get down!" yelled Ireheart, dropping to the floor. Out of the corner of his eye, he saw Rodario's horse struck on the haunches with an arrow. The animal whinnied with the shock and made a leap into the air and over the edge of the canyon. With the actor on its back!

Strangely enough, it occurred to Ireheart at that moment that the archer must have a twisted sense of humor. Almost like a dwarf.

Balyndar tied his neckerchief around his mouth and nose as protection against the smoke. It had already served him well in the desert when there was sand to contend with. His horse was rearing up, so he reined it in and stopped before it could throw him off. "Wait! The horse is spooked by the fire," he called.

"Let's leave the horses here." Coïra dismounted and Tungdil followed suit.

"We have to get over to the tower. The last inhabitants of Dsôn will have taken refuge there to escape the magus." The one-eyed dwarf put his hands on his hips and stared into the wind at the dancing flames. "What do you reckon, maga?"

Coïra shut her eyes and murmured a simple spell to investigate the quality of the flames that were raging in front of them as high as a house. "I don't want to waste energy now—I'll need it for Lot-Ionan," she explained. "So we can't fly." She felt the fire was being fed by magic and thus could not be extinguished by an elementary spell.

Balyndar regarded his ax carefully. "Wouldn't Keenfire protect me from magic?"

"But not from molten metal; it will burn your feet," replied Tungdil darkly.

Coïra had noted the large loose round pebbles that lay scattered around. She smiled. "I've got an idea," she said, and wove a simple hovering spell.

The stones lifted themselves up and formed a raised causeway that led safely over the inferno.

Balyndar did not hesitate. He walked along the gangway she had created, the head of his ax shimmering and forming a protective sphere around him that was large enough to encompass Coïra and Tungdil. The maga had to tilt her head and walk along hunched over in an uncomfortable posture, but at least the flames could not harm her.

Coïra secured their progress by repeatedly magicking the stones behind them to whizz round to form a roadway in front. The heat made things difficult for her, but Tungdil displayed no discomfort. Balyndar occasionally had to wipe sweat off his brow but, as a dwarf, he was used to the temperatures in a forge.

They made their way along the broad causeway toward the mountain. They had no time to consider the dying beauty of the place. Not that there was much left of Dsôn's charms; all the wooden buildings had gone.

Tungdil, Coïra and Balyndar reached the steps leading up to the basalt tower. They knew it would be an extremely strenuous ascent but the only way was to take it one step at a time.

They climbed, with the dwarves having to make an extra effort because the steps had been designed for the legs of älfar, not those of the children of the Smith. As they climbed they looked around them to check no one was following.

The crater edge where Ireheart and the others were waiting was veiled in smoke and even the top of the tower was enveloped in acrid clouds. They would not be visible to their friends.

Gasping for air and with protesting leg muscles they finally reached the platform where they had seen Lot-Ionan. The headless älf corpse lay where it had fallen, surrounded by a pool of black blood.

"I wonder if they use their own blood in their paintings," Balyndar said scornfully.

"There won't be any of them left to try," Tungdil replied, hurrying off to the gate that led to the interior of the tower. They stepped through one after another, with the one-eyed dwarf and the fifthling in front, followed by the maga.

It was cool and quiet inside. Coïra closed and bolted the door behind them. The rattle of the bolts sliding home echoed throughout the building. The sound of the fire, the flash of sparks, and the crash of falling timbers and walls—all this was outside. Given the silence, it felt as if the tower had been built on some distant lonely mountain peak. Peaceful and welcoming.

Coïra could smell the stone and an overlay of incense and strong spice.

"To the staircase," Tungdil held Bloodthirster steady in his firm hands and stomped up the spiral stairway.

It was Balyndar and not Coïra who asked to take a break after they had gone up countless twisting steps. "I can't feel my feet anymore," he explained quietly. "I don't know how you manage with your heavy armor, Goldhand, but I can't go any further."

"You *can't*?" Tungdil came down toward him, grabbing him by the collar. "This is not some petty quarrel between the älfar and a wizard. This is about the fate of Girdlegard. And the future of the dwarves!" He dragged him upright and gave him a shove with the hilt of Bloodthirster. "Get in front! If you slow down, I'll stab you."

Coïra did not know how to take this threat. But it was enough to stop Balyndar complaining any further. Her own physical exhaustion distressed her but her brain was on high alert. She was expecting an älf to appear at any second. Or Lot-Ionan himself.

Small blue glowing crystals set into the walls gave some illumination. The tower had no windows.

After climbing a hundred steps they arrived in an anteroom in which they found four dead älfar. Their ribcages had been torn open. Their shredded leather armor had offered no protection against the magic attack.

"We're getting closer," Balyndar whispered excitedly, taking a firmer hold on Keenfire.

Tungdil marched through the hall and strode over to the far side of the tower.

They had located the throne room that the Dsôn Aklán had wanted for themselves, rather than surrendering it to Aiphatòn. The room was dark, ten paces high, with filigree metal columns supporting the ceiling, although these seemed too thin and fragile to be able to bear the weight of all the upper floors.

Between the pillars ropes were tied from which floor-length

banners were suspended, guiding the visitor's gaze to the great throne that stood on a raised platform. Seven steps led up to the throne itself, which was constructed out of tionium and palandium, thus combining the two elements that represented good and evil.

Seven more dead älfar lay on the floor, displaying scorch marks and burns on their bodies; their weapons had melted or burst under the influence of some mighty power.

Balyndar was about to ask a question but there came a sudden crackle and through the swathes of material they perceived a dazzling flash. A loud scream rang out, followed by a second voice laughing. Then a clank sounded as a weapon of some kind hit the floor.

Tungdil ground his teeth. "You know what that means," he whispered to the maga and fifthling. "We need to distract his attention. Coïra, you wrestle him to the ground when he's whipped himself into a frenzy against us." His one brown eye fixed its gaze on her. "Do not kill him!" he emphasized. "Forget revenge. He's our last chance, the only means we have to save the realm from a fate worse than anything ten dragons could come up with." He gave Balyndar the sign to proceed.

The maga waited until they disappeared behind the first hanging lengths of material, then she followed. Her arms were half raised, so her fingers would be ready to draw the necessary shapes in the air. Her heart was beating faster than normal and sweat coursed down her spine. She was frightened. The sheltered life of a princess had been no preparation for these tasks.

She had, of course, always wanted to be given an opportunity to use her magic skills to destroy Lohasbrand, to turn his orc army to dust and to rain down punishments on his vassals. But to meet a magus in battle was another kettle of fish entirely: A completely new challenge.

Coïra had never had the chance to compete against another magician. Her mother, due to her imprisonment, had been unable to teach her any of the required skills, so she had gathered much of her knowledge from Wey's historical archive, and whenever she had needed to ask something she had been forced to couch her queries in generalized terms so as not to arouse the suspicions of the soldiers guarding her mother.

All this and memories of the dangerous journey they had endured, taxing her beyond endurance much of the time—all this flew through her mind, making it hard for her to prepare confidently for what would be a baptism of fire.

Then she heard Balyndar call, followed by a hiss and an explosion heralded by a lilac flash. The shock waves blew the banners aside, allowing her to see that the dwarves had confronted the magus!

Balyndar was again protected by his sphere, while the magus sustained a magic ray attacking the shield; lightning flashes issued from his onyx-headed walking staff, shooting toward Tungdil, whose armor runes were fully ablaze. Then the wind created by the force of the explosion dropped, and the flags and banners fell back into place, concealing events from her once more.

Coïra was afraid. To create a double spell and to keep both going simultaneously, surely that was not possible! Lot-Ionan's powers must be enormous.

She pulled herself together. "I can't abandon them," the young woman told herself, and she ran off to join the dwarves.

So far Lot-Ionan had no idea there was a maga present who might represent a danger. This was presumably a considerable advantage. "Be with me, Mother," she prayed as she drew the first of the hanging fabric screens aside.

She did not see the älf standing diagonally behind the curtain until it was too late; she had been concentrating on the magus.

It was Sisaroth! He was bleeding from wounds on his neck, shoulder, and left arm; the right leg appeared only as a piece of burned and blackened meat surrounded by scraps of armor.

But he did not hesitate.

He immediately stabbed at her with his two-handed sword, piercing her abdomen.

The pain made the spell on her lips fade away. As she attempted it a second time, Sisaroth twisted his sword round and wrenched it upwards through her. The blade left an appalling wound in her fragile body: Blood and other fluids gushed and her intestines tumbled out. The maga fell, feeling him withdraw his sword.

"What a surprise! An unhoped for pleasure," said the älf with satisfaction. "My heart rejoices to be able to avenge my sister's death!" He knelt down and drew out his double-edged dagger. "Your death bears the name of Sisaroth," he whispered into her right ear as he placed the knife at her throat. "Your soul is lost forever, sorceress." With obvious enjoyment he pressed the weapon slowly through her skin into the flesh, relishing the fear in her widening eyes as she whimpered and moaned. "I would love to stay to see your spirit leave," he whispered as tenderly as a lover as he pulled the dagger carefully out of her throat. Then he got up and limped off, past the dying woman, over to the doorway.

Coïra lay on the basalt flagstones gasping for breath, wondering why she felt so little pain. She tried a healing incantation. But her injured lung did not permit her to pronounce a single word.

Ireheart threw himself down onto the mud and looked at Mallenia, who was staring at him with shocked eyes, trying to sit up and pull the arrow from her back. He could see she was extremely confused.

"No, stay down!" he called.

But she did not listen to him. She sat up and turned her head to find the arrow sticking out of her. Her fingers were about to clasp it and break off the shaft when a second arrow came whirring through the air, striking her in the throat. She tipped to one side, gurgling. Another crash and a Zhadár screamed.

"Slîn!" Ireheart yelled, incensed. *We haven't come this far and survived all those dangers only to have some stupid cowardly älf pick us off.* "Shoot the wretched black-eyes, confound you!"

"I can't see him," came a voice at his side. "He's hidden in the grass."

"Curses! I shit on Tion and all his creatures!" Ireheart bellowed, feeling his battle-fury take over. But, of course, the unwisest of options when attacked by a hidden bowman was to get up and start running toward him.

With a metallic clink an arrow hit his helmet, knocking it off. Ireheart thought the arrow tip had grazed his skin.

"Slîn!"

"I can't see where he is!! I can't see him, damn it!" the fourthling called back in desperation.

Ireheart looked over his shoulder to the edge of the crater. He had been hoping Rodario might somehow have managed to appear, but there was no sign. The actor must have fallen to his death on the back of that terrified plunging horse. *Bloody stupid kind of death* . . . His fury grew more heated yet. "Hey, black-eyes! A challenge! How about a duel? You and me?"

"Patience," came an älf voice. "First I want to eliminate your backup."

There were two more arrow strikes, this time hitting Slîn and the remaining Zhadár.

"That should do it," Ireheart heard the älf say. The dwarf saw the älf standing thirty paces away in waist-high grass. It was a relaxed Tirîgon, holding his two-hander propped against his shoulder. "Ready?"

"And how!" snarled Ireheart, getting to his feet. He tossed his black hair braid back and raised his crow's beak, realizing he was the only one of the party who had not been shot. He rushed over to the älf.

Tirîgon did not move, which seemed provocative in the extreme. "I had hoped the kordrion would eat you and the emperor. It seems I must do everything myself. I shall have death take you."

"You won't." Ireheart allowed rage to take possession of him. The world was drenched in a red mist, his head felt hot and his muscles were sheer bursting with the need to plunge the crow's beak spike into the opponent's face.

Yet he held back.

He had to use his brain and make sure the älf could not

take advantage of his longer reach and the two-handed sword. Strength was good, fury was better, but not until the opponent's two strong points had been counterbalanced. He was going to try to achieve that by causing him serious damage.

Ireheart had got ten paces closer and increased his pace. "Now I'll thrash that grin off your face with my weapon!"

Tirîgon was still smiling and unperturbed, his long sword resting against his shoulder. "Tell me, you short-legged piece of scum: What makes you think it was me that shot those arrows?"

No quiver, no arrows, no bow. Too late Ireheart realized his mistake.

XXIX

Girdlegard,
Älfar Realm of Dsôn Balsur,
Dsôn,
Late Spring, 6492nd Solar Cycle

Through the sphere Balyndar caught sight of Lot-Ionan. The magus was exactly as they had so recently seen him portrayed. The sturdy dwarf needed all his strength to keep hold of Keenfire and brace it against the pressure stemming from the magic attack. Tungdil's armor, as far as Balyndar could see, was doing its job well in protecting its bearer from lightning bolts delivered by the magus.

"Coïra!" Balyndar shouted in warning to the young woman; conscious, however, this would rob them of the element of surprise. He did not know how long he and Keenfire would be able to maintain their defense.

But there was no sign of their maga.

The assault ended and the magic barrier around him died away. "Vraccas!" he called, to give himself courage as he charged toward Lot-Ionan, blade upraised.

The magus stared at the ax, then looked at Tungdil and executed a swift movement. Above the dwarf's head the ropes anchoring the lengths of fabric gave way and the banners unfurled about Tungdil's ears. Balyndar understood: Lot-Ionan wanted to confront his attackers one by one.

An extra burst of speed took him nearly up to the magus. As Lot-Ionan brandished the onyx-headed staff at him an orange-colored beam shot out, striking the stone panels around him and tearing them out of their fixtures. The magus, having understood that his adversaries were immune to direct magic attack, forced the young dwarf ten paces into the air directly in the path of the falling stone.

And Balyndar was falling now.

He struck out with Keenfire and hit one of the horizontal flag supports. The ax head hooked itself over and he swung to and fro on the banner as if on a rope. Serious injury or death would result from a fall from this height.

Balyndar looked down at Coïra and froze in horror. The wound he saw in her body had to be fatal, surely, but how had it occurred? Too late he remembered that Lot-Ionan had been fighting an älf when they arrived. The älf must have used the chance to escape and have attacked the maga.

However distraught he was about Coïra, he had to act.

Gathering the material in his hands, he locked both arms around it and used the flag to slide safely down to ground level.

On the way down he witnessed Tungdil and Lot-Ionan talking together! He could not hear what they were saying because he was too far away, but they were standing face to face, neither attacking the other. *What did it mean?*

Tungdil leaped forward and swept Bloodthirster at the magus, who laughed as he made a gesture that had the dwarf suddenly enveloped by one of the flags; then he reached out at full stretch to land a blow on Tungdil with his staff.

Hardly had the onyx stone touched the embroidered material than the fabric turned into a gigantic snake wrapping its coils around Tungdil's body. Muscles worked feverishly

and the armor creaked in protest but the dwarf was unable
to move.

Balyndar was on the ground by this time and rushed over
toward Lot-Ionan, Keenfire at the ready. The diamonds and
inlay pattern shone with inner fire and the heat it gave out
was like being in a forge.

Bald-headed Lot-Ionan saw him coming and turned to
face him. "So what are the children of the Smith doing,
coming to the aid of the älfar?" The ends of his beard waggled
and the sharp-featured face was an uncanny picture of malice.

"We're not here on their behalf." Balyndar leaped at the
magus, swinging Keenfire in a powerful stroke; Lot-Ionan
did not have to know that he only intended to hit him with
the flat side of the weapon.

The magus sidestepped with surprising agility, raising his
own staff to strike Balyndar.

Keenfire and onyx clashed in mid-air.

The explosion that ensued stunned and dazzled Balyndar.
He could hear a rattling sound as if pebbles were being
dropped. Blinded, he stumbled forward under the impetus
of his own attack and staggered into a pillar, which broke
his fall.

He ducked and whirled round, holding Keenfire in front
of himself as protection. Gradually his sight returned.

Tungdil was still locked in the clutches of the enormous
snake.

Lot-Ionan waved the remains of his broken staff accusingly
in Balyndar's direction. The top end had snapped off and
the onyx jewel lay in fragments around the throne.

"By Samusin!" gasped the magus, flinging the broken
pieces at him. "By Samusin!" he shrieked in fury, lifting his

arms. "If only you were a mere stain on the ground as I intended!" Invisible powers must still have been issuing from the magus, for the flagstones, the pillars and everything near Balyndar started to shake and move toward him. "I shall squash you like squeezing a lemon, dwarf! Your bones will be ground to powder and be banished to eternal oblivion with the rest of the tower."

With a loud roar Tungdil tore the snake in two with his bare hands, not needing Bloodthirster. He kicked the weapon up with his foot, catching it adroitly to go in for the attack.

The quaking walls round Balyndar ceased their movement. The young dwarf breathed a sigh of relief and threw himself on the magus. "For Girdlegard!"

But to his surprise Tungdil ran past the wizard, heading instead straight for *him*!

Ireheart did not hesitate.

Grim and stubborn, he ran full tilt at the älf, not wasting a thought on the fact that a black arrow could strike at any second.

"Parry this if you can!" he bawled, slamming his crow's beak down murderously, the spike targeting the älf's left flank.

Tirîgon acted swiftly. He brought down his two-handed sword, plunging the tip into the earth, thus blocking the first attack; then, supporting himself on his parrying stick, he dealt a two-footed kick into Ireheart's face.

The dwarf staggered back, spitting blood. His nose was broken and already swelling up. He could see the white of the exposed bone. Two of his teeth were loose. "You've made me bite my tongue," he raged at the älf.

"It won't be your last injury." Tirîgon leaned on the parrying stick, staring at the flames engulfing the city. "That destruction is hardly all down to you."

"I wish it was." Ireheart came up to his adversary and feigned a strike at his head, but altered direction, aiming the flat edge of the crow's beak at the älf's right thigh.

Tirîgon took an evasive sidestep and placed a hand on his sword, pulling it to one side. Once more the dwarf-weapon clashed on steel. And again the älf launched a mighty kick, striking Ireheart in the neck.

With a curse Ireheart charged forward, landing on his knees in the dust. "This is not a proper fight!" he yelled angrily. "Come on, fight like a decent warrior!"

"But I'm not fighting against a decent warrior, so why should I?" the älf returned scornfully, leaning on his tall sword. "I always thought the famous Ireheart was an excellent fighter, but I'm disappointed to find him as lame as an orc." He put his head on one side and winked. "I'll grant you one wish: How would you like to die?"

Ireheart whirled the crow's beak. "Drinking a beer, black-eyes!" He pushed forward. "As you don't have any beer with you, I'm safe." This time he struck diagonally.

Tirîgon ducked and used the two-hander again to block the blow.

But in his arrogance he had underestimated the dwarf's furious strength. The blow thrust the älf back onto the ground and, although the weapon itself did not strike him, the sharp end of his own parrying stick was forced right into his shoulder.

I've got you! Ireheart followed through swiftly, striking at Tirîgon and missing his head by the breadth of a beard hair.

The älf executed a backwards somersault, intending to grab his two-hander, but the dwarf stamped on the sword, grinning.

Tirîgon grinned arrogantly back and drew out both his double-daggers at the speed of light; the stabs ensued in a flowing movement.

Ireheart saw the two arms with their four blades heading for him. He had to decide which to parry. He blocked one with his weapon haft and the blades swished past his face. But the second knife hit him.

The double blade did not penetrate the chain-mail shirt, but the blow winded him badly.

The next assault followed fast and Ireheart tried to back away from Tirîgon.

The älf did not let up, but kept attacking with the daggers. Still with a smile on his finely chiseled features, he appeared not to have exerted himself at all.

Ireheart's hands were cut, as was his face and every part of his body that was not covered in chain mail.

"You see, I'm out to cut you, not to kill you," the älf explained with a laugh. "Are you getting tired, dwarf? If you collapse and breathe your last before my very eyes I shall watch carefully and store up the moment in my memory. I can use it in a picture? Or a drawing?"

"You're only slashing at me because you are not fast enough to catch me properly, black-eyes!" Ireheart had detected a pattern to the attacks. *I know what you are going to do next.* "And anyway," he taunted, dodging the dagger thrust and plunging the spike of his crow's beak directly into the älf's belly. "You won't be doing any more painting." He tossed the paralyzed Tirîgon onto his back and tore the weapon downwards in his flesh to widen the entry wound. "Except in the dirt here, clawing with your fingers!" He levered the weapon out of the body cavity, tearing the guts. He studied the bloodied tip with satisfaction. "You guys really aren't anything special. You're just big, that's all." Ireheart kicked him viciously in the face, heard the bones crack, then spat at him. "That's for breaking my nose." Then he turned round.

He stared at Slîn in horror. He was sitting up and aiming his crossbow at him. He had only pretended to be wounded! "What . . .!"

"I should have done this a long time ago," snarled the fourthling. And fired.

Keenfire and Bloodthirster clashed, sparks flying in all directions, fizzling against the dwarves and on the floor.

Tungdil's weapon could not deny its origins as the sword of an Unslayable. Any other blade would have shattered under the impact of Keenfire, but Bloodthirster stood up to the onslaught defiantly.

The diamonds on the ax head increased their brilliance, infuriated not to be able to destroy Bloodthirster.

Balyndar felt that Tungdil surpassed him in physical strength several times over. He was being forced backwards against a pillar. "You traitor!" he screamed at the one-eyed dwarf, attempting to knee him in the groin. "I always suspected you were closer to your foster-father than you were to your own folk!"

Tungdil kicked his knee away and head-butted him, sending his skull crashing back into the pillar.

Balyndar saw nothing but stars; the pressure on Keenfire

lessened. Tungdil had moved away. Now his sight was clearing.

The one-eyed dwarf stood in front of Lot-Ionan as if wanting to protect him. "Calm down," he said. "He has agreed to help us."

The fifthling shook his head to clear it. "*Help?*" He looked from Tungdil to the wizard and back again incredulously. "Lot-Ionan, who has oppressed the south of Girdlegard for many cycles, and whose apprentices have wiped out the population in great swathes of the land, is going to *help* us? And of his own *free will*?"

"He knows he can't defeat both of us." Tungdil lowered Bloodthirster. "To save himself pain and humiliation he is prepared to accept my offer."

Balyndar gulped. "You sound like his spokesman, not his enemy." It was hard to believe what he was hearing. Behind Lot-Ionan he suddenly made out a vague slim shape moving. "No, don't!" he shouted.

Tungdil and the magus both turned.

Coïra stood behind them, her arms half raised as she prepared a spell. Over her breast her clothing hung in blood-soaked tatters and the naked skin revealed below the garments was lighter in some places than in others.

Even if nothing remained of the terrible wound, Balyndar could see by looking at Coïra's widened eyes that she had not recovered from the shock. She seemed determined Lot-Ionan should pay for the injury inflicted on her. Could she have forgotten that their mission needed him alive?

Do we really need him? The thought came flying into his mind from somewhere and it started to take root. He looked at his magic ax which had served so well against magi and monsters of all kinds. *Why would it not work against Tungdil Goldhand's master?*

Tungdil looked at the young woman. "Maga, stop whatever it is you are doing! No force is needed. He will come with us to the Black Abyss."

Coïra's lips were moving. Her palms glowed red and a beam three fingers wide was released, hissing, toward Lot-Ionan, who held out an arm, the hand turned upwards, pointing at the ceiling. The beam collided with the palm of his hand and dissipated, with smaller rays diverted in all directions. And so the duel ended.

And that was how she was planning to vanquish him? Given this pitiful performance on the part of the maga Balyndar was glad that they had settled the matter without her help.

Tungdil changed position and came to stand between Coïra and Lot-Ionan.

Balyndar went up to her. "Can you hear me, Majesty?" he asked gently, holding Keenfire so that he could use it to defend himself against a spell.

The young woman lowered her head until she could look him directly in the eyes. "I nearly died," she declared blankly, and he could see fresh blood on her lips. "I nearly died, but . . ." She looked down at herself. "I am not decent. The älf tore off my clothes and . . ." Coïra sobbed. "I have failed against Lot-Ionan, because I used up my magic to heal myself." She buried her face in her hands, weeping hysterically. Her words were for the most part unintelligible but the name Sisaroth occurred again and again.

Balyndar looked helplessly at Tungdil. "What's wrong with her?"

"What would be wrong with her, do you think? Death had her in its hands and she was in pain great enough to unman any stout warrior and make him lose his senses." The one-eyed dwarf put Bloodthirster away. "It may be a long time before her mind recovers."

"Or maybe it never will." Balyndar watched her sadly. Taking her in his arms to offer consolation would not be right for him. And not only because of the difference in their heights.

"All the more vital that we have Lot-Ionan." Tungdil bent down to pick up one of the splinters from the onyx jewel. "You broke his staff. That weakens him, he tells me, but he is still capable of creating powerful spells."

Balyndar studied the magus. The man was not looking at him and his eyes were wandering past him as if he were some trivial object. "Can't he speak for himself?"

"Not with you or any other. He does not consider you to be of equal status."

"But you are?" Balyndar's retort was louder than he had intended, and more scornful.

"I am his foster-son."

"If we want to know something we have to speak through you?" Balyndar could not grasp it. Tungdil had found yet another way to make all of them dependent on him, dwarves and Girdlegarders alike.

The one-eyed dwarf nodded. "Exactly. I don't like it either but that's the way he wants it."

"*He wants it!*" Balyndar laughed outright. "It's not up to him to *want* it! He is our prisoner!"

"He surrendered voluntarily. It's different."

"Then let's *make* him our prisoner." Balyndar swung

Keenfire. "I can knock him down. This weapon gives me the power and he won't be able to do anything to defend himself."

Tungdil was angry now. "You know that is not true. He could have you buried under the collapsing tower and Keenfire would have to let it happen."

"But . . ."

Tungdil took a step toward him. "Control yourself, Balyndar Steelfinger! You are an excellent warrior with a legendary weapon, but I am the high king! Do what I tell you or I will give you a lesson in respect. And by all that is infamous: I will do it!" He looked at the doorway. "We have not finished here. The älf Sisaroth has got away. He nearly robbed us of our maga." He marched off. Lot-Ionan followed him, not even glancing at Balyndar.

Balyndar went up to Coïra and touched her arm. "Forgive me, Majesty, but we must leave," he told her gently.

She wiped her face on her sleeve to dry her tears, then smiled bravely and followed the others. As she went, her eyes searched the dark corners of the hall in fear.

Balyndar noticed that she stayed very close to him. She was terribly afraid of the älf who had escaped.

In a state of high alert they left the throne room where, until recently, Aiphatòn had resided. That was all in the past. Like the kordrion. Like the Dragon Lohasbrand and his vassals. Balyndar thought Lot-Ionan's name would fit nicely in the list of dead monsters.

While the group made their way down the stairs, he placed his right hand on the sigurdacia wood handle. He would ensure the magus did not return alive to Girdlegard after the battle at the Black Abyss.

Balyndar could see Lot-Ionan's bald head in front of him.

There were such stories about him. The originally affable magus had turned into an evil despot whose cruel deeds and indifference to the suffering of others were well known. And he had practically annihilated the entire tribe of secondling dwarves.

This thought alone was enough to bring Balyndar's rage to boiling point, making him snort with fury. He did not believe now and would not in a hundred cycles ever believe that Lot-Ionan had joined forces with them without having evil in mind. *He and Tungdil have come up with a plot.* Perhaps they had decided to split Girdlegard between the two of them? What he would have given to have been able to overhear those negotiations.

Lost in thought he was suddenly made aware by Keenfire that an ambush threatened.

The inlay pattern flared up and Balyndar whirled round with a shout, the ax lifted ready to strike dead the älf who had crept up on him. "May Tion take you!"

But nobody was there.

A sharp pain burned its way down through his shoulder.

Balyndar dropped to the floor, thus freeing his body from the sword that had skewered him. He rolled onto his back, just in time to see the second thrust coming and to avert it with his own ax; the sword tip clattered onto the basalt floor tiles, leaving a furrow in the stone.

Sisaroth was suspended *above* him!

The älf had braced his feet against two of the ceiling arches on the stairway and had been lying in wait there like a falcon. Now he sprang down to land behind Balyndar, stabbing over the top of him at the maga's retreating back and injuring her afresh. Then he dragged his long sword downwards. Coïra stumbled and fell.

Quickly the dwarf moved to avoid the blade slicing into his flesh. But the parrying stick stabbed him painfully under the collarbone. With a growl he hefted Keenfire upwards, but Sisaroth dodged the blade and kicked Balyndar's hands, so that he almost lost his grip on his weapon. There was a crack. Some bone somewhere had fractured but as yet he felt nothing. The wound in his shoulder hurt too badly for him to be aware of any other pain. *In spite of his many injuries he is lethal and he is fast. Confounded creature!*

The älf took two swift steps and sprang up against the wall to run up along the ceiling to attack Lot-Ionan.

Tungdil and the magus had been alerted by the sound of fighting and the maga's scream as she collapsed on the stairs. But Coïra had fallen against Lot-Ionan, knocking him off balance. Fortunately this caused Sisaroth's attack to fail, otherwise the blade would have struck the magus on the head. Tungdil parried the first blow with a swift movement, then Sisaroth landed in front of him and thrust at him again.

Tungdil arrested the blow just above his head, kept his weapon raised and approached the älf. The raucous scrape of metal on metal as the blades met made Balyndar's hair stand on end.

Sisaroth dodged the charging dwarf, taking two steps to the right and then to the left, planning to run up to the ceiling again, but Tungdil speared his wounded leg with an upward stroke that took him by surprise. Blood flowed out of the gaping wound, where the bone was now exposed.

With a shout, Sisaroth fell on the basalt stairs and lost his sword. The dwarf expedited the weapon down the stairs with a hefty kick.

The älf was far from having given up. He hurled the first

of his double-daggers at the one-eyed dwarf—but the magic decorations on the armor blazed out and the weapon was stopped in mid-flight before it could touch the tionium. It fell harmlessly onto the stone floor.

Sisaroth had already drawn his second dagger but was hesitating. The sight of Tungdil's armor seemed to distract him or bring home to him perhaps that this was a foe he would not be able to defeat. But then he gave a sudden laugh and spoke an incantation in his own language.

The runes flared one after another and Tungdil, who had been about to attack the älf, froze like a statue and fell. He rolled down the stairs with a terrible clatter, keeping tight hold of Bloodthirster and making no attempt to save himself.

Sisaroth was still laughing and turned, knife in hand, to Lot-Ionan. "Who would have thought the tide would turn?"

The magus, bleeding from a wound on his brow from when he had hit the wall after colliding with Coïra, found himself hampered by the veil of blood.

Balyndar clenched his teeth and gathered himself for a mighty throw.

Keenfire started its arced flight and went straight at the älf.

Ireheart saw the bolt flying toward him and could not believe his eyes. There was no time to react—the shot was upon him . . .

. . . and missed his left eye socket by a finger's width. The dwarf heard it whirr and felt the wind of its passing. Then it thudded home behind him.

Ireheart knew what that meant. He ducked down, twirling round, his crow's beak held at head height. He saw the arm with the double-bladed knife swipe above his head and then his own metal spike thudded deep into Tirîgon's left side.

"It's time you knew when to give up and die, black-eyes!" he yelled at the älf, in whose heart the crossbow bolt was buried.

Without a sound Tirîgon fell to his knees and tipped on his side.

"I'm not taking any chances this time," growled Ireheart, hammering the älf's skull flat with the crow's beak. He dragged the corpse to the edge of the crater and tossed it over. "Have a good flight!" He watched as the body fell three miles down, bashing against the rocks on the way before crashing into the ground. No one could survive a fall such as that.

"At last!" He heard the relief in Rodario's voice. The actor was hanging from his badly bent sword, which had got stuck in a cleft in the rocks; he had rammed it into a crevice as he fell, thus saving himself.

"Ho! And what have you done with your horse?" Ireheart had to ask, grinning in spite of himself. "Why didn't you grab hold of it with those long legs of yours?"

"Ireheart! I need your help!" Slîn called. "Mallenia's badly hurt. We have to bandage her."

He looked down to where Rodario hung. "The sword will hold for a bit. I have to look to your darling girl," he shouted and rushed off to the fourthling, who was kneeling at the woman's side, assessing her injuries.

Ireheart could see that she was still breathing. The arrow in her neck might have cut through flesh and sinews but, to judge from the bleeding, it had not touched an artery. He was more worried about the arrow in her back.

"There's nothing we can do except try to keep her alive until

Coïra comes back to heal her magically," he told Slîn, helping him to apply bandaging. "Keep talking to keep her awake. I'll see what I can do for the actor before the steel snaps and he follows black-eyes down into the crater." He put his hand on the fourthling's shoulder. "Thank you. I am in your debt."

"No. You're not," said Slîn. "We are a group and everyone looks after everyone else." He hesitated. "At least we children of the Smith must always try to."

"You're right." Ireheart stood up and took the horses' reins, knotting them together to make a long rope. While he was doing so, Balodil came over. He had bandaged his own injured arm. Tossing a drinking flask to Ireheart, he said, "The owner won't be needing this anymore. But you will." Then he sat down and, in spite of his injury, helped Ireheart tie the reins together.

They walked over to the edge and lowered the leather rope down to Rodario, who was swinging to and fro in the breeze. "High time!" he greeted the dwarves. "I can't hold on much longer."

"If you had kept the horse between your knees it would have been harder still. Catch hold," called Ireheart. "We'll pull you up."

Balodil and Ireheart managed to liberate Rodario from his precarious situation; the actor was able also to save his bent sword, having yanked it out of the crevice.

"What will you use that for?" wondered Ireheart. "Attacking round corners?"

"I'll keep it. As a souvenir." Rodario went pale when he saw Mallenia on the ground. He ran over and cushioned her head on his knee. "We must do something . . ." he said in desperation.

"We can only wait," said Ireheart. "The injury is too grave, and none of us is a healer. We need the maga to come and close up the wounds."

Rodario swallowed hard and nodded.

The wind changed and the inferno in Dsôn died down. Ireheart looked across at the tower where his friend was, with Coïra and Balyndar, hoping to subdue Lot-Ionan. "Vraccas, let them succeed," he prayed, and looked at Balodil, who was kneeling next to the body of his dead comrade, muttering a prayer which, if he had heard aright, the Zhadár was also addressing to the god Vraccas.

Keenfire struck Sisaroth in the right shoulder, knocking him off his feet and onto his back. The älf hurtled down several steps until he came slithering to a halt.

Fighting for breath, Balyndar ran up to Sisaroth to finish him off. The älf was just struggling upright, Keenfire still embedded in his shoulder, dark blood streaming from the wound and down over his armor.

Balyndar opened his mouth in a yell and vaulted forward, gripping the hilt of Sisaroth's sword ready to use it and holding on to the parrying stick.

Sisaroth attempted to dodge but his own blade caught him in the groin. It pierced the armor with a grinding noise and he screamed out in agony.

Balyndar laughed and grabbed Keenfire by the haft. "That's the sound for me!" He snatched the ax back while Sisaroth tried a final stab at his throat, but the dwarf cut his head clean off his shoulders. A fountain of blood shot up all the way to the vaulted ceiling and the decapitated älf fell back down the stairs.

Still gasping for air, Balyndar had to sit down. He felt

dizzy and his limbs were like lead. He could hardly move. Keenfire weighed more than four full sacks of gold.

A shadow fell on him. It was Lot-Ionan, staring down at him, a malicious smile on his lips.

Balyndar thought there was no earthly chance of stopping the magus if he wanted to kill them all. He felt exhausted. Tungdil was nowhere to be seen and Coïra presented no danger to the man. "Don't even think of it," he threatened Lot-Ionan nevertheless.

The magus seemed to shake his fingers, and suddenly a blue flame shimmered over to Balyndar, creeping inside his mouth and nose.

A warmth overcame him; it felt like being granted shelter, love and joy. His body received new strength and his wounds tickled and fizzed. When these sensations ceased he saw that his skin where the injuries had been was now without blemish, as if he had never been touched by a sword.

Lot-Ionan passed him by without a further glance.

Meanwhile Coïra, groaning, struggled to sit up, holding her head. She saw the dead älf, then Balyndar, and followed the magus with her eyes until he had disappeared down the spiral staircase. "What happened?"

"A lot," the dwarf replied crisply, getting to his feet. He felt as if he had slept through half an orbit and was awakening refreshed. Lot-Ionan had kept to his side of the bargain and healed him. "And a small miracle, too. Come on, let's find Goldhand!"

Together they hurried down the tower steps.

Tungdil Goldhand lay in his rigid armor next to an exhausted Mallenia by the campfire a mile north of the crater.

Lot-Ionan had transported the paralyzed dwarf out of Dsôn and up onto the plateau by magic, while Coïra had ministered to the wounded of their party with her remaining powers. She was not able to restore the blood that Mallenia had lost and thus the freedom-fighter was as weak as a little child.

Rodario looked after her tenderly, but they knew Mallenia could not accompany them any longer. Speed was of the essence on their journey and she could not travel. They planned to leave her to be cared for at the nearest farmstead. She would follow on as soon as she was sufficiently recovered.

Ireheart pushed Tungdil's visor up and rubbed his beard thoughtfully. "So this time it was the älf?"

"Yes. He recited a formula." Tungdil tried to lift his arm. "Nothing."

Balodil stood on the far side and uttered some strange dark words. Not a single rune shone out. He shrugged his shoulders regretfully and stomped back to the fire.

Ireheart grinned and raised his crow's beak. "You know what that means?"

"Yes," replied his friend roughly. "And I don't like it."

"Wait!" called Coïra. "Do we know what kind of phrase was used?"

Ireheart explained concisely what had happened the previous time, leaving out any details that the maga did not need to know.

Her face became thoughtful. "But if the Zhadár could not help this time it won't have been the same phrase." She leaned over Tungdil and asked, "Can you give us any hint?"

Ireheart suspected Tungdil had not told him the whole truth when relating the origins and peculiarities of the suit of armor. *Perhaps on purpose*, buzzed the lonely doubter inside his head. *He didn't want you to know where he is vulnerable. And look where that has got him.*

"He'd be able to tell me now," he told the doubting voice. Unfortunately he said it out loud, causing Coïra to look surprised. "Nothing important. I was talking to myself," said Ireheart, motioning Coïra to step aside. "Right there! Mind out!" he bellowed for everyone's benefit. "There'll be lightning flashes, so shield your eyes or look the other way."

He positioned himself, legs wide apart, over Tungdil, lifted his weapon and slammed it down using the flat side like he had done before, in the Outer Lands.

There was a dull thud and Tungdil groaned. Despite its hardness the tionium showed a dent in the breastplate.

"What is wrong, for Vraccas's sake?" Ireheart swung the crow's beak up again and tensed the muscles in his upper body to put all his strength into the next blow. "You'll start next time I touch you!"

Another crash and the armor buckled and dented again. But no flash ensued and the armor lost none of its rigidity. Tungdil groaned and gasped.

"Charming! We're in trouble here," remarked Slîn superfluously.

"I can see that!" snarled Ireheart. "Does it hurt a lot, Scholar?" he asked kindly.

"Only when I laugh," coughed the dwarf. "Don't hit me again, Ireheart. Or if you do, aim somewhere else. Or I'll suffocate."

"I think . . . the älf has . . . turned off the magic. Except for the . . . safety cut-out." Ireheart ran his fingers over the dents in the metal. "All this hammering is no help at all."

"We must get a cart for him," Rodario suggested. "And that way, since we'll only be going slowly, we can take Mallenia along, too."

"No," protested Tungdil. "We'll find a way to force the armor to wake up. And we'll do it tonight."

"Well, charming," murmured Slîn. "Why doesn't Balyndar have a go with Keenfire?"

"Has the sense of all your ancestors completely deserted you? You might as well shoot him in the eye," said Ireheart. "It could kill him!"

"How so?" asked Balyndar. "He is not one of our enemies." He got to his feet at the campfire, chucked away the rabbit bones he'd been gnawing at, and picked up his ax. As always, the inlay pattern and diamonds glowed, giving off a faint sheen. "Let's see. Or has anybody got any objections?"

Slîn and Ireheart exchanged glances. Even Tungdil remained silent.

XXX

The Outer Lands,
The Black Abyss,
Early Summer, 6492nd Solar Cycle

As they rode up to the Evildam fortress they saw flags and banners wafting proudly in the wind. But the walls had suffered damage.

Ireheart turned to Tungdil, who, with Lot-Ionan's help, was now able to move again in his armor, "What can have been happening?"

He recalled how the magus, recently, had maliciously let them all spend the whole night puzzling over the frozen armor before getting up at dawn, executing two swift gestures and throwing a dark purple veil over the tionium. After that the armor had worked perfectly, even repairing the dents to its own bodywork, whereas previously it had failed to respond even to Keenfire. The magus gave no explanation for what he had done. Not even to his foster-son.

Afterwards everything had moved fast.

They had left Mallenia and Rodario back at a farmstead and headed off in a breathless gallop toward the Brown Mountains, crossing directly through to the Outer Lands. They stopped for nothing and were answerable to no one— Tungdil was high king and did not have to justify his actions. His word was law.

Ireheart glanced at the magus. *We're going to have trouble with him.*

Tungdil had also noted the cracks in the fortress walls. "As long as Evildam is still standing we have not lost," he said, relief in his voice. "The most important thing is that we aren't too late."

Trumpets heralded their approach. A detachment of ubariu and dwarves marched out to accompany the high king's troop as behoved their status, leading them to the tower, now newly equipped with additional supports, while the garrison cheered.

Ireheart saw many more children of the Smith on the battlements than expected. "Are my eyes deceiving me?" he asked Slîn, drawing his attention to the soldiers.

"No. There are some standards up there I don't recognize."

"Or perhaps these are banners you never wanted to see," Balyndar added. "Those are the thirdling clans."

"By Vraccas!" said Ireheart in astonishment. "So they've come to support us!" He turned to Tungdil. "Your own tribe has come to lend arms to the high king." He laughed in relief.

"It was a good trick, choosing the one-eyed dwarf as high king," Balyndar muttered.

"It wasn't a trick," protested Ireheart angrily. "It was . . ."

"There's Goda," Slîn interrupted. "Are you going to greet your wife, General, or shall I do it for you?"

Ireheart reined in his pony, jumped off and ran to his spouse, embracing her, even letting go of his crow's beak for once to do so. "I'm holding all the happiness of the world in my arms," he whispered in her ear, feeling his throat constrict. "I have missed you so, Goda!"

She hid her face in his shoulder and pressed him to her. "At last," she murmured. "I nearly died of worry and couldn't let the others see." She looked at Tungdil, still on his horse, and saw Lot-Ionan beside him. "You've done it!"

"It was easier than we'd thought," he told her, freeing himself from the embrace. "Let's talk about it inside. There is a great deal to tell."

"Here, too." She looked him straight in the eyes. "Sadly, none of it good, my husband."

Anxiously, Ireheart hurried to reach the conference hall. The dwarves, Coïra and Lot-Ionan followed and Goda gave the order to fetch their guests.

On all sides dwarves knelt in homage to Tungdil, proffering their weapons to him as a mark of respect and unconditional obedience. Ireheart could tell Goda did not appreciate this gesture. *Well, there's a surprise.*

The rejoicing in Evildam was unstinting. From the other three gates came bugle calls and the clatter of axes on shields. A storm of euphoria broke over them, with everyone involved in the celebration: Dwarves, humans, undergroundlings and ubariu alike.

Ireheart walked tall and proud as never before. Back straight, crow's beak shouldered, legs splayed, he waved at the crowds, a smile on his face. It was the same for Slîn and Balyndar. They relished being treated as heroes. And rightly so.

Only his wife's stony expression troubled the warrior's mood. But only slightly.

The double doors leading to the conference chamber were opened for them by the ubariu sentries.

Ireheart's jaw dropped: Dwarves were seated at the table! Dozens of dwarves, all of them clan leaders, and the flags that hung on the walls behind them denoted which delegates had come.

"By Vraccas!" he exclaimed, his heart racing with joy. "Scholar, do you see that?" He wanted to grab him by the shoulder and shake him wildly in his excitement, but he thought better of it.

"Stay near me, all of you," Tungdil told his friends quietly. "I want them to remember the faces of their greatest heroes forever." He walked in, slow and dignified.

A clanking and clattering sounded out as the dwarves knelt before their high king, holding up their swords in the age-old oath of allegiance. All the tribes were represented; even the thirdlings and freelings had come to pledge fealty and to follow Tungdil's command.

Nobody spoke. It was a weighty moment, the greatest event in the history of the children of the Smith.

The impressive sight brought tears to Ireheart's eyes. His Scholar had achieved what no high king before him had ever accomplished. He was not ashamed of the salty drops on his cheeks and he could see the same emotion on the faces of many gathered there.

"Long live High King Tungdil Goldhand!" he shouted, raising his crow's beak before falling on one knee. Affected by the spectacle, Slîn and Balyndar followed suit. Goda was the last to bow the knee to the one-eyed dwarf.

"You have responded to my call." Tungdil raised his deep voice, covering the audience with the essence of his royal authority. "For this I thank you. The definitive battle for Girdlegard will be fought in the Black Abyss, because the war that started two hundred and fifty cycles ago has not yet ended." He let his gaze wander over the assembled dwarves. "This is why I have returned: To help my people."

"That's a lie," hissed Goda, but only Ireheart heard her.

He flashed his eyes in warning and she bit her lip.

"You can see that I have changed, but in my heart I am still a child of the Smith. Without my friends," and he gestured toward the dwarves behind him, "my first task would never have succeeded. It is clearer than ever now that we will meet the second challenge triumphantly." He indicated to the assembly that all should rise. "I bear the title of high king because the fourthlings and fifthlings elected me. Many may see it as a fault that I was not chosen by all the tribes." Tungdil raised his arms. "I ask you, each and every one of you, every clan leader and every king, for this very reason, once more: Do you wish me to lead you?"

The thunder of agreement made the room rock, and Ireheart felt a jolt to his spine. *Such unity!*

Tungdil bowed to the dwarves. "I swear that I shall serve my folk and that you shall never regret your choice." Then he turned his brown eye to the thirdlings. "Step forward, king of the thirdlings, and announce what we have agreed."

To Ireheart's surprise Rognor Mortalblow stepped back and gave way to a familiar figure. "Hargorin Deathbringer!" he exclaimed. He had not expected that.

The sturdy dwarf placed both hands on his belt. "My name is feared as leader of the Black Squadron, but my deeds served but one goal: To allow my tribe to survive in the hope that an opportunity like today would arrive when we could sit with our brothers and our sisters round one table. And fight evil," he declared. "Rognor was my chancellor, carrying out my commands. He would have given his life for me if the älfar had attacked, aiming to kill the king of the thirdlings." He pointed to Balodil. "And it was by my orders that coura-geous warriors transformed themselves into Zhadár, to learn the secrets of the älfar and deploy their own tricks against them."

The first decent thirdling. Apart from the Scholar.

Ireheart listened agog, like all the others present in the chamber.

"We have made preparations. And we are sick," Hargorin went on, "we are sick of fighting our own brothers and sisters. Even though it would have been easy to eradicate the remaining tribes because we are superior in number, and because, thanks to the Invisibles, we knew the secrets of all of the strongholds, we would not have attacked you. It was enough to know we could have defeated you had we so wished." He took a deep breath. "I, Hargorin Deathbringer of the clan of Death Bringers, now declare the blood-feud ended between us and the other dwarves of Girdlegard, whether they belong to a tribe or designate themselves as free! No dwarf need go in fear of his or her life when entering the Black Mountains or on meeting one of us." He tapped his weapon. "This shall never taste dwarf blood. I swear by Vraccas! We are a united folk, all children of the Smith!"

Ireheart stood thunderstruck. He looked at Tungdil, then at Goda and finally at Hargorin. "Peace?" he mumbled. "The thirdlings are making peace with us?"

Hargorin smiled at him. "Peace," he affirmed.

In that moment anyone could have heard the fall of a sparrow's tail feather.

The kings and clan leaders stared at Hargorin and his delegation. They had heard the words but as yet did not believe them.

Ireheart knew how they felt. He, too, was speechless. The prospect of hundreds, no, thousands more cycles of warfare and hatred had been removed with those few sentences, and no endless negotiations had been necessary! All made possible by a single dwarf: Tungdil Goldhand.

That is his great achievement, he thought. *There will be no greater high king to come after him. There will be statues showing him as the bringer of unification. Desperate returnee has become unassailable warrior and high king of all the tribes.* Ireheart's breathing sped up with the excitement and, when nobody in the chamber voiced a response, he cried out: "Smash us with the sacred hammer of Vraccas—is no one going to cheer?"

A hurricane of voices broke out, assailing the ears and outdoing the thunder of jubilation they had heard on entering the fortress. Dwarves on all sides shouted out in joy and relief, waving weapons in the air and running up to the thirdlings. Not to attack them but to shake hands.

Tungdil remained where he was, Bloodthirster in one hand, the other on his hip, smiling as he surveyed the scene.

Ireheart could contain himself no longer: He embraced his friend with a laugh, slapping him on the back over and over. "You were amazing, Scholar!"

"Without you, old friend, none of this would have been possible," the one-eyed dwarf replied, holding out his hand. Then he turned to Slîn, Balodil and Balyndar. "Without each and every one of you it would not have been possible. You all shared in our success." Finally he turned to address the assembly. "We can celebrate later," he said, waiting for quiet. "Let us think now of those who have given their lives in this mission and have been welcomed into the eternal forge of Vraccas."

To Ireheart's astonishment Tungdil reeled off every single name of the fallen, from the dwarves to the Zhadár.

"And now," he said to Goda, "I want to hear what has happened here since we have been gone."

The maga made her report. She told of the attack the monsters had launched, of their own counterattack, the appearance of the enemy magus, the abduction of her daughter, the injury to her son. She told of all the events round the Black Abyss.

Ireheart's euphoric mood plummeted and concern for his children made him start to his feet.

But Goda held him back with her eyes, warning him not to leave the assembly. "They are both safe now. Go and see them when the audience is over," she told him. "There has been no change since my daughter escaped and returned to us. The monsters have rebuilt their towers taller than before. Their camp has now regained its former size," she summed up. "But there has been no sighting of their magus."

Tungdil nodded. "You have heard now why we need Lot-Ionan to combat the dwarf who calls himself Vraccas. In the cycles I spent in the Black Abyss I made him my mortal enemy, but I assure you he would have broken out some time or other even without my provocation. His thirst for power is insatiable." He had them bring out the scale model of the ravine, which showed the locations of all the tents and towers. "He is our prime target. Once he is dead the beasts will lose heart. Then it will be an easy fight and we will be in a position to make the rocks collapse on top of them, making sure no evil ever escapes again!"

"When do we start fighting?" Hargorin asked, puzzling over the model.

"In two orbits' time. I need to rest after my journey." Tungdil tapped the glass dome that represented the barrier.

It shattered. "Lot-Ionan will do that for us and he will ride into battle at my side. We'll finish the monsters off, and as soon as the dwarf-magus notices he's nearing defeat, he'll come out." He gave the assembled kings a piercing warning look and urged them, "No one is to confront him! He belongs to me and Lot-Ionan. No one else could stop him. Goda has already described his power. Nobody would stand a chance."

"Apart from me," interrupted Balyndar. He pulled Keenfire out of its sheath and showed it to the assembly. A loud murmur ran through the crowd. "The weapon which vanquished the demon, which defeated Nôd'onn and many of Girdlegard's foes, has returned to its own kind. And it will serve us once more."

"The diamonds are glowing," one of the dwarves called out in alarm. "Who is among us? The ax is trying to warn us."

The Zhadár stepped forward. "It's me," he chuckled. "I may look like a dwarf, but I changed ages ago. The älfar implanted the seed of evil in me but I used its power to do good. That," he whistled softly, indicating Keenfire, "is why it is sparkling so nicely. It can sense my presence."

Goda looked at Tungdil and was about to say something but Ireheart gestured emphatically to her to keep silent. He guessed she was going to cast new doubts on the integrity of the Scholar. *Not now*, he mouthed.

"He is the last of his kind," said Tungdil. "His friends and comrades have all fallen, fighting the good fight and giving their lives for Girdlegard. With his help we can find and kill every last älf, wherever he may be hiding, as soon as we have our victory here in the Outer Lands."

The assembled dwarves applauded or clattered their weapons on the table.

"Then go back to your warriors, and tell them what is to happen the orbit after next. And take your rest." The high king bowed his head to them. "Vraccas will be with you." Turning, he nodded to Ireheart and left the chamber.

Goda came over to her husband. "You heard it."

"What?"

"Vraccas will be with *us*." She watched Tungdil's retreating back. "But who is with *him*?"

"Oh, come now, Goda." Ireheart sighed and shook his head. He left her standing there and went to see his children.

One orbit later, when Ireheart had stretched out for a nap, there was a knock at the door and a messenger asked him to go to the conference chamber. The high king had summoned him.

Ireheart made his way there as quickly as he could. He was thinking through the next orbit's battle. Evildam echoed to the sound of blades being sharpened on whetstones, and the clink of hammer on metal where armor was being repaired. Final preparations were underway. They were agreed on tactics. Nothing would be changed now.

He worried less about himself and his own survival; he was concerned for Sanda in particular. *I would give anything for her to recover from what has happened*. While his injured son was obviously getting better, he had seen in his daughter's eyes that Sanda had not got over her treatment in captivity.

He had noticed a similar effect in Coïra, who had still not recovered from her near-death experience at Sisaroth's hands. For this reason he had put the two of them together, hoping they would share confidences and help each other.

Balyndar was another problem. Ireheart feared the fifthling might do something reckless with Keenfire, endangering the outcome for the dwarves. The looks that Balyndar and Goda had exchanged were almost conspiratorial. It would be no use trying to talk sense to his spouse. She had made up her mind and was not going to change it. All Tungdil's achievements meant nothing to her.

"Vraccas, why did you make us so stubborn?" he complained under his breath before going down the corridor that led to the conference chamber. Coïra was also on her way there.

He lifted his arm in greeting and she slowed her pace. She was wearing a dark-blue robe with long sleeves, and a black cap on her head. Ireheart recognized Weyurn's coat of arms in the embroidery on the sleeves. "How are you, Majesty?"

"Well, thank you." She smiled. "You'll be wanting to know if I've spoken to your daughter?"

Ireheart tilted his head and his braid fell forward. "I'm so worried about her . . . she's so low and seems very confused. So different."

Coïra frowned. "Have your wife's suspicions taken hold of you, too?"

"What suspicions?"

"That it is not really your daughter."

Ireheart threw up his hands. "Is she saying that? First it was the Scholar she had doubts about and now she thinks her own daughter has been replaced! It's persecution mania!"

"Yes, yes," said Coïra mildly, to calm the dwarf down. "It obviously is your daughter. She has told me many personal details." She stopped at the door. "She has endured the most terrible thing that a woman can ever go through. The dwarf that abducted her announced his intentions and put the blame squarely on Goda for not accepting his conditions. Her spirit has been damaged by the thought of this betrayal." She placed her hand on his shoulder. "I can do nothing for her, Boïndil Doubleblade. My fate was harmless in comparison."

Ireheart could find no reply, so great was the hatred raging in his soul. Hatred for the enemy in the vraccasium armor, against whom all his fighting prowess would be useless in battle. *I shall desecrate his corpse.*

In a fury he stepped into the hall with Coïra—but stopped dead in his tracks: As well as Tungdil, Slîn, Balyndar and Balodil there were two white-clad elves in the room, wearing light palandium armor under their robes.

They carried swords and shields on their backs and long daggers hung from their belts. The male was dark, while the female's hair was almost white; both looked too tall for Ireheart's taste, too thin and too pretty. *As with the älfar; they don't come in the fat and ugly format at all. If only one of them would just fart like a pony so they weren't always so damn perfect.*

Tungdil asked the maga and Ireheart to come in, and introduced the elves. "These are the last two heroes to whom you owe the annihilation of the Girdlegard älfar. They were as much a part of it as I was myself." He said their names, then indicated the elves. "This is Ilahín and his wife Fiëa. When the rebellion started in the älfar regions they left their hiding place and led the humans to where the black-eyes were."

"But we would never have been able to do that without your preparatory work," Fiëa said sweetly in typical singsong elf tones. Dwarves had never liked the way the elves spoke. Nor the way they admired the humans.

"So you've heard?" said Ireheart, baring his teeth and looking at the tips of their ears.

Ilahín laughed. "I've missed all those dwarf-jokes."

Ireheart stopped. "You like being made fun of?"

"He's an exception," Fiëa said, not sounding quite so friendly now. "I'm not fond of it at all."

"Stop right now, old friend," said Tungdil, motioning to him and Coïra to sit down. "They have come to thank us and to bring news from Girdlegard."

Ilahín waited until everyone was seated. "Aiphatòn's action and your own involvement have meant that it is safe for us to appear once more and for us elves to take some part in the liberation of our homeland. As we are not able or willing to give our thanks to the Unslayables' offspring, because of who he is descended from, this makes it all the more important for us to thank you." He lifted a chest from the floor and opened it. It contained daggers made of a white metal. "They are made of pure palandium and can cut through anything. They have the power of the elf goddess in them and will equip you for the coming battle."

Fiëa handed a knife to each of them.

Ireheart had to admit that the workmanship was excellent, even if they could not compare with dwarf-weapons. He could see the elves employed different procedures when tempering and forging metal. *Children's toys*. But he did not want to be disagreeable so he thanked them politely for their gift and tucked his new dagger in his belt. It was quite something to have an elf weapon hanging on a dwarf's combat belt.

"We have also destroyed wide swathes of Dsôn Bhará, as well as Phôseon Dwhamant. The area has been given back its old name of Âlandur. The humans will make sure that nothing remains to remind them of älfar occupation." Ilahín pointed to his wife. "Fiëa and I will return to the Golden Plain to found a settlement. We are convinced the elves will return to Girdlegard when the news of the victory gets out into the Outer Lands. We want them to find a home waiting when they arrive." The elf smiled.

"How charming. But there are only two of you," commented Slîn.

"We live long enough to get a lot done," was Ilahín's reply.

"And we shall not die before the other elves have arrived," added Fiëa determinedly.

"The daggers are not their only gift. They have offered to fight with us against the monsters," Tungdil explained.

"Isn't that rather dangerous if you are keen to start a new homeland for your people?" Slîn asked, not noticing until after he spoke that his words could be construed as an insult of sorts. "I'm not doubting your skill in a fight, Fiëa and Ilahín, but . . . it will be a fierce battle and many will be injured, many will be killed. Of course it is nothing compared to the campaign you fought against the älfar in Girdlegard."

Fiëa looked at him. "Your concern is touching, but we know how to fight, Slîn." She bowed. "Permit us to retire. We must rest to be ready for the morrow." She and Ilahín left the room.

"Well, what do you know?" Balyndar had the dagger on the table in front of him. "The elves have emerged from their forest haunts." Slîn and Balodil laughed quietly.

"They know when a battle is hopeless and can assess when victory is possible." Tungdil stared at them sharply, tying his new dagger to his belt. "Ask the fifthlings and firstlings. They have used similar strategies in past cycles, as far as I can make out. There is a difference between strategic withdrawal and the cowardice you seem to be accusing them of." He walked to the door. "We meet tomorrow. I am not to be disturbed until sun-up, when we attack the beasts."

Ireheart also took his leave and disappeared.

Slîn studied the model of the ravine and fortress. "Right, so tomorrow it is." He glanced at Coïra. "You will cope, maga?"

"With Lot-Ionan and Goda's support there should be no problem getting the mountain to collapse in on the abyss," she answered. "On my own I would never manage it, but with the three of us I'm sure it's possible."

"But what if you have to use up your energy in the battle?" Balyndar tipped over some of the little figures in the evil camp.

"I don't think we'll have to. Lot-Ionan is the one who'll have to cast most of the spells. His magic reserve is incredible. I don't know how he does it. Even though Balyndar damaged his onyx staff." She suppressed a yawn. "We'll attack and defeat the army of darkness. If we run out of missiles for the new catapults, then it's your turn. Together with the ubariu, the undergroundlings and the humans it should be easier than . . ." she flicked another of the little figures off the board ". . . doing that." With these words she took her leave and left the chamber; the Zhadár disappeared without a farewell.

Slîn looked first at Balyndar, then back to Keenfire. "Don't do anything silly," he warned, as he got to his feet. He held his crossbow in such a way that it could be construed as a threat. "I shan't let you out of my sight on the battlefield and should I see you up to any treachery directed against the properly elected high king . . ." He left the sentence unfinished and strode out, his weapon shouldered.

Balyndar sat alone in the chamber, his eyes on the model of the abyss and his right hand on the hilt of Keenfire. "I'll do whatever I think is right," he said, leaning forward. He had discovered a figure that looked very like Tungdil.

He reached out for it, tossed it into the air and chopped it in half with Keenfire's blade.

Ireheart made sure that he could not be seen, then knocked at the door.

Ilahín opened up, looking surprised. "Well, what brings you here, Boïndil Doubleblade? What can I . . . ?"

"Let me in," Ireheart said, pushing past the elf. "Forgive my coming unannounced, but there's a very . . . unpleasant matter I need your help with." He sat down, his shoulders drooping. "Help me, Ilahín."

The elf shut the door and pulled out a chair for himself facing the dwarf. "You know, friend dwarf, that I will gladly help you. What's on your mind?"

Ireheart took out the drinking pouch that Balodil had given him. "Smell that and maybe you can understand. This used to belong to a Zhadár and I drank out of it by mistake."

Ilahín took the vessel, opened it and fanned the air to get the scent. All his amiable helpfulness disappeared. "This is . . . elf blood!"

"And it's the reason the älfar hunted you all down. They needed it to brew a concoction that turned selected thirdling warriors into Zhadár," he explained, looking at the elf. "My drinking it was a mistake," he insisted. "One of the Zhadár told me only an elf would be able to liberate me from the curse of having drunk it." He rubbed his nose awkwardly.

Ilahín gave no answer. Instead he called Fiëa, held the pouch out to her and pointed to Ireheart. There followed a long and involved exchange that grew more and more heated. The dwarf got the impression the two elves did not agree. *But about what?*

"Forgive me if I interrupt you," he called out after a long tense wait. "Is there any remedy against the thirst or not?"

The elves stared at him.

Ilahín took a deep breath. "The thing is, Boïndil Doubleblade, we don't really know," he admitted. "Your guilt is very serious."

"Ho, damn it! But I had no idea."

"That is neither here nor there," said Fiëa sharply. "If you kill a human and then say you didn't know it was wrong, the other humans will still hunt you down and bring you to trial, won't they?"

Ireheart had to nod in agreement.

"What you've done is to commit blasphemy and the fact you did it unwittingly does not help. That's unfortunately the fact of the matter," said Ilahín in friendlier tones. "However, you are one of our folk's benefactors, so we believe the goddess will perhaps be merciful in your case and reduce the punishment."

"I don't understand. What's going to happen? What have I got to do?"

Fiëa took the leather pouch and cut it open. The dark viscous liquid spilt onto the floor and formed a stain. "You will have to pray to Sitalia, Boïndil Doubleblade, and beg her to release you from the curse."

"But . . ." He saw the stain growing in size until the elf-woman covered it with a cloth to wipe it up. Then the cloth flew into the fire and there was a hissing sound. Black flames shot out and then the nightmare was over. "But I need . . ."

"No, Boïndil Doubleblade." Ilahín interrupted him. "Each new sip of that liquid would take you one step nearer damnation."

Ireheart tugged at the silver and black hairs on his scalp in frustration. "It's the only way to combat the thirst! You have no idea how it burns!"

They looked at each other again. Fiëa took a small bag from her belt. "In here are some herbs, Boïndil Doubleblade, which will help you with the symptoms. But the thirst will only disappear if Sitalia pardons you. Pray to her, that is what we counsel. Pray with fervor and humility."

"But I did nothing wrong!" Ireheart felt a fool constantly reiterating his innocence, but he did not know what else to do.

"Tell Sitalia," advised Fiëa. "We believe you. Your deeds speak for you."

Ilahín touched the despairing dwarf on the brow. "You must convince the goddess. She will show herself to you if you do things properly."

"Or else?" he asked uncertainly.

"The herbs will not help you forever, and you . . ." Fiëa grimaced. "You know what will happen, friend dwarf." They looked at him, challenge in their eyes. He understood.

He got up, dragged himself to the door and went out. "Thank you," he said as he turned on the threshold. "Praying to Sitalia," he muttered under his breath. "Begging the pointy-ears' goddess for favors! It's come to that! I'm *innocent*!" Depression and prevarication had given way to the familiar stubborn resistance. "Then I'd rather die a hero's death in battle! So there! That's all the elves will get out of me!"

He stomped off down the corridor to his own chambers with grim determination. *Vraccas will help* me.

XXXI

The Outer Lands,
The Black Abyss,
Early Summer, 6492nd Solar Cycle

It was pouring down.

A violent storm had broken out overnight, deluging fortress and ravine alike as if to wash the defending forces from the very battlements and to flood the chasm of the evil beasts.

By daybreak the thunder and lightning had passed but the rain remained. The attack was still scheduled to take place. Tungdil had insisted on this.

The units stood ready behind each of the four gates. This time they were strictly divided: Humans at the eastern gate, the ubariu to the west, undergroundlings north and the dwarves in the south. The intention was to confuse the beasts by disguising the direction of the major attack.

And this main focus was to be from the south, with Tungdil, Balyndar, Ireheart, Goda, Coïra, Lot-Ionan and the dwarf contingents. The humans would divert and feign an attack together with the undergroundlings at the northern entry point, while the ubariu were to come to the dwarf-army flank in support.

Ireheart stood up in his stirrups to survey the massed army of male and female warriors. Their banners and standards high in the gray air displayed their pride in the newfound harmony among the children of the Smith. A victory would unite them still more firmly. "I thank you, Vraccas," he murmured and turned to the gate. *Even if I find my own death today.*

Around him were gathered the heroes of the first mission, as well as Goda and Lot-Ionan. The dwarf-woman would not look at the magus and always kept her distance. She would have refused to speak a single word to her former master even if he had wished it.

Ireheart saw from his wife's expression that she would rather have been confronting the magus in combat than the beasts from the ravine. Again he noted Goda and Balyndar exchanging rapid glances. The fifthling looked at Slîn, who was observing him intently and tapping the shaft of his crossbow, as if by chance.

Ireheart scratched his silvery black beard. *What are they up to?* There was something he was not privy to and it worried him. He would not be able to stop in the heat of battle to play nursemaid to them in order to head off some harebrained scheme.

He was about to wheel his pony toward Tungdil, but the one-eyed dwarf was already giving the signal to attack.

The double doors of the mighty gate swung wide open and Ireheart knew the same would be happening at the other three entrances, sending these disparate armies on their way. If he had got it right there would be one thousand humans fighting under the leadership of the elves, four thousand undergroundlings, a solid ten thousand ubariu and then another force of ten thousand dwarves, of which the six thousand thirdlings made up the largest section.

But before any of them could set foot on the plain the first stroke had to be successful.

Lot-Ionan stepped forward to study the dark-red barrier edge. He placed his left hand on it and spoke a short sentence, suddenly crying out loud and tensing his whole body.

White lightning flashed through the shield, causing it to dissolve. The barrier disappeared with a high-pitched whine!

"For Girdlegard!" came Tungdil's rallying cry. He sounded his bugle. All four armies started their advance, while the fortress catapults went into action, raining down havoc on the bewildered monsters.

Rocks, arrows and spears hurtled through the air, crashing and thumping down; burning petroleum bombs and red-hot iron balls shot over into the monsters' unprotected camp, striking the tents to kill and maim those inside. They struck the siege towers, the battering rams, the storm ladders, all the military equipment the beasts had placed ready on the plain.

As fire erupted, the crackling of bursting wood could be heard above the screams of the beleaguered creatures. At that moment the clouds parted and the rain stopped. It was as if the gods were sending them propitious weather. But all of a sudden a second barrier appeared twenty paces further on. The projectiles bounced off it harmlessly.

"Shields!" bellowed Ireheart to the forces behind him, reaching for his own.

The first of the deflected missiles started to strike the dwarves, who had quickly brought up their shields to protect their heads. They hid until the lethal hail of projectiles had ceased. The catapult crews on the battlements had reacted swiftly and stopped firing to prevent hitting their own ranks, but some of the missiles had been in mid-flight.

Ireheart felt a light blow and then a stronger one that

tumbled him out of the saddle. He rolled over, keeping under his shield. This proved the saving of him when, a moment later, something soft thudded into the shield, causing a burst of flame. He flung his burning shield away and bounded away from the fire. Had the bag of petroleum touched his body he would have perished in the flames.

Ireheart saw Goda smiling happily at the sun, lifting her bugle to her lips to play a rapid succession of notes whose significance he did not understand.

All around the battlements of Evildam dazzling light flared out.

He could see the soldiers hefting vast burnished metal mirrors into place. The sun was reflected hundreds of times, dancing over the ground and focusing on the largest of the enemy siege towers where the beasts were getting ready to fire catapults. These beams of light pierced the magic barrier without hindrance.

Confused, the monsters shut their eyes. Ireheart saw them waving their arms about and then the first of them caught fire!

Ireheart was amazed. *The mirrors are catching the power of the mighty orb and are relaying it a hundredfold in strength!* Even damp wood was catching fire; then, suddenly, the petroleum for the beasts' fire arrows ignited, sending up a burst of flame. The base of the siege tower was engulfed by the blaze.

Goda whooped with excitement and Kiras hugged her. Ireheart felt proud that his wife had come up with such a trick. *She's a little scholar herself. Not only a maga*, he thought, hurrying to join Tungdil and Balyndar.

The mirrors were adjusted anew to attack the next tower

with their dazzling rays. The force of the beam was enough to make all the beasts there quickly evacuate the construction. They could guess what would happen if they stood their ground when the first of the rays started to converge: The whole erection would turn into a blazing inferno, burying many of their number under the burning rubble as it collapsed.

Ireheart's initial optimism that they might carry the day became a stout conviction. But not yet utter unshakeable certainty.

Lot-Ionan was at the barrier, forcing it to disintegrate once more, but this time the fortress catapult crews held back, fearing the shield might re-form further along, thus causing death and injury to their own soldiers when shots were deflected.

Ireheart attended to his wounded warriors and calculated how many casualties the dwarves had suffered. Some lay on the ground, bleeding, others, with dented helmets and body armor, stayed bravely on their feet.

Tungdil sprang off his pony. "Forward!" he yelled frenetically, brandishing Bloodthirster. "Mow them down!" Then he stormed off, ax gripped in both hands.

The dwarf-army followed him, taking courage from their war-cry chorus, which resounded off the walls of the fortress.

The beasts were rushing into battle formation, obviously in panic.

Reinforcements arriving from the ravine did nothing to calm the enemy's frenzied endeavors. The recently arrived monsters were infected by their comrades' nervousness, prompting their furious officers to lash out at their own troops with their long whips, almost as if they were fighting the foe.

The dwarves were now less than a hundred paces from

the enemy front rank; suddenly the kordrion's monstrous head showed itself above the edge of the ravine.

Ireheart immediately recognized it as the one that Tungdil had attacked on his re-emergence from the Black Abyss. The scars and missing eye were obvious.

Swiftly, he placed wax plugs in his ears, as did the others, the surrounding roar of battle immediately being muffled as if coming from a distance.

The kordrion opened its mouth to bellow, and came further up out of the cleft in the rocks.

Ireheart grinned. None of the dwarves had halted. The roar still sounded frightening but it was no longer able to paralyze them, a lack of reaction that clearly disturbed the monsters more than anything.

And their own riposte soon followed. Lot-Ionan fired two bright blue beams at the kordrion, striking him in the neck. Flames erupted, and the creature's gray flesh blistered from the heat, burning black. The skin burst open and bluish black blood splattered down onto the beasts beneath.

The kordrion charged, screaming, out of the chasm, trampling its own monster-soldiers under its claws. It pushed up, spreading its massive wings, but was hit by a second wave of magic—this time from Goda. A crackling yellow flash of lightning bored its way into the creature's flank, leaving a hole the size of a mill wheel.

With a yell, the kordrion catapulted itself aloft with powerful movements of its wings, heading high into the sky, spilling its blood on the ground below. It made no attempt to bombard the magus or the maga with white fire; the pain and shock had been too sudden. It had never met an attack of this nature.

The dwarves cheered when they saw their greatest adversary take flight. But if they expected this setback to discourage the monsters they were disappointed. Having overcome their initial panic they now clashed with the dwarves in full combat, shields held in front of themselves in battle formation.

Again Lot-Ionan showed why he was rightly feared by all the inhabitants of Girdlegard: He spread his arms wide as if trying to encompass a wall and gave a high-pitched whistle.

A terrible gust of wind arose and whirled off to meet the monsters' phalanx. For a length of forty paces the fighting beasts were scattered by the blast, thrown into the air and hurled backwards to be spiked on the raised weapons of their own fighters, before the ranks behind in their turn were blown into the air. The magus kept up this mighty gale until a swathe thirty paces wide had been cleared.

And it was into this gap that Tungdil led the dwarf-army. "I'll take the left." He raced off and let Bloodthirster do its worst among the remaining ranks of the enemy.

Ireheart grinned and broadened his chest proudly. "Follow me!" he bawled, hammering his weapon into the repulsive head of a monster that looked like a gugul on long legs. A mass of jelly spattered out and the beast fell over. "For Girdlegard!" came their cry.

The army split into sections, driving the weakened enemy before it. Axes sliced and crashed through shields, armor and trunks, shattering weapons and bones, sending opponents bleeding to the sodden ground.

The children of the Smith were letting nothing stop their onslaught; they clambered over corpses, battering and slaying anything in their path. Ireheart had Goda at his side and she increased the enemy's confusion with a few strokes of magic;

Coïra and Lot-Ionan were with Tungdil and Balyndar was nearby. Ireheart expected Slîn must be behind somewhere, sending out death with his crossbow bolts.

Ireheart surrendered to his battle-fury, yelling and laughing like a madman, wielding his crow's beak with irresistible force.

The weapon's spike cracked open every type of armor plating, smashing every shield and bone it touched; the blunt side hammered helmets, ribs and kneecaps flat and rendered faces a jellied pulp. Finally Ireheart's rampaging was halted somewhat by the amount of enemy blood clouding his vision. He had to stop and wipe his face with his beard.

That was when he realized he had led his section of the army right through to the last ranks of the foe. There was no more resistance to face.

Ireheart swung his crow's beak up in triumph and trumpeted a wild resounding "Vraccas," taken up by the voices of all the dwarves at his side. He turned to see how Tungdil was doing.

At that moment the figure of a lone dwarf emerged from the ravine. His vraccasium armor glowed golden red in the sunlight.

His appearance brought everything to a halt, smothering their joy at their initial victory as surely as if a bucket of manure had been emptied on their heads.

Ireheart found himself compelled to stare at the dwarf and forgot the commands he had been about to give. The others reacted similarly on seeing their weird new opponent. He was imposing in spite of being so small in comparison with the beasts, and an aura of dark power enveloped him, notwithstanding the brightness of his armor.

The dwarf raised an arm and, at his signal, monsters marched out of the abyss behind him, all fully a head taller than the largest ubariu.

The monsters wore heavy gray metal armor topped with dark animal skins and helmets sporting the horns of wild beasts, with visors in the shape of ugly masks to hide their faces. In one hand they bore mighty swords or huge axes, while in the other they held long shields as protection against arrows.

Ireheart counted a hundred of them. *One hundred particularly large challenges.*

They came to a halt behind the dwarf and, at a shouted command, rammed the points of their shields down into the earth so that it shook at the impact. Then a second unit came marching out of the abyss, similarly armored, taking up position behind the front line. These beasts were holding scythe-like weapons; the shafts were reinforced with iron bands and the top ends were equipped with spikes the length of a finger.

The dwarf in vraccasium armor waited until the clash and clank had ceased, then took his two hammers and slammed them into one another, creating a cacophonous metallic noise, loud and extraordinarily unpleasant. Ireheart shook his head to deal with it. Wax plugs were no help. He looked at Tungdil, who had also led his troops in the first phase of the battle to victory. Thus roughly eight thousand fighting-fit children of the Smith were confronting two hundred opponents. This should be pure slaughter. But the size of their adversaries was no clue to their skill in combat.

One of the giant soldiers stepped up next to his master. "He who bears many names demands to know," his voice echoed over the battlefield, "where the thief is who stole his armor. Who betrayed him. Who tried to kill him as a coward kills."

At that, Goda put her bugle to her lips and gave the guards on the battlements a new command. At once the mirrored rays focused on the unknown dwarf, aiming to cook him inside his own armor!

Balyndar had fought his way through the enemy ranks at Tungdil's side. He would never have considered himself a clumsy or unwieldy fighter, but that was the way he came across next to the agility of the one-eyed dwarf. While the fifthling was still busy dealing with extricating Keenfire out of enemy flesh after one deadly strike, Tungdil had already sliced up two opponents and was hurling himself on the third. Bloodthirster was a frightening weapon and was giving all honor to its name.

Balyndar had tried his level best but was unable to keep up.

Coïra and Lot-Ionan, preserving their strength, were leaving all the vanquishing up to the dwarves. The fifthling thought this strategy eminently sensible.

Their victory had been shockingly easy and they had allowed themselves a few moments' respite before marching onwards to the Black Abyss.

Balyndar tried to locate Slîn but could see no sign of him. The threat the fourthling had made against him was not going to stop him doing what he and Goda had planned. Girdlegard had to be made safe for the next thousand cycles and that would only happen if every source of danger were eradicated. *Every single one!*

He noted that it had grown quieter but then a painfully loud cry assaulted his ears, making him start. Balyndar turned and saw the dwarf in red-gold armor in front of new adversaries. Quickly he pushed through to reach Tungdil's side. Lot-Ionan and Coïra joined them.

He could see the maga was frightened. This would be her first real experience of warfare, and that encounter with Sisaroth had left her with mental scars that had yet to heal. All the blood, the stink from steaming torn guts, the debris and the shouts were all hard to bear for the young woman.

Balyndar reckoned she would soon withdraw to seek safety in the fortress. So he touched her gently on the elbow and smiled at her encouragingly. It did not occur to him that he was no reassuring sight with his filthy smeared face and Keenfire dripping blood.

Coïra's smile was more of a grimace, and he noticed that her leather armor bore traces of vomit.

There was movement on the other side of the battlefield. One of the gigantic warriors had stepped up next to the dwarf in vraccasium armor. "He who bears many names," so echoed the voice, "demands to know where the thief is who stole his armor. Who betrayed him. Who tried to kill him as a coward kills."

Tungdil lifted his visor and opened his mouth to reply, but a bugle sounded.

The mirrors focused the beams and targeted the unknown dwarf, whose armor glowed in response.

"Excellent!" cheered Balyndar. Magic would be no help here, as the monsters had recently found out behind their seemingly impregnable barrier. "He'll be stewed like a rabbit in a pot."

"What infernal idiocy," Tungdil exclaimed, shouting out his orders. The dwarves were to gather into a single army, with himself, Lot-Ionan, Coïra and Balyndar at the head of it.

"Why? Do you call it idiocy because it wasn't you who thought it up?" Balyndar was proud that Goda had come up with the trick with the mirrors.

"She ought to have asked me," snarled Tungdil, sounding as dangerous as a wild animal. "This is exactly what I didn't want to have happen." He pointed to the dwarf. "Now he will use all his energy to make us pay."

"Your instruction was that no one should confront him," Balyndar began, wanting to excuse Goda's action.

The one brown eye flashed in fury and Balyndar could see it change color as Tungdil glared at him! Uncanny green clouds and spirals whirled and black spidery lines shot out across the skin under the golden eye patch. "Trying to kill him: Would you not call that *confronting him*? It certainly is in my book."

Balyndar was still reeling from shock. He had never seen weird black lines like these except on an älf: Never on a dwarf before. "Proof, at last," he murmured, watching Keenfire's diamonds sparkle. "My conscience will be clear."

The vraccasium-clad dwarf clashed his hammers one against the other, and hardly had the noise rung out than the burnished shields on the battlements disintegrated. The soldiers who had been holding them and directing the light were suddenly blasted with sharp fragments and fell in chaotic disarray. Loud cries of fear and agony rang out.

"That," Tungdil told Balyndar darkly, "was only the beginning. An initial flash of lightning before the storm proper." He nodded to Lot-Ionan and stepped forward.

As the two sections of the dwarf-army came together, the one-eyed dwarf and magus moved away, heading toward the enemy.

Balyndar followed, pulling Coïra along by the sleeve; from the other side he could see Goda and Ireheart approach. Of Slîn there was still no sign.

The monster warrior who had served the enemy dwarf as a mouthpiece raised his voice once more: "He who bears many names laughs at your pathetic attempt to harm him. For the present he will be lenient and not impose harsher punishment. He will spare the fortress and all the lands on this and the other side of the mountains. If the thief is surrendered . . ."

"Save your breath," Tungdil retorted. "You will neither pardon nor be lenient. You are here to kill." He held Bloodthirster out. "Once, this weapon spared your life. It will not happen a second time."

Ireheart watched the ranks of enemy warriors. *They must carry special powers or why else would they confront our vastly superior numbers?* Or perhaps they were extremely stupid. "What do you know about these soldiers?" he said under his breath to Tungdil.

"No idea," his friend replied, without turning his head. "But even in those relatively small numbers they'll be dangerous. Or he wouldn't have brought them out."

"He who bears many names will make this offer only once. Everything that subsequently happens will be your own fault," the spokesman called out, while his master stood motionless at his side, hammers held loosely in his hands.

The undergroundlings appeared at the army's flank and saw that they had arrived too late for the first battle. Kiras, their leader, called them to a halt. A few thousand more adversaries to confront the fighters from the ravine.

Is that all there's going to be? Ireheart kept expecting another wave of Tion's monsters to surge up out of the Black Abyss, maybe another kordrion, a dragon or two, anything that would stand at the side of these pitiful two hundred creatures for the inevitable battle. He was getting ever more concerned that no extra troops were appearing on the other side. "When's it going to start?" he whispered. "Scholar, how long do we wait?"

Tungdil took two paces forward. "Here stands a famulus to challenge his master!" he called. "Let us see who prevails. After that, the armies can meet in battle if they still care to."

Thundering and clanking, the contingent of humans appeared and the ubariu army crested the wall of rock. They, too, took up their formations. Thus the pincer movement was complete and the last two hundred and one enemies were surrounded.

Ireheart found the tension unbearable. "How can he remain so calm?" he asked.

"Goldhand or the other one?" responded Balyndar.

"The other one." Ireheart scanned the gathered forces of humans, ubariu, undergroundlings and dwarves. "Even I would be a bit nervous faced with this lot."

"Not if you had a pact with your supposed enemy," Balyndar remarked, glancing at Goda. "It could be that we are the victims of the most scurrilous, duplicitous plot in the history of Girdlegard."

"Nonsense," grunted Ireheart. "The Scholar would never do a thing like that." His fingers tightened on the shaft of his ax. "May Vraccas be my witness: If the two of them don't start fighting soon, I will."

Tungdil advanced toward the vraccasium-clad dwarf, his left arm stretched out in a gesture of challenge.

His opponent gave a harsh growl and stomped forward, lifting both hammers and twirling them playfully.

The armies watched closely what their leaders were doing and waited, tense and alert, for the duel to begin: Famulus versus master.

Ireheart glanced over at Lot-Ionan. The magus twitched his fingers almost imperceptibly and his lips moved in a silent incantation. *What is he up to?*

Before the two opponents had reached each other, the dwarf in vraccasium uttered a further sound and pointed one of his hammers at Tungdil.

The fact that nothing happened seemed to disturb both of them, as Ireheart could see from their body posture. The Scholar was the first to recover composure: He made a swift leap forward, swinging Bloodthirster at his opponent's head.

It took a while for Ireheart to work out what had occurred. The opposing dwarf had tried to freeze the tionium armor and paralyze Tungdil, but it had not happened! Ireheart spotted a satisfied expression on the face of their own magus. Had he counteracted the spell? Had the course of action been agreed in advance with the Scholar . . . or was it the overture to an act of treachery?

The master warded off Tungdil's strike, halting it with his crossed hammers, pushing back the attacker, who spun on his heel and forced the blade up against the evil dwarf's throat.

Again the hammers were crossed, forming scissors, then their master turned them and hooked the hammer heads together so that Tungdil was prevented from extracting

Bloodthirster. The dwarf-magus ducked down, wrenching back Tungdil's lethal blade.

The maneuver was successful and the united armies let out a horrified cry as Bloodthirster flew through the air and got stuck in a bog ten paces away from Tungdil. Hollow laughter rang out from under the master's helmet and he pushed his visor up. The repulsive sight of the disfigured face made Ireheart retch.

A whirring sound—and suddenly a bolt flew from out of the midst of the assembled dwarves, hitting the dwarf-master in the face. Slîn had obviously been waiting for precisely the right moment.

Ireheart could see clearly that the projectile had penetrated the nose plate. Blood oozed out, the injured dwarf swayed and took two steps to the side, to be caught by one of his own troops hurrying to his aid. He uttered a loud groan and made useless gestures with the hammers. Tungdil raced over to retrieve Bloodthirster while Lot-Ionan raised his arms to cast a spell.

"By Vraccas! *Now* it's going to start," said Ireheart.

Girdlegard,
Kingdom of Urgon,
Passview, in the Northeast,
Thirty-one miles from the Entrance to the Realm of the Fourthlings,
In the Brown Mountains,
Early Summer, 6492nd Solar Cycle

Rodario was just about to scold Mallenia for having got up, but then he fell silent and sat down on the edge of the bed to watch her.

She was standing at the window in her nightgown looking out over the hills of Urgon and over to Borwôl, where the troll realm had once been. The light from the window made the fabric of her night attire transparent, showing an appealing silhouette; in spite of her muscular build she still had feminine curves. In his arms, Mallenia always felt quite different from Coïra. Rodario was aware of his outstanding good fortune.

"I'm amazed," said the Ido girl, half turning to him.

"Are you? What about?"

"How you ever managed to survive. You've no idea how to move silently, Rodario."

"I wasn't trying to," he said with a smile. "I didn't want to startle you." He tried to put on a stern face. "You should be in bed. You're supposed to be resting. The journey tired you."

"That's what journeys do. I don't want to miss the outcome of the battle. In all of Girdlegard there's talk of nothing else." She leaned out again, watching the people in the streets outside the inn. "Some of the men are going off to volunteer for the army."

Rodario got up and came to stand behind her, wrapping his arms around her body and holding her tight. "The humans are drunk on their victories and their newfound freedom! It's great! But it'll be even better if it's all over before they get there." He followed her gaze; a company of young men in armor were setting off under a standard bearing the coat of arms of their town. "If they have to fight monsters they will lose."

Mallenia turned in his arms. "Is that why we are making such slow progress? Are you trying to keep me safe?" Her eyes challenged his. "Tell me the truth, actor."

"We're going slowly because the coach cannot travel any faster," he assured her. "I want to find out how Coïra is and I don't want to leave her alone any longer."

Mallenia nodded. "Yes, that's what I thought. So she needs your protection more than I do."

"When she left with Tungdil and the rest it was the other way around. You were too weak even to lift a knife," he objected.

"That's all changed now," she said, grinning. She gave him a playful shove that took him off balance.

"So I see," he said, laughing. He kissed her hand. "So let's get going." He collected their things while she changed out of her nightgown in front of him with no false modesty, putting on her leather armor and picking up her swords. Her movements were still slow and she had some difficulty fastening all the buckles but she managed in the end.

Their bags were ready and Rodario called the innkeeper's boy to help with carrying the luggage.

Together they loaded the coach Rodario had hired, stowing provisions on board for themselves and the coachman, and oats for the horses.

Rodario was about to help Mallenia up into the carriage when the innkeeper emerged. He held his errand boy roughly by the scruff of the neck. "One moment!" he said sharply. "This ne'er-do-well has a confession to make."

"Must I really?" the boy whimpered.

A slap in the face convinced him. "You deserve to have your hand cut off. That's what will happen if the fine lady and gentleman insist on the proper penalty," he yelled at the boy. "You bring shame to my establishment! And you will pay for it with pain."

Rodario had been feeling in his pockets to see if anything was missing. Neither he nor Mallenia seemed to have been robbed. "Tell me what you found on him, my good man."

The landlord let go of the boy's ear and cuffed him on the nape of the neck. With his other hand he reached into his apron pocket and handed a surprised Rodario an object wrapped in cloth.

The actor immediately recognized the cloth as being his own; after all, his initials were embroidered in the corner. But he had no idea what could be wrapped in it. He took the proffered item and exchanged glances with Mallenia before carefully unpacking it.

"He said he found it on the floor in your room. Under the bed where the lady was sleeping," he blurted out. "There's no way I'll believe that, the scoundrel! Things have been going missing ever since he started here." He boxed the boy's ears again. "I swear by the gods I'll chop your hand off myself if these good people insist! It'll be a pleasure!"

The boy sobbed and tried to lie his way out of trouble.

Rodario had finished unwinding the cloth and stared at the dull stone that lay there. "It isn't mine," he whispered to Mallenia, who looked as shocked as he was.

"A turquoise smoke diamond. What do you think it's worth?" she replied.

So far, neither the landlord nor errand boy had noticed their surprise, so the actor wrapped their find up again.

"Thank you for being so vigilant," he said, fishing some coins out of his purse. "Here, as a reward." He gestured toward the youth magnanimously "Let him go. It will be a lesson to him. If he doesn't mend his ways, chop his feet off. Then he can still work in the kitchen for you."

The innkeeper's face brightened. "Thank you, sire! Very generous of you indeed!" He gave the boy a few kicks on the backside to propel him back inside.

Rodario unwrapped the stone again. "A smoke diamond. It really is," he said, enthralled. But how did it get to be wrapped up in my handkerchief?"

Mallenia took the diamond, turning it in her hand. Dark shards of metal fell from the cloth onto the floor.

Rodario picked them up and handed them to the girl. "What do you think those are?"

"Perhaps they're part of the original setting?" She examined the fragments. "This is tionium!"

"Apart from the fact that the stone is not mine, I haven't even got a tionium pendant it could have hung on." Rodario stroked his pointed beard, then smoothed down his mustache.

Mallenia laughed. "For a clever man you can be quite slow at times."

He folded his arms across his chest. "Really?"

She held the smoke diamond out to him. "Tionium?"

Rodario studied the stone, then her face, and then he snatched it up. "All I can think of is Tungdil's armor . . ." He hesitated. "You think this may be his?"

"But who cut the stone out and hid it in your things? And why?"

"To accuse me of theft, I suppose." He leaned back against the carriage, tossing the diamond up into the air and catching it. "But it doesn't make sense. Everyone knows I don't need to steal."

"Perhaps the real thief wanted to escape notice."

"Then why not just chuck the stone away?" His eyes

followed the diamond as he juggled it. "Perhaps they wanted to sow discord among our group on the mission."

"But how would they know the group would split up?" Mallenia continued. "So he got what he wanted anyway."

Rodario popped the stone in his glove and tied some string round it to stop it falling out. "Let's assume it's from Tungdil's armor. What's it for, do you think?. I can't remember having seen it before."

"It may have been under a flap . . . or on the inside."

"We must restore it to Tungdil," said Rodario, about to spring up into the carriage.

Mallenia held him back. "That will be too slow. We'll have to ride."

"We?" He kissed her on the forehead. "*I* will ride, Mallenia. You stay here or you can follow in the carriage."

She frowned. "So do you fancy being knocked down by a woman in full view of all these worthy citizens?"

Rodario sniffed to show his displeasure. "To underestimate the physical prowess of one's companion is not a good basis for a successful relationship, my dear."

"Exactly. It was just a question. No more than that." Mallenia grinned and called the landlord to get them two good horses.

They waited impatiently in the inn, taking a simple meal of ham with bread, washed down with water.

"Do you think," asked Rodario, taking a large bite, "that we could be responsible for bringing about a successful end to the battle?" He sighed. "Oh, this would make a great play. My forefather would have been proud of me! I seem to be walking in his footsteps when it comes to being instrumental in saving Girdlegard." He chewed his food and reached for another slice of bread. "And then, of course, there's my work as the bard of freedom."

He tipped his chair backwards and forwards, staring up at the ceiling. "Maybe I'll even have earned myself a royal position!"

"Do you want to rule Idoslane?" she teased him. "Then you would have to defeat me. You can't do that. But Urgon's throne is empty. Why don't you apply?"

Rodario laughed. "It would be a considerable promotion in status. Quite incredible to think . . ."

". . . of you as the new Incredible Rodario," she said, completing the thought and standing up. The landlord waved them over. "I'll believe it when I see it happen."

They went out, paid the innkeeper and swung themselves up into the saddle on their chestnut mares.

"Do you know what I'd do first if I were king of Urgon?" He checked to ensure the diamond was still fastened securely at his wrist.

"No."

"I'd conquer Idoslane and make you my personal slave." Rodario grinned and rode off.

"Men!" Mallenia laughed and jabbed her heels into her horse's flanks.

XXXII

I reheart was burning to give the command to attack, but it was not his place, even if the duel between famulus and master had now ended. Slîn's action had been against all the rules but had certainly decided the outcome. He had no objection to what the fourthling had done.

Tungdil reached Bloodthirster and was pulling it out of the muddy swamp with both hands when suddenly the warriors of the vraccasium-clad dwarf turned invisible. "Armies! Attack!" ordered the one-eyed dwarf. "Attack and kill!"

The dwarf-army charged forward, racing to where the opponents had been. All were uneasy, knowing they might be struck by blades they could sense but not see.

The ubariu, humans and undergroundlings moved swiftly in.

Lot-Ionan's fingers sent blue energy flashes at the master, but the badly injured dwarf raised his right hand for long enough to catch the beams in the smoke diamond of his gauntlet; the gem glowed, but that was all that happened.

Ireheart saw their own magus grow paler by the moment and heard him call out to Coïra. *Confound it, so things are getting hard for him?* She nodded reluctantly and pointed her left arm at the enemy. Lot-Ionan did the same. *They must be wanting to combine forces on this.*

The first of the transformed enemies must have reached the ranks of the army where fighting could now be seen. Their terror-inducing scythe-like weapons were coming into their own, the cutting edge slicing through soldiers, mowing them down, severing flesh, sinew and bone in one lethal semicircle after another. Heaps of mutilated warriors piled up all around. The invisible creatures worked their way through the army as if it were a cornfield at harvest time. Those struck not by blade but by spiked shaft were thrown off their feet and tossed, mortally wounded, through the air, landing among their own comrades. The enemy could not be seen.

The effect on the army was obvious.

On all four fronts the advance halted, many warriors turning tail in terror as they heard the whirr of approaching scythes.

The second battalion of opponents, armed with axes and swords, seemed to have formed small groups and were rampaging through the army lines, making inroads through the throng. None survived their blows.

How can these fiends be tackled? Ireheart saw that the warriors next to Coïra were being hurled through the air. Holy forge-fire! One of the invisible enemies must be approaching the maga! Lot-Ionan was still immersed in fabricating his spell as she stopped what she was doing and sprang aside with a shout.

Ireheart ran over to defend Coïra, puzzling over how he could make their opponents visible again.

The battle raged around them, the warriors desperately trying to defend themselves against their invisible adversaries but only succeeding in laying a few of them low. Hard to locate and harder still to fight. Worse still, it took an incredible number of blows to bring them down; as well as their invisibility they had their armor and shields for protection.

Ireheart had lost sight of Tungdil while trying to help the maga. Coïra possessed the power to defend herself but was retreating from the fray, shrieking in terror. Hers was no warrior spirit.

Lot-Ionan, meanwhile, had sent his magic force against the fallen master—the rays were met once again by a freshly erected barrier! Flames licked around the sides of a bright red dome before dying out.

"Stupid fool! See what you've done through your cowardice!" The magus cursed Coïra, who had tripped over the hem of her dress, tumbling to the boggy ground. The accident fortuitously saved her from the invisible sweep of the scythes, for to her right and left dwarves were felled mercilessly, injured and mutilated. Blood and severed limbs abounded.

Ireheart had almost reached her but could not believe how Lot-Ionan was behaving—ignoring Coïra instead of helping her up. He was making for the magic barrier behind which Tungdil's former master was already pulling the crossbow bolt out of his head. The wound closed up as soon as the tip of the bolt had left the skull and he jumped to his feet as if nothing had happened. He could not be slain with ordinary weapons.

"Vraccas, we need your assistance!" Ireheart saw more dwarves cut to ribbons while others plunged frantically into the swamp; blood and mud splashed up. He stared at the ground and noted the huge footprints of his opponents.

"I've got you," he growled, taking a running leap to aim

a blow at where he supposed the creature's neck to be. He brought down the crow's beak with all his might. The spike shattered something and a loud cry rang out. Thudding into metal, the dwarf held on to the shaft of his weapon as firmly as he could while his adversary bucked and tossed under him like an unbroken horse trying to throw off a rider.

But Ireheart was having none of that. Refusing to loosen his grip, he hung suspended with his feet a pace and a half above the ground, swinging wildly and cackling with laughter. "Rear and buck all you like! It's no use! You won't get rid of me!" He quickly drew his knife out with one hand, clamping it between his teeth. Then he pulled himself up with both hands along the shaft of his crow's beak until he reached the ax head, then plunged his knife into the wound until the blood ran free. "How do you like that, long legs?" he growled, rootling around in the flesh until he got through to a bone, where he anchored the knife.

"Off to Tion with you!" Ireheart clung onto the dagger in order to gain leverage to extract the crow's beak, which he wielded in an upward swing.

There was a clang as the spike met and pierced metal. The bucking motion ceased and the dwarf was pitched forward and down as the invisible warrior crashed down at Coïra's feet. Ireheart picked himself up and stood on the creature's neck, hands around the crow's beak. "Ho! That was none too easy," he called out to the maga, as he pulled his weapon out of the body of the fallen foe. Visible now in death, its enormous dimensions could be fully seen.

Ireheart stepped over the head and hopped down to where the maga was standing on the soft ground. "Girdlegard needs you!" he urged her, proffering his bloodied gloved hand. "Get over your fear and concentrate on your magic powers or things will end badly." He pointed to the barrier. "Help Lot-Ionan!"

Coïra's eyes fluttered; she was in a panic, not even daring to grasp the dwarf's hand. "I can't," she whispered. "I'm too frightened."

With a hissing sound the swamp started to boil and bubble. Jets spurted up twenty paces high all over the battlefield, deluging the warriors. The impact knocked many of them over and the soft mud covered their armor, helmets, eyes . . . It also covered the invisible giant hordes! The coat of dirt made them instantly detectable and the dwarves made immediate use of this fact.

That will have been Goda's work! thought Ireheart, proud as could be.

Coïra was still staring at him blankly, refusing to budge, so he turned and ran to the barrier. *Stupid human women!* Out of the corner of his eye he saw Balyndar, Tungdil and Lot-Ionan hurrying over to her.

Ireheart grinned. The quartet would surely prove too much for the dwarf in the posh armor. "You've been a master, now you'll be an ex-master," he smirked.

One by one they too arrived at the barrier, through which they spied the master and the last of his followers.

"Go on," Ireheart urged the magus. "Get the barrier down so we can do for him!"

Lot-Ionan paid no attention. His fingers were making shapes in the air.

Tungdil stepped up to the barrier and banged on it with Bloodthirster. It pinged like glass. "Our duel is not yet over. Your fighters are being defeated, as you can see. Would it not spur you on to see me dead even if you have lost them all?"

"He who bears many names," the nearest enemy fighter spoke up, "announces that the battle is not over. But until then," and suddenly the barrier moved to encompass Tungdil, locking him in, "he will fight you and punish you." Then he lifted his black bugle and blew a blast on it. Numerous holes in the instrument allowed him to play a range of notes, as if on a flute.

"No!" called Ireheart, smashing his crow's beak into the shield. It hummed but did not disintegrate. "Let me in!"

Balyndar grabbed him by the shoulder and forced him to look at the ravine. "What do we do now?"

Ireheart pulled himself out of Balyndar's grip. "Don't you touch me . . ." Then he noticed what all the others were staring at.

Another kordrion had appeared in the cleft. The head was smaller than the fully grown version—but then one head after another popped up. The beast revealed itself to the armies of Girdlegard.

"A kordrion with four heads," groaned Ireheart.

Tungdil had taken up the fight with his former master while the shimmering protective shield expanded in size once more. The dwarves and Lot-Ionan had to step back.

Ireheart cursed and looked at the magus, who was still casting spells but having no success on his own. "Goda!" he called. "Goda, we need you!"

"Disappear!" Balyndar struck the magic hemisphere, but Keenfire had no effect. It bounced off and nearly injured its owner with the spike.

The giant bugler sounded another range of notes and, in

response, the kordrion hissed and charged the nearest ubariu soldiers, breathing a sea of white fire over them. Spewing out flames in three directions at once, the four-headed creature was inflicting carnage on the troops. At a further signal it unfolded its wings, took off and landed in the very heart of the ubariu, crushing many of the valiant warriors; two of the creature's heads snapped and bit at them while the other two sent out the deadly white fire.

"Come, on, wizard!" Ireheart bellowed at Lot-Ionan. "We need to get that trumpet thing."

Meanwhile, the bout between Tungdil and his master was progressing; they were well matched. Neither was gaining the upper hand, each succeeding in inflicting cuts and dents on the armor of the other. The runes stayed still. Ireheart did not know why.

Goda turned up, breathing heavily. "I can only do one last spell," she admitted.

"And that's just the one I need," said Lot-Ionan, facing forward without even glancing at her. "Do you know the Sarifanie words?"

"Remember, you taught me that one shortly before I quit," she replied. "It is not good magic."

"That doesn't matter," Ireheart fumed at her. "Not now, Goda! Help him to break down the barrier or the kordrion will destroy one army after another!" He waved his weapon, noticing how the blood had dried on it.

The dwarf-woman was obviously extremely reluctant but she stepped up next to her former mentor and put her left hand in his right. Each of them pointed at the barrier with the forefinger of their free hand, then shut their eyes.

At that moment Tungdil was stunned by a hammer blow

to the head that hurled him right over to the edge of the barrier, barely a hand's breadth away from Ireheart. His helmet had fallen off and blood was coursing down from a cut on the forehead.

What . . . ? Eyes wide in horror Ireheart stared at his friend's face: It was covered in black lines, just like an enraged älf, the lines spreading out from the golden eye patch. Ireheart half expected the whole face to shatter into pieces like broken pottery.

Tungdil shook himself and warded off the next blow, striking the master in the face with the jagged edge of Bloodthirster. The sharp tips stabbed through the skin to the bone beneath, lodging fast.

The dwarf in the vraccasium armor hit out blindly and Tungdil grabbed his hand, broke the wrist and snatched the hammer. Then he swerved aside. Smashing it down on Bloodthirster's blade, he drove the sharpened tips further into his opponent's face.

The master fell on his back and tried to crawl away from Tungdil, blood pouring from the neck wound and staining the ground.

A further signal was sounded on the enemy bugle.

Dropping its pursuit of the decimated ubariu, the four-headed kordrion launched itself onto the group of humans, wings flapping. They did not even try to offer resistance, but took flight at once.

The catapults on the battlements had started up. Losses among their own troops should shots go astray were regrettable but a four-headed kordrion could not be allowed to survive. Clouds of arrows and spears darkened the battlefield as battle raged against the beast.

Ireheart paid no attention to the battle. He wanted to be with his friend, and it *was* his friend under the magic dome. *I have to get in there!*

The final monster warrior drew his sword, about to intercede in the duel.

Tungdil kept his cool and raised the hammer. With all his might he slammed the hammer down—once, twice, three times—onto Bloodthirster, driving the blade right through the skull of the convulsing enemy, until the head was split in two. The sharp movements of arms and legs ceased; the limbs flopped back and were still. The famulus had taken the life of his master.

"*Huzzah!*" yelled Ireheart, beside himself. "*He's done it!*"

Smiling grimly, Tungdil pulled Bloodthirster out of the carcass and aimed the tip of it at the final enemy, whose approaching steps were slowing now.

A loud high sound, like a storm whistling through a canyon, reverberated around them and the barrier flickered and disappeared.

"Scholar, leave Long Legs to me!" bellowed Ireheart, charging with his weapon raised high at the enemy. The monster, having been unable to save his leader's life, raised the fateful bugle to his lips once more, forcing Ireheart to an action dwarves only contemplate if they are carrying a second weapon on their person: He hurled the crow's beak.

The weapon hummed across toward the opponent, its spike striking him just as he was about to sound the first note, penetrating his helmet and destroying his brain. The giant fell, bugle clattering to the ground and bursting into tiny pieces.

"Ha!" rejoiced Ireheart, fists in the air, as he turned toward his friends. "Did you see that . . ." His jaw dropped.

Goda had sunk to her knees in front of Lot-Ionan; their hands were still joined. She was convulsed in pain, her face a grimace, and her breath coming in rapid gasps.

Lot-Ionan's other arm was pointing forward, with a lilac ball of energy floating above his palm emitting rays of light in sudden jets. Then the color turned to deep green.

"I knew the dwarves would be able to manage without me," he said, laughing. "I saved my magic for now."

Balyndar was about to fall on the magus, but suddenly all the discarded weapons rose up out of the swamp and aimed themselves at him.

"Nobody comes near me unless I permit them to." Lot-Ionan looked at the kordrion. "A useful animal. It is keeping the army occupied for me so I'll have less killing to do before I go back to Girdlegard. My dream of reigning supreme is coming true." He made a bow to Tungdil. "Thanks to you, foster-son. Without you I should never have achieved all this."

"There you are," Balyndar crowed. "He is a traitor!"

"No. Quite the opposite," continued the magus. Lightning flashed out of the sphere, hitting Tungdil's armor. Not a single rune shimmered in defensive warning. The energy struck his breast and hurled him backwards, where he fell next to the corpse of his former master. "He meant what he said. Only I don't hold with making bargains and pacts with creatures who are not worthy of my discourse. However, he gave me the opportunity to concern myself more closely with the protective spells on the armor." Lot-Ionan smirked. "Very helpfully."

"I'm going to cut you right out of your stupid hood." Ireheart took a threatening step forward.

"Take one more step and your wife will be blown into tiny pieces," the magus warned him calmly.

Ireheart stopped short. "What are you waiting for then? Why don't you go ahead and kill us both now?"

"I may need you again." Lot-Ionan followed the kordrion's movements as it rampaged through the undergroundlings' ranks, killing its victims with swift bites. "On the other hand it should be sufficient if I just have you stuffed."

The swords floating in front of Balyndar advanced. He managed to deflect three blades, but then the next ones dug into his flesh, stabbing him in the body, arms and legs. Only neck and head remained whole. He tipped over into the swamp, moaning, and lost consciousness.

"Enough!" thundered a clear voice. "I can stop you, Lot-Ionan. Your days as an insane magus are over at last!"

Ireheart was flabbergasted to see Rodario on the battlefield. In his right hand he was holding a smoke diamond . . . the very smoke diamond Ireheart had once handed back to Tungdil after it had been dropped in Evildam!

"This artifact will seal your destruction!" The actor spoke clearly, enunciating his words and projecting his voice as if this were the climax of a tragedy on stage. As he approached the small group he said, "I know its power and shall use it without a second thought, no matter how you may have served us in the past." He held the stone out in front of himself as if it were a shield.

Lot-Ionan raised his eyebrows then laughed outright. "An actor, am I right? Looks like Rodario and talks like him. An excellent performance. But completely useless." He sent a magic beam that focused precisely on the stone.

The smoke diamond flared up in Rodario's fingers and crumbled instantly to black powder.

"By Samusin! I could have sworn it was going to be really important," said a disappointed Rodario.

"No, it wasn't," gloated the magus. "Let us bring this to an end, before . . ."

Half a dozen red flashes shot out, crackling behind him. Lot-Ionan was forced forward and stumbled over Goda; she tore herself free and drew her dagger to stab the magus in the throat, but his sphere of energy halted her action by thrusting itself against her forehead. She collapsed without a word.

"Goda!" Ireheart raced forward, forgetting that his crow's beak was still stuck in the enemy he had been fighting.

Covered in filth, Coïra was less than ten paces away from them waving her hands for another spell. Finally she had been able to overcome her paralyzing terror.

Lot-Ionan stayed on his knees, also working on a spell.

There was a humming sound and a crossbow bolt slammed through the magus's back into his heart. Slîn had scored once more, but Lot-Ionan was still alive, the danger that he might loose a final violent magic strike still remaining.

Shrieking with fury, Ireheart raced over, snatching up Keenfire as he passed. Whirling it above his head he followed through with a horizontal blow to Lot-Ionan's throat.

A sparkling trail appeared in the ax-head's wake and a wave of heat wafted back to the dwarf—and then he hit home!

The sharply polished diamonds cleaved the wizard's neck so that the head flew off in a wide arc. The torso fell to one side and landed in the dirt, stump-side down.

"Vraccas!" cried Ireheart with a gasp, not quite able to take in the significance of his heroic deed. He stared at

Lot-Ionan's head and saw that the lips were still moving and a smile had appeared on the features; then the eyes rolled up into the skull and the sheen of life was extinguished. "What? Did he . . . ?"

Tungdil was suddenly at his side. There was no evidence now in his countenance of those horrific black lines. "Break him open!" he demanded through clenched teeth, his right hand clutching the hole in his own breastplate armor. "Didn't you hear me?" When the astonished dwarf failed to react, Tungdil grabbed the dagger and brutally slit the dead man's body from top to bottom.

A green glow flared in the carcass, getting steadily stronger and making the red flesh transparent. Smoke curled up with a smell of burning.

"By all the infamous ones!" Tungdil searched in the steaming guts, arms up to his elbows covered in blood. Then his fist closed and he pulled something out, together with a handful of flesh.

Ireheart could hear hissing inside the gauntleted grip, like the sound of water sizzling on a red-hot stove. "What, by Vraccas, is that?"

"It's the fragment of malachite," his friend replied briskly as he got to his feet. "All of you, run to the fortress," he commanded as he charged off to the ravine.

"What? Why, Scholar, why?"

"Run as far and fast as you can!" shouted Tungdil, charging on down the path to the abyss until he was swallowed up in the shadows. Ireheart attempted to help Goda up but she did not move, so he threw her across his shoulder. "Hey there, actor! Go and get Balyndar!" He snatched his bugle from his belt and gave the dwarves the signal to retreat.

Coïra watched the ravine in disbelief. "He has made fools of all of us!"

"What do you mean?" said Ireheart, looking at the kordrion which, though weighed down by a mass of spears and arrows, was still continuing to wreak havoc on the troops in its vicinity. Spreading its wings it climbed the rocks of the Black Abyss, then slid down in an attempt to launch itself into the air above the plain. There seemed no way for them to prevent its escape.

"He has taken the force of the magus with him!" The maga gulped. "There was immense power in that crystal splinter. That was how Lot-Ionan was able to store up all his magic!"

Meanwhile, Rodario had hauled Balyndar out of the swamp and tossed him onto his shoulder like a sack of flour. "You lot and your armor," he complained. "It just adds to the weight."

The dwarf-army obeyed Ireheart's clarion call and the remaining soldiers retreated from the field of battle.

"Yes, but what's he going to do with it?" protested Boïndil in defense of his friend, countering the queen's accusations. "He has surely proved he is on our side . . ."

Before Coïra could reply there was an enormous crash in the Black Abyss, followed by a quaking of the earth that threw them all off their feet; then came the explosion.

Ireheart twisted round to see what was happening.

Parts of the fortress had collapsed, with great wall sections falling down, taking the men on the battlements to their doom.

The chasm was suffused with a ghostly dark-green incandescent glow. A broad beam shot up vertically toward the sky and then a second detonation occurred, lifting rocks around the ravine's edges. Finally the earth subsided, bringing the cliffs down with it.

It all happened so quickly that the kordrion had not been able to reach a safe distance. As it flapped wildly to get away it was struck by hurtling debris that half buried it. It disappeared with a screech into the collapsing ravine, turning to ash when it came into contact with the glare.

A third explosion hurled molten rock into the air. It spattered as far as the fleeing armies, creating new victims. Smoke and steam rose up, obscuring the view.

The battlefield was silent now.

"No." Ireheart stared into the veil of steam and dirt. "Coïra, can you get rid of this fog? I have to know what's happening." He stood up, groaning, and laid Goda down on her cloak. She was still breathing, so he was less concerned about her than about the welfare of his friend.

The maga did what he had requested and called up a mild breeze to waft away the curtain, even though clouds of dirt and steam still persisted.

The Black Abyss had gone; lava bubbled in its place, the black heart-blood of the mountains sealing up the chasm. Evildam had lost a good third of its walls and, as far as he could make out through the smoke, only a few of the human and ubariu warriors were still alive. The dwarf-fighters, men and women alike, had done better than the others because the kordrion had never reached their ranks.

"He has made the ultimate sacrifice," he muttered gruffly. "The Scholar knew what would happen and gave his life for us!" Tears filled his eyes. "Vraccas, you have admitted the greatest of your heroes to your eternal forge today."

"There!" cried Rodario with a happy laugh. "Can you see what I see?"

Ireheart glanced to the left—and gave a shout of joy: Through the smoke and ash a dwarf came swaying and stumbling, clad in battered tionium; he was using Bloodthirster as a crutch and limping over toward them.

"Scholar!" Ireheart rejoiced. "Oh, Vraccas, if I ever strike it rich I'll offer all my wealth at your shrine! It'll be worth it! Worth it a thousand times over!"

The armies on the plain and fortress walls had seen Tungdil. The chorus of voices cheering their hero was louder than any shouts of joy Ireheart had heard before. He wept with emotion.

Tungdil was badly burned; lava had cooled and hardened on his chest, and blood was pouring from a gaping wound in his side. But still he had walked smiling out of the inferno and was now waving to the humans, the ubariu, the undergroundlings and his own folk.

"That's my Scholar," sobbed Ireheart.

"I knew we'd do it," said Slîn, shaking hands with Ireheart. "A good job we trusted him."

The dwarves, injured or otherwise, sank to their knees before the high king: Even Ireheart and Slîn, who was putting a new bolt in his bow to be on the safe side, bowed to show respect.

The wave spread.

Humans, elves, ubariu and undergroundlings bowed before Tungdil Goldhand as the trumpets blared. Tungdil walked steadily onward until he had nearly reached his friend.

I knew it! Ireheart was the first to get to his feet, intending to give Tungdil a hearty embrace, high king or no.

Suddenly Kiras sprang past him and he felt a jerk at his arm as she raced toward the Scholar. He realized too late that the undergroundling had grabbed Keenfire out of his grasp.

"This is not Tungdil Goldhand! This weapon can't be fooled like you can." Kiras shrieked, holding the legendary ax in both hands. "See how the diamonds sparkle! What more proof do we need?" She delivered a strike.

Slîn uttered a curse and lifted his weapon, aiming and firing in one smooth movement.

The bolt struck Kiras from behind, finding her heart, but at the same time the ax sliced through the tionium armor, through the ribs and into Tungdil's heart. They fell dying into each other's arms, to sink into the swamp.

The trumpeting stopped abruptly and a mass cry of horror resounded on all sides.

"No!" Ireheart ran up. He dragged the undergroundling's body off Tungdil, levered Keenfire out of the wound and surveyed the horrific injury, which was pouring blood. A conventional healer would be unable to do anything at all.

"Coïra," he yelled, beside himself. "Come here and save him, maga!"

She stepped forward slowly and shook her head sorrowfully. With a voice thick with tears she said, "I can't. I have nothing left. I used it all to produce the wind you asked for . . ."

Ireheart lifted his friend's head and washed away the mud from his face using water from his drinking pouch. "This must not be allowed to happen, ye gods," he shouted. "You cannot let the hero of Girdlegard and the Outer Lands die!"

"It . . . was . . . not . . . Tungdil," breathed Kiras, contorting her body and moaning. "The gems on the ax . . . I had to do it . . ." Her eyes dimmed.

"IT WAS HIM!" cried Ireheart, staring at Keenfire. The diamonds were still glowing but Boïndil knew that the cause was him—a result of the elf curse—not Tungdil. "It *was* him!" he echoed quietly, weeping at the death of his friend.

Goda opened her eyes.

She had heard everything and had only pretended to be in a swoon so that her husband would not be able to demand that she save the creature's life.

When she sat up she noticed something sparkling in the cuff of her sleeve.

She reached and pulled out the last of the lost diamond splinters. It had been with her all along!

Goda saw Ireheart hunched over the corpse of the dead dwarf. It would have been so easy for her to keep him alive . . .

Epilogue

Hargorin Deathbringer looked at the sixth of the vrac-casium caskets—the one that had the thirdling runes embossed on the side.

Inside were some of Tungdil Goldhand's ashes from the extremely moving cremation ceremony. In a departure from normal dwarf-tradition, the tribes and freeling dwarves had each been given a commemorative portion of the ashes of this, the mightiest and most worthy dwarf high king who had ever lived, so that they could conserve and honor his memory in their own land. This was the agreement the kings and queens had reached.

Ireheart pushed the box over the table to him, then handed the others to Xamtor, to Balyndis, who had now recovered from her fever, to Frandibar, and to Gordislan the Younger from the freeling city. He did not touch the last box, which had the sign of the secondlings on it.

They had all gathered in the assembly hall of the fortress round a small table to discuss what had happened and what the immediate future might hold for the children of the Smith. All those present were distraught at the recent death of their hero and the atmosphere was distinctly gloomy.

Hargorin looked at the others, then slid the little casket back to Ireheart. "They have chosen you as their king. It is yours. Take it with you to the Blue Mountains and put up a worthy monument to your friend."

Ireheart looked at the box. Part of him was still refusing to accept the idea that the Scholar was now dead. Another part of him embraced the notion that it had not been Tungdil but his doppelganger who had died. And the third and strongest part of him knew who it was they had committed to the fire while the trumpets had sounded, the dwarf-choirs had sung and prayers to Vraccas had been spoken. Balyndis told them all that it had indeed been Tungdil. Ireheart's inner being had told him the same thing.

I should have listened to my own feelings right from the beginning. He had allowed himself to be influenced by those like Goda and Kiras who had been led astray. There were still those among the tribes who were secretly waiting for Tungdil's return. *I know better.*

He stretched his hand out slowly and placed his fingers on the reddish golden metal. "I shall do that, Hargorin." He took a long breath. "I shall leave soon, together with those of my tribe who had fled to the freelings. We will put things to rights and will clear the last of the black-eyes' corpses from the tunnels."

Balyndis gave him an encouraging smile. "You will be more than capable, Boïndil. I know from our previous acquaintance that you always love a challenge."

Ireheart gave a faint grin in response. "Let's hope Vraccas is listening, Queen Balyndis."

"We still have to settle the matter of appointing our next high king," said Frandibar thoughtfully.

"Let's leave that question open. For the next twenty cycles," suggested Xamtor. "I don't think it would be fitting to choose a replacement for Tungdil Goldhand in a rush. Let the throne remain empty for now. We shall see who proves worthy of the high office of supreme leader of all the dwarf-tribes."

"If it were up to me," Hargorin said, indicating Boïndil, "it would be him."

Ireheart raised his hand, rejecting the honor. "I thank you for your nomination but I should not want to accept the title. Xamtor's suggestion is the best. Let us meet once a cycle and report what occurs in each of our dwarf realms. In twenty cycles' time we will summon the clan leaders and let them decide." His speech was greeted with applause.

Frandibar looked at the model of the Black Abyss, which still showed the rocks and fortress. "Evildam will be left in the care of the ubariu and undergroundlings, Boïndil."

"Yes. There is no reason to hold on to the fortress or repair it. They can let the fortress decay or use the materials to build something else. I heard talk about erecting a statue to Tungdil's memory." He consulted the lined faces round him. "Is there anything else we need to discuss?"

Nobody had any new issues to bring to the table and so the assembly broke up, with the delegates taking leave of each other before making their way back to their own realms. Frandibar would have the shortest journey, Xamtor the longest.

Ireheart strolled off through Evildam, the casket under his arm. He was deep in thought. Cracks had appeared on all the walls. It was time for the rest of the garrison to leave; other parts of the building were threatening to cave in, despite the engineering supports hurriedly put in place.

The last Zhadár suddenly stood in front of him with a

demonic grin, as if he had been spat out by the darkness. "Are you off home?"

Ireheart contemplated the dark armor that the dwarf, who called himself Balodil, had never taken off. "Yes, what about you? You are a thirdling . . ."

He denied it vehemently. "No, I'm a Zhadár, created by the älfar. And I want to hunt them down until I've smoked the last of them out of their hidey holes."

"Aiphatòn was going to take that on. If you're going to do it, at least take a party of the former Black Squadron along under your command."

"Aiphatòn would never be able to find them all. I know their secrets but he doesn't. They tricked their own emperor; he seems keen to forget that. I'll go alone. The thirdlings are good fighters but they're not the right ones to hunt down the älfar." Balodil took his flask off his belt. "This is for you."

Ireheart stared at the gift and reached out for it. "But . . . I thought you need it yourself?" He looked around carefully to see if he could be observed.

The Zhadár chuckled, then barked like a dog, though he soon seemed quite normal again. "I can make my own stuff." He leaned forward. "From älfar blood," he said in a voice as deep as a well. "I squash them like you squeeze fruit to get the juice out." He ran his tongue over his lips and his eyes glittered.

Ireheart could not deny that he found Balodil weird. "What will you do after you've found them all?"

He shrugged his shoulders and puffed out the air in his lungs, looking like a dwarf-child being told off by its mother. "This and that. Perhaps I'll go to the freelings, perhaps I'll leave Girdlegard, perhaps I'll jump off a cliff." He gurgled and rubbed his beard. "Or perhaps I'll go to the Outer Lands and look for an army to invade Girdlegard with." He watched Ireheart's face carefully. "Well?"

"You wouldn't do that." Ireheart studied him. "You know there are too many heroes who can stop you." Now Ireheart bent forward. "And I know your weak point: Tungdil's son could never destroy his own father's inheritance."

Balodil jerked back and gave a malicious laugh. "No, I was never his son. I picked up the story and liked the idea of joking around with the name." He giggled again. "It fooled you, didn't it?"

"Nearly," Boïndil admitted, relieved. "I wish you luck with your plans."

The Zhadár saluted. "If you ever need me, call my name to the east wind. The wind is my friend and will send me your message," he said earnestly, stepping out into the outer corridor, where the torches had suddenly been extinguished. "May your god protect you." And with that he was gone.

Almost too late Ireheart remembered. "Where did you hear Balodil's story?"

"A friend told me," came the answer out of the darkness. "The one you called the Growler. He claimed he was Tungdil's son."

The dwarf felt his blood run cold. "What?" He followed the Zhadár into the dark. "Is that true?"

There was no answer.

With a head full of thoughts Boïndil went back to his quarters. Some dwarves were leaving, carrying heavy boxes and wooden chests.

The move was underway. Everything had been packed and was ready to go to its real home.

It's really a bit of a shame. Ireheart was beginning to feel nostalgic and passed his hand over the granite of the walls. Evildam had been built according to his plans and had been home to him, his children having grown up here. *I shall often come back, even if the journey's only in my mind.*

He entered the room where his family were sitting with Coïra, Mallenia and Rodario. His wife was talking with the maga and waved him to come in as soon as she noticed him.

Ireheart knew she had attended the funeral for Kiras: A swift and simple ceremony. He had not gone, himself. The murderess of his best friend could expect neither pity nor respect.

"Ho! Have the magae been dividing up Girdlegard?" he joked, putting casket and flask on the table.

"No. We shall live in peace and harmony with one another," Coïra answered. "We have decided that I shall use and guard the magic source in the former älfar realm. I shall do this together with the two elves. It is regrettable but I shall have to govern Weyurn from a distance. Goda will protect the source in the Blue Mountains."

"The new king of Gauragar may not like that idea."

"She will," said Mallenia. "The new king is going to be a queen."

"You?" Ireheart bowed in her direction. "You have really earned it after so many cycles fighting for freedom. I offer my hearty congratulations, Queen Mallenia. Is our actor friend going to be taking Idoslane under his wing perhaps?" He winked.

"No. I'm happy for her to reign in both those lands. I'm

applying for Urgon," Rodario answered calmly. "The assembly there is interviewing candidates; I'll address it on my way home. What with my heroic deeds and the legendary theater tours I've undertaken, the throne should be in my pocket."

Mallenia and Coïra both laughed at him. "And he really believes it, the poor thing," the Ido woman teased.

"Yes, I do!" Rodario pouted. "You'll see! I'll be ruler there!"

"In your dreams or your next life," joked Coïra. "You should have enough on your plate, going to and fro between your two women. You wouldn't have time for such an important office." She put on a sad face. "Or are you saying that we don't mean as much to you as a throne?"

Rodario burst out laughing. "If you ever get fed up with running a country and being a maga you can always get a job in my theater."

Mallenia only grinned, one hand on the hilt of her sword. "Let's go. Goda and Ireheart must have things to talk about."

The two women and Rodario shook hands with the others and left.

"The long-uns are a strange lot," said Ireheart, kissing Goda on the forehead. "Sometimes just the one of you is too much for me, but the actor wants to take on two women."

Goda grinned and sent the children out to help with the packing. "You will make a good king. Your children will support you." She kissed him. "As I do."

"Do you?" he blurted out the question.

She started to reply but instead stroked his silvery black hair. "It is the only issue we disagree on, dear husband. Kiras was right to do what she did."

Ireheart looked deep into her eyes. "You know I see things

very differently. We won't mention it again." He turned away, teeth clenched, so as not to say more, not to hurt her. He loved her too much for that.

Ireheart heard her sigh and leave the room.

Relieved to be alone with his thoughts he turned to the table, where two items waited for his attention: The casket and the drinking pouch.

He strode over, touching first the cool vraccasium and then the leather drinking vessel. He took his own flask out from under his chain mail and was disgusted to hear the black liquid inside swill thickly about.

It's this stuff that caused Tungdil's death. This and the curse that rests on me.

Ireheart took his crow's beak, stepped over to the huge fireplace and started to feed the blaze, putting log after log on the pile of burning wood until the flames rose high. He went over the events of recent orbits in his mind. So many of his questions would stay unanswered forever. *You and I shall meet again in the eternal forge. Then we shall have time to talk.*

"I don't need to ask the elf goddess for mercy," he said quietly, throwing his own drinking pouch into the flames. The heat scorched and blackened the leather and the black liquid seeped out. When it touched the glowing wood it bubbled away to dark smoke. "I am Boïndil Doubleblade of the clan of the Ax Swingers, a child of the Smith and king, from the tribe of secondling dwarves." He hurled the second vessel into the fire. "Vraccas made us out of stone and gave us life. I will overcome the curse on my own, as true as I stand here!"

He watched fascinated as the second vessel was devoured

by the flames. Resting his hands on top of the crow's beak, he drew himself up tall and straightened his back, looking every inch the born ruler.

Then he turned round and went back to the table, contemplating the vraccasium urn that shone in the reflected firelight, as if it had an inner strength. He placed a hand on it and felt its warmth.

"I shall miss you, Scholar," he whispered. Then, picking up the urn he left the room without looking round. The Blue Mountains were waiting for their king.

Dramatis Personae

DWARVES

Firstling Kingdom
Xamtor Boldface, king of the Firstlings, from the clan of the Bold Faces of Borengar's firstling folk.

Secondling Kingdom
Boïndil Doubleblade, also known as **Ireheart,** from the clan of the Swinging Axes, warrior.
Boëndalin Powerthrust, his eldest son.

Thirdling Kingdom
Tungdil Goldhand, warrior and scholar.
Goda Flameheart, warrior.
Sanda and **Bandaál,** two of Goda's children.
Hargorin Deathbringer, leader of the Black Squadron.
Jarkalín Blackfist, horseman with the Black Squadron.
Rognor Mortalblow, king of the thirdlings.

Fourthling Kingdom
Frandibar Gemholder of the clan of the Gold Beaters, king of the fourthlings.

Goïmslîn Fastdraw (Slîn) of the clan of the Sapphire Finders, descended from Goïmdil's fourthling folk.

Fifthling Kingdom
Balyndis Steelfinger of the clan of the Steel Fingers, queen.
Balyndar Steelfinger of the clan of the Steel Fingers, her son.

Freelings
Gordislan Starfist, king of Trovegold.
Barskalín, sytràp (commander) of the Zhadár (älfar name for the Invisibles).

HUMANS

Rodario the Incomparable, actor.
Rodario the Seventh, actor.
Mallenia, freedom-fighter.

Queen Wey XI, deposed queen of Weyurn.
Princess Coïra Weytana, her daughter.
Count Loytan Loytansberg, a noble in Weyurn.
Duke Amtrin, ruler in Gauragar; a vassal of the älfar.

Enslin Rotha, mayor of Hangtower.
Tilda Cooperstone, town councilor in Hangtower.
Tilman Berbusch, rebel.
Hindrek, gamekeeper.
Cobert, his eldest son.
Ortram, his youngest son.
Qelda, his wife.
Duke Pawald, vassal of the älfar.

Wislaf, Gerobert, Vlatin and **Diederich,** Pawald's men.

Frederik, butcher in Topholiton.

Zedrik, sentry in Topholiton.

Uwo, fishmonger in Topholiton.

Arnfried, blacksmith in Topholiton.

Girín, official, deputy for Lohasbrand.

Rilde, farmer (f.) of large estate.

Xara, her daughter.

Mila, farmer (f.).

Grolf and **Lirf,** farmhands.

Lombrecht, the old farmer, Rilde's father.

Franek, famulus.

Droman, Vot and **Bumina,** two famuli and one famula.

OTHERS

Aiphatòn, emperor of the älfar.

Sisaroth, Tirîgon and **Firûsha,** älfar triplets, also known as the Dsôn Aklán, the gods of Dsôn (Bhará).

Ùtsintas, älf in Dsôn Bhará.

Wielgar, Lohasbrander, henchman of Lohasbrand.

Pashbar, orc guard.

Yagur, ubari army officer in Evildam.

Pfalgur, ubari army officer in Evildam.

Fanaríl and **Alysante,** elves.

Ilahín, elf.

Fiëa, an elf, wife of Ilahín.

Afterword

After the third volume I was convinced I had finished Tungdil Goldhand's story. Well . . .

Could I have guessed that what I considered the end of the matter would have aroused so much curiosity and so many requests for the saga to be continued? It certainly took me by surprise: Eighteen months of endless emails all on the same topic. At readings (no matter which book I was reading from) people would ask about volume four. And people all wanted to know about that joke (which still has not been explained, and now never will be. There are some secrets that have to stay secret. This is the author's revenge.)

It was tremendous fun thinking up these new adventures and placing the old friends in fresh battles. For the very last time.

I am no fan of Happy Ends in the conventional sense. This ending is unambiguous, at least it is from my viewpoint. The dwarves have passed their final test and have earned peace and quiet.

In order to forestall tons of emails asking about a possible fifth volume, I must emphasize: ***Nothing is planned!*** Anyway, tetralogies are unusual enough. Another fine reason.

What's next?

The world of fantasy still has me in its grip and the universe won't undergo any major change: It's the turn of the älfar now! Evil demands the balance be redressed and wants the right to report from its point of view. There are a few issues to bring to light.

When this will all be ready to read I cannot say at the moment. But the älfar won't be patient for long. Although, I must admit it would be fun to write a whole series about a clumsy fat farting elf . . .

Acknowledgments

My thanks go first of all to the many, many dwarf-fans whose loyalty and enthusiasm I find fascinating! It has made me very happy to entertain my readers with stories about the "Small People."

I should like also to thank the numerous test-readers, Michael "LudoCreatrix," Palm and Barbara Beckmann, Piper Verlag my publishers, and my editors Angela Kuepper and Carsten Polzin, both with Piper. Piper let me do whatever I want. Let's hope that lasts! I don't want to omit the Alten Bahnhof, where I spent so many creatively inspiring and entertaining evenings.

And this is for those who enjoy statistics. During the writing of this book the author used up 223 candles, 359 liters of tea (Assam Hazelbank, Assam Mokalbarie, East Frisian blend, spiced tea, English blend, English Breakfast tea) and twice that amount of tap water, 91 joss sticks (various fragrances) and absolutely no drugs, legal or otherwise. None of the above-mentioned teas are drugs!

No animals were harmed in the making of this book. Unless they might possibly and without my knowledge have come too close to the candles, the hot tea, the water or the joss sticks.

extras

www.orbitbooks.net

about the author

Markus Heitz was born in 1971 in Germany. He studied history, German language, and literature and won the German Fantasy Award in 2003 for his debut novel, *Shadows Over Ulldart*. His *Dwarves* series is a bestseller in Europe. Markus Heitz lives in Zweibrücken.

Find out more about Markus Heitz and other Orbit authors by registering for the free monthly newsletter at www.orbitbooks.net

if you enjoyed
THE FATE OF THE DWARVES

look out for

SEVEN PRINCES

by

John R. Fultz

I

City of Men and Giants

In the twenty-sixth year of his reign madness came to the King of New Udurum. It did not fall upon him like a flood, but grew like a creeping fungus in the hollows of his mind. At first he hid the madness from his Queen, his children, and his subjects, but eventually he could no longer steady his shaking hands or hold the gaze of his advisors during council.

Udurum was a city of both Men and Giants. The power of King Vod had fostered an era of peace between the two races for almost three decades. Vod himself was both Man *and* Giant, and therefore the city's perfect monarch. He was born as a Giant, grew into a sorcerer, and became a man to marry a human girl. He slew Omagh the Serpent-Father and rebuilt the fallen city of Giantkind, Now, twenty-five years after he forged a path through the mountains and began the reconstruction of New Udurum, his children were grown and he felt the call of an old curse. This was the source of his madness.

The children of King Vod and Queen Shaira were neither Giant nor human, but a new breed all their own. His first son Fangodrel was pale of skin, with sable hair and the anguished soul of a poet. These were altogether human qualities. His second and third sons likewise stood no taller than average Men, but they carried the strength of Giants in their modest frames, and their skins were the color of tempered bronze. These were Tadarus and Vireon, whom many called his "true sons". His daughter, youngest of the brood, was named Sharadza. She took after Queen Shaira, almost a mirror image of her mother, yet in her fifteenth year was already as tall as her brothers.

When Vod began ignoring his royal duties, his court began to grumble. Both Men and Giants feared his dissolution as an effective monarch. His uncle, the Giant called Fangodrim the Gray, tried to quell the fears of the court as best he could. But even he knew that Vod's rule sat in peril.

When the chill of early fall began to invade the warmth of late summer, Vod called for his children. "Bring them all before me," he told Fangodrim. A cadre of servants ran along the gigantic corridors of the palace in search of Vod's offspring.

Sharadza sat beneath the spreading arms of a great oak, listening to the Storyteller. The leaves had turned from green to orange and red; the rest of the courtyard's lush foliage was following suit. All the colors of the rainbow revealed themselves in this miniature version of the deep forest beyond the city walls. She was not permitted to exit the gates of New Udurum, not without the escort of her father, and he had not taken her into the forest since last season. Here, beneath trees grown safely within the palace grounds, she got a taste of those wild autumn colors, but in her heart she longed to walk among the colossal Uyga trees once again. The sun shone brightly through the turning leaves, but had lost its heat. The faintest breath of winter blew on the wind today. She sat on a stone bench as the old man finished his tale.

"So the God of the Sky had no choice but to recognize the Sea God as his equal. But still sometimes the Sky and Sea fight one another, and these battles Men call hurricanes. Doomed is the ship that ventures across the waves while these two deities are in dispute." The old man turned his head to better meet the eyes of the Princess. "Are you troubled, Majesty?" he asked.

Sharadza had been distracted by the varicolored leaves blown upon the wind. Beyond the tops of the palace walls, gray clouds poured across the sky. Soon the season of storms would be upon them, and then the crystal purity of winter. She did not mind that chilliest of seasons, but fall was her favorite. Each tree seemed hung with fabulous jewels. She smiled at the old man. It really was not fair to invite him here and pay less than full attention to his stories.

"Forgive me, Fellow," she said. "I am somewhat distracted these days."

The old man smiled. He ran a hand through his short white beard and nodded. "You are growing up," he sighed. "Mayhap you do not care for my stories any longer."

"No, don't think that," she said, taking his wrinkled hand in hers. "I treasure your visits, I really do. You know so many tales that I could never find in the library."

Old Fellow grinned. "Would you have another?" he asked.

Sharadza rose and walked about the oak tree, trailing her fingers along its rough bark. "Tell me what you know of my father," she said. "Tell me about Old Udurum. Before I was born."

"Ah," said the Storyteller. "You had better ask the King for stories of his youth. He would tell them better than I."

"But you know he won't talk to me," she said, blinking her green eyes at him. "I hardly see him . . . He's always in a meeting, or in council, or off brooding in the forest with his Giant cousins. He forgets I even exist."

"Nonsense, Majesty," said Fellow, rising from his stone seat. His back was slightly bent, and he supported himself with a tall, roughly carved cane. His robes were a patchwork of motley, as if he wore all the shades of the fall leaves, a myriad of colors spread across the fabric of his flowing raiment. Yet Fellow wore such colors all year round. He had very little taste when it came to matters of style. She had given him gifts of silken tunics, delicate scarves woven in Shar Dni, and other garments worthy of a nobleman's closet, but he refused to wear any of them. He would, however, accept whatever jewels or coins she managed to wheedle from her parents. Even Storytellers had to eat, and Fellow was little more than a vagabond. Yet he was so much more.

"Your father cherishes you, as does your kind mother," said Fellow in the tone of an encouraging schoolmaster, which he was not. Sharadza's tutors were never so informal with her, nor did she relish spending time with them the way she savored her every rendezvous with the Storyteller. He wandered the streets of the city between visits, telling his stories on street corners and in wine shops, earning his daily bread by weaving tales for the weary Men and Giants of Udurum.

"What do you know of him?" she asked, challenging Fellow to spill any secrets he might possess.

The old man licked his dry lips. "I know that he built New Udurum on the ruins of the old city, after the Lord of Serpents destroyed it."

"Everyone knows that."

"Yes, but did you know the young Vod was born a Giant but was raised by human parents?"

Sharadza nodded, sitting back down on the cold bench. Thunder rolled low in the distance, like the pounding of great breakers at the edge of a distant sea. She had heard rumors of her father's human parents, but he never spoke of them to her.

"Oh, they did not know he was a Giant at first, just a very large baby," said the Storyteller. "But they soon found out when he grew too fast." His voice sank to a whisper. "They say his human father abandoned him, but his mother never did. She died not long after the building of the new city."

"She would have been my grandmother," said Sharadza.

"Not entirely," said Fellow, "for she was never related to your father by blood."

"What about the Serpent Lord? Is it true my father slew him?"

"Yes," said the Storyteller. "By virtue of his sorcery, the same powers that make him both Giant and Man, your father destroyed the oldest enemy of Giant-kind. His magic made him tall as the Grim Mountains, and he wrestled with the Great Wyrm, his flesh burned by the great fires that it spit in his face. Their battle took place right here, among the ruins of Old Udurum. Nearly all the Giants had been slain and their city toppled. When young Vod crushed the life out of the monster, he vowed to rebuild the city. That is why we have this capital of Giants and Men. Your father brought peace to the Great Ones and the Small Ones. He is a hero. Never forget that."

Sharadza nodded. How could she ever forget the legacy of her father? But there was much she still did not understand. The wind caught up her long black curls, and she brushed them away from her face.

"Is it true the Giants are dying?" she asked.

The Storyteller frowned at her. "Since the destruction of Old Udurum, no Giantess has borne a child. Some say the dying Serpent Lord put a curse on his enemies, and that is the reason why the she-Giants are barren. If your father had not fallen in love with your mother, a human, you and your brothers might never have been born at all! The Giants who live among us now are old. Yes, they are a dying breed, and they know it. Little more than a thousand still walk the world, and by the time your own children are grown someday, they may all be gone."

"Is there nothing we can do?" Sharadza asked. Such finality made her want to cry. Her cousins were Giants, so if they died a part of her died with them. Her father's best friend was his uncle Fangodrim, who was uncle to her as well.

"Likely not," said Fellow. "These things are decided by higher powers than you or I. But remember that it is not death that counts in the end, but a life lived well."

Sharadza smiled through her brimming tears. Fellow was always saying things like that. "Jewels of wisdom" he sometimes called them. It was one of the things she loved about him.

"Fellow," she said, "I have another question for you."

"Of course, Majesty."

"How did my father learn sorcery? Was he born with it?"

Fellow sat quietly for a moment. Sharadza heard the moaning wind and a peal of approaching thunder.

"I'd best tell that story another time," said the old man.

"Why?"

"Because your mother is coming."

"Oh! You must hide. I'm not supposed to be listening to your tales. She says you're a liar and not to be trusted."

Fellow smiled at her, the skin about his gray eyes wrinkling. "Do you believe that, Princess?"

She kissed his cheek. "Of course not. Now go. I hear her steps along the walk."

Fellow turned toward the tall hedge and disappeared into the leaves. He would find his way back out onto the streets of New Udurum by a hidden path she had shown him months ago. She could not explain her mother's distrust of the Storyteller, but she knew in her heart it was baseless, so she smuggled him into the royal gardens whenever she could, at least once a week. She began to think of him as her grandfather, albeit a grandfather she could never publicly acknowledge. She had learned much from his stories, and there was much more to discover.

Queen Shaira rounded the corner of the hedge maze with two palace guards in tow. Shaira was not a tall woman, but her presence loomed as that of a Giantess. Her hair was dark and her eyes bright as emeralds, both like her daughter's. Looking at her mother, standing there in her gown of purple silk and white brocade, a crown of silver and diamond circling her brow, Sharadza knew exactly what she would look like when she was grown. There could be no doubt that she would be the spitting image of her beautiful and regal mother. At the age of forty-five, Shaira retained every bit of her beauty, and this gave Sharadza no small comfort.

Her mother called her name, and smiled at her in that loving way that nobody else could ever smile. In the warmth of that smile, the day felt a bit less cool. The blaze of summer lived in her mother's green eyes. Maybe it was the fact that Shaira had grown up in a desert kingdom, or maybe her love itself was the source of the heat.

Sharadza ran to embrace the Queen.

"What are you doing out here, Little One?" asked Shaira. Even though Sharadza stood taller than her mother already, Shaira still called her by that nickname. She felt comfortably small in her mother's arms. It had always been so.

"Admiring the leaves," she answered. "Aren't they beautiful?" She cast her gaze upward at the splendid fall colors.

Her mother gave her a quizzical look, as if suspecting that she told only part of the truth. "Your father summons you before the throne," she said, running her hands along Sharadza's hair, smoothing the dark curls.

"Me?" Sharadza asked, stunned by the news.

"You and your brothers," said her mother, and the Princess saw a worried look pass across her face like a shadow passing across the face of the sun.

"What is the matter?" Sharadza asked.

"Come," said the Queen. "We shall soon know."

She followed her mother across the grand courtyard as big wet drops of rain began to fall. The sound of the drops hitting the leaves was a chorus of whispers. Then a blast of thunder split the sky, and she entered the palace proper.

Mother and daughter walked toward the King's hall as the storm broke against monolithic walls built by the hands of Giants.

Not far from Udurum's gates, beneath the branches of enormous trees, a gathering of Giants stood in a circle about two struggling figures. By the purple cloaks and blackened bronze they wore, these Uduru were known to all as the King's Warriors. They howled and leaped and shouted curses, but their great axes, swords, and hammers hung sheathed on their backs. Their eyes focused on the two man-sized combatants at their center.

Among the brown leaves lying big as shields on the forest floor, two sinewy, broad-chested youths rolled in a contest of power and stamina. Straining muscles gleamed with sweat, and the wrestlers breathed through gritted teeth. A pulp of leaves and mud smeared their bodies. The Giants, each standing three times the height of the wrestlers, shouted and waved bags of gold above the peaks of black war helms.

'Tadarus!' some shouted.

'Vireon!' cried others.

On the ground, Vireon stared up into his brother's face, feeling the weight of him like a boulder against his chest. Their arms locked together like the trunks of young oaks. Vireon's legs shot upward, his heels dug into Tadarus' abdomen, and his brother went flying. The giants roared. Now both brothers stood on their feet, coiled in the manner of crouching tigers. Tadarus laughed. Vireon smiled back at him.

"My little brother!" roared Tadarus. "You know I will beat you. I always do."

Now Vireon laughed to show his defiance. "You are but one year my senior. And youth has its advantages."

Shoulders slammed together and the Giants reeled from the sheer force of their collision. Once more the brothers stood locked in stalemate.

Vireon wondered who would tire first. If he could simply outlast his brother, he would win. The Giants would never underestimate him again.

They might have been twins, these two, but for Vireon's more narrow face and slightly lesser height. They shared the same jet-black hair, the same sky-blue eyes, and the strength of raging Uduru.

Tadarus slammed Vireon's back against a tree trunk. The monolithic Uyga trunk trembled, bark exploded, and the last of the tree's faded leaves fell in a slow rain about the brothers as they wrestled. The Giants howled at this display of strength, and Vireon leapt forward, flipping over his brother's head. They rolled together longwise through a debris of branch, bark, and leaf. Dead wood cracked beneath their bodies.

At the end of the roll, Vireon arose first, his arms still locked on his brother's shoulders. He took advantage of Tadarus' split second of disorientation and hurled him through the air, screaming after him. Tadarus crashed through a pine tree as thick as his waist, shearing it in half. Both he and the upper half of the tree fell with a double crash into the forest beyond the ring of bewildered Giants.

Vireon stood panting in the center of the chattering Uduru. The thrill of victory was a momentary sensation, replaced by instant worry for his brother, who lay somewhere in the shadows of the great trees.

"What excellence!" growled Boroldun the Bear-Fang. "The younger triumphs at last!"

"Hail, Vireon the Younger!" bellowed Danthus the Sharp-Tooth. "I knew your day would come!"

The Giants exchanged bags of gold, precious jewels, and other baubles as the supporters of Vireon claimed their winnings. Vireon payed them no attention, but leaped across the stump of the felled tree to find his brother. Tadarus lay among a knot of big ferns growing about a wedge-shaped boulder. Vireon feared the big rock had brained his brother.

Gods of Earth and Sky, let him be well.

Vireon bent low over his brother. "Tadarus?"

Without opening his eyes, Tadarus sprang up and knocked Vireon off his feet with the force of his shoulder. Vireon's posterior met the ground, and he stared up into the grinning face of his brother.

"Did you think you had actually *hurt* me?" Tadarus said. A few Giants came tromping near, flattening the undergrowth with their every step. Some of them shouted to their fellows that Tadarus was fine – of course. The elder brother offered his hand, and Vireon took it. Now they stood together as the Giants looked upon them with admiration.

"I beat you," said Vireon.

"So you did," said Tadarus, smiling. "And you killed a tree."

The Giants laughed, thunder among the redwoods.

"I say your next bout should be fought on the plains of the Stormlands, or perhaps the top of a mountain!" said the Sharp-Tooth. "To avoid more casualties of nature!"

The Giants and Tadarus laughed. Vireon saw no humor. He regretted the felling of the pine. He would carry it back to the palace for the woodcarvers, or at the least to stoke the fires of the kitchens. Even a tree's death must serve a purpose.

"I am proud of you, brother," said Tadarus. Once more he placed his hands on Vireon's shoulders, warmly this time. His white teeth showed in the forest gloom as he looked his brother in the eye. "You have proven yourself my equal this day. And won a ton of loot for old Sharp-Tooth!"

Vireon at last smiled. His beefy chest swelled. He loved his brother. Only praise from his father could find more currency in his heart.

"I stand amazed, yet again," said the Sharp-Tooth to his fellows. Most of the Giants wandered toward the city gates as drops of rain began to fall, but three of the Sharp-Tooth's fellows lingered, his steadfast drinking companions, Dabruz the Flame-Heart, Grodulum the Hammer, and Hrolgar the Iron-Foot. "These whelps are sturdy as Uduru, though they could pass for Men in any kingdom south of the Grim."

"The True Sons of Vod!" said the Iron-Foot. "They are both men and giants."

"Perhaps we're neither," said Tadarus, sharing a gourd of cool water with Vireon. "Perhaps we are something new. Mother said we carry the best of both races in our blood. Perhaps there is no name for what we are."

"Aye," said Danthus. "You speak with your father's wisdom.

But here, Vireon, take you this hammer won from Ohlung the Bear-Slayer." He held the great weapon out to Vireon. The length of it was greater than half the youth's body, but he grabbed its haft and lifted it above his head, testing its balance. It was a Giant's weapon, forged in the smithies of Old Udurum, before the coming of the Serpent Father. Its pitted head was carved into the likeness of a grinning demon, and a band of beaten bronze wound about the dark stone.

"It is a good hammer," said Vireon, admiring the ancient signs of the Uduru carved into the back of the demon-head. "But too unsubtle for me. I think my brother should have it."

Vireon passed the hammer to Tadarus, who grinned at him again and took the war hammer, swinging it about him a few times playfully. "A fine weapon," said Tadarus. "But you won. It should be yours!" He offered it back to Vireon.

"And as mine, it is also mine to give!" Vireon rammed his elbow into Tadarus' tight stomach. Tadarus grunted, then laughed. He nodded, and the argument was done.

The rain fell now in pleasant sheets, so the brothers washed the earth from their bodies while cold winds blew through the upper leaves. The Giants stood counting their loot, heedless of the rising storm.

"Now," said Tadarus, banging his fists together with fresh vigor. "Which one of you Uduru will challenge me and my brother? Let's have a *real* wrestling match!"

The Giants roared their mirth at him, and Vireon went to fetch the felled tree. "None will wrestle you, Prince," said the Sharp-Tooth. "For there is the off chance that you might win. And no Giant could stand being bested by such a small thing."

Tadarus laughed. "Then flee, Giants! Or face my wrath!" He lunged at the Uduru, and they scattered among the trees, laughing at his temerity, dropping coins and jewels in their wake. Vireon joined his brother, the slain tree slung over one shoulder. Tadarus took up his hammer.

"Thank you, Brother," said Tadarus. "For the hammer."

Vireon grinned. "It was the least I could do after humiliating you in front of the Uduru."

Tadarus looked at his brother with a semblance of anger on his handsome face.

"Do you imply that you could best me twice?" he asked.

Vireon grinned. "Three times, even."

Tadarus threw down his hammer, and Vireon his tree trunk. Again they faced each other, crouching ready to spring. The rain pelted them and thunder rolled among the deeps of the forest.

A different thunder, that of a horse's hooves pounding the wet earth, met Vireon's ears. He turned his head just as Tadarus slammed into him. They rolled through the mud for a short while until the voice calling them rose above the sound of the storm.

"Prince Tadarus! Prince Vireon! The King commands your presence!" The hooded cloak of the King's Messenger shone brightly violet during a brief flare of lightning. A black steed, caparisoned in jewels and silk, had carried the rider to them. His name was Tumond, a good man. And he only carried important messages for the King of New Udurum. For Father to summon them in such a manner, the matter must be of great urgency.

Tadarus knew these things as well as Vireon. The brothers rose from their mud-fight, took up hammer and tree, and ran beside the horse as it galloped across the field toward the black towers of the city.

Lightning bolts hurtled madly across the black sky as the brothers ran. Orange watch-fires burned along the city wall in gigantic braziers. The Princes followed the herald onto the wide street called Giant's Way. All eyes large and small turned to catch a glimpse as they jogged toward the spires of jet and basalt that marked the palace of Vod, living heart of the City of Men and Giants.

The eldest Prince of New Udurum stood near a north-facing window high in a tower of the gargantuan palace. Fangodrel watched the thunderheads rolling in and casting their shadows across the great forest. The rolling landscape was a panoply of colors as far as the eye could see, an ocean of autumn leaves in every shade of the rainbow save one. All the green had bled away from the world, and the myriad hues of autumn stood triumphant. A chill wind stole through the open window and raked his chest with icy fingers.

The wide chamber lay shrouded in the gloom of a small brazier topped with low-burning flames. On the bed behind him the servant girl Yazmilla lay senseless among the silken pillows. Her flesh had not been enough to quench his restless hunger. At least her ceaseless yammering had stopped, now that she was unconscious. Now he might have chance for concentration.

He turned his attention to the parchment on his writing table. The poem was almost finished. A few more lines would bring the piece to a transcendent climax. Forty-two lines were ideal. The first thirty had taken a month of agonizing introspection . . . long walks beneath the cold moon . . . a hundred meditations in the moldy air of the city graveyard. Every line was a piece of his soul, a shard of truth, jagged and dangerous to the touch. The splinters of his essential self. This would be his greatest work, a poem that would shame all the hundreds that came before it. His crowning achievement in the realm of verse. If he could only finish it.

He took up a white-feathered quill and dipped its point into a cup of black ink. The point hovered over his parchment. His mind reeled with blank frustration. He hesitated. A drop of ink fell onto the page, blotting like black blood. His left fist clenched, fingernails digging into his palm, and he bit his lip until it bled. His red eyes watered, and he threw the quill across the room like a dart. He stuffed the unfinished poem into the drawer of the table, slamming it shut.

Inspiration is a fickle whore.

The sleeping girl would wake soon, whimpering and crying, begging for more of the bloodflower. He lifted to his lips the long pipe, carved from white oak into the shape of a many-legged Serpent of legend. Touching a candle's flame to the round bowl in the back of the Serpent's skull, he inhaled the sweet crimson vapor. It sang in his veins and sent sparks flying behind his eyes, so that he imagined it was his skull, not the Serpent's, to which he touched the flame. Leaning his head back, he slumped onto a divan of burgundy velvet. From his reclining position he watched the stormclouds moving toward the window. A few wet drops blew in to kiss his naked skin.

The lights of the city were kindled below as the day turned to night; a million tiny jewels spread in secret patterns far below the tower chamber. He drew another lungful of the bloodflower smoke into his lungs, and watched lightning caper among the thunderheads. He enjoyed the advent of a storm, the casting of light into darkness, the warm air growing cold, the faint stench of fear that rose from the streets as the commoners fled for shelter. He brought the Serpent's tail to his lips once more. Now thunder rang inside his skull, shaking his very bones with its violence. He fell prone on the divan, trembling, moaning his pleasure to the corners of the dim chamber.

The girl must have heard him. She raised bleary eyes toward him and staggered to his side on the narrow couch. She placed a long-nailed hand upon his white breast. He flicked it away. He would touch her only when he pleased. She was merely a servant, and should know better than to touch him when *she* chose.

"My Prince," she mumbled, her pouting lips close to his ear. "Let me taste the smoke with you again."

He passed her the pipe and the candle. She inhaled, coughing, and lay back on the couch beside him. The candle fell from her fingers and singed the rug. He rushed to grab it, but its flame had scored a black mark into the vermilion fabric. He grabbed her by the neck and slapped her face. She awoke, staring into his black jewel eyes, timid as a cornered hare. Her fear reignited his desire.

"I could have you whipped for that," he whispered in the breathy tone of a lover, but his threat was a bludgeon of iron. "Or thrown from the roof of this tower."

"I'm so sorry, My Prince," she muttered. Silly wench, nothing but a scullery maid he'd pulled from the kitchens a week ago. She made an interesting plaything for a while, but he had grown bored of her. She was barely seventeen years and knew nothing. He was Fangodrel, and had celebrated his manhood at fifteen – ten years ago.

"Perhaps," he told her, "you can earn my favor once again."

He took her, this time on the divan, and far more roughly than before. The rain fell in silver sheets beyond the window as the black clouds moved in to separate palace and sky. He wrapped his hands about her throat, the bloodflower singing in his veins. Flames seemed to burst from his eyes as he took his pleasure. His body moved of its own volition, while his mind floated in a miasma of swirling crimson. The bloodflower danced in his vision, telling its tale of endless secrets. He listened . . . at the edge of awareness . . . he burned . . . he almost, almost understood. The flames faded.

When he was finished, cold rain blew in through the window and the storm still raged. The girl lay limp in his hands. He pulled away. Her neck bore a purple ring, and his fingers were numb.

Lightning threw mock daylight into the chamber, and for an instant he saw himself in the oval mirror on his far wall. A pale, emaciated figure bending over the pink and lifeless carcass of a slain animal. He stared into his own eyes for an eternal instant. Then the chamber plunged into darkness again. The coals in the brazier had burned out, moistened by the big raindrops blowing through the window.

He stood and fastened the obsidian panes into place, shutting out the storm. He re-lit the candle with a tinder stick and held it over the body of Yazmilla. So beautiful she was, even in death. More beautiful even, for the absolute stillness of her features, the cool pleasantness of her pallid skin.

A pounding at his chamber door brought him out of the trance, and he turned from the dead girl to face the oak-and-bronze portal.

"What is it?" he bellowed.

"My Prince, your Lord-King Father summons you." A thin, reedy voice. "Even now he gathers in the Chamber of Audience all those of his household."

Fangodrel watched the candle flame dance in the dead girl's eyes, twin rubies captured in orbs of glass.

"My Prince?" came the voice again, through the heavy door.

"Rathwol, is that you?"

"Yes, My Lord. So sorry to trouble you. The summons comes from the King's Viceroy."

He stumbled to the door and unfastened the heavy chain. Opening it just enough, he motioned his body servant inside.

Rathwol entered, a slight man with a hawkish nose, his lavender tunic reeking of turnips, sweat, and sour ale. His bald pate was covered by a leather skullcap, and his tunic bore the fine gold trim of a palace servant, though it needed a good washing. He appeared to have crawled out of a gopher's burrow somewhere. The man was an offense to royal sensibility, but he was very useful.

"Light a brazier," Fangodrel commanded him, handing over the candle.

Rathwol followed the order, using a fine oil to ignite some coals in a dry bowl of hammered iron. His close-set eyes immediately fell upon the body of Yazmilla, lying on the soiled couch. Another man might have screamed in shock or revulsion, but Rathwol had seen much worse. He had prowled the streets of Uurz for twenty years before finagling his way onto the palace staff in New Udurum. Most likely he had fled his native city to avoid imprisonment. Fangodrel had never asked what crimes he may have committed, and he did not care. He only knew that Rathwol was a loyal subject, and a man who could keep his many secrets.

Fangodrel scrubbed himself with a towel and bowl of lemon-water. Rathwol bent to examine the dead girl's neck, checking for a pulse.

"Oh, My Prince," he muttered. "Here was a tasty bit of flesh for the nobbin . . ."

"Get rid of her," said Fangodrel, pulling on a pair of doe-skin leggings and boots of black leather. "*Discreetly.*"

Rathwol looked up at his master. "Into the furnace? Same as the others?"

"Need you ask, fool?" Fangodrel pulled on a high-collared tunic of green and silver, fastening it along the sternum with engraved buttons. "There's a palm-weight sapphire in it for you."

"My Lord is generous," said Rathwol, his eyes turning back to the dead girl's face.

"Get rid of that carpet, too," said Fangodrel. "She *burned* it."

Rain pelted against the window panes, like claws scratching at the inner hood of a coffin. Such thoughts made him wince, but it was only the lingering effect of the bloodflower. It always made him a bit morbid.

Rathwol laid the girl's body gently on the ruined carpet and rolled it up.

"Get her clothes too," said Fangodrel, motioning toward the bed.

Fangodrel checked himself in the big mirror. He combed his narrow mustache and groomed his short black beard into a single point in the style of Shar Dni. He wore his dark hair short, and he brushed it back from his forehead, running a handful of lamb grease through it and wiping his fingers clean on the towel. He hung an amulet of opal and emerald about his neck, and placed a thin circlet of platinum set with a single onyx on his forehead. This was the crown of the Eldest Prince, the Heir-Apparent to the throne of New Udurum. A cloak of green and silver completed his raiment.

His pale skin did not matter, he told himself. It did not matter that his lean, V-shaped face in no way resembled the broad, roughhewn visage of his father, nor that his physical strength was a mere fraction of Tadarus or Vireon. None of these things mattered, for he was the Eldest Prince. *Let men continue to call me Fangodrel the Pale*, he told himself, *for my skin will never be the umber shade of my brothers. But none can deny that I am the heir to Vod, King of Men and Giants.*

Rathwol carried his burden to the door. There was no sign of the girl now inside the thick roll of carpet. Fangodrel, grimacing at the faint touch of dirty nails, slipped a jewel into the man's sweaty hand just before he exited.

The Prince waited a moment after his body servant left, lingering just long enough to drink a gulp of red wine from a crystal goblet. Lightning flared outside the opaque windows, bolts of fire dripping from the Sky God's fingertips.

Thunder boomed above the soaring towers as he left the chamber and descended a spiral staircase. As he walked he thought one last time of pretty Yazmilla. The girl had been a simpleton but she was not entirely without charms. Tonight he must find a replacement for her.

But first an audience with his noble father.

What could the old fool possibly want of him?

VISIT THE ORBIT BLOG AT

www.orbitbooks.net

FEATURING

BREAKING NEWS
FORTHCOMING RELEASES
LINKS TO AUTHOR SITES
EXCLUSIVE INTERVIEWS
EARLY EXTRACTS

**AND COMMENTARY FROM
OUR EDITORS**

With regular updates from our team,
orbitbooks.net is your source
for all things orbital

●

While you're there, join our e-mail list
to receive information on special offers,
giveaways, and more

●

Find us on Facebook at www.facebook.com/orbitbooks
Follow us on Twitter @orbitbooks

imagine. explore. engage.

orbit

www.orbitbooks.net